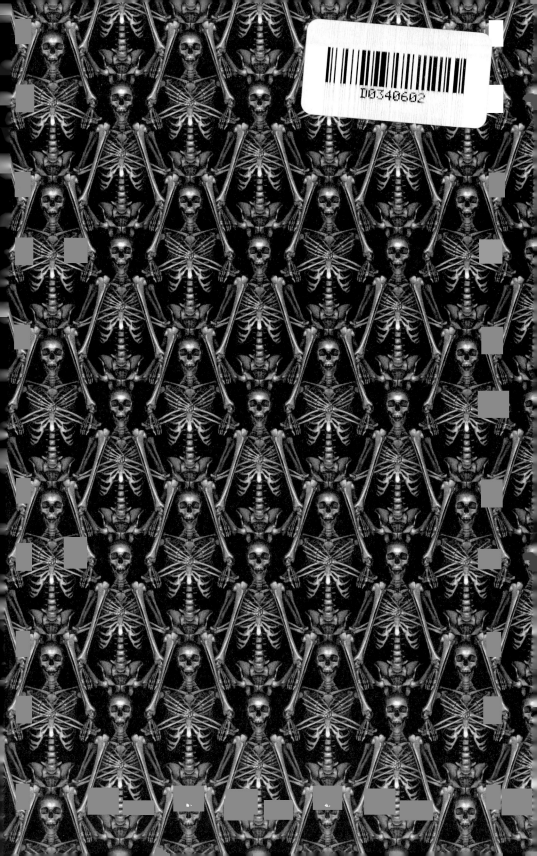

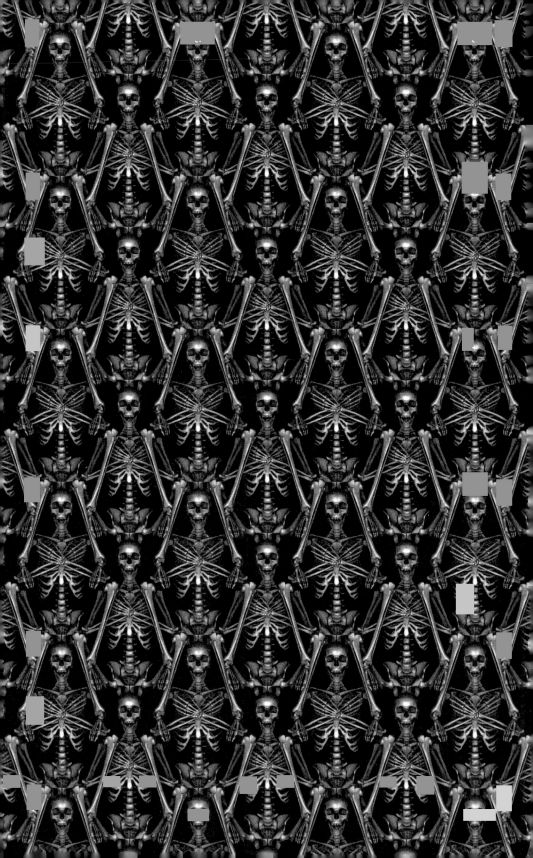

THE SCREAMING SKULL
and Other Classic Horror Stories

Compiled by
Michael Kelahan

THE SCREAMING SKULL
and Other
Classic Horror Stories

FALL RIVER PRESS

Book design by Maria Mann

Fall River Press
122 Fifth Avenue
New York, NY 10011

ISBN: 978-1-4351-2498-1

Printed and bound in the United States of America

1 3 5 7 9 10 8 6 4 2

FOR S.T. JOSHI

For reasons that should be obvious

CONTENTS

INTRODUCTION

"THE OLDEST AND STRONGEST EMOTION OF MANKIND IS FEAR,
AND THE OLDEST AND STRONGEST KIND OF FEAR IS FEAR OF THE
UNKNOWN. THESE FACTS FEW PSYCHOLOGISTS WILL DISPUTE,
AND THEIR ADMITTED TRUTH MUST ESTABLISH FOR ALL TIME
THE GENUINENESS AND DIGNITY OF THE WEIRDLY HORRIBLE TALE
AS A LITERARY FORM."

When twentieth-century horror master H.P. Lovecraft introduced his landmark essay "Supernatural Horror in Literature" with these observations, he was acknowledging both the validity of the horror story as a serious literary form and the universality of its appeal over time and across cultures. Lovecraft wrote his essay in 1927 at the height of the American pulp magazine era, when the bulk of horror fiction being written was ghettoized in cheap magazines with lurid covers that were considered disposable by most readers. At that time, however, the literary tradition of horror fiction was more than a century-and-a-half old and, as the contents of this volume show, the best examples of the form measured up to the best work of the era's top literary writers—if, for no other reason, because they were being written by those very writers.

The literary tradition of horror begins in earnest with the Gothic era, whose origins are typically traced to the publication of Horace Walpole's *The Castle of Otranto* in 1765. Flamboyantly macabre and larded with set pieces and characters that would become clichés of the Gothic genre—a crumbling ancestral castle, an ancient family curse, a psychologically tormented villain, a virtuous heroine, supernatural manifestations as inexplicable as they were outrageous—Walpole's novel was the first trickle of what would eventually become a torrent of Gothic fiction that flooded the marketplace over the next half century. The roots of the Gothic have been traced back several decades previous to the mortality-minded school of British "Graveyard Poets" and to philosophers whose aesthetic theories of the sublime explored the intensification of beauty by its juxtaposition to the grotesque. Why such morbid writing should prove so popular is anyone's guess. However, the Gothic and its immediate antecedents emerged at the height of the neoclassical era and it is largely assumed that the depravity, primitivism, and sensational thrills that became hallmarks of the form were a direct response to the rationality and reason that defined the Age of Enlightenment. The Gothic was both an acknowledgment and a celebration of irrepressible emotions and impulses that the more refined literature of the day denied.

In the ensuing decades, the Gothic developed along two major avenues of expression. In the rationalized Gothic typified by Anne Radcliffe's *The Mysteries of Udolpho* (1794), threats of an apparently supernatural nature are ultimately revealed to be schemes of entirely human invention. The imperiled heroines of these stories resist seemingly insuperable threats to their innocence and virtue and are justly rewarded for their moral steadfastness. The world in these tales shows its dark side, but it is always the bright side that triumphs. This permutation of the Gothic was more consistent in spirit with the non-Gothic romances and historical novels of the day. In the supernatural Gothic, represented at its most extreme by Matthew Gregory Lewis's *The Monk* (1796), the supernatural is a force of irrationality that overwhelms and disorders the hitherto secure and predictable world of the characters. Evil flourishes and often triumphs, despite the goodness and godliness of the most virtuous characters, casting doubt on the moral order of the universe. These two predominant Gothic story types became the model for most horror fiction written in the two centuries since.

By the end of the eighteenth century, the public's insatiable appetite for sensational fiction had encouraged a glut of cheap abridgements and knock-offs of the better-known Gothics. Dubbed the shilling-shockers, these short booklets reduced the labyrinthine plots of their models to basic formulae and their atmospheric set pieces and scenarios to stock props and furniture. The shilling-shockers were unintentional self-parodies that paved the way for more lighthearted satires of the Gothics including Jane Austen's *Northanger Abbey* (1818) and Thomas Love Peacock's *Nightmare Abbey* (1818). More important, they singled out key motifs and themes by which Gothic horror was recognized and in their own inelegant way helped to define the signifiers of the horror genre.

The Gothic era breathed its last gasp in the early decades of the nineteenth century through such landmark novels as Mary Shelley's *Frankenstein* (1818) and Charles Robert Maturin's *Melmoth the Wanderer* (1820), which used the Gothic novel format as a foundation for provocative philosophical, theological, and metaphysical speculation. These books were outgrowths of the Romantic movement, which was typified by ideas and concerns in the poetry of William Wordsworth, Samuel Taylor Coleridge, Lord Byron, and Percy Bysshe Shelley in England and the fiction of Nathaniel Hawthorne, Edgar Allan Poe, Washington Irving, and Herman Melville in America. The Gothic was closely intertwined with Romanticism, especially in its rejection of scientific rationalism and emphasis on personal experience shaped by intense emotions including awe and terror, and Gothic elements appeared in the work of numerous writers in America and England who forged the Romantic tradition through their short stories and novels. The Gothic was not entirely supplanted by the literary movements that followed it, but rather translated into a sensibility that continued to inform literature, including but not exclusive to the tale of horror.

Prior to the nineteenth century tales of Gothic horror were largely British or continental in origin and ran almost exclusively to novel-length. That changed tremendously with the evolution of the American literary tradition. Following the lead of Charles Brockden Brown, who had transplanted the traditional European Gothic to American settings in *Wieland* (1798), *Edgar Huntly* (1799), and other novels, American writers began looking to their own country for source material for tales of the supernatural. In "Rip Van Winkle" and "The Legend of Sleepy Hollow," Washington Irving explored fanciful legends of the new nation's old Dutch settlers. Nathaniel Hawthorne took a different approach in his fiction, seeing in the untamed wilderness of America a perfect landscape in which to externalize the moral turmoil experienced by the nation's Puritan founders. Hawthorne's contemporary, Edgar Allan Poe, found in the horror story the perfect literary form for artistic explorations of morbid and moody states of mind, intense and often troubling emotions, and perverse quirks of characters and their manifestations. Each of these writers showed the creative possibilities inherent in the horror story form when literary writers turned their attention to it.

And it should be remembered that, in the nineteenth century, there was neither a horror "genre" and nor horror writers. Although some writers specialized in stories that dwelt on dark and disturbing subject matter, horror was still regarded as a particular mood or one sensibility among the many that a writer might choose to emphasize in a work. Horror and the supernatural were primarily considered tools by which writers might seek to articulate or emphasize a particular emotion or idea in their work. Stories a writer shaped with those tools were read with the same regard as those that were not. To be sure, there were writers who specialized in writing tales of the macabre, or whose horror stories are remembered today because they have aged better than the other types of fiction they wrote, among them W.W. Jacobs, F. Marion Crawford, Vernon Lee, Robert W. Chambers, Oliver Onions, and Edward Lucas White (to name but a few represented in this book). But nearly every distinguished writer of the late nineteenth and early twentieth century—Hawthorne, Edith Wharton, Henry James, Robert Louis Stevenson, and Charles Dickens, among others—at some point tried his or her hand at a ghost story or tale of the uncanny.

The century in which the fiction in this volume was written represents the richest and most imaginative century for the tale of horror. Certain iconic monsters came into existence then, among them the vampire, whose literary debut dates to John Polidori's "The Vampyre" (1819) and whose persona was perfected in Bram Stoker's *Dracula* (1897), the novel that established the "rules" for literary treatments of the vampire thereafter. Ground-breaking tales featuring mummies (Sir Arthur Conan Doyle's "Lot No. 249" and "The Ring of Thoth") and werewolves (G.W.M. Reynolds's *Wagner, the Wehr-Wolf* and Clemence Housman's "The Were-Wolf") also saw publication in this period. By far the most popular story type was the ghost tale, whose leading exponents included J. Sheridan Le Fanu and M.R. James. In the tales collected as *Ghost Stories of an Antiquary* (1904) and his writings on ghost fiction, James codified the rules of the modern ghost story, notably in his assertions ghosts should be malevolent and that the settings of ghost stories should be modern and rendered with a verisimilitude to suspend reader disbelief.

In the nineteenth century, in both England and America, the term "ghost story" was a catch-all used to describe nearly all tales of the supernatural. In part, this was because a vocabulary for describing the many facets and subgenres of horror fiction had yet to emerge. As an increasing number of writers began exploring and extending the imaginative possibilities of the horror story, the idea of a horror genre that could encompass many subgenres began to evolve.

The variety of horror story types that engaged the imaginations of writers in this century is manifest in the contents of this volume. Edgar Allan Poe's "The Masque of the Red Death" and Ralph Adams Cram's "No. 252 Rue M. le Prince," separated by nearly a century, show the lingering influence of the traditional Gothic. Nathaniel Hawthorne's "Young Goodman Brown" and J. Sheridan Le Fanu's "Sir Dominick's Bargain" are both stories about deals with the devil and their unfortunate outcomes. Edith Nesbit's "Man-Size in Marble," M.R. James's "Canon Alberic's Scrap-book," Saki's "The Music on the Hill," and John Buchan's "The Grove of Ashtaroth" all feature unnatural survivals of the historical past into the present. W.W. Jacobs's "The Monkey's Paw" is a simple tale of wish-fulfillment and its terrible price. Guy de Maupassant's "Was it a Dream?" Robert W. Chambers's "The Yellow Sign," Ambrose Bierce's "The Death of Halpin Frayser," and William Fryer Harvey's "August Heat" all are concerned with the unsettling intersection of dreams and reality. The metaphysics of strange and disturbing alternate realities color the events of John Metcalfe's "The Bad Lands," Gertrude Atherton's "The Striding Place," and Oliver Onions's "Rooum." The classic ghost story gets a gruesome makeover in Perceval Landon's "Thurnley Abbey," while subject matter that might have been fit for childish fantasy takes a diabolic turn in Arthur Machen's "The White People." The awe and mystery of the natural world give rise to horrors incomprehensible to human understanding in Algernon Blackwood's "The Willows." F. Marion Crawford's "The Screaming Skull" is a tale of supernatural vengeance from beyond the grave. Monsters that straddle the boundary between the natural and the supernatural feature in E.F. Benson's "The Horror Horn," William Hope Hodgson's "The Voice in the Night," and A. Merritt's "The People of the Pit." Ordinary people experience the horror of being thrust into extraordinarily surreal situations in M.P. Shiel's "Huguenin's Wife" and Edward Lucas White's "The Snout." And horror grows out of non-supernatural scenarios in Maurice Level's "In the Light of the Red Lamp" and Tod Robbins's "Silent, White and Beautiful."

It is worth pointing out that all of these stories were written during, or in the shadow of, the Victorian era, which we traditionally think of as an age of emotional reserve, proper decorum, and cultural sophistication. Much as Gothic fiction called attention to emotions and impulses that ran deep beneath the orderly facades of the neoclassic era, so do these horror stories give expression to some of the fears and anxieties readers entertained at the time of their popularity.

The last story in this book, H.P. Lovecraft's "The Outsider," was published at the height of America's pulp fiction era. The pulps were the twentieth century's equivalent of the eighteenth century shilling-shocker and the Victorian penny-dreadful. They provided inexpensive entertainment for readers with less sophisticated tastes, and they mark the growing division between so-called high and low culture. The earliest pulp magazines published between the 1890s and the 1920s were, for the most part, general fiction magazines whose contents included all varieties of fiction: romance, historical, adventure, western, mystery, fantasy, and occasionally horror. As the popularity of these magazines increased, publishers began targeting readers with specific interests, and genre magazines devoted to a specific story type came into existence. *Weird Tales*, the first magazine devoted exclusively to tales of fantasy and horror, was launched in 1923 and published until 1954. In its pages, the modern horror genre was defined.

Weird Tales and the other pulp magazines that followed its lead changed the approach to horror fiction by publishing a type of tale written to commercially proven formulas that satisfied reader expectations for horror fiction. The pulp era thus marks a turning point from the stories collected in *The Screaming Skull and Other Classic Horror Stories*. If, as Lovecraft concluded in "Supernatural Horror in the Literature," the tale of horror "will chiefly appeal as always to a limited audience with keen special sensibilities," then the stories in this volume can be thought of as the broad foundation that supports the specialized literature of horror. They helped to determine the architecture of the contemporary tale of horror, and they will continue to influence the shape of horror fiction for ages to come.

—Michael Kelahan

YOUNG GOODMAN BROWN

NATHANIEL HAWTHORNE

In the fiction of Nathaniel Hawthorne (1804–1864), guilt and sin exert a near-supernatural power over characters and cast a pall of the uncanny over their experiences. Hawthorne was particularly interested in the Puritan heritage of his native New England and this story, first published in the April 1835 issue of *New England Magazine*, expresses the sensibility of many Puritan thinkers who saw in the wild and untamed wilderness of colonial America a mirror for the spiritual wilderness inside the individual.

Young Goodman Brown came forth at sunset into the street at Salem village, but put his head back, after crossing the threshold, to exchange a parting kiss with his young wife. And Faith, as the wife was aptly named, thrust her own pretty head into the street, letting the wind play with the pink ribbons of her cap, while she called to Goodman Brown.

"Dearest heart," whispered she, softly and rather sadly, when her lips were close to his ear, "pr'y thee put off your journey until sunrise and sleep in your own bed to-night. A lone woman is troubled with such dreams and such thoughts that she's afeard of herself sometimes. Pray tarry with me this night, dear husband, of all nights in the year."

"My love and my Faith," replied young Goodman Brown, "of all nights in the year, this one night must I tarry away from thee. My journey, as thou callest it, forth and back again, must needs be done 'twixt now and sunrise. What, my sweet, pretty wife, dost thou doubt me already, and we but three months married!"

"Then God bless you!" said Faith, with the pink ribbons; "and may you find all well when you come back."

"Amen!" cried Goodman Brown. "Say thy prayers, dear Faith, and go to bed at dusk, and no harm will come to thee."

So they parted; and the young man pursued his way until, being about to turn the corner by the meeting-house, he looked back and saw the head of Faith still peeping after him with a melancholy air, in spite of her pink ribbons.

"Poor little Faith!" thought he, for his heart smote him. "What a wretch am I, to leave her on such an errand! She talks of dreams, too. Methought, as she spoke, there was trouble in her face, as if a dream had warned her what work is to be done to-night. But no, no! 't would kill her to think it. Well, she's a blessed angel on earth; and after this one night I'll cling to her skirts and follow her to Heaven."

With this excellent resolve for the future, Goodman Brown felt himself justified in making more haste on his present evil purpose. He had taken a dreary road, darkened by all the gloomiest trees of the forest, which barely stood aside to let the narrow path creep through, and closed immediately behind. It was all as lonely as could be; and there is this peculiarity in such a solitude, that the traveller knows not who may be concealed by the innumerable trunks and the thick boughs overhead; so that with lonely footsteps he may yet be passing through an unseen multitude.

"There may be a devilish Indian behind every tree," said Goodman Brown to himself; and he glanced fearfully behind him as he added, "What if the devil himself should be at my very elbow!"

His head being turned back, he passed a crook of the road, and, looking forward again, beheld the figure of a man, in grave and decent attire, seated at the foot of an old tree. He arose at Goodman Brown's approach and walked onward side by side with him.

"You are late, Goodman Brown," said he. "The clock of the Old South was striking as I came through Boston; and that is full fifteen minutes agone."

"Faith kept me back a while," replied the young man, with a tremor in his voice, caused by the sudden appearance of his companion, though not wholly unexpected.

It was now deep dusk in the forest, and deepest in that part of it where these two were journeying. As nearly as could be discerned, the second traveller was about fifty years old, apparently in the same rank of life as Goodman Brown, and bearing a considerable resemblance to him, though perhaps more in expression than features. Still they might have been taken for father and son. And yet, though the elder person was as simply clad as the younger, and as simple in manner too, he had an indescribable air of one who knew the world, and who would not have felt abashed at the governor's dinner table or in King William's court, were it possible that his affairs should call him thither. But the only thing about him that could be fixed upon as remarkable was his staff, which bore the likeness of a great black snake, so curiously wrought that it might almost be seen to twist and wriggle itself like a living serpent. This, of course, must have been an ocular deception, assisted by the uncertain light.

"Come, Goodman Brown," cried his fellow-traveller, "this is a dull pace for the beginning of a journey. Take my staff, if you are so soon weary."

"Friend," said the other, exchanging his slow pace for a full stop, "having kept covenant by meeting thee here, it is my purpose now to return whence I came. I have scruples touching the matter thou wot'st of."

"Sayest thou so?" replied he of the serpent, smiling apart. "Let us walk on, nevertheless, reasoning as we go; and if I convince thee not thou shalt turn back. We are but a little way in the forest, yet."

"Too far, too far!" exclaimed the goodman, unconsciously resuming his walk. "My father never went into the woods on such an errand, nor his father before him. We have been a race of honest men and good Christians since the days of the martyrs; and shall I be the first of the name of Brown that ever took this path and kept—"

"Such company, thou wouldst say," observed the elder person, interpreting his pause. "Well said, Goodman Brown! I have been as well acquainted with your family as with ever a one among the Puritans; and that's no trifle to say. I helped your grandfather, the constable, when he lashed the Quaker woman so smartly through the streets of Salem; and it was I that brought your father a pitch-pine knot, kindled at my own hearth, to set fire to an Indian village, in King Philip's war. They were my good friends, both; and many a pleasant walk have we had along this path, and returned merrily after midnight. I would fain be friends with you for their sake."

"If it be as thou sayest," replied Goodman Brown, "I marvel they never spoke of these matters. Or, verily, I marvel not, seeing that the least rumor of the sort would have driven them from New England. We are a people of prayer, and good works to boot, and abide no such wickedness."

"Wickedness or not," said the traveller with the twisted staff, "I have a very general acquaintance here in New-England. The deacons of many a church have drunk the communion wine with me; the selectmen, of divers, towns make me their chairman; and a majority of the Great and General Court are firm supporters of my interest. The governor and I, too—but these are state-secrets."

"Can this be so!" cried Goodman Brown, with a stare of amazement at his undisturbed companion. "Howbeit, I have nothing to do with the governor and council; they have their own ways, and are no rule for a simple husbandman like me. But, were I to go on with thee, how should I meet the eye of that good old man, our minister, at Salem village? Oh, his voice would make me tremble both Sabbath-day and lecture-day."

Thus far the elder traveller had listened with due gravity; but now burst into a fit of irrepressible mirth, shaking himself so violently, that his snake-like staff actually seemed to wriggle in sympathy.

"Ha! ha! ha!" shouted he, again and again; then composing himself, "Well, go on, Goodman Brown, go on; but, pr'y thee, don't kill me with laughing!"

"Well, then, to end the matter at once," said Goodman Brown, considerably nettled, "there is my wife, Faith. It would break her dear little heart; and I'd rather break my own!"

"Nay, if that be the case," answered the other, "e'en go thy ways, Goodman Brown. I would not, for twenty old women, like the one hobbling before us that Faith should come to any harm."

As he spoke, he pointed his staff at a female figure on the path, in whom Goodman Brown recognized a very pious and exemplary dame, who had taught him his catechism, in youth, and was still his moral and spiritual adviser, jointly with the minister and Deacon Gookin.

"A marvel, truly, that Goody Cloyse should be so far in the wilderness at night-fall," said he. "But with your leave, friend, I shall take a cut through the woods until we have left this Christian woman behind. Being a stranger to you, she might ask whom I was consorting with, and whither I was going."

"Be it so," said his fellow-traveller. "Betake you to the woods, and let me keep the path."

Accordingly the young man turned aside, but took care to watch his companion, who advanced softly along the road until he had come within a staff's length of the old dame. She, meanwhile, was making the best of her way, with singular speed for so aged a woman, and mumbling some indistinct words, a prayer, doubtless, as she went. The traveller put forth his staff and touched her withered neck with what seemed the serpent's tail.

"The devil!" screamed the pious old lady.

"Then Goody Cloyse knows her old friend?" observed the traveller, confronting her and leaning on his writhing stick.

"Ah, forsooth, and is it your worship indeed?" cried the good dame. "Yea, truly is it, and in the very image of my old gossip, Goodman Brown, the grandfather of the silly fellow that now is. But—would your worship believe it?—my broomstick hath strangely disappeared, stolen, as I suspect, by that unhanged witch, Goody

4

Cory, and that, too, when I was all anointed with the juice of smallage and cinque-foil, and wolf's-bane—"

"Mingled with fine wheat and the fat of a new-born babe," said the shape of old Goodman Brown.

"Ah, your worship knows the receipt," cried the old lady, cackling aloud. "So, as I was saying, being all ready for the meeting, and no horse to ride on, I made up my mind to foot it; for they tell me, there is a nice young man to be taken into communion to-night. But now your good worship will lend me your arm, and we shall be there in a twinkling."

"That can hardly be," answered her friend. "I may not spare you my arm, Goody Cloyse; but here is my staff, if you will."

So saying, he threw it down at her feet, where, perhaps, it assumed life, being one of the rods which its owner had formerly lent to the Egyptian Magi. Of this fact, however, Goodman Brown could not take cognizance. He had cast up his eyes in astonishment, and, looking down again, beheld neither Goody Cloyse nor the serpentine staff, but his fellow-traveller alone, who waited for him as calmly as if nothing had happened.

"That old woman taught me my catechism!" said the young man; and there was a world of meaning in this simple comment.

They continued to walk onward, while the elder traveller exhorted his companion to make good speed and persevere in the path, discoursing so aptly, that his arguments seemed rather to spring up in the bosom of his auditor, than to be suggested by himself. As they went, he plucked a branch of maple, to serve for a walking-stick, and began to strip it of the twigs and little boughs, which were wet with evening dew. The moment his fingers touched them, they became strangely withered and dried up, as with a week's sunshine. Thus the pair proceeded, at a good free pace, until suddenly, in a gloomy hollow of the road, Goodman Brown sat himself down on the stump of a tree and refused to go any farther.

"Friend," said he, stubbornly, "my mind is made up. Not another step will I budge on this errand. What if a wretched old woman do choose to go to the devil, when I thought she was going to Heaven! Is that any reason why I should quit my dear Faith, and go after her?"

"You will think better of this by-and-by," said his acquaintance, composedly. "Sit here and rest yourself a while; and when you feel like moving again, there is my staff to help you along."

Without more words, he threw his companion the maple stick, and was as speedily out of sight, as if he had vanished into the deepening gloom. The young man sat a few moments, by the road-side, applauding himself greatly, and thinking with how clear a conscience he should meet the minister, in his morning-walk, nor shrink from the eye of good old Deacon Gookin. And what calm sleep would be his, that very night, which was to have been spent so wickedly, but so purely and sweetly now, in the arms of Faith! Amidst these pleasant and praiseworthy meditations, Goodman Brown heard the tramp of horses along the road, and deemed it advisable to conceal himself within the verge of the forest, conscious of the guilty purpose that had brought him thither, though now so happily turned from it.

On came the hoof-tramps and the voices of the riders, two grave old voices, conversing soberly as they drew near. These mingled sounds appeared to pass along the road, within a few yards of the young man's hiding-place; but, owing doubtless to the depth of the gloom at that particular spot, neither the travellers nor their steeds were visible. Though their figures brushed the small boughs by the way-side, it could not be seen that they intercepted, even for a moment, the faint gleam from the strip of bright sky athwart which they must have passed. Goodman Brown alternately crouched and stood on tiptoe, pulling aside the branches and thrusting forth his head as far as he durst without discerning so much as a shadow. It vexed him the more, because he could have sworn, were such a thing possible, that he recognized the voices of the minister and Deacon Gookin, jogging along quietly, as they were wont to do, when bound to some ordination or ecclesiastical council. While yet within hearing, one of the riders stopped to pluck a switch.

"Of the two, reverend Sir," said the voice like the deacon's, "I had rather miss an ordination-dinner than to-night's meeting. They tell me that some of our community are to be here from Falmouth and beyond, and others from Connecticut and Rhode Island; besides several of the Indian powwows, who, after their fashion, know almost as much deviltry as the best of us. Moreover, there is a goodly young woman to be taken into communion."

"Mighty well, Deacon Gookin!" replied the solemn old tones of the minister. "Spur up, or we shall be late. Nothing can be done, you know, until I get on the ground."

The hoofs clattered again, and the voices, talking so strangely in the empty air, passed on through the forest, where no church had ever been gathered, nor solitary Christian prayed. Whither, then, could these holy men be journeying so deep into the heathen wilderness? Young Goodman Brown caught hold of a tree for support, being ready to sink down on the ground, faint and overburthened with the heavy sickness of his heart. He looked up to the sky, doubting whether there really was a Heaven above him. Yet, there was the blue arch, and the stars brightening in it.

"With Heaven above, and Faith below, I will yet stand firm against the devil!" cried Goodman Brown.

While he still gazed upward, into the deep arch of the firmament, and had lifted his hands to pray, a cloud, though no wind was stirring, hurried across the zenith, and hid the brightening stars. The blue sky was still visible, except directly overhead, where this black mass of cloud was sweeping swiftly northward. Aloft in the air, as if from the depths of the cloud, came a confused and doubtful sound of voices. Once, the listener fancied that he could distinguish the accents of towns-people of his own, men and women, both pious and ungodly, many of whom he had met at the communion-table, and had seen others rioting at the tavern. The next moment, so indistinct were the sounds, he doubted whether he had heard aught but the murmur of the old forest, whispering without a wind. Then came a stronger swell of those familiar tones, heard daily in the sunshine at Salem village, but never, until now, from a cloud of night. There was one voice of a young woman, uttering lamentations, yet with an uncertain sorrow, and entreating for some favor, which, perhaps, it would grieve her to obtain. And all the unseen multitude, both saints and sinners, seemed to encourage her onward.

"Faith!" shouted Goodman Brown, in a voice of agony and desperation; and the echoes of the forest mocked him, crying—"Faith! Faith!" as if bewildered wretches were seeking her all through the wilderness.

The cry of grief, rage, and terror was yet piercing the night, when the unhappy husband held his breath for a response. There was a scream, drowned immediately in a louder murmur of voices, fading into far-off laughter, as the dark cloud swept away, leaving the clear and silent sky above Goodman Brown. But something fluttered lightly down through the air and caught on the branch of a tree. The young man seized it, and beheld a pink ribbon.

"My Faith is gone!" cried he, after one stupefied moment. "There is no good on earth; and sin is but a name. Come, devil; for to thee is this world given."

And maddened with despair, so that he laughed loud and long, did Goodman Brown grasp his staff and set forth again, at such a rate, that he seemed to fly along the forest-path, rather than to walk or run. The road grew wilder and drearier, and more faintly traced, and vanished at length, leaving him in the heart of the dark wilderness, still rushing onward with the instinct that guides mortal man to evil. The whole forest was peopled with frightful sounds; the creaking of the trees, the howling of wild beasts, and the yell of Indians; while sometimes the wind tolled like a distant church-bell, and sometimes gave a broad roar around the traveller, as if all Nature were laughing him to scorn. But he was himself the chief horror of the scene, and shrank not from its other horrors.

"Ha! ha! ha!" roared Goodman Brown when the wind laughed at him. "Let us hear which will laugh loudest. Think not to frighten me with your deviltry. Come witch, come wizard, come Indian powwow, come devil himself! and here comes Goodman Brown. You may as well fear him as he fear you."

In truth, all through the haunted forest, there could be nothing more frightful than the figure of Goodman Brown. On he flew among the black pines, brandishing his staff with frenzied gestures, now giving vent to an inspiration of horrid blasphemy, and now shouting forth such laughter, as set all the echoes of the forest laughing like demons around him. The fiend in his own shape is less hideous, than when he rages in the breast of man. Thus sped the demoniac on his course, until, quivering among the trees, he saw a red light before him, as when the felled trunks and branches of a clearing have been set on fire, and throw up their lurid blaze against the sky, at the hour of midnight. He paused, in a lull of the tempest that had driven him onward, and heard the swell of what seemed a hymn, rolling solemnly from a distance with the weight of many voices. He knew the tune; it was a familiar one in the choir of the village meeting-house. The verse died heavily away, and was lengthened by a chorus, not of human voices, but of all the sounds of the benighted wilderness, pealing in awful harmony together. Goodman Brown cried out, and his cry was lost to his own ear, by its unison with the cry of the desert.

In the interval of silence he stole forward until the light glared full upon his eyes. At one extremity of an open space, hemmed in by the dark wall of the forest, arose a rock, bearing some rude, natural resemblance either to an alter or a pulpit, and surrounded by four blazing pines, their tops aflame, their stems untouched, like candles at an evening meeting. The mass of foliage that had overgrown the summit of the rock was all on fire, blazing high into the night and fitfully illuminating the whole field. Each pendent twig and leafy festoon was in a blaze. As the red light arose and fell, a numerous congregation alternately shone forth, then disappeared in shadow, and again grew, as it were, out of the darkness, peopling the heart of the solitary woods at once.

"A grave and dark-clad company," quoth Goodman Brown.

In truth they were such. Among them, quivering to-and-fro, between gloom and splendor, appeared faces that would be seen, next day, at the council-board of the province, and others which, Sabbath after Sabbath, looked devoutly heavenward, and benignantly over the crowded pews, from the holiest pulpits in the land.

Some affirm, that the lady of the governor was there. At least, there were high dames well known to her, and wives of honored husbands, and widows, a great multitude, and ancient maidens, all of excellent repute, and fair young girls, who trembled lest their mothers should espy them. Either the sudden gleams of light, flashing over the obscure field, bedazzled Goodman Brown, or he recognized a score of the church-members of Salem village famous for their especial sanctity. Good old Deacon Gookin had arrived, and waited at the skirts of that venerable saint, his revered pastor. But, irreverently consorting with these grave, reputable, and pious people, these elders of the church, these chaste dames and dewy virgins, there were men of dissolute lives and women of spotted fame, wretches given over to all mean and filthy vice, and suspected even of horrid crimes. It was strange to see, that the good shrank not from the wicked, nor were the sinners abashed by the saints. Scattered also among their pale-faced enemies were the Indian priests, or powows, who had often scared their native forest with more hideous incantations than any known to English witchcraft.

"But where is Faith?" thought Goodman Brown; and, as hope came into his heart, he trembled.

Another verse of the hymn arose, a slow and mournful strain, such as the pious love, but joined to words which expressed all that our nature can conceive of sin, and darkly hinted at far more. Unfathomable to mere mortals is the lore of fiends. Verse after verse was sung; and still the chorus of the desert swelled between like the deepest tone of a mighty organ; and with the final peal of that dreadful anthem there came a sound, as if the roaring wind, the rushing streams, the howling beasts, and every other voice of the unconcerted wilderness, were mingling and according with the voice of guilty man, in homage to the prince of all. The four blazing pines threw up a loftier flame, and obscurely discovered shapes and visages of horror on the smoke-wreaths, above the impious assembly. At the same moment, the fire on the rock shot redly forth and formed a glowing arch above its base, where now appeared a figure. With reverence be it spoken, the figure bore no slight similitude, both in garb and manner, to some grave divine of the New England churches.

"Bring forth the converts!" cried a voice that echoed through the field and rolled into the forest.

At the word, Goodman Brown stepped forth from the shadow of the trees and approached the congregation, with whom he felt a loathful brotherhood, by the sympathy of all that was wicked in his heart. He could have well-nigh sworn that the shape of his own dead father beckoned him to advance, looking downward from a smoke wreath, while a woman, with dim features of despair, threw out her hand to warn him back. Was it his mother? But he had no power to retreat one step, nor to resist, even in thought, when the minister and good old Deacon Gookin seized his arms, and led him to the blazing rock. Thither came also the slender form of a veiled female, led between Goody Cloyse, that pious teacher of the catechism, and Martha Carrier, who had received the devil's promise to be queen of hell. A rampant hag was she! And there stood the proselytes, beneath the canopy of fire.

"Welcome, my children," said the dark figure, "to the communion of your race. Ye have found thus young your nature and your destiny. My children, look behind you!"

They turned; and flashing forth, as it were, in a sheet of flame, the fiend-worshippers were seen; the smile of welcome gleamed darkly on every visage.

"There," resumed the sable form, "are all whom ye have reverenced from youth. Ye deemed them holier than yourselves, and shrank from your own sin, contrasting it with their lives of righteousness, and prayerful aspirations heavenward. Yet, here are they all, in my worshipping assembly. This night it shall be granted you to know their secret deeds; how hoary-bearded elders of the church have whispered wanton words to the young maids of their households; how many a woman, eager for widows' weeds, has given her husband a drink at bedtime and let him sleep his last sleep in her bosom; how beardless youths have made haste to inherit their fathers' wealth; and how fair damsels—blush not, sweet ones—have dug little graves in the garden, and bidden me, the sole guest, to an infant's funeral. By the sympathy of your human hearts for sin ye shall scent out all the places—whether in church, bed-chamber, street, field, or forest—where crime has been committed, and shall exult to behold the whole earth one stain of guilt, one mighty blood-spot. Far more than this! It shall be yours to penetrate, in every bosom, the deep mystery of sin, the fountain of all wicked arts, and which inexhaustibly supplies more evil impulses than human power—than my power at its utmost—can make manifest in deeds. And now, my children, look upon each other."

They did so; and, by the blaze of the hell-kindled torches, the wretched man beheld his Faith, and the wife her husband, trembling before that unhallowed altar.

"Lo, there ye stand, my children," said the figure, in a deep and solemn tone, almost sad with its despairing awfulness, as if his once angelic nature could yet mourn for our miserable race. "Depending upon one another's hearts, ye had still hoped that virtue were not all a dream. Now are ye undeceived. Evil is the nature of mankind. Evil must be your only happiness. Welcome again, my children, to the communion of your race."

"Welcome," repeated the fiend-worshippers, in one cry of despair and triumph.

And there they stood, the only pair, as it seemed, who were yet hesitating on the verge of wickedness, in this dark world. A basin was hollowed, naturally, in the rock. Did it contain water, reddened by the lurid light? or was it blood? or, perchance, a liquid flame? Herein did the Shape of Evil dip his hand and prepare to lay the mark of baptism upon their foreheads, that they might be partakers of the mystery of sin, more conscious of the secret guilt of others, both in deed and thought, than they could now be of their own. The husband cast one look at his pale wife, and Faith at him. What polluted wretches would the next glance show them to each other, shuddering alike at what they disclosed and what they saw!

"Faith! Faith!" cried the husband. "Look up to heaven, and resist the wicked one."

Whether Faith obeyed he knew not. Hardly had he spoken when he found himself amid calm night and solitude, listening to a roar of the wind which died heavily away through the forest. He staggered against the rock, and felt it chill and damp; while a hanging twig, that had been all on fire, besprinkled his cheek with the coldest dew.

The next morning young Goodman Brown came slowly into the street of Salem village, staring around him like a bewildered man. The good old minister was taking a walk along the grave-yard, to get an appetite for breakfast and meditate his sermon, and bestowed a blessing, as he passed, on Goodman Brown. He shrank from the venerable saint, as if to avoid an anathema. Old Deacon Gookin was at domestic worship, and the holy words of his prayer were heard through the open window. "What God doth the wizard pray to?" quoth Goodman Brown. Goody Cloyse, that excellent old Christian, stood in the early sunshine at her own lattice, catechising a little girl, who had brought her a pint of morning's milk. Goodman Brown snatched away the child, as from the grasp of the fiend himself. Turning the corner by the meeting-house, he spied the head of Faith, with the pink ribbons, gazing anxiously forth, and bursting into such joy at sight of him that she skipped along the street and almost kissed her husband before the whole village. But, Goodman Brown looked sternly and sadly into her face, and passed on without a greeting.

Had Goodman Brown fallen asleep in the forest and only dreamed a wild dream of a witch-meeting?

Be it so if you will; but, alas! it was a dream of evil omen for young Goodman Brown. A stern, a sad, a darkly meditative, a distrustful, if not a desperate man did he become from the night of that fearful dream. On the Sabbath-day, when the congregation were singing a holy psalm, he could not listen, because an anthem of sin rushed loudly upon his ear, and drowned all the blessed strain. When the minister spoke from the pulpit with power and fervid eloquence, and, with his hand on the open Bible, of the sacred truths of our religion, and of saint-like lives and triumphant deaths, and of future bliss or misery unutterable, then did Goodman Brown turn pale, dreading lest the roof should thunder down upon the gray blasphemer and his hearers. Often, waking suddenly at midnight, he shrank from the bosom of Faith, and at morning or eventide, when the family knelt down at prayer, he scowled and muttered to himself, and gazed sternly at his wife, and turned away. And when he had lived long, and was borne to his grave a hoary corpse, followed by Faith, an aged woman, and children and grandchildren, a goodly procession, besides neighbors not a few, they carved no hopeful verse upon his tombstone, for his dying hour was gloom.

THE MASQUE
OF THE RED DEATH

EDGAR ALLAN POE

MASTER OF THE TALE OF PSYCHOLOGICAL HORROR, EDGAR
ALLAN POE (1809-1849) WROTE STORIES STEEPED IN GLOOM
AND SUFFUSED WITH AN OVERPOWERING SENSE OF HUMAN
MORTALITY. ALTHOUGH POE WAS A QUINTESSENTIAL AMERICAN
AUTHOR, MANY OF HIS TALES, INCLUDING THIS ONE, FIRST
PUBLISHED IN THE MAY 1842 ISSUE OF *GRAHAM'S LADY'S AND
GENTLEMAN'S MAGAZINE,* EXHIBIT FLAMBOYANT FLOURISHES
OF THE EUROPEAN GOTHIC TRADITION. THIS ALLEGORICAL
REFLECTION ON THE IMMINENCE AND INESCAPABILITY OF DEATH
IS ONE OF HIS FEW OVERTLY SUPERNATURAL STORIES.

The "RED DEATH" had long devastated the country. No pestilence had ever been so fatal, or so hideous. Blood was its Avatar and its seal—the redness and the horror of blood. There were sharp pains, and sudden dizziness, and then profuse bleeding at the pores, with dissolution. The scarlet stains upon the body and especially upon the face of the victim, were the pest ban which shut him out from the aid and from the sympathy of his fellow-men. And the whole seizure, progress and termination of the disease, were the incidents of half an hour.

But the Prince Prospero was happy and dauntless and sagacious. When his dominions were half depopulated, he summoned to his presence a thousand hale and light-hearted friends from among the knights and dames of his court, and with these retired to the deep seclusion of one of his castellated abbeys. This was an extensive and magnificent structure, the creation of the prince's own eccentric yet august taste. A strong and lofty wall girdled it in. This wall had gates of iron. The courtiers, having entered, brought furnaces and massy hammers and welded the bolts. They resolved to leave means neither of ingress or egress to the sudden impulses of despair or of frenzy from within. The abbey was amply provisioned. With such precautions the courtiers might bid defiance to contagion. The external world could take care of itself. In the meantime it was folly to grieve, or to think. The prince had provided all the appliances of pleasure. There were buffoons, there were improvisatori, there were ballet-dancers, there were musicians, there was Beauty, there was wine. All these and security were within. Without was the "Red Death."

It was toward the close of the fifth or sixth month of his seclusion, and while the pestilence raged most furiously abroad, that the Prince Prospero entertained his thousand friends at a masked ball of the most unusual magnificence.

It was a voluptuous scene, that masquerade. But first let me tell of the rooms in which it was held. There were seven—an imperial suite. In many palaces, however, such suites form a long and straight vista, while the folding doors slide back nearly to the walls on either hand, so that the view of the whole extent is scarcely impeded. Here the case was very different; as might have been expected from the duke's love of the *bizarre*. The apartments were so irregularly disposed that the vision embraced but little more than one at a time. There was a sharp turn at every twenty or thirty yards, and at each turn a novel effect. To the right and left, in the middle of each wall, a tall and narrow Gothic window looked out upon a closed corridor which pursued the windings of the suite. These windows were of stained glass whose color varied in accordance with the prevailing hue of the decorations of the chamber into which it opened. That at the eastern extremity was hung, for example, in blue—and vividly blue were its windows. The second chamber was purple in its ornaments and tapestries, and here the panes were purple. The third was green throughout, and so were the casements. The fourth was furnished and lighted with orange—the fifth with white—the sixth with violet. The seventh apartment was closely shrouded in black velvet tapestries that hung all over the ceiling and down the walls, falling in heavy folds upon a carpet of the same material and hue. But in this chamber only, the color of the windows failed to correspond with the decorations. The panes here were scarlet—a deep blood color. Now in no one of the seven apartments was there any lamp or candelabrum, amid the profusion of golden ornaments that lay scattered to and fro or depended from the roof. There was no light of any kind emanating from lamp or candle within the suite of chambers. But in the corridors that followed the suite, there stood, opposite to each window, a heavy tripod, bearing a brazier of fire that protected its rays through the tinted glass and so glaringly illumined the room. And thus were produced a multitude of gaudy and fantastic appearances. But in the western or black chamber the effect of the fire-light that streamed upon the dark hangings through the blood-tinted panes, was ghastly in the extreme, and produced so wild a look upon the countenances of those who entered, that there were few of the company bold enough to set foot within its precincts at all.

It was in this apartment, also, that there stood against the western wall, a gigantic clock of ebony. Its pendulum swung to and fro with a dull, heavy, monotonous clang; and when the minute-hand made the circuit of the face, and the hour was to be stricken, there came from the brazen lungs of the clock a sound which was clear and loud and deep and exceedingly musical, but of so peculiar a note and emphasis that, at each lapse of an hour, the musicians of the orchestra were constrained to pause, momentarily, in their performance, to hearken to the sound; and thus the waltzers perforce ceased their evolutions; and there was a brief disconcert of the whole gay company; and, while the chimes of the clock yet rang, it was observed that the giddiest grew pale, and the more aged and sedate passed their hands over their brows as if in confused reverie or meditation. But when the echoes had fully ceased, a light laughter at once pervaded the assembly; the musicians looked at each other and smiled as if at their own nervousness and folly, and made whispering vows, each to the other, that the next chiming of the clock should produce in them no similar emotion; and then, after the lapse of sixty minutes (which embrace three thousand and six hundred seconds of the Time that flies), there came yet another chiming of the clock, and then were the same disconcert and tremulousness and meditation as before.

But, in spite of these things, it was a gay and magnificent revel. The tastes of the duke were peculiar. He had a fine eye for colors and effects. He disregarded the *decora* of mere fashion. His plans were bold and fiery, and his conceptions glowed with barbaric luster. There are some who would have thought him mad. His followers felt that he was not. It was necessary to hear and see and touch him to be *sure* that he was not.

He had directed, in great part, the moveable embellishments of the seven chambers, upon occasion of this great *fête*; and it was his own guiding taste which had given character to the masqueraders. Be sure they were grotesque. There were much glare and glitter and piquancy and phantasm—much of what has been since seen in "Hernani." There were arabesque figures with unsuited limbs and appointments. There were delirious fancies such as the madman fashions. There was much of the beautiful, much of the wanton, much of the *bizarre*, something of the terrible, and not a little of that which might have excited disgust. To and fro in the seven chambers there stalked, in fact, a multitude of dreams. And these—the dreams—writhed in and about, taking hue from the rooms, and causing the wild music of the orchestra to seem as the echo of their steps. And, anon, there strikes the ebony clock which stands in the hall of the velvet. And then, for a moment, all is still, and all is silent save the voice of the clock. The dreams are stiff-frozen as they stand. But the echoes of the chime die away—they have endured but an instant—and a light, half-subdued laughter floats after them as they depart. And now again the music swells, and the dreams live, and writhe to and fro more merrily than ever, taking hue from the many tinted windows through which stream the rays from the tripods. But to the chamber which lies most westwardly of the seven, there are now none of the maskers who venture; for the night is waning away; and there flows a ruddier light through the blood-colored panes; and the blackness of the sable drapery appalls; and to him whose foot falls upon the sable carpet, there comes from the near clock of ebony a muffled peal more solemnly emphatic than any which reaches *their* ears who indulge in the more remote gaieties of the other apartments.

But these other apartments were densely crowded, and in them beat feverishly the heart of life. And the revel went whirlingly on, until at length there commenced the sounding of midnight upon the clock. And then the music ceased, as I have told; and the evolutions of the waltzers were quieted; and there was an uneasy cessation of all things as before. But now there were twelve strokes to be sounded by the bell of the clock; and thus it happened, perhaps, that more of thought crept, with more of time, into the meditations of the thoughtful among those who reveled. And thus, too, it happened, perhaps, that before the last echoes of the last chime had utterly sunk into silence, there were many individuals in the crowd who had found leisure to become aware of the presence of a masked figure which had arrested the attention of no single individual before. And the rumor of this new presence having spread itself whisperingly around, there arose at length from the whole company a buzz, or murmur, expressive of disapprobation and surprise—then, finally, of terror, of horror, and of disgust.

In an assembly of phantasms such as I have painted, it may well be supposed that no ordinary appearance could have excited such sensation. In truth the mas-querade license of the night was nearly unlimited; but the figure in question had out-Heroded Herod, and gone beyond the bounds of even the prince's indefinite decorum. There are chords in the hearts of the most reckless which cannot be touched without emotion. Even with the utterly lost, to whom life and death are equally jests, there are matters of which no jest can be made. The whole company, indeed, seemed now deeply to feel that in the costume and bearing of the stranger neither wit nor propriety existed. The figure was tall and gaunt, and shrouded from head to foot in the habiliments of the grave. The mask which concealed the visage was made so nearly to resemble the countenance of a stiffened corpse that the closest scrutiny must have had difficulty in detecting the cheat. And yet all this might have been endured, if not approved, by the mad revelers around. But the mummer had gone so far as to assume the type of the Red Death. His vesture was dabbled in *blood*—and his broad brow, with all the features of the face, was besprinkled with the scarlet horror.

When the eyes of Prince Prospero fell upon this spectral image (which with a slow and solemn movement, as if more fully to sustain its *rôle,* stalked to and fro among the waltzers) he was seen to be convulsed, in the first moment with a strong shudder either of terror or distaste; but, in the next, his brow reddened with rage.

"Who dares?" he demanded hoarsely of the courtiers who stood near him—"who dares insult us with this blasphemous mockery? Seize him and unmask him—that we may know whom we have to hang at sunrise, from the battlements!"

It was in the eastern or blue chamber in which stood the Prince Prospero as he uttered these words. They rang throughout the seven rooms loudly and clearly—for the prince was a bold and robust man, and the music had become hushed at the waving of his hand.

It was in the blue room where stood the prince, with a group of pale courtiers by his side. At first, as he spoke, there was a slight rushing movement of this group in the direction of the intruder, who at the moment was also near at hand, and now, with deliberate and stately step, made closer approach to the speaker. But from a certain nameless awe with which the mad assumptions of the mummer had inspired the whole party, there were found none who put forth hand to seize him; so that, unimpeded, he passed within a yard of the prince's person; and, while the vast assembly, as if with one impulse, shrank from the centers of the rooms to the walls, he made his way uninterruptedly, but with the same solemn and measured step which had distinguished him from the first, through the blue chamber to the purple—through the purple to the green—through the green to the orange—through this again to the white—and even thence to the violet, ere a decided movement had been made to arrest him. It was then, however, that the Prince Prospero, maddening with rage and the shame of his own momentary cowardice, rushed hurriedly through the six chambers, while none followed him on account of a deadly terror that had seized upon all. He bore aloft a drawn dagger, and had approached, in rapid impetuosity, to within three or four feet of the retreating figure, when the latter, having attained the extremity of the velvet apartment, turned suddenly and confronted his pursuer. There was a sharp cry—and the dagger dropped gleaming upon the sable carpet, upon which, instantly afterwards, fell prostrate in death the Prince

Prospero. Then, summoning the wild courage of despair, a throng of the revelers at once threw themselves into the black apartment, and, seizing the mummer, whose tall figure stood erect and motionless within the shadow of the ebony clock, gasped in unutterable horror at finding the grave-cerements and corpse-like mask which they handled with so violent a rudeness, untenanted by any tangible form.

And now was acknowledged the presence of the Red Death. He had come like a thief in the night. And one by one dropped the revelers in the blood-bedewed halls of their revel, and died each in the despairing posture of his fall. And the life of the ebony clock went out with that of the last of the gay. And the flames of the tripods expired. And Darkness and Decay and the Red Death held illimitable dominion over all.

THE MOONSTONE MASS

HARRIET PRESCOTT SPOFFORD

THE SEARCH FOR A NORTHWEST PASSAGE THAT WOULD
ALLOW SHIPS TO NAVIGATE THROUGH, RATHER THAN AROUND,
THE LAND MASS OF THE NORTH AND SOUTH AMERICAN
CONTINENTS, SPURRED MANY EXPLORATORY EXPEDITIONS
FROM THE FIFTEENTH THROUGH TWENTIETH CENTURIES.
IN THE NINETEENTH AND TWENTIETH CENTURIES, IT
INSPIRED MANY TALES OF FANTASY AND HORROR ABOUT THE
PERILS THAT MIGHT BE ENCOUNTERED ON SUCH VOYAGES,
INCLUDING THIS STORY BY AMERICAN WRITER HARRIET
PRESCOTT SPOFFORD (1835–1921), FIRST PUBLISHED IN
THE OCTOBER 1868 ISSUE OF *HARPER'S MONTHLY*.

There was a certain weakness possessed by my ancestors, though in nowise peculiar to them, and of which, in common with other more or less undesirable traits, I have come into the inheritance.

It was the fear of dying in poverty. That, too, in the face of a goodly share of pelf stored in stocks, and lands, and copper-bottomed clippers, or what stood for copper-bottomed clippers, or rather sailed for them, in the clumsy commerce of their times.

There was one old fellow in particular—his portrait is hanging over the hall stove to-day, leaning forward, somewhat blistered by the profuse heat and wasted fuel there, and as if as long as such an outrageous expenditure of caloric was going on he meant to have the full benefit of it—who is said to have frequently shed tears over the probable price of his dinner, and on the next day to have sent home a silver dish to eat it from at a hundred times the cost. I find the inconsistencies of this individual constantly cropping out in myself; and although I could by no possibility be called a niggard, yet I confess that even now my prodigalities make me shiver.

Some years ago I was the proprietor of the old family estate, unencumbered by any thing except timber, that is worth its weight in gold yet, as you might say; alone in the world, save for an unloved relative; and with a sufficiently comfortable income, as I have since discovered, to meet all reasonable wants. I had, moreover, promised me in marriage the hand of a woman without a peer, and which, I believe now, might have been mine on any day when I saw fit to claim it.

That I loved Eleanor tenderly and truly you can not doubt; that I desired to bring her home, to see her flitting here and there in my dark old house, illuminating it with her youth and beauty, sitting at the head of my table that sparkled with its gold and silver heir-looms, making my days and nights like one delightful dream, was just as true.

And yet I hesitated. I looked over my bankbook—I cast up my accounts. I have enough for one, I said; I am not sure that it is enough for two. Eleanor, daintily nurtured, requires as dainty care for all time to come; moreover, it is not two alone to be considered, for should children come, there is their education, their maintenance, their future provision and portion to be found. All this would impoverish us, and unless we ended by becoming mere dependents, we had, to my excited vision, only the cold charity of the world and the work-house to which to look forward. I do not believe that Eleanor thought me right in so much of the matter as I saw fit to explain, but in maiden pride her lips perforce were scaled. She laughed though, when I confessed my work-house fear, and said that for her part she was thankful there was such a refuge at all, standing as it did on its knoll in the midst of green fields, and shaded by broad-limbed oaks—she had always envied the old women sitting there by their evening fireside, and mumbling over their small affairs to one another. But all her words seemed merely idle badinage—so I delayed. I said—when this ship sails in, when that dividend is declared, when I see how this speculation turns out—the days were long that added up the count of years, the nights were dreary; but I believed that I was actuated by principle, and took pride to myself for my strength and self-denial.

Moreover, old Paul, my great-uncle on my mother's side, and the millionaire of the family, was a bitter misogynist, and regarded women and marriage and household cares as the three remediless mistakes of an overruling Providence. He knew of my engagement to, Eleanor, but so long as it remained in that stage he had nothing to say. Let me once marry, and my share of his million would be best represented by a cipher. However, he was not a man to adore, and he could not live forever.

Still, with all my own effort, I amassed wealth but slowly, according to my standard; my various ventures had various luck; and one day my old Uncle Paul, always intensely interested in the subject, both scientifically and from a commercial point of view, too old and feeble to go himself, but fain to send a proxy, and desirous of money in the family, made me an offer of that portion of his wealth on my return which would be mine on his demise, funded safely subject to my order, provided I made one of those who sought the discovery of the Northwest Passage.

I went to town, canvassed the matter with the experts—I had always an adventurous streak, as old Paul well knew—and having given many hours to the pursuit of the smaller sciences, had a turn for danger and discovery as well. And when the *Albatross* sailed—in spite of Eleanor's shivering remonstrance and prayers and tears, in spite of the grave looks of my friends—I was one of those that clustered on her deck, prepared for either fate. They—my companions—it is true, were led by nobler lights; but as for me, it was much as I told Eleanor—my affairs were so regulated that they would go on uninterruptedly in my absence; I should be no worse off for going, and if I returned, letting alone the renown of the thing, my Uncle Paul's donation was to be appropriated; every thing then was assured, and we stood possessed of lucky lives. If I had any keen or eager desire of search, any purpose to aid the growth of the world or to penetrate the secrets of its formation, as indeed I think I must have had, I did not at that time know any thing about it. But I was to learn that death and stillness have no kingdom on this globe, and that even in the extremest bitterness of cold and ice perpetual interchange and motion is taking place. So we went, all sails set on favorable winds, bounding over blue sea, skirting frowning coasts, and ever pushing our way up into the dark mystery of the North.

I shall not delay here to tell of Danish posts and the hospitality of summer settlements in their long afternoon of arctic daylight; nor will I weary you with any description of the succulence of the radishes that grew under the panes of glass in the Governor's scrap of moss and soil, scarcely of more size than a lady's parlor fernery, and which seemed to our dry mouths full of all the earth's cool juices—but advance, as we ourselves hastened to do, while that chill and crystalline sun shone, up into the ice-cased dens and caverns of the Pole. By the time that the long, blue twilight fell, when the rough and rasping cold sheathed all the atmosphere, and the great stars pricked themselves out on the heavens like spears' points, the *Albatross* was hauled up for winter-quarters, banked and boarded, heaved high on fields of ice; and all her inmates, during the wintry dark, led the life that prepared them for further exploits in higher latitudes the coming year, learning the dialects of the Esquimaux, the tricks of the seal and walrus, making long explorations with the dogs and Glipnu, their master, breaking ourselves in for business that had no play about it.

Then, at last, the August suns set us free again; inlets of tumultuous water traversed the great ice-floes; the *Albatross,* refitted, ruffled all her plumage and spread her wings once more for the North—for the secret that sat there domineering all its substance.

It was a year since we had heard from home; but who staid to think of that while our keel spurned into foam the sheets of steely seas, and day by day brought us nearer to the hidden things we sought? For myself I confess that, now so close to the end as it seemed, curiosity and research absorbed every other faculty; Eleanor might be mouldering back to the parent earth—I could not stay to meditate on such a possibility; my Uncle Paul's donation might enrich itself with gold-dust instead of the gathered dust of idle days—it was nothing to me. I had but one thought, one ambition, one desire in those days—the discovery of the clear seas and open passage. I endured all our hardships as if they had been luxuries: I made light of scurvy, banqueted off train-oil, and met that cold for which there is no language framed, and which might be a new element; or which, rather, had seemed in that long night like the vast void of ether beyond the uttermost star, where was neither air nor light nor heat, but only bitter negation and emptiness. I was hardly conscious of my body; I was only a concentrated search in myself.

The recent explorers had announced here, in the neighborhood of where our third summer at last found us, the existence of an immense space of clear water. One even declared that he had seen it.

My Uncle Paul had pronounced the declaration false, and the sight an impossibility. The North he believed to be the breeder of icebergs, an ever-welling fountain of cold; the great glaciers there forever form, forever fall; the ice-packs line the gorges from year to year unchanging; peaks of volcanic rock drop their frozen mantles like a scale only to display the fresher one beneath. The whole region, said he, is Plutonic, blasted by a primordial convulsion of the great forces of creation; and though it may be a few miles nearer to the central fires of the earth, allowing that there are such things, yet that would not in itself detract from the frigid power of its sunless solitudes, the more especially when it is remembered that the spinning of the earth, while in its first plastic material, which gave it greater circumference and thinness of shell at its equator, must have thickened the shell correspondingly at the poles; and the character of all the waste and wilderness there only signifies the impenetrable wall between its surface and centre, through which wall no heat could enter or escape. The great rivers, like the White and the Mackenzie, emptying to the north of the continents, so far from being enough in themselves to form any body of ever fresh and flowing water, can only pierce the opposing ice-fields in narrow streams and bays and inlets as they seek the Atlantic and the Pacific seas. And as for the theory of the currents of water heated in the tropics and carried by the rotary motion of the planet to the Pole, where they rise and melt the ice-floes into this great supposititious sea, it is simply an absurdity on the face of it, he argued, when you remember that warm water being in its nature specifically lighter than cold it would have risen to the surface long before it reached there. No, thought my Uncle Paul, who took nothing for granted; it is as I said, an absurdity on the face of it; my nephew shall prove it, and I stake half the earnings of my life upon it.

To tell the truth, I thought much the same as he did; and now that such a mere trifle of distance intervened between me and the proof, I was full of a feverish impatience that almost amounted to insanity.

We had proceeded but a few days, coasting the crushing capes of rock that every where seemed to run out in a diablerie of tusks and horns to drive us from the region that they warded, now cruising through a runlet of blue water just wide enough for our keel, with silver reaches of frost stretching away into a ghastly horizon—now plunging upon tossing seas, the sun wheeling round and round, and never sinking from the strange, weird sky above us, when again to our look-out a glimmer in the low horizon told its awful tale—a sort of smoky lustre like that which might ascend from an army of spirits—the fierce and fatal spirits tented on the terrible field of the ice-floe.

We were alone, our single little ship speeding ever upward in the midst of that untraveled desolation. We spoke seldom to one another, oppressed with the sense of our situation. It was a loneliness that seemed more than a death in life, a solitude that was supernatural. Here and now it was clear water; ten hours later and we were, caught in the teeth of the cold, wedged in the ice that had advanced upon us and surrounded us, fettered by another winter in latitudes where human life had never before been supported.

We found, before the hands of the dial had taught us the lapse of a week, that this would be something not to be endured. The sun sank lower every day behind the crags and silvery horns; the heavens grew to wear a hue of violet, almost black, and yet unbearably dazzling; as the notes of our voices fell upon the atmosphere they assumed a metallic tone, as if the air itself had become frozen from the beginning of the world and they tinkled against it; our sufferings had mounted in their intensity till they were too great to be resisted.

It was decided at length—when the one long day had given place to its answering night, and in the jet-black heavens the stars, like knobs of silver, sparkled so large and close upon us that we might have grasped them in our hands—that I should take a sledge with Glipnu and his dogs, and see if there were any path to the westward by which, if the *Albatross* were forsaken, those of her crew that remained might follow it, and find an escape to safety. Our path was on a frozen sea; if we discovered land we did not know that the foot of man had ever trodden it; we could hope to find no *caché* of snow-buried food—neither fish nor game lived in this desert of ice that was so devoid of life in any shape as to seem dead itself. But, well provisioned, furred to the eyes, and essaying to nurse some hopefulness of heart, we set out on our way through this Valley of Death, relieving one another, and traveling day and night.

Still night and day to the west rose the black coast, one interminable height; to the east extended the sheets of unbroken ice; sometimes a huge glacier hung pendulous from the precipice; once we saw, by the starlight, a white, foaming, rushing river arrested and transformed to ice in its flight down that steep. A south wind began to blow behind us; we traveled on the ice; three days, perhaps, as days are measured among men, had passed, when we found that we made double progress, for the ice traveled too; the whole field, earned by some northward-bearing current, was afloat; it began to be crossed and cut by a thousand crevasses; the cakes, an acre each, tilted up and down, and made wide waves with their ponderous plashing in the black body of the sea; we could hear them grinding distantly in the clear dark against the coast, against each other. There was no retreat—there was no advance; we were on the ice, and the ice was breaking up. Suddenly we rounded a tongue of the primeval rock, and recoiled before a narrow gulf—one sharp shadow, as deep as despair, as full of aguish fears. It was just wide enough for the sledge to span. Glipnu made the dogs leap; we could be no worse off if they drowned. They touched the opposite block; it careened; it went under; the sledge went with it; I was left alone where I had stood. Two dogs broke loose, and scrambled up beside me; Glipnu and the others I never saw again. I sank upon the ice; the dogs crouched beside me; sometimes I think they saved my brain from total ruin, for without them I could not have withstood the enormity of that loneliness, a loneliness that it was impossible should be broken—floating on and on with that vast journeying company of spectral ice. I had food enough to support life for several days to come, in the pouch at my belt; the dogs and I shared it—for, last as long as it would, when it should be gone there was only death before us—no reprieve—sooner or later that; as well sooner as later—the living terrors of this icy hell were all about us, and death could be no worse.

Still the south wind blew, the rapid current carried us, the dark skies grew deep and darker, the lanes and avenues between the stars were crowded with forebodings—for the air seemed full of a new power, a strange and invisible influence, as if a king of unknown terrors here held his awful state. Sometimes the dogs stood tip and growled and bristled their shaggy hides; I, prostrate on the ice, in all my frame was stung with a universal tingle. I was no longer myself. At this moment my blood seemed to sing and bubble in my veins; I grew giddy with a sort of delirious and inexplicable ecstasy; with another moment unutterable horror seized me; I was plunged and weighed down with a black and suffocating load, while evil things seemed to flap their wings in my face, to breathe in my mouth, to draw my soul out of my body and carry it careering through the frozen realm of that murky heaven, to restore it with a shock of agony. Once as I lay there, still floating, floating northward, out of the dim dark rim of the water-world, a lance of piercing light shot tip the zenith; it divided the heavens like a knife; they opened out in one blaze, and the fire fell sheetingly down before my face—cold fire, curdingly cold—light robbed of heat, and set free in a preternatural anarchy of the elements; its fringes swung to and fro before my face, pricked it with flaming spiculæ, dissolving in a thousand colors that spread every where over the low field, flashing, flickering, creeping, reflecting, gathering again in one long serpentine line of glory that wavered in slow convolutions across the cuts and crevasses of the ice, wreathed ever nearer, and, lifting its head at last, became nothing in the darkness hut two great eyes like glowing coals, with which it stared me to a stound, till I threw myself face down to hide me in the ice; and the whining, bristling dogs cowered backward, and were dead.

I should have supposed myself to be in the region of the magnetic pole of the sphere, if I did not know that I had long since left it behind me. My pocket-compass had become entirely useless, and every scrap of metal that I had about me had become a loadstone. The very ice, as if it were congealed from water that held large quantities of iron in solution; iron escaping from whatever solid land there was beneath or around, the Plutonic rock that such a region could have alone veined and seamed with metal. The very ice appeared to have a magnetic quality; it held me so that I changed my position upon it with difficulty, and, as if it established a battery by the aid of the singular atmosphere above it, frequently sent thrills quivering through and through me till my flesh seemed about to resolve into all the jarring atoms of its original constitution; and again soothed me, with a velvet touch, into a state which, if it were not sleep, was at least haunted by visions that I dare not believe to have been realities, and from which I always awoke with a start to find myself still floating, floating. My watch had long since ceased to beat. I felt an odd persuasion that I had died when that stood still, and only this slavery of the magnet, of the cold, this power that locked every thing in invisible fetters and let nothing loose again, held my soul still in the bonds of my body. Another idea, also, took possession of me, for my mind was open to whatever visitant chose to enter, since utter despair of safety or release had left it vacant of a hope or fear. These enormous days and nights, swinging in their arc six months long, were the pendulum that dealt time in another measure than that dealt by the sunlight of lower zones; they told the time of what interminable years, the years of what vast generations far beyond the span that covered the ago of the primeval men of Scripture—they measured time on this gigantic and enduring scale for what wonderful and mighty beings, old as the everlasting hills, as destitute as they of mortal sympathy, cold and inscrutable, handling the two-edged javelins of frost and magnetism, and served by all the unknown polar agencies. I fancied that I saw their far-reaching cohorts, marshaling and manœuvring at times in the field of an horizon that was boundless, the glitter of their spears and casques, the sheen of their white banners; and again, sitting in fearful circle with their phantasmagoria they shut and hemmed me in and watched me writhe like a worm before them.

I had a fancy that the perpetual play of magnetic impulses here gradually disintegrated the expanse of ice, as sunbeams might have done. If it succeeded in unseating me from my cold station I should drown, and there would be an end of me; it would be all one; for though I clung to life I did not cling to suffering. Something of the wild beast seemed to spring up in my nature; that ignorance of any moment but the present. I felt a certain kinship to the bear in her comfortable snowiness whom I had left in the parallels far below this unreal tract of horrors. I remembered traditions of such metempsychoses; the thought gave me a pang that none of these fierce and subtle elements had known how to give before. But all the time my groaning, cracking ice was moving with me, splitting now through all its leagues of length along the darkness, with an explosion like a cannon's shot, that echoed again and again in every gap and chasm of its depth, and seemed to be caught up and repeated by a thousand airy sprites, and snatched on from one to another till it fell dead through the frozen thickness of the air.

It was at about this time that I noticed another species of motion than that which had hitherto governed it seizing this journeying ice. It bent and bent, as a glacier does in its viscous flow between mountains; it crowded, and loosened, and rent apart, and at last it broke in every direction, and every fragment was crushed and jammed together again; and the whole mass was following, as I divined, the curve of some enormous whirlpool that swept it from beneath. It might have been a day and night, it might have been an hour, that we traveled on this vast curve—I had no more means of knowing than if I had veritably done with time. We were one expanse of shadow; not a star above us, only a sky of impenetrable gloom received the shimmering that now and again the circling ice cast off. It was a strange slow motion, yet with such a steadiness and strength about it that it had the effect of swiftness. It was long since any water, or the suspicion of any, had been visible; we might have been grinding through some gigantic hollow for all I could have told; snow had never fallen here; the mass moved you knew as if you felt the prodigious hand that grasped and impelled it from beneath. Whither was it tending, in the eddy of what huge stream that went, with the smoke of its fall hovering on the brink, to plunge a tremendous cataract over the limits of the earth into the unknown abyss of space? Far in advance there was a faint glimmering, a sort of powdery light glancing here and there. As we approached it—the ice and I—it grew fainter, and was, by-and-by, lost in a vast twilight that surrounded us on all sides; at the same time it became evident that we had passed under a roof, an immense and yaultcd roof. As crowding, stretching, rending, we passed on, uncanny gleams were playing distantly above us and around us, now and then overlaying all things with a sheeted illumination as deathly as a grave-light, now and then shooting up in spires of blood-red radiance that disclosed the terrible aurora. I was in a cavern of ice, as wide and as high as the heavens; these flashes of glory, alternated with equal flashes of darkness, as you might say, taught me to perceive. Perhaps tremendous tide after tide had hollowed it with all its fantastic recesses; or had that Titanic race of the interminable years built it as a palace for their monarch, a temple for their deity, with its domes that sprung far up immeasurable heights and hung palely shining like mock heavens of hazy stars; its aisles that stretched away down colonnades of crystal columns into unguessed darkness; its high-heaved arches, its pierced and open sides? Now an aurora burned up like a blue-light, and went skimming under all the vaults far off into far and farther hollows, revealing, as it went, still loftier heights and colder answering radiances. Then these great arches glowed like blocks of beryl. Wondrous tracery of delicate vines and leaves, greener than the greenest moss, wandered over them, wreathed the great pillars, and spread round them in capitals of flowers; roses crimson as a carbuncle; hyacinths like bedded cubes of amethyst; violets bluer than sapphires—all as if the flowers had been turned to flame, yet all so cruelly cold, as if the power that wrought such wonders could simulate a sparkle beyond even the lustre of light, but could not give it heat, that principle of life, that fountain of first being. Yonder a stalactite of clustered ruby—that kept the aurora and glinted faintly, and more faintly, till the thing came again, when it grasped a whole body-full of splendor—hung downward and dropped a thread-like stem and a blossom of palest pink, like a transfigured Linnæa, to meet the snow-drop in its sheath of green that shot up from a spire of aqua marine below. Here living rainbows flew from buttress to buttress and frolicked in the domes—the only things that dared to live and sport where beauty was frozen into horror. It seemed as if that shifting death-light of the aurora photographed all these things upon my memory, for I noted none of them at the time. I only wondered idly whither we were tending as we drove in deeper and deeper under that ice-roof, and curved more and more circlingly upon our course while the silent flashes sped on overhead. Now we were in the dark again crashing onward; now a cold blue radiance burst from every icicle, from every crevice, and I saw that the whole enormous mass of our motion bent and swept around a single point—a dark yet glittering form that sat as if upon the apex of the world. Was it one of those mightier than the Anakim, more than the sons of God, to whom all the currents of this frozen world converged? Sooth I know not—for presently I imagined that my vision made only an exaggeration of some brown Esquimaux sealed up and left in his snow-house to die. A thin sheathing of ice appeared to clothe him and give the glister to his duskiness. Insensible as I had thought myself to any further fear, I cowered beneath the stare of those dead and icy eyes. Slowly we rounded, and ever rounded; the inside, on which my place was, moving less slowly than the outer circle of the sheeted mass in its viscid flow; and as we moved, by some fate my eye was caught by the substance on which this figure sat. It was no figure at all now, but a bare jag of rock rising in the centre of this solid whirlpool, and carrying on its summit something which held a light that not one of these icy freaks, pranking in the dress of gems and flowers, had found it possible to assume. It was a thing so real, so genuine, my breath became suspended; my heart ceased to beat; my brain, that had been a lump of ice, seemed to move in its skull; hope, that had deserted me, suddenly sprung up like a second life within me; the old passion was not dead, if I was. It rose stronger than life or death or than myself. If I could but snatch that mass of moonstone, that inestimable wealth! It was nothing deceptive, I declared to myself. What more natural home could it have than this region, thrown up here by the old Plutonic powers of the planet, as the same substance in smaller shape was thrown up on the peaks of the Mount St. Gothard, when the Alpine aiguilles first sprang into the day? There it rested, limpid with its milky pearl, casting out flakes of flame and azure, of red and leaf-green light, and holding yet a sparkle of silver in the reflections and refractions of its inner axis—the splendid Turk's-eye of the lapidaries, the cousin of the water-opal and the girasole, the precious essence of feldspar. Could I break it, I would find clusters of great hemitrope crystals. Could I obtain it, I should have a jewel in that mass of moonstone such as the world never saw! The throne of Jemschid could not cast a shadow beside it.

Then the bitterness of my fate overwhelmed me. Here, with this treasure of a kingdom, this jewel that could not be priced, this wealth beyond an Emperor's—and here only to die! My stolid apathy vanished, old thoughts dominated once more, old habits, old desires. I thought of Eleanor then in her warm, sunny home, the blossoms that bloomed around her, the birds that sang, the cheerful evening fires, the longing thoughts for one who never came, who never was to come. But I would! I cried, where human voice had never cried before. I would return! I would take this treasure with| me! I would not be defrauded! Should not I, a man, conquer this inanimate blind matter? I reached out my hands to seize it. Slowly it receded—slowly, and less slowly; or was the motion of the ice still carrying me onward? Had we encircled this apex? and were we driving out into the open and uncovered North, and so down the seas and out to the open main of black water again? If so—if I could live through it—I must have this thing!

I rose, and as well as I could, with my cramped and stiffened limbs, I moved to go back for it. It was useless; the current that carried us was growing invincible, the gaping gulfs of the outer seas were sucking us toward them. I fell; I scrambled to my feet; I would still have gone back, but, as I attempted it, the ice whereon I was inclined ever so slightly, tipped more boldly, gave way, and rose in a billow, broke, and piled over on another mass beneath. Then the cavern was behind us, and I comprehended that this ice-stream, having doubled its central point, now in its outward movement encountered the still incoming body, and was to pile above and pass over it, the whole expanse bending, cracking, breaking, crowding, and compressing, till its rearing tumult made bergs more mountainous than the offshot glaciers of the Greenland continent, that should ride safely down to crumble in the surging seas below. As block after block of the rent ice rose in the air, lighted by the blue and bristling aurora-points, toppled and mounted higher, it seemed to me that now indeed I was battling with those elemental agencies in the dreadful fight I had desired—one man against the might of matter. I sprang from that block to another; I gained my balance on a third, climbing, shouldering, leaping, straggling, holding with my hands, catching with my feet, crawling, stumbling, tottering, rising high and higher with the mountain ever making underneath; power unknown to my foes coming to my aid, a blessed rushing warmth that glowed on all the surface of my skin, that set the blood to racing in my veins, that made my heart beat with newer hope, sink with newer despair, rise buoyant with new determination. Except when the shaft of light pierced the shivering sky I could not see or guess, the height that I had gained. I was vaguely aware of chasms that were bottomless, of precipices that opened on them, of pinnacles rising round me in aerial spires, when suddenly the shelf, on which I must have stood, yielded, as if it were pushed by great hands, swept down a steep incline like an avalanche, stopped halfway, but sent me flying on, sliding, glancing, like a shooting-star, down, down the slippery side, breathless, dizzy, smitten with blistering pain by awful winds that whistled by me, far out upon the level ice below that tilted up and down again with the great resonant plash of open water, and conscious for a moment that I lay at last upon a fragment that the mass behind urged on, I knew and I remembered nothing more.

Faces were bending over me when I opened my eyes again, rough, uncouth, and bearded faces, but no monsters of the pole. Whalemen rather, smelling richly of train-oil, but I could recall nothing in all my life one fraction so beautiful as they; the angels on whom I hope to open my eyes when Death has really taken me will scarcely seem sights more blest than did those rude whalers of the North Pacific Sea. The North Pacific Sea—for it was there that I was found, explain it how you may— whether the *Albatross* had pierced farther to the west than her sailing-master knew, and had lost her reckoning with a disordered compass-needle under new stars—or whether I had really been the sport of the demoniac beings of the ice, tossed by them from zone to zone in a dozen hours. The whalers, real creatures enough, had discovered me on a block of ice, they said; nor could I, in their opinion, have been many days undergoing my dreadful experience, for there was still food in my wallet when they opened it. They would never believe a word of my story, and so far from regarding me as one who had proved the Northwest Passage in my own person, they considered me a mere idle maniac, as uncomfortable a thing to have on shipboard as a ghost or a dead body, wrecked and unable to account for myself, and gladly transferred me to a homeward-bound Russian man-of-war, whose officers afforded me more polite but quite as decided skepticism. I have never to this day found any one who believed my story when I told it—so you can take it for what it is worth. Even my Uncle Paul flouted it, and absolutely refused to surrender the sum on whose expectation I had taken ship; while my old ancestor, who hung peeling over the hall fire, dropped from his frame in disgust at the idea of one of his hard-cash descendants turning romancer. But all I know is that the *Albatross* never sailed into port again, and that if I open my knife to-day and lay it on the table it will wheel about till the tip of its blade points full at the North Star.

I have never found any one to believe me, did I say? Yes, there is one—Eleanor never doubted a word of my narration, never asked me if cold and suffering had not shaken my reason. But then, after the first recital, she has never been willing to hear another word about it, and if I ever allude to my lost treasure or the possibility of instituting search for it, she asks me if I need more lessons to be content with the treasure that I have, and gathers up her work and gently leaves the room. So that, now I speak of it so seldom, if I had not told the thing to you it might come to pass that I should forget altogether the existence of my mass of moonstone. My mass of moonshine, old Paul calls it. I let him have his say; he can not have that nor any thing else much longer; but when all is done I recall Galileo and I mutter to myself, "*Per si muove*—it *was* a mass of moonstone! With these eyes I saw it, with these hands I touched it, with this heart I longed for it, with this will I mean to have it yet!"

SIR DOMINICK'S BARGAIN
A LEGEND OF DUNORAN

J. SHERIDAN LE FANU

One of the most influential writers of ghost and Gothic stories, Joseph Sheridan Le Fanu (1814–1873) mixed supernatural marvels and mysteries with the history and folklore of his native Ireland. Originally published in 1838 under the title "The Fortunes of Sir Robert Ardagh," this deal–with–devil story was revised for publication in the July 6, 1872 issue of *All the Year Round*, then under the editorship of Charles Dickens.

In the early autumn of the year 1838, business called me to the south of Ireland. The weather was delightful, the scenery and people were new to me, and sending my luggage on by the mail-coach route in charge of a servant, I hired a serviceable nag at a posting-house, and, full of the curiosity of an explorer, I commenced a leisurely journey of five-and-twenty miles on horseback, by sequestered cross-roads, to my place of destination. By bog and hill, by plain and ruined castle, and many a winding stream, my picturesque road led me.

I had started late, and having made little more than half my journey, I was thinking of making a short halt at the next convenient place, and letting my horse have a rest and a feed, and making some provision also for the comforts of his rider.

It was about four o'clock when the road ascending a gradual steep, found a passage through a rocky gorge between the abrupt termination of a range of mountain to my left and a rocky hill, that rose dark and sudden at my right. Below me lay a little thatched village, under a long line of gigantic beech-trees, through the boughs of which the lowly chimneys sent up their thin turf-smoke. To my left, stretched away for miles, ascending the mountain range I have mentioned, a wild park, through whose sward and ferns the rock broke, timeworn and lichen-stained. This park was studded with straggling wood, which thickened to something like a forest, behind and beyond the little village I was approaching, clothing the irregular ascent of the hillsides with beautiful, and in some places discoloured foliage.

As you descend, the road winds slightly, with the grey park-wall, built of loose stone, and mantled here and there with ivy, at its left, and crosses a shallow ford; and as I approached the village, through breaks in the woodlands, I caught glimpses of the long front of an old ruined house, placed among the trees, about half-way up the picturesque mountain-side.

The solitude and melancholy of this ruin piqued my curiosity. When I had reached the rude thatched public-house, with the sign of St. Columbkill, with robes, mitre, and crosier displayed over its lintel, having seen to my horse, and made a good meal myself on a rasher and eggs, I began to think again of the wooded park and the ruinous house, and resolved on a ramble of half an hour among its sylvan solitudes.

The name of the place, I found, was Dunoran; and beside the gate a stile admitted to the grounds, through which, with a pensive enjoyment, I began to saunter towards the dilapidated mansion.

A long grass-grown road, with many turns and windings, led up to the old house, under the shadow of the wood.

The road, as it approached the house, skirted the edge of a precipitous glen, clothed with hazel, dwarf-oak, and thorn, and the silent house stood with its wide-open hall-door facing this dark ravine, the further edge of which was crowned with towering forest; and great trees stood about the house and its deserted court-yard and stables.

I walked in and looked about me, through passages overgrown with nettles and weeds; from room to room with ceilings rotted, and here and there a great beam dark and worn, with tendrils of ivy trailing over it. The tall walls with rotten plaster were stained and mouldy, and in some rooms the remains of decayed wainscoting crazily swung to and fro. The almost sashless windows were darkened also with ivy, and about the tall chimneys the jackdaws were wheeling, while from the huge trees that overhung the glen in sombre masses at the other side, the rooks kept up a ceaseless cawing.

As I walked through these melancholy passages—peeping only into some of the rooms, for the flooring was quite gone in the middle, and bowed down toward the centre, and the house was very nearly unroofed, a state of things which made the exploration a little critical—I began to wonder why so grand a house, in the midst of scenery so picturesque, had been permitted to go to decay; I dreamed of the hospitalities of which it had long ago been the rallying place, and I thought what a scene of Redgauntlet revelries it might disclose at midnight.

The great staircase was of oak, which had stood the weather wonderfully, and I sat down upon its steps, musing vaguely on the transitoriness of all things under the sun.

Except for the hoarse and distant clamour of the rooks, hardly audible where I sat, no sound broke the profound stillness of the spot. Such a sense of solitude I have seldom experienced before. The air was stirless, there was not even the rustle of a withered leaf along the passage. It was oppressive. The tall trees that stood close about the building darkened it, and added something of awe to the melancholy of the scene.

In this mood I heard, with an unpleasant surprise, close to me, a voice that was drawling, and, I fancied, sneering, repeat the words: "Food for worms, dead and rotten; God over all."

There was a small window in the wall, here very thick, which had been built up, and in the dark recess of this, deep in the shadow, I now saw a sharp-featured man, sitting with his feet dangling. His keen eyes were fixed on me, and ho was smiling cynically, and before I had well recovered my surprise, he repeated the distich:

> "If death was a thing that money could buy,
> The rich they would live, and the poor they would die.

"It was a grand house in its day, sir," he continued, "Dunoran House, and the Sarsfields. Sir Dominick Sarsfield was the last of the old stock. He lost his life not six foot away from where you are sitting."

As he thus spoke he let himself down, with a little jump, on to the ground.

He was a dark-faced, sharp-featured, little hunchback, and had a walking-stick in his hand, with the end of which he pointed to a rusty stain in the plaster of the wall.

"Do you mind that mark, sir?" he asked.

"Yes," I said, standing up, and looking at it, with a curious anticipation of something worth hearing.

"That's about seven or eight foot from the ground, sir, and you'll not guess what it is."

"I dare say not," said I, "unless it is a stain from the weather?"

"'Tis nothing so lucky, sir," he answered, with the same cynical smile and a wag of his head, still pointing at the mark with his stick. "That's a splash of brains and blood. It's there this hundherd years; and it will never leave it while the wall stands."

"He was murdered, then?"

"Worse than that, sir," he answered.

"He killed himself, perhaps?"

"Worse than that, itself, this cross between us and harm! I'm oulder than I look, sir; you wouldn't guess my years."

He became silent, and looked at me, evidently inviting a guess.

"Well, I should guess you to be about five-and-fifty."

He laughed, and took a pinch of snuff, and said:

"I'm that, your honour, and something to the back of it. I was seventy last Candlemas. You would not a' thought that, to look at me."

"Upon my word I should not; I can hardly believe it even now. Still, you don't remember Sir Dominick Sarsfield's death?" I said, glancing up at the ominous stain on the wall.

"No, sir, that was a long while before I was born. But my grandfather was butler here long ago, and many a time I heard tell how Sir Dominick came by his death. There was no masther in the great house ever sinst that happened. But there was two sarvants in care of it, and my aunt was one o' them; and she kep' me here wid her till I was nine year old, and she was lavin' the place to go to Dublin; and from that time it was let to go down. The wind sthript the roof, and the rain rotted the timber, and little by little, in sixty years time, it kem to what you see. But I have a likin' for it still, for the sake of ould times; and I never come this way but I take a look in. I don't think it's many more times I'll be turnin' in to see the ould place, for I'll be undher the sod myself before long."

"You'll outlive younger people," I said. And, quitting that trite subject, I ran on: "I don't wonder that you like this old place; it is a beautiful spot, such noble trees."

"I wish ye seen the glin when the nuts is ripe; they're the sweetest nuts in all Ireland, I think," he rejoined, with a practical sense of the picturesque. "You'd fill your pockets while you'd be lookin' about you."

"These are very fine old woods," I remarked. "I have not seen any in Ireland I thought so beautiful."

"Eiah! your honour, the woods about here is nothing to what they wor. All the mountains along here was wood when my father was a gossoon, and Murroa Wood was the grandest of them all. All oak mostly, and all cut down as bare as the road. Not one loft here that's fit to compare with them. Which way did your honour come hither—from Limerick?"

"No. Killaloe."

"Well, then, you passed the ground where Murroa Wood was in former times. You kem undher Lisnavourra, the steep knob of a hill about a mile above the village here. 'Twas near that Murroa Wood was, and 'twas there Sir Dominick Sarsfield first met the devil, the Lord between us and harm, and a bad meeting it was for him and his."

I had become interested in the adventure which had occurred in the very scenery which had so greatly attracted me, and my new acquaintance, the little hunchback, was easily entreated to tell me the story, and spoke thus, so soon as we had each resumed his seat:

It was a fine estate when Sir Dominick came into it; and grand doings there was entirely, feasting and fiddling, free quarters for all the pipers in the counthry round, and a welcome for every one that liked to come. There was wine, by the hogshead, for the quality; and potteen enough to set a town a-fire, and beer and cidher enough to float a navy, for the boys and girls, and the likes o' me. It was kep' up the best part of a month, till the weather broke, and the rain spoilt the sod for the moneen jigs, and the fair of Allybally Killudeen comin' on they wor obliged to give over their divarsion, and attind to the pigs.

But Sir Dominick was only beginnin' when they wor lavin' off. There was no way of gettin' rid of his money and estates he did not try—what with drinkin', dicin', racin', cards, and all soarts, it was not many years before the estates wor in debt, and Sir Dominick a distressed man. He shewed a bold front to the world as long as he could; and then he sould off his dogs, and most of the horses, and gev out he was going to thravel in France, and the like; and so off with him for awhile; and no one in these parts heard tale or tidings of him for two or three years. Till at last quite unexpected, one night there comes a rapping at the big kitchen window. It was past ten o'clock, and old Connor Hanlon, the butler, my grandfather, was sittin' by the fire alone, warming his shins over it. There was a keen cast wind blowing along the mountains that night, and whistling cowld enough, through the tops of the trees, and soundin' lonesome through the long chimneys.

(And the story-teller glanced up at the nearest stack visible from his seat.)

So he wasn't quite sure of the knockin' at the window, and up he gets, and sees his master's face.

My grandfather was glad to see him safe, for it was a long time since there was any news of him; but he was sorry, too, for it was a changed place, and only himself and old Juggy Broadrick in charge of the house, and a man in the stables, and it was a poor thing to see him comin' back to his own like that.

He shook Con by the hand, and says he:

"I came here to say a word to you. I left my horse with Dick in the stable; I may want him again before morning, or I may never want him."

And with that he turns into the big kitchen, and draws a stool, and sits down to take an air of the fire.

"Sit down, Connor, opposite me, and listen to what I tell you, and don't be afeard to say what you think."

He spoke all the time lookin' into the fire, with his hands stretched over it, and a tired man he looked.

"An' why should I be afeard, Masther Dominick?" says my grandfather. "Yourself was a good masther to me, and so was your father, rest his soul, before you, and I'll say the truth, and dar' the devil, and more than that, for any Sarsfield of Dunoran, much less yourself, and a good right I'd have."

"It's all over with me, Con," says Sir Dominick.

"Heaven forbid!" says my grandfather.

"'Tis past praying for," says Sir Dominick. "The last guinea's gone; the ould place will follow it. It must be sold, and I'm come here, I don't know why, like a ghost, to have a last look round me, and go off in the dark again."

And with that he tould him to be sure, in case he should hear of his death, to give the oak box, in the closet off his room, to his cousin, Pat Sarsfield, in Dublin, and the sword and pistols his grandfather carried at Aughrim, and two or three thrifling things of the kind.

And says he, "Con, they say if the divil gives you money overnight, you'll find nothing but a bagful of pebbles, and chips, and nutshells, in the morning. If I thought he played fair, I'm in the humour to make a bargain with him to-night."

"Lord forbid!" says my grandfather, standing up, with a start, and crossing himself.

"They say the country's full of men, listin' sogers for the King o' France. If I light on one o' them, I'll not refuse his offer. How contrary things goes! How long is it since me and Captain Waller fought the jewel at New Castle?"

"Six years, Masther Dominick, and ye broke his thigh with the bullet the first shot."

"I did, Con," says he, "and I wish, instead, he had shot me through the heart. Have you any whisky?"

My grandfather took it out of the buffet, and the masther pours out some into a bowl, and drank it off.

"I'll go out and have a look at my horse," says he, standing up. There was a sort of a stare in his eyes, as he pulled his riding-cloak about him, as if there was something bad in his thoughts.

"Sure, I'won't be a minute runnin' out myself to the stable, and looking after the horse for you myself," says my grandfather.

"I'm not goin' to the stable," says Sir Dominick; "I may as well tell you, for I see you found it out already—I'm goin' across the deer-park; if I come back you'll see me in an hour's time. But, anyhow, you'd better not follow me, for if you do I'll shoot you, and that 'id be a bad ending to our friendship."

And with that he walks down this passage here, and turns the key in the side door at that end of it, and out wid him on the sod into the moonlight and the cowld wind; and my grandfather seen him walkin' hard towards the park-wall, and then he comes in and closes the door with a heavy heart.

Sir Dominick stopped to think when he got to the middle of the deer-park, for he had not made np his mind when he left the house, and the whisky did not clear his head, only it gev him courage.

He did not feel the cowld wind now, nor fear death, nor think much of anything but the shame and fall of the old family.

And he made up his mind, if no better thought came to him between that and there, so soon as he came to Murroa Wood, he'd hang himself from one of the oak branches with his cravat.

It was a bright moonlight night, there was just a bit of a cloud driving across the moon now and then, but, only for that, as light a'most as day.

Down he goes, right for the wood of Murroa. It seemed to him every step he took was as long as three, and it was no time till he was among the big oak-trees with their roots spreading from one to another, and their branches stretching overhead like the timbers of a naked roof, and the moon shining down through them, and casting their shadows thick and twisted abroad on the ground as black as my shoe.

He was sobering a bit by this time, and he slacked his pace, and he thought 'twould be better to list in the French king's army, and thry what that might do for him, for he knew a man might take his own life any time, but it would puzzle him to take it back again when he liked.

Just as he made up his mind not to make away with himself, what should he hear but a step clinkin' along the dry ground under the trees, and soon he sees a grand gentleman right before him comin' up to meet him.

He was a handsome young man like himself, and he wore a cocked-hat with gold-lace round it, such as officers wears on their coats, and he had on a dress the same as French officers wore in them times.

He stopped opposite Sir Dominick, and *he* cum to a standstill also.

The two gentlemen took off their hats to one another, and says the stranger:

"I am recruiting, sir," says he, "for my sovereign, and you'll find my money won't turn into pebbles, chips, and nutshells, by to-morrow."

At the same time he pulls out a big purse full of gold.

The minute he set eyes on that gentleman, Sir Dominick had his own opinion of him; and at those words he felt the very hair standing up on his head.

"Don't be afraid," says he, "the money won't burn you. If it proves honest gold, and if it prospers with you, I'm willing to make a bargain. This is the last day of February," says he; "I'll serve you seven years, and at the end of that time you shall serve me, and I'll come for you when the seven years is over, when the clock turns the minute between February and March; and the first of March ye'll come away with me, or never. You'll not find me a bad master, any more than a bad servant. I love my own; and I command all the pleasures and the glory of the world. The bargain dates from this day, and the lease is out at midnight on the last day I told you; and in the year"—he told him the year, it was easy reckoned, but I forget it—"and if you'd rather wait," he says, "for eight months and twenty-eight days, before you sign the writin', you may, if you meet me here. But I can't do a great deal for you in the mean time; and if you don't sign then, all you get from me, up to that time, will vanish away, and you'll be just as you are to-night, and ready to hang yourself on the first tree you meet."

Well, the end of it was, Sir Dominick chose to wait, and he came back to the house with a big bag full of money, as round as your hat a'most.

My grandfather was glad enough, you may be sure, to see the master safe and sound again so soon. Into the kitchen he bangs again, and swings the bag o' money on the table; and he stands up straight, and heaves up his shoulders like a man that has just got shut of a load; and he looks at the bag, and my grandfather looks at him, and from him to it, and back again. Sir Dominick looked as white as a sheet, and says he:

"I don't know, Con, what's in it: it's the heaviest load I ever carried."

He seemed shy of openin' the bag; and he made my grandfather heap up a roaring fire of turf and wood, and then, at last, he opens it, and, sure enough, 'twas stuffed full o' golden guineas, bright and new, as if they were only that minute out o' the Mint.

Sir Dominick made my grandfather sit at his elbow while he counted every guinea in the bag.

When he was done countin', and it wasn't far from daylight when that time came, Sir Dominick made my grandfather swear not to tell a word about it. And a close secret it was for many a day after.

When the eight months and twenty-eight days were pretty near spent and ended, Sir Dominick returned to the house here with a troubled mind, in doubt what was best to be done, and no one alive but my grandfather knew anything about the matter, and he not half what had happened.

As the day drew near, towards the end of October, Sir Dominick grew only more and more troubled in mind.

One time he made up his mind to have no more to say to such things, nor to speak again with the like of them he met with in the wood of Murroa. Then, again, his heart failed him when he thought of his debts, and he not knowing where to turn. Then, only a week before the day, everything began to go wrong with him. One man wrote from London to say that Sir Dominick paid three thousand pounds to the wrong man, and must pay it over again; another demanded a debt he never heard of before; and another, in Dublin, denied the payment of a tundherin' big bill, and Sir Dominick could nowhere find the receipt, and so on, wid fifty other things as bad.

Well, by the time the night of the 28th of October came round, he was a'most ready to lose his senses with all the demands that was risin' up again him on all sides, and nothing to meet them but the help of the one dhreadful friend he had to depind on at night in the oak-wood down there below.

So there was nothing for it but to go through with the business that was begun already, and about the same hour as he went last, he takes off the little crucifix he wore round his neck, for he was a Catholic, and his gospel, and his bit o' the thrue cross that he had in a locket, for since he took the money from the Evil One he was growin' frightful in himself, and got all he could to guard him from the power of the devil. But to-night, for his life, he daren't take them with him. So he gives them into my grandfather's hands without a word, only he looked as white as a sheet o' paper; and he takes his hat and sword, and telling my grandfather to watch for him, away he goes, to try what would come of it.

It was a fine still night, and the moon—not so bright, though, now as the first time—was shinin' over heath and rock, and down on the lonesome oak-wood below him.

His heart beat thick as he drew near it. There was not a sound, not even the distant bark of a dog from the village behind him. There was not a lonesomer spot in the country round, and if it wasn't for his debts and losses that was drivin' him on half mad, in spite of his fears for his soul and his hopes of paradise, and all his good angel was whisperin' in his ear, he would a' turned back, and sent for his clargy, and made his confession and his penance, and changed his ways, and led a good life, for he was frightened enough to have done a great dale.

Softer and slower he stept as he got, once more, in undher the big branches of the old oak-threes; and when he got in a bit, near where he met with the bad spirit before, he stopped and looked round him, and felt himself, every bit, turning as cowld as a dead man, and you may be sure he did not feel much betther when he seen the same man steppin' from behind the big tree that was touchin' his elbow a'most.

"You found the money good," says he, "but it was not enough. No matter, you shall have enough and to spare. I'll see after your luck, and I'll give you a hint whenever it can serve you; and any time you want to see me you have only to come down here, and call my face to mind, and wish me present. You shan't owe a shilling by the end of the year, and you shall never miss the right card, the best throw, and the winning horse. Are you willing?"

The young gentleman's voice almost stuck in his throat, and his hair was rising on his head, but he did get out a word or two to signify that he consented; and with that the Evil One handed him a needle, and bid him give him three drops of blood from his arm; and he took them in the cup of an acorn, and gave him a pen, and bid him write some words that ho repeated, and that Sir Dominick did not understand, on two thin slips of parchment. He took one himself, and the other he sunk in Sir Dominiek's arm at the place where he drew the blood, and he closed the flesh over it. And that's as true as you're sittin' there!

Well, Sir Dominick went home. He was a frightened man, and well he might be. But in a little time he began to grow aisier in his mind. Anyhow, he got out of debt very quick, and money came tumbling in to make him richer, and everything he took in hand prospered, and he never made a wager, or played a game, but he won; and for all that, there was not a poor man on the estate that was not happier than Sir Dominick.

So he took again to his old ways: for, when the money came back, all came back, and there was hounds and horses, and wine galore, and no end of company, and grand doin's, and divarsion, up here at the great house. And some said Sir Dominick was thinkin' of gettin' married; and more said he wasn't. But, anyhow, there was somethin' throublin' him more than common, and so one night, unknownst to all, away he goes to the lonesome oakwood. It was something, maybe, my grandfather thought was troublin' him about a beautiful young lady he was jealous of, and mad in love with her. But that was only guess.

Well, when Sir Dominick got into the wood this time, he grew more in dread than ever; and he was on the point of turnin' and lavin' the place, when who should he see, close beside him, but my gentleman, seated on a big stone undher one of the trees. In place of looking the fine young gentleman in goold lace and grand clothes he appeared before, he was now in rags, he looked twice the size he had been, and his face smutted with soot, and he had a murtherin' big steel hammer, as heavy as a half-hundred, with a handle a yard long, across his knees. It was so dark under the tree, he did not see him quite clear for some time.

He stood up, and he looked awful tall entirely. And what passed between them in that discourse my grandfather never heered. But Sir Dominick was as black as night afterwards, and hadn't a laugh for anything nor a word a'most for any one, and he only grew worse and worse, and darker and darker. And now this thing, whatever it was, used to come to him of its own accord, whether he wanted it or no; sometimes in one shape, and sometimes in another, in lonesome places, and sometimes at his side by night when he'd be ridin' home alone, until at last he lost heart altogether and sent for the priest.

The priest was with him a long time, and when he heered the whole story, he rode off all the way for the bishop, and the bishop came here to the great house next day, and he gev Sir Dominick a good advice. He toult him he must give over dicin', and swearin', and drinkin', and all bad company, and live a vartuous steady life until the seven years' bargain was out, and if the divil didn't come for him the minute afther the stroke of twelve the first mornin' of the month of March, he was safe out of the bargain. There was not more than eight or ten months to run now before the seven years wor out, and he lived all the time according to the bishop's advice, as strict as if he was "in retreat."

Well, you may guess he felt quare enough when the mornin' of the 28th of February came.

The priest came up by appointment, and Sir Dominick and his raverence wor together in the room you see there, and kep' up their prayers together till the clock struck twelve, and a good hour after, and not a sign of a disturbance, nor nothing came near them, and the priest slep' that night in the house in the room next Sir Dominick's, and all went over as comfortable as could be, and they shook hands and kissed like two comrades after whining a battle.

So, now, Sir Dominick thought he might as well have a pleasant evening, after all his fastin' and praying; and he sent round to half a dozen of the neighbouring gentlemen to come and dine with him, and his raverence stayed and dined also, and a roarin' bowl o' punch they had, and no end o' wine, and the swearin' and dice, and cards, and guineas changing hands, and songs and stories, that wouldn't do any one good to hear, and the good priest slipped away, when he seen the turn things was takin', and it was not far from the stroke of twelve when Sir Dominick, sitting at the head of his table, swears, "this is the best first of March I ever sat down with my friends."

"It ain't the first o' March," says Mr. Hiffernan of Ballyvoreen. He was a scholard, and always kep' an almanack.

"What is it, then?" says Sir Dominick, startin' up, and dhroppin' the ladle into the bowl, and starin' at him as if he had two heads.

"'Tis the twenty-ninth of February, leap year," says he.

And just as they were talkin', the clock strikes twelve; and my grandfather, who was half asleep in a chair by the fire in the hall, openin' his eyes, sees a short square fellow, with a cloak on, and long black hair bushin' out from under his hat, standin' just there where you see the bit o' light shinin' again' the wall.

(My hunchbacked friend pointed with his stick to a little patch of red sunset light that relieved the deepening shadow of the passage.)

"Tell your master," says he, in an awful voice, like the growl of a baist, "that I'm here by appointment, and expect him down-stairs this minute."

Up goes my grandfather, by these very steps you are sittin' on.

"Tell him I can't come down yet," says Sir Dominick, and he turns to the company in the room, and says he, with a cold sweat shinin' on his face, "for God's sake, gentlemen, will any of you jump from the window, and bring the priest here?" One looked at another, and no one knew what to make of it, and in the mean time, up comes my grandfather again, and says he, tremblin', "He says, sir, unless you go down to him, he'll come up to you."

"I don't understand this, gentlemen, I'll see what it means," says Sir Dominick, trying to put a face on it, and walkin' out o' the room like a man through the press-room, with the hangman waitin' for him outside. Down the stairs he comes, and two or three of the gentlemen peeping over the banisters, to see. My grandfather was walking six or eight steps behind him, and he seen the stranger take a stride out to meet Sir Dominick, and catch him up in his arms, and whirl his head against the wall, and wi' that the hall-doore flies open, and out goes the candles, and the turf and wood-ashes flyin' with the wind out o' the hall-fire, ran in a drift o' sparks along the floore by his feet.

Down runs the gintlemen. Bang goes the hall-doore. Some comes runnin' up, and more runnin' down, with lights. It was all over with Sir Dominick. They lifted up the corpse, and put its shoulders again' the wall; but there was not a gasp left in him. He was cowld and stiffenin' already.

Pat Donovan was comin' up to the great house late that night, and after he passed the little brook, that the carriage track up to the house crosses, and about fifty steps to this side of it, his dog, that was by his side, makes a sudden wheel, and springs over the wall, and sets up a yowlin' inside you'd hear a mile away; and that minute two men passed him by in silence, goin' down from the house, one of them short and square, and the other like Sir Dominick in shape, but there was little light under the trees where he was, and they looked only like shadows; and as they passed him by he could not hear the sound of their feet, and he drew back to the wall frightened; and when he got up to the great house, he found all in confusion, and the master's body, with the head smashed to pieces, lying just on *that spot*.

The narrator stood up and indicated with the point of his stick the exact site of the body, and, as I looked, the shadow deepened, the red stain of sunlight vanished from the wall, and the sun had gone down behind the distant hill of New Castle, leaving the haunted scene in the deep grey of darkening twilight.

So I and the story-teller parted, not without good wishes on both sides, and a little "tip," which seemed not unwelcome, from me.

It was dusk and the moon up by the time I reached the village, remounted my nag, and looked my last on the scene of the terrible legend of Dunoran.

WAS IT A DREAM?

GUY DE MAUPASSANT

In the macabre stories of French writer Guy de Maupassant (1850–1893), it is often hard to distinguish genuine supernatural experience from experiences colored by the emotional duress or madness of their narrators. This devastating tales of horror was first published in 1887.

I had loved her madly!

"Why does one love? Why does one love? How queer it is to see only one being in the world, to have only one thought in one's mind, only one desire in the heart, and only one name on the lips—a name which comes up continually, rising, like the water in a spring, from the depths of the soul to the lips, a name which one repeats over and over again, which one whispers ceaselessly, everywhere, like a prayer.

"I am going to tell you our story, for love only has one, which is always the same. I met her and loved her; that is all. And for a whole year I had lived on her tenderness, on her caresses, in her arms, in her dresses, on her words, so completely wrapped up, bound, and absorbed in everything which came from her, that I no longer cared whether it was day or night, or whether I was dead or alive, on this old earth of ours.

"And then she died. How? I do not know; I no longer know anything. But one evening she came home wet, for it was raining heavily, and the next day she coughed, and she coughed for about a week, and took to her bed. What happened I do not remember now, but doctors came, wrote, and went away. Medicines were brought, and some women made her drink them. Her hands were hot, her fore-head was burning, and her eyes bright and sad. When I spoke to her, she answered me, but I do not remember what she said. I have forgotten everything, everything,

everything! She died, and I very well remember her slight, feeble sigh. The nurse said:'Ah!' and I understood, I understood!

"I knew nothing more, nothing. I saw a priest, who said: 'Your mistress?' and it seemed to me as if he were insulting her. As she was dead, nobody had the right to say that any longer, and I turned him out. Another came who was very kind and tender, and I shed tears when he spoke to me about her.

"They consulted me about the funeral, but I do not remember anything that they said, though I recollect the coffin, and the sound of the hammer when they nailed her down in it. Oh! God, God!

"She was buried! Buried! She! In that hole! Some people came—female friends. I made my escape and ran away. I ran, and then walked through the streets, went home, and the next day started on a journey.

★ ★ ★

"Yesterday I returned to Paris, and when I saw my room again—our room, our bed, our furniture, everything that remains of the life of a human being after death—I was seized by such a violent attack of fresh grief, that I felt like opening the window and throwing myself out into the street. I could not remain any longer among these things, between those walls which had inclosed and sheltered her, which retained a thousand atoms of her, of her skin and of her breath in their imperceptible crevices. I took up my hat to make my escape, and just as I reached the door, I passed the large glass in the hall, which she had put there so that she might look at herself every day from head to foot as she went out, to see if her toilette looked well, and was correct and pretty, from her little boots to her bonnet.

"I stopped short in front of that looking-glass in which she had so often been reflected—so often, so often, that it must have retained her reflection. I was standing there, trembling, with my eyes fixed on the glass—on that flat, profound, empty glass—which had contained her entirely, and had possessed her as much as I, as my passionate looks had. I felt as if I loved that glass. I touched it; it was cold. Oh! the recollection! sorrowful mirror, burning mirror, horrible mirror, to make men suffer such torments! Happy is the man whose heart forgets everything that it has contained, everything that has passed before it, everything that has looked at itself in it, or has been reflected in its affection, in its love! How I suffer!

"I went out without knowing it, without wishing it, and toward the cemetery. I found her simple grave, a white marble cross, with these few words:

"'She loved, was loved, and died.'

"She is there, below, decayed! How horrible! I sobbed with my forehead on the ground and I stopped there for a long time, a long time. Then I saw that it was getting dark, and a strange, mad wish, the wish of a despairing lover, seized me. I wished to pass the night, the last night, in weeping on her grave. But I should be seen and driven out. How was I to manage? I was cunning, and got up and began to roam about in that city of the dead. I walked and walked. How small this city is, in comparison with the other, the city in which we live. And yet, how much more umerous the dead are than the living. We want high houses, wide streets and much room for the four generations who see the daylight at the same time, drink water from the spring, and wine from the vines, and eat bread from the plains.

"And for all the generations of the dead, for all that ladder of humanity that has descended to us here, there is scarcely anything, scarcely anything! The earth takes them back, and oblivion effaces them. Adieu!

"At the end of the cemetery, I suddenly perceived that I was in its oldest part, where those who had been dead a long time are mingling with the soil, where the crosses themselves are decayed, where possibly newcomers will be put to-morrow. It is full of untended roses, of strong and dark cypress-trees, a sad and beautiful garden, nourished on human flesh.

"I was alone, perfectly alone. So I crouched in a green tree and hid myself there completely amid the thick and somber branches. I waited, clinging to the stem, as a shipwrecked man clings to a plank.

"When it was quite dark, I left my refuge and began to walk softly, slowly, inaudibly, through that ground full of dead people. I wandered about for a long time, but could not find her tomb again. I went on with extended arms, knocking against the tombs with my hands, my feet, my knees, my chest, even with my head, without being able to find her. I groped about like a blind man finding his way; I felt the stones, the crosses, the iron railings, the metal wreaths, and the wreaths of faded flowers! I read the names with my fingers, by passing them over the letters. What a night! What a night! I could not find her again!

"There was no moon! What a night! 1 was frightened, horribly frightened in these narrow paths, between two rows of graves. Graves! graves! graves! nothing but graves! On my right, on my left, in front of me, around me, everywhere there were graves! I sat down on one of them, for I could not walk any longer, my knees were so weak. I could hear by heart beat! And I heard something else as well. What? A confused, nameless noise. Was the noise in my head, in the impenetrable night, or beneath the mysterious earth, the earth sown with human corpses? I looked all around me, but I cannot say how long I remained there; I was paralyzed with terror, cold with fright, ready to shout out, ready to die.

"Suddenly, it seemed to me that the slab of marble on which I was sitting was moving. Certainly it was moving, as if it were being raised. With a bound, I sprang upon the neighboring tomb, and I saw, yes, I distinctly saw the stone which I had just quitted rise upright. Then the dead person appeared, a naked skeleton, pushing the stone back with its bent back. I saw it quite clearly, although the night was so dark. On the cross I could read:

"'Here lies Jacques Olivant, who died at the age of fifty-one. He loved his family, was kind and honorable, and died in the grace of the Lord.'

"The dead man also read what was inscribed on his tombstone; then he picked up a stone off the path, a little, pointed stone, and began to scrape the letters carefully. He slowly effaced them, and with the hollows of his eyes he looked at the places where they had been engraved. Then, with the tip of the bone that had been his forefinger, he wrote in luminous letters, like those lines which boys trace on walls with the tip of a lucifer match:

"'Here reposes Jacques Olivant, who died at the age of fifty-one. He hastened his father's death by his unkindness, as he wished to inherit his fortune; he tortured his wife, tormented his children, deceived his neighbors, robbed everyone he could, and died wretched.'

"When he had finished writing, the dead man stood motionless, looking at his work. On turning round I saw that all the graves were open, that all the dead bodies had emerged from them, and that all had effaced the lies inscribed on the gravestones by their relations, substituting the truth instead. And I saw that all had been the tormentors of their neighbors—malicious, dishonest, hypocrites, liars, rogues, calumniators, envious; that they had stolen, deceived, performed every disgraceful, every abominable action, these good fathers, these faithful wives, these devoted sons, these chaste daughters, these honest tradesmen, these men and women who were called irreproachable. They were all writing at the same time, on the threshold of their eternal abode, the truth, the terrible and the holy truth of which everybody was ignorant, or pretended to be ignorant, while they were alive. "I thought that she also must have written something on her tombstone, and now running without any fear among the half-open coffins, among the corpses and skeletons, I went toward her, sure that I should find her immediately. I recognized her at once, without seeing her face, which was covered by the winding-sheet, and on the marble cross, where shortly before I had read:

"'She loved, was loved, and died.'

I now saw:

"'Having gone out in the rain one day, in order to deceive her lover, she caught cold and died.'

★ ★ ★

"It appears that they found me at daybreak, lying on the grave unconscious."

MAN-SIZE IN MARBLE

E. NESBIT

BEFORE SHE WROTE *FIVE CHILDREN AND IT, THE RAILWAY CHILDREN,* AND OTHER CLASSICS OF CHILDREN'S LITERATURE, ENGLISH AUTHOR EDITH NESBIT (1858-1924) WROTE SEVERAL COLLECTIONS OF MACABRE TALES FOR ADULT READERS, INCLUDING *GRIM TALES,* WHERE THIS STORY APPEARED IN 1893. SET ON HALLOWEEN, IT FEATURES A UNIQUE HORROR FROM ENGLAND'S HISTORICAL PAST.

Although every word of this story is as true as despair, I do not expect people to believe it. Nowadays a "rational explanation" is required before belief is possible. Let me then, at once, offer the "rational explanation" which finds most favour among those who have heard the tale of my life's tragedy. It is held that we were "under a delusion," Laura and I, on that 31st of October; and that this supposition places the whole matter on a satisfactory and believable basis. The reader can judge, when he, too, has heard my story, how far this is an "explanation," and in what sense it is "rational." There were three who took part in this: Laura and I and another man. The other man still lives, and can speak to the truth of the least credible part of my story.

★ ★ ★

I never in my life knew what it was to have as much money as I required to supply the most ordinary needs—good colours, books, and cab-fares—and when we were married we knew quite well that we should only be able to live at all by "strict punctuality and attention to business." I used to paint in those days, and Laura used to write, and we felt sure we could keep the pot at least simmering. Living in town was out of the question, so we went to look for a cottage in the country, which should be at once sanitary and picturesque. So rarely do these two qualities meet in one cottage that our search was for some time quite fruitless. We tried advertisements, but most of the desirable rural residences which we did look at proved to be lacking in both essentials, and when a cottage chanced to have drains it always had stucco as well and was shaped like a tea-caddy. And if we found a vine or rose-covered porch, corruption invariably lurked within. Our minds got so befogged by the eloquence of house-agents and the rival disadvantages of the fever-traps and outrages to beauty which we had seen and scorned, that I very much doubt whether either of us, on our wedding morning, knew the difference between a house and a haystack. But when we got away from friends and house-agents, on our honeymoon, our wits grew clear again, and we knew a pretty cottage when at last we saw one. It was at Brenzett—a little village set on a hill over against the southern marshes. We had gone there, from the seaside village where we were staying, to see the church, and two fields from the church we found this cottage. It stood quite by itself, about two miles from the village. It was a long, low building, with rooms sticking out in unexpected places. There was a bit of stone-work—ivy-covered and moss-grown, just two old rooms, all that was left of a big house that had once stood there—and round this stone-work the house had grown up. Stripped of its roses and jasmine it would have been hideous. As it stood it was charming, and after a brief examination we took it. It was absurdly cheap. The rest of our honeymoon we spent in grubbing about in second-hand shops in the county town, picking up bits of old oak and Chippendale chairs for our furnishing. We wound up with a run up to town and a visit to Liberty's, and soon the low oak-beamed lattice-windowed rooms began to be home. There was a jolly old-fashioned garden, with grass paths, and no end of hollyhocks and sunflowers, and big lilies. From the window you could see the marsh-pastures, and beyond them the blue, thin line of the sea. We were as happy as the summer was glorious, and settled down into work sooner than we ourselves expected. I was never tired of sketching the view and the wonderful cloud effects from the open lattice, and Laura would sit at the table and write verses about them, in which I mostly played the part of foreground.

We got a tall old peasant woman to do for us. Her face and figure were good, though her cooking was of the homeliest; but she understood all about gardening, and told us all the old names of the coppices and cornfields, and the stories of the smugglers and highwaymen, and, better still, of the "things that walked," and of the "sights" which met one in lonely glens of a starlight night. She was a great comfort to us, because Laura hated housekeeping as much as I loved folklore, and we soon came to leave all the domestic business to Mrs. Dorman, and to use her legends in little magazine stories which brought in the jingling guinea.

We had three months of married happiness, and did not have a single quarrel. One October evening I had been down to smoke a pipe with the doctor—our only neighbour—a pleasant young Irishman. Laura had stayed at home to finish a comic sketch of a village episode for the *Monthly Marplot*. I left her laughing over her own jokes, and came in to find her a crumpled heap of pale muslin weeping on the window seat.

"Good heavens, my darling, what's the matter?" I cried, taking her in my arms. She leaned her little dark head against my shoulder and went on crying. I had never seen her cry before—we had always been so happy, you see—and I felt sure some frightful misfortune had happened.

"What is the matter? Do speak."

"It's Mrs. Dorman," she sobbed.

"What has she done?" I inquired, immensely relieved.

"She says she must go before the end of the month, and she says her niece is ill; she's gone down to see her now, but I don't believe that's the reason, because her niece is always ill. I believe someone has been setting her against us. Her manner was so queer—"

"Never mind, Pussy," I said; "whatever you do, don't cry, or I shall have to cry too, to keep you in countenance, and then you'll never respect your man again!"

She dried her eyes obediently on my handkerchief, and even smiled faintly.

"But you see," she went on, "it is really serious, because these village people are so sheepy, and if one won't do a thing you may be quite sure none of the others will. And I shall have to cook the dinners, and wash up the hateful greasy plates; and you'll have to carry cans of water about, and clean the boots and knives—and we shall never have any time for work, or earn any money, or anything. We shall have to work all day, and only be able to rest when we are witing for the kettle to boil!"

I represented to her that even if we had to perform these duties, the day would still present some margin for other toils and recreations. But she refused to see the matter in any but the greyest light. She was very unreasonable, my Laura, but I could not have loved her any more if she had been as reasonable as Whately.

"I'll speak to Mrs. Dorman when she comes back, and see if I can't come to terms with her," I said. "Perhaps she wants a rise in her screw. It will be all right. Let's walk up to the church."

The church was a large and lonely one, and we loved to go there, especially upon bright nights. The path skirted a wood, cut through it once, and ran along the crest of the hill through two meadows, and round the churchyard wall, over which the old yews loomed in black masses of shadow. This path, which was partly paved, was called "the bier-balk," for it had long been the way by which the corpses had been carried to burial. The churchyard was richly treed, and was shaded by great elms which stood just outside and stretched their majestic arms in benediction over the happy dead. A large, low porch let one into the building by a Norman doorway and a heavy oak door studded with iron. Inside, the arches rose into darkness, and between them the reticulated windows, which stood out white in the moonlight. In the chancel, the windows were of rich glass, which showed in faint light their noble colouring, and made the black oak of the choir pews hardly more solid than the shadows. But on each side of the altar lay a grey marble figure of a knight in full plate armour lying upon a low slab, with hands held up in everlasting prayer, and these figures, oddly enough, were always to be seen if there was any glimmer of light in the church. Their names were lost, but the peasants told of them that they had been fierce and wicked men, marauders by land and sea, who had been the scourge of their time, and had been guilty of deeds so foul that the house they had lived in—the big house, by the way, that had stood on the site of our cottage—had been stricken by lightning and the vengeance of Heaven. But for all that, the gold of their heirs had bought them a place in the church. Looking at the bad hard faces reproduced in the marble, this story was easily believed.

The church looked at its best and weirdest on that night, for the shadows of the yew trees fell through the windows upon the floor of the nave and touched the pillars with tattered shade. We sat down together without speaking, and watched the solemn beauty of the old church, with some of that awe which inspired its early builders. We walked to the chancel and looked at the sleeping warriors. Then we rested some time on the stone seat in the porch, looking out over the stretch of quiet moonlit meadows, feeling in every fibre of our being the peace of the night and of our happy love; and came away at last with a sense that even scrubbing and blackleading were but small troubles at their worst.

Mrs. Dorman had come back from the village, and I at once invited her to a *tête-à-tête*.

"Now, Mrs. Dorman," I said, when I had got her into my painting room, "what's all this about your not staying with us?"

"I should be glad to get away, sir, before the end of the month," she answered, with her usual placid dignity.

"Have you any fault to find, Mrs. Dorman?"

"None at all, sir; you and your lady have always been most kind, I'm sure—"

"Well, what is it? Are your wages not high enough?"

"No, sir, I gets quite enough."

"Then why not stay?"

"I'd rather not"—with some hesitation—"my niece is ill."

"But your niece has been ill ever since we came."

No answer. There was a long and awkward silence. I broke it.

"Can't you stay for another month?" I asked.

"No, sir. I'm bound to go by Thursday."

And this was Monday!

"Well, I must say, I think you might have let us know before. There's no time now to get any one else, and your mistress is not fit to do heavy housework. Can't you stay till next week?"

"I might be able to come back next week."

I was now convinced that all she wanted was a brief holiday, which we should have been willing enough to let her have, as soon as we could get a substitute.

"But why must you go this week?" I persisted. "Come, out with it."

Mrs. Dorman drew the little shawl, which she always wore, tightly across her bosom, as though she were cold. Then she said, with a sort of effort—

"They say, sir, as this was a big house in Catholic times, and there was a many deeds done here."

The nature of the "deeds" might be vaguely inferred from the inflection of Mrs. Dorman's voice—which was enough to make one's blood run cold. I was glad that Laura was not in the room. She was always nervous, as highly-strung natures are, and I felt that these tales about our house, told by this old peasant woman, with her impressive manner and contagious credulity, might have made our home less dear to my wife.

"Tell me all about it, Mrs. Dorman," I said; "you needn't mind about telling me. I'm not like the young people who make fun of such things."

Which was partly true.

"Well, sir"—she sank her voice—"you may have seen in the church, beside the altar, two shapes."

"You mean the effigies of the knights in armour," I said cheerfully.

"I mean them two bodies, drawed out man-size in marble," she returned, and I had to admit that her description was a thousand times more graphic than mine, to say nothing of a certain weird force and uncanniness about the phrase "drawed out man-size in marble."

"They do say, as on All Saints' Eve them two bodies sits up on their slabs, and gets off of them, and then walks down the aisle, *in their marble*"—(another good phrase, Mrs. Dorman)—"and as the church clock strikes eleven they walks out of the church door, and over the graves, and along the bier-balk, and if it's a wet night there's the marks of their feet in the morning."

"And where do they go?" I asked, rather fascinated.

"They comes back here to their home, sir, and if any one meets them—"

"Well, what then?" I asked.

But no—not another word could I get from her, save that her niece was ill and she must go. After what I had heard I scorned to discuss the niece, and tried to get from Mrs. Dorman more details of the legend. I could get nothing but warnings.

"Whatever you do, sir, lock the door early on All Saints' Eve, and make the cross-sign over the doorstep and on the windows."

"But has any one ever seen these things?" I persisted.

"That's not for me to say. I know what I know, sir."

"Well, who was here last year?"

"No one, sir; the lady as owned the house only stayed here in summer, and she always went to London a full month afore the night. And I'm sorry to inconvenience you and your lady, but my niece is ill and I must go on Thursday."

I could have shaken her for her absurd reiteration of that obvious fiction, after she had told me her real reasons.

She was determined to go, nor could our united entreaties move her in the least.

I did not tell Laura the legend of the shapes that "walked in their marble," partly because a legend concerning our house might perhaps trouble my wife, and partly, I think, from some more occult reason. This was not quite the same to me as any other story, and I did not want to talk about it till the day was over. I had very soon ceased to think of the legend, however. I was painting a portrait of Laura, against the lattice window, and I could not think of much else. I had got a splendid background of yellow and grey sunset, and was working away with enthusiasm at her lace. On Thursday Mrs. Dorman went. She relented, at parting, so far as to say—

"Don't you put yourself about too much, ma'am, and if there's any little thing I can do next week, I'm sure I shan't mind."

From which I inferred that she wished to come back to us after Hallowe'en. Up to the last she adhered to the fiction of the niece with touching fidelity.

Thursday passed off pretty well. Laura showed marked ability in the matter of steak and potatoes, and I confess that my knives, and the plates, which I insisted upon washing, were better done than I had dared to expect.

Friday came. It is about what happened on that Friday that this is written. I wonder if I should have believed it, if any one had told it to me. I will write the story of it as quickly and plainly as I can. Everything that happened on that day is burnt into my brain. I shall not forget anything, nor leave anything out.

I got up early, I remember, and lighted the kitchen fire, and had just achieved a smoky success, when my little wife came running down, as sunny and sweet as the clear October morning itself. We prepared breakfast together, and found it very good fun. The housework was soon done, and when brushes and brooms and pails were quiet again, the house was still indeed. It is wonderful what a difference one makes in a house. We really missed Mrs. Dorman, quite apart from considerations concerning pots and pans. We spent the day in dusting our books and putting them straight, and dined gaily on cold steak and coffee. Laura was, if possible, brighter and gayer and sweeter than usual, and I began to think that a little domestic toil was really good for her. We had never been so merry since we were married, and the walk we had that afternoon was, I think, the happiest time of all my life. When we had watched the deep scarlet clouds slowly pale into leaden grey against a pale-green sky, and saw the white mists curl up along the hedgerows in the distant marsh, we came back to the house, silently, hand in hand.

"You are sad, my darling," I said, half-jestingly, as we sat down together in our little parlour. I expected a disclaimer, for my own silence had been the silence of complete happiness. To my surprise she said—

"Yes. I think I am sad, or rather I am uneasy. I don't think I'm very well. I have shivered three or four times since we came in, and it is not cold, is it?"

"No," I said, and hoped it was not a chill caught from the treacherous mists that roll up from the marshes in the dying light. No—she said, she did not think so. Then, after a silence, she spoke suddenly—

"Do you ever have presentiments of evil?"

"No," I said, smiling, "and I shouldn't believe in them if I had."

"I do," she went on; "the night my father died I knew it, though he was right away in the north of Scotland." I did not answer in words.

She sat looking at the fire for some time in silence, gently stroking my hand. At last she sprang up, came behind me, and, drawing my head back, kissed me.

"There, it's over now," she said. "What a baby I am! Come, light the candles, and we'll have some of these new Rubinstein duets."

And we spent a happy hour or two at the piano.

At about half-past ten I began to long for the good-night pipe, but Laura looked so white that I felt it would be brutal of me to fill our sitting-room with the fumes of strong cavendish.

"I'll take my pipe outside," I said.

"Let me come, too."

"No, sweetheart, not to-night; you're much too tired. I shan't be long. Get to bed, or I shall have an invalid to nurse to-morrow as well as the boots to clean."

I kissed her and was turning to go, when she flung her arms round my neck, and held me as if she would never let me go again. I stroked her hair.

"Come, Pussy, you're over-tired. The housework has been too much for you."

She loosened her clasp a little and drew a deep breath.

"No. We've been very happy to-day, Jack, haven't we? Don't stay out too long."

"I won't, my dearie."

I strolled out of the front door, leaving it unlatched. What a night it was! The jagged masses of heavy dark cloud were rolling at intervals from horizon to horizon, and thin white wreaths covered the stars. Through all the rush of the cloud river, the moon swam, breasting the waves and disappearing again in the darkness. When now and again her light reached the woodlands they seemed to be slowly and noiselessly waving in time to the swing of the clouds above them. There was a strange grey light over all the earth; the fields had that shadowy bloom over them which only comes from the marriage of dew and moonshine, or frost and starlight.

I walked up and down, drinking in the beauty of the quiet earth and the changing sky. The night was absolutely silent. Nothing seemed to be abroad. There was no scurrying of rabbits, or twitter of the half-asleep birds. And though the clouds went sailing across the sky, the wind that drove them never came low enough to rustle the dead leaves in the woodland paths. Across the meadows I could see the church tower standing out black and grey against the sky. I walked there thinking over our three months of happiness—and of my wife, her dear eyes, her loving ways. Oh, my little girl! my own little girl; what a vision came then of a long, glad life for you and me together!

I heard a bell-beat from the church. Eleven already! I turned to go in, but the night held me. I could not go back into our little warm rooms yet. I would go up to the church. I felt vaguely that it would be good to carry my love and thankfulness to the sanctuary whither so many loads of sorrow and gladness had been borne by the men and women of the dead years.

I looked in at the low window as I went by. Laura was half lying on her chair in front of the fire. I could not see her face, only her little head showed dark against the pale blue wall. She was quite still. Asleep, no doubt. My heart reached out to her, as I went on. There must be a God, I thought, and a God who was good. How otherwise could anything so sweet and dear as she have ever been imagined?

I walked slowly along the edge of the wood. A sound broke the stillness of the night, it was a rustling in the wood. I stopped and listened. The sound stopped too. I went on, and now distinctly heard another step than mine answer mine like an echo. It was a poacher or a wood-stealer, most likely, for these were not unknown in our Arcadian neighbourhood. But whoever it was, he was a fool not to step more lightly. I turned into the wood, and now the footstep seemed to come from the path I had just left. It must be an echo, I thought. The wood looked perfect in the moonlight. The large dying ferns and the brushwood showed where through thinning foliage the pale light came down. The tree trunks stood up like Gothic columns all around me. They reminded me of the church, and I turned into the bier-balk, and passed through the corpse-gate between the graves to the low porch. I paused for a moment on the stone seat where Laura and I had watched the fading landscape. Then I noticed that the door of the church was open, and I blamed myself for having left it unlatched the other night. We were the only people who ever cared to come to the church except on Sundays, and I was vexed to think that through our carelessness the damp autumn airs had had a chance of getting in and injuring the old fabric. I went in. It will seem strange, perhaps, that I should have gone half-way up the aisle before I remembered—with a sudden chill, followed by as sudden a rush of self-contempt—that this was the very day and hour when, according to tradition, the "shapes drawed out man-size in marble" began to walk.

Having thus remembered the legend, and remembered it with a shiver, of which I was ashamed, I could not do otherwise than walk up towards the altar, just to look at the figures—as I said to myself; really what I wanted was to assure myself, first, that I did not believe the legend, and, secondly, that it was not true. I was rather glad that I had come. I thought now I could tell Mrs. Dorman how vain her fancies were, and how peacefully the marble figures slept on through the ghastly hour. With my hands in my pockets I passed up the aisle. In the grey dim light the eastern end of the church looked larger than usual, and the arches above the two tombs looked larger too. The moon came out and showed me the reason. I stopped short, my heart gave a leap that nearly choked me, and then sank sickeningly.

The "bodies drawed out man-size" *were gone*, and their marble slabs lay wide and bare in the vague moonlight that slanted through the east window.

Were they really gone? or was I mad? Clenching my nerves, I stooped and passed my hand over the smooth slabs, and felt their flat unbroken surface. Had some one taken the things away? Was it some vile practical joke? I would make sure, anyway. In an instant I had made a torch of a newspaper, which happened to be in my pocket, and lighting it held it high above my head. Its yellow glare illumined the dark arches and those slabs. The figures were gone. And I was alone in the church; or was I alone?

And then a horror seized me, a horror indefinable and indescribable—an overwhelming certainty of supreme and accomplished calamity. I flung down the torch and tore along the aisle and out through the porch, biting my lips as I ran to keep myself from shrieking aloud. Oh, was I mad—or what was this that possessed me? I leaped the churchyard wall and took the straight cut across the fields, led by the light from our windows. Just as I got over the first stile, a dark figure seemed to spring out of the ground. Mad still with that certainty of misfortune, I made for the thing that stood in my path, shouting, "Get out of the way, can't you!"

But my push met with a more vigorous resistance than I had expected. My arms were caught just above the elbow and held as in a vice, and the raw-boned Irish doctor actually shook me.

"Would ye?" he cried, in his own unmistakable accents—"would ye, then?"

"Let me go, you fool," I gasped. "The marble figures have gone from the church; I tell you they've gone."

He broke into a ringing laugh. "I'll have to give ye a draught to-morrow, I see. Ye've bin smoking too much and listening to old wives' tales."

"I tell you, I've seen the bare slabs."

"Well, come back with me. I'm going up to old Palmer's—his daughter's ill; we'll look in at the church and let me see the bare slabs."

"You go, if you like," I said, a little less frantic for his laughter; "I'm going home to my wife."

"Rubbish, man," said he; "d'ye think I'll permit of that? Are ye to go saying all yer life that ye've seen solid marble endowed with vitality, and me to go all me life saying ye were a coward? No, sir—ye shan't do ut!"

The night air—a human voice—and I think also the physical contact with this six feet of solid common sense, brought me back a little to my ordinary self, and the word "coward" was a mental shower-bath.

"Come on, then," I said sullenly; "perhaps you're right."

He still held my arm tightly. We got over the stile and back to the church. All was still as death. The place smelt very damp and earthy. We walked up the aisle. I am not ashamed to confess that I shut my eyes: I knew the figures would not be there. I heard Kelly strike a match.

"Here they are, ye see, right enough; ye've been dreaming or drinking, asking yer pardon for the imputation."

I opened my eyes. By Kelly's expiring vesta I saw two shapes lying "in their marble" on their slabs. I drew a deep breath, and caught his hand.

"I'm awfully indebted to you," I said. "It must have been some trick of light, or I have been working rather hard, perhaps that's it. Do you know, I was quite convinced they were gone."

"I'm aware of that," he answered rather grimly; "ye'll have to be careful of that brain of yours, my friend, I assure ye."

He was leaning over and looking at the right-hand figure, whose stony face was the most villainous and deadly in expression.

"By Jove," he said, "something has been afoot here—this hand is broken."

And so it was. I was certain that it had been perfect the last time Laura and I had been there.

"Perhaps some one has *tried* to remove them," said the young doctor.

"That won't account for my impression," I objected.

"Too much painting and tobacco will account for that, well enough."

"Come along," I said, "or my wife will be getting anxious. You'll come in and have a drop of whisky and drink confusion to ghosts and better sense to me."

"I ought to go up to Palmer's, but it's so late now I'd best leave it till the morning," he replied. "I was kept late at the Union, and I've had to see a lot of people since. All right, I'll come back with ye."

I think he fancied I needed him more than did Palmer's girl, so, discussing how such an illusion could have been possible, and deducing from this experience large generalities concerning ghostly apparitions, we walked up to our cottage. We saw, as we walked up the garden-path, that bright light streamed out of the front door, and presently saw that the parlour door was open too. Had she gone out?

"Come in," I said, and Dr. Kelly followed me into the parlour. It was all ablaze with candles, not only the wax ones, but at least a dozen guttering, glaring tallow dips, stuck in vases and ornaments in unlikely places. Light, I knew, was Laura's remedy for nervousness. Poor child! Why had I left her? Brute that I was.

We glanced round the room, and at first we did not see her. The window was open, and the draught set all the candles flaring one way. Her chair was empty and her handkerchief and book lay on the floor. I turned to the window. There, in the recess of the window, I saw her. Oh, my child, my love, had she gone to that window to watch for me? And what had come into the room behind her? To what had she turned with that look of frantic fear and horror? Oh, my little one, had she thought that it was I whose step she heard, and turned to meet—what?

She had fallen back across a table in the window, and her body lay half on it and half on the window-seat, and her head hung down over the table, the brown hair loosened and fallen to the carpet. Her lips were drawn back, and her eyes wide, wide open. They saw nothing now. What had they seen last?

The doctor moved towards her, but I pushed him aside and sprang to her; caught her in my arms and cried—

"It's all right, Laura! I've got you safe, dear."

She fell into my arms in a heap. I clasped her and kissed her, and called her by all her pet names, but I think I knew all the time that she was dead. Her hands were tightly clenched. In one of them she held something fast. When I was quite sure that she was dead, and that nothing mattered at all any more, I let him open her hand to see what she held.

It was a grey marble finger.

THE DEATH OF
HALPIN FRAYSER

AMBROSE BIERCE

A JOURNALIST AND CRITIC BY PROFESSION, AMBROSE BIERCE
(1842–1914?) WAS RENOWNED FOR HIS SARDONIC SENSIBILITY,
WHICH INTENSIFIED THE HORRORS OF HIS STORIES OF THE
SUPERNATURAL AND GAVE A SHARP DRAMATIC EDGE TO HIS
TALES OF THE CIVIL WAR. THIS STORY, WHICH WAS FIRST
PUBLISHED IN THE DECEMBER 19, 1891 ISSUE OF *THE WAVE,*
IS ONE OF BIERCE'S MORE UNCOMMON TALES OF THE MACABRE,
SHOWING AN AMBIGUOUS APPROACH TO ITS HORRORS THAT
SEEMS APPROPRIATE FOR ITS BLEND OF DREAMS AND REALITY.

I

For by death is wrought greater change than hath been shown. Whereas in
general the spirit that removed cometh back upon occasion, and is sometimes seen of those in flesh (appearing in the form of the body it bore) yet
it hath happened that the veritable body without the spirit hath walked.
And it is attested of those encountering who have lived to speak thereon
that a lich so raised up hath no natural affection, nor remembrance thereof,
but only hate. Also, it is known that some spirits which in life were benign
become by death evil altogether.—*Hali.*

One dark night in midsummer a man waking from a dreamless sleep in a forest
lifted his head from the earth, and staring a few moments into the blackness,
said: "Catherine Larue." He said nothing more; no reason was known to him why
he should have said so much.

The man was Halpin Frayser. He lived in St. Helena, but where he lives now is uncertain, for he is dead. One who practices sleeping in the woods with nothing under him but the dry leaves and the damp earth, and nothing over him but the branches from which the leaves have fallen and the sky from which the earth has fallen, cannot hope for great longevity, and Frayser had already attained the age of thirty-two. There are persons in this world, millions of persons, and far and away the best persons, who regard that as a very advanced age. They are the children. To those who view the voyage of life from the port of departure the bark that has accomplished any considerable distance appears already in close approach to the farther shore. However, it is not certain that Halpin Frayser came to his death by exposure.

He had been all day in the hills west of the Napa Valley, looking for doves and such small game as was in season. Late in the afternoon it had come on to be cloudy, and he had lost his bearings; and although he had only to go always downhill— everywhere the way to safety when one is lost—the absence of trails had so impeded him that he was overtaken by night while still in the forest. Unable in the darkness to penetrate the thickets of manzanita and other undergrowth, utterly bewildered and overcome with fatigue, he had lain down near the root of a large madrono and fallen into a dreamless sleep. It was hours later, in the very middle of the night, that one of God's mysterious messengers, gliding ahead of the incalculable host of his companions sweeping westward with the dawn line, pronounced the awakening word in the ear of the sleeper, who sat upright and spoke, he knew not why, a name, he knew not whose.

Halpin Frayser was not much of a philosopher, nor a scientist. The circumstance that, waking from a deep sleep at night in the midst of a forest, he had spoken aloud a name that he had not in memory and hardly had in mind did not arouse an enlightened curiosity to investigate the phenomenon. He thought it odd, and with a little perfunctory shiver, as if in deference to a seasonal presumption that the night was chill, he lay down again and went to sleep. But his sleep was no longer dreamless.

He thought he was walking along a dusty road that showed white in the gathering darkness of a summer night. Whence and whither it led, and why he traveled it, he did not know, though all seemed simple and natural, as is the way in dreams; for in the Land Beyond the Bed surprises cease from troubling and the judgment is at rest. Soon he came to a parting of the ways; leading from the highway was a road less traveled, having the appearance, indeed, of having been long abandoned, because, he thought, it led to something evil; yet he turned into it without hesitation, impelled by some imperious necessity.

As he pressed forward he became conscious that his way was haunted by invisible existences whom he could not definitely figure to his mind. From among the trees on either side he caught broken and incoherent whispers in a strange tongue which yet he partly understood. They seemed to him fragmentary utterances of a monstrous conspiracy against his body and soul.

It was now long after nightfall, yet the interminable forest through which he journeyed was lit with a wan glimmer having no point of diffusion, for in its mysterious lumination nothing cast a shadow. A shallow pool in the guttered depression of an old wheel rut, as from a recent rain, met his eye with a crimson gleam. He stooped and plunged his hand into it. It stained his fingers; it was blood! Blood, he then observed, was about him everywhere. The weeds growing rankly by the roadside showed it in blots and splashes on their big, broad leaves. Patches of dry dust between the wheelways were pitted and spattered as with a red rain. Defiling the trunks of the trees were broad maculations of crimson, and blood dripped like dew from their foliage.

All this he observed with a terror which seemed not incompatible with the fulfillment of a natural expectation. It seemed to him that it was all in expiation of some crime which, though conscious of his guilt, he could not rightly remember. To the menaces and mysteries of his surroundings the consciousness was an added horror. Vainly he sought by tracing life backward in memory, to reproduce the moment of his sin; scenes and incidents came crowding tumultuously into his mind, one picture effacing another, or commingling with it in confusion and obscurity, but nowhere could he catch a glimpse of what he sought. The failure augmented his terror; he felt as one who has murdered in the dark, not knowing whom nor why. So frightful was the situation—the mysterious light burned with so silent and awful a menace; the noxious plants, the trees that by common consent are invested with a melancholy or baleful character, so openly in his sight conspired against his peace; from overhead and all about came so audible and startling whispers and the sighs of creatures so obviously not of earth—that he could endure it no longer, and with a great effort to break some malign spell that bound his faculties to silence and inaction, he shouted with the full strength of his lungs! His voice broken, it seemed, into an infinite multitude of unfamiliar sounds, went babbling and stammering away into the distant reaches of the forest, died into silence, and all was as before. But he had made a beginning at resistance and was encouraged. He said:

"I will not submit unheard. There may be powers that are not malignant traveling this accursed road. I shall leave them a record and an appeal. I shall relate my wrongs, the persecutions that I endure—I, a helpless mortal, a penitent, an unoffending poet!" Halpin Frayser was a poet only as he was a penitent: in his dream.

Taking from his clothing a small red-leather pocketbook, one-half of which was leaved for memoranda, he discovered that he was without a pencil. He broke a twig from a bush, dipped it into a pool of blood and wrote rapidly. He had hardly touched the paper with the point of his twig when a low, wild peal of laughter broke out at a measureless distance away, and growing ever louder, seemed approaching ever nearer; a soulless, heartless, and unjoyous laugh, like that of the loon, solitary by the lakeside at midnight; a laugh which culminated in an unearthly shout close at hand, then died away by slow gradations, as if the accursed being that uttered it had withdrawn over the verge of the world whence it had come. But the man felt that this was not so—that it was near by and had not moved.

A strange sensation began slowly to take possession of his body and his mind. He could not have said which, if any, of his senses was affected; he felt it rather as a consciousness—a mysterious mental assurance of some overpowering presence—some supernatural malevolence different in kind from the invisible existences that swarmed about him, and superior to them in power. He knew that it had uttered that hideous laugh. And now it seemed to be approaching him; from what direction he did not know—dared not conjecture. All his former fears were forgotten or merged in the gigantic terror that now held him in thrall. Apart from that, he had but one thought: to complete his written appeal to the benign powers who, traversing the haunted wood, might some time rescue him if he should be denied the blessing of annihilation. He wrote with terrible rapidity, the twig in his fingers rilling blood without renewal; but in the middle of a sentence his hands denied their service to his will, his arms fell to his sides, the book to the earth; and powerless to move or cry out, he found himself staring into the sharply drawn face and blank, dead eyes of his own mother, standing white and silent in the garments of the grave!

II

In his youth Halpin Frayser had lived with his parents in Nashville, Tennessee. The Fraysers were well-to-do, having a good position in such society as had survived the wreck wrought by civil war. Their children had the social and educational opportunities of their time and place, and had responded to good associations and instruction with agreeable manners and cultivated minds. Halpin being the youngest and not over robust was perhaps a trifle "spoiled." He had the double disadvantage of a mother's assiduity and a father's neglect. Frayser *père* was what no Southern man of means is not—a politician. His country, or rather his section and State, made demands upon his time and attention so exacting that to those of his family he was compelled to turn an ear partly deafened by the thunder of the political captains and the shouting, his own included.

Young Halpin was of a dreamy, indolent and rather romantic turn, somewhat more addicted to literature than law, the profession to which he was bred. Among those of his relations who professed the modern faith of heredity it was well understood that in him the character of the late Myron Bayne, a maternal great-grandfather, had revisited the glimpses of the moon—by which orb Bayne had in his lifetime been sufficiently affected to be a poet of no small Colonial distinction. If not specially observed, it was observable that while a Frayser who was not the proud possessor of a sumptuous copy of the ancestral "poetical works" (printed at the family expense, and long ago withdrawn from an inhospitable market) was a rare Frayser indeed, there was an illogical indisposition to honor the great deceased in the person of his spiritual successor. Halpin was pretty generally deprecated as an intellectual black sheep who was likely at any moment to disgrace the flock by bleating in meter. The Tennessee Fraysers were a practical folk—not practical in the popular sense of devotion to sordid pursuits, but having a robust contempt for any qualities unfitting a man for the wholesome vocation of politics.

In justice to young Halpin it should be said that while in him were pretty faithfully reproduced most of the mental and moral characteristics ascribed by history and family tradition to the famous Colonial bard, his succession to the gift and faculty divine was purely inferential. Not only had he never been known to court the muse, but in truth he could not have written correctly a line of verse to save himself from the Killer of the Wise. Still, there was no knowing when the dormant faculty might wake and smite the lyre.

In the meantime the young man was rather a loose fish, anyhow. Between him and his mother was the most perfect sympathy, for secretly the lady was herself a devout disciple of the late and great Myron Bayne, though with the tact so generally and justly admired in her sex (despite the hardy calumniators who insist that it is essentially the same thing as cunning) she had always taken care to conceal her weakness from all eyes but those of him who shared it. Their common guilt in respect of that was an added tie between them. If in Halpin's youth his mother had "spoiled" him, he had assuredly done his part toward being spoiled. As he grew to such manhood as is attainable by a Southerner who does not care which way elections go the attachment between him and his beautiful mother—whom from early childhood he had called Katy—became yearly stronger and more tender. In these two romantic natures was manifest in a signal way that neglected phenomenon, the dominance of the sexual element in all the relations of life, strengthening, softening, and beautifying even those of consanguinity. The two were nearly inseparable, and by strangers observing their manner were not infrequently mistaken for lovers.

Entering his mother's boudoir one day Halpin Frayser kissed her upon the forehead, toyed for a moment with a lock of her dark hair which had escaped from its confining pins, and said, with an obvious effort at calmness:

"Would you greatly mind, Katy, if I were called away to California for a few weeks?"

It was hardly needful for Katy to answer with her lips a question to which her telltale cheeks had made instant reply. Evidently she would greatly mind; and the tears, too, sprang into her large brown eyes as corroborative testimony.

"Ah, my son," she said, looking up into his face with infinite tenderness, "I should have known that this was coming. Did I not lie awake a half of the night weeping because, during the other half, Grandfather Bayne had come to me in a dream, and standing by his portrait—young, too, and handsome as that—pointed to yours on the same wall? And when I looked it seemed that I could not see the features; you had been painted with a face cloth, such as we put upon the dead. Your father has laughed at me, but you and I, dear, know that such things are not for nothing. And I saw below the edge of the cloth the marks of hands on your throat—forgive me, but we have not been used to keep such things from each other. Perhaps you have another interpretation. Perhaps it does not mean that you will go to California. Or maybe you will take me with you?"

It must be confessed that this ingenious interpretation of the dream in the light of newly discovered evidence did not wholly commend itself to the son's more logical mind; he had, for the moment at least, a conviction that it foreshadowed a more simple and immediate, if less tragic, disaster than a visit to the Pacific Coast. It was Halpin Frayser's impression that he was to be garroted on his native heath.

"Are there not medicinal springs in California?" Mrs. Frayser resumed before he had time to give her the true reading of the dream—"places where one recovers from rheumatism and neuralgia? Look—my fingers feel so stiff; and I am almost sure they have been giving me great pain while I slept."

She held out her hands for his inspection. What diagnosis of her case the young man may have thought it best to conceal with a smile the historian is unable to state, but for himself he feels bound to say that fingers looking less stiff, and showing fewer evidences of even insensible pain, have seldom been submitted for medical inspection by even the fairest patient desiring a prescription of unfamiliar scenes.

The outcome of it was that of these two odd persons having equally odd notions of duty, the one went to California, as the interest of his client required, and the other remained at home in compliance with a wish that her husband was scarcely conscious of entertaining.

While in San Francisco Halpin Frayser was walking one dark night along the water front of the city, when, with a suddenness that surprised and disconcerted him, he became a sailor. He was in fact "shanghaied" aboard a gallant, gallant ship, and sailed for a far countree. Nor did his misfortunes end with the voyage; for the ship was cast ashore on an island of the South Pacific, and it was six years afterward when the survivors were taken off by a venturesome trading schooner and brought back to San Francisco.

Though poor in purse, Frayser was no less proud in spirit than he had been in the years that seemed ages and ages ago. He would accept no assistance from strangers, and it was while living with a fellow survivor near the town of St. Helena, awaiting news and remittances from home, that he had gone gunning and dreaming.

III

The apparition confronting the dreamer in the haunted wood—the thing so like, yet so unlike his mother—was horrible! It stirred no love nor longing in his heart; it came unattended with pleasant memories of a golden past—inspired no sentiment of any kind; all the finer emotions were swallowed up in fear. He tried to turn and run from before it, but his legs were as lead; he was unable to lift his feet from the ground. His arms hung helpless at his sides; of his eyes only he retained control, and these he dared not remove from the lusterless orbs of the apparition, which he knew was not a soul without a body, but that most dreadful of all existences infesting that haunted wood—a body without a soul! In its blank stare was neither love, nor pity, nor intelligence—nothing to which to address an appeal for mercy. "An appeal will not lie," he thought, with an absurd reversion to professional slang, making the situation more horrible, as the fire of a cigar might light up a tomb.

For a time, which seemed so long that the world grew gray with age and sin, and the haunted forest, having fulfilled its purpose in this monstrous culmination of its terrors, vanished out of his consciousness with all its sights and sounds, the apparition stood within a pace, regarding him with the mindless malevolence of a wild brute; then thrust its hands forward and sprang upon him with appalling ferocity! The act released his physical energies without unfettering his will; his mind was still spellbound, but his powerful body and agile limbs, endowed with a blind, insensate life of their own, resisted stoutly and well. For an instant he seemed to see this unnatural contest between a dead intelligence and a breathing mechanism only as a spectator—such fancies are in dreams; then he regained his identity almost as if by a leap forward into his body, and the straining automaton had a directing will as alert and fierce as that of its hideous antagonist.

But what mortal can cope with a creature of his dream? The imagination creating the enemy is already vanquished; the combat's result is the combat's cause. Despite his struggles—despite his strength and activity, which seemed wasted in a void, he felt the cold fingers close upon his throat. Borne backward to the earth, he saw above him the dead and drawn face within a hand's breadth of his own, and then all was black. A sound as of the beating of distant drums—a murmur of swarming voices, a sharp, far cry signing all to silence, and Halpin Frayser dreamed that he was dead.

IV

A warm, clear night had been followed by a morning of drenching fog. At about the middle of the afternoon of the preceding day a little whiff of light vapor—a mere thickening of the atmosphere, the ghost of a cloud—had been observed clinging to the western side of Mount St. Helena, away up along the barren altitudes near the summit. It was so thin, so diaphanous, so like a fancy made visible, that one would have said: "Look quickly! in a moment it will be gone."

In a moment it was visibly larger and denser. While with one edge it clung to the mountain, with the other it reached farther and farther out into the air above the lower slopes. At the same time it extended itself to north and south, joining small patches of mist that appeared to come out of the mountainside on exactly the same level, with an intelligent design to be absorbed. And so it grew and grew until the summit was shut out of view from the valley, and over the valley itself was an ever-extending canopy, opaque and gray. At Calistoga, which lies near the head of the valley and the foot of the mountain, there were a starless night and a sunless morning. The fog, sinking into the valley, had reached southward, swallowing up ranch after ranch, until it had blotted out the town of St. Helena, nine miles away. The dust in the road was laid; trees were adrip with moisture; birds sat silent in their coverts; the morning light was wan and ghastly, with neither color nor fire.

Two men left the town of St. Helena at the first glimmer of dawn, and walked along the road northward up the valley toward Calistoga. They carried guns on their shoulders, yet no one having knowledge of such matters could have mistaken them for hunters of bird or beast. They were a deputy sheriff from Napa and a detective from San Francisco—Holker and Jaralson, respectively. Their business was man-hunting.

"How far is it?" inquired Holker, as they strode along, their feet stirring white the dust beneath the damp surface of the road.

"The White Church? Only a half mile farther," the other answered. "By the way," he added, "it is neither white nor a church; it is an abandoned schoolhouse, gray with age and neglect. Religious services were once held in it—when it was white, and there is a graveyard that would delight a poet. Can you guess why I sent for you, and told you to come heeled?"

"Oh, I never have bothered you about things of that kind. I've always found you communicative when the time came. But if I may hazard a guess, you want me to help you arrest one of the corpses in the graveyard."

"You remember Branscom?" said Jaralson, treating his companion's wit with the inattention that it deserved.

"The chap who cut his wife's throat? I ought; I wasted a week's work on him and had my expenses for my trouble. There is a reward of five hundred dollars, but none of us ever got a sight of him. You don't mean to say—"

"Yes, I do. He has been under the noses of you fellows all the time. He comes by night to the old graveyard at the White Church."

"The devil! That's where they buried his wife."

"Well, you fellows might have had sense enough to suspect that he would return to her grave some time."

"The very last place that anyone would have expected him to return to."

"But you had exhausted all the other places. Learning your failure at them, I 'laid for him' there."

"And you found him?"

"Damn it! he found *me*. The rascal got the drop on me—regularly held me up and made me travel. It's God's mercy that he didn't go through me. Oh, he's a good one, and I fancy the half of that reward is enough for me if you're needy."

Holker laughed good humoredly, and explained that his creditors were never more importunate.

"I wanted merely to show you the ground, and arrange a plan with you," the detective explained. "I thought it as well for us to be heeled, even in daylight."

"The man must be insane," said the deputy sheriff. "The reward is for his capture and conviction. If he's mad he won't be convicted."

Mr. Holker was so profoundly affected by that possible failure of justice that he involuntarily stopped in the middle of the road, then resumed his walk with abated zeal.

"Well, he looks it," assented Jaralson. "I'm bound to admit that a more unshaven, unshorn, unkempt, and uneverything wretch I never saw outside the ancient and honorable order of tramps. But I've gone in for him, and can't make up my mind to let go. There's glory in it for us, anyhow. Not another soul knows that he is this side of the Mountains of the Moon."

70

"All right," Holker said; "we will go and view the ground," and he added, in the words of a once favorite inscription for tombstones: " 'where you must shortly lie'—I mean, if old Branscom ever gets tired of you and your impertinent intrusion. By the way, I heard the other day that 'Branscom' was not his real name."

"What is?"

"I can't recall it. I had lost all interest in the wretch, and it did not fix itself in my memory—something like Pardee. The woman whose throat he had the bad taste to cut was a widow when he met her. She had come to California to look up some relatives—there are persons who will do that sometimes. But you know all that."

"Naturally."

"But not knowing the right name, by what happy inspiration did you find the right grave? The man who told me what the name was said it had been cut on the headboard."

"I don't know the right grave." Jaralson was apparently a trifle reluctant to admit his ignorance of so important a point of his plan. "I have been watching about the place generally. A part of our work this morning will be to identify that grave. Here is the White Church."

For a long distance the road had been bordered by fields on both sides, but now on the left there was a forest of oaks, madronos, and gigantic spruces whose lower parts only could be seen, dim and ghostly in the fog. The undergrowth was, in places, thick, but nowhere impenetrable. For some moments Holker saw nothing of the building, but as they turned into the woods it revealed itself in faint gray outline through the fog, looking huge and far away. A few steps more, and it was within an arm's length, distinct, dark with moisture, and insignificant in size. It had the usual country-schoolhouse form—belonged to the packing-box order of architecture; had an underpinning of stones, a moss-grown roof, and blank window spaces, whence both glass and sash had long departed. It was ruined, but not a ruin—a typical Californian substitute for what are known to guide-bookers abroad as "monuments of the past." With scarcely a glance at this uninteresting structure Jaralson moved on into the dripping undergrowth beyond.

"I will show you where he held me up," he said. "This is the graveyard."

Here and there among the bushes were small inclosures containing graves, sometimes no more than one. They were recognized as graves by the discolored stones or rotting boards at head and foot, leaning at all angles, some prostrate; by the ruined picket fences surrounding them; or, infrequently, by the mound itself showing its gravel through the fallen leaves. In many instances nothing marked the spot where lay the vestiges of some poor mortal—who, leaving "a large circle of sorrowing

friends," had been left by them in turn—except a depression in the earth, more last-
ing than that in the spirits of the mourners. The paths, if any paths had been, were
long obliterated; trees of a considerable size had been permitted to grow up from the
graves and thrust aside with root or branch the inclosing fences. Over all was that
air of abandonment and decay which seems nowhere so fit and significant as in a
village of the forgotten dead.

As the two men, Jaralson leading, pushed their way through the growth of young
trees, that enterprising man suddenly stopped and brought up his shotgun to the
height of his breast, uttered a low note of warning, and stood motionless, his eyes
fixed upon something ahead. As well as he could, obstructed by brush, his companion,
though seeing nothing, imitated the posture and so stood, prepared for what might
ensue. A moment later Jaralson moved cautiously forward, the other following.

Under the branches of an enormous spruce lay the dead body of a man. Standing
silent above it they noted such particulars as first strike the attention—the face, the
attitude, the clothing; whatever most promptly and plainly answers the unspoken
question of a sympathetic curiosity.

The body lay upon its back, the legs wide apart. One arm was thrust upward, the
other outward; but the latter was bent acutely, and the hand was near the throat. Both
hands were tightly clenched. The whole attitude was that of desperate but ineffectual
resistance to—what?

Near by lay a shotgun and a game bag through the meshes of which was seen the
plumage of shot birds. All about were evidences of a furious struggle; small sprouts
of poison-oak were bent and denuded of leaf and bark; dead and rotting leaves had
been pushed into heaps and ridges on both sides of the legs by the action of other
feet than theirs; alongside the hips were unmistakable impressions of human knees.

The nature of the struggle was made clear by a glance at the dead man's throat
and face. While breast and hands were white, those were purple—almost black. The
shoulders lay upon a low mound, and the head was turned back at an angle otherwise impossible, the expanded eyes staring blankly backward in a direction opposite
to that of the feet. From the froth filling the open mouth the tongue protruded,
black and swollen. The throat showed horrible contusions; not mere finger-marks,
but bruises and lacerations wrought by two strong hands that must have buried
themselves in the yielding flesh, maintaining their terrible grasp until long after
death. Breast, throat, face, were wet; the clothing was saturated; drops of water, con-
densed from the fog, studded the hair and mustache.

All this the two men observed without speaking—almost at a glance. Then
Holker said:

"Poor devil! he had a rough deal."

Jaralson was making a vigilant circumspection of the forest, his shotgun held in both hands and at full cock, his finger upon the trigger.

"The work of a maniac," he said, without withdrawing his eyes from the inclosing wood. "It was done by Branscom—Pardee."

Something half hidden by the disturbed leaves on the earth caught Holker's attention. It was a red-leather pocketbook. He picked it up and opened it. It contained leaves of white paper for memoranda, and upon the first leaf was the name "Halpin Frayser." Written in red on several succeeding leaves—scrawled as if in haste and barely legible—were the following lines, which Holker read aloud, while his companion continued scanning the dim gray confines of their narrow world and hearing matter of apprehension in the drip of water from every burdened branch:

> "Enthralled by some mysterious spell, I stood
> In the lit gloom of an enchanted wood.
> The cypress there and myrtle twined their boughs,
> Significant, in baleful brotherhood.
>
> "The brooding willow whispered to the yew;
> Beneath, the deadly nightshade and the rue,
> With immortelles self-woven into strange
> Funereal shapes, and horrid nettles grew.
>
> "No song of bird nor any drone of bees,
> Nor light leaf lifted by the wholesome breeze:
> The air was stagnant all, and Silence was
> A living thing that breathed among the trees.
>
> "Conspiring spirits whispered in the gloom,
> Half-heard, the stilly secrets of the tomb.
> With blood the trees were all adrip; the leaves
> Shone in the witch-light with a ruddy bloom.
>
> "I cried aloud!—the spell, unbroken still,
> Rested upon my spirit and my will.
> Unsouled, unhearted, hopeless and forlorn,
> I strove with monstrous presages of ill!
>
> "At last the viewless—"

Holker ceased reading; there was no more to read. The manuscript broke off in the middle of a line.

"That sounds like Bayne," said Jaralson, who was something of a scholar in his way. He had abated his vigilance and stood looking down at the body.

"Who's Bayne?" Holker asked rather incuriously.

"Myron Bayne, a chap who flourished in the early years of the nation—more than a century ago. Wrote mighty dismal stuff; I have his collected works. That poem is not among them, but it must have been omitted by mistake."

"It is cold," said Holker; "let us leave here; we must have up the coroner from Napa."

Jaralson said nothing, but made a movement in compliance. Passing the end of the slight elevation of earth upon which the dead man's head and shoulders lay, his foot struck some hard substance under the rotting forest leaves, and he took the trouble to kick it into view. It was a fallen headboard, and painted on it were the hardly decipherable words, "Catharine Larue."

"Larue, Larue!" exclaimed Holker, with sudden animation. "Why, that is the real name of Branscom—not Pardee. And—bless my soul! how it all comes to me—the murdered woman's name had been Frayser!"

"There is some rascally mystery here," said Detective Jaralson. "I hate anything of that kind."

There came to them out of the fog—seemingly from a great distance—the sound of a laugh, a low, deliberate, soulless laugh, which had no more of joy than that of a hyena night-prowling in the desert; a laugh that rose by slow gradation, louder and louder, clearer, more distinct and terrible, until it seemed barely outside the narrow circle of their vision; a laugh so unnatural, so unhuman, so devilish, that it filled those hardy man-hunters with a sense of dread unspeakable! They did not move their weapons nor think of them; the menace of that horrible sound was not of the kind to be met with arms. As it had grown out of silence, so now it died away; from a culminating shout which had seemed almost in their ears, it drew itself away into the distance, until its failing notes, joyless and mechanical to the last, sank to silence at a measureless remove.

HUGUENIN'S WIFE

M. P. SHIEL

Matthew Phipps Shiel (1865-1947), author of the classic apocalyptic science fiction novel *The Purple Cloud,* often wrote in a baroque, surreal style redolent with excesses common to the work of many writers during England's "yellow nineties." Shiel greatly admired the fiction of Edgar Allan Poe and this story, first published in the April 1895 issue of the *Pall Mall Magazine,* evokes the spirit of Poe's macabre masterpiece "The Fall of the House of Usher."

Huguenin, my friend—the man of Art and thrills and impulses,—the finished *boulevardier,* the *persifleur*—must, I concluded with certainty, be frenzied. So, at least, I reasoned when, after long years of silence, I received from him this letter:—

"'*Sdili,*' my friend; that is the name by which they now call this ancient Delos. Wherefore has it been written, 'so passeth the glory of the world.'

"Ah! but to me it is—as to *her* it was—still Delos, the Sacred Island, the birthplace of Apollo, son of Leto! On the summit of Cynthus I look from my dwelling, and within the wide reach of the Cyclades perceive even yet the fruity offerings arriving from Syria, from Sicily, from Egypt; I see the barks that bring the sacred envoys of Pan-Ionium to festival—I note the flutter of their hallowed garments—on the breeze once more floats to me their 'Songs of Deliverance.'

"The island now belongs almost entirely to me. I am, too, almost its sole inhabitant. It is, you know, only four miles long, and half as broad, and I have purchased every available foot of its surface. On the flat top of the granite Cynthus I live, and here, my friend, shall I die. Chains more inexorable and horrible than any which the limbs of Prometheus ever knew bind me to this crag.

"A friend! a friend! That is the thing after which my sick spirit pants. A *living man:* of the dead I have enough; of living monsters, ah, too much! An aged servant or two, who seem persistently to shun me—this is all I possess of human fellowship. Would that I dared to ask you, an old companion, to come to the solace of a sinking man in this place of desolation!"

The letter continued long in this strain of mingled rhapsody and despair, containing, moreover, a lengthy disquisition on the Pythagorean doctrine of the metempsychosis of the soul. Three times did the words "living monsters" occur. Such a communication, coming from *him,* did not fail to excite my utmost curiosity and pity.

From London to Delos is no inconsiderable journey; yet, conquered during the course of a long vacation by an irresistible impulse, and the fond memories of other days, I actually found myself, on a starry night, disembarking on the sands that bound the once famous harbour of the tiny Greek island. My arrival may be dated by the fact that it fell out just two months before the very extraordinary natural phenomena of which Delos was the scene during the night of August 13th, 1880. I crossed the ring of flat land which nearly encircles the islet, and began the ascent of the central mountain. The slumberous air languished with the wild breath of rose and jessamine and almond; the pipe of the cicala and the gleam of the firefly were not wanting to add to the narcotic charms of this land of dreams. In less than an hour I walked into a tangled garden, and placed my hand on the shoulder of a tall, stooping man, dressed in Attic attire, who walked solitary under the trees.

With a fearful start he turned and faced me.

"Oh," he said, panting, and placing both his hands upon his chest, "I was greatly surprised! My heart—"

He could utter no more. It was Huguenin, and yet not he. The heavy beard rolling down his white woollen garments was, I could see, still black as ever; but the masses of unkempt hair which floated with every zephyr about his face and neck were bleached to the whiteness of snow. He stared at me through the dull and cavernous eyes of a man long dead.

We walked into the house together. The mere sight of the building was enough to convince me that in some mysterious way, to some morbid degree, the Past had fettered and darkened the intellect of my friend. The mansion was of the purely Hellenic type, but nothing less than inconceivable in extent—a wilderness rather than a habitation. I found myself in an ancient Greek house—only, a Greek house multiplied many times over into an endless, continuous congeries of Greek houses. It consisted of a single story, though here and there on the vast flat roof there rose a second layer of apartments. These latter were reached by ladders. We walked through a door—opening inwards—into a passage, which in turn led us to an oblong marble court-yard; this was the *aule,* surrounded by Corinthian pillars, and having in the centre an altar of stone to *Zeus Herkeios.* Around this court on every hand was ranged a series of halls, chambers, *thalamoi,* hung with rich velvets; and the whole mighty house—made up of a hundred and a hundred reproductions of such court-yards with their surrounding chambers—formed a trackless desert of rooms, through whose uniform labyrinths the most cunning would assuredly fail to find his way.

"This building," said Huguenin to me, some days after my arrival, "this building—every stone, plank, drapery of it—was the creation of my wife's wild and restless fancy."

I stared at him.

"You doubt that I have, or had, a wife? Come, then, with me; you shall—you shall—see her face."

He led the way through the dark and windowless house, lighted throughout the day and night by the dim purple radiance shed from many small, open lamps of earthenware filled with the fragrant *nardinum,* an oil pressed from the flower of the Arabian grass *nardus.*

I followed the emaciated figure of Huguenin through a great number of the gloomy chambers. As he moved slowly forward, visibly panting, I noticed that he kept his form bent downward, seeming to seek for something; and this something I soon found to be a scarlet thread, laid down to afford guidance for the feet through the mazes of the house, and running along the black floor. Suddenly he stopped before the door of one of the apartments called *amphithalamoi,* and, himself remaining without, motioned to me to enter.

I am not a man of what might be called "a tremulous diathesis," yet not without a tremor did I glance round the room. For a time I could discern nothing under the sombre glimmer radiated from a single *lampas* pendent from wrought brazen chains. But at length a great painting in oils, unframed, occupying nearly one whole side of the chamber, grew upon my sight. It was the picture of a woman. My heart throbbed with a most strange, deep excitement as I gazed upon her lineaments.

She stood erect, robed in a flowing, crimson, embroidered *peplos,* with head slightly thrown back, and one hand and arm pointing stiffly outward and upward. The countenance was not merely Grecian—ancient Grecian, as distinct from modern—but it was so in a highly exaggerated and unlifelike degree. Was the woman, I asked myself, more lovely than ever mortal was before—or more hideous? She was the one or the other, or both; but the riddle baffled me. The Lamia of Keats arose before me—that "shape of gorgeous hue, vermilion-spotted, golden, green and blue." A hardly-breathing surprise of eyes held me fixed as the image slowly took possession of my vision. Here, then, I muttered, was the Gorgon's head, whose hair was serpents and her eye a basilisk's; and as I so thought, I reflected, too, on the myth of how from the dripping blood of Medusa's head strange creatures sprang to life; and then, with a shuddering abhorrence, I remembered Huguenin's childish ravings about "monsters." I drew nearer, in order to analyse the impression almost of dread wrought upon me, and I quickly found—or thought I found—the key. It lay, surely, in the woman's eyes. They were the very eyes of the tiger: circular, green, large, with glittering yellow radii. I hurried from the room.

"You have seen her?" asked Huguenin, with a cunning, eager distortion of his ashen face.

"Yes, Huguenin, I have seen her. She is very beautiful."

"She painted it herself," he said in a whisper.

"Really!"

"She considered herself—she *was*—the greatest painter who has lived since Apelles."

"But now—where is she now? "

He brought his lips quite close to my ear.

"She is dead. You, at any rate, would call her so."

This ambiguity appeared to me only the more singular when I discovered that it was his habit, at stated intervals, to make regular and stealthy visits to distant parts of the dwelling. Our bed-chambers being contiguous, I could not fail, as time passed, to notice that he would rise in the dead of night, when he supposed me asleep, and gathering together the fragments of our last meal, depart rapidly and silently with them through the dim and vast house, led always in one particular direction by the scarlet thread of silk which ran along the floor.

I now set myself strenuously to the study of Huguenin. The nature of his physical malady, at least, was clear. He laboured under the singular affection to which physicians have given the name of Cheyne Stoke's Respiration, the disease manifesting itself at intervals by compelling him to lie back in a perfect agony of inhalation, and groan for air; the bones of his cheeks seemed on the point of appearing through their sere wrapping of mummy-skin; the *alæ* of his nose never rested from an extravagance of expansion and retraction. But even this ruin of a body might, I considered, be made partially whole, were it not that to lull the rage and fever of such a *mind* the world contained no anodyne. For one thing, a most curious belief in some unnamed fate hanging over the island on which he lived haunted him. Again and again he recalled to me all that in the long past had been written about Delos: the strange notion contained both in the Homeric and the Alexandrian hymns to the Delian Apollo that the island was *floating;* or that it was merely secured by chains; or that it had only been thrown up from the deeps as a temporary resting-place for Ortygia in her travail; or that it might *sink* before the spurning foot of the new-born god. He was never tired, through long hours, of pursuing, as if in soliloquy, a kind of somnolent, mystical exegesis of such passages as we read together. "Do you know," he said, "that the ancients really supposed the streams of Delos to rise and fall with the rise and fall of the Nile? Could anything point more clearly to a belief in the extraordinary nature of the island, its far-reaching volcanic affinities, occult geologic eccentricities?" Often would he repeat the punning hexameter line of the very ancient Sibylline prophecy—

"And Samos shall be sand, and Delos (the far-seen) sink from sight."

often, too, having repeated it, he would strike from the repining chords of an Æolian lyre the air of a threnody which, as he told me, his wife had composed to suit the verse; and when to the funeral wail of this dirge—so wild, so mournful, that I could never hear it without a shudder—Huguenin added the melancholy note of his now hollow and plaintive voice, the intensity of effect produced on me reached the intolerable degree, and I was glad of the dubious and pallid and purple gloaming of the mansion, which partially hid my face from him.

"Observe, however," he added one day, "the meaning of the implied epithet 'far-seen' as applied to Delos: it means 'glorious,' 'illustrious'—far-seen to the spiritual rather than to the bodily eye, for the island is not very mountainous. The words 'sink from sight' must therefore be supposed to have the corresponding significance of an extinction of this glory. And now judge whether or no this prophecy has not been already fulfilled, when I tell you that this sacrosanct land, which no dog's foot was once allowed to touch, on which no man was permitted to be born or to die, bears at this moment on its bosom a monster fouler than the brain of demon ever conceived. A fearful literal and physical fulfilment of the prophecy cannot, I consider, be far distant."

That all this esotericism was not native to Huguenin I was certain. His mind, I was convinced, had been ploughed into by some tremendous energy, before ever this rank growth had choked it. I drew him on, little by little, to speak of his wife.

She was, he told me, of a very antique Athenian family, which by constant effort had conserved its purity of blood. It was while passing southward through Greece in a world-weary mood, some years before my visit, that he came one night to the village of Castri; and there, on the site of the ancient Delphi, in the centre of an angry crowd of Greeks and Turks, who threatened to rend her to pieces, he first saw Andromeda, his wife. "This incredible courage," he said, "this vast originality was hers, to take upon herself the part of a modern Hypatia—to venture on the task of the bringing back of the gods, in the rnidst of a fanatical people, at the latter end of a century like the present. The furious mob from which I rescued her was standing around her in front of the vestibule of a just completed temple to Apollo, whose worship she was then and there attempting to restore."

The love of the woman fastened on her preserver with passionate intensity. Huguenin felt himself constrained by the impulse of an irresistible Will. They were united, and came at her bidding to live in the grey abode of her creation at Delos. In this solitude, under this shadow, the man and the woman faced each other. As the months passed the husband found that he had married a seer of visions and a dreamer of dreams. And visions of what hue! and dreams of what madness! He confessed to me that he was greatly awed by her, and with this awe was blended a feeling which, if it was not fear, was akin to fear. That he loved her not at all he now knew, while the excess of her passion for him he grew to regard with the hate which men feel for the distilled elixir of the hemlock. Yet his mind inevitably took on the lurid hue of hers. He drank in unfailingly all her creeds. He followed her in the same way that a satellite follows a world. When for days together she hid herself from him and disappeared, he would wander desolate and full of search over the pathless house. Finding that she habitually yielded her body to the lotus delights of certain opiate seeds produced on the island, he found the courage to frown and warn, and ended by himself becoming a bond-slave to the drowsy *ganja* of India. So too with the most strange fascination she exercised over the animal world: he disliked it—he dreaded it; regarded it as excessive and unnatural; but he looked on only with the furtive, pale eye of suspicion, and said nothing. When she walked she was accompanied by a long magnetised *queue* of living things, felines in particular, and birds of large size. Dogs, on the contrary, shunned her, bristling. She had brought with her from the mainland a collection of these followers, of which Huguenin had never seen the half; they were imprisoned in unknown nooks of the building; ever and anon she would vanish from the house, to reappear with new companions. Her kindness to these dumb creatures should, I presume, have been amply sufficient to account for her power over them; but Huguenin's mind, already grown morbid, probed darkly after some other explanation. The primary *motif* of this unquietness doubtless lay in his wife's fanaticism on the subject of the Pythagorean theory of the transmigration of souls. On this theme Andromeda, it was clear, was violently deranged. She would stand, he declared, with outstretched arm, with eye wild-staring, with rigid body, and in a rapid, guttural recitative—like a rapt, delirious Pythoness—would prophesy of the eternal mutations prepared for the spirit of man. She would dwell, above all, with a kind of contempt, on the limitations of animal forms in the actual world, and would indignantly insist that the spirit of an extraordinary and original man, disembodied, *should and must* re-embody itself in a correspondingly extraordinary and original form. "And," she would often add, "such forms do really exist on the earth, but the God, willing to save the race from frenzy, hides them from the eyes of common men."

It was long, however, before I could induce Huguenin to speak of the final catastrophe of his singular wedded life. He related it in these words:—

"You now know that Andromeda was among the great painters of the world—you have seen her picture of herself. One day, after dilating, as was her wont, on the narrow limitation of forms, she said suddenly, 'But you, too, shall be of the initiated: come, come, you shall see *something.*' She went swiftly forward, beckoning, looking back repeatedly to smile on me a loving patronage, with the condescension of a priestess to a neophyte; I followed, till before a lately finished painting she stopped, pointing. I will not attempt—the attempt would be folly—to tell you what thing of horror and madness I saw before me on the canvas; nor can I explain in words the tempest of anger, of loathing and disgust, that stirred within me at the sight. Kindled by the blasphemy of her fancy, I raised my hand to strike her head; and to this hour I know not if I struck her. My hand, it is true, felt the sensation of contact with something soft and yielding; but the blow, if blow there were, was surely too slight to harm the frame of a creature far feebler than the human. Yet she fell; the film of coming death grew over her dull, upbraiding eyes; one last word only she spoke, pointing to the Uncleanness: 'In the flesh you may yet behold it!' and so, still pointing, pointing, she passed away.

"I bore her body, embalmed in the Greek manner by an expert of Corinth, to one of the smaller apartments on the roof of the house. I saw, as I turned to leave her in the gloom of the strait and lonely chamber, the mortal smile on her waxen face within the open coffin. Two weeks later I went again to visit her. My friend, she had vanished utterly—save that the bones remained; and from the vacant coffin, above the now fleshless skull, two eyes—living—the very eyes of Andromeda's soul, but full of a new-born, intenser light—the eyes, too, of the pictured horror whose whole form I now discerned in the darkness—gleamed out upon me. I slammed to the door, and fainted on the floor."

"The suggestion," I said, "which you seem to wish to convey is that of a transition of forms from the human to the animal; but, surely, the explanation that the monster, brought secretly by your wife into the house, imprisoned unawares by you with the dead, and maddened by hunger, fed on the uncovered body, is, if not less horrible, at least less improbable."

He looked doubtingly at me for a moment, and then replied: "There was no monster imprisoned with the dead. Be not rash with 'explanations.' You do not require me to tell you, what you must know, that there are many more things in earth—to say nothing of heaven—than were ever dreamt of in your philosophy."

But at least, I urged, he would see the necessity of flying from that place. He answered with the extraordinary avowal that it was no longer doubtful to him, from the effect which any neglect to minister to the creature's wants produced on his own bodily health, that his life was intimately bound up with the life of the being he stayed to maintain; that with the *second* murder of which he should be guilty—nay, with the very attempt to commit it, as, for example, by flight from the house—his own life would inevitably be forfeited.

I accordingly formed the resolution to work the deliverance of my friend in spite of himself. Two months had now passed; the end of my visit was drawing near; yet his maladies of brain and body were not alleviated. It tortured me to think of leaving him once more alone, a prey to the manias which distracted him.

That very day, while he slept his damp, unquiet, opiate slumbers, I started out on the track indicated by the scarlet thread. So far it led—and the rooms through which it passed were of such uniformity, and the path so serpentine, and the sameness of construction on every hand so unbroken—that I could not doubt but that, the clue once snapped at any point, the journey to the desired end could be accomplished only by the most improbable good fortune. I followed the thread to its termination: it stopped at the foot of a ladder-like stair, which I ascended. At the top of the stair, and close to it, I was faced by a narrow wall, in which was a closed wooden door; in the door a hole large enough to admit the hand. As I placed my foot on the topmost step, a long, low, plaintive whine, with a sickening likeness to a human wail, broke upon my ear.

I hurriedly descended the steps. Some little distance from them I broke the silken thread, and, gathering it up in my hand as I went, again broke it near the region of the house which we occupied.

"Hereby," I said, as I held the gathered portion to the flame of a lamp, "shall a soul be saved alive."

I watched him later on through half-closed lids, as he departed, haggard and shivering, on his nightly errand. My heart throbbed under an agony of disquiet while I awaited his long-delayed return.

He came swiftly and softly into my room, and shook me by the shoulder. On his face was a look of unusual calmness, of dignity and mystery.

"Wake up," he said. "I wish you—I am a sorry host, am I not?—I wish you to leave me to-night, at once; to leave the island—*now.*"

"But tell me—" I gasped.

"Nay, nay; I will take no refusal. Trust me this once, and go. There is a danger here. Destiny is against me—an impudent destiny, careless even to conceal its hand. Go. One or two of the fisher-folk of the harbour will convey you over to Rhenea before the morning light, and you will be saved."

"But saved from what?"

"From what? I cannot tell you: from the destiny, whatever it be, which awaits me. Do you know—can you dream—that the thread on which my life depends is *snapped?* "

"But suppose I tell you—"

"You can tell me nothing. Ah you hear that?"

He held up his hand and listened. It was a sudden shriek of the wind around the house.

"It is but the rising wind," I muttered, starting up.

"Ah, but that—that which followed. Did you not *feel* it? "

"Huguenin, I felt nothing."

He had clasped with both arms a marble pillar, against which his forehead rested, while with one foot he gently and mechanically patted the floor. In this posture, now utterly demoralised and craven, he remained for some minutes. The wail of the wind was heard at intervals. Suddenly he turned towards me, with a ghastly face and the scream of a frightened woman.

"Now—now at least—*you feel it!* "

I could no longer deny. It was as if the whole island had gently rocked to and fro on a pivot.

Thoroughly unnerved myself, trembling more with awe than with terror, I seized Huguenin's arm, and sought to draw him from the pillar, which, muttering low, he still embraced. He sullenly refused to stir; and I, resolved in any event to stay by him, sat near. The seismic agitation increased. But he seemed to take no further note of anything,—only, with the regularity of a clock's oscillations, the tripudi-ary automatic motion of his foot persisted. In this way an hour, two hours, passed. At the end of that time the rocking movement of the earth had become intense, rapid and continuous.

There came a moment when, overwhelmed by a new panic, I sprang to my feet and shook him.

"Headstrong man!" I cried, "have you then parted with every sense? Do you not smell—can you not feel—that the house is in flames?"

His eyes, which had grown dark and dull, blazed up instantly with a new madness.

"Then," he shouted, with the roar of a clarion,—"then she shall—I say she *shall* be saved! The cheetah—*the feathered cheetah!*"

Before I could lay hold of the now foaming maniac, he had dashed past me into a corridor. I followed behind in hottest pursuit. The carpets and hangings, as yet but dully glowing, filled the passages with the smoke of Tophet. I hoped that Huguenin, weak of lung, would fall choked and exhausted. Some power seemed to lend him strength—he rushed onward like the wind; some sure, mysterious instinct seemed to guide him—not once did he falter or hesitate.

The long chase through the cracking house, burning now on every side, was over. The just intuitions of insanity had not failed the madman—he reached the goal for which he panted. I saw him hasten up the half-consumed ladder, whose foot was already in a lake of flame. He rushed to the smouldering wooden door of the tomb of Andromeda, and tore it wide open. And now from out the vault there burst—above the roaring of the fire, and the whistle of the tempest, and the thousandfold rattle of the earthquake—a shrill and raucous shriek, which turned my blood to ice; and I saw proceeding from the darkness a creature whose native loathsomeness human language has no vocabulary to describe. For if I say that it was a cheetah—of very large size—its eyes a yellow liquid conflagration—its fat and boneless body swathed in a thick panoply of dark grey feathers, vermilion-tipped—with a simili-tude of miniature wings on its back—with a wide, vast, downward-sweeping tail like the tail of a bird of paradise,—how by such words can I image forth all the retching nausea, all the bottomless hate and fear, with which I looked? The fire, it was evident, had already reached the body of the beast; already it flamed. I saw it fly, rather than spring, at Huguenin's head; the burial of its fangs in his flesh, the meeting of its teeth about his windpipe, I saw. He tottered—gurgling—tearing at the feathery horror—backward over the spot where a moment before the stair had stood; together they fell into the sea of flame beneath.

I ran in headlong haste from the house, discovering by good chance an egress. The night was clear, yet all the winds seemed to tumble in disenchained ecstacy about the islet. As I descended I noted the scathed and scorched aspect of the trees and of certain of the rocks; at one spot a multitude of deep, smooth, conical openings, edged with grey, glowing scoriæ, riveted my attention. Still lower, I stood on a bluff promontory and looked sheer into the sea. The sight was sublime and appalling. The deep—without billow or foam or ripple—luminous far down with phosphorescences—rushed, like some lambent lamina yoked to the fiery steeds of Diomedes, with a steady, intense, almost dazzling impetuosity towards the island. Delos, indeed, seemed to *float*—to swim, painfully struggling, like a little doomed bird, against the all-engulfing element. I passed with the earliest light from this mystic shrine of ancient piety. Among the last sights that greeted my gaze was the still ascending reek of the blighted and accursed dwelling of Huguenin.

CANON ALBERIC'S
SCRAP-BOOK

M.R. JAMES

MONTAGUE RHODES JAMES (1862-1936) IS CREDITED WITH
HAVING LAID DOWN THE GROUND RULES OF THE MODERN
GHOST STORY, PARTICULARLY IN HIS STIPULATIONS THAT
GHOSTS SHOULD BE MALEVOLENT AND THAT EVERY ASPECT OF A
GHOST STORY HAD TO LEND CREDIBILITY TO THEIR EXISTENCE.
JAMES'S SPECIALTY WAS THE ANTIQUARIAN GHOST TALE WHOSE
SUPERNATURAL MENACE IS OFTEN AN UNHALLOWED SURVIVAL
FROM A MORE SUPERSTITIOUS PAST. THE DEMONIC ENTITY
THAT MANIFESTS IN THIS STORY, FIRST PUBLISHED IN THE
MARCH 1895 ISSUE OF ENGLAND'S *NATIONAL REVIEW* AND
COLLECTED IN HIS LANDMARK COMPILATION *GHOST STORIES
OF AN ANTIQUARY*, STRETCHES THE DEFINITION OF A "GHOST,"
THOUGH ITS MALEVOLENCE IS INDISPUTABLE.

St. Bertrand de Comminges is a decayed town on the spurs of the Pyrenees, not very far from Toulouse, and still nearer to Bagneres-de-Luchon. It was the site of a bishopric until the Revolution, and has a cathedral which is visited by a certain number of tourists. In the spring of 1883 an Englishman arrived at this old-world place—I can hardly dignify it with the name of city, for there are not a thousand inhabitants. He was a Cambridge man, who had come specially from Toulouse to see St. Bertrand's Church, and had left two friends, who were less keen archaeologists than himself, in their hotel at Toulouse, under promise to join him on the following morning. Half an hour at the church would satisfy *them*, and all three could then pursue their journey in the direction of Auch. But our Englishman had come early on the day in question, and proposed to himself to fill a note-book and to use several dozens of plates in the process of describing and photographing every corner of the wonderful church that dominates the little hill of Comminges. In order to carry out this design satisfactorily, it was necessary to monopolize the verger of the church for the day. The verger or sacristan (I prefer the latter appellation, inaccurate as it may be) was accordingly sent for by the somewhat brusque lady who keeps the inn of the Chapeau Rouge; and when he came, the Englishman found him an unexpectedly interesting object of study. It was not in the personal appearance of the little, dry, wizened old man that the interest lay, for he was precisely like dozens of other church-guardians in France, but in a curious furtive or rather hunted and oppressed air which he had. He was per-petually half glancing behind him; the muscles of his back and shoulders seemed to be hunched in a continual nervous contraction, as if he were expecting every moment to find himself in the clutch of an enemy. The Englishman hardly knew whether to put him down as a man haunted by a fixed delusion, or as one oppressed by a guilty conscience, or as an unbearably henpecked husband. The probabilities, when reck-oned up, certainly pointed to the last idea; but, still, the impression conveyed was that of a more formidable persecutor even than a termagant wife.

However, the Englishman (let us call him Dennistoun) was soon too deep in his note-book and too busy with his camera to give more than an occasional glance to the sacristan. Whenever he did look at him, he found him at no great distance, either huddling himself back against the wall or crouching in one of the gorgeous stalls. Dennistoun became rather fidgety after a time. Mingled suspicions that he was keeping the old man from his *dejeuner*, that he was regarded as likely to make away with St Bertrand's ivory crozier, or with the dusty stuffed crocodile that hangs over the font, began to torment him.

"Won't you go home?" he said at last; "I'm quite well able to finish my notes alone; you can lock me in if you like. I shall want at least two hours more here, and it must be cold for you, isn't it?"

"Good heavens!" said the little man, whom the suggestion seemed to throw into a state of unaccountable terror, "such a thing cannot be thought of for a moment. Leave monsieur alone in the church? No, no; two hours, three hours, all will be the same to me. I have breakfasted, I am not at all cold, with many thanks to monsieur."

"Very well, my little man," quoth Dennistoun to himself: "you have been warned, and you must take the consequences."

Before the expiration of the two hours, the stalls, the enormous dilapidated organ, the choir-screen of Bishop John de Mauléon, the remnants of glass and tapestry, and the objects in the treasure-chamber had been well and truly examined; the sacristan still keeping at Dennistoun's heels, and every now and then whipping round as if he had been stung, when one or other of the strange noises that trouble a large empty building fell on his ear. Curious noises they were, sometimes.

"Once," Dennistoun said to me, "I could have sworn I heard a thin metallic voice laughing high up in the tower. I darted an inquiring glance at my sacristan. He was white to the lips. 'It is he—that is—it is no one; the door is locked,' was all he said, and we looked at each other for a full minute."

Another little incident puzzled Dennistoun a good deal. He was examining a large dark picture that hangs behind the altar, one of a series illustrating the miracles of St Bertrand. The composition of the picture is well-nigh indecipherable, but there is a Latin legend below, which runs thus:

Qualiter S. Bertrandus liberavit hominem quem diabolus diu volebat strangulare. (How St. Bertrand delivered a man whom the Devil long sought to strangle.)

Dennistoun was turning to the sacristan with a smile and a jocular remark of some sort on his lips, but he was confounded to see the old man on his knees, gazing at the picture with the eye of a suppliant in agony, his hands tightly clasped, and a rain of tears on his cheeks. Dennistoun naturally pretended to have noticed nothing, but the question would not go away from him, "Why should a daub of this kind affect anyone so strongly?" He seemed to himself to be getting some sort of clue to the reason of the strange look that had been puzzling him all the day: the man must be a monomaniac; but what was his monomania?

It was nearly five o'clock; the short day was drawing in, and the church began to fill with shadows, while the curious noises—the muffled footfalls and distant talking voices that had been perceptible all day—seemed, no doubt because of the fading light and the consequently quickened sense of hearing, to become more frequent and insistent.

The sacristan began for the first time to show signs of hurry and impatience. He heaved a sigh of relief when camera and note-book were finally packed up and stowed away, and hurriedly beckoned Dennistoun to the western door of the church, under the tower. It was time to ring the Angelus. A few pulls at the reluctant rope, and the great bell Bertrande, high in the tower, began to speak, and swung her voice up among the pines and down to the valleys, loud with mountain-streams, calling the dwellers on those lonely hills to remember and repeat the salutation of the angel to her whom he called Blessed among women. With that a profound quiet seemed to fall for the first time that day upon the little town, and Dennistoun and the sacristan went out of the church.

On the doorstep they fell into conversation.

"Monsieur seemed to interest himself in the old choir-books in the sacristy."

"Undoubtedly. I was going to ask you if there were a library in the town."

"No, monsieur; perhaps there used to be one belonging to the Chapter, but it is now such a small place—" Here came a strange pause of irresolution, as it seemed; then, with a sort of plunge, he went on: "But if monsieur is *amateur des vieux livres*, I have at home something that might interest him. It is not a hundred yards."

At once all Dennistoun's cherished dreams of finding priceless manuscripts in untrodden corners of France flashed up, to die down again the next moment. It was probably a stupid missal of Plantin's printing, about 1580. Where was the likelihood that a place so near Toulouse would not have been ransacked long ago by collectors? However, it would be foolish not to go; he would reproach himself for ever after if he refused. So they set off. On the way the curious irresolution and sudden determination of the sacristan recurred to Dennistoun, and he wondered in a shamefaced way whether he was being decoyed into some purlieu to be made away with as a supposed rich Englishman. He contrived, therefore, to begin talking with his guide, and to drag in, in a rather clumsy fashion, the fact that he expected two friends to join him early the next morning. To his surprise, the announcement seemed to relieve the sacristan at once of some of the anxiety that oppressed him.

"That is well," he said quite brightly—"that is very well. Monsieur will travel in company with his friends: they will be always near him. It is a good thing to travel thus in company—sometimes."

The last word appeared to be added as an afterthought and to bring with it a relapse into gloom for the poor little man.

They were soon at the house, which was one rather larger than its neighbours, stone-built, with a shield carved over the door, the shield of Alberic de Mauléon, a collateral descendant, Dennistoun tells me, of Bishop John de Mauléon. This Alberic was a Canon of Comminges from 1680 to 1701. The upper windows of the mansion were boarded up, and the whole place bore, as does the rest of Comminges, the aspect of decaying age.

Arrived on his doorstep, the sacristan paused a moment.

"Perhaps," he said, "perhaps, after all, monsieur has not the time?"

"Not at all—lots of time—nothing to do till tomorrow. Let us see what it is you have got."

The door was opened at this point, and a face looked out, a face far younger than the sacristan's, but bearing something of the same distressing look: only here it seemed to be the mark, not so much of fear for personal safety as of acute anxiety on behalf of another. Plainly the owner of the face was the sacristan's daughter; and, but for the expression I have described, she was a handsome girl enough. She brightened up considerably on seeing her father accompanied by an able-bodied stranger. A few remarks passed between father and daughter of which Dennistoun only caught these words, said by the sacristan: "He was laughing in the church," words which were answered only by a look of terror from the girl.

But in another minute they were in the sitting-room of the house, a small, high chamber with a stone floor, full of moving shadows cast by a wood-fire that flickered on a great hearth. Something of the character of an oratory was imparted to it by a tall crucifix, which reached almost to the ceiling on one side; the figure was painted of the natural colours, the cross was black. Under this stood a chest of some age and solidity, and when a lamp had been brought, and chairs set, the sacristan went to this chest, and produced therefrom, with growing excitement and nervousness, as Dennistoun thought, a large book, wrapped in a white cloth, on which cloth a cross was rudely embroidered in red thread. Even before the wrapping had been removed, Dennistoun began to be interested by the size and shape of the volume. "Too large for a missal," he thought, "and not the shape of an antiphoner; perhaps it may be something good, after all." The next moment the book was open, and Dennistoun felt that he had at last lit upon something better than good. Before him lay a large folio, bound, perhaps, late in the seventeenth century, with the arms of Canon Alberic de Mauléon stamped in gold on the sides. There may have been a hundred and fifty leaves of paper in the book, and on almost every one of them was fastened a leaf from an illuminated manuscript. Such a collection Dennistoun had hardly dreamed of in his wildest moments. Here were ten leaves from a copy of Genesis, illustrated with pictures, which could not be later than A.D. 700. Further on was a complete set of pictures from a Psalter, of English execution, of the very finest kind that the thirteenth century could produce; and, perhaps best of all, there were twenty leaves of uncial writing in Latin, which, as a few words seen here and there told him at once, must belong to some very early unknown patristic treatise. Could it possibly be a fragment of the copy of Papias "On the Words of Our Lord," which was known to have existed as late as the twelfth century at Nîmes?* In any case, his mind was made up; that book must return to Cambridge with him, even if

---

*We now know that these leaves did contain a considerable fragment of that work, if not of that actual copy of it.

he had to draw the whole of his balance from the bank and stay at St. Bertrand till the money came. He glanced up at the sacristan to see if his face yielded any hint that the book was for sale. The sacristan was pale, and his lips were working.

"If monsieur will turn on to the end," he said.

So monsieur turned on, meeting new treasures at every rise of a leaf; and at the end of the book he came upon two sheets of paper, of much more recent date than anything he had seen yet, which puzzled him considerably. They must be contemporary, he decided, with the unprincipled Canon Alberic, who had doubtless plundered the Chapter library of St. Bertrand to form this priceless scrap-book. On the first of the paper sheets was a plan, carefully drawn and instantly recognizable by a person who knew the ground, of the south aisle and cloisters of St Bertrand's. There were curious signs looking like planetary symbols, and a few Hebrew words in the corners; and in the north-west angle of the cloister was a cross drawn in gold paint. Below the plan were some lines of writing in Latin, which ran thus:

> *Responsa 12^{mi} Dec. 1694. Interrogatum est: Inveniamne? Responsum est: Invenies. Fiamne dives? Fies. Vivamne invidendus? Vives. Moriarne in lecto meo? Ita.* (Answers of the 12th of December, 1694. It was asked: Shall I find it? Answer: Thou shalt. Shall I become rich? Thou wilt. Shall I live an object of envy? Thou wilt. Shall I die in my bed? Thou wilt.)

"A good specimen of the treasure-hunter's record—quite reminds one of Mr Minor-Canon Quatremain in 'Old St. Paul's,'" was Dennistoun's comment, and he turned the leaf.

What he then saw impressed him, as he has often told me, more than he could have conceived any drawing or picture capable of impressing him. And, though the drawing he saw is no longer in existence, there is a photograph of it (which I possess) which fully bears out that statement. The picture in question was a sepia drawing at the end of the seventeenth century, representing, one would say at first sight, a Biblical scene; for the architecture (the picture represented an interior) and the figures had that semi-classical flavour about them which the artists of two hundred years ago thought appropriate to illustrations of the Bible. On the right was a king on his throne, the throne elevated on twelve steps, a canopy overhead, soldiers on either side—evidently King Solomon. He was bending forward with outstretched sceptre, in attitude of command; his face expressed horror and disgust, yet there was in it also the mark of imperious command and confident power. The left half of the picture was the strangest, however. The interest plainly centred there.

On the pavement before the throne were grouped four soldiers, surrounding a crouching figure which must be described in a moment. A fifth soldier lay dead on the pavement, his neck distorted, and his eye-balls starting from his head. The four surrounding guards were looking at the King. In their faces, the sentiment of horror was intensified; they seemed, in fact, only restrained from flight by their implicit trust in their master. All this terror was plainly excited by the being that crouched in their midst.

I entirely despair of conveying by any words the impression which this figure makes upon anyone who looks at it. I recollect once showing the photograph of the drawing to a lecturer on morphology—a person of, I was going to say, abnormally sane and unimaginative habits of mind. He absolutely refused to be alone for the rest of that evening, and he told me afterwards that for many nights he had not dared to put out his light before going to sleep. However, the main traits of the figure I can at least indicate.

At first you saw only a mass of coarse, matted black hair; presently it was seen that this covered a body of fearful thinness, almost a skeleton, but with the muscles standing out like wires. The hands were of a dusky pallor, covered, like the body, with long, coarse hairs, and hideously taloned. The eyes, touched in with a burning yellow, had intensely black pupils, and were fixed upon the throned King with a look of beast-like hate. Imagine one of the awful bird-catching spiders of South America translated into human form, and endowed with intelligence just less than human, and you will have some faint conception of the terror inspired by the appalling effigy. One remark is universally made by those to whom I have shown the picture: "It was drawn from the life."

As soon as the first shock of his irresistible fright had subsided, Dennistoun stole a look at his hosts. The sacristan"s hands were pressed upon his eyes; his daughter, looking up at the cross on the wall, was telling her beads feverishly.

At last the question was asked: "Is this book for sale?"

There was the same hesitation, the same plunge of determination that he had noticed before, and then came the welcome answer: "If monsieur pleases."

"How much do you ask for it?"

"I will take two hundred and fifty francs."

This was confounding. Even a collector"s conscience is sometimes stirred, and Dennistoun"s conscience was tenderer than a collector"s.

"My good man!" he said again and again, "your book is worth far more than two hundred and fifty francs. I assure you—far more."

But the answer did not vary: "I will take two hundred and fifty francs—not more."

There was really no possibility of refusing such a chance. The money was paid, the receipt signed, a glass of wine drunk over the transaction, and then the sacristan seemed to become a new man. He stood upright, he ceased to throw those suspicious glances behind him, he actually laughed or tried to laugh. Dennistoun rose to go.

"I shall have the honour of accompanying monsieur to his hotel?" said the sacristan.

"Oh, no, thanks! it isn't a hundred yards. I know the way perfectly, and there is a moon."

The offer was pressed three or four times and refused as often.

"Then, monsieur will summon me if—if he finds occasion; he will keep the middle of the road, the sides are so rough."

"Certainly, certainly," said Dennistoun, who was impatient to examine his prize by himself; and he stepped out into the passage with his book under his arm.

Here he was met by the daughter; she, it appeared, was anxious to do a little business on her own account; perhaps, like Gehazi, to "take somewhat" from the foreigner whom her father had spared.

"A silver crucifix and chain for the neck; monsieur would perhaps be good enough to accept it?"

Well, really, Dennistoun hadn't much use for these things. What did mademoiselle want for it?

"Nothing—nothing in the world. Monsieur is more than welcome to it."

The tone in which this and much more was said was unmistakably genuine, so that Dennistoun was reduced to profuse thanks, and submitted to have the chain put round his neck. It really seemed as if he had rendered the father and daughter some service which they hardly knew how to repay. As he set off with his book they stood at the door looking after him, and they were still looking when he waved them a last good night from the steps of the Chapeau Rouge.

Dinner was over, and Dennistoun was in his bedroom, shut up alone with his acquisition. The landlady had manifested a particular interest in him since he had told her that he had paid a visit to the sacristan and bought an old book from him. He thought, too, that he had heard a hurried dialogue between her and the said sacristan in the passage outside the *salle à manger*, some words to the effect that "Pierre and Bertrand would be sleeping in the house" had closed the conversation.

All this time a growing feeling of discomfort had been creeping over him— nervous reaction, perhaps, after the delight of his discovery. Whatever it was, it resulted in a conviction that there was someone behind him, and that he was far more comfortable with his back to the wall. All this, of course, weighed light in the balance as against the obvious value of the collection he had acquired. And now, as I said, he was alone in his bedroom, taking stock of Canon Alberic's treasures, in which every moment revealed something more charming.

"Bless Canon Alberic! " said Dennistoun, who had an inveterate habit of talking to himself. "I wonder where he is now? Dear me! I wish that landlady would learn to laugh in a more cheering manner; it makes one feel as if there was someone dead in the house. Half a pipe more, did you say? I think perhaps you are right. I wonder what that crucifix is that the young woman insisted on giving me? Last century, I suppose. Yes, probably. It is rather a nuisance of a thing to have round one's neck— just too heavy. Most likely her father has been wearing it for years. I think I might give it a clean up before I put it away."

He had taken the crucifix off, and laid it on the table, when his attention was caught by an object lying on the red cloth just by his left elbow. Two or three ideas of what it might be flitted through his brain with their own incalculable quickness.

"A penwiper? No, no such thing in the house. A rat? No, too black. A large spider? I trust to goodness not—no. Good God! a hand like the hand in that picture!"

In another infinitesimal flash he had taken it in. Pale, dusky skin, covering nothing but bones and tendons of appalling strength; coarse black hairs, longer than ever grew on a human hand; nails rising from the ends of the fingers and curving sharply down and forward, grey, horny, and wrinkled.

He flew out of his chair with deadly, inconceivable terror clutching at his heart. The shape, whose left hand rested on the table, was rising to a standing posture behind his seat, its right hand crooked above his scalp. There was black and tattered drapery about it; the coarse hair covered it as in the drawing. The lower jaw was thin—what can I call it?—shallow, like a beast's; teeth showed behind the black lips; there was no nose; the eyes, of a fiery yellow, against which the pupils showed black and intense, and the exulting hate and thirst to destroy life which shone there, were the most horrifying features in the whole vision. There was intelligence of a kind in them—intelligence beyond that of a beast, below that of a man.

The feelings which this horror stirred in Dennistoun were the intensest physical fear and the most profound mental loathing. What did he do? What could he do? He has never been quite certain what words he said, but he knows that he spoke, that he grasped blindly at the silver crucifix, that he was conscious of a movement towards him on the part of the demon, and that he screamed with the voice of an animal in hideous pain.

Pierre and Bertrand, the two sturdy little serving-men, who rushed in, saw nothing, but felt themselves thrust aside by something that passed out between them, and found Dennistoun in a swoon. They sat up with him that night, and his two friends were at St. Bertrand by nine 'clock next morning. He himself, though still shaken and nervous, was almost himself by that time, and his story found credence with them, though not until they had seen the drawing and talked with the sacristan.

Almost at dawn the little man had come to the inn on some pretence, and had listened with the deepest interest to the story retailed by the landlady. He showed no surprise.

"It is he—it is he! I have seen him myself," was his only comment; and to all questionings but one reply was vouchsafed: "Deux fois je l'ai vu: mille fois je l'ai senti." He would tell them nothing of the provenance of the book, nor any details of his experiences. "I shall soon sleep, and my rest will be sweet. Why should you trouble me?" he said.*

We shall never know what he or Canon Alberic de Mauléon suffered. At the back of that fateful drawing were some lines of writing which may be supposed to throw light on the situation:

> Contradictio Salomonis cum demonio nocturno.
> Albericus de Mauleone delineavit.
> V. Deus in adiutorium. Ps. Qui habitat.
> Sancte Bertrande, demoniorum effugator, intercede pro me miserrimo.
> Primum uidi nocte 12(mi) Dec. 1694:
> uidebo mox ultimum. Peccaui et passus
> sum, plura adhuc passurus. Dec. 29, 1701†

I have never quite understood what was Dennistoun's view of the events I have narrated. He quoted to me once a text from Ecclesiasticus: "Some spirits there be

---

*He died that summer; his daughter married, and settled at St Papoul. She never understood the circumstances of her father's "obsession".

†I.e., The Dispute of Solomon with a demon of the night. Drawn by Alberic de Mauléon. Versicle. O Lord, make haste to help me. Psalm. Whoso dwelleth (xci.)

Saint Bertrand, who puttest devils to flight, pray for me most unhappy. I saw it first on the night of Dec. 12, 1694: soon I shall see it for the last time. I have sinned and suffered, and have more to suffer yet. Dec. 29, 1701.

The "Gallia Christiana" gives the date of the Canon's death as December 31, 1701, "in bed, of a sudden seizure." Details of this kind are not common in the great work of the Sammarthani.

that are created for vengeance, and in their fury lay on sore strokes." On another occasion he said: "Isaiah was a very sensible man; doesn't he say something about night monsters living in the ruins of Babylon? These things are rather beyond us at present."

Another confidence of his impressed me rather, and I sympathized with it. We had been, last year, to Comminges, to see Canon Alberic's tomb. It is a great marble erection with an effigy of the Canon in a large wig and soutane, and an elaborate eulogy of his learning below. I saw Dennistoun talking for some time with the Vicar of St Bertrand's, and as we drove away he said to me: "I hope it isn't wrong: you know I am a Presbyterian—but I—I believe there will be 'saying of Mass and singing of dirges' for Alberic de Mauléon's rest." Then he added, with a touch of the Northern British in his tone, "I had no notion they came so dear."

★ ★ ★

The book is in the Wentworth Collection at Cambridge. The drawing was photographed and then burnt by Dennistoun on the day when he left Comminges on the occasion of his first visit.

THE YELLOW SIGN

ROBERT W. CHAMBERS

ROBERT W. CHAMBERS (1865–1933) ABANDONED A CAREER AS
AN ARTIST AND BECAME ONE OF THE BEST-SELLING WRITERS
OF POPULAR FICTION IN THE EARLY TWENTIETH CENTURY. THIS
STORY, WHICH ANCHORED HIS 1895 COLLECTION *THE KING IN
YELLOW,* SHARES WITH SEVERAL OF HIS OTHER TALES A DARK
MYTHOLOGY RELATED TO A SCANDALOUS AND DANGEROUS BOOK
THAT BEARS THE SAME TITLE AS HIS COLLECTION. SET IN THE
BOHEMIAN ART WORLD OF NEW YORK CITY AT THE TURN OF
THE TWENTIETH CENTURY, "THE YELLOW SIGN" PRESENTS AN
UNFORGETTABLE PORTRAIT OF A WORLD WHERE DECADENCE AND
DEATH ARE INTIMATELY BOUND UP WITH ONE ANOTHER.

> "Let the red dawn surmise
> What we shall do,
> When this blue starlight dies
> And all is through."

I

There are so many things which are impossible to explain! Why should certain chords in music make me think of the brown and golden tints of autumn foliage? Why should the Mass of Sainte Cecile bend my thoughts wandering among caverns whose walls blaze with ragged masses of virgin silver? What was it in the roar and turmoil of Broadway at six o'clock that flashed before my eyes the picture of a still Breton forest where sunlight filtered through spring foliage and Sylvia bent, half curiously, half tenderly, over a small green lizard, murmuring: "To think that this also is a little ward of God!"

When I first saw the watchman his back was toward me. I looked at him in-differently until he went into the church. I paid no more attention to him than I had to any other man who lounged through Washington Square that morning, and when I shut my window and turned back into my studio I had forgotten him. Late in the afternoon, the day being warm, I raised the window again and leaned out to get a sniff of air. A man was standing in the courtyard of the church, and I noticed him again with as little interest as I had that morning. I looked across the square to where the fountain was playing and then, with my mind filled with vague impres-sions of trees, asphalt drives, and the moving groups of nursemaids and holiday-makers, I started to walk back to my easel. As I turned, my listless glance included the man below in the church-yard. His face was toward me now, and with a perfectly involuntary movement I bent to see it. At the same moment he raised his head and looked at me. Instantly I thought of a coffin-worm. Whatever it was about the man that repelled me I did not know, but the impression of a plump white grave-worm was so intense and nauseating that I must have shown it in my expression, for he turned his puffy face away with a movement which made me think of a disturbed grub in a chestnut.

I went back to my easel and motioned the model to resume her pose. After working a while I was satisfied that I was spoiling what I had done as rapidly as pos-sible, and I took up a palette knife and scraped the color out again. The flesh tones were sallow and unhealthy, and I did not understand how I could have painted such sickly color into a study which before that had glowed with healthy tones.

I looked at Tessie. She had not changed, and the clear flush of health dyed her neck and cheeks as I frowned.

"Is it something I've done?" she said.

"No; I've made a mess of this arm, and for the life of me I can't see how I came to paint such mud as that into the canvas," I replied.

"Don't I pose well?" she insisted.

"Of course, perfectly."

"Then it's not my fault?"

"No. It's my own."

"I am very sorry," she said.

I told her she could rest while I applied rag and turpentine to the plague spot on my canvas, and she went off to smoke a cigarette and look over the illustrations in the *Courier Français*.

I did not know whether it was something in the turpentine or a defect in the canvas, but the more I scrubbed the more that gangrene seemed to spread. I worked like a beaver to get it out, and yet the disease appeared to creep from limb to limb of the study before me. Alarmed, I strove to arrest it, but now the color on the breast changed and the whole figure seemed to absorb the infection as a sponge soaks up water. Vigorously I plied palette-knife, turpentine, and scraper, thinking all the time what a séance I should hold with Duval who had sold me the canvas; but soon I noticed that it was not the canvas which was defective nor yet the colors of Edward. "It must be the turpentine," I thought angrily, "or else my eyes have become so blurred and confused by the afternoon light that I can't see straight." I called Tessie, the model. She came and leaned over my chair blowing rings of smoke into the air.

"What *have* you been doing to it?" she exclaimed

"Nothing," I growled, "it must be this turpentine!"

"What a horrible color it is now," she continued. "Do you think my flesh resembles green cheese?"

"No, I don't," I said angrily; "did you ever know me to paint like that before?"

"No, indeed!"

"Well, then!"

"It must be the turpentine, or something," she admitted.

She slipped on a Japanese robe and walked to the window. I scraped and rubbed until I was tired, and finally picked up my brushes and hurled them through the canvas with a forcible expression, the tone alone of which reached Tessie's ears.

Nevertheless she promptly began: "That's it! Swear and act silly and ruin your brushes! You have been three weeks on that study, and now look! What's the good of ripping the canvas? What creatures artists are!"

I felt about as much ashamed as I usually did after such an outbreak, and I turned the ruined canvas to the wall. Tessie helped me clean my brushes, and then danced away to dress. From the screen she regaled me with bits of advice concerning whole or partial loss of temper, until, thinking, perhaps, I had been tormented sufficiently, she came out to implore me to button her waist where she could not reach it on the shoulder.

"Everything went wrong from the time you came back from the window and talked about that horrid-looking man you saw in the church-yard," she announced.

"Yes, he probably bewitched the picture," I said, yawning. I looked at my watch.

"It's after six, I know," said Tessie, adjusting her hat before the mirror.

"Yes," I replied, "I didn't mean to keep you so long." I leaned out of the window but recoiled with disgust, for the young man with the pasty face stood below in the church-yard. Tessie saw my gesture of disapproval and leaned from the window.

"Is that the man you don't like?" she whispered.

I nodded.

"I can't see his face, but he does look fat and soft. Someway or other," she continued, turning to look at me, "he reminds me of a dream—an awful dream—I once had. Or," she mused, looking down at her shapely shoes, "was it a dream after all?"

"How should I know?" I smiled.

Tessie smiled in reply.

"You were in it," she said, "so perhaps you might know something about it."

"Tessie! Tessie!" I protested, "don't you dare flatter by saying that you dream about me!"

"But I did," she insisted; "shall I tell you about it?"

"Go ahead," I replied, lighting a cigarette.

Tessie leaned back on the open window-sill and began very seriously.

"One night last winter I was lying in bed thinking about nothing at all in particular. I had been posing for you and I was tired out, yet it seemed impossible for me to sleep. I heard the bells in the city ring ten, eleven, and midnight. I must have fallen asleep about midnight because I don't remember hearing the bells after that. It seemed to me that I had scarcely closed my eyes when I dreamed that something impelled me to go to the window. I rose, and raising the sash leaned out. Twenty-fifth Street was deserted as far as I could see. I began to be afraid; everything outside seemed so—so black and uncomfortable. Then the sound of wheels in the distance came to my ears, and it seemed to me as though that was what I must wait for. Very slowly the wheels approached, and, finally, I could make out a vehicle moving along the street. It came nearer and nearer, and when it passed beneath my window I saw it was a hearse. Then, as I trembled with fear, the driver turned and looked straight at me. When I awoke I was standing by the open window shivering with cold, but the black-plumed hearse and the driver were gone. I dreamed this dream again in March last, and again awoke beside the open window. Last night the dream came again. You remember how it was raining; when I awoke, standing at the open window, my night-dress was soaked."

"But where did I come into the dream?" I asked.

"You—you were in the coffin; but you were not dead."

"In the coffin?"

"Yes."

"How did you know? Could you see me?"

"No; I only knew you were there."

"Had you been eating Welsh rarebits, or lobster salad?" I began, laughing, but the girl interrupted me with a frightened cry.

"Hello! What's up?" I said, as she shrank into the embrasure by the window.

"The—the man below in the church-yard; he drove the hearse."

"Nonsense," I said, but Tessie's eyes were wide with terror. I went to the window and looked out. The man was gone. "Come, Tessie," I urged, "don't be foolish. You have posed too long; you are nervous."

"Do you think I could forget that face?" she murmured. "Three times I saw the hearse pass below my window, and every time the driver turned and looked up at me. Oh, his face was so white and—and soft? It looked dead—it looked as if it had been dead a long time."

I induced the girl to sit down and swallow a glass of Marsala. Then I sat down beside her, and tried to give her some advice.

"Look here, Tessie," I said, "you go to the country for a week or two, and you'll have no more dreams about hearses. You pose all day, and when night comes your nerves are upset. You can't keep this up. Then again, instead of going to bed when your day's work is done, you run off to picnics at Sulzer's Park, or go to the Eldorado or Coney Island, and when you come down here next morning you are fagged out. There was no real hearse. There was a soft-shell crab dream."

She smiled faintly.

"What about the man in the church-yard?"

"Oh, he's only an ordinary unhealthy, every-day creature."

"As true as my name is Tessie Reardon, I swear to you, Mr. Scott, that the face of the man below in the church-yard is the face of the man who drove the hearse!"

"What of it?" I said. "It's an honest trade."

"Then you think I *did* see the hearse?"

"Oh," I said diplomatically, "if you really did, it might not be unlikely that the man below drove it. There is nothing in that."

Tessie rose, unrolled her scented handkerchief, and taking a bit of gum from a knot in the hem, placed it in her mouth. Then drawing on her gloves she offered me her hand, with a frank, "Good-night, Mr. Scott," and walked out.

II

The next morning, Thomas, the bell-boy, brought me the *Herald* and a bit of news. The church next door had been sold. I thanked Heaven for it, not that being a Catholic I had any repugnance for the congregation next door, but because my nerves were shattered by a blatant exhorter, whose every word echoed through the aisle of the church as if it had been my own rooms, and who insisted on his r's with a nasal persistence which revolted my every instinct. Then, too, there was a fiend in human shape, an organist, who reeled off some of the grand old hymns with an interpretation of his own, and I longed for the blood of a creature who could play the "Doxology" with an amendment of minor chords which one hears only in a quartet of very young undergraduates. I believe the minister was a good man, but when he bellowed: "And the Lorrrd said unto Moses, the Lorrrd is a man of war; the Lorrrd his name. My wrath shall wax hot and I will kill you with the sworrrrd!" I wondered how many centuries of purgatory it would take to atone for such a sin.

"Who bought the property?" I asked Thomas.

"Nobody that I knows, sir. They do say the gent wot owns this 'ere 'Amilton flats was lookin' at it. 'E might be a bildin' more studios."

I walked to the window. The young man with the unhealthy face stood by the church-yard gate, and at the mere sight of him the same overwhelming repugnance took possession of me.

"By the way, Thomas," I said, "who is that fellow down there?"

Thomas sniffed. "That there worm, sir? 'Es night-watchman of the church, sir. 'E maikes me tired a-sittin' out all night on them steps and lookin' at you insultin' like. I'd a punched 'is 'ed, sir—beg pardon, sir—"

"Go on, Thomas."

"One night a comin' 'ome with 'Arry, the other English boy, I sees 'im a sittin' there on them steps. We 'ad Molly and Jen with us, sir, the two girls on the tray service, an' 'e looks so insultin' at us that I up and sez, 'Wat you looking hat, you fat slug?'—beg pardon, sir, but that's 'ow I sez, sir. Then 'e don't say nothin' and I sez: 'Come out and I'll punch that puddin' 'ed.' Then I hopens the gate an' goes in, but 'e don't say nothin', only looks insultin' like. Then I 'its 'im one, but, ugh! 'is 'ed was that cold and mushy it ud sicken you to touch 'im."

"What did he do then?" I asked curiously.

"'Im? Nawthin'."

"And you, Thomas?"

The young fellow flushed with embarrassment and smiled uneasily.

"Mr. Scott, sir, I ain't no coward, an' I can't make it out at all why I run. I was in the 5th Lawncers, sir, bugler at Tel-el-Kebir, an' was shot by the wells."

"You don't mean to say you ran away?"

"Yes, sir; I run."

"Why?"

"That's just what I want to know, sir. I grabbed Molly an' run, an' the rest was as frightened as I."

"But what were they frightened at?"

Thomas refused to answer for a while, but now my curiosity was aroused about the repulsive young man below and I pressed him. Three years' sojourn in America had not only modified Thomas' cockney dialect but had given him the American's fear of ridicule.

"You won't believe me, Mr. Scott, sir?"

"Yes, I will."

"You will lawf at me, sir?"

"Nonsense!"

He hesitated. "Well, sir, it's Gawd's truth that when I 'it 'im 'e grabbed me wrists, sir, and when I twisted 'is soft, mushy fist one of 'is fingers come off in me 'and."

The utter loathing and horror of Thomas' face must have been reflected in my own, for he added:

"It's orful, an' now when I see 'im I just go away. 'E maikes me hill."

When Thomas had gone I went to the window. The man stood beside the church-railing with both hands on the gate, but I hastily retreated to my easel again, sickened and horrified, for I saw that the middle finger of his right hand was missing.

At nine o'clock Tessie appeared and vanished behind the screen with a merry "Good morning, Mr. Scott." When she had reappeared and taken her pose upon the model-stand I started a new canvas, much to her delight. She remained silent as long as I was on the drawing, but as soon as the scrape of the charcoal ceased and I took up my fixative she began to chatter.

"Oh, I had such a lovely time last night. We went to Tony Pastor's."

"Who are 'we'?" I demanded.

"Oh, Maggie, you know, Mr. Whyte's model, and Pinkie McCormick—we call her Pinkie because she's got that beautiful red hair you artists like so much—and Lizzie Burke."

I sent a shower of spray from the fixative over the canvas, and said: "Well, go on."

"We saw Kelly and Baby Barnes the skirt-dancer and—and all the rest. I made a mash."

"Then you have gone back on me, Tessie?"

She laughed and shook her head.

"He's Lizzie Burke's brother, Ed. He's a perfect gen'l'man."

I felt constrained to give her some parental advice concerning mashing, which she took with a bright smile.

"Oh, I can take care of a strange mash," she said, examining her chewing gum, "but Ed is different. Lizzie is my best friend."

Then she related how Ed had come back from the stocking mill in Lowell, Massachusetts, to find her and Lizzie grown up, and what an accomplished young man he was, and how he thought nothing of squandering half-a-dollar for ice-cream and oysters to celebrate his entry as clerk into the woollen department of Macy's. Before she finished I began to paint, and she resumed the pose, smiling and chattering like a sparrow. By noon I had the study fairly well rubbed in and Tessie came to look at it.

"That's better," she said.

I thought so too, and ate my lunch with a satisfied feeling that all was going well. Tessie spread her lunch on a drawing table opposite me and we drank our claret from the same bottle and lighted our cigarettes from the same match. I was very much attached to Tessie. I had watched her shoot up into a slender but exquisitely formed woman from a frail, awkward child. She had posed for me during the last three years, and among all my models she was my favourite. It would have troubled me very much indeed had she become "tough" or "fly," as the phrase goes, but I never noticed any deterioration of her manner, and felt at heart that she was all right. She and I never discussed morals at all, and I had no intention of doing so, partly because I had none myself, and partly because I knew she would do what she liked in spite of me. Still I did hope she would steer clear of complications, because I wished her well, and then also I had a selfish desire to retain the best model I had. I knew that mashing, as she termed it, had no significance with girls like Tessie, and that such things in America did not resemble in the least the same things in Paris. Yet, having lived with my eyes open, I also knew that somebody would take Tessie away some day, in one manner or another, and though I professed to myself that marriage was nonsense, I sincerely hoped that, in this case, there would be a priest at the end of the vista. I am a Catholic. When I listen to high mass, when I sign myself, I feel that everything, including myself, is more cheerful, and when I confess, it does me good. A man who lives as much alone as I do, must confess to somebody. Then, again, Sylvia was Catholic, and it was reason enough for me. But I was speaking of Tessie, which is very different. Tessie also was Catholic and much more devout than I, so, taking it all in all, I had little fear for my pretty model until she should fall in love. But *then* I knew that fate alone would decide her future for her, and I prayed inwardly that fate would keep her away from men like me and throw into her path nothing but Ed Burkes and Jimmy McCormicks, bless her sweet face!

Tessie sat blowing rings of smoke up to the ceiling and tinkling the ice in her tumbler.

"Do you know that I also had a dream last night?" I observed.

"Not about that man," she laughed.

"Exactly. A dream similar to yours, only much worse."

It was foolish and thoughtless of me to say this, but you know how little tact the average painter has.

"I must have fallen asleep about ten o'clock," I continued, "and after a while I dreamt that I awoke. So plainly did I hear the midnight bells, the wind in the tree-branches, and the whistle of steamers from the bay, that even now I can scarcely believe I was not awake. I seemed to be lying in a box which had a glass cover. Dimly I saw the street lamps as I passed, for I must tell you, Tessie, the box in which I reclined appeared to lie in a cushioned wagon which jolted me over a stony pavement. After a while I became impatient and tried to move, but the box was too narrow. My hands were crossed on my breast, so I could not raise them to help myself. I listened and then tried to call. My voice was gone. I could hear the trample of the horses attached to the wagon, and even the breathing of the driver. Then another sound broke upon my ears like the raising of a window sash. I managed to turn my head a little, and found I could look, not only through the glass cover of my box, but also through the glass panes in the side of the covered vehicle. I saw houses, empty and silent, with neither light nor life about any of them excepting one. In that house a window was open on the first floor, and a figure all in white stood looking down into the street. It was you."

Tessie had turned her face away from me and leaned on the table with her elbow.

"I could see your face," I resumed, "and it seemed to me to be very sorrowful. Then we passed on and turned into a narrow black lane. Presently the horses stopped. I waited and waited, closing my eyes with ear and impatience, but all was silent as the grave. After what seemed to me hours, I began to feel uncomfortable. A sense that somebody was close to me made me unclose my eyes. Then I saw the white face of the hearse-driver looking at me through the coffin-lid—"

A sob from Tessie interrupted me. She was trembling like a leaf. I saw I had made an ass of myself and attempted to repair the damage.

"Why, Tess," I said, "I only told you this to show you what influence your story might have on another person's dreams. You don't suppose I really lay in a coffin, do you? What are you trembling for? Don't you see that your dream and my unreasonable dislike for that inoffensive watchman of the church simply set my brain working as soon as I fell asleep?"

She laid her head between her arms, and sobbed as if her heart would break. What a precious triple donkey I had made of myself! But I was about to break my record. I went over and put my arm about her.

"Tessie dear, forgive me," I said; "I had no business to frighten you with such nonsense. You are too sensible a girl, too good a Catholic to believe in dreams."

Her hand tightened on mine and her head fell back upon my shoulder, but she still trembled and I petted her and comforted her.

"Come, Tess, open your eyes and smile."

Her eyes opened with a slow languid movement and met mine, but their expression was so queer that I hastened to reassure her again.

"It's all humbug, Tessie; you surely are not afraid that any harm will come to you because of that."

"No," she said, but her scarlet lips quivered.

"Then, what's the matter? Are you afraid?"

"Yes. Not for myself."

"For me, then?" I demanded gaily.

"For you," she murmured in a voice almost inaudible. "I—I care for you."

At first I started to laugh, but when I understood her, a shock passed through me, and I sat like one turned to stone. This was the crowning bit of idiocy I had committed. During the moment which elapsed between her reply and my answer I thought of a thousand responses to that innocent confession. I could pass it by with a laugh, I could misunderstand her and assure her as to my health, I could simply point out that it was impossible she could love me. But my reply was quicker than my thoughts, and I might think and think now when it was too late, for I had kissed her on the mouth.

That evening I took my usual walk in Washington Park, pondering over the occurrences of the day. I was thoroughly committed. There was no back out now, and I stared the future straight in the face. I was not good, not even scrupulous, but I had no idea of deceiving either myself or Tessie. The one passion of my life lay buried in the sunlit forests of Brittany. Was it buried for ever? Hope cried "No!" For three years I had been listening to the voice of Hope, and for three years I had waited for a footstep on my threshold. Had Sylvia forgotten? "No!" cried Hope.

I said that I was no good. That is true, but still I was not exactly a comic opera villain. I had led an easy-going reckless life, taking what invited me of pleasure, deploring and sometimes bitterly regretting consequences. In one thing alone, except my painting, was I serious, and that was something which lay hidden if not lost in the Breton forests.

It was too late for me to regret what had occurred during the day. Whatever it had been, pity, a sudden tenderness for sorrow, or the more brutal instinct of gratified vanity, it was all the same now, and unless I wished to bruise an innocent heart, my path lay marked before me. The fire and strength, the depth of passion of a love which I had never even suspected, with all my imagined experience in the world, left me no alternative but to respond or send her away. Whether because I am so cowardly about giving pain to others, or whether it was that I have little of the gloomy Puritan in me, I do not know, but I shrank from disclaiming responsibility for that thoughtless kiss, and in fact had no time to do so before the gates of her heart opened and the flood poured forth. Others who habitually do their duty and find a sullen satisfaction in making themselves and everybody else unhappy, might have withstood it. I did not. I dared not. After the storm had abated I did tell her that she might better have loved Ed Burke and worn a plain gold ring, but she would not hear of it, and I thought perhaps as long as she had decided to love somebody she could not marry, it had better be me. I, at least, could treat her with an intelligent affection, and whenever she became tired of her infatuation she could go none the worse for it. For I was decided on that point although I knew how hard it would be. I remembered the usual termination of Platonic *liaisons*, and thought how disgusted I had been whenever I heard of one. I knew I was undertaking a great deal for so unscrupulous a man as I was, and I dreamed the future, but never for one moment did I doubt that she was safe with me. Had it been anybody but Tessie I should not have bothered my head about scruples. For it did not occur to me to sacrifice Tessie as I would have sacrificed a woman of the world. I looked the future squarely in the face and saw the several probable endings to the affair. She would either tire of the whole thing, or become so unhappy that I should have either to marry her or go away. If I married her we would be unhappy. I with a wife unsuited to me, and she with a husband unsuitable for any woman. For my past life could scarcely entitle me to marry. If I went away she might either fall ill, recover, and marry some Eddie Burke, or she might recklessly or deliberately go and do something foolish. On the other hand, if she tired of me, then her whole life would be before her with beautiful vistas of Eddie Burkes and marriage rings and twins and Harlem flats and Heaven knows what. As I strolled along through the trees by the Washington Arch, I decided that she should find a substantial friend in me, anyway, and the future could take care of itself. Then I went into the house and put on my evening dress, for the little faintly-perfumed note on my dresser said, "Have a cab at the stage door at eleven," and the note was signed "Edith Carmichel, Metropolitan Theatre."

I took supper that night, or rather we took supper, Miss Carmichel and I, at Solari's, and the dawn was just beginning to gild the cross on the Memorial Church as I entered Washington Square after leaving Edith at the Brunswick. There was not a soul in the park as I passed along the trees and took the walk which leads from the Garibaldi statue to the Hamilton Apartment House, but as I passed the church-yard I saw a figure sitting on the stone steps. In spite of myself a chill crept over me at the sight of the white puffy face, and I hastened to pass. Then he said something which might have been addressed to me or might merely have been a mutter to himself, but a sudden furious anger flamed up within me that such a creature should address me. For an instant I felt like wheeling about and smashing my stick over his head, but I walked on, and entering the Hamilton went to my apartment. For some time I tossed about the bed trying to get the sound of his voice out of my ears, but could not. It filled my head, that muttering sound, like thick oily smoke from a fat-rendering vat or an odour of noisome decay. And as I lay and tossed about, the voice in my ears seemed more distinct, and I began to understand the words he had muttered. They came to me slowly as if I had forgotten them, and at last I could make some sense out of the sounds. It was this:

"Have you found the Yellow Sign?"

"Have you found the Yellow Sign?"

"Have you found the Yellow Sign?"

I was furious. What did he mean by that? Then with a curse upon him and his I rolled over and went to sleep, but when I awoke later I looked pale and haggard, for I had dreamed the dream of the night before, and it troubled me more than I cared to think.

I dressed and went down into my studio. Tessie sat by the window, but as I came in she rose and put both arms around my neck for an innocent kiss. She looked so sweet and dainty that I kissed her again and then sat down before the easel.

"Hello! Where's the study I began yesterday?" I asked.

Tessie looked conscious, but did not answer. I began to hunt among the piles of canvases, saying, "Hurry up, Tess, and get ready; we must take advantage of the morning light."

When at last I gave up the search among the other canvases and turned to look around the room for the missing study I noticed Tessie standing by the screen with her clothes still on.

"What's the matter," I asked, "don't you feel well?"

"Yes."

"Then hurry."

"Do you want me to pose as—as I have always posed?"

Then I understood. Here was a new complication. I had lost, of course, the best nude model I had ever seen. I looked at Tessie. Her face was scarlet. Alas! Alas! We had eaten of the tree of knowledge, and Eden and native innocence were dreams of the past—I mean for her.

I suppose she noticed the disappointment on my face, for she said: "I will pose if you wish. The study is behind the screen here where I put it."

"No," I said, "we will begin something new"; and I went into my wardrobe and picked out a Moorish costume which fairly blazed with tinsel. It was a genuine costume, and Tessie retired to the screen with it enchanted. When she came forth again I was astonished. Her long black hair was bound above her forehead with a circlet of turquoises, and the ends, curled about her glittering girdle. Her feet were encased in the embroidered pointed slippers and the skirt of her costume, curiously wrought with arabesques in silver, fell to her ankles. The deep metallic blue vest embroidered with silver and the short Mauresque jacket spangled and sewn with turquoises became her wonderfully. She came up to me and held up her face smiling. I slipped my hand into my pocket, and drawing out a gold chain with a cross attached, dropped it over her head.

"It's yours, Tessie."

"Mine?" she faltered.

"Yours. Now go and pose," Then with a radiant smile she ran behind the screen and presently reappeared with a little box on which was written my name.

"I had intended to give it to you when I went home to-night," she said, "but I can't wait now."

I opened the box. On the pink cotton inside lay a clasp of black onyx, on which was inlaid a curious symbol or letter in gold. It was neither Arabic nor Chinese, nor, as I found afterwards, did it belong to any human script.

"It's all I had to give you for a keepsake," she said timidly.

I was annoyed, but I told her how much I should prize it, and promised to wear it always. She fastened it on my coat beneath the lapel.

"How foolish, Tess, to go and buy me such a beautiful thing as this," I said.

"I did not buy it," she laughed.

"Where did you get it?"

Then she told me how she had found it one day while coming from the Aquarium in the Battery, how she had advertised it and watched the papers, but at last gave up all hopes of finding the owner.

"That was last winter," she said, "the very day I had the first horrid dream about the hearse."

I remembered my dream of the previous night but said nothing, and presently my charcoal was flying over a new canvas, and Tessie stood motionless on the model-stand.

III

The day following was a disastrous one for me. While moving a framed canvas from one easel to another my foot slipped on the polished floor, and I fell heavily on both wrists. They were so badly sprained that it was useless to attempt to hold a brush, and I was obliged to wander about the studio, glaring at unfinished drawings and sketches, until despair seized me and I sat down to smoke and twiddle my thumbs with rage. The rain blew against the windows and rattled on the roof of the church, driving me into a nervous fit with its interminable patter. Tessie sat sewing by the window, and every now and then raised her head and looked at me with such innocent compassion that I began to feel ashamed of my irritation and looked about for something to occupy me. I had read all the papers and all the books in the library, but for the sake of something to do I went to the bookcases and shoved them open with my elbow. I knew every volume by its color and examined them all, passing slowly around the library and whistling to keep up my spirits. I was turning to go into the dining-room when my eye fell upon a book bound in serpent skin, standing in a corner of the top shelf of the last bookcase. I did not remember it, and from the floor could not decipher the pale lettering on the back, so I went to the smoking-room and called Tessie. She came in from the studio and climbed up to reach the book.

"What is it?" I asked.

"*The King in Yellow.*"

I was dumfounded. Who had placed it there? How came it in my rooms? I had long ago decided that I should never open that book, and nothing on earth could have persuaded me to buy it. Fearful lest curiosity might tempt me to open it, I had never even looked at it in book-stores. If I ever had had any curiosity to read it, the awful tragedy of young Castaigne, whom I knew, prevented me from exploring its wicked pages. I had always refused to listen to any description of it, and indeed, nobody ever ventured to discuss the second part aloud, so I had absolutely no knowledge of what those leaves might reveal. I stared at the poisonous mottled binding as I would at a snake.

"Don't touch it, Tessie," I said; "come down."

Of course my admonition was enough to arouse her curiosity, and before I could prevent it she took the book and, laughing, danced off into the studio with it. I called to her, but she slipped away with a tormenting smile at my helpless hands, and I followed her with some impatience.

"Tessie!" I cried, entering the library, "listen, I am serious. Put that book away. I do not wish you to open it!" The library was empty. I went into both drawing-rooms, then into the bedrooms, laundry, kitchen, and finally returned to the library and began a systematic search. She had hidden herself so well that it was half-an-hour later when I discovered her crouching white and silent by the latticed window in the store-room above. At the first glance I saw she had been punished for her foolishness. *The King in Yellow* lay at her feet, but the book was open at the second part. I looked at Tessie and saw it was too late. She had opened *The King in Yellow*. Then I took her by the hand and led her into the studio. She seemed dazed, and when I told her to lie down on the sofa she obeyed me without a word. After a while she closed her eyes and her breathing became regular and deep, but I could not determine whether or not she slept. For a long while I sat silently beside her, but she neither stirred nor spoke, and at last I rose, and, entering the unused store-room, took the book in my least injured hand. It seemed heavy as lead, but I carried it into the studio again, and sitting down on the rug beside the sofa, opened it and read it through from beginning to end.

When, faint with excess of my emotions, I dropped the volume and leaned wearily back against the sofa, Tessie opened her eyes and looked at me.

★ ★ ★

We had been speaking for some time in a dull monotonous strain before I realized that we were discussing *The King in Yellow*. Oh the sin of writing such words—words which are clear as crystal, limpid and musical as bubbling springs, words which sparkle and glow like the poisoned diamonds of the Medicis! Oh the wickedness, the hopeless damnation of a soul who could fascinate and paralyze human creatures with such words—words understood by the ignorant and wise alike, words which are more precious than jewels, more soothing than music, more awful than death!

We talked on, unmindful of the gathering shadows, and she was begging me to throw away the clasp of black onyx quaintly inlaid with what we now knew to be the Yellow Sign. I never shall know why I refused, though even at this hour, here in my bedroom as I write this confession, I should be glad to know *what* it was that prevented me from tearing the Yellow Sign from my breast and casting it into the fire. I am sure I wished to do so, and yet Tessie pleaded with me in vain. Night fell and the hours dragged on, but still we murmured to each other of the King and the Pallid Mask, and midnight sounded from the misty spires in the fog-wrapped city. We spoke of Hastur and of Cassilda, while outside the fog rolled against the blank window-panes as the cloud waves roll and break on the shores of Hali.

The house was very silent now, and not a sound came up from the misty streets. Tessie lay among the cushions, her face a grey blot in the gloom, but her hands were clasped in mine, and I knew that she knew and read my thoughts as I read hers, for we had understood the mystery of the Hyades and the Phantom of Truth was laid. Then as we answered each other, swiftly, silently, thought on thought, the shadows stirred in the gloom about us, and far in the distant streets we heard a sound. Nearer and nearer it came, the dull crunching of wheels, nearer and yet nearer, and now, outside before the door it ceased, and I dragged myself to the window and saw a black-plumed hearse. The gate below opened and shut, and I crept shaking to my door and bolted it, but I knew no bolts, no locks, could keep that creature out who was coming for the Yellow Sign. And now I heard him moving very softly along the hall. Now he was at the door, and the bolts rotted at his touch. Now he had entered. With eyes starting from my head I peered into the darkness, but when he came into the room I did not see him. It was only when I felt him envelope me in his cold soft grasp that I cried out and struggled with deadly fury, but my hands were useless and he tore the onyx clasp from my coat and struck me full in the face. Then, as I fell, I heard Tessie's soft cry and her spirit fled: and even while falling I longed to follow her, for I knew that the King in Yellow had opened his tattered mantle and there was only God to cry to now.

I could tell more, but I cannot see what help it will be to the world. As for me, I am past human help or hope. As I lie here, writing, careless even whether or not I die before I finish, I can see the doctor gathering up his powders and phials with a vague gesture to the good priest beside me, which I understand.

They will be very curious to know the tragedy—they of the outside world who write books and print millions of newspapers, but I shall write no more, and the father confessor will seal my last words with the seal of sanctity when his holy office is done. They of the outside world may send their creatures into wrecked homes and death-smitten firesides, and their newspapers will batten on blood and tears, but with me their spies must halt before the confessional. They know that Tessie is dead and that I am dying. They know how the people in the house, aroused by an infernal scream, rushed into my room and found one living and two dead, but they do not know what I shall tell them now; they do not know that the doctor said as he pointed to a horrible decomposed heap on the floor—the livid corpse of the watchman from the church: "I have no theory, no explanation. That man must have been dead for months!"

I think I am dying. I wish the priest would—

NO. 252 RUE M. LE PRINCE

RALPH ADAMS CRAM

BEFORE HE BECAME A WORLD-FAMOUS ARCHITECT WHOSE
COMMISSIONS WOULD INCLUDE THE CATHEDRAL OF ST. JOHN
THE DIVINE IN NEW YORK CITY, RALPH ADAMS CRAM
(1863-1942) WROTE A SLIM VOLUME OF GHOST STORIES,
BLACK SPIRITS AND WHITE (1895), WHOSE SETTINGS WERE
INSPIRED BY HIS TRAVELS IN EUROPE. THE DESCRIPTIVE
ARCHITECTURAL DETAIL THAT GROUNDS THE SUPERNATURAL
HORRORS OF THIS STORY IN REALITY SHOWS WHY CRAM WENT
ON TO BECOME A LEADING EXPONENT OF THE GOTHIC
TRADITION IN HIS WORK AS AN ARCHITECT.

When in May, 1886, I found myself at last in Paris, I naturally determined to throw myself on the charity of an old chum of mine, Eugene Marie d'Ardeche, who had forsaken Boston a year or more ago on receiving word of the death of an aunt who had left him such property as she possessed. I fancy this windfall surprised him not a little, for the relations between the aunt and nephew had never been cordial, judging from Eugene's remarks touching the lady, who was, it seems, a more or less wicked and witch-like old person, with a penchant for black magic, at least such was the common report.

Why she should leave all her property to d'Ardeche, no one could tell, unless it was that she felt his rather hobbledehoy tendencies towards Buddhism and occultism might some day lead him to her own unhallowed height of questionable illumination. To be sure d'Ardeche reviled her as a bad old woman, being himself in that state of enthusiastic exaltation which sometimes accompanies a boyish fancy for occultism; but in spite of his distant and repellent attitude, Mlle. Blaye de Tartas made him her sole heir, to the violent wrath of a questionable old party known to infamy as the Sar Torrevieja, the "King of the Sorcerers." This malevolent old portent, whose gray and crafty face was often seen in the Rue M. le Prince during the life of Mlle. de Tartas had, it seems, fully expected to enjoy her small wealth after her death; and when it appeared that she had left him only the contents of the gloomy old house in the Quartier Latin, giving the house itself and all else of which she died possessed to her nephew in America, the Sar proceeded to remove everything from the place, and then to curse it elaborately and comprehensively, together with all those who should ever dwell therein.

Whereupon he disappeared.

This final episode was the last word I received from Eugene, but I knew the number of the house, 252 Rue M. le Prince. So, after a day or two given to a first cursory survey of Paris, I started across the Seine to find Eugene and compel him to do the honors of the city.

Every one who knows the Latin Quarter knows the Rue M. le Prince, running up the hill towards the Garden of the Luxembourg. It is full of queer houses and odd corners—or was in '86—and certainly No. 252 was, when I found it, quite as queer as any. It was nothing but a doorway, a black arch of old stone between and under two new houses painted yellow. The effect of this bit of seventeenth-century masonry, with its dirty old doors, and rusty broken lantern sticking gaunt and grim out over the narrow sidewalk, was, in its frame of fresh plaster, sinister in the extreme.

I wondered if I had made a mistake in the number; it was quite evident that no one lived behind those cobwebs. I went into the doorway of one of the new hotels and interviewed the concierge.

No, M. d'Ardeche did not live there, though to be sure he owned the mansion; he himself resided in Meudon, in the country house of the late Mlle. de Tartas. Would Monsieur like the number and the street?

Monsieur would like them extremely, so I took the card that the concierge wrote for me, and forthwith started for the river, in order that I might take a steam-boat for Meudon. By one of those coincidences which happen so often, being quite inexplicable, I had not gone twenty paces down the street before I ran directly into the arms of Eugene d'Ardeche. In three minutes we were sitting in the queer little garden of the Chien Bleu, drinking vermouth and absinthe, and talking it all over.

"You do not live in your aunt's house?" I said at last, interrogatively.

"No, but if this sort of thing keeps on I shall have to. I like Meudon much better, and the house is perfect, all furnished, and nothing in it newer than the last century. You must come out with me to-night and see it. I have got a jolly room fixed up for my Buddha. But there is something wrong with this house opposite. I can't keep a tenant in it—not four days. I have had three, all within six months, but the stories have gone around and a man would as soon think of hiring the Cour des Comptes to live in as No. 252. It is notorious. The fact is, it is haunted the worst way."

I laughed and ordered more vermouth.

"That is all right. It is haunted all the same, or enough to keep it empty, and the funny part is that no one knows *how* it is haunted. Nothing is ever seen, nothing heard. As far as I can find out, people just have the horrors there, and have them so bad they have to go to the hospital afterwards. I have one ex-tenant in the Bicêtre now. So the house stands empty, and as it covers considerable ground and is taxed for a lot, I don't know what to do about it. I think I'll either give it to that child of sin, Torrevieja, or else go and live in it myself. I shouldn't mind the ghosts, I am sure."

"Did you ever stay there?"

"No, but I have always intended to, and in fact I came up here to-day to see a couple of rake-hell fellows I know, Fargeau and Duchesne, doctors in the Clinical Hospital beyond here, up by the Parc Mont Souris. They promised that they would spend the night with me some time in my aunt's house—which is called around here, you must know, 'la Bouche d'Enfer'—and I thought perhaps they would make it this week, if they can get off duty. Come up with me while I see them, and then we can go across the river to Véfour's and have some luncheon, you can get your things at the Chatham, and we will go out to Meudon, where of course you will spend the night with me."

The plan suited me perfectly, so we went up to the hospital, found Fargeau, who declared that he and Duchesne were ready for anything, the nearer the real "bouche d'enfer" the better; that the following Thursday they would both be off duty for the night, and that on that day they would join in an attempt to outwit the devil and clear up the mystery of No. 252.

"Does M. l'Américain go with us?" asked Fargeau.

"Why of course," I replied, "I intend to go, and you must not refuse me, d'Ardeche; I decline to be put off. Here is a chance for you to do the honors of your city in a manner which is faultless. Show me a real live ghost, and I will forgive Paris for having lost the Jardin Mabille."

So it was settled.

Later we went down to Meudon and ate dinner in the terrace room of the villa, which was all that d'Ardeche had said, and more, so utterly was its atmosphere that of the seventeenth century. At dinner Eugene told me more about his late aunt, and the queer goings on in the old house.

Mlle. Blaye lived, it seems, all alone, except for one female servant of her own age; a severe, taciturn creature, with massive Breton features and a Breton tongue, whenever she vouchsafed to use it. No one ever was seen to enter the door of No. 252 except Jeanne the servant and the Sar Torrevieja, the latter coming constantly from none knew whither, and always entering, *never leaving*. Indeed, the neighbors, who for eleven years had watched the old sorcerer sidle crab-wise up to the bell almost every day, declared vociferously that *never* had he been seen to leave the house. Once, when they decided to keep absolute guard, the watcher, none other than Maitre Garceau of the Chien Bleu, after keeping his eyes fixed on the door from ten o'clock one morning when the Sar arrived until four in the afternoon, during which time the door was unopened (he knew this, for had he not gummed a ten-centime stamp over the joint and was not the stamp unbroken) nearly fell down when the sinister figure of Torrevieja slid wickedly by him with a dry "Pardon, Monsieur!" and disappeared again through the black doorway.

This was curious, for No. 252 was entirely surrounded by houses, its only windows opening on a courtyard into which no eye could look from the hotels of the Rue M. le Prince and the Rue de l'Ecole, and the mystery was one of the choice possessions of the Latin Quarter.

Once a year the austerity of the place was broken, and the denizens of the whole quarter stood open-mouthed watching many carriages drive up to No. 252, many of them private, not a few with crests on the door panels, from all of them descending veiled female figures and men with coat collars turned up. Then followed curious sounds of music from within, and those whose houses joined the blank walls of No. 252 became for the moment popular, for by placing the ear against the wall strange music could distinctly be heard, and the sound of monotonous chanting voices now and then. By dawn the last guest would have departed, and for another year the hotel of Mlle. de Tartas was ominously silent.

Eugene declared that he believed it was a celebration of "Walpurgisnacht," and certainly appearances favored such a fancy.

"A queer thing about the whole affair is," he said, "the fact that every one in the street swears that about a month ago, while I was out in Concarneau for a visit, the music and voices were heard again, just as when my revered aunt was in the flesh. The house was perfectly empty, as I tell you, so it is quite possible that the good people were enjoying an hallucination."

I must acknowledge that these stories did not reassure me; in fact, as Thursday came near, I began to regret a little my determination to spend the night in the house. I was too vain to back down, however, and the perfect coolness of the two doctors, who ran down Tuesday to Meudon to make a few arrangements, caused me to swear that I would die of fright before I would flinch. I suppose I believed more or less in ghosts, I am sure now that I am older I believe in them, there are in fact few things I can *not* believe. Two or three inexplicable things had happened to me, and, although this was before my adventure with Rendel in Paestum, I had a strong predisposition to believe some things that I could not explain, wherein I was out of sympathy with the age.

Well, to come to the memorable night of the twelfth of June, we had made our preparations, and after depositing a big bag inside the doors of No. 252, went across to the Chien Bleu, where Fargeau and Duchesne turned up promptly, and we sat down to the best dinner Pere Garceau could create.

I remember I hardly felt that the conversation was in good taste. It began with various stories of Indian fakirs and Oriental jugglery, matters in which Eugene was curiously well read, swerved to the horrors of the great Sepoy mutiny, and thus to reminiscences of the dissecting-room. By this time we had drunk more or less, and Duchesne launched into a photographic and Zolaesque account of the only time (as he said) when he was possessed of the panic of fear; namely, one night many years ago, when he was locked by accident into the dissecting-room of the Loucine, together with several cadavers of a rather unpleasant nature. I ventured to protest mildly against the choice of subjects, the result being a perfect carnival of horrors, so that when we finally drank our last *crème de cacao* and started for "la Bouche d'Enfer," my nerves were in a somewhat rocky condition.

It was just ten o'clock when we came into the street. A hot dead wind drifted in great puffs through the city, and ragged masses of vapor swept the purple sky; an unsavory night altogether, one of those nights of hopeless lassitude when one feels, if one is at home, like doing nothing but drink mint juleps and smoke cigarettes.

Eugene opened the creaking door, and tried to light one of the lanterns; but the gusty wind blew out every match, and we finally had to close the outer doors before we could get a light. At last we had all the lanterns going, and I began to look around curiously. We were in a long, vaulted passage, partly carriageway, partly footpath, perfectly bare but for the street refuse which had drifted in with eddying winds. Beyond lay the courtyard, a curious place rendered more curious still by the fitful moonlight and the flashing of four dark lanterns. The place had evidently been once a most noble palace. Opposite rose the oldest portion, a three-story wall of the time of Francis I., with a great wisteria vine covering half. The wings on either side were more modern, seventeenth century, and ugly, while towards the street was nothing but a flat unbroken wall.

The great bare court, littered with bits of paper blown in by the wind, fragments of packing cases, and straw, mysterious with flashing lights and flaunting shadows, while low masses of torn vapor drifted overhead, hiding, then revealing the stars, and all in absolute silence, not even the sounds of the streets entering this prison-like place, was weird and uncanny in the extreme. I must confess that already I began to feel a slight disposition towards the horrors, but with that curious inconsequence which so often happens in the case of those who are deliberately growing scared, I could think of nothing more reassuring than those delicious verses of Lewis Carroll's:—

> "Just the place for a Snark! I have said it twice,
> That alone should encourage the crew.
> Just the place for a Snark! I have said it thrice,
> What I tell you three times is true,"—

which kept repeating themselves over and over in my brain with feverish insistence.

Even the medical students had stopped their chaffing, and were studying the surroundings gravely.

"There is one thing certain," said Fargeau, "*anything* might have happened here without the slightest chance of discovery. Did ever you see such a perfect place for lawlessness?"

"And *anything* might happen here now, with the same certainty of impunity," continued Duchesne, lighting his pipe, the snap of the match making us all start. "D'Ardeche, your lamented relative was certainly well fixed; she had full scope here for her traditional experiments in demonology."

"Curse me if I don't believe that those same traditions were more or less founded on fact," said Eugene. "I never saw this court under these conditions before, but I could believe anything now. What's that!"

"Nothing but a door slamming," said Duchesne, loudly.

"Well, I wish doors wouldn't slam in houses that have been empty eleven months."

"It is irritating," and Duchesne slipped his arm through mine; "but we must take things as they come. Remember we have to deal not only with the spectral lumber left here by your scarlet aunt, but as well with the supererogatory curse of that hell-cat Torrevieja. Come on! let's get inside before the hour arrives for the sheeted dead to squeak and gibber in these lonely halls. Light your pipes, your tobacco is a sure protection against 'your whoreson dead bodies'; light up and move on."

We opened the hall door and entered a vaulted stone vestibule, full of dust, and cobwebby.

"There is nothing on this floor," said Eugene, "except servants' rooms and offices, and I don't believe there is anything wrong with them. I never heard that there was, any way. Let's go up stairs."

So far as we could see, the house was apparently perfectly uninteresting inside, all eighteenth-century work, the facade of the main building being, with the vestibule, the only portion of the Francis I work.

"The place was burned during the Terror," said Eugene, "for my great-uncle, from whom Mlle. de Tartas inherited it, was a good and true Royalist; he went to Spain after the Revolution, and did not come back until the accession of Charles X., when he restored the house, and then died, enormously old. This explains why it is all so new."

The old Spanish sorcerer to whom Mlle. de Tartas had left her personal property had done his work thoroughly. The house was absolutely empty, even the wardrobes and bookcases built in had been carried away; we went through room after room, finding all absolutely dismantled, only the windows and doors with their casings, the parquet floors, and the florid Renaissance mantels remaining.

"I feel better," remarked Fargeau. "The house may be haunted, but it don't look it, certainly; it is the most respectable place imaginable."

"Just you wait," replied Eugene. "These are only the state apartments, which my aunt seldom used, except, perhaps, on her annual 'Walpurgisnacht.' Come up stairs and I will show you a better *mise en scène.*"

On this floor, the rooms fronting the court, the sleeping-rooms, were quite small—("They are the bad rooms all the same," said Eugene)—four of them, all just as ordinary in appearance as those below. A corridor ran behind them connecting with the wing corridor, and from this opened a door, unlike any of the other doors in that it was covered with green baize, somewhat moth-eaten. Eugene selected a key from the bunch he carried, unlocked the door, and with some difficulty forced it to swing inward; it was as heavy as the door of a safe.

"We are now," he said, "on the very threshold of hell itself; these rooms in here were my scarlet aunt's unholy of unholies. I never let them with the rest of the house, but keep them as a curiosity. I only wish Torrevieja had kept out; as it was, he looted them, as he did the rest of the house, and nothing is left but the walls and ceiling and floor. They are something, however, and may suggest what the former condition must have been. Tremble and enter."

The first apartment was a kind of anteroom, a cube of perhaps twenty feet each way, without windows, and with no doors except that by which we entered and another to the right. Walls, floor, and ceiling were covered with a black lacquer, brilliantly polished, that flashed the light of our lanterns in a thousand intricate reflections. It was like the inside of an enormous Japanese box, and about as empty. From this we passed to another room, and here we nearly dropped our lanterns. The room was circular, thirty feet or so in diameter, covered by a hemispherical dome; walls and ceiling were dark blue, spotted with gold stars; and reaching from floor to floor across the dome stretched a colossal figure in red lacquer of a nude woman kneeling, her legs reaching out along the floor on either side, her head touching the lintel of the door through which we had entered, her arms forming its sides, with the fore arms extended and stretching along the walls until they met the long feet. The most astounding, misshapen, absolutely terrifying thing, I think, I ever saw. From the navel hung a great white object, like the traditional roe's egg of the Arabian Nights. The floor was of red lacquer, and in it was inlaid a pentagram the size of the room, made of wide strips of brass. In the centre of this pentagram was a circular disk of black stone, slightly saucer-shaped, with a small outlet in the middle.

The effect of the room was simply crushing, with this gigantic red figure crouched over it all, the staring eyes fixed on one, no matter what his position. None of us spoke, so oppressive was the whole thing.

The third room was like the first in dimensions, but instead of being black it was entirely sheathed with plates of brass, walls, ceiling, and floor—tarnished now, and turning green, but still brilliant under the lantern light. In the middle stood an oblong altar of porphyry, its longer dimensions on the axis of the suite of rooms, and at one end, opposite the range of doors, a pedestal of black basalt.

This was all. Three rooms, stranger than these, even in their emptiness, it would be hard to imagine. In Egypt, in India, they would not be entirely out of place, but here in Paris, in a commonplace *hôtel*, in the Rue M. le Prince, they were incredible.

We retraced our steps, Eugene closed the iron door with its baize covering, and we went into one of the front chambers and sat down, looking at each other.

"Nice party, your aunt," said Fargeau. "Nice old party, with amiable tastes; I am glad we are not to spend the night in *those* rooms."

"What do you suppose she did there?" inquired Duchesne. "I know more or less about black art, but that series of rooms is too much for me."

"My impression is," said d'Ardeche, "that the brazen room was a kind of sanctuary containing some image or other on the basalt base, while the stone in front was really an altar—what the nature of the sacrifice might be I don't even guess. The round room may have been used for invocations and incantations. The pentagram looks like it. Any way it is all just about as queer and *fin de siècle* as I can well imagine. Look here, it is nearly twelve, let's dispose of ourselves, if we are going to hunt this thing down."

The four chambers on this floor of the old house were those said to be haunted, the wings being quite innocent, and, so far as we knew, the floors below. It was arranged that we should each occupy a room, leaving the doors open with the lights burning, and at the slightest cry or knock we were all to rush at once to the room from which the warning sound might come. There was no communication between the rooms to be sure, but, as the doors all opened into the corridor, every sound was plainly audible.

The last room fell to me, and I looked it over carefully.

It seemed innocent enough, a commonplace, square, rather lofty Parisian sleeping-room, finished in wood painted white, with a small marble mantel, a dusty floor of inlaid maple and cherry, walls hung with an ordinary French paper, apparently quite new, and two deeply embrasured windows looking out on the court.

I opened the swinging sash with some trouble, and sat down in the window seat with my lantern beside me trained on the only door, which gave on the corridor.

The wind had gone down, and it was very still without—still and hot. The masses of luminous vapor were gathering thickly overhead, no longer urged by the gusty wind. The great masses of rank wisteria leaves, with here and there a second blossoming of purple flowers, hung dead over the window in the sluggish air. Across the roofs I could hear the sound of a belated *fiacre* in the streets below. I filled my pipe again and waited.

For a time the voices of the men in the other rooms were a companionship, and at first I shouted to them now and then, but my voice echoed rather unpleasantly through the long corridors, and had a suggestive way of reverberating around the left wing beside me, and coming out at a broken window at its extremity like the voice of another man. I soon gave up my attempts at conversation, and devoted myself to the task of keeping awake.

It was not easy; why did I eat that lettuce salad at Père Garceau's? I should have known better. It was making me irresistibly sleepy, and wakefulness was absolutely necessary. It was certainly gratifying to know that I could sleep, that my courage was by me to that extent, but in the interests of science I must keep awake. But almost never, it seemed, had sleep looked so desirable. Half a hundred times, nearly, I would doze for an instant, only to awake with a start, and find my pipe gone out. Nor did the exertion of relighting it pull me together. I struck my match mechanically, and with the first puff dropped off again. It was most vexing. I got up and walked around the room. It was most annoying. My cramped position had almost put both my legs to sleep. I could hardly stand. I felt numb, as though with cold. There was no longer any sound from the other rooms, nor from without. I sank down in my window seat. How dark it was growing! I turned up the lantern. That pipe again, how obstinately it kept going out! and my last match was gone. The lantern, too, was *that* going out? I lifted my hand to turn it up again. It felt like lead, and fell beside me.

Then I awoke—absolutely. I remembered the story of "The Haunters and the Haunted." *This* was the Horror. I tried to rise, to cry out. My body was like lead, my tongue was paralyzed. I could hardly move my eyes. And the light was going out. There was no question about that. Darker and darker yet; little by little the pattern of the paper was swallowed up in the advancing night. A prickling numbnessgathered in every nerve, myright arm slipped without feeling from my lap to my side, and I could not raise it—it swung helpless. A thin, keen humming began in my head, like the cicadas on a hillside in September. The darkness was coming fast.

Yes, this was it. Something was subjecting me, body and mind, to slow paralysis. Physically I was already dead. If I could only hold my mind, my consciousness, I might still be safe, but could I? Could I resist the mad horror of this silence, the deepening dark, the creeping numbness? I knew that, like the man in the ghost story, my only safety lay here.

It had come at last. My body was dead, I could no longer move my eyes. They were fixed in that last look on the place where the door had been, now only a deepening of the dark.

Utter night: the last flicker of the lantern was gone. I sat and waited; my mind was still keen, but how long would it last? There was a limit even to the endurance of the utter panic of fear.

Then the end began. In the velvet blackness came two white eyes, milky, opalescent, small, far away—awful eyes, like a dead dream. More beautiful than I can describe, the flakes of white flame moving from the perimeter inward, disappearing in the centre, like a never ending flow of opal water into a circular tunnel. I could not have moved my eyes had I possessed the power: they devoured the fearful, beautiful things that grew slowly, slowly larger, fixed on me, advancing, growing more beautiful, the white flakes of light sweeping more swiftly into the blazing vortices, the awful fascination deepening in its insane intensity as the white, vibrating eyes grew nearer, larger.

123

Like a hideous and implacable engine of death the eyes of the unknown Horror swelled and expanded until they were close before me, enormous, terrible, and I felt a slow, cold, wet breath propelled with mechanical regularity against my face, enveloping me in its fetid mist, in its charnel-house deadliness.

With ordinary fear goes always a physical terror, but with me in the presence of this unspeakable Thing was only the utter and awful terror of the mind, the mad fear of a prolonged and ghostly nightmare. Again and again I tried to shriek, to make some noise, but physically I was utterly dead. I could only feel myself go mad with the terror of hideous death. The eyes were close on me,—their movement so swift that they seemed to be but palpitating flames, the dead breath was around me like the depths of the deepest sea.

Suddenly a wet, icy mouth, like that of a dead cuttle-fish, shapeless, jelly-like, fell over mine. The horror began slowly to draw my life from me, but, as enormous and shuddering folds of palpitating jelly swept sinuously around me, my will came back, my body awoke with the reaction of final fear, and I closed with the nameless death that enfolded me.

What was it that I was fighting? My arms sunk through the unresisting mass that was turning me to ice. Moment by moment new folds of cold jelly swept round me, crushing me with the force of Titans. I fought to wrest my mouth from this awful Thing that sealed it, but, if ever I succeeded and caught a single breath, the wet, sucking mass closed over my face again before I could cry out. I think I fought for hours, desperately, insanely, in a silence that was more hideous than any sound,—fought until I felt final death at hand, until the memory of all my life rushed over me like a flood, until I no longer had strength to wrench my face from that hellish succubus, until with a last mechanical struggle I fell and yielded to death.

* * *

Then I heard a voice say, "If he is dead, I can never forgive myself; I was to blame."

Another replied, "He is not dead, I know we can save him if only we reach the hospital in time. Drive like hell, *cocher*! twenty francs for you, if you get there in three minutes."

Then there was night again, and nothingness, until I suddenly awoke and stared around. I lay in a hospital ward, very white and sunny, some yellow *fleurs-de-lis* stood beside the head of the pallet, and a tall sister of mercy sat by my side.

To tell the story in a few words, I was in the Hotel Dieu, where the men had taken me that fearful night of the twelfth of June. I asked for Fargeau or Duchesne, and by and by the latter came, and sitting beside the bed told me all that I did not know.

It seems that they had sat, each in his room, hour after hour, hearing nothing, very much bored, and disappointed. Soon after two o'clock Fargeau, who was in the next room, called to me to ask if I was awake. I gave no reply, and, after shouting once or twice, he took his lantern and came to investigate. The door was locked on the inside! He instantly called d'Ardeche and Duchesne, and together they hurled themselves against the door. It resisted. Within they could hear irregular footsteps dashing here and there, with heavy breathing. Although frozen with terror, they fought to destroy the door and finally succeeded by using a great slab of marble that formed the shelf of the mantel in Fargeau's room. As the door crashed in, they were suddenly hurled back against the walls of the corridor, as though by an explosion, the lanterns were extinguished, and they found themselves in utter silence and darkness.

As soon as they recovered from the shock, they leaped into the room and fell over my body in the middle of the floor. They lighted one of the lanterns, and saw the strangest sight that can be imagined. The floor and walls to the height of about six feet were running with something that seemed like stagnant water, thick, glutinous, sickening. As for me, I was drenched with the same cursed liquid. The odor of musk was nauseating. They dragged me away, stripped off my clothing, wrapped me in their coats, and hurried to the hospital, thinking me perhaps dead. Soon after sunrise d'Ardeche left the hospital, being assured that I was in a fair way to recovery, with time, and with Fargeau went up to examine by daylight the traces of the adventure that was so nearly fatal. They were too late. Fire engines were coming down the street as they passed the Academie. A neighbor rushed up to d'Ardeche: "O Monsieur! what misfortune, yet what fortune! It is true *la Bouche d'Enfer*—I beg pardon, the residence of the lamented Mlle. de Tartas—was burned, but not wholly, only the ancient building. The wings were saved, and for that great credit is due the brave firemen. Monsieur will remember them, no doubt."

It was quite true. Whether a forgotten lantern, overturned in the excitement, had done the work, or whether the origin of the fire was more supernatural, it was certain that "the Mouth of Hell" was no more. A last engine was pumping slowly as d'Ardeche came up; half a dozen limp, and one distended, hose stretched through the *porte cochère*, and within only the facade of Francis I remained, draped still with the black stems of the wisteria. Beyond lay a great vacancy, where thin smoke was rising slowly. Every floor was gone, and the strange halls of Mlle. Blaye de Tartas were only a memory.

With d'Ardeche I visited the place last year, but in the stead of the ancient walls was then only a new and ordinary building, fresh and respectable; yet the wonderful stories of the old *Bouche d'Enfer* still lingered in the quarter, and will hold there, I do not doubt, until the Day of Judgment.

THE STRIDING PLACE

GERTRUDE ATHERTON

A PROLIFIC WRITER OF HISTORICAL NOVELS AND REGIONAL
FICTION, CALIFORNIAN GERTRUDE ATHERTON (1857–1948)
WROTE AT A TIME WHEN MANY MAINSTREAM WRITERS
EXPLORED SUPERNATURAL THEMES IN THEIR WORK REGARDLESS
OF GENRE IDENTIFICATION. THIS STORY, WHICH WAS PUBLISHED
IN *THE SPEAKER* IN 1896 AND LATER COLLECTED IN HER
SHORT-FICTION COMPILATION *THE BELL IN THE FOG AND
OTHER STORIES* (1905), SHOWS HOW EFFECTIVELY A STRONG
LITERARY SENSIBILITY CAN SHAPE HORRIFIC SUBJECT MATTER.

Weigall, continental and detached, tired early of grouse-shooting. To stand propped against a sod fence while his host's workmen routed up the birds with long poles and drove them towards the waiting guns, made him feel himself a parody on the ancestors who had roamed the moors and forests of this West Riding of Yorkshire in hot pursuit of game worth the killing. But when in England in August he always accepted whatever proffered for the season, and invited his host to shoot pheasants on his estates in the South. The amusements of life, he argued, should be accepted with the same philosophy as its ills.

It had been a bad day. A heavy rain had made the moor so spongy that it fairly sprang beneath the feet. Whether or not the grouse had haunts of their own, wherein they were immune from rheumatism, the bag had been small. The women, too, were an unusually dull lot, with the exception of a new-minded *débutante* who bothered Weigall at dinner by demanding the verbal restoration of the vague paintings on the vaulted roof above them.

But it was no one of these things that sat on Weigall's mind as, when the other men went up to bed, he let himself out of the castle and sauntered down to the river. His intimate friend, the companion of his boyhood, the chum of his college days, his fellow-traveller in many lands, the man for whom he possessed stronger affection than for all men, had mysteriously disappeared two days ago, and his track might have sprung to the upper air for all trace he had left behind him. He had been a guest on the adjoining estate during the past week, shooting with the fervor of the true sportsman, making love in the intervals to Adeline Cavan, and apparently in the best of spirits. As far as was known there was nothing to lower his mental mercury, for his rent-roll was a large one, Miss Cavan blushed whenever he looked at her, and, being one of the best shots in England, he was never happier than in August. The suicide theory was preposterous, all agreed, and there was as little reason to believe him murdered. Nevertheless, he had walked out of March Abbey two nights ago without hat or overcoat, and had not been seen since.

The country was being patrolled night and day. A hundred keepers and workmen were beating the woods and poking the bogs on the moors, but as yet not so much as a handkerchief had been found.

Weigall did not believe for a moment that Wyatt Gifford was dead, and although it was impossible not to be affected by the general uneasiness, he was disposed to be more angry than frightened. At Cambridge Gifford had been an incorrigible practical joker, and by no means had outgrown the habit; it would be like him to cut across the country in his evening clothes, board a cattle-train, and amuse himself touching up the picture of the sensation in West Riding.

However, Weigall's affection for his friend was too deep to companion with tranquillity in the present state of doubt, and, instead of going to bed early with the other men, he determined to walk until ready for sleep. He went down to the river and followed the path through the woods. There was no moon, but the stars sprinkled their cold light upon the pretty belt of water flowing placidly past wood and ruin, between green masses of overhanging rocks or sloping banks tangled with tree and shrub, leaping occasionally over stones with the harsh notes of an angry scold, to recover its equanimity the moment the way was clear again.

It was very dark in the depths where Weigall trod. He smiled as he recalled a remark of Gifford's: "An English wood is like a good many other things in life—very promising at a distance, but a hollow mockery when you get within. You see daylight on both sides, and the sun freckles the very bracken. Our woods need the night to make them seem what they ought to be—what they once were, before our ancestors' descendants demanded so much more money, in these so much more various days."

Weigall strolled along, smoking, and thinking of his friend, his pranks—many of which had done more credit to his imagination than this—and recalling conversations that had lasted the night through. Just before the end of the London season they had walked the streets one hot night after a party, discussing the various theories of the soul's destiny. That afternoon they had met at the coffin of a college friend whose mind had been a blank for the past three years. Some months previously they had called at the asylum to see him. His expression had been senile, his face imprinted with the record of debauchery. In death the face was placid, intelligent, without ignoble lineation—the face of the man they had known at college. Weigall and Gifford had had no time to comment there, and the afternoon and evening were full; but, coming forth from the house of festivity together, they had reverted almost at once to the topic.

"I cherish the theory," Gifford had said, "that the soul sometimes lingers in the body after death. During madness, of course, it is an impotent prisoner, albeit a conscious one. Fancy its agony, and its horror! What more natural than that, when the life-spark goes out, the tortured soul should take possession of the vacant skull and triumph once more for a few hours while old friends look their last? It has had time to repent while compelled to crouch and behold the result of its work, and it has shrived itself into a state of comparative purity. If I had my way, I should stay inside my bones until the coffin had gone into its niche, that I might obviate for my poor old comrade the tragic impersonality of death. And I should like to see justice done to it, as it were—to see it lowered among its ancestors with the ceremony and solemnity that are its due. I am afraid that if I dissevered myself too quickly, I should yield to curiosity and hasten to investigate the mysteries of space."

"You believe in the soul as an independent entity, then—that it and the vital principle are not one and the same?"

"Absolutely. The body and soul are twins, life comrades—sometimes friends, sometimes enemies, but always loyal in the last instance. Some day, when I am tired of the world, I shall go to India and become a mahatma, solely for the pleasure of receiving proof during life of this independent relationship."

"Suppose you were not sealed up properly, and returned after one of your astral flights to find your earthly part unfit for habitation? It is an experiment I don't think I should care to try, unless even juggling with soul and flesh had palled."

"That would not be an uninteresting predicament. I should rather enjoy experimenting with broken machinery."

The high wild roar of water smote suddenly upon Weigall's ear and checked his memories. He left the wood and walked out on the huge slippery stones which nearly close the River Wharfe at this point, and watched the waters boil down into the narrow pass with their furious untiring energy. The black quiet of the woods rose high on either side. The stars seemed colder and whiter just above. On either hand the perspective of the river might have run into a rayless cavern. There was no lonelier spot in England, nor one which had the right to claim so many ghosts, if ghosts there were.

Weigall was not a coward, but he recalled uncomfortably the tales of those that had been done to death in the Strid.* Wordsworth's Boy of Egremond had been disposed of by the practical Whitaker; but countless others, more venturesome than wise, had gone down into that narrow boiling course, never to appear in the still pool a few yards beyond. Below the great rocks which form the walls of the Strid was believed to be a natural vault, on to whose shelves the dead were drawn. The spot had an ugly fascination. Weigall stood, visioning skeletons, uncoffined and green, the home of the eyeless things which had devoured all that had covered and filled that rattling symbol of man's mortality; then fell to wondering if any one had attempted to leap the Strid of late. It was covered with slime; he had never seen it look so treacherous.

He shuddered and turned away, impelled, despite his manhood, to flee the spot. As he did so, something tossing in the foam below the fall—something as white, yet independent of it—caught his eye and arrested his step. Then he saw that it was describing a contrary motion to the rushing water—an upward backward motion. Weigall stood rigid, breathless; he fancied he heard the crackling of his hair. Was that a hand? It thrust itself still higher above the boiling foam, turned sidewise, and four frantic fingers were distinctly visible against the black rock beyond.

Weigall's superstitious terror left him. A man was there, struggling to free himself from the suction beneath the Strid, swept down, doubtless, but a moment before his arrival, perhaps as he stood with his back to the current.

He stepped as close to the edge as he dared. The hand doubled as if in imprecation, shaking savagely in the face of that force which leaves its creatures to immutable law; then spread wide again, clutching, expanding, crying for help as audibly as the human voice.

Weigall dashed to the nearest tree, dragged and twisted off a branch with his strong arms, and returned as swiftly to the Strid. The hand was in the same place, still

---

*"This striding place is called the 'Strid,'
A name which it took of yore;
A thousand years hath it borne the name,
And it shall a thousand more."

gesticulating as wildly; the body was undoubtedly caught in the rocks below, perhaps already half-way along one of those hideous shelves. Weigall let himself down upon a lower rock, braced his shoulder against the mass beside him, then, leaning out over the water, thrust the branch into the hand. The fingers clutched it convulsively. Weigall tugged powerfully, his own feet dragged perilously near the edge. For a moment he produced no impression, then an arm shot above the waters.

The blood sprang to Weigall's head; he was choked with the impression that the Strid had him in her roaring hold, and he saw nothing. Then the mist cleared. The hand and arm were nearer, although the rest of the body was still concealed by the foam. Weigall peered out with distended eyes. The meagre light revealed in the cuffs links of a peculiar device. The fingers clutching the branch were as familiar.

Weigall forgot the slippery stones, the terrible death if he stepped too far. He pulled with passionate will and muscle. Memories flung themselves into the hot light of his brain, trooping rapidly upon each other's heels, as in the thought of the drowning. Most of the pleasures of his life, good and bad, were identified in some way with this friend. Scenes of college days, of travel, where they had deliberately sought adventure and stood between one another and death upon more occasions than one, of hours of delightful companionship among the treasures of art, and others in the pursuit of pleasure, flashed like the changing particles of a kaleidoscope. Weigall had loved several women; but he would have flouted in these moments the thought that he had ever loved any woman as he loved Wyatt Gifford. There were so many charming women in the world, and in the thirty-two years of his life he had never known another man to whom he had cared to give his intimate friendship.

He threw himself on his face. His wrists were cracking, the skin was torn from his hands. The fingers still gripped the stick. There was life in them yet.

Suddenly something gave way. The hand swung about, tearing the branch from Weigall's grasp. The body had been liberated and flung outward, though still submerged by the foam and spray.

Weigall scrambled to his feet and sprang along the rocks, knowing that the danger from suction was over and that Gifford must be carried straight to the quiet pool. Gifford was a fish in the water and could live under it longer than most men. If he survived this, it would not be the first time that his pluck and science had saved him from drowning.

Weigall reached the pool. A man in his evening clothes floated on it, his face turned towards a projecting rock over which his arm had fallen, upholding the body. The hand that had held the branch hung limply over the rock, its white reflection visible in the black water. Weigall plunged into the shallow pool, lifted Gifford in his arms and returned to the bank. He laid the body down and threw off his coat that he might be the freer to practise the methods of resuscitation. He was glad of the moment's respite. The valiant life in the man might have been exhausted in that last struggle. He had not dared to look at his face, to put his ear to the heart. The hesitation lasted but a moment. There was no time to lose.

He turned to his prostrate friend. As he did so, something strange and disagreeable smote his senses. For a half-moment he did not appreciate its nature. Then his teeth clacked together, his feet, his outstretched arms pointed towards the woods. But he sprang to the side of the man and bent down and peered into his face. There was no face.

MARSYAS IN FLANDERS

VERNON LEE

VERNON LEE WAS THE PSEUDONYM OF ENGLISH WRITER VIOLET
PAGET (1856–1935), A DISTINGUISHED *BELLE LETTRIST* AND
CRITIC OF CULTURE AND THE ARTS. MUCH OF HER SHORT
SUPERNATURAL FICTION IS BASED ON THE FOLKLORE AND
HISTORY OF THE EUROPEAN CONTINENT, INCLUDING THIS
STORY FROM 1900, WHICH COMMENTS WRYLY ON PAGAN AND
CHRISTIAN INFLUENCES ON THE ARTS.

I

You are right. This is not the original crucifix at all. Another one has been put instead. *Il y a eu substitution,*" and the little old Antiquary of Dunes nodded mysteriously, fixing his ghostseer's eyes upon mine.

He said it in a scarce audible whisper. For it happened to be the vigil of the Feast of the Crucifix, and the once famous church was full of semi-clerical persons decorating it for the morrow, and of old ladies in strange caps, clattering about with pails and brooms. The Antiquary had brought me there the very moment of my arrival, lest the crowd of faithful should prevent his showing me everything next morning.

The famous crucifix was exhibited behind rows and rows of unlit candles and surrounded by strings of paper flowers and coloured muslin and garlands of sweet resinous maritime pine; and two lighted chandeliers illumined it.

"There has been an exchange," he repeated, looking round that no one might hear him. "Il y a eu substitution."

For I had remarked, as anyone would have done, at the first glance, that the crucifix had every appearance of French work of the thirteenth century, boldly realistic, whereas the crucifix of the legend, which was a work of St. Luke, which had hung for centuries in the Holy Sepulchre at Jerusalem and been miraculously cast ashore

133

at Dunes in 1195, would surely have been a more or less Byzantine image, like its miraculous companion of Lucca.

"But why should there have been a substitution?" I inquired innocently.

"Hush, hush," answered the Antiquary, frowning, "not here—later, later—"

He took me all over the church, once so famous for pilgrimages; but from which, even like the sea which has left it in a salt marsh beneath the cliffs, the tide of devotion has receded for centuries. It is a very dignified little church, of charmingly restrained and shapely Gothic, built of a delicate pale stone, which the sea damp has picked out, in bases and capitals and carved foliation, with stains of a lovely bright green. The Antiquary showed me where the transept and belfry had been left unfinished when the miracles had diminished in the fourteenth century. And he took me up to the curious warder's chamber, a large room up some steps in the triforium; with a fireplace and stone seats for the men who guarded the precious crucifix day and night. There had even been beehives in the window, he told me, and he remembered seeing them still as a child.

"Was it usual, here in Flanders, to have a guardroom in churches containing important relics?" I asked, for I could not remember having seen anything similar before.

"By no means," he answered, looking round to make sure we were alone, "but it was necessary here. You have never heard in what the chief miracles of this church consisted?"

"No," I whispered back, gradually infected by his mysteriousness, "unless you allude to the legend that the figure of the Saviour broke all the crosses until the right one was cast up by the sea?"

He shook his head but did not answer, and descended the steep stairs into the nave, while I lingered a moment looking down into it from the warder's chamber. I have never had so curious an impression of a church. The chandeliers on either side of the crucifix swirled slowly round, making great pools of light which were broken by the shadows of the clustered columns, and among the pews of the nave moved the flicker of the sacristan's lamp. The place was full of the scent of resinous pine branches, evoking dunes and mountainsides; and from the busy groups below rose a subdued chatter of women's voices, and a splash of water and clatter of pattens. It vaguely suggested preparations for a witches' sabbath.

"What sort of miracles did they have in this church?" I asked, when we had passed into the dusky square, "and what did you mean about their having exchanged the crucifix—about a *substitution?*"

It seemed quite dark outside. The church rose black, a vague lopsided mass of buttresses and high-pitched roofs, against the watery, moonlit sky; the big trees of the churchyard behind wavering about in the seawind; and the windows shone yellow, like flaming portals, in the darkness.

"Please remark the bold effect of the gargoyles," said the Antiquary pointing upwards.

They jutted out, vague wild beasts, from the roof-line; and, what was positively frightening, you saw the moonlight, yellow and blue through the open jaws of some of them. A gust swept through the trees, making the weathercock clatter and groan.

"Why, those gargoyle wolves seem positively to howl," I exclaimed.

The old Antiquary chuckled. "Aha," he answered, "did I not tell you that this church has witnessed things like no other church in Christendom? And it still remembers them! There—have you ever known such a wild, savage church before?"

And as he spoke there suddenly mingled with the sough of the wind and the groans of the weather-vane, a shrill quavering sound as of pipers inside.

"The organist trying his vox humana for tomorrow," remarked the Antiquary.

II

Next day I bought one of the printed histories of the miraculous crucifix which they were hawking all round the church; and next day also, my friend the Antiquary was good enough to tell me all that he knew of the matter. Between my two informants, the following may be said to be the true story.

In the autumn of 1195, after a night of frightful storm, a boat was found cast upon the shore of Dunes, which was at that time a fishing village at the mouth of the Nys, and exactly opposite a terrible sunken reef.

The boat was broken and upset; and close to it, on the sand and bent grass, lay a stone figure of the crucified Saviour, without its cross and, as seems probable, also without its arms, which had been made of separate blocks. A variety of persons immediately came forward to claim it; the little church of Dunes, on whose glebe it was found; the Barons of Cröy, who had the right of jetsam on that coast, and also the great Abbey of St. Loup of Arras, as possessing the spiritual overlordship of the place. But a holy man who lived close by in the cliffs, had a vision which settled the dispute. St. Luke in person appeared and told him that he was the original maker of the figure; that it had been one of three which had hung round the Holy Sepulchre of Jerusalem; that three knights, a Norman, a Tuscan, and a man of Arras, had with the permission of Heaven stolen them from the Infidels and placed them on unmanned boats that one of the images had been cast upon the Norman coast near Salenelles; that the second had run aground not far from the city of Lucca, in

Italy and that this third was the one which had been embarked by the knight from Artois. As regarded its final resting place, the hermit, on the authority of St. Luke, recommended that the statue should be left to decide the matter itself. Accordingly the crucified figure was solemnly cast back into the sea. The very next day it was found once more in the same spot, among the sand and bent grass at the mouth of the Nys. It was therefore deposited in the little church of Dunes; and very soon indeed the flocks of pious persons who brought it offerings from all parts made it necessary and possible to rebuild the church thus sanctified by its presence.

The Holy Effigy of Dunes—Sacra Dunarum Effigies as it was called—did not work the ordinary sort of miracles. But its fame spread far and wide by the unexampled wonders which became the constant accompaniment of its existence. The Effigy, as above mentioned, had been discovered without the cross to which it had evidently been fastened, nor had any researches or any subsequent storms brought the missing blocks to light, despite the many prayers which were offered for the purpose. After some time therefore, and a deal of discussion, it was decided that a new cross should be provided for the effigy to hang upon. And certain skilful stonemasons of Arras were called to Dunes for this purpose. But behold! the very day after the cross had been solemnly erected in the church, an unheard of and terrifying fact was discovered. The Effigy, which had been hanging perfectly straight the previous evening, had shifted its position, and was bent violently to the right, as if in an effort to break loose.

This was attested not merely by hundreds of laymen, but by the priests of the place, who notified the fact in a document, existing in the episcopal archives of Arras until 1790, to the Abbot of St. Loup their spiritual overlord.

This was the beginning of a series of mysterious occurrences which spread the fame of the marvellous crucifix all over Christendom. The Effigy did not remain in the position into which it had miraculously worked itself: it was found, at intervals of time, shifted in some other manner upon its cross, and always as if it had gone through violent contortions. And one day, about ten years after it had been cast up by the sea, the priests of the church and the burghers of Dunes discovered the Effigy hanging in its original outstretched, symmetrical attitude, but O wonder! with the cross, broken in three pieces, lying on the steps of its chapel.

Certain persons, who lived in the end of the town nearest the church, reported to have been roused in the middle of the night by what they had taken for a violent clap of thunder, but which was doubtless the crash of the Cross falling down, or perhaps, who knows? the noise with which the terrible Effigy had broken loose and spurned the alien cross from it. For that was the secret: the Effigy, made by a saint

136

and come to Dunes by miracle, had evidently found some trace of unholiness in the stone to which it had been fastened. Such was the ready explanation afforded by the Prior of the church, in answer to an angry summons of the Abbot of St. Loup, who expressed his disapproval of such unusual miracles. Indeed, it was discovered that the piece of marble had not been cleaned from sinful human touch with the necessary rites before the figure was fastened on; a most grave, though excusable oversight. So a new cross was ordered, although it was noticed that much time was lost about it; and the consecration took place only some years later.

Meanwhile the Prior had built the warder's chamber, with the fireplace and recess, and obtained permission from the Pope himself that a clerk in orders should watch day and night, on the score that so wonderful a relic might be stolen. For the relic had by this time entirely cut out all similar crucifixes, and the village of Dunes, through the concourse of pilgrims, had rapidly grown into a town, the property of the now fabulously wealthy Priory of the Holy Cross.

The Abbots of St. Loup, however, looked upon the matter with an unfavourable eye. Although nominally remaining their vassals, the Priors of Dunes had contrived to obtain gradually from the Pope privileges which rendered them virtually independent, and in particular, immunities which sent to the treasury of St. Loup only a small proportion of the tribute money brought by the pilgrims. Abbot Walterius in particular, showed himself actively hostile. He accused the Prior of Dunes of having employed his warders to trump up stories of strange movements and sounds on the part of the still crossless Effigy, and of suggesting, to the ignorant, changes in its attitude which were more credulously believed in now that there was no longer the straight line of the cross by which to verify. So finally the new cross was made, and consecrated, and on Holy Cross Day of the year, the Effigy was fastened to it in the presence of an immense concourse of clergy and laity. The Effigy, it was now supposed, would be satisfied, and no unusual occurrences would increase or perhaps fatally compromise its reputation for sanctity.

These expectations were violently dispelled. In November, 1293, after a year of strange rumours concerning the Effigy, the figure was again discovered to have moved, and continued moving, or rather (judging from the position on the cross) writhing; and on Christmas Eve of the same year, the cross was a second time thrown down and dashed in pieces. The priest on duty was, at the same time, found, it was thought, dead, in his warder's chamber. Another cross was made and this time privately consecrated and put in place, and a hole in the roof made a pretext to close the church for a while, and to perform the rites of purification necessary after its pollution by workmen. Indeed, it was remarked that on this occasion the Prior of Dunes took as much trouble to diminish and if possible to hide away the miracles, as his predecessor had done his best to blazon the preceding ones abroad. The priest who had been on duty on the eventful Christmas Eve disappeared mysteriously, and it was thought by many persons that he had gone mad and was confined in the Prior's prison, for fear of the revelations he might make. For by this time, and not without some encouragement from the Abbots at Arras, extraordinary stories had begun to circulate about the goings-on in the church of Dunes. This church, be it remembered, stood a little above the town, isolated and surrounded by big trees. It was surrounded by the precincts of the Priory and, save on the water side, by high walls. Nevertheless, persons there were who affirmed that, the wind having been in that direction, they had heard strange noises come from the church of nights. During storms, particularly, sounds had been heard which were variously described as howls, groans, and the music of rustic dancing. A master mariner affirmed that one Halloween, as his boat approached the mouth of the Nys, he had seen the church of Dunes brilliantly lit up, its immense windows flaming. But he was suspected of being drunk and of having exaggerated the effect of the small light shining from the warder's chamber. The interest of the townsfolk of Dunes coincided with that of the Priory, since they prospered greatly by the pilgrimages, so these tales were promptly hushed up. Yet they undoubtedly reached the ear of the Abbot of St. Loup. And at last there came an event which brought them all back to the surface.

For, on the Vigil of All Saints, 1299, the church was struck by lightning. The new warder was found dead in the middle of the nave, the cross broken in two; and oh, horror! the Effigy was missing. The indescribable fear which overcame everyone was merely increased by the discovery of the Effigy lying behind the high altar, in an attitude of frightful convulsion, and, it was whispered, blackened by lightning.

This was the end of the strange doings at Dunes.

An ecclesiastical council was held at Arras, and the church shut once more for nearly a year. It was opened this time and re-consecrated by the Abbot of St. Loup, whom the Prior-of Holy Cross served humbly at mass. A new chapel had been built, and in it the miraculous crucifix was displayed, dressed in more splendid brocade and gems than usual, and its head nearly hidden by one of the most gorgeous crowns ever seen before; a gift, it was said, of the Duke of Burgundy.

All this new splendour, and the presence of the great Abbot himself was presently explained to the faithful, when the Prior came forward to announce that a last and greatest miracle had now taken place. The original cross, on which the figure had hung in the Church of the Holy Sepulchre, and for which the Effigy had spurned all others made by less holy hands, had been cast on the shore of Dunes, on the very spot where, a hundred years before, the figure of the Saviour had been discovered in the sands. "This," said the Prior, "was the explanation of the terrible occurrences which had filled all hearts with anguish. The Holy Effigy was now satisfied, it would rest in peace and its miraculous powers would be engaged only in granting the prayers of the faithful."

One-half of the forecast came true: from that day forward the Effigy never shifted its position, but from that day forward also, no considerable miracle was ever registered; the devotion of Dunes diminished, other relics threw the Sacred Effigy into the shade; and the pilgrimages dwindling to mere local gatherings, the church was never brought to completion.

What had happened? No one ever knew, guessed, or perhaps even asked. But, when in 1790 the Archiepiscopal palace of Arras was sacked, a certain notary of the neighbourhood bought a large portion of the archives at the price of waste paper, either from historical curiosity, or expecting to obtain thereby facts which might gratify his aversion to the clergy. These documents lay unexamined for many years, till my friend the Antiquary bought them. Among them taken helter skelter from the Archbishop's palace, were sundry papers referring to the suppressed Abbey of St. Loup of Arras, and among these latter, a series of notes concerning the affairs of the church of Dunes; they were, so far as their fragmentary nature explained, the minutes of an inquest made in 1309, and contained the deposition of sundry witnesses. To understand their meaning it is necessary to remember that this was the time when witch trials had begun, and when the proceedings against the Templars had set the fashion of inquests which could help the finances of the country while furthering the interests of religion.

What appears to have happened is that after the catastrophe of the Vigil of All Saints, October, 1299, the Prior, Urbain de Luc, found himself suddenly threatened with a charge of sacrilege and witchcraft, of obtaining miracles of the Effigy by devilish means, and of converting his church into a chapel of the Evil One.

Instead of appealing to high ecclesiastical tribunals, as the privileges obtained from the Holy See would have warranted, Prior Urbain guessed that this charge came originally from the wrathful Abbot of St. Loup, and, dropping all his pretensions in order to save himself, he threw himself upon the mercy of the Abbot whom he had hitherto flouted. The Abbot appears to have been satisfied by his submission, and the matter to have dropped after a few legal preliminaries, of which the notes found among the archiepiscopal archives of Arras represented a portion. Some of these notes my friend the Antiquary kindly allowed me to translate from the Latin, and I give them here, leaving the reader to make what he can of them.

"Item. The Abbot expresses himself satisfied that His Reverence the Prior has had no personal knowledge of or dealings with the Evil One (Diabolus). Nevertheless, the gravity of the charge requires . . ."—here the page is torn.

"Hugues Jacquot, Simon le Couvreur, Pierre Denis, burghers of Dunes, being interrogated, witness:

"That the noises from the Church of the Holy Cross always happened on nights of bad storms, and foreboded shipwrecks on the coast; and were very various, such as terrible rattling, groans, howls as of wolves, and occasional flute playing. A certain Jehan, who has twice been branded and flogged for lighting fires on the coast and otherwise causing ships to wreck at the mouth of the Nys, being promised immunity, after two or three slight pulls on the rack, witnesses as follows: That the band of wreckers to which he belongs always knew when a dangerous storm was brewing, on account of the noises which issued from the church of Dunes. Witness has often climbed the walls and prowled round in the churchyard, waiting to hear such noises. He was not unfamiliar with the howlings and roarings mentioned by the previous witnesses. He has heard tell by a countryman who passed in the night that the howling was such that the countryman thought himself pursued by a pack of wolves, although it is well known that no wolf has been seen in these parts for thirty years. But the witness himself is of the opinion that the most singular of all the noises, and the one which always accompanied or foretold the worst storms, was a noise of flutes and pipes (quod vulgo dicuntur flustes et musettes) so sweet that the King of France could not have sweeter at his Court. Being interrogated whether he had ever seen anything? the witness answers: 'That he has seen the church brightly lit up from the sands; but on approaching found all dark, save the light from the warder's chamber. That once, by moonlight, the piping and fluting and howling being uncommonly loud, he thought he had seen wolves, and a human figure on the roof, but that he ran away from fear, and cannot be sure.'

"Item. His Lordship the Abbot desires the Right Reverend Prior to answer truly, placing his hand on the Gospels, whether or not he had himself heard such noises.

"The Right Reverend Prior denies ever having heard anything similar. But, being threatened with further proceedings (the rack?) acknowledges that he had frequently been told of these noises by the Warder on duty.

"Query: Whether the Right Reverend Prior was ever told anything else by the Warder?

"*Answer:* Yes; but under the seal of confession. The last Warder, moreover, the one killed by lightning, had been a reprobate priest, having committed the greatest crimes and obliged to take asylum, whom the Prior had kept there on account of the difficulty of finding a man sufficiently courageous for the office.

"*Query:* Whether the Prior has ever questioned previous Warders?

"*Answer:* That the Warders were bound to reveal only in confession whatever they had heard, that the Prior's predecessors had kept the seal of confession inviolate, and that though unworthy, the Prior himself desired to do alike.

"*Query:* What had become of the Warder who had been found in a swoon after the occurrences of Hallow Even?

"*Answer:* That the Prior does not know. The Warder was crazy. The Prior believes he was secluded for that reason."

A disagreeable surprise had been, apparently, arranged for Prior Urbain de Luc. For the next entry states that:

"Item. By order of His Magnificence the Lord Abbot, certain servants of the Lord Abbot aforesaid introduce Robert Baudouin priest, once Warder in the Church of the Holy Cross, who has been kept ten years in prison by His Reverence the Prior, as being of unsound mind. Witness manifests great terror on finding himself in the presence of their Lordships, and particularly of His Reverence the Prior. And refuses to speak, hiding his face in his hands and uttering shrieks. Being comforted with kind words by those present, nay even most graciously by My Lord the Abbot himself, *etiam* threatened with the rack if he continue obdurate, this witness deposes as follows, not without much lamentation, shrieking and senseless jabber after the manner of mad men.

"*Query:* Can he remember what happened on the Vigil of All Saints, in the church of Dunes, before he swooned on the floor of the church?

"*Answer:* He cannot. It would be sin to speak of such things before great spiritual Lords. Moreover he is but an ignorant man, and also mad. Moreover his hunger is great.

"Being given white bread from the Lord Abbot's own table, witness is again cross-questioned.

"*Query:* What can he remember of the events of the Vigil of All Saints?

"Answer: Thinks he was not always mad. Thinks he has not always been in prison. Thinks he once went in a boat on sea, etc.

"*Query:* Does witness think he has ever been in the church of Dunes?

141

"*Answer:* Cannot remember. But is sure that he was not always in prison.

"*Query:* Has witness ever heard anything like that? (My Lord the Abbot having secretly ordered that a certain fool in his service, an excellent musician, should suddenly play the pipes behind the Arras.)

"At which sound witness began to tremble and sob and fall on his knees, and catch hold of the robe even of My Lord the Abbot, hiding his head therein.

"*Query:* Wherefore does he feel such terror, being in the fatherly presence of so clement a prince as the Lord Abbot?

"*Answer:* That witness cannot stand that piping any longer. That it freezes his blood. That he has told the Prior many times that he will not remain any longer in the warder's chamber. That he is afraid for his life. That he dare not make the sign of the Cross nor say his prayers for fear of the Great Wild Man. That the Great Wild Man took the Cross and broke it in two and played at quoits with it in the nave. That all the wolves trooped down from the roof howling, and danced on their hind legs while the Great Wild man played the pipes on the high altar. That witness had surrounded himself with a hedge of little crosses, made of broken rye straw, to keep off the Great Wild Man from the warder's chamber. Ah—ah—ah! He is piping again! The wolves are howling! He is raising the tempest.

"Item. That no further information can be extracted from witness who falls on the floor like one possessed and has to be removed from the presence of His Lordship the Abbot and His Reverence the Prior."

III

Here the minutes of the inquest break off. Did those great spiritual dignitaries ever get to learn more about the terrible doings in the church of Dunes? Did they ever guess at their cause?

"For there was a cause," said the Antiquary, folding his spectacles after reading me these notes, "or more strictly the cause still exists. And you will understand, though those learned priests of six centuries ago could not."

And rising, he fetched a key from a shelf and preceded me into the yard of his house, situated on the Nys, a mile below Dunes.

Between the low steadings one saw the salt marsh, lilac with sea lavender, the Island of Birds, a great sandbank at the mouth of the Nys, where every kind of sea fowl gathers; and beyond, the angry whitecrested sea under an angry orange afterglow. On the other side, inland, and appearing above the farm roofs, stood the church of Dunes, its pointed belfry and jagged outlines of gables and buttresses and gargoyles and wind-warped pines black against the easterly sky of ominous livid red.

"I told you," said the Antiquary, stopping with the key in the lock of a big out-house, "that there had been a *substitution*; that the crucifix at present at Dunes is not the one miraculously cast up by the storm of 1195. I believe the present one may be identified as a life-size statue, for which a receipt exists in the archives of Arras, furnished to the Abbot of St. Loup by Estienne Le Mas and Guillaume Pernel, stonemasons, in the year 1299, that is to say the year of the inquest and of the cessation of all supernatural occurrences at Dunes. As to the original effigy, you shall see it and understand everything."

The Antiquary opened the door of a sloping, vaulted passage, lit a lantern and led the way. It was evidently the cellar of some mediaeval building, and a scent of wine, of damp wood, and of fir branches from innumerable stacked up faggots, filled the darkness among thickset columns.

"Here," said the Antiquary, raising his lantern, "he was buried beneath this vault and they had run an iron stake through his middle, like a vampire, to prevent his rising."

The Effigy was erect against the dark wall, surrounded by brushwood. It was more than life-size, nude, the arms broken off at the shoulders, the head, with stubbly beard and clotted hair, drawn up with an effort, the face contracted with agony; the muscles dragged as of one hanging crucified, the feet bound together with a rope. The figure was familiar to me in various galleries. I came forward to examine the ear: it was leaf-shaped.

"Ah, you have understood the whole mystery," said the Antiquary.

"I have understood," I answered, not knowing how far his thought really went, "that this supposed statue of Christ is an antique satyr, a Marsyas awaiting his punishment."

The Antiquary nodded. "Exactly," he said drily, "that is the whole explanation. Only I think the Abbot and the Prior were not so wrong to drive the iron stake through him when they removed him from the church."

THE MONKEY'S PAW

W. W. JACOBS

IN HIS LIFETIME, WILLIAM WYMARK JACOBS (1863–1943) WAS
BEST KNOWN FOR HIS HUMOROUS STORIES AND TALES OF SAILORS
AND THE SEA. TODAY, HE IS REMEMBERED ALMOST EXCLUSIVELY
FOR THIS MASTERPIECE ABOUT THE INELUCTABILITY OF FATE
AND THE CONSEQUENCES OF TRYING TO CIRCUMVENT IT.
"THE MONKEY'S PAW" FIRST APPEARED IN THE SEPTEMBER 1902
ISSUE OF *HARPER'S MONTHLY* AND IS PROOF THAT NOT ALL
OF THE BEST HORROR STORIES WERE WRITTEN BY SPECIALISTS
IN THE GENRE.

I

Without, the night was cold and wet, but in the small parlour of Laburnam Villa the blinds were drawn and the fire burned brightly. Father and son were at chess, the former, who possessed ideas about the game involving radical changes, putting his king into such sharp and unnecessary perils that it even provoked comment from the white-haired old lady knitting placidly by the fire.

"Hark at the wind," said Mr. White, who, having seen a fatal mistake after it was too late, was amiably desirous of preventing his son from seeing it.

"I'm listening," said the latter, grimly surveying the board as he stretched out his hand. "Check."

"I should hardly think that he'd come to-night," said his father, with his hand poised over the board.

"Mate," replied the son.

"That's the worst of living so far out," bawled Mr. White, with sudden and unlooked-for violence; "of all the beastly, slushy, out-of-the-way places to live in, this is the worst. Pathway's a bog, and the road's a torrent. I don't know what people are thinking about. I suppose because only two houses in the road are let, they think it doesn't matter."

"Never mind, dear," said his wife, soothingly; "perhaps you'll win the next one."

Mr. White looked up sharply, just in time to intercept a knowing glance between mother and son. The words died away on his lips, and he hid a guilty grin in his thin grey beard.

"There he is," said Herbert White, as the gate banged to loudly and heavy footsteps came toward the door.

The old man rose with hospitable haste, and opening the door, was heard condoling with the new arrival. The new arrival also condoled with himself, so that Mrs. White said, "Tut, tut!" and coughed gently as her husband entered the room, followed by a tall, burly man, beady of eye and rubicund of visage.

"Sergeant-Major Morris," he said, introducing him.

The sergeant-major shook hands, and taking the proffered seat by the fire, watched contentedly while his host got out whiskey and tumblers and stood a small copper kettle on the fire.

At the third glass his eyes got brighter, and he began to talk, the little family circle regarding with eager interest this visitor from distant parts, as he squared his broad shoulders in the chair and spoke of wild scenes and doughty deeds; of wars and plagues and strange peoples.

"Twenty-one years of it," said Mr. White, nodding at his wife and son. "When he went away he was a slip of a youth in the warehouse. Now look at him."

"He don't look to have taken much harm," said Mrs. White, politely.

"I'd like to go to India myself," said the old man, "just to look round a bit, you know."

"Better where you are," said the sergeant-major, shaking his head. He put down the empty glass, and sighing softly, shook it again.

"I should like to see those old temples and fakirs and jugglers," said the old man. "What was that you started telling me the other day about a monkey's paw or something, Morris?"

"Nothing," said the soldier, hastily. "Leastways nothing worth hearing."

"Monkey's paw?" said Mrs. White, curiously.

"Well, it's just a bit of what you might call magic, perhaps," said the sergeant-major, offhandedly.

His three listeners leaned forward eagerly. The visitor absent-mindedly put his empty glass to his lips and then set it down again. His host filled it for him.

"To look at," said the sergeant-major, fumbling in his pocket, "it's just an ordinary little paw, dried to a mummy."

He took something out of his pocket and proffered it. Mrs. White drew back with a grimace, but her son, taking it, examined it curiously.

"And what is there special about it?" inquired Mr. White as he took it from his son, and having examined it, placed it upon the table.

"It had a spell put on it by an old fakir," said the sergeant-major, "a very holy man. He wanted to show that fate ruled people's lives, and that those who interfered with it did so to their sorrow. He put a spell on it so that three separate men could each have three wishes from it."

His manner was so impressive that his hearers were conscious that their light laughter jarred somewhat.

"Well, why don't you have three, sir?" said Herbert White, cleverly.

The soldier regarded him in the way that middle age is wont to regard presumptuous youth. "I have," he said, quietly, and his blotchy face whitened.

"And did you really have the three wishes granted?" asked Mrs. White.

"I did," said the sergeant-major, and his glass tapped against his strong teeth.

"And has anybody else wished?" persisted the old lady.

"The first man had his three wishes. Yes," was the reply; "I don't know what the first two were, but the third was for death. That's how I got the paw."

His tones were so grave that a hush fell upon the group.

"If you've had your three wishes, it's no good to you now, then, Morris," said the old man at last. "What do you keep it for?"

The soldier shook his head. "Fancy, I suppose," he said, slowly. "I did have some idea of selling it, but I don't think I will. It has caused enough mischief already. Besides, people won't buy. They think it's a fairy tale; some of them, and those who do think anything of it want to try it first and pay me afterward."

"If you could have another three wishes," said the old man, eyeing him keenly, "would you have them?"

"I don't know," said the other. "I don't know."

He took the paw, and dangling it between his forefinger and thumb, suddenly threw it upon the fire. White, with a slight cry, stooped down and snatched it off.

"Better let it burn," said the soldier, solemnly.

"If you don't want it, Morris," said the other, "give it to me."

"I won't," said his friend, doggedly. "I threw it on the fire. If you keep it, don't blame me for what happens. Pitch it on the fire again like a sensible man."

The other shook his head and examined his new possession closely. "How do you do it?" he inquired.

"Hold it up in your right hand and wish aloud," said the sergeant-major, "but I warn you of the consequences."

"Sounds like the *Arabian Nights*," said Mrs. White, as she rose and began to set the supper. "Don't you think you might wish for four pairs of hands for me?"

Her husband drew the talisman from pocket, and then all three burst into laughter as the sergeant-major, with a look of alarm on his face, caught him by the arm.

"If you must wish," he said, gruffly, "wish for something sensible."

Mr. White dropped it back in his pocket, and placing chairs, motioned his friend to the table. In the business of supper the talisman was partly forgotten, and afterward the three sat listening in an enthralled fashion to a second instalment of the soldier's adventures in India.

"If the tale about the monkey's paw is not more truthful than those he has been telling us," said Herbert, as the door closed behind their guest, just in time for him to catch the last train, "we sha'nt make much out of it."

"Did you give him anything for it, father?" inquired Mrs. White, regarding her husband closely.

"A trifle," said he, colouring slightly. "He didn't want it, but I made him take it. And he pressed me again to throw it away."

"Likely," said Herbert, with pretended horror. "Why, we're going to be rich, and famous and happy. Wish to be an emperor, father, to begin with; then you can't be henpecked."

He darted round the table, pursued by the maligned Mrs. White armed with an antimacassar.

Mr. White took the paw from his pocket and eyed it dubiously. "I don't know what to wish for, and that's a fact," he said, slowly. "It seems to me I've got all I want."

"If you only cleared the house, you'd be quite happy, wouldn't you?" said Herbert, with his hand on his shoulder. "Well, wish for two hundred pounds, then; that'll just do it."

His father, smiling shamefacedly at his own credulity, held up the talisman, as his son, with a solemn face, somewhat marred by a wink at his mother, sat down at the piano and struck a few impressive chords.

"I wish for two hundred pounds," said the old man distinctly.

A fine crash from the piano greeted the words, interrupted by a shuddering cry from the old man. His wife and son ran toward him.

"It moved," he cried, with a glance of disgust at the object as it lay on the floor. "As I wished, it twisted in my hand like a snake."

"Well, I don't see the money," said his son as he picked it up and placed it on the table, "and I bet I never shall."

"It must have been your fancy, father," said his wife, regarding him anxiously.

He shook his head. "Never mind, though; there's no harm done, but it gave me a shock all the same."

They sat down by the fire again while the two men finished their pipes. Outside, the wind was higher than ever, and the old man started nervously at the sound of a door banging upstairs. A silence unusual and depressing settled upon all three, which lasted until the old couple rose to retire for the night.

"I expect you'll find the cash tied up in a big bag in the middle of your bed," said Herbert, as he bade them good-night, "and something horrible squatting up on top of the wardrobe watching you as you pocket your ill-gotten gains."

He sat alone in the darkness, gazing at the dying fire, and seeing faces in it. The last face was so horrible and so simian that he gazed at it in amazement. It got so vivid that, with a little uneasy laugh, he felt on the table for a glass containing a little water to throw over it. His hand grasped the monkey's paw, and with a little shiver he wiped his hand on his coat and went up to bed.

II

In the brightness of the wintry sun next morning as it streamed over the breakfast table he laughed at his fears. There was an air of prosaic wholesomeness about the room which it had lacked on the previous night, and the dirty, shrivelled little paw was pitched on the sideboard with a carelessness which betokened no great belief in its virtues.

"I suppose all old soldiers are the same," said Mrs. White. "The idea of our listening to such nonsense! How could wishes be granted in these days? And if they could, how could two hundred pounds hurt you, father?"

"Might drop on his head from the sky," said the frivolous Herbert.

"Morris said the things happened so naturally," said' his father, "that you might if you so wished attribute it to coincidence."

"Well, don't break into the money before I come back," said Herbert as he rose from the table. "I'm afraid it'll turn you into a mean, avaricious man, and we shall have to disown you."

His mother laughed, and following him to the door, watched him down the road; and returning to the breakfast table, was very happy at the expense of her husband's credulity. All of which did not prevent her from scurrying to the door at the postman's knock, nor prevent her from referring somewhat shortly to retired sergeant-majors of bibulous habits when she found that the post brought a tailor's bill.

"Herbert will have some more of his funny remarks, I expect, when he comes home," she said, as they sat at dinner.

"I dare say," said Mr. White, pouring himself out some beer; "but for all that, the thing moved in my hand; that I'll swear to."

"You thought it did," said the old lady soothingly.

"I say it did," replied the other. "There was no thought about it; I had just— What's the matter?"

His wife made no reply. She was watching the mysterious movements of a man outside, who, peering in an undecided fashion at the house, appeared to be trying to make up his mind to enter. In mental connection with the two hundred pounds, she noticed that the stranger was well dressed, and wore a silk hat of glossy newness. Three times he paused at the gate, and then walked on again. The fourth time he stood with his hand upon it, and then with sudden resolution flung it open and walked up the path. Mrs. White at the same moment placed her hands behind her, and hurriedly unfastening the strings of her apron, put that useful article of apparel beneath the cushion of her chair.

She brought the stranger, who seemed ill at ease, into the room. He gazed at her furtively, and listened in a preoccupied fashion as the old lady apologized for the appearance of the room, and her husband's coat, a garment which he usually reserved for the garden. She then waited as patiently as her sex would permit, for him to broach his business, but he was at first strangely silent.

"I—was asked to call," he said at last, and stooped and picked a piece of cotton from his trousers. "I come from 'Maw and Meggins.'"

The old lady started. "Is anything the matter?" she asked, breathlessly. "Has anything happened to Herbert? What is it? What is it?"

Her husband interposed. "There, there, mother," he said, hastily. "Sit down, and don't jump to conclusions. You've not brought bad news, I'm sure, sir;" and he eyed the other wistfully.

"I'm sorry—" began the visitor.

"Is he hurt?" demanded the mother, wildly.

The visitor bowed in assent. "Badly hurt," he said, quietly, "but he is not in any pain."

"Oh, thank God!" said the old woman, clasping her hands. "Thank God for that! Thank—"

She broke off suddenly as the sinister meaning of the assurance dawned upon her and she saw the awful confirmation of her fears in the other's perverted face. She caught her breath, and turning to her slower-witted husband, laid her trembling old hand upon his. There was a long silence.

"He was caught in the machinery," said the visitor at length in a low voice.

"Caught in the machinery," repeated Mr. White, in a dazed fashion, "yes."

He sat staring blankly out at the window, and taking his wife's hand between his own, pressed it as he had been wont to do in their old courting-days nearly forty years before.

"He was the only one left to us," he said, turning gently to the visitor. "It is hard."

The other coughed, and rising, walked slowly to the window. "The firm wished me to convey their sincere sympathy with you in your great loss," he said, without looking round. "I beg that you will understand I am only their servant and merely obeying orders."

There was no reply; the old woman's face was white, her eyes staring, and her breath inaudible; on the husband's face was a look such as his friend the sergeant might have carried into his first action.

"I was to say that Maw and Meggins disclaim all responsibility," continued the other. "They admit no liability at all, but in consideration of your son's services, they wish to present you with a certain sum as compensation."

Mr. White dropped his wife's hand, and rising to his feet, gazed with a look of horror at his visitor. His dry lips shaped the words, "How much?"

"Two hundred pounds," was the answer.

Unconscious of his wife's shriek, the old man smiled faintly, put out his hands like a sightless man, and dropped, a senseless heap, to the floor.

III

In the huge new cemetery, some two miles distant, the old people buried their dead, and came back to a house steeped in shadow and silence. It was all over so quickly that at first they could hardly realize it, and remained in a state of expectation as though of something else to happen—something else which was to lighten this load, too heavy for old hearts to bear.

But the days passed, and expectation gave place to resignation—the hopeless resignation of the old, sometimes miscalled, apathy. Sometimes they hardly exchanged a word, for now they had nothing to talk about, and their days were long to weariness.

It was about a week after that the old man, waking suddenly in the night, stretched out his hand and found himself alone. The room was in darkness, and the sound of subdued weeping came from the window. He raised himself in bed and listened.

"Come back," he said, tenderly. "You will be cold."

"It is colder for my son," said the old woman, and wept afresh.

The sound of her sobs died away on his ears. The bed was warm, and his eyes heavy with sleep. He dozed fitfully, and then slept until a sudden wild cry from his wife awoke him with a start.

"The paw!" she cried wildly. "The monkey's paw!"

He started up in alarm. "Where? Where is it? What's the matter?"

She came stumbling across the room toward him. "I want it," she said, quietly. "You've not destroyed it?"

"It's in the parlour, on the bracket," he replied, marvelling. "Why?"

She cried and laughed together, and bending over, kissed his cheek.

"I only just thought of it," she said, hysterically. "Why didn't I think of it before? Why didn't you think of it?"

"Think of what?" he questioned.

"The other two wishes," she replied, rapidly.

"We've only had one."

"Was not that enough?" he demanded, fiercely.

"No," she cried, triumphantly; "we'll have one more. Go down and get it quickly, and wish our boy alive again."

The man sat up in bed and flung the bedclothes from his quaking limbs. "Good God, you are mad!" he cried, aghast.

"Get it," she panted; "get it quickly, and wish—Oh, my boy, my boy!"

Her husband struck a match and lit the candle. "Get back to bed," he said, unsteadily. "You don't know what you are saying."

"We had the first wish granted," said the old woman, feverishly; "why not the second?"

"A coincidence," stammered the old man.

"Go and get it and wish," cried his wife, quivering with excitement.

The old man turned and regarded her, and his voice shook. "He has been dead ten days, and besides he—I would not tell you else, but—I could only recognize him by his clothing. If he was too terrible for you to see then, how now?"

"Bring him back," cried the old woman, and dragged him toward the door. "Do you think I fear the child I have nursed?"

He went down in the darkness, and felt his way to the parlour, and then to the mantelpiece. The talisman was in its place, and a horrible fear that the unspoken wish might bring his mutilated son before him ere he could escape from the room seized upon him, and he caught his breath as he found that he had lost the direction of the door. His brow cold with sweat, he felt his way round the table, and groped along the wall until he found himself in the small passage with the unwholesome thing in his hand.

Even his wife's face seemed changed as he entered the room. It was white and expectant, and to his fears seemed to have an unnatural look upon it. He was afraid of her.

"*Wish!*" she cried, in a strong voice.

"It is foolish and wicked," he faltered.

"*Wish!*" repeated his wife.

He raised his hand. "I wish my son alive again."

The talisman fell to the floor, and he regarded it fearfully. Then he sank trembling into a chair as the old woman, with burning eyes, walked to the window and raised the blind.

He sat until he was chilled with the cold, glancing occasionally at the figure of the old woman peering through the window. The candle-end, which had burned below the rim of the china candlestick, was throwing pulsating shadows on the ceiling and walls, until, with a flicker larger than the rest, it expired. The old man, with an unspeakable sense of relief at the failure of the talisman, crept back to his bed, and a minute or two afterward the old woman came silently and apathetically beside him.

Neither spoke, but lay silently listening to the ticking of the clock. A stair creaked, and a squeaky mouse scurried noisily through the wall. The darkness was oppressive, and after lying for some time screwing up his courage, he took the box of matches, and striking one, went downstairs for a candle.

At the foot of the stairs the match went out, and he paused to strike another; and at the same moment a knock, so quiet and stealthy as to be scarcely audible, sounded on the front door.

The matches fell from his hand and spilled in the passage. He stood motionless, his breath suspended until the knock was repeated. Then he turned and fled swiftly back to his room, and closed the door behind him. A third knock sounded through the house.

"What's that?" cried the old woman, starting up.

"A rat," said the old man in shaking tones—"a rat. It passed me on the stairs."

His wife sat up in bed listening. A loud knock resounded through the house.

"It's Herbert!" she screamed. "It's Herbert!"

She ran to the door, but her husband was before her, and catching her by the arm, held her tightly.

"What are you going to do?" he whispered hoarsely.

"It's my boy; it's Herbert!" she cried, struggling mechanically. "I forgot it was two miles away. What are you holding me for? Let go. I must open the door."

"For God's sake don't let it in," cried the old man, trembling.

"You're afraid of your own son," she cried, struggling. "Let me go. I'm coming, Herbert; I'm coming."

There was another knock, and another. The old woman with a sudden wrench broke free and ran from the room. Her husband followed to the landing, and called after her appealingly as she hurried downstairs. He heard the chain rattle back and the bottom bolt drawn slowly and stiffly from the socket. Then the old woman's voice, strained and panting.

"The bolt," she cried, loudly. "Come down. I can't reach it."

But her husband was on his hands and knees groping wildly on the floor in search of the paw. If he could only find it before the thing outside got in. A perfect fusillade of knocks reverberated through the house, and he heard the scraping of a chair as his wife put it down in the passage against the door. He heard the creaking of the bolt as it came slowly back, and at the same moment he found the monkey's paw, and frantically breathed his third and last wish.

The knocking ceased suddenly, although the echoes of it were still in the house. He heard the chair drawn back, and the door opened. A cold wind rushed up the staircase, and a long loud wail of disappointment and misery from his wife gave him courage to run down to her side, and then to the gate beyond. The street lamp flickering opposite shone on a quiet and deserted road.

THE WHITE PEOPLE

ARTHUR MACHEN

A TITANIC FIGURE IN THE HISTORY OF SUPERNATURAL
LITERATURE, ARTHUR MACHEN (1863-1947) WROTE STORIES
IN WHICH THE EVERYDAY ORDINARINESS OF OUR WORLD IS
REVEALED TO BE A VEIL MERCIFULLY CLOAKING TRUTHS OF A
DARKER REALITY THAT HAVE COME DOWN TO US IN ATTENUATED
FORM AS MYTHS, LEGENDS, AND FOLKLORE. OCCASIONALLY,
THAT VEIL IS RIPPED ASIDE, AS IN THIS STORY, IN WHICH THE
INCOMPREHENSIBLE EVIL OF THE UNDERLYING HORROR IS FILTERED
THROUGH THE NAÏVE PERCEPTIONS OF AN INNOCENT CHILD
BEING INITIATED INTO ITS RITES AND RITUALS. "THE WHITE
PEOPLE" WAS FIRST PUBLISHED IN THE JANUARY 1904 ISSUE OF
HORLICK'S MAGAZINE AND COLLECTED IN MACHEN'S SEMINAL
VOLUME OF WEIRD FICTION *THE HOUSE OF SOULS* (1906).

PROLOGUE

S orcery and sanctity," said Ambrose, "these are the only realities. Each is an ecstasy,
a withdrawal from the common life."

Cotgrave listened, interested. He had been brought by a friend to this mouldering house in a northern suburb, through an old garden to the room where Ambrose
the recluse dozed and dreamed over his books.

"Yes," he went on, "magic is justified of her children. There are many, I think,
who eat dry crusts and drink water, with a joy infinitely sharper than anything
within the experience of the 'practical' epicure."

"You are speaking of the saints?"

"Yes, and of the sinners, too. I think you are falling into the very general error
of confining the spiritual world to the supremely good; but the supremely wicked,

necessarily, have their portion in it. The merely carnal, sensual man can no more be a great sinner than he can be a great saint. Most of us are just indifferent, mixed-up creatures; we muddle through the world without realizing the meaning and the inner sense of things, and, consequently, our wickedness and our goodness are alike second-rate, unimportant."

"And you think the great sinner, then, will be an ascetic, as well as the great saint?"

"Great people of all kinds forsake the imperfect copies and go to the perfect originals. I have no doubt but that many of the very highest among the saints have never done a 'good action' (using the words in their ordinary sense). And, on the other hand, there have been those who have sounded the very depths of sin, who all their lives have never done an 'ill deed.'"

He went out of the room for a moment, and Cotgrave, in high delight, turned to his friend and thanked him for the introduction.

"He's grand," he said. "I never saw that kind of lunatic before."

Ambrose returned with more whisky and helped the two men in a liberal manner. He abused the teetotal sect with ferocity, as he handed the seltzer, and pouring out a glass of water for himself, was about to resume his monologue, when Cotgrave broke in—

"I can't stand it, you know," he said, "your paradoxes are too monstrous. A man may be a great sinner and yet never do anything sinful! Come!"

"You're quite wrong," said Ambrose. "I never make paradoxes; I wish I could. I merely said that a man may have an exquisite taste in Romanee Conti, and yet never have even smelt four ale. That's all, and it's more like a truism than a paradox, isn't it? Your surprise at my remark is due to the fact that you haven't realized what sin is. Oh, yes, there is a sort of connexion between Sin with the capital letter, and actions which are commonly called sinful: with murder, theft, adultery, and so forth. Much the same connexion that there is between the A, B, C and fine literature. But I believe that the misconception—it is all but universal—arises in great measure from our looking at the matter through social spectacles. We think that a man who does evil to *us* and to his neighbours must be very evil. So he is, from a social standpoint; but can't you realize that Evil in its essence is a lonely thing, a passion of the solitary, individual soul? Really, the average murderer, *quâ* murderer, is not by any means a sinner in the true sense of the word. He is simply a wild beast that we have to get rid of to save our own necks from his knife. I should class him rather with tigers than with sinners."

"It seems a little strange."

"I think not. The murderer murders not from positive qualities, but from negative ones; he lacks something which non-murderers possess. Evil, of course, is wholly positive—only it is on the wrong side. You may believe me that sin in its proper sense is very rare; it is probable that there have been far fewer sinners than saints. Yes, your standpoint is all very well for practical, social purposes; we are naturally inclined to think that a person who is very disagreeable to us must be a very great sinner! It is very disagreeable to have one's pocket picked, and we pronounce the thief to be a very great sinner. In truth, he is merely an undeveloped man. He cannot be a saint, of course; but he may be, and often is, an infinitely better creature than thousands who have never broken a single commandment. He is a great nuisance to *us*, I admit, and we very properly lock him up if we catch him; but between his troublesome and unsocial action and evil—Oh, the connexion is of the weakest."

It was getting very late. The man who had brought Cotgrave had probably heard all this before, since he assisted with a bland and judicious smile, but Cotgrave began to think that his "lunatic" was turning into a sage.

"Do you know," he said, "you interest me immensely? You think, then, that we do not understand the real nature of evil?"

"No, I don't think we do. We over-estimate it and we under-estimate it. We take the very numerous infractions of our social 'bye-laws'—the very necessary and very proper regulations which keep the human company together—and we get frightened at the prevalence of 'sin' and 'evil.' But this is really nonsense. Take theft, for example. Have you any *horror* at the thought of Robin Hood, of the Highland caterans of the seventeenth century, of the moss-troopers, of the company promoters of our day?

"Then, on the other hand, we underrate evil. We attach such an enormous importance to the 'sin' of meddling with our pockets (and our wives) that we have quite forgotten the awfulness of real sin."

"And what is sin?" said Cotgrave.

"I think I must reply to your question by another. What would your feelings be, seriously, if your cat or your dog began to talk to you, and to dispute with you in human accents? You would be overwhelmed with horror. I am sure of it. And if the roses in your garden sang a weird song, you would go mad. And suppose the stones in the road began to swell and grow before your eyes, and if the pebble that you noticed at night had shot out stony blossoms in the morning?

"Well, these examples may give you some notion of what sin really is."

"Look here," said the third man, hitherto placid, "you two seem pretty well wound up. But I'm going home. I've missed my tram, and I shall have to walk."

Ambrose and Cotgrave seemed to settle down more profoundly when the other had gone out into the early misty morning and the pale light of the lamps.

"You astonish me," said Cotgrave. "I had never thought of that. If that is really so, one must turn everything upside down. Then the essence of sin really is——"

"In the taking of heaven by storm, it seems to me," said Ambrose. "It appears to me that it is simply an attempt to penetrate into another and higher sphere in a forbidden manner. You can understand why it is so rare. There are few, indeed, who wish to penetrate into other spheres, higher or lower, in ways allowed or forbidden. Men, in the mass, are amply content with life as they find it. Therefore there are few saints, and sinners (in the proper sense) are fewer still, and men of genius, who partake sometimes of each character, are rare also. Yes; on the whole, it is, perhaps, harder to be a great sinner than a great saint."

"There is something profoundly unnatural about sin? Is that what you mean?"

"Exactly. Holiness requires as great, or almost as great, an effort; but holiness works on lines that *were* natural once; it is an effort to recover the ecstasy that was before the Fall. But sin is an effort to gain the ecstasy and the knowledge that pertain alone to angels, and in making this effort man becomes a demon. I told you that the mere murderer is not *therefore* a sinner; that is true, but the sinner is sometimes a murderer. Gilles de Raiz is an instance. So you see that while the good and the evil are unnatural to man as he now is—to man the social, civilized being—evil is unnatural in a much deeper sense than good. The saint endeavours to recover a gift which he has lost; the sinner tries to obtain something which was never his. In brief, he repeats the Fall."

"But are you a Catholic?" said Cotgrave.

"Yes; I am a member of the persecuted Anglican Church."

"Then, how about those texts which seem to reckon as sin that which you would set down as a mere trivial dereliction?"

"Yes; but in one place the word 'sorcerers' comes in the same sentence, doesn't it? That seems to me to give the key-note. Consider: can you imagine for a moment that a false statement which saves an innocent man's life is a sin? No; very good, then, it is not the mere liar who is excluded by those words; it is, above all, the 'sorcerers' who use the material life, who use the failings incidental to material life as instruments to obtain their infinitely wicked ends. And let me tell you this: our higher senses are so blunted, we are so drenched with materialism, that we should probably fail to recognize real wickedness if we encountered it."

"But shouldn't we experience a certain horror—a terror such as you hinted we would experience if a rose tree sang—in the mere presence of an evil man?"

"We should if we were natural: children and women feel this horror you speak of, even animals experience it. But with most of us convention and civilization and education have blinded and deafened and obscured the natural reason. No, sometimes we may recognize evil by its hatred of the good—one doesn't need much penetration to guess at the influence which dictated, quite unconsciously, the 'Blackwood' review of Keats—but this is purely incidental; and, as a rule, I suspect that the Hierarchs of Tophet pass quite unnoticed, or, perhaps, in certain cases, as good but mistaken men."

"But you used the word 'unconscious' just now, of Keats' reviewers. Is wickedness ever unconscious?"

"Always. It must be so. It is like holiness and genius in this as in other points; it is a certain rapture or ecstasy of the soul; a transcendent effort to surpass the ordinary bounds. So, surpassing these, it surpasses also the understanding, the faculty that takes note of that which comes before it. No, a man may be infinitely and horribly wicked and never suspect it. But I tell you, evil in this, its certain and true sense, is rare, and I think it is growing rarer."

"I am trying to get hold of it all," said Cotgrave. "From what you say, I gather that the true evil differs generically from that which we call evil?"

"Quite so. There is, no doubt, an analogy between the two; a resemblance such as enables us to use, quite legitimately, such terms as the 'foot of the mountain' and the 'leg of the table.' And, sometimes, of course, the two speak, as it were, in the same language. The rough miner, or 'puddler,' the untrained, undeveloped 'tiger-man,' heated by a quart or two above his usual measure, comes home and kicks his irritating and injudicious wife to death. He is a murderer. And Gilles de Raiz was a murderer. But you see the gulf that separates the two? The 'word,' if I may so speak, is accidentally the same in each case, but the 'meaning' is utterly different. It is flagrant 'Hobson Jobson' to confuse the two, or rather, it is as if one supposed that Juggernaut and the Argonauts had something to do etymologically with one another. And no doubt the same weak likeness, or analogy, runs between all the 'social' sins and the real spiritual sins, and in some cases, perhaps, the lesser may be 'schoolmasters' to lead one on to the greater—from the shadow to the reality. If you are anything of a Theologian, you will see the importance of all this."

"I am sorry to say," remarked Cotgrave, "that I have devoted very little of my time to theology. Indeed, I have often wondered on what grounds theologians have claimed the title of Science of Sciences for their favourite study; since the 'theological' books I have looked into have always seemed to me to be concerned with feeble and obvious pieties, or with the kings of Israel and Judah. I do not care to hear about those kings."

Ambrose grinned.

"We must try to avoid theological discussion," he said. "I perceive that you would be a bitter disputant. But perhaps the 'dates of the kings' have as much to do with theology as the hobnails of the murderous puddler with evil."

"Then, to return to our main subject, you think that sin is an esoteric, occult thing?"

"Yes. It is the infernal miracle as holiness is the supernal. Now and then it is raised to such a pitch that we entirely fail to suspect its existence; it is like the note of the great pedal pipes of the organ, which is so deep that we cannot hear it. In other cases it may lead to the lunatic asylum, or to still stranger issues. But you must never confuse it with mere social misdoing. Remember how the Apostle, speaking of the 'other side,' distinguishes between 'charitable' actions and charity. And as one may give all one's goods to the poor, and yet lack charity; so, remember, one may avoid every crime and yet be a sinner."

"Your psychology is very strange to me," said Cotgrave, "but I confess I like it, and I suppose that one might fairly deduce from your premises the conclusion that the real sinner might very possibly strike the observer as a harmless personage enough?"

"Certainly; because the true evil has nothing to do with social life or social laws, or if it has, only incidentally and accidentally. It is a lonely passion of the soul—or a passion of the lonely soul—whichever you like. If, by chance, we understand it, and grasp its full significance, then, indeed, it will fill us with horror and with awe. But this emotion is widely distinguished from the fear and the disgust with which we regard the ordinary criminal, since this latter is largely or entirely founded on the regard which we have for our own skins or purses. We hate a murderer, because we know that we should hate to be murdered, or to have any one that we like murdered. So, on the 'other side,' we venerate the saints, but we don't 'like' them as we like our friends. Can you persuade yourself that you would have 'enjoyed' St. Paul''s company? Do you think that you and I would have "got on" with Sir Galahad?

"So with the sinners, as with the saints. If you met a very evil man, and recognized his evil; he would, no doubt, fill you with horror and awe; but there is no reason why you should 'dislike' him. On the contrary, it is quite possible that if you could succeed in putting the sin out of your mind you might find the sinner capital company, and in a little while you might have to reason yourself back into horror.

Still, how awful it is. If the roses and the lilies suddenly sang on this coming morning; if the furniture began to move in procession, as in De Maupassant's tale!"

"I am glad you have come back to that comparison," said Cotgrave, "because I wanted to ask you what it is that corresponds in humanity to these imaginary feats of inanimate things. In a word—what is sin? You have given me, I know, an abstract definition, but I should like a concrete example."

"I told you it was very rare," said Ambrose, who appeared willing to avoid the giving of a direct answer. "The materialism of the age, which has done a good deal to suppress sanctity, has done perhaps more to suppress evil. We find the earth so very comfortable that we have no inclination either for ascents or descents. It would seem as if the scholar who decided to "specialize" in Tophet, would be reduced to purely antiquarian researches. No palaeontologist could show you a *live* pterodactyl."

"And yet you, I think, have "specialized," and I believe that your researches have descended to our modern times."

"You are really interested, I see. Well, I confess, that I have dabbled a little, and if you like I can show you something that bears on the very curious subject we have been discussing."

Ambrose took a candle and went away to a far, dim corner of the room. Cotgrave saw him open a venerable bureau that stood there, and from some secret recess he drew out a parcel, and came back to the window where they had been sitting.

Ambrose undid a wrapping of paper, and produced a green pocket-book.

"You will take care of it?" he said. "Don't leave it lying about. It is one of the choicer pieces in my collection, and I should be very sorry if it were lost."

He fondled the faded binding.

"I knew the girl who wrote this," he said. "When you read it, you will see how it illustrates the talk we have had to-night. There is a sequel, too, but I won't talk of that."

"There was an odd article in one of the reviews some months ago," he began again, with the air of a man who changes the subject. "It was written by a doctor—Dr. Coryn, I think, was the name. He says that a lady, watching her little girl playing at the drawing-room window, suddenly saw the heavy sash give way and fall on the child's fingers. The lady fainted, I think, but at any rate the doctor was summoned, and when he had dressed the child's wounded and maimed fingers he was summoned to the mother. She was groaning with pain, and it was found that three fingers of her hand, corresponding with those that had been injured on the child's hand, were swollen and inflamed, and later, in the doctor's language, purulent sloughing set in."

Ambrose still handled delicately the green volume.

"Well, here it is," he said at last, parting with difficulty, it seemed, from his treasure.

"You will bring it back as soon as you have read it," he said, as they went out into the hall, into the old garden, faint with the odour of white lilies.

There was a broad red band in the east as Cotgrave turned to go, and from the high ground where he stood he saw that awful spectacle of London in a dream.

THE GREEN BOOK

The morocco binding of the book was faded, and the colour had grown faint, but there were no stains nor bruises nor marks of usage. The book looked as if it had been bought "on a visit to London" some seventy or eighty years ago, and had somehow been forgotten and suffered to lie away out of sight. There was an old, delicate, lingering odour about it, such an odour as sometimes haunts an ancient piece of furniture for a century or more. The end-papers, inside the binding, were oddly decorated with coloured patterns and faded gold. It looked small, but the paper was fine, and there were many leaves, closely covered with minute, painfully formed characters.

I found this book (the manuscript began) in a drawer in the old bureau that stands on the landing. It was a very rainy day and I could not go out, so in the afternoon I got a candle and rummaged in the bureau. Nearly all the drawers were full of old dresses, but one of the small ones looked empty, and I found this book hidden right at the back. I wanted a book like this, so I took it to write in. It is full of secrets. I have a great many other books of secrets I have written, hidden in a safe place, and I am going to write here many of the old secrets and some new ones; but there are some I shall not put down at all. I must not write down the real names of the days and months which I found out a year ago, nor the way to make the Aklo letters, or the Chian language, or the great beautiful Circles, nor the Mao Games, nor the chief songs. I may write something about all these things but not the way to do them, for peculiar reasons. And I must not say who the Nymphs are, or the Dols, or Jeelo, or what voolas mean. All these are most secret secrets, and I am glad when I remember what they are, and how many wonderful languages I know, but there are some things that I call the secrets of the secrets of the secrets that I dare not think of unless I am quite alone, and then I shut my eyes, and put my hands over them and whisper the word, and the Alala comes. I only do this at night in my room or in certain woods that I know, but I must not describe them, as they are secret woods. Then there are the Ceremonies, which are all of them important, but some are more delightful than others—there are the White Ceremonies, and the Green Ceremonies, and the Scarlet Ceremonies. The Scarlet Ceremonies are the best, but there is only one place where they can be performed properly, though there is a very nice imitation which I have done in other places. Besides these, I have the dances, and the Comedy, and I have done the Comedy sometimes when the others were looking, and they didn't understand anything about it. I was very little when I first knew about these things.

When I was very small, and mother was alive, I can remember remembering things before that, only it has all got confused. But I remember when I was five or six I heard them talking about me when they thought I was not noticing. They were saying how queer I was a year or two before, and how nurse had called my mother to come and listen to me talking all to myself, and I was saying words that nobody could understand. I was speaking the Xu language, but I only remember a very few of the words, as it was about the little white faces that used to look at me when I was lying in my cradle. They used to talk to me, and I learnt their language and talked to them in it about some great white place where they lived, where the trees and the grass were all white, and there were white hills as high up as the moon, and a cold wind. I have often dreamed of it afterwards, but the faces went away when I was very little. But a wonderful thing happened when I was about five. My nurse was carrying me on her shoulder; there was a field of yellow corn, and we went through it, it was very hot. Then we came to a path through a wood, and a tall man came after us, and went with us till we came to a place where there was a deep pool, and it was very dark and shady. Nurse put me down on the soft moss under a tree, and she said: "She can't get to the pond now." So they left me there, and I sat quite still and watched, and out of the water and out of the wood came two wonderful white people, and they began to play and dance and sing. They were a kind of creamy white like the old ivory figure in the drawing-room; one was a beautiful lady with kind dark eyes, and a grave face, and long black hair, and she smiled such a strange sad smile at the other, who laughed and came to her. They played together, and danced round and round the pool, and they sang a song till I fell asleep. Nurse woke me up when she came back, and she was looking something like the lady had looked, so I told her all about it, and asked her why she looked like that. At first she cried, and then she looked very frightened, and turned quite pale. She put me down on the grass and stared at me, and I could see she was shaking all over. Then she said I had been dreaming, but I knew I hadn't. Then she made me promise not to say a word about it to anybody, and if I did I should be thrown into the black pit. I was not frightened at all, though nurse was, and I never forgot about it, because when I shut my eyes and it was quite quiet, and I was all alone, I could see them again, very faint and far away, but very splendid; and little bits of the song they sang came into my head, but I couldn't sing it.

I was thirteen, nearly fourteen, when I had a very singular adventure, so strange that the day on which it happened is always called the White Day. My mother had been dead for more than a year, and in the morning I had lessons, but they let me go out for walks in the afternoon. And this afternoon I walked a new way, and a little brook led me into a new country, but I tore my frock getting through some of the difficult places, as the way was through many bushes, and beneath the low branches of trees, and up thorny thickets on the hills, and by dark woods full of creeping thorns. And it was a long, long way. It seemed as if I was going on for ever and ever, and I had to creep by a place like a tunnel where a brook must have been, but all the water had dried up, and the floor was rocky, and the bushes had grown overhead till they met, so that it was quite dark. And I went on and on through that dark place; it was a long, long way. And I came to a hill that I never saw before. I was in a dismal thicket full of black twisted boughs that tore me as I went through them, and I cried out because I was smarting all over, and then I found that I was climbing, and I went up and up a long way, till at last the thicket stopped and I came out crying just under the top of a big bare place, where there were ugly grey stones lying all about on the grass, and here and there a little twisted, stunted tree came out from under a stone, like a snake. And I went up, right to the top, a long way. I never saw such big ugly stones before; they came out of the earth some of them, and some looked as if they had been rolled to where they were, and they went on and on as far as I could see, a long, long way. I looked out from them and saw the country, but it was strange. It was winter time, and there were black terrible woods hanging from the hills all round; it was like seeing a large room hung with black curtains, and the shape of the trees seemed quite different from any I had ever seen before. I was afraid. Then beyond the woods there were other hills round in a great ring, but I had never seen any of them; it all looked black, and everything had a voor over it. It was all so still and silent, and the sky was heavy and grey and sad, like a wicked voorish dome in Deep Dendo. I went on into the dreadful rocks. There were hundreds and hundreds of them. Some were like horrid-grinning men; I could see their faces as if they would jump at me out of the stone, and catch hold of me, and drag me with them back into the rock, so that I should always be there. And there were other rocks that were like animals, creeping, horrible animals, putting out their tongues, and others were like words that I could not say, and others like dead people lying on the grass. I went on among them, though they frightened me, and my heart was full of wicked songs that they put into it; and I wanted to make faces and twist myself about in the way they did, and I went on and on a long way till at last I liked the rocks, and they didn't frighten me any more. I sang the songs I thought of; songs full of words that must not be spoken or written down. Then I made faces like the faces on the rocks, and I twisted myself about like the twisted ones, and I lay down flat on the ground like the dead ones, and I went up to one that was grinning, and put my arms round him and hugged him. And so I went on and on through the rocks till I came to a round mound in the middle of them. It was higher than a mound, it was nearly as high as our house, and it was like a great basin turned upside down, all smooth and round and green, with one stone, like a post, sticking up at the top. I climbed up the sides, but they were so steep I had to stop or I should have rolled all the way down again, and I should have knocked against the stones at the bottom, and perhaps been killed. But I wanted to get up to the very top of the big round mound, so I lay down flat on my face, and took hold of the grass with my hands and drew myself up, bit by bit, till I was at the top. Then I sat down on the stone in the middle, and looked all round about. I felt I had come such a long, long way, just as if I were a hundred miles from home, or in some other country, or in one of the strange places I had read about in the "Tales of the Genie" and the "Arabian Nights," or as if I had gone across the sea, far away, for years and I had found another world that nobody had ever seen or heard of before, or as if I had somehow flown through the sky and fallen on one of the stars I had read about where every-thing is dead and cold and grey, and there is no air, and the wind doesn't blow. I sat on the stone and looked all round and down and round about me. It was just as if I was sitting on a tower in the middle of a great empty town, because I could see nothing all around but the grey rocks on the ground. I couldn't make out their shapes any more, but I could see them on and on for a long way, and I looked at them, and they seemed as if they had been arranged into patterns, and shapes, and figures. I knew they couldn't be, because I had seen a lot of them coming right out of the earth, joined to the deep rocks below, so I looked again, but still I saw nothing but circles, and small circles inside big ones, and pyramids, and domes, and spires, and they seemed all to go round and round the place where I was sitting, and the more I looked, the more I saw great big rings of rocks, getting bigger and bigger, and I stared so long that it felt as if they were all moving and turning, like a great wheel, and I was turning, too, in the middle. I got quite dizzy and queer in the head, and everything began to be hazy and not clear, and I saw little sparks of blue light, and the stones looked as if they were springing and dancing and twisting as they went round and round and round. I was frightened again, and I cried out loud, and jumped up from the stone I was sitting on, and fell down. When I got up I was so glad they all looked still, and I sat down on the top and slid down the mound, and went on again. I danced as I went in the peculiar way the rocks had danced when I got giddy, and I was so glad I could do it quite well, and I danced and danced along, and sang extraordinary songs that came into my head. At last I came to the edge of that great flat hill, and there were no more rocks, and the way went again through a dark thicket in a hollow. It was just as bad as the other one I went through climbing up, but I didn't mind this one, because I was so glad I had seen those singular dances and could imitate them. I went down, creeping through the bushes, and a tall nettle stung me on my leg, and made me burn, but I didn't mind it, and I tingled with the boughs and the thorns, but I only laughed and sang. Then I got out of the thicket into a close valley, a little secret place like a dark passage that nobody ever knows of, because it was so narrow and deep and the woods were so thick round it. There is a steep bank with trees hanging over it, and there the ferns keep green all through the winter, when they are dead and brown upon the hill, and the ferns there have a sweet, rich smell like what oozes out of fir trees. There was a little stream of water running down this valley, so small that I could easily step across it. I drank the water with my hand, and it tasted like bright, yellow wine, and it sparkled and bubbled as it ran down over beautiful red and yellow and green stones, so that it seemed alive and all colours at once. I drank it, and I drank more with my hand, but I couldn't drink enough, so I lay down and bent my head and sucked the water up with my lips. It tasted much better, drinking it that way, and a ripple would come up to my mouth and give me a kiss, and I laughed, and drank again, and pretended there was a nymph, like the one in the old picture at home, who lived in the water and was kissing me. So I bent low down to the water, and put my lips softly to it, and whispered to the nymph that I would come again. I felt sure it could not be common water, I was so glad when I got up and went on; and I danced again and went up and up the valley, under hanging hills. And when I came to the top, the ground rose up in front of me, tall and steep as a wall, and there was nothing but the green wall and the sky. I thought of "for ever and for ever, world without end, Amen"; and I thought I must have really found the end of the world, because it was like the end of everything, as if there could be nothing at all beyond, except the kingdom of Voor, where the light goes when it is put out, and the water goes when the sun takes it away. I began to think of all the long, long way I had journeyed, how I had found a brook and followed it, and followed it on, and gone through bushes and thorny thickets, and dark woods full of creeping thorns. Then I had crept up a tunnel under trees, and climbed a thicket, and seen all the grey rocks, and sat in the middle of them when they turned round, and then I had gone on through the grey rocks and come down the hill through the stinging thicket and up the dark valley, all a long, long way. I wondered how I should get home again, if I could ever find the way, and if my home was there any more, or if it were turned and everybody in it into grey rocks, as in the "Arabian Nights." So I sat down on the grass and thought what I should do next. I was tired, and my feet were hot with walking, and as I looked about I saw there was a wonderful well just under the high, steep wall of grass. All the ground round it was covered with bright, green, dripping moss; there was every kind of moss there, moss like beautiful little ferns, and like palms and fir trees, and it was all green as jewellery, and drops of water hung on it like diamonds. And in the middle was the great well, deep and shining and beautiful, so clear that it looked as if I could touch the red sand at the bottom, but it was far below. I stood by it and looked in, as if I were looking in a glass. At the bottom of the well, in the middle of it, the red grains of sand were moving and stirring all the time, and I saw how the water bubbled up, but at the top it was quite smooth, and full and brimming. It was a great well, large like a bath, and with the shining, glittering green moss about it, it looked like a great white jewel, with green jewels all round. My feet were so hot and tired that I took off my boots and stockings, and let my feet down into the water, and the water was soft and cold, and when I got up I wasn't tired any more, and I felt I must go on, farther and farther, and see what was on the other side of the wall. I climbed up it very slowly, going sideways all the time, and when I got to the top and looked over, I was in the queerest country I had seen, stranger even than the hill of the grey rocks. It looked as if earth-children had been playing there with their spades, as it was all hills and hollows, and castles and walls made of earth and covered with grass. There were two mounds like big beehives, round and great and solemn, and then hollow basins, and then a steep mounting wall like the ones I saw once by the seaside where the big guns and the soldiers were. I nearly fell into one of the round hollows, it went away from under my feet so suddenly, and I ran fast down the side and stood at the bottom and looked up. It was strange and solemn to look up. There was nothing but the grey, heavy sky and the sides of the hollow; every-thing else had gone away, and the hollow was the whole world, and I thought that at night it must be full of ghosts and moving shadows and pale things when the moon shone down to the bottom at the dead of the night, and the wind wailed up above. It was so strange and solemn and lonely, like a hollow temple of dead heathen gods. It reminded me of a tale my nurse had told when I was quite little; it was the same nurse that took me into the wood where I saw the beautiful white people. And I remembered how nurse had told me the story one winter night, when the wind was beating the trees against the wall, and crying and moaning in the nursery chimney. She said there was, somewhere or other, a hollow pit, just like the one I was standing in, everybody was afraid to go into it or near it, it was such a bad place. But once upon a time there was a poor girl who said she would go into the hollow pit, and everybody tried to stop her, but she would go. And she went down into the pit and came back laughing, and said there was nothing there at all, except green grass and red stones, and white stones and yellow flowers. And soon after people saw she had most beautiful emerald earrings, and they asked how she got them, as she and her mother were quite poor. But she laughed, and said her earrings were not made of emeralds at all, but only of green grass. Then, one day, she wore on her breast the reddest ruby that any one had ever seen, and it was as big as a hen's egg, and glowed and sparkled like a hot burning coal of fire. And they asked how she got it, as she and her mother were quite poor. But she laughed, and said it was not a ruby at all, but only a red stone. Then one day she wore round her neck the loveliest necklace that any one had ever seen, much finer than the queen's finest, and it was made of great bright diamonds, hundreds of them, and they shone like all the stars on a night in June. So they asked her how she got it, as she and her mother were quite poor. But she laughed, and said they were not diamonds at all, but only white stones. And one day she went to the Court, and she wore on her head a crown of pure angel-gold, so nurse said, and it shone like the sun, and it was much more splendid than the crown the king was wearing himself, and in her ears she wore the emeralds, and the big ruby was the brooch on her breast, and the great diamond necklace was sparkling on her neck. And the king and queen thought she was some great princess from a long way off, and got down from their thrones and went to meet her, but somebody told the king and queen who she was, and that she was quite poor. So the king asked why she wore a gold crown, and how she got it, as she and her mother were so poor. And she laughed, and said it wasn't a gold crown at all, but only some yellow flowers she had put in her hair. And the king thought it was very strange, and said she should stay at the Court, and they would see what would happen next. And she was so lovely that everybody said that her eyes were greener than the emeralds, that her lips were redder than the ruby, that her skin was whiter than the diamonds, and that her hair was brighter than the golden crown. So the king's son said he would marry her, and the king said he might. And the bishop married them, and there was a great supper, and afterwards the king's son went to his wife's room. But just when he had his hand on the door, he saw a tall, black man, with a dreadful face, standing in front of the door, and a voice said—

> Venture not upon your life,
> This is mine own wedded wife.

Then the king's son fell down on the ground in a fit. And they came and tried to get into the room, but they couldn't, and they hacked at the door with hatchets, but the wood had turned hard as iron, and at last everybody ran away, they were so frightened at the screaming and laughing and shrieking and crying that came out of the room. But next day they went in, and found there was nothing in the room but thick black smoke, because the black man had come and taken her away. And on the bed there were two knots of faded grass and a red stone, and some white stones, and some faded yellow flowers. I remembered this tale of nurse's while I was standing at the bottom of the deep hollow; it was so strange and solitary there, and I felt afraid. I could not see any stones or flowers, but I was afraid of bringing them away without knowing, and I thought I would do a charm that came into my head to keep the black man away. So I stood right in the very middle of the hollow, and I made sure that I had none of those things on me, and then I walked round the place, and touched my eyes, and my lips, and my hair in a peculiar manner, and whispered some queer words that nurse taught me to keep bad things away. Then I felt safe and climbed up out of the hollow, and went on through all those mounds and hollows and walls, till I came to the end, which was high above all the rest, and I could see that all the different shapes of the earth were arranged in patterns, something like the grey rocks, only the pattern was different. It was getting late, and the air was indistinct, but it looked from where I was standing something like two great figures of people lying on the grass. And I went on, and at last I found a certain wood, which is too secret to be described, and nobody knows of the passage into it, which I found out in a very curious manner, by seeing some little animal run into the wood through it. So I went after the animal by a very narrow dark way, under thorns and bushes, and it was almost dark when I came to a kind of open place in the middle. And there I saw the most wonderful sight I have ever seen, but it was only for a minute, as I ran away directly, and crept out of the wood by the passage I had come by, and ran and ran as fast as ever I could, because I was afraid, what I had seen was so wonderful and so strange and beautiful. But I wanted to get home and think of it, and I did not know what might not happen if I stayed by the wood. I was hot all over and trembling, and my heart was beating, and strange cries that I could not help came from me as I ran from the wood. I was glad that a great white moon came up from over a round hill and showed me the way, so I went back through the mounds and hollows and down the close valley, and up through the thicket over the place of

168

the grey rocks, and so at last I got home again. My father was busy in his study, and the servants had not told about my not coming home, though they were frightened, and wondered what they ought to do, so I told them I had lost my way, but I did not let them find out the real way I had been. I went to bed and lay awake all through the night, thinking of what I had seen. When I came out of the narrow way, and it looked all shining, though the air was dark, it seemed so certain, and all the way home I was quite sure that I had seen it, and I wanted to be alone in my room, and be glad over it all to myself, and shut my eyes and pretend it was there, and do all the things I would have done if I had not been so afraid. But when I shut my eyes the sight would not come, and I began to think about my adventures all over again, and I remembered how dusky and queer it was at the end, and I was afraid it must be all a mistake, because it seemed impossible it could happen. It seemed like one of nurse's tales, which I didn't really believe in, though I was frightened at the bottom of the hollow; and the stories she told me when I was little came back into my head, and I wondered whether it was really there what I thought I had seen, or whether any of her tales could have happened a long time ago. It was so queer; I lay awake there in my room at the back of the house, and the moon was shining on the other side towards the river, so the bright light did not fall upon the wall. And the house was quite still. I had heard my father come upstairs, and just after the clock struck twelve, and after the house was still and empty, as if there was nobody alive in it. And though it was all dark and indistinct in my room, a pale glimmering kind of light shone in through the white blind, and once I got up and looked out, and there was a great black shadow of the house covering the garden, looking like a prison where men are hanged; and then beyond it was all white; and the wood shone white with black gulfs between the trees. It was still and clear, and there were no clouds on the sky. I wanted to think of what I had seen but I couldn't, and I began to think of all the tales that nurse had told me so long ago that I thought I had forgotten, but they all came back, and mixed up with the thickets and the grey rocks and the hollows in the earth and the secret wood, till I hardly knew what was new and what was old, or whether it was not all dreaming. And then I remembered that hot summer afternoon, so long ago, when nurse left me by myself in the shade, and the white people came out of the water and out of the wood, and played, and danced, and sang, and I began to fancy that nurse told me about something like it before I saw them, only I couldn't recollect exactly what she told me. Then I wondered whether she had been the white lady, as I remembered she was just as white and beautiful, and had the same dark eyes and black hair; and sometimes she smiled and looked like the lady had looked, when she was telling me some of her stories, beginning with

"Once on a time," or "In the time of the fairies." But I thought she couldn't be the lady, as she seemed to have gone a different way into the wood, and I didn't think the man who came after us could be the other, or I couldn't have seen that wonderful secret in the secret wood. I thought of the moon: but it was afterwards when I was in the middle of the wild land, where the earth was made into the shape of great figures, and it was all walls, and mysterious hollows, and smooth round mounds, that I saw the great white moon come up over a round hill. I was wondering about all these things, till at last I got quite frightened, because I was afraid something had happened to me, and I remembered nurse's tale of the poor girl who went into the hollow pit, and was carried away at last by the black man. I knew I had gone into a hollow pit too, and perhaps it was the same, and I had done something dreadful. So I did the charm over again, and touched my eyes and my lips and my hair in a peculiar manner, and said the old words from the fairy language, so that I might be sure I had not been carried away. I tried again to see the secret wood, and to creep up the passage and see what I had seen there, but somehow I couldn't, and I kept on thinking of nurse's stories. There was one I remembered about a young man who once upon a time went hunting, and all the day he and his hounds hunted everywhere, and they crossed the rivers and went into all the woods, and went round the marshes, but they couldn't find anything at all, and they hunted all day till the sun sank down and began to set behind the mountain. And the young man was angry because he couldn't find anything, and he was going to turn back, when just as the sun touched the mountain, he saw come out of a brake in front of him a beautiful white stag. And he cheered to his hounds, but they whined and would not follow, and he cheered to his horse, but it shivered and stood stock still, and the young man jumped off the horse and left the hounds and began to follow the white stag all alone. And soon it was quite dark, and the sky was black, without a single star shining in it, and the stag went away into the darkness. And though the man had brought his gun with him he never shot at the stag, because he wanted to catch it, and he was afraid he would lose it in the night. But he never lost it once, though the sky was so black and the air was so dark, and the stag went on and on till the young man didn't know a bit where he was. And they went through enormous woods where the air was full of whispers and a pale, dead light came out from the rotten trunks that were lying on the ground, and just as the man thought he had lost the stag, he would see it all white and shining in front of him, and he would run fast to catch it, but the stag always ran faster, so he did not catch it. And they went through the enormous woods, and they swam across rivers, and they waded through black marshes where the ground bubbled, and the air was full of will-o'-the-wisps, and the stag fled away down into rocky narrow valleys, where the air was like the smell of a vault, and the man went after it. And they went over the great mountains and the man heard the wind come down from the sky, and the stag went on and the man went after. At last the sun rose and the young man found he was in a country that he had never seen before; it was a beautiful valley with a bright stream running through it, and a great, big round hill in the middle. And the stag went down the valley, towards the hill, and it seemed to be getting tired and went slower and slower, and though the man was tired, too, he began to run faster, and he was sure he would catch the stag at last. But just as they got to the bottom of the hill, and the man stretched out his hand to catch the stag, it vanished into the earth, and the man began to cry; he was so sorry that he had lost it after all his long hunting. But as he was crying he saw there was a door in the hill, just in front of him, and he went in, and it was quite dark, but he went on, as he thought he would find the white stag. And all of a sudden it got light, and there was the sky, and the sun shining, and birds singing in the trees, and there was a beautiful fountain. And by the fountain a lovely lady was sitting, who was the queen of the fairies, and she told the man that she had changed herself into a stag to bring him there because she loved him so much. Then she brought out a great gold cup, covered with jewels, from her fairy palace, and she offered him wine in the cup to drink. And he drank, and the more he drank the more he longed to drink, because the wine was enchanted. So he kissed the lovely lady, and she became his wife, and he stayed all that day and all that night in the hill where she lived, and when he woke he found he was lying on the ground, close to where he had seen the stag first, and his horse was there and his hounds were there waiting, and he looked up, and the sun sank behind the mountain. And he went home and lived a long time, but he would never kiss any other lady because he had kissed the queen of the fairies, and he would never drink common wine any more, because he had drunk enchanted wine. And sometimes nurse told me tales that she had heard from her great-grandmother, who was very old, and lived in a cottage on the mountain all alone, and most of these tales were about a hill where people used to meet at night long ago, and they used to play all sorts of strange games and do queer things that nurse told me of, but I couldn't understand, and now, she said, everybody but her great-grandmother had forgotten all about it, and nobody knew where the hill was, not even her great-grandmother. But she told me one very strange story about the hill, and I trembled when I remembered it. She said that people always went there in summer, when it was very hot, and they had to dance a good deal. It would be all dark at first, and there were trees there, which made it much darker, and people would come, one by one, from all directions, by a secret path which nobody else knew, and two persons would keep the gate, and every one as they came up had to give a very curious sign, which nurse showed me as well as she could, but she said she couldn't show me properly. And all kinds of people would come; there would be gentle folks and village folks, and some old people and boys and girls, and quite small children, who sat and watched. And it would all be dark as they came in, except in one corner where some one was burning something that smelt strong and sweet, and made them laugh, and there one would see a glaring of coals, and the smoke mounting up red. So they would all come in, and when the last had come there was no door any more, so that no one else could get in, even if they knew there was anything beyond. And once a gentleman who was a stranger and had ridden a long way, lost his path at night, and his horse took him into the very middle of the wild country, where everything was upside down, and there were dreadful marshes and great stones everywhere, and holes underfoot, and the trees looked like gibbet-posts, because they had great black arms that stretched out across the way. And this strange gentleman was very frightened, and his horse began to shiver all over, and at last it stopped and wouldn't go any farther, and the gentleman got down and tried to lead the horse, but it wouldn't move, and it was all covered with a sweat, like death. So the gentleman went on all alone, going farther and farther into the wild country, till at last he came to a dark place, where he heard shouting and singing and crying, like nothing he had ever heard before. It all sounded quite close to him, but he couldn't get in, and so he began to call, and while he was calling, something came behind him, and in a minute his mouth and arms and legs were all bound up, and he fell into a swoon. And when he came to himself, he was lying by the roadside, just where he had first lost his way, under a blasted oak with a black trunk, and his horse was tied beside him. So he rode on to the town and told the people there what had happened, and some of them were amazed; but others knew. So when once everybody had come, there was no door at all for anybody else to pass in by. And when they were all inside, round in a ring, touching each other, some one began to sing in the darkness, and some one else would make a noise like thunder with a thing they had on purpose, and on still nights people would hear the thundering noise far, far away beyond the wild land, and some of them, who thought they knew what it was, used to make a sign on their breasts when they woke up in their beds at dead of night and heard that terrible deep noise, like thunder on the mountains. And the noise and the singing would go on and on for a long time, and the people who were in a ring swayed a little to and fro; and the song was in an old, old language that nobody knows now, and the tune was queer. Nurse said her great-grandmother had known some one who remembered a little of it, when she was quite a little girl, and nurse tried to sing some of it to me, and it was so strange a tune that I turned all cold and my flesh crept as if I had put my hand on something dead. Sometimes it was a man that sang and sometimes it was a woman, and sometimes the one who sang it did it so well that two or three of the people who were there fell to the ground shrieking and tearing with their hands. The singing went on, and the people in the ring kept swaying to and fro for a long time, and at last the moon would rise over a place they called the Tole Deol, and came up and showed them swinging and swaying from side to side, with the sweet thick smoke curling up from the burning coals, and floating in circles all around them. Then they had their supper. A boy and a girl brought it to them; the boy carried a great cup of wine, and the girl carried a cake of bread, and they passed the bread and the wine round and round, but they tasted quite different from common bread and common wine, and changed everybody that tasted them. Then they all rose up and danced, and secret things were brought out of some hiding place, and they played extraordinary games, and danced round and round and round in the moonlight, and sometimes people would suddenly disappear and never be heard of afterwards, and nobody knew what had happened to them. And they drank more of that curious wine, and they made images and worshipped them, and nurse showed me how the images were made one day when we were out for a walk, and we passed by a place where there was a lot of wet clay. So nurse asked me if I would like to know what those things were like that they made on the hill, and I said yes. Then she asked me if I would promise never to tell a living soul a word about it, and if I did I was to be thrown into the black pit with the dead people, and I said I wouldn't tell anybody, and she said the same thing again and again, and I promised. So she took my wooden spade and dug a big lump of clay and put it in my tin bucket, and told me to say if any one met us that I was going to make pies when I went home. Then we went on a little way till we came to a little brake growing right down into the road, and nurse stopped, and looked up the road and down it, and then peeped through the hedge into the field on the other side, and then she said, "Quick!" and we ran into the brake, and crept in and out among the bushes till we had gone a good way from the road. Then we sat down under a bush, and I wanted so much to know what nurse was going to make with the clay, but before she would begin she made me promise again not to say a word about it, and she went again and peeped through the bushes on every side, though the lane was so small and deep that hardly anybody ever went there. So we sat down, and nurse took the clay out of the bucket, and began to knead it with her hands, and do queer things with it, and turn it about. And she hid it under a big dock-leaf for a minute or two and then she brought it out again, and then she stood up and sat down, and walked round the clay in a peculiar manner, and all the time she was softly singing a sort of rhyme, and her face got very red. Then she sat down again, and took the clay in her hands and began to shape it into a doll, but not like the dolls I have at home, and she made the queerest doll I had ever seen, all out of the wet clay, and hid it under a bush to get dry and hard, and all the time she was making it she was singing these rhymes to herself, and her face got redder and redder. So we left the doll there, hidden away in the bushes where nobody would ever find it. And a few days later we went the same walk, and when we came to that narrow, dark part of the lane where the brake runs down to the bank, nurse made me promise all over again, and she looked about, just as she had done before, and we crept into the bushes till we got to the green place where the little clay man was hidden. I remember it all so well, though I was only eight, and it is eight years ago now as I am writing it down, but the sky was a deep violet blue, and in the middle of the brake where we were sitting there was a great elder tree covered with blossoms, and on the other side there was a clump of meadowsweet, and when I think of that day the smell of the meadowsweet and elder blossom seems to fill the room, and if I shut my eyes I can see the glaring blue sky, with little clouds very white floating across it, and nurse who went away long ago sitting opposite me and looking like the beautiful white lady in the wood. So we sat down and nurse took out the clay doll from the secret place where she had hidden it, and she said we must "pay our respects," and she would show me what to do, and I must watch her all the time. So she did all sorts of queer things with the little clay man, and I noticed she was all streaming with perspiration, though we had walked so slowly, and then she told me to "pay my respects," and I did everything she did because I liked her, and it was such an odd game. And she said that if one loved very much, the clay man was very good, if one did certain things with it, and if one hated very much, it was just as good, only one had to do different things, and we played with it a long time, and pretended all sorts of things. Nurse said her great-grandmother had told her all about these images, but what we did was no harm at all, only a game. But she told me a story about these images that frightened me very much, and that was what I remembered that night when I was lying awake in my room in the pale, empty darkness, thinking of what I had seen and the secret wood. Nurse said there was once a young lady of the high gentry, who lived in a great castle. And she was so beautiful that all the gentlemen wanted to marry her, because she was the loveliest lady that anybody had ever seen, and she was kind to everybody, and everybody thought she was very good. But though she was polite to all the gentlemen who wished to marry her, she put them off, and said she couldn't make up her mind, and she wasn't sure she wanted to marry anybody at all. And her father, who was a very great lord, was angry, though he was so fond of her, and he asked her why she wouldn't choose a bachelor out of all the handsome young men who came to the castle. But she only said she didn't love any of them very much, and she must wait, and if they pestered her, she said she would go and be a nun in a nunnery. So all the gentlemen said they would go away and wait for a year and a day, and when a year and a day were gone, they would come back again and ask her to say which one she would marry. So the day was appointed and they all went away; and the lady had promised that in a year and a day it would be her wedding day with one of them. But the truth was, that she was the queen of the people who danced on the hill on summer nights, and on the proper nights she would lock the door of her room, and she and her maid would steal out of the castle by a secret passage that only they knew of, and go away up to the hill in the wild land. And she knew more of the secret things than any one else, and more than any one knew before or after, because she would not tell anybody the most secret secrets. She knew how to do all the awful things, how to destroy young men, and how to put a curse on people, and other things that I could not understand. And her real name was the Lady Avelin, but the dancing people called her Cassap, which meant somebody very wise, in the old language. And she was whiter than any of them and taller, and her eyes shone in the dark like burning rubies; and she could sing songs that none of the others could sing, and when she sang they all fell down on their faces and worshipped her. And she could do what they called shib-show, which was a very wonderful enchantment. She would tell the great lord, her father, that she wanted to go into the woods to gather flowers, so he let her go, and she and her maid went into the woods where nobody came, and the maid would keep watch. Then the lady would lie down under the trees and begin to sing a particular song, and she stretched out her arms, and from every part of the wood great serpents would come, hissing and gliding in and out among the trees, and shooting out their forked tongues as they crawled up to the lady. And they all came to her, and twisted round her, round her body, and her arms, and her neck, till she was covered with writhing serpents, and there was only her head to be seen. And she whispered to them, and she sang to them, and they writhed round and round, faster and faster, till she told them to go. And they all went away directly, back to their holes, and on the lady's breast there would be a most curious, beautiful stone, shaped something like an egg, and coloured dark blue and yellow, and red, and green, marked like a serpent's scales. It was called a glame stone, and with it one could do all sorts of wonderful things, and nurse said her great-grandmother had seen a glame stone with her own eyes, and it was for all the world shiny and scaly like a snake. And the lady could do a lot of other things as well, but she was quite fixed that she would not be married. And there were a great many gentlemen who wanted to marry her, but there were five of them who were chief, and their names were Sir Simon, Sir John, Sir Oliver, Sir Richard, and Sir Rowland. All the others believed she spoke the truth, and that she would choose one of them to be her man when a year and a day was done; it was only Sir Simon, who was very crafty, who thought she was deceiving them all, and he vowed he would watch and try if he could find out anything. And though he was very wise he was very young, and he had a smooth, soft face like a girl's, and he pretended, as the rest did, that he would not come to the castle for a year and a day, and he said he was going away beyond the sea to foreign parts. But he really only went a very little way, and came back dressed like a servant girl, and so he got a place in the castle to wash the dishes. And he waited and watched, and he listened and said nothing, and he hid in dark places, and woke up at night and looked out, and he heard things and he saw things that he thought were very strange. And he was so sly that he told the girl that waited on the lady that he was really a young man, and that he had dressed up as a girl because he loved her so very much and wanted to be in the same house with her, and the girl was so pleased that she told him many things, and he was more than ever certain that the Lady Avelin was deceiving him and the others. And he was so clever, and told the servant so many lies, that one night he managed to hide in the Lady Avelin"s room behind the curtains. And he stayed quite still and never moved, and at last the lady came. And she bent down under the bed, and raised up a stone, and there was a hollow place underneath, and out of it she took a waxen image, just like the clay one that I and nurse had made in the brake. And all the time her eyes were burning like rubies. And she took the little wax doll up in her arms and held it to her breast, and she whispered and she murmured, and she took it up and she laid it down again, and she held it high, and she held it low, and she laid it down again. And she said, "Happy is he that begat the bishop, that ordered the clerk, that married the man, that had the wife, that fashioned the hive, that harboured the bee, that gathered the wax that my own true love was made of." And she brought out of an aumbry a great golden bowl, and she brought out of a closet a great jar of wine, and she poured some of the wine into the bowl, and she laid her mannikin very gently in the wine, and washed it in the wine all over. Then she went to a cupboard and took a small round cake and laid it on the image's mouth, and then she bore it softly and covered it up. And Sir Simon, who was watching all the time, though he was terribly frightened, saw the lady bend down and stretch out her arms and whisper and sing, and then Sir Simon saw beside her a handsome young man, who kissed her on the lips.

And they drank wine out of the golden bowl together, and they ate the cake together. But when the sun rose there was only the little wax doll, and the lady hid it again under the bed in the hollow place. So Sir Simon knew quite well what the lady was, and he waited and he watched, till the time she had said was nearly over, and in a week the year and a day would be done. And one night, when he was watching behind the curtains in her room, he saw her making more wax dolls. And she made five, and hid them away. And the next night she took one out, and held it up, and filled the golden bowl with water, and took the doll by the neck and held it under the water. Then she said—

> Sir Dickon, Sir Dickon, your day is done,
> You shall be drowned in the water wan.

And the next day news came to the castle that Sir Richard had been drowned at the ford. And at night she took another doll and tied a violet cord round its neck and hung it up on a nail. Then she said—

> Sir Rowland, your life has ended its span,
> High on a tree I see you hang.

And the next day news came to the castle that Sir Rowland had been hanged by robbers in the wood. And at night she took another doll, and drove her bodkin right into its heart. Then she said—

> Sir Noll, Sir Noll, so cease your life,
> Your heart pierced with the knife.

And the next day news came to the castle that Sir Oliver had fought in a tavern, and a stranger had stabbed him to the heart. And at night she took another doll, and held it to a fire of charcoal till it was melted. Then she said—

> Sir John, return, and turn to clay,
> In fire of fever you waste away.

And the next day news came to the castle that Sir John had died in a burning fever. So then Sir Simon went out of the castle and mounted his horse and rode away to the bishop and told him everything. And the bishop sent his men, and they took the Lady Avelin, and everything she had done was found out. So on the day after the year and a day, when she was to have been married, they carried her through the town in her smock, and they tied her to a great stake in the market-place, and burned her alive before the bishop with her wax image hung round her neck. And people said the wax man screamed in the burning of the flames. And I thought of this story again and again as I was lying awake in my bed, and I seemed to see the Lady Avelin in the market-place, with the yellow flames eating up her beautiful white body. And I thought of it so much that I seemed to get into the story myself, and I fancied I was the lady, and that they were coming to take me to be burnt with fire, with all the people in the town looking at me. And I wondered whether she cared, after all the strange things she had done, and whether it hurt very much to be burned at the stake. I tried again and again to forget nurse's stories, and to remember the secret I had seen that afternoon, and what was in the secret wood, but I could only see the dark and a glimmering in the dark, and then it went away, and I only saw myself running, and then a great moon came up white over a dark round hill. Then all the old stories came back again, and the queer rhymes that nurse used to sing to me; and there was one beginning "Halsy cumsy Helen musty," that she used to sing very softly when she wanted me to go to sleep. And I began to sing it to myself inside of my head, and I went to sleep.

The next morning I was very tired and sleepy, and could hardly do my lessons, and I was very glad when they were over and I had had my dinner, as I wanted to go out and be alone. It was a warm day, and I went to a nice turfy hill by the river, and sat down on my mother's old shawl that I had brought with me on purpose. The sky was grey, like the day before, but there was a kind of white gleam behind it, and from where I was sitting I could look down on the town, and it was all still and quiet and white, like a picture. I remembered that it was on that hill that nurse taught me to play an old game called "Troy Town," in which one had to dance, and wind in and out on a pattern in the grass, and then when one had danced and turned long enough the other person asks you questions, and you can't help answering whether you want to or not, and whatever you are told to do you feel you have to do it. Nurse said there used to be a lot of games like that that some people knew of, and there was one by which people could be turned into anything you liked, and an old man her great-grandmother had seen had known a girl who had been turned into a large snake. And there was another very ancient game of dancing and winding and turning, by which you could take a person out of himself and hide him away as long as you liked, and his body went walking about quite empty, without any sense in it. But I came to that hill because I wanted to think of what had happened the day before, and of the secret of the wood. From the place where I was sitting I could see beyond the town, into the opening I had found, where a little brook had led me into an unknown country. And I pretended I was following the brook over again, and I went all the way in my mind, and at last I found the wood, and crept into it under the bushes, and then in the dusk I saw something that made me feel as if I were filled with fire, as if I wanted to dance and sing and fly up into the air, because I was changed and wonderful. But what I saw was not changed at all, and had not grown old, and I wondered again and again how such things could happen, and whether nurse's stories were really true, because in the daytime in the open air everything seemed quite different from what it was at night, when I was frightened, and thought I was to be burned alive. I once told my father one of her little tales, which was about a ghost, and asked him if it was true, and he told me it was not true at all, and that only common, ignorant people believed in such rubbish. He was very angry with nurse for telling me the story, and scolded her, and after that I promised her I would never whisper a word of what she told me, and if I did I should be bitten by the great black snake that lived in the pool in the wood. And all alone on the hill I wondered what was true. I had seen something very amazing and very lovely, and I knew a story, and if I had really seen it, and not made it up out of the dark, and the black bough, and the bright shining that was mounting up to the sky from over the great round hill, but had really seen it in truth, then there were all kinds of wonderful and lovely and terrible things to think of, so I longed and trembled, and I burned and got cold. And I looked down on the town, so quiet and still, like a little white picture, and I thought over and over if it could be true. I was a long time before I could make up my mind to anything; there was such a strange fluttering at my heart that seemed to whisper to me all the time that I had not made it up out of my head, and yet it seemed quite impossible, and I knew my father and everybody would say it was dreadful rubbish. I never dreamed of telling him or anybody else a word about it, because I knew it would be of no use, and I should only get laughed at or scolded, so for a long time I was very quiet, and went about thinking and wondering; and at night I used to dream of amazing things, and sometimes I woke up in the early morning and held out my arms with a cry. And I was frightened, too, because there were dangers, and some awful thing would happen to me, unless I took great care, if the story were true. These old tales were always in my head, night and morning, and I went over them and told them to myself over and over again, and went for walks in the places where nurse had told them to me; and when I sat in the nursery by the fire in the evenings I used to fancy nurse was sitting in the other chair, and telling me some wonderful story in a low voice, for fear anybody should be listening. But she used to like best to tell me about things when we were right out in the country, far from the house, because she said she was telling me such secrets, and walls have ears. And if it was something more than ever secret, we had to hide in brakes or woods; and I used to think it was such fun creeping along a hedge, and going very softly, and then we would get behind the bushes or run into the wood all of a sudden, when we were sure that none was watching us; so we knew that we had our secrets quite all to ourselves, and nobody else at all knew anything about them. Now and then, when we had hidden ourselves as I have described, she used to show me all sorts of odd things. One day, I remember, we were in a hazel brake, overlooking the brook, and we were so snug and warm, as though it was April; the sun was quite hot, and the leaves were just coming out. Nurse said she would show me something funny that would make me laugh, and then she showed me, as she said, how one could turn a whole house upside down, without anybody being able to find out, and the pots and pans would jump about, and the china would be broken, and the chairs would tumble over of themselves. I tried it one day in the kitchen, and I found I could do it quite well, and a whole row of plates on the dresser fell off it, and cook''s little work-table tilted up and turned right over "before her eyes," as she said, but she was so frightened and turned so white that I didn't do it again, as I liked her. And after-wards, in the hazel copse, when she had shown me how to make things tumble about, she showed me how to make rapping noises, and I learnt how to do that, too. Then she taught me rhymes to say on certain occasions, and peculiar marks to make on other occasions, and other things that her great-grandmother had taught her when she was a little girl herself. And these were all the things I was thinking about in those days after the strange walk when I thought I had seen a great secret, and I wished nurse were there for me to ask her about it, but she had gone away more than two years before, and nobody seemed to know what had become of her, or where she had gone. But I shall always remember those days if I live to be quite old, because all the time I felt so strange, wondering and doubting, and feeling quite sure at one time, and making up my mind, and then I would feel quite sure that such things couldn't happen really, and it began all over again. But I took great care not to do certain things that might be very dangerous. So I waited and wondered for a long time, and though I was not sure at all, I never dared to try to find out. But one day I became sure that all that nurse said was quite true, and I was all alone when I found it out. I trembled all over with joy and terror, and as fast as I could I ran into one of the old brakes where we used to go—it was the one by the lane, where nurse made the little clay man—and I ran into it, and I crept into it; and when I came to the place where the elder was, I covered up my face with my hands and lay down flat on the grass, and I stayed there for two hours without moving, whispering to myself delicious, terrible things, and saying some words over and over again. It was all true and wonderful and splendid, and when I remembered the story I knew and thought of what I had really seen, I got hot and I got cold, and the air seemed full of scent, and flowers, and singing. And first I wanted to make a little clay man, like the one nurse had made so long ago, and I had to invent plans and stratagems, and to look about, and to think of things beforehand, because nobody must dream of anything that I was doing or going to do, and I was too old to carry clay about in a tin bucket. At last I thought of a plan, and I brought the wet clay to the brake, and did everything that nurse had done, only I made a much finer image than the one she had made; and when it was finished I did everything that I could imagine and much more than she did, because it was the likeness of something far better. And a few days later, when I had done my lessons early, I went for the second time by the way of the little brook that had led me into a strange country. And I followed the brook, and went through the bushes, and beneath the low branches of trees, and up thorny thickets on the hill, and by dark woods full of creeping thorns, a long, long way. Then I crept through the dark tunnel where the brook had been and the ground was stony, till at last I came to the thicket that climbed up the hill, and though the leaves were coming out upon the trees, everything looked almost as black as it was on the first day that I went there. And the thicket was just the same, and I went up slowly till I came out on the big bare hill, and began to walk among the wonderful rocks. I saw the terrible voor again on everything, for though the sky was brighter, the ring of wild hills all around was still dark, and the hanging woods looked dark and dreadful, and the strange rocks were as grey as ever; and when I looked down on them from the great mound, sitting on the stone, I saw all their amazing circles and rounds within rounds, and I had to sit quite still and watch them as they began to turn about me, and each stone danced in its place, and they seemed to go round and round in a great whirl, as if one were in the middle of all the stars and heard them rushing through the air. So I went down among the rocks to dance with them and to sing extraordinary songs; and I went down through the other thicket, and drank from the bright stream in the close and secret valley, putting my lips down to the bubbling water; and then I went on till I came to the deep, brimming well among the glittering moss, and I sat down. I looked before me into the secret darkness of the valley, and behind me was the great high wall of grass, and all around me there were the hanging woods that made the valley such a secret place. I knew there was nobody here at all besides myself, and that no one could see me. So I took off my boots and stockings, and let my feet down into the water, saying the words that I knew. And it was not cold at all, as I expected, but warm and very pleasant, and when my feet were in it I felt as if they were in silk, or as if the nymph were kissing them. So when I had done, I said the other words and made the signs, and then I dried my feet with a towel I had brought on purpose, and put on my stockings and boots. Then I climbed up the steep wall, and went into the place where there are the hollows, and the two beautiful mounds, and the round ridges of land, and all the strange shapes. I did not go down into the hollow this time, but I turned at the end, and made out the figures quite plainly, as it was lighter, and I had remembered the story I had quite forgotten before, and in the story the two figures are called Adam and Eve, and only those who know the story understand what they mean. So I went on and on till I came to the secret wood which must not be described, and I crept into it by the way I had found. And when I had gone about halfway I stopped, and turned round, and got ready, and I bound the handkerchief tightly round my eyes, and made quite sure that I could not see at all, not a twig, nor the end of a leaf, nor the light of the sky, as it was an old red silk handkerchief with large yellow spots, that went round twice and covered my eyes, so that I could see nothing. Then I began to go on, step by step, very slowly. My heart beat faster and faster, and something rose in my throat that choked me and made me want to cry out, but I shut my lips, and went on. Boughs caught in my hair as I went, and great thorns tore me; but I went on to the end of the path. Then I stopped, and held out my arms and bowed, and I went round the first time, feeling with my hands, and there was nothing. I went round the second time, feeling with my hands, and there was nothing. Then I went round the third time, feeling with my hands, and the story was all true, and I wished that the years were gone by, and that I had not so long a time to wait before I was happy for ever and ever.

Nurse must have been a prophet like those we read of in the Bible. Everything that she said began to come true, and since then other things that she told me of have happened. That was how I came to know that her stories were true and that I had not made up the secret myself out of my own head. But there was another thing that happened that day. I went a second time to the secret place. It was at the deep brimming well, and when I was standing on the moss I bent over and looked in, and then I knew who the white lady was that I had seen come out of the water in the wood long ago when I was quite little. And I trembled all over, because that told me other things. Then I remembered how sometime after I had seen the white people in the wood, nurse asked me more about them, and I told her all over again, and she listened, and said nothing for a long, long time, and at last she said, "You will see her again." So I understood what had happened and what was to happen. And I understood about the nymphs; how I might meet them in all kinds of places, and they would always help me, and I must always look for them, and find them in all sorts of strange shapes and appearances. And without the nymphs I could never have found the secret, and without them none of the other things could happen. Nurse had told me all about them long ago, but she called them by another name, and I did not know what she meant, or what her tales of them were about, only that they were very queer. And there were two kinds, the bright and the dark, and both were very lovely and very wonderful, and some people saw only one kind, and some only the other, but some saw them both. But usually the dark appeared first, and the bright ones came afterwards, and there were extraordinary tales about them. It was a day or two after I had come home from the secret place that I first really knew the nymphs. Nurse had shown me how to call them, and I had tried, but I did not know what she meant, and so I thought it was all nonsense. But I made up my mind I would try again, so I went to the wood where the pool was, where I saw the white people, and I tried again. The dark nymph, Alanna, came, and she turned the pool of water into a pool of fire . . .

EPILOGUE

"That's a very queer story," said Cotgrave, handing back the green book to the recluse, Ambrose. "I see the drift of a good deal, but there are many things that I do not grasp at all. On the last page, for example, what does she mean by 'nymphs?' "

"Well, I think there are references throughout the manuscript to certain 'processes' which have been handed down by tradition from age to age. Some of these processes are just beginning to come within the purview of science, which has arrived at them—or rather at the steps which lead to them—by quite different paths. I have interpreted the reference to 'nymphs' as a reference to one of these processes."

"And you believe that there are such things?"

"Oh, I think so. Yes, I believe I could give you convincing evidence on that point. I am afraid you have neglected the study of alchemy? It is a pity, for the symbolism, at all events, is very beautiful, and moreover if you were acquainted with certain books on the subject, I could recall to your mind phrases which might explain a good deal in the manuscript that you have been reading."

"Yes; but I want to know whether you seriously think that there is any foundation of fact beneath these fancies. Is it not all a department of poetry; a curious dream with which man has indulged himself?"

"I can only say that it is no doubt better for the great mass of people to dismiss it all as a dream. But if you ask my veritable belief—that goes quite the other way. No; I should not say belief, but rather knowledge. I may tell you that I have known cases in which men have stumbled quite by accident on certain of these 'processes,' and have been astonished by wholly unexpected results. In the cases I am thinking of there could have been no possibility of 'suggestion' or sub-conscious action of any kind. One might as well suppose a schoolboy 'suggesting' the existence of Æschylus to himself, while he plods mechanically through the declensions.

"But you have noticed the obscurity," Ambrose went on, "and in this particular case it must have been dictated by instinct, since the writer never thought that her manuscripts would fall into other hands. But the practice is universal, and for most excellent reasons. Powerful and sovereign medicines, which are, of necessity, virulent poisons also, are kept in a locked cabinet. The child may find the key by chance, and drink herself dead; but in most cases the search is educational, and the phials contain precious elixirs for him who has patiently fashioned the key for himself."

"You do not care to go into details?"

"No, frankly, I do not. No, you must remain unconvinced. But you saw how the manuscript illustrates the talk we had last week?"

"Is this girl still alive?"

"No. I was one of those who found her. I knew the father well; he was a lawyer, and had always left her very much to herself. He thought of nothing but deeds and leases, and the news came to him as an awful surprise. She was missing one morning; I suppose it was about a year after she had written what you have read. The servants were called, and they told things, and put the only natural interpretation on them—a perfectly erroneous one.

"They discovered that green book somewhere in her room, and I found her in the place that she described with so much dread, lying on the ground before the image."

"It was an image?"

"Yes, it was hidden by the thorns and the thick undergrowth that had surrounded it. It was a wild, lonely country; but you know what it was like by her description, though of course you will understand that the colours have been heightened. A child's imagination always makes the heights higher and the depths deeper than they really are; and she had, unfortunately for herself, something more than imagination. One might say, perhaps, that the picture in her mind which she succeeded in a measure in putting into words, was the scene as it would have appeared to an imaginative artist. But it is a strange, desolate land."

"And she was dead?"

"Yes. She had poisoned herself—in time. No; there was not a word to be said against her in the ordinary sense. You may recollect a story I told you the other night about a lady who saw her child's fingers crushed by a window?"

"And what was this statue?"

"Well, it was of Roman workmanship, of a stone that with the centuries had not blackened, but had become white and luminous. The thicket had grown up about it and concealed it, and in the Middle Ages the followers of a very old tradition had known how to use it for their own purposes. In fact it had been incorporated into the monstrous mythology of the Sabbath. You will have noted that those to whom a sight of that shining whiteness had been vouchsafed by chance, or rather, perhaps, by apparent chance, were required to blindfold themselves on their second approach. That is very significant."

"And is it there still?"

"I sent for tools, and we hammered it into dust and fragments."

"The persistence of tradition never surprises me," Ambrose went on after a pause. "I could name many an English parish where such traditions as that girl had listened to in her childhood are still existent in occult but unabated vigour. No, for me, it is the 'story' not the 'sequel,' which is strange and awful, for I have always believed that wonder is of the soul."

THE SCREAMING SKULL

F. MARION CRAWFORD

An American expatriate who lived in Italy for most of
his adult life, Francis Marion Crawford (1854–1909)
was a popular writer of historical romances who
occasionally dabbled in supernatural fiction. This
dramatic monlogue, from the July 11, 1908 issue of
Collier's, is interesting for its stream-of-consciousness
narrative style that helps to keep the horrors at bay
until the final paragraphs.

I have often heard it scream. No, I am not nervous, I am not imaginative, and I never believed in ghosts, unless that thing is one. Whatever it is, it hates me almost as much as it hated Luke Pratt, and it screams at me.

If I were you, I would never tell ugly stories about ingenious ways of killing people, for you never can tell but that some one at the table may be tired of his or her nearest and dearest. I have always blamed myself for Mrs. Pratt's death, and I suppose I was responsible for it in a way, though heaven knows I never wished her anything but long life and happiness. If I had not told that story she might be alive yet. That is why the thing screams at me, I fancy.

She was a good little woman, with a sweet temper, all things considered, and a nice gentle voice; but I remember hearing her shriek once when she thought her little boy was killed by a pistol that went off, though every one was sure that it was not loaded. It was the same scream; exactly the same, with a sort of rising quaver at the end; do you know what I mean? Unmistakable.

The truth is, I had not realised that the doctor and his wife were not on good terms. They used to bicker a bit now and then when I was here, and I often noticed that little Mrs. Pratt got very red and bit her lip hard to keep her temper, while Luke grew pale and said the most offensive things. He was that sort when he was in the nursery, I remember, and afterward at school. He was my cousin, you know; that is how I came by this house; after he died, and his boy Charley was killed in South Africa, there were no relations left. Yes, it's a pretty little property, just the sort of thing for an old sailor like me who has taken to gardening.

One always remembers one's mistakes much more vividly than one's cleverest things, doesn't one? I've often noticed it. I was dining with the Pratts one night, when I told them the story that afterwards made so much difference. It was a wet night in November, and the sea was moaning. Hush!—if you don't speak you will hear it now. . . .

Do you hear the tide? Gloomy sound, isn't it? Sometimes, about this time of year—hallo!—there it is! Don't be frightened, man—it won't eat you—it's only a noise, after all! But I'm glad you've heard it, because there are always people who think it's the wind, or my imagination, or something. You won't hear it again to-night, I fancy, for it doesn't often come more than once. Yes—that's right. Put another stick on the fire, and a little more stuff into that weak mixture you're so fond of. Do you remember old Blauklot the carpenter, on that German ship that picked us up when the *Clontarf* went to the bottom? We were hove to in a howling gale one night, as snug as you please, with no land within five hundred miles, and the ship coming up and falling off as regularly as clockwork—"Biddy te boor beebles ashore tis night, poys!" old Blauklot sang out, as he went off to his quarters with the sail-maker. I often think of that, now that I'm ashore for good and all.

Yes, it was on a night like this, when I was at home for a spell, waiting to take the *Olympia* out on her first trip—it was on the next voyage that she broke the record, you remember—but that dates it. Ninety-two was the year, early in November.

The weather was dirty, Pratt was out of temper, and the dinner was bad, very bad indeed, which didn't improve matters, and cold, which made it worse. The poor little lady was very unhappy about it, and insisted on making a Welsh rarebit on the table to counteract the raw turnips and the half-boiled mutton. Pratt must have had a hard day. Perhaps he had lost a patient. At all events, he was in a nasty temper.

"My wife is trying to poison me, you see!" he said. "She'll succeed some day." I saw that she was hurt, and I made believe to laugh, and said that Mrs. Pratt was much too clever to get rid of her husband in such a simple way; and then I began to tell them about Japanese tricks with spun glass and chopped horsehair and the like.

Pratt was a doctor, and knew a lot more than I did about such things, but that only put me on my mettle, and I told a story about a woman in Ireland who did for three husbands before any one suspected foul play.

Did you never hear that tale? The fourth husband managed to keep awake and caught her, and she was hanged. How did she do it? She drugged them, and poured melted lead into their ears through a little horn funnel when they were asleep. . . . No—that's the wind whistling. It's backing up to the southward again. I can tell by the sound. Besides, the other thing doesn't often come more than once in an evening even at this time of year—when it happened. Yes, it was in November. Poor Mrs. Pratt died suddenly in her bed not long after I dined here. I can fix the date, because I got the news in New York by the steamer that followed the *Olympia* when I took her out on her first trip. You had the *Leofric* the same year? Yes, I remember. What a pair of old buffers we are coming to be, you and I. Nearly fifty years since we were apprentices together on the *Clontarf*. Shall you ever forget old Blauklot? "Biddy te boor beebles ashore, poys!" Ha, ha! Take a little more, with all that water. It's the old Hulstkamp I found in the cellar when this house came to me, the same I brought Luke from Amsterdam five-and-twenty years ago. He had never touched a drop of it. Perhaps he's sorry now, poor fellow.

Where did I leave off? I told you that Mrs. Pratt died suddenly—yes. Luke must have been lonely here after she was dead, I should think; I came to see him now and then, and he looked worn and nervous, and told me that his practice was growing too heavy for him, though he wouldn't take an assistant on any account. Years went on, and his son was killed in South Africa, and after that he began to be queer. There was something about him not like other people. I believe he kept his senses in his profession to the end; there was no complaint of his having made bad mistakes in cases, or anything of that sort, but he had a look about him—

Luke was a red-headed man with a pale face when he was young, and he was never stout; in middle age he turned a sandy grey, and after his son died he grew thinner and thinner, till his head looked like a skull with parchment stretched over it very tight, and his eyes had a sort of glare in them that was very disagreeable to look at.

He had an old dog that poor Mrs. Pratt had been fond of, and that used to follow her everywhere. He was a bull-dog, and the sweetest tempered beast you ever saw, though he had away of hitching his upper lip behind one of his fangs that frightened strangers a good deal. Sometimes, of an evening, Pratt and Bumble—that was the dog's name—used to sit and look at each other a long time, thinking about old tunes, I suppose, when Luke's wife used to sit in that chair you've got. That was always her place, and this was the doctor's, where I'm sitting. Bumble used to climb up by the footstool—he was old and fat by that time, and could not jump much, and his teeth were getting shaky. He would look steadily at Luke, and Luke looked steadily at the dog, his face growing more and more like a skull with two little coals for eyes; and after about five minutes or so, though it may have been less, old Bumble would suddenly begin to shake all over, and all on l a sudden he would set up an awful howl, as if he 'had been shot, and tumble out of the easy-chair and trot away, and hide himself under the sideboard, and lie there making odd noises.

Considering Pratt's looks in those last months, the thing is not surprising, you know. I'm not nervous or imaginative, but I can quite believe he might have sent a sensitive woman into hysterics—his head looked so much like a skull in parchment.

At last I came down one day before Christmas, when my ship was in dock and I had three weeks off. Bumble was not about, and I said casually that I supposed the old dog was dead.

"Yes," Pratt answered, and I thought there was something odd in his tone even before he went on after a little pause. "I killed him," he said presently. "I could not stand it any longer."

I asked what it was that Luke could not stand, though I guessed well enough.

"He had a way of sitting in her chair and glaring at me, and then howling." Luke shivered a little. "He didn't suffer at all, poor old Bumble," he went on in a hurry, as if he thought I might imagine he had been cruel. "I put dionine into his drink to make him sleep soundly, and then I chloroformed him gradually, so that he could not have felt suffocated even if he was dreaming. It's been quieter since then."

I wondered what he meant, for the words slipped out as if he could not help saying them. I've understood since. He meant that he did not hear that noise so often after the dog was out of the way. Perhaps he thought at first that it was old Bumble in the yard howling at the moon, though it's not that kind of noise, is it? Besides, I know what it is, if Luke didn't. It's only a noise, after all, and a noise never hurt anybody yet. But he was much more imaginative than I am. No doubt there really is something about this place that I don't understand; but when I don't understand a thing, I call it a phenomenon, and I don't take it for granted that it's going to kill me, as he did. I don't understand everything, by long odds, nor do you, nor does any man who has been to sea. We used to talk of tidal waves, for instance, and we could not account for them; now we account for them by calling them submarine earthquakes, and we branch off into fifty theories, any one of which might make earthquakes quite comprehensible if we only knew what they are. I fell in with one of them once, and the inkstand flew straight up from the table against the ceiling of my cabin. The same thing happened to Captain Lecky—I dare say you've read about it in his "Wrinkles." Very good. If that sort of thing took place ashore, in this room for instance, a nervous person would talk about spirits and levitation and fifty things that mean nothing, instead of just quietly setting it down as a "phenomenon" that has not been explained yet. My view of that voice, you see.

Besides, what is there to prove that Luke killed his wife? I would not even suggest such a thing to any one but you. After all, there was nothing but the coincidence that poor little Mrs. Pratt died suddenly in her bed a few days after I told that story at dinner. She was not the only woman who ever died like that. Luke got the doctor over from the next parish, and they agreed that she had died of something the matter with her heart. Why not? It's common enough.

Of course, there was the ladle. I never told anybody about that, and it made me start when I found it in the cupboard in the bedroom. It was new, too—a little tinned iron ladle that had not been in the fire more than once or twice, and there was some lead in it that had been melted, and stuck to the bottom of the bowl, all grey, with hardened dross on it. But that proves nothing. A country doctor is generally a handy man, who does everything for himself, and Luke may have had a dozen reasons for melting a little lead in a ladle. He was fond of sea-fishing, for instance, and he may have cast a sinker for a night-line; perhaps it was a weight for the hall clock, or something like that. All the same, when I found it I had a rather queer sensation, because it looked so much like the thing I had described when I told them the story. Do you understand? It affected me unpleasantly, and I threw it away; it's at the bottom of the sea a mile from the Spit, and it will be jolly well rusted beyond recognising if it's ever washed up by the tide.

You see, Luke must have bought it in the village, years ago, for the man sells just such ladles still. I suppose they are used in cooking. In any case, there was no reason why an inquisitive housemaid should find such a thing lying about, with lead in it, and wonder what it was, and perhaps talk to the maid who heard me tell the story at dinner—for that girl married the plumber's son in the village, and may remember the whole thing.

You understand me, don't you? Now that Luke Pratt is dead and gone, and lies buried beside his wife, with an honest man's tombstone at his head, I should not care to stir up anything that could hurt his memory. They are both dead, and their son, too. There was trouble enough about Luke's death, as it was.

How? He was found dead on the beach one morning, and there was a coroner's inquest. There were marks on his throat, but he had not been robbed. The verdict was that he had come to his end "by the hands or teeth of some person or animal unknown," for half the jury thought it might have been a big dog that had thrown him down and gripped his windpipe, though the skin of his throat was not broken. No one knew at what time he had gone out, nor where he had been. He was found lying on his back above high-water mark, and an old card-board bandbox that had belonged to his wife lay under his hand, open. The lid had fallen off. He seemed to have been carrying home a skull in the box—doctors are fond of collecting such things. It had rolled out and lay near his head, and it was a remarkably fine skull, rather small, beautifully shaped and very white, with perfect teeth. That is to say, the upper jaw was perfect, but there was no lower one at all, when I first saw it.

Yes, I found it here when I came. You see, it was very white and polished, like a thing meant to be kept under a glass case, and the people did not know where it came from, nor what to do with it; so they put it back into the bandbox and set it on the shelf of the cupboard in the best bedroom, and of course they showed it to me when I took possession. I was taken down to the beach, too, to be shown the place where Luke was found, and the old fisherman explained just how he was lying, and the skull beside him. The only point he could not explain was why the skull had rolled up the sloping sand toward Luke's head instead of rolling downhill to his feet. It did not seem odd to me at the time, but I have often thought of it since, for the place is rather steep. I'll take you there to-morrow if you like—I made a sort of cairn of stones there afterward.

When he fell down, or was thrown down—whichever happened—the bandbox struck the sand, and the lid came off, and the thing came out and ought to have rolled down. But it didn't. It was close to his head, almost touching it, and turned with the face toward it. I say it didn't strike me as odd when the man told me; but I could not help thinking about it afterward, again and again, till I saw a picture of it all when I closed my eyes; and then I began to ask myself why the plaguey thing had rolled up instead of down, and why it had stopped near Luke's head instead of anywhere else, a yard away, for instance.

You naturally want to know what conclusion I reached, don't you? None that at all explained the rolling, at all events. But I got something else into my head, after a time, that made me feel downright uncomfortable.

Oh, I don't mean as to anything supernatural! There may be ghosts, or there may not be. If there are, I'm not inclined to believe that they can hurt living people except by frightening them, and, for my part, I would rather face any shape of ghost than a fog in the Channel when it's crowded. No. What bothered me was just a foolish idea, that's all, and I cannot tell how it began, nor what made it grow till it turned into a certainty.

I was thinking about Luke and his poor wife one evening over my pipe and a dull book, when it occurred to me that the skull might possibly be hers, and I have never got rid of the thought since. You'll tell me there's no sense in it, no doubt; that Mrs. Pratt was buried like a Christian and is lying in the churchyard where they put her, and that it's perfectly monstrous to suppose her husband kept her skull in her old bandbox in his bedroom. All the same, in the face of reason, and common sense, and probability, I'm convinced that he did. Doctors do all sorts of queer things that would make men like you and me feel creepy, and those are just the things that don't seem probable, nor logical, nor sensible to us.

Then, don't you see?—if it really was her skull, poor woman, the only way of accounting for his having it is that he really killed her, and did it in that way, as the woman killed her husbands in the story, and that he was afraid there might be an examination some day which would betray him. You see, I told that too, and I believe it had really happened some fifty or sixty years ago. They dug up the three skulls, you know, and there was a small lump of lead rattling about in each one. That was what hanged the woman. Luke remembered that, I'm sure. I don't want to know what he did when he thought of it; my taste never ran in the direction of horrors, and I don't fancy you care for them either, do you? No. If you did, you might supply what is wanting to the story.

It must have been rather grim, eh? I wish I did not see the whole thing so distinctly, just as everything must have happened. He took it the night before she was buried, I'm sure, after the coffin had been shut, and when the servant girl was asleep. I would bet anything, that when he'd got it, he put something under the sheet in its place, to fill up and look like it. What do you suppose he put there, under the sheet?

I don't wonder you take me up on what I'm saying! First I tell you that I don't want to know what happened, and that I hate to think about horrors, and then I describe the whole thing to you as if I had seen it. I'm quite sure that it was her work-bag that he put there. I remember the bag very well, for she always used it of an evening; it was made of brown plush, and when it was stuffed full it was about the size of—you understand. Yes, there I am, at it again! You may laugh at me, but you don't live here alone, where it was done, and you didn't tell Luke the story about the melted lead. I'm not nervous, I tell you, but sometimes I begin to feel that I understand why some people are. I dwell on all this when I'm alone, and I dream of it, and when that thing screams—well, frankly, I don't like the noise any more than you do, though I should be used to it by this time.

I ought not to be nervous. I've sailed in a haunted ship. There was a Man in the Top, and two-thirds of the crew died of the West Coast fever inside of ten days after we anchored; but I was all right, then and afterward. I have seen some ugly sights, too, just as you have, and all the rest of us. But nothing ever stuck in my head in the way this does.

You see, I've tried to get rid of the thing, but it doesn't like that. It wants to be there in its place, in Mrs. Pratt's bandbox in the cupboard in the best bedroom. It's not happy anywhere else. How do I know that? Because I've tried it. You don't suppose that I've not tried, do you? As long as it's there it only screams now and then, generally at this time of year, but if I put it out of the house it goes on all night, and no servant will stay here twenty-four hours. As it is, I've often been left alone and have been obliged to shift for myself for a fortnight at a time. No one from the village would ever pass a night under the roof now, and as for selling the place, or even letting it, that's out of the question. The old women say that if I stay here I shall come to a bad end myself before long.

I'm not afraid of that. You smile at the mere idea that any one could take such nonsense seriously. Quite right. It's utterly blatant nonsense, I agree with you. Didn't I tell you that it's only a noise after all when you started and looked round as if you expected to see a ghost standing behind your chair?

I may be all wrong about the skull, and I like to think that I am—when I can. It may be just a fine specimen which Luke got somewhere long ago, and what rattles about inside when you shake it may be nothing but a pebble, or a bit of hard clay, or anything. Skulls that have lain long in the ground generally have something inside them that rattles, don't they? No, I've never tried to get it out, whatever it is; I'm afraid it might be lead, don't you see? And if it is, I don't want to know the fact, for I'd much rather not be sure. If it really is lead, I killed her quite as much as if I had done the deed myself. Anybody must see that, I should think. As long as I don't know for certain, I have the consolation of saying that it's all utterly ridiculous nonsense, that Mrs. Pratt died a natural death and that the beautiful skull belonged to Luke when he was a student in London. But if I were quite sure, I believe I should have to leave the house; indeed I do, most certainly. As it is, I had to give up trying to sleep in the best bedroom where the cupboard is.

You ask me why I don't throw it into the pond—yes, but please don't call it a "confounded bugbear"—it doesn't like being called names.

There! Lord, what a shriek! I told you so! You're quite pale, man. Fill up your pipe and draw your chair nearer to the fire, and take some more drink. Old Hollands never hurt anybody yet. I've seen a Dutchman in Java drink half a jug of Hulstkamp in a morning without turning a hair. I don't take much rum myself, because it doesn't agree with my rheumatism, but you are not rheumatic and it won't damage you. Besides, it's a very damp night outside. The wind is howling again, and it will soon be in the southwest; do you hear how the windows rattle? The tide must have turned too, by the moaning.

We should not have heard the thing again if you had not said that. I'm pretty sure we should not. Oh yes, if you choose to describe it as a coincidence, you are quite welcome, but I would rather that you should not call the thing names again, if you don't mind. It may be that the poor little woman hears, and perhaps it hurts her, don't you know? Ghost? No! You don't call anything a ghost that you can take in your hands and look at in broad daylight, and that rattles when you shake it. Do you, now? But it's something that hears and understands; there's no doubt about that.

I tried sleeping in the best bedroom when I first came to the house, just because it was the best and the most comfortable, but I had to give it up. It was their room, and there's the big bed she died in, and the cupboard is in the thickness of the wall, near the head, on the left. That's where it likes to be kept, in its bandbox. I only used the room for a fortnight after I came, and then I turned out and took the little room downstairs, next to the surgery, where Luke used to sleep when he expected to be called to a patient during the night.

I was always a good sleeper ashore; eight hours is my dose, eleven to seven when I'm alone, twelve to eight when I have a friend with me. But I could not sleep after three o'clock in the morning in that room—a quarter past, to be accurate—as a matter of fact, I timed it with my old pocket chronometer, which still keeps good time, and it was always at exactly seventeen minutes past three. I wonder whether that was the hour when she died?

It was not what you have heard. If it had been that I could not have stood it two nights. It was just a start and a moan and hard breathing for a few seconds in the cupboard, and it could never have waked me under ordinary circumstances, I'm sure. I suppose you are like me in that, and we are just like other people who have been to sea. No natural sounds disturb us at all, not all the racket of a square-rigger hove to in a heavy gale, or rolling on her beam ends before the wind. But if a lead pencil gets adrift and rattles in the drawer of your cabin table you are awake in a moment. Just so—you always understand. Very well, the noise in the cupboard was no louder than that, but it waked me instantly.

I said it was like a "start." I know what I mean, but it's hard to explain without seeming to talk nonsense. Of course you cannot exactly "hear" a person "start"; at the most, you might hear the quick drawing of the breath between the parted lips and closed teeth, and the almost imperceptible sound of clothing that moved suddenly though very slightly. It was like that.

You know how one feels what a sailing vessel is going to do, two or three seconds before she does it, when one has the wheel. Riders say the same of a horse, but that's less strange, because the horse is a live animal with feelings of its own, and only poets and landsmen talk about a ship being alive, and all that. But I have always felt somehow that besides being a steaming machine or a sailing machine for carrying weights, a vessel at sea is a sensitive instrument, and a means of communication between nature and man, and most particularly the man at the wheel, if she is steered by hand. She takes her impressions directly from wind and sea, tide and stream, and transmits them to the man's hand, just as the wireless telegraph picks up the interrupted currents aloft and turns them out below in the form of a message.

You see what I am driving at; I felt that something started in the cupboard, and I felt it so vividly that I heard it, though there may have been nothing to hear, and the sound inside my head waked me suddenly. But I really heard the other noise. It was as if it were muffled inside a box, as far away as if it came through a long-distance telephone; and yet I knew that it was inside the cupboard near the head of my bed. My hair did not bristle and my blood did not run cold that time. I simply resented being waked up by something that had no business to make a noise, any more than a pencil should rattle in the drawer of my cabin table on board ship. For I did not understand; I just supposed that the cupboard had some communication with the outside air, and that the wind had got in and was moaning through it with a sort of very faint screech. I struck a light and looked at my watch, and it was seventeen minutes past three. Then I turned over and went to sleep on my right ear. That's my good one; I'm pretty deaf with the other, for I struck the water with it when I was a lad in diving from the foretopsail yard. Silly thing to do, it was, but the result is very convenient when I want to go to sleep when there's a noise.

That was the first night, and the same thing happened again and several times afterward, but not regularly, though it was always at the same time, to a second; perhaps I was sometimes sleeping on my good ear, and sometimes not. I overhauled the cupboard and there was no way by which the wind could get in, or anything else, for the door makes a good fit, having been meant to keep out moths, I suppose; Mrs. Pratt must have kept her winter things in it, for it still smells of camphor and turpentine.

After about a fortnight I had had enough of the noises. So far I had said to myself that it would be silly to yield to it and take the skull out of the room. Things always look differently by daylight, don't they? But the voice grew louder—I suppose one may call it a voice—and it got inside my deaf ear, too, one night. I realised that when I was wide awake, for my good ear was jammed down on the pillow, and

I ought not to have heard a fog-horn in that position. But I heard that, and it made me lose my temper, unless it scared me, for sometimes the two are not far apart. I struck a light and got up, and I opened the cupboard, grabbed the bandbox and threw it out of the window, as far as I could.

Then my hair stood on end. The thing screamed in the air, like a shell from a twelve-inch gun. It fell on the other side of the road. The night was very dark, and I could not see it fall, but I know it fell beyond the road. The window is just over the front door, it's fifteen yards to the fence, more or less, and the road is ten yards wide. There's a quickset hedge beyond, along the glebe that belongs to the vicarage.

I did not sleep much more that night. It was not more than half an hour after I had thrown the bandbox out when I heard a shriek outside—like what we've had to-night, but worse, more despairing, I should call it; and it may have been my imagination, but I could have sworn that the screams came nearer and nearer each time. I lit a pipe, and walked up and down for a bit, and then took a book and sat up reading, but I'll be hanged if I can remember what I read nor even what the book was, for every now and then a shriek came up that would have made a dead man turn in his coffin.

A little before dawn some one knocked at the front door. There was no mistaking that for anything else, and I opened my window and looked down, for I guessed that some one wanted the doctor, supposing that the new man had taken Luke's house. It was rather a relief to hear a human knock after that awful noise.

You cannot see the door from above, owing to the little porch. The knocking came again, and I called out, asking who was there, but nobody answered, though the knock was repeated. I sang out again, and said that the doctor did not live here any longer. There was no answer, but it occurred to me that it might be some old countryman who was stone deaf. So I took my candle and went down to open the door. Upon my word, I was not thinking of the thing yet, and *I* had almost forgotten the other noises. I went down convinced that I should find somebody outside, on the doorstep, with a message. I set the candle on the hall table, so that the wind should not blow it out when I opened. While I was drawing the old-fashioned bolt I heard the knocking again. It was not loud, and it had a queer, hollow sound, now that I was close to it, I remember, but I certainly thought it was made by some person who wanted to get in.

It wasn't. There was nobody there, but as I opened the door inward, standing a little on one side, so as to see out at once, something rolled across the threshold and stopped against my foot.

I drew back as I felt it, for I knew what it was before I looked down. I cannot tell you how I knew, and it seemed unreasonable, for I am still quite sure that I had thrown it across the road. It's a French window, that opens wide, and I got a good swing when I flung it out. Besides, when I went out early in the morning, I found the bandbox beyond the thickset hedge.

You may think it opened when I threw it, and that the skull dropped out; but that's impossible, for nobody could throw an empty cardboard box so far. It's out of the question; you might as well try to fling a ball of paper twenty-five yards, or a blown bird's egg.

To go back, I shut and bolted the hall door, picked the thing up carefully, and put it on the table beside the candle. I did that mechanically, as one instinctively does the right thing in danger without thinking at all—unless one does the opposite. It may seem odd, but I believe my first thought had been that somebody might come and find me there on the threshold while it was resting against my foot, lying a little on its side, and turning one hollow eye up at my face, as if it meant to accuse me. And the light and shadow from the candle played in the hollows of the eyes as it stood on the table, so that they seemed to open and shut at me. Then the candle went out quite unexpectedly, though the door was fastened and there was not the least draught; and I used up at least half a dozen matches before it would burn again.

I sat down rather suddenly, without quite knowing why. Probably I had been badly frightened, and perhaps you will admit there was no great shame in being scared. The thing had come home, and it wanted to go upstairs, back to its cupboard. I sat still and stared at it for a bit, till I began to feel very cold; then I took it and carried it up and set it in its place, and I remember that I spoke to it, and promised that it should have its bandbox again in the morning.

You want to know whether I stayed in the room till daybreak? Yes, but I kept a light burning, and sat up smoking and reading, most likely out of fright; plain, undeniable fear, and you need not call it cowardice either, for that's not the same thing. I could not have stayed alone with that thing in the cupboard; I should have been scared to death, though I'm not more timid than other people. Confound it all, man, it had crossed the road alone, and had got up the doorstep and had knocked to be let in.

When the dawn came, I put on my boots and went out to find the bandbox. I had to go a good way round, by the gate near the highroad, and I found the box open and hanging on the other side of the hedge. It had caught on the twigs by the string, and the lid had fallen off and was lying on the ground below it. That shows that it did not open till it was well over; and if it had not opened as soon as it left my hand, what was inside it must have gone beyond the road too.

That's all. I took the box upstairs to the cupboard, and put the skull back and locked it up. When the girl brought me my breakfast she said she was sorry, but that she must go, and she did not care if she lost her month's wages. I looked at her, and her face was a sort of greenish, yellowish white. I pretended to be surprised, and asked what was the matter; but that was of no use, for she just turned on me and wanted to know whether I meant to stay in a haunted house, and how long I expected to live if I did, for though she noticed I was sometimes a little hard of hearing, she did not believe that even I could sleep through those screams again— and if I could, why had I been moving about the house and opening and shutting the front door, between three and four in the morning? There was no answering that, since she had heard me, so off she went, and I was left to myself. I went down to the village during the morning and found a woman who was willing to come and do the little work there is and cook my dinner, on condition that she might go home every night. As for me, I moved downstairs that day, and I have never tried to sleep in the best bedroom since. After a little while I got a brace of middle-aged Scotch servants from London, and things were quiet enough for a long time. I began by telling them that the house was in a very exposed position, and that the wind whistled round it a good deal in the autumn and winter, which had given it a bad name in the village, the Cornish people being inclined to superstition and telling ghost stories. The two hard-faced, sandy-haired sisters almost smiled, and they answered with great contempt that they had no great opinion of any Southern bogey whatever, having been in service in two English haunted houses, where they had never seen so much as the Boy in Gray, whom they reckoned no very particular rarity in Forfarshire.

They stayed with me several months, and while they were in the house we had peace and quiet. One of them is here again now, but she went away with her sister within the year. This one—she was the cook—married the sexton, who works in my garden. That's the way of it. It's a small village and he has not much to do, and he knows enough about flowers to help me nicely, besides doing most of the hard work; for though I'm fond of exercise, I'm getting a little stiff in the hinges. He's a sober, silent sort of fellow, who minds his own business, and he was a widower when I came here—Trehearn is his name, James Trehearn. The Scotch sisters would not admit that there was anything wrong about the house, but when November came they gave me warning that they were going, on the ground that the chapel was such a long walk from here, being in the next parish, and that they could not possibly go to our church. But the younger one came back in the spring, and as soon as the banns could be published she was married to James Trehearn by the vicar, and she seems to have had no scruples about hearing him preach since then. I'm quite satisfied, if she is! The couple live in a small cottage that looks over the churchyard.

I suppose you are wondering what all this has to do with what I was talking about. I'm alone so much that when an old friend comes to see me, I sometimes go on talking just for the sake of hearing my own voice. But in this case there is really a connection of ideas. It was James Trehearn who buried poor Mrs. Pratt, and her husband after her in the same grave, and it's not far from the back of his cottage. That's the connection in my mind, you see. It's plain enough. He knows something; I'm quite sure that he does, by his manner, though he's such a reticent beggar.

Yes, I'm alone in the house at night now, for Mrs. Trehearn does everything her-self, and when I have a friend the sexton's niece comes in to wait on the table. He takes his wife home every evening in winter, but in summer, when there's light, she goes by herself. She's not a nervous woman, but she's less sure than she used to be that there are no bogies in England worth a Scotchwoman's notice. Isn't it amusing, the idea that Scotland has a monopoly of the supernatural? Odd sort of national pride, I call that, don't you?

That's a good fire, isn't it? When driftwood gets started at last there's nothing like it, I think. Yes, we get lots of it, for I'm sorry to say there are still a great many wrecks about here. It's a lonely coast, and you may have all the wood you want for the trouble of bringing it in. Trehearn and I borrow a cart now and then, and load it between here and the Spit. I hate a coal fire when I can get wood of any sort. A log is company, even if it's only a piece of a deck-beam or timber sawn off, and the salt in it makes pretty sparks. See how they fly, like Japanese hand-fireworks! Upon my word, with an old friend and a good fire and a pipe, one forgets all about that thing upstairs, especially now that the wind has moderated. It's only a lull, though, and it will blow a gale before morning.

You think you would like to see the skull? I've no objection. There's no reason why you shouldn't have a look at it, and you never saw a more perfect one in your life, except that there are two front teeth missing in the lower jaw.

Oh yes—I had not told you about the jaw yet. Trehearn found it in the garden last spring when he was digging a pit for a new asparagus bed. You know we make asparagus beds six or eight feet deep here. Yes, yes—I had forgotten to tell you that. He was digging straight down, just as he digs a grave; if you want a good asparagus bed made, I advise you to get a sexton to make it for you. Those fellows have a wonderful knack at that sort of digging.

Trehearn had got down about three feet when he cut into a mass of white lime in the side of the trench. He had noticed that the earth was a little looser there, though he says it had not been disturbed for a number of years. I suppose he thought that even old lime might not be good for asparagus, so he broke it out and threw it up. It was pretty hard, he says, in biggish lumps, and out of sheer force of habit he cracked the lumps with his spade as they lay outside the pit beside him; the jawbone of a skull dropped out of one of the pieces. He thinks he must have knocked out the two front teeth in breaking up the lime, but he did not see them anywhere. He's a very experienced man in such things, as you may imagine, and he said at once that the jaw had probably belonged to a young woman, and that the teeth had been complete when she died. He brought it to me, and asked me if I wanted to keep it; if I did not, he said he would drop it into the next grave he made in the churchyard, as he supposed it was a Christian jaw, and ought to have decent burial, wherever the rest of the body might be. I told him that doctors often put bones into quicklime to whiten them nicely, and that I supposed Dr. Pratt had once had a little lime pit in the garden for that purpose, and had forgotten the jaw. Trehearn looked at me quietly.

"Maybe it fitted that skull that used to be in the cupboard upstairs, sir," he said. "Maybe Dr. Pratt had put the skull into the lime to clean it, or something, and when he took it out he left the lower jaw behind. There's some human hair sticking in the lime, sir."

I saw there was, and that was what Trehearn said. If he did not suspect something, why in the world should he have suggested that the jaw might fit the skull? Besides, it did. That's proof that he knows more than he cares to tell. Do you suppose he looked before she was buried? Or perhaps—when he buried Luke in the same grave—

Well, well, it's of no use to go over that, is it? I said I would keep the jaw with the skull, and I took it upstairs and fitted it into its place. There's not the slightest doubt about the two belonging together, and together they are.

Trehearn knows several things. We were talking about plastering the kitchen a while ago, and he happened to remember that it had not been done since the very week when Mrs. Pratt died. He did not say that the mason must have left some lime on the place, but he thought it, and that it was the very same lime he had found in the asparagus pit. He knows a lot. Trehearn is one of your silent beggars who can put two and two together. That grave is very near the back of his cottage, too, and he's one of the quickest men with a spade I ever saw. If he wanted to know the truth, he could, and no one else would ever be the wiser unless he chose to tell. In a quiet village like ours, people don't go and spend the night in the churchyard to see whether the sexton potters about by himself between ten o'clock and daylight.

What is awful to think of, is Luke's deliberation, if he did it; his cool certainty that no one would find him out; above all, his nerve, for that must have been extraordinary. I sometimes think it's bad enough to live in the place where it was done, if it really was done. I always put in the condition, you see, for the sake of his memory, and a little bit for my own sake, too.

I'll go upstairs and fetch the box in a minute. Let me light my pipe; there's no hurry! We had supper early, and it's only half-past nine o'clock. I never let a friend go to bed before twelve, or with less than three glasses—you may have as many more as you like, but you shan't have less, for the sake of old times.

It's breezing up again, do you hear? That was only a lull just now, and we are going to have a bad night.

A thing happened that made me start a little when I found that the jaw fitted exactly. I'm not very easily startled in that way myself, but I have seen people make a quick movement, drawing their breath sharply, when they had thought they were alone and suddenly turned and saw some one very near them. Nobody can call that fear. You wouldn't, would you? No. Well, just when I had set the jaw in its place under the skull, the teeth closed sharply on my finger. It felt exactly as if it were biting me hard, and I confess that I jumped before I realised that I had been pressing the jaw and the skull together with my other hand. I assure you I was not at all nervous. It was broad daylight, too, and a fine day, and the sun was streaming into the best bedroom. It would have been absurd to be nervous, and it was only a quick mistaken impression, but it really made me feel queer. Somehow it made me think of the funny verdict of the coroner's jury on Luke's death, "by the hand or teeth of some person or animal unknown." Ever since that I've wished I had seen those marks on his throat, though the lower jaw was missing then.

I have often seen a man do insane things with his hands that he does not realise at all. I once saw a man hanging on by an old awning stop with one hand, leaning backward, outboard, with all his weight on it, and he was just cutting the stop with the knife in his other hand when I got my arms round him. We were in mid-ocean, going twenty knots. He had not the smallest idea what he was doing; neither had I when I managed to pinch my finger between the teeth of that thing. I can feel it now. It was exactly as if it were alive and were trying to bite me. It would if it could, for I know it hates me, poor thing! Do you suppose that what rattles about inside is really a bit of lead? Well, I'll get the box down presently, and if whatever it is happens to drop out into your hands that's your affair. If it's only a clod of earth or a pebble, the whole matter would be off my mind, and I don't believe I should ever think of the skull again; but somehow I cannot bring myself to shake out the bit of hard stuff myself. The mere idea that it may be lead makes me confoundedly uncomfortable, yet I've got the conviction that I shall know before long. I shall certainly know. I'm sure Trehearn knows, but he's such a silent beggar.

I'll go upstairs now and get it. What? You had better go with me? Ha, ha! do you think I'm afraid of a bandbox and a noise? Nonsense!

Bother the candle, it won't tight! As if the ridiculous thing understood what it's wanted for! Look at that—the third match. They light fast enough for my pipe. There, do you see? It's a fresh box, just out of the tin safe where I keep the supply on account of the dampness. Oh, you think the wick of the candle may be damp, do you? All right, I'll light the beastly thing in the fire. That won t go out, at all events. Yes, it sputters a bit, but it will keep lighted now. It burns just like any other candle, doesn't it? The fact is, candles are not very good about here. I don't know where they come from, but they have a way of burning low occasionally, with a greenish flame that spits tiny sparks, and I'm often annoyed by their going out of themselves. It cannot be helped, for it will be long before we have electricity in our village. It really is rather a poor light, isn't it?

You think I had better leave you the candle and take the lamp, do you? I don't like to carry lamps about, that's the truth. I never dropped one in my life, but I have always thought I might, and it's so confoundedly dangerous if you do. Besides, I am pretty well used to these rotten candles by this time.

You may as well finish that glass while I'm getting it, for I don't mean to let you off with less than three before you go to bed. You won't have to go upstairs, either, for I've put you in the old study next to the surgery—that's where I live myself. The fact is, I never ask a friend to sleep upstairs now. The last man who did was Crackenthorpe, and he said he was kept awake all night. You remember old Crack, don't you? He stuck to the Service, and they've just made him an admiral. Yes, I'm off now—unless the candle goes out. I couldn't help asking if you remembered Crackenthorpe. If any one had told us that the skinny little idiot he used to be was to turn out the most successful of the lot of us, we should have laughed at the idea, shouldn't we? You and I did not do badly, it's true—but I'm really going now. I don't mean to let you think that I've been putting it off by talking! As if there were anything to be afraid of! If I were scared, I should tell you so quite frankly, and get you to go upstairs with me.

★ ★ ★

Here's the box. I brought it down very carefully, so as not to disturb it, poor thing. You see, if it were shaken, the jaw might get separated from it again, and I'm sure it wouldn't like that. Yes, the candle went out as I was coming downstairs, but that was the draught from the leaky window on the landing. Did you hear anything? Yes, there was another scream. Am I pale, do you say? That's nothing. My heart is a little queer sometimes, and I went upstairs too fast. In fact, that's one reason why I really prefer to live altogether on the ground floor.

Wherever that shriek came from, it was not from the skull, for I had the box in my hand when I heard the noise, and here it is now; so we have proved definitely that the screams are produced by something else. I've no doubt I shall find out some day what makes them. Some crevice in the wall, of course, or a crack in a chimney, or a chink in the frame of a window. That's the way all ghost stories end in real life. Do you know, I'm jolly glad I thought of going up and bringing it down for you to see, for that last shriek settles the question. To think that I should have been so weak as to fancy that the poor skull could really cry out like a living thing!

Now I'll open the box, and we'll take it out and look at it under the bright light. It's rather awful to think that the poor lady used to sit there, in your chair, evening after evening, in just the same light, isn't it? But then—I've made up my mind that it's all rubbish from beginning to end, and that it's just an old skull that Luke had when he was a student; and perhaps he put it into the lime merely to whiten it, and could not find the jaw.

I made a seal on the string, you see, after I had put the jaw in its place, and I wrote on the cover. There's the old white label on it still, from the milliner's, addressed to Mrs. Pratt when the hat was sent to her, and as there was room I wrote on the edge: "A skull, once the property of the late Luke Pratt, M.D." I don't quite know why I wrote that, unless it was with the idea of explaining how the thing happened to be in my possession. I cannot help wondering sometimes what sort of hat it was that came in the bandbox. What colour was it, do you think? Was it a gay spring hat with a bobbing feather and pretty ribands? Strange that the very same box should hold the head that wore the finery—perhaps. No—we made up our minds that it just came from the hospital in London where Luke did his time. It's far better to look at it in that light, isn't it? There's no more connection between that skull and poor Mrs. Pratt than there was between my story about the lead and—

Good Lord! Take the lamp—don't let it go out, if you can help it—I'll have the window fastened again in a second—I say, what a gale! There, it's out! I told you so! Never mind, there's the firelight—I've got the window shut—the bolt was only half down. Was the box blown off the table? Where the deuce is it? There! That won't open again, for I've put up the bar. Good dodge, an old-fashioned bar—there's nothing like it. Now, you find the band box while I light the lamp. Confound those wretched matches! Yes, a pipe spill is better—it must light in the fire—I hadn't thought of it—thank you—there we are again. Now, where's the box? Yes, put it back on the table, and we'll open it.

That's the first time I have ever known the wind to burst that window open; but it was partly carelessness on my part when I last shut it. Yes, of course I heard the scream. It seemed to go all round the house before it broke in at the window. That proves that it's always been the wind and nothing else, doesn't it? When it was not the wind, it was my imagination. I've always been a very imaginative man: I must have been, though I did not know it. As we grow older we understand ourselves better, don't you know?

I'll have a drop of the Hulstkamp neat, by way of an exception, since you are filling up your glass. That damp gust chilled me, and with my rheumatic tendency I'm very much afraid of a chill, for the cold sometimes seems to stick in my joints all winter when it once gets in.

By George, that's good stuff! I'll just light a fresh pipe, now that everything is snug again, and then we'll open the box. I'm so glad we heard that last scream together, with the skull here on the table between us, for a thing cannot possibly be in two places at the same time, and the noise most certainly came from outside, as any noise the wind makes must. You thought you heard it scream through the room after the window was burst open? Oh yes, so did I, but that was natural enough when everything was open. Of course we heard the wind. What could one expect?

Look here, please. I want you to see that the seal is intact before we open the box together. Will you take my glasses? No, you have your own. All right. The seal is sound, you see, and you can read the words of the motto easily. "Sweet and low"—that's it—because the poem goes on "Wind of the Western sea," and says, " blow him again to me," and all that. Here is the seal on my watch-chain, where it's hung for more than forty years. My poor little wife gave it to me when I was courting, and I never had any other. It was just like her to think of those words—she was always fond of Tennyson.

It's of no use to cut the string, for it's fastened to the box, so I'll just break the wax and untie the knot, and afterward we'll seal it up again. You see, I like to feel that the thing is safe in its place, and that nobody can take it out. Not that I should suspect Trehearn of meddling with it, but I always feel that he knows a lot more than he tells.

You see, I've managed it without breaking the string, though when I fastened it I never expected to open the bandbox again. The lid comes off easily enough. There! Now look!

What? Nothing in it? Empty? It's gone, man, the skull is gone!

★ ★ ★

No, there's nothing the matter with me. I'm only trying to collect my thoughts. It's so strange. I'm positively certain that it was inside when I put on the seal last spring. I can't have imagined that: it's utterly impossible. If I ever took a stiff glass with a friend now and then, I would admit that I might have made some idiotic mistake when I had taken too much. But I don't, and I never did. A pint of ale at supper and half a go of rum at bedtime was the most I ever took in my good days. I believe it's always we sober fellows who get rheumatism and gout! Yet there was my seal, and there is the empty bandbox. That's plain enough.

I say, I don't half like this. It's not right. There's something wrong about it, in my opinion. You needn't talk to me about supernatural manifestations, for I don't believe in them, not a little bit! Somebody must have tampered with the seal and stolen the skull Sometimes, when I go out to work in the garden in summer, I leave my watch and chain on the table. Trehearn must have taken the seal then, and used it, for he would be quite sure that I should not come in for at least an hour.

If it was not Trehearn—oh, don't talk to me about the possibility that the thing has got out by itself! If it has, it must be somewhere about the house, in some out-of-the-way corner, waiting. We may come upon it anywhere, waiting for us, don't you know?—just waiting in the dark. Then it will scream at me; it will shriek at me in the dark, for it hates me, I tell you!

The bandbox is quite empty. We are not dreaming, either of us. There, I turn it upside down.

What's that? Something fell out as I turned it over. It's on the floor, it's near your feet, I know it is, and we must find it. Help me to find it, man. Have you got it? For God's sake, give it to me, quickly!

Lead! I knew it when I heard it fall. I knew it couldn't be anything else by the little thud it made on the hearth-rug. So it was lead after all, and Luke did it.

I feel a little bit shaken up—not exactly nervous, you know, but badly shaken up, that's the fact. Anybody would, I should think. After all, you cannot say that it's fear of the thing, for I went up and brought it down—at least, I believed I was bringing it down, and that's the same thing, and by George, rather than give in to such silly nonsense, I'll take the box upstairs again and put it back in its place. It's not that. It's the certainty that the poor little woman came to her end in that way, by my fault, because I told the story. That's what is so dreadful. Somehow, I had always hoped that I should never be quite sure of it, but there is no doubting it now. Look at that!

Look at it! That little lump of lead with no particular shape. Think of what it did, man! Doesn't it make you shiver? He gave her something to make her sleep, of course, but there must have been one moment of awful agony. Think of having boiling lead poured into your brain. Think of it. She was dead before she could scream, but only think of—oh! there it is again—it's just outside—I know it's just outside—I can't keep it out of my head!—oh!—oh!

* * *

You thought I had fainted? No, I wish I had, for it would have stopped sooner. It's all very well to say that it's only a noise, and that a noise never hurt anybody—you're as white as a shroud yourself. There's only one thing to be done, if we hope to close an eye to-night. We must find it and put it back into its bandbox and shut it up in the cupboard, where it likes to be. I don't know how it got out, but it wants to get in again. That's why it screams so awfully to-night—it was never so bad as this—never since I first—

Bury it? Yes, if we can find it, we'll bury it, if it takes us all night. We'll bury it six feet deep and ram down the earth over it, so that it shall never get out again, and if it screams, we shall hardly hear it so deep down. Quick, we'll get the lantern and look for it. It cannot be far away; I'm sure it's just outside—it was coming in when I shut the window, I know it.

Yes, you're quite right. I'm losing my senses, and I must get hold of myself. Don't speak to me for a minute or two; I'll sit quite still and keep my eyes shut and repeat something I know. That's the best way.

"Add together the altitude, the latitude, and the polar distance, divide by two and subtract the altitude from the half-sum; then add the logarithm of the secant of the latitude, the cosecant of the polar distance, the cosine of the half-sum and the sine of the half-sum minus the altitude"—there! Don't say that I'm out of my senses, for my memory is all right, isn't it?

Of course, you may say that it's mechanical, and that we never forget the things we learned when we were boys and have used almost every day for a lifetime. But that's the very point. When a man is going crazy, it's the mechanical part of his mind that gets out of order and won't work right; he remembers things that never happened, or he sees things that aren't real, or he hears noises when there is perfect silence. That's not what is the matter with either of us, is it?

Come, we'll get the lantern and go round the house. It's not raining—only blowing like old boots, as we used to say. The lantern is in the cupboard under the stairs in the hall, and I always keep it trimmed in case of a wreck.

No use to look for the thing? I don't see how you can say that. It was nonsense to talk of burying it, of course, for it doesn't want to be buried; it wants to go back into its bandbox and be taken upstairs, poor thing! Trehearn took it out, I know, and made the seal over again. Perhaps he took it to the churchyard, and he may have meant well. I daresay he thought that it would not scream any more if it were quietly laid in consecrated ground, near where it belongs. But it has come home. Yes, that's it. He's not half a bad fellow, Trehearn, and rather religiously inclined, I think. Does not that sound natural, and reasonable, and well meant? He supposed it screamed because it was not decently buried—with the rest. But he was wrong. How should he know that it screams at me because it hates me, and because it's my fault that there was that little lump of lead in it?

No use to look for it, anyhow? Nonsense! I tell you it wants to be found—Hark! what's that knocking? Do you hear it? Knock—knock—knock—three times, then a pause, and then again. It has a hollow sound, hasn't it?

It has come home. I've heard that knock before. It wants to come in and be taken upstairs, in its box. It's at the front door.

Will you come with me? We'll take it in. Yes, I own that I don't like to go alone and open the door. The thing will roll in and stop against my foot, just as it did before, and the light will go out. I'm a good deal shaken by finding that bit of lead, and, besides, my heart isn't quite right—too much strong tobacco, perhaps. Besides, I'm quite willing to own that I'm a bit nervous to-night, if I never was before in my life.

That's right, come along! I'll take the box with me, so as not to come back. Do you hear the knocking? It's not like any other knocking I ever heard. If you will hold this door open, I can find the lantern under the stairs by the light from this room without bringing the lamp into the hall—it would only go out.

The thing knows we are coming—hark! It's impatient to get in. Don't shut the door till the lantern is ready, whatever you do. There will be the usual trouble with the matches, I suppose—no, the first one, by Jove! I tell you it wants to get in, so there's no trouble. All right with that door now; shut it, please. Now come and hold the lantern, for it's blowing so hard outside that I shall have to use both hands. That's it, hold the light low. Do you hear the knocking still? Here goes—I'll open just enough with my foot against the bottom of the door—now!

Catch it! it's only the wind that blows it across the floor, that's all—there's half a hurricane outside, I tell you! Have you got it? The bandbox is on the table. One minute, and I'll have the bar up. There!

Why did you throw it into the box so roughly? It doesn't like that, you know.

What do you say? Bitten your hand? Nonsense, man! You did just what I did. You pressed the jaws together with your other hand and pinched yourself. Let me see. You don't mean to say you have drawn blood? You must have squeezed hard, by Jove, for the skin is certainly torn. I'll give you some carbolic solution for it before we go to bed, for they say a scratch from a skull's tooth may go bad and give trouble.

Come inside again and let me see it by the lamp. I'll bring the bandbox—never mind the lantern, it may just as well burn in the hall, for I shall need it presently when I go up the stairs. Yes, shut the door if you will; it makes it more cheerful and bright. Is your finger still bleeding? I'll get you the carbolic in an instant; just let me see the thing.

Ugh! There's a drop of blood on the upper jaw. It's on the eye-tooth. Ghastly, isn't it? When I saw it running along the floor of the hall, the strength almost went out of my hands, and I felt my knees bending; then I understood that it was the gale, driving it over the smooth boards. You don't blame me? No, I should think not! We were boys together, and we've seen a thing or two, and we may just as well own to each other that we were both in a beastly funk when it slid across the floor at you. No wonder you pinched your finger picking it up, after that, if I did the same thing out of sheer nervousness, in broad daylight, with the sun streaming in on me.

Strange that the jaw should stick to it so closely, isn't it? I suppose it's the dampness, for it shuts like a vice—I have wiped off the drop of blood, for it was not nice to look at. I'm not going to try to open the jaws, don't be afraid! I shall not play any tricks with the poor thing, but I'll just seal the box again, and we'll take it upstairs and put it away where it wants to be. The wax is on the writing-table by the window. Thank you. It will be long before I leave my seal lying about again, for Trehearn to use, I can tell you. Explain? I don't explain natural phenomena, but if you choose to think that Trehearn had hidden it somewhere in the bushes, and that the gale blew it to the house against the door, and made it knock, as if it wanted to be let in, you're not thinking the impossible, and I'm quite ready to agree with you.

Do you see that? You can swear that you've actually seen me seal it this time, in case anything of the kind should occur again. The wax fastens the strings to the lid, which cannot possibly be lifted, even enough to get in one finger. You're quite satisfied, aren't you? Yes. Besides, I shall lock the cupboard and keep the key in my pocket hereafter.

Now we can take the lantern and go upstairs. Do you know? I'm very much inch'ned to agree with your theory that the wind blew it against the house. I'll go ahead, for I know the stairs; just hold the lantern near my feet as we go up. How the wind howls and whistles! Did you feel the sand on the floor under your shoes as we crossed the hall?

Yes—this is the door of the best bedroom. Hold up the lantern, please. This side, by the head of the bed. I left the cupboard open when I got the box. Isn't it queer how the faint odour of women's dresses will hang about an old closet for years? This is the shelf. You've seen me set the box there, and now you see me turn the key and put it into my pocket. So that's done!

★ ★ ★

Good-night. Are you sure you're quite comfortable? It's not much of a room, but I daresay you would as soon sleep here as upstairs to-night. If you want anything, sing out; there's only a lath and plaster partition between us. There's not so much wind on this side by half. There's the Hollands on the table, if you'll have one more nightcap. No? Well, do as you please. Good-night again, and don't dream about that thing, if you can.

★ ★ ★

The following paragraph appeared in the *Penraddon News,* 23rd November, 1906:

MYSTERIOUS DEATH OF A RETIRED SEA CAPTAIN

"The village of Tredcombe is much disturbed by the strange death of Captain Charles Braddock, and all sorts of impossible stories are circulating with regard to the circumstances, which certainly seem difficult of explanation. The retired captain, who had successfully commanded in his time the largest and fastest liners belonging to one of the principal transatlantic steamship companies, was found dead in his bed on Tuesday morning in his own cottage, a quarter of a mile from the village. An examination was made at once by the local practitioner, which revealed the horrible fact that the deceased had been bitten in the throat by a human assailant, with such amazing force as to crush the windpipe and cause death. The marks of the teeth of both jaws were so plainly visible on the skin that they could be counted, but the perpetrator of the deed had evidently lost the two lower middle incisors. It is hoped that this peculiarity may help to identify the murderer, who can only be a dangerous escaped maniac. The deceased, though over sixty-five years of age, is said to have been a hale man of considerable physical strength, and it is remarkable that no signs of any struggle were visible in the room, nor could it be ascertained how the murderer had entered the house. Warning has been sent to all the insane asylums in the United Kingdom, but as yet no information has been received regarding the escape of any dangerous patient.

"The coroner's jury returned the somewhat singular verdict that Captain Braddock came to his death 'by the hands or teeth of some person unknown.' The local surgeon is said to have expressed privately the opinion that the maniac is a woman, a view he deduces from the small size of the jaws, as shown by the marks of the teeth. The whole affair is shrouded in mystery. Captain Braddock was a widower, and lived alone. He leaves no children."

[*Note.*—Students of ghost lore and haunted houses will find the foundation of the foregoing story in the legends about a skull which is still preserved in the farm-house called Bettiscombe Manor, situated, I believe, on the Dorsetshire coast.]

IN THE LIGHT
OF THE RED LAMP

MAURICE LEVEL

French writer Maurice Level (1875-1926) earned recognition as a master of the non–supernatural *conte cruel* through his collection of stories translated into English in 1909 as *The Grip of Fear*. This tale was first published in *Le Journal* in 1906, and American editors George Jean Nathan and H.L. Mencken regarded it highly enough to reprint in the May 1920 issue of their pulp fiction magazine *Black Mask*.

Seated in a large armchair near the fire, his elbows on his knees, his hands held out to the warmth, he was talking slowly, interrupting himself abruptly now and again with a murmured: "Yes . . . yes . . ." as if he were trying to gather up, to make sure of his memories: then he would continue his sentence.

The table beside him was littered with papers, books, odds and ends of various kinds. The lamp was turned low: I could see nothing of him except his pallid face and his hands, long and thin in the fire-light.

The purring of a cat that lay on the hearth-rug and the crackling of the logs that sent up strangely-shaped flames were the only sounds that broke the silence. He was speaking in a faraway voice as a man might in his dream.

"Yes . . . yes . . . It was the great, the greatest misfortune of my life. I could have borne the loss of every penny I possess, of my health . . . anything . . . everything . . . but not that! To have lived for ten years with the woman you adore, and then to watch her die and be left to face life alone . . . quite alone . . . it was almost more than I could bear! . . . It is six months since I lost her . . . How long ago it seems! And how short the days used to be . . . If only she had been ill for some time, if only there had been some warning . . . It seems a horrible thing to say, but when you know beforehand the mind gets prepared, doesn't it? . . . Little by little the heart readjusts its outlook . . . you grow used to the idea . . . but as it was . . ."

"But I thought she had been ill for some time?" I said.

He shook his head. "Not at all, not at all . . . It was quite sudden . . . The doctors were never even able to find out what was the matter with her . . . It all happened and was over in two days. Since then I don't know how or why I have gone on living. All day long I wander round the house looking for some reminder of her that I never find, imagining that she will appear to me from behind the hangings, that a breath of her scent will come to me in the empty rooms . . ."

He stretched out his hand towards the table.

"Look, yesterday I found that . . . this veil, in one of my pockets. She gave it to me to carry one evening when we were at the theatre, and I try to believe it still smells of her perfume, is still warm from its contact with her face . . . But no! Nothing remains . . . except sorrow . . . *though there is something,* only it . . . it . . . In the first shock of grief you sometimes have extraordinary ideas . . . Can you believe that I photographed her lying on her death-bed? I took my camera into the white, silent room, and lit the magnesium wire: yes, overwhelmed as I was with grief, I did with the most scrupulous precaution and care things from which I should shrink to-day, revolting things . . . Yet it is a great consolation to know she is there, that I shall be able to see her again as she looked that last day."

"Where is this photograph!" I asked.

Leaning forward, he replied in a low voice: "I haven't got it, or rather, I have it . . . I have the plate, but I have never had the courage to touch it . . . Yet how I have longed to see it!"

He laid his hand on my arm: "Listen . . . to-night . . . your visit . . . the way I have been able to talk about her . . . it makes me feel better, almost strong again . . . would you, will you come with me to the dark room! Will you help me develop the plate!"

He looked into my face with the anxious, questioning expression of a child who fears he may be refused something he longs to have.

"Of course I will," I answered.

He rose quickly. "Yes . . . with you it will be different. With you I shall keep calm . . . and it will do me good . . . I shall be much happier . . . you'll see . . ."

We went to the dark room, a closet with bottles ranged round on shelves. A trestle-table littered with dishes, glasses and books ran along one side of the wall.

By the light of a candle that threw flickering shadows round him, he silently examined the labels on the bottles and rubbed some dishes.

Presently he lit a lamp with red glass, blew out the candle, and said to me: "Shut the door."

There was something dramatic about the darkness relieved only by the blood-red light. Unexpected reflections touched the sides of the bottles, played on his wrinkled cheeks, on his hollow temples.

He said: "Is the door closely shut? Then I will begin."

He opened a dark slide and took out the plate. Holding it carefully at the corners between his thumb and first fingers, he looked at it intently for a long time as if trying to see the invisible picture which was so soon to appear.

With great care he let it glide into the bath and began to rock the dish. I cannot say why, but it seemed to me that the tapping of the porcelain on the boards at regular intervals made a curiously mournful sound: the monotonous lapping of the liquid suggested a vague sobbing, and I could not lift my eyes from the milk-colored piece of glass which was slowly taking on a darker line round its edges.

I looked at my friend. His lips were trembling as he murmured words and sentences which I failed to catch.

He drew out the plate, held it up to the level of his eyes, and said as I leaned over his shoulder:

"It's coming up . . . slowly . . . My developer is rather weak . . . But that's nothing . . . Look, the high lights are coming . . . Wait! . . . you'll see . . ."

He put the plate back, and it sank into the developer with a soft, sucking sound. The gray color had spread uniformly over the whole plate. His head bent over it, he explained:

"That dark rectangle is the bed . . . up above, that square," he pointed it out with a motion of his chin, "is the pillow: and in the middle, that lighter part with the pale streak outlined on the background . . . that is . . . Look, there is the crucifix I put between her fingers. My poor little one . . . my darling!"

His voice was hoarse with emotion: the tears were running down his cheeks as his chest rose and fell.

"The details are coming up," he said presently, trying to control himself. "I can see the lighted candles and the flowers . . . her hair, which was so beautiful . . . the hands of which she was so proud . . . and the little white rosary that I found in her Book of Hours . . . *Mon Dieu,* how it hurts to see it all again, yet somehow it makes me happy . . . very happy . . . I am looking at her again, my poor darling . . ."

Feeling that emotion was overcoming him and wishing to soothe, I said:

"Don't you think the plate is ready now!" He held it up near the lamp, examined it closely, and put it back in the bath. After a short interval he drew it out afresh, re-examined it, and again put it back, murmuring:

"No . . . no . . ."

Something in the tone of his voice and the abruptness of his gesture struck me, but I had no time to think, for he at once began to speak again.

"There are still some details to come up . . . It's rather long, but as I told you my developer is weak . . . so they only come up one by one."

He counted: "One . . . two . . . three . . . four . . . five . . . This time it will do. If I force it, I shall spoil it . . ."

He took out the plate, waved it vertically up and down, dipped it in clean water, and held it towards me:

"Look!"

But as I was stretching out my hand he started and bent forward, holding the plate up to the lamp, and his face, lit up by the light, had suddenly become so ghastly that I cried:

"What is it? What's the matter!"

His eyes were fixed in a wide terrified stare, his lips were drawn back and showed teeth that were chattering: I could hear his heart beating in a way that made his whole body rock backwards and forwards.

I put my hand on his shoulder, and unable to imagine what could possibly cause such terrible anguish, I cried for the second time:

"But what is it? Tell me. What's the matter?"

He turned his face to me, so drawn it no longer seemed human, and as his blood-shot eyes looked into mine he seized me by the wrist with a grip that sent his nails into my flesh.

Thrice he opened his mouth trying to speak; then brandishing the plate above his head, he shrieked into the crimson-lit darkness:

"The matter? . . . the matter? . . . I have murdered her! . . . She wasn't dead! . . . the eyes have moved! . ."

214

THE WILLOWS

ALGERNON BLACKWOOD

English writer Algernon Blackwood (1869–1951) wrote tales of the supernatural featuring most of the iconic monsters of horror. In his best work, though, Blackwood evoked the awesome incomprehensibility of the natural world. This story, which was first published in his collection *The Listener and Other Stories* (1907), is a landmark of supernatural fiction and an unforgettable example of how much horror can be conveyed by what is suggested rather than shown.

I

After leaving Vienna, and long before you come to Budapest, the Danube enters a region of singular loneliness and desolation, where its waters spread away on all sides regardless of a main channel, and the country becomes a swamp for miles upon miles, covered by a vast sea of low willow-bushes. On the big maps this deserted area is painted in a fluffy blue, growing fainter in colour as it leaves the banks, and across it may be seen in large straggling letters the word *Sümpfe*, meaning marshes.

In high flood this great acreage of sand, shingle-beds, and willow-grown islands is almost topped by the water, but in normal seasons the bushes bend and rustle in the free winds, showing their silver leaves to the sunshine in an ever-moving plain of bewildering beauty. These willows never attain to the dignity of trees; they have no rigid trunks; they remain humble bushes, with rounded tops and soft outline, swaying on slender stems that answer to the least pressure of the wind; supple as grasses, and so continually shifting that they somehow give the impression that the entire plain is moving and alive. For the wind sends waves rising and falling over the whole surface, waves of leaves instead of waves of water, green swells like the sea,

215

too, until the branches turn and lift, and then silvery white as their underside turns to the sun.

Happy to slip beyond the control of the stern banks, the Danube here wanders about at will among the intricate network of channels intersecting the islands everywhere with broad avenues down which the waters pour with a shouting sound; making whirlpools, eddies, and foaming rapids; tearing at the sandy banks; carrying away masses of shore and willow-clumps; and forming new islands innumerably which shift daily in size and shape and possess at best an impermanent life, since the flood-time obliterates their very existence.

Properly speaking, this fascinating part of the river's life begins soon after leaving Pressburg, and we, in our Canadian canoe, with gipsy tent and frying-pan on board, reached it on the crest of a rising flood about mid-July. That very same morning, when the sky was reddening before sunrise, we had slipped swiftly through still-sleeping Vienna, leaving it a couple of hours later a mere patch of smoke against the blue hills of the Wienerwald on the horizon; we had breakfasted below Fischeramend under a grove of birch trees roaring in the wind; and had then swept on the tearing current past Orth, Hainburg, Petronell (the old Roman Carnuntum of Marcus Aurelius), and so under the frowning heights of Thelsen on a spur of the Carpathians, where the March steals in quietly from the left and the frontier is crossed between Austria and Hungary.

Racing along at twelve kilometers an hour soon took us well into Hungary, and the muddy waters—sure sign of flood—sent us aground on many a shingle-bed, and twisted us like a cork in many a sudden belching whirlpool before the towers of Pressburg (Hungarian, Poszóny) showed against the sky; and then the canoe, leaping like a spirited horse, flew at top speed under the grey walls, negotiated safely the sunken chain of the Fliegende Brucke ferry, turned the corner sharply to the left, and plunged on yellow foam into the wilderness of islands, sandbanks, and swamp-land beyond—the land of the willows.

The change came suddenly, as when a series of bioscope pictures snaps down on the streets of a town and shifts without warning into the scenery of lake and forest. We entered the land of desolation on wings, and in less than half an hour there was neither boat nor fishing-hut nor red roof, nor any single sign of human habitation and civilization within sight. The sense of remoteness from the world of humankind, the utter isolation, the fascination of this singular world of willows, winds, and waters, instantly laid its spell upon us both, so that we allowed laughingly to one another that we ought by rights to have held some special kind of passport to admit us, and that we had, somewhat audaciously, come without asking leave into a separate little kingdom of wonder and magic—a kingdom that was reserved for the use of others who had a right to it, with everywhere unwritten warnings to trespassers for those who had the imagination to discover them.

Though still early in the afternoon, the ceaseless buffetings of a most tempestuous wind made us feel weary, and we at once began casting about for a suitable camping-ground for the night. But the bewildering character of the islands made landing difficult; the swirling flood carried us in shore and then swept us out again; the willow branches tore our hands as we seized them to stop the canoe, and we pulled many a yard of sandy bank into the water before at length we shot with a great sideways blow from the wind into a backwater and managed to beach the bows in a cloud of spray. Then we lay panting and laughing after our exertions on the hot yellow sand, sheltered from the wind, and in the full blaze of a scorching sun, a cloudless blue sky above, and an immense army of dancing, shouting willow bushes, closing in from all sides, shining with spray and clapping their thousand little hands as though to applaud the success of our efforts.

"What a river!" I said to my companion, thinking of all the way we had traveled from the source in the Black Forest, and how he had often been obliged to wade and push in the upper shallows at the beginning of June.

"Won't stand much nonsense now, will it?" he said, pulling the canoe a little farther into safety up the sand, and then composing himself for a nap.

I lay by his side, happy and peaceful in the bath of the elements—water, wind, sand, and the great fire of the sun—thinking of the long journey that lay behind us, and of the great stretch before us to the Black Sea, and how lucky I was to have such a delightful and charming traveling companion as my friend, the Swede.

We had made many similar journeys together, but the Danube, more than any other river I knew, impressed us from the very beginning with its *aliveness*. From its tiny bubbling entry into the world among the pinewood gardens of Donaueschingen, until this moment when it began to play the great river-game of losing itself among the deserted swamps, unobserved, unrestrained, it had seemed to us like following the growth of some living creature. Sleepy at first, but later developing violent desires as it became conscious of its deep soul, it rolled, like some huge fluid being, through all the countries we had passed, holding our little craft on its mighty shoulders, playing roughly with us sometimes, yet always friendly and well-meaning, till at length we had come inevitably to regard it as a Great Personage.

How, indeed, could it be otherwise, since it told us so much of its secret life? At night we heard it singing to the moon as we lay in our tent, uttering that odd sibilant note peculiar to itself and said to be caused by the rapid tearing of the pebbles along its bed, so great is its hurrying speed. We knew, too, the voice of its gurgling whirlpools, suddenly bubbling up on a surface previously quite calm; the roar of its shallows and swift rapids; its constant steady thundering below all mere surface sounds; and that ceaseless tearing of its icy waters at the banks. How it stood up and shouted when the rains fell flat upon its face! And how its laughter roared out when the wind blew up-stream and tried to stop its growing speed! We knew all its sounds and voices, its tumblings and foamings, its unnecessary splashing against the bridges; that self-conscious chatter when there were hills to look on; the affected dignity of its speech when it passed through the little towns, far too important to laugh; and all these faint, sweet whisperings when the sun caught it fairly in some slow curve and poured down upon it till the steam rose.

It was full of tricks, too, in its early life before the great world knew it. There were places in the upper reaches among the Swabian forests, when yet the first whispers of its destiny had not reached it, where it elected to disappear through holes in the ground, to appear again on the other side of the porous limestone hills and start a new river with another name; leaving, too, so little water in its own bed that we had to climb out and wade and push the canoe through miles of shallows!

And a chief pleasure, in those early days of its irresponsible youth, was to lie low, like Brer Fox, just before the little turbulent tributaries came to join it from the Alps, and to refuse to acknowledge them when in, but to run for miles side by side, the dividing line well marked, the very levels different, the Danube utterly declining to recognize the newcomer. Below Passau, however, it gave up this particular trick, for there the Inn comes in with a thundering power impossible to ignore, and so pushes and incommodes the parent river that there is hardly room for them in the long twist-ing gorge that follows, and the Danube is shoved this way and that against the cliffs, and forced to hurry itself with great waves and much dashing to and fro in order to get through in time. And during the fight our canoe slipped down from its shoulder to its breast, and had the time of its life among the struggling waves. But the Inn taught the old river a lesson, and after Passau it no longer pretended to ignore new arrivals.

This was many days back, of course, and since then we had come to know other aspects of the great creature, and across the Bavarian wheat plain of Straubing she wandered so slowly under the blazing June sun that we could well imagine only the surface inches were water, while below there moved, concealed as by a silken mantle, a whole army of Undines, passing silently and unseen down to the sea, and very leisurely too, lest they be discovered.

Much, too, we forgave her because of her friendliness to the birds and animals that haunted the shores. Cormorants lined the banks in lonely places in rows like short black palings; grey crows crowded the shingle-beds; storks stood fishing in the vistas of shallower water that opened up between the islands, and hawks, swans, and marsh birds of all sorts filled the air with glinting wings and singing, petulant cries. It was impossible to feel annoyed with the river's vagaries after seeing a deer leap with a splash into the water at sunrise and swim past the bows of the canoe; and often we saw fawns peering at us from the underbrush, or looked straight into the brown eyes of a stag as we charged full tilt round a corner and entered another reach of the river. Foxes, too, everywhere haunted the banks, tripping daintily among the driftwood and disappearing so suddenly that it was impossible to see how they managed it.

But now, after leaving Pressburg, everything changed a little, and the Danube became more serious. It ceased trifling. It was half-way to the Black Sea, within seeming distance almost of other, stranger countries where no tricks would be permitted or understood. It became suddenly grown-up, and claimed our respect and even our awe. It broke out into three arms, for one thing, that only met again a hundred kilometers farther down, and for a canoe there were no indications which one was intended to be followed.

"If you take a side channel," said the Hungarian officer we met in the Pressburg shop while buying provisions, "you may find yourselves, when the flood subsides, forty miles from anywhere, high and dry, and you may easily starve. There are no people, no farms, no fishermen. I warn you not to continue. The river, too, is still rising, and this wind will increase."

The rising river did not alarm us in the least, but the matter of being left high and dry by a sudden subsidence of the waters might be serious, and we had consequently laid in an extra stock of provisions. For the rest, the officer's prophecy held true, and the wind, blowing down a perfectly clear sky, increased steadily till it reached the dignity of a westerly gale.

It was earlier than usual when we camped, for the sun was a good hour or two from the horizon, and leaving my friend still asleep on the hot sand, I wandered about in desultory examination of our hotel. The island, I found, was less than an acre in extent, a mere sandy bank standing some two or three feet above the level of the river. The far end, pointing into the sunset, was covered with flying spray which the tremendous wind drove off the crests of the broken waves. It was triangular in shape, with the apex up stream.

I stood there for several minutes, watching the impetuous crimson flood bearing down with a shouting roar, dashing in waves against the bank as though to sweep it bodily away, and then swirling by in two foaming streams on either side. The ground seemed to shake with the shock and rush, while the furious movement of the willow bushes as the wind poured over them increased the curious illusion that the island itself actually moved. Above, for a mile or two, I could see the great river descending upon me; it was like looking up the slope of a sliding hill, white with foam, and leaping up everywhere to show itself to the sun.

The rest of the island was too thickly grown with willows to make walking pleasant, but I made the tour, nevertheless. From the lower end the light, of course, changed, and the river looked dark and angry. Only the backs of the flying waves were visible, streaked with foam, and pushed forcibly by the great puffs of wind that fell upon them from behind. For a short mile it was visible, pouring in and out among the islands, and then disappearing with a huge sweep into the willows, which closed about it like a herd of monstrous antediluvian creatures crowding down to drink. They made me think of gigantic sponge-like growths that sucked the river up into themselves. They caused it to vanish from sight. They herded there together in such overpowering numbers.

Altogether it was an impressive scene, with its utter loneliness, its bizarre suggestion; and as I gazed, long and curiously, a singular emotion began to stir somewhere in the depths of me. Midway in my delight of the wild beauty, there crept, unbidden and unexplained, a curious feeling of disquietude, almost of alarm.

A rising river, perhaps, always suggests something of the ominous; many of the little islands I saw before me would probably have been swept away by the morning; this resistless, thundering flood of water touched the sense of awe. Yet I was aware that my uneasiness lay deeper far than the emotions of awe and wonder. It was not that I felt. Nor had it directly to do with the power of the driving wind—this shouting hurricane that might almost carry up a few acres of willows into the air and scatter them like so much chaff over the landscape. The wind was simply enjoying itself, for nothing rose out of the flat landscape to stop it, and I was conscious of sharing its great game with a kind of pleasurable excitement. Yet this novel emotion had nothing to do with the wind. Indeed, so vague was the sense of distress I experienced, that it was impossible to trace it to its source and deal with it accordingly, though I was aware somehow that it had to do with my realization of our utter insignificance before this unrestrained power of the elements about me. The huge-grown river had something to do with it too—a vague, unpleasant idea that we had somehow trifled with these great elemental forces in whose power we lay helpless every hour of the day and night. For here, indeed, they were gigantically at play together, and the sight appealed to the imagination.

But my emotion, so far as I could understand it, seemed to attach itself more particularly to the willow bushes, to these acres and acres of willows, crowding, so thickly growing there, swarming everywhere the eye could reach, pressing upon the river as though to suffocate it, standing in dense array mile after mile beneath the sky, watching, waiting, listening. And, apart quite from the elements, the willows connected themselves subtly with my malaise, attacking the mind insidiously somehow by reason of their vast numbers, and contriving in some way or other to represent to the imagination a new and mighty power, a power, moreover, not altogether friendly to us.

Great revelations of nature, of course, never fail to impress in one way or another, and I was no stranger to moods of the kind. Mountains overawe and oceans terrify, while the mystery of great forests exercises a spell peculiarly its own. But all these, at one point or another, somewhere link on intimately with human life and human experience. They stir comprehensible, even if alarming, emotions. They tend on the whole to exalt.

With this multitude of willows, however, it was something far different, I felt. Some essence emanated from them that besieged the heart. A sense of awe awakened, true, but of awe touched somewhere by a vague terror. Their serried ranks, growing everywhere darker about me as the shadows deepened, moving furiously yet softly in the wind, woke in me the curious and unwelcome suggestion that we had trespassed here upon the borders of an alien world, a world where we were intruders, a world where we were not wanted or invited to remain—where we ran grave risks perhaps!

The feeling, however, though it refused to yield its meaning entirely to analysis, did not at the time trouble me by passing into menace. Yet it never left me quite, even during the very practical business of putting up the tent in a hurricane of wind and building a fire for the stew-pot. It remained, just enough to bother and perplex, and to rob a most delightful camping-ground of a good portion of its charm. To my companion, however, I said nothing, for he was a man I considered devoid of imagination. In the first place, I could never have explained to him what I meant, and in the second, he would have laughed stupidly at me if I had.

There was a slight depression in the center of the island, and here we pitched the tent. The surrounding willows broke the wind a bit.

"A poor camp," observed the imperturbable Swede when at last the tent stood upright, "no stones and precious little firewood. I'm for moving on early to-morrow—eh? This sand won't hold anything."

But the experience of a collapsing tent at midnight had taught us many devices, and we made the cozy gipsy house as safe as possible, and then set about collecting a store of wood to last till bed-time. Willow bushes drop no branches, and driftwood was our only source of supply. We hunted the shores pretty thoroughly. Everywhere the banks were crumbling as the rising flood tore at them and carried away great portions with a splash and a gurgle.

"The island's much smaller than when we landed," said the accurate Swede. "It won't last long at this rate. We'd better drag the canoe close to the tent, and be ready to start at a moment's notice. *I* shall sleep in my clothes."

He was a little distance off, climbing along the bank, and I heard his rather jolly laugh as he spoke.

"By Jove!" I heard him call, a moment later, and turned to see what had caused his exclamation. But for the moment he was hidden by the willows, and I could not find him.

"What in the world's this?" I heard him cry again, and this time his voice had become serious.

I ran up quickly and joined him on the bank. He was looking over the river, pointing at something in the water.

"Good heavens, it's a man's body!" he cried excitedly. "Look!"

A black thing, turning over and over in the foaming waves, swept rapidly past. It kept disappearing and coming up to the surface again. It was about twenty feet from the shore, and just as it was opposite to where we stood it lurched round and looked straight at us. We saw its eyes reflecting the sunset, and gleaming an odd yellow as the body turned over. Then it gave a swift, gulping plunge, and dived out of sight in a flash.

"An otter, by gad!" we exclaimed in the same breath, laughing.

It *was* an otter, alive, and out on the hunt; yet it had looked exactly like the body of a drowned man turning helplessly in the current. Far below it came to the surface once again, and we saw its black skin, wet and shining in the sunlight.

Then, too, just as we turned back, our arms full of driftwood, another thing happened to recall us to the river bank. This time it really was a man, and what was more, a man in a boat. Now a small boat on the Danube was an unusual sight at any time, but here in this deserted region, and at flood time, it was so unexpected as to constitute a real event. We stood and stared.

Whether it was due to the slanting sunlight, or the refraction from the wonderfully illumined water, I cannot say, but, whatever the cause, I found it difficult to focus my sight properly upon the flying apparition. It seemed, however, to be a man standing upright in a sort of flat-bottomed boat, steering with a long oar, and being carried down the opposite shore at a tremendous pace. He apparently was looking across in our direction, but the distance was too great and the light too uncertain for us to make out very plainly what he was about. It seemed to me that he was gesticulating and making signs at us. His voice came across the water to us shouting something furiously, but the wind drowned it so that no single word was audible. There was something curious about the whole appearance—man, boat, signs, voice—that made an impression on me out of all proportion to its cause.

"He's crossing himself!" I cried. "Look, he's making the sign of the Cross!"

"I believe you're right," the Swede said, shading his eyes with his hand and watching the man out of sight. He seemed to be gone in a moment, melting away down there into the sea of willows where the sun caught them in the bend of the river and turned them into a great crimson wall of beauty. Mist, too, had begun to rise, so that the air was hazy.

"But what in the world is he doing at nightfall on this flooded river?" I said, half to myself. "Where is he going at such a time, and what did he mean by his signs and shouting? D'you think he wished to warn us about something?"

"He saw our smoke, and thought we were spirits probably," laughed my companion. "These Hungarians believe in all sorts of rubbish; you remember the shopwoman at Pressburg warning us that no one ever landed here because it belonged to some sort of beings outside man's world! I suppose they believe in fairies and elementals, possibly demons, too. That peasant in the boat saw people on the islands for the first time in his life," he added, after a slight pause, "and it scared him, that's all."

The Swede's tone of voice was not convincing, and his manner lacked something that was usually there. I noted the change instantly while he talked, though without being able to label it precisely.

"If they had enough imagination," I laughed loudly—I remember trying to make as much noise as I could—"they might well people a place like this with the old gods of antiquity. The Romans must have haunted all this region more or less with their shrines and sacred groves and elemental deities."

The subject dropped and we returned to our stew-pot, for my friend was not given to imaginative conversation as a rule. Moreover, just then I remember feeling distinctly glad that he was not imaginative; his stolid, practical nature suddenly seemed to me welcome and comforting. It was an admirable temperament, I felt; he could steer down rapids like a red Indian, shoot dangerous bridges and whirlpools better than any white man I ever saw in a canoe. He was a grand fellow for an adventurous trip, a tower of strength when untoward things happened. I looked at his strong face and light curly hair as he staggered along under his pile of driftwood (twice the size of mine!), and I experienced a feeling of relief. Yes, I was distinctly glad just then that the Swede was—what he was, and that he never made remarks that suggested more than they said.

"The river's still rising, though," he added, as if following out some thoughts of his own, and dropping his load with a gasp. "This island will be under water in two days if it goes on."

"I wish the *wind* would go down," I said. "I don't care a fig for the river."

The flood, indeed, had no terrors for us; we could get off at ten minutes' notice, and the more water the better we liked it. It meant an increasing current and the obliteration of the treacherous shingle-beds that so often threatened to tear the bottom out of our canoe.

Contrary to our expectations, the wind did not go down with the sun. It seemed to increase with the darkness, howling overhead and shaking the willows round us like straws. Curious sounds accompanied it sometimes, like the explosion of heavy guns, and it fell upon the water and the island in great flat blows of immense power. It made me think of the sounds a planet must make, could we only hear it, driving along through space.

But the sky kept wholly clear of clouds, and soon after supper the full moon rose up in the east and covered the river and the plain of shouting willows with a light like the day.

We lay on the sandy patch beside the fire, smoking, listening to the noises of the night round us, and talking happily of the journey we had already made, and of our plans ahead. The map lay spread in the door of the tent, but the high wind made it hard to study, and presently we lowered the curtain and extinguished the lantern. The firelight was enough to smoke and see each other's faces by, and the sparks flew about overhead like fireworks. A few yards beyond, the river gurgled and hissed, and from time to time a heavy splash announced the falling away of further portions of the bank.

Our talk, I noticed, had to do with the faraway scenes and incidents of our first camps in the Black Forest, or of other subjects altogether remote from the present setting, for neither of us spoke of the actual moment more than was necessary— almost as though we had agreed tacitly to avoid discussion of the camp and its incidents. Neither the otter nor the boatman, for instance, received the honor of a single mention, though ordinarily these would have furnished discussion for the greater part of the evening. They were, of course, distinct events in such a place.

The scarcity of wood made it a business to keep the fire going, for the wind, that drove the smoke in our faces wherever we sat, helped at the same time to make a forced draught. We took it in turn to make some foraging expeditions into the darkness, and the quantity the Swede brought back always made me feel that he took an absurdly long time finding it; for the fact was I did not care much about being left alone, and yet it always seemed to be my turn to grub about among the bushes or scramble along the slippery banks in the moonlight. The long day's battle with wind and water—such wind and such water!—had tired us both, and an early bed was the obvious program. Yet neither of us made the move for the tent. We lay there, tending the fire, talking in desultory fashion, peering about us into the dense willow bushes, and listening to the thunder of wind and river. The loneliness of the place had entered our very bones, and silence seemed natural, for after a bit the sound of our voices became a trifle unreal and forced; whispering would have been the fitting mode of communication, I felt, and the human voice, always rather absurd amid the roar of the elements, now carried with it something almost illegitimate. It was like talking out loud in church, or in some place where it was not lawful, perhaps not quite *safe*, to be overheard.

The eeriness of this lonely island, set among a million willows, swept by a hurricane, and surrounded by hurrying deep waters, touched us both, I fancy. Untrodden by man, almost unknown to man, it lay there beneath the moon, remote from human influence, on the frontier of another world, an alien world, a world tenanted by willows only and the souls of willows. And we, in our rashness, had dared to invade it, even to make use of it! Something more than the power of its mystery stirred in me as I lay on the sand, feet to fire, and peered up through the leaves at the stars. For the last time I rose to get firewood.

"When this has burnt up," I said firmly, "I shall turn in," and my companion watched me lazily as I moved off into the surrounding shadows.

For an unimaginative man I thought he seemed unusually receptive that night, unusually open to suggestion of things other than sensory. He too was touched by the beauty and loneliness of the place. I was not altogether pleased, I remember, to recognize this slight change in him, and instead of immediately collecting sticks, I made my way to the far point of the island where the moonlight on plain and river could be seen to better advantage. The desire to be alone had come suddenly upon me; my former dread returned in force; there was a vague feeling in me I wished to face and probe to the bottom.

When I reached the point of sand jutting out among the waves, the spell of the place descended upon me with a positive shock. No mere "scenery" could have produced such an effect. There was something more here, something to alarm.

I gazed across the waste of wild waters; I watched the whispering willows; I heard the ceaseless beating of the tireless wind; and, one and all, each in its own way, stirred in me this sensation of a strange distress. But the *willows* especially; for ever they went on chattering and talking among themselves, laughing a little, shrilly crying out, sometimes sighing—but what it was they made so much to-do about belonged to the secret life of the great plain they inhabited. And it was utterly alien to the world I knew, or to that of the wild yet kindly elements. They made me think of a host of beings from another plane of life, another evolution altogether, perhaps, all discussing a mystery known only to themselves. I watched them moving busily together, oddly shaking their big bushy heads, twirling their myriad leaves even when there was no wind. They moved of their own will as though alive, and they touched, by some incalculable method, my own keen sense of the *horrible*.

There they stood in the moonlight, like a vast army surrounding our camp, shaking their innumerable silver spears defiantly, formed all ready for an attack.

The psychology of places, for some imaginations at least, is very vivid; for the wanderer, especially, camps have their "note" either of welcome or rejection. At first it may not always be apparent, because the busy preparations of tent and cooking prevent, but with the first pause—after supper usually—it comes and announces itself. And the note of this willow-camp now became unmistakably plain to me; we were interlopers, trespassers; we were not welcomed. The sense of unfamiliarity grew upon me as I stood there watching. We touched the frontier of a region where our presence was resented. For a night's lodging we might perhaps be tolerated; but for a prolonged and inquisitive stay—No! by all the gods of the trees and wilderness, no! We were the first human influences upon this island, and we were not wanted. *The willows were against us.*

Strange thoughts like these, bizarre fancies, borne I know not whence, found lodgment in my mind as I stood listening. What, I thought, if, after all, these crouching willows proved to be alive; if suddenly they should rise up, like a swarm of living creatures, marshaled by the gods whose territory we had invaded, sweep towards us off the vast swamps, booming overhead in the night—and then settle down! As I looked it was so easy to imagine they actually moved, crept nearer, retreated a little, huddled together in masses, hostile, waiting for the great wind that should finally start them a-running. I could have sworn their aspect changed a little, and their ranks deepened and pressed more closely together.

The melancholy shrill cry of a night-bird sounded overhead, and suddenly I nearly lost my balance as the piece of bank I stood upon fell with a great splash into the river, undermined by the flood. I stepped back just in time, and went on hunting for firewood again, half laughing at the odd fancies that crowded so thickly into my mind and cast their spell upon me. I recalled the Swede's remark about moving on next day, and I was just thinking that I fully agreed with him, when I turned with a start and saw the subject of my thoughts standing immediately in front of me. He was quite close. The roar of the elements had covered his approach.

"You've been gone so long," he shouted above the wind, "I thought something must have happened to you."

But there was that in his tone, and a certain look in his face as well, that conveyed to me more than his usual words, and in a flash I understood the real reason for his coming. It was because the spell of the place had entered his soul too, and he did not like being alone.

"River still rising," he cried, pointing to the flood in the moonlight, "and the wind's simply awful."

He always said the same things, but it was the cry for companionship that gave the real importance to his words.

"Lucky," I cried back, "our tent's in the hollow. I think it'll hold all right." I added something about the difficulty of finding wood, in order to explain my absence, but the wind caught my words and flung them across the river, so that he did not hear, but just looked at me through the branches, nodding his head.

"Lucky if we get away without disaster!" he shouted, or words to that effect; and I remember feeling half angry with him for putting the thought into words, for it was exactly what I felt myself. There was disaster impending somewhere, and the sense of presentiment lay unpleasantly upon me.

We went back to the fire and made a final blaze, poking it up with our feet. We took a last look round. But for the wind the heat would have been unpleasant. I put this thought into words, and I remember my friend's reply struck me oddly: that he would rather have the heat, the ordinary July weather, than this "diabolical wind."

Everything was snug for the night; the canoe lying turned over beside the tent, with both yellow paddles beneath her; the provision sack hanging from a willow-stem, and the washed-up dishes removed to a safe distance from the fire, all ready for the morning meal.

We smothered the embers of the fire with sand, and then turned in. The flap of the tent door was up, and I saw the branches and the stars and the white moonlight. The shaking willows and the heavy buffetings of the wind against our taut little house were the last things I remembered as sleep came down and covered all with its soft and delicious forgetfulness.

II

Suddenly I found myself lying awake, peering from my sandy mattress through the door of the tent. I looked at my watch pinned against the canvas, and saw by the bright moonlight that it was past twelve o'clock—the threshold of a new day—and I had therefore slept a couple of hours. The Swede was asleep still beside me; the wind howled as before; something plucked at my heart and made me feel afraid. There was a sense of disturbance in my immediate neighbourhood.

I sat up quickly and looked out. The trees were swaying violently to and fro as the gusts smote them, but our little bit of green canvas lay snugly safe in the hollow, for the wind passed over it without meeting enough resistance to make it vicious. The feeling of disquietude did not pass, however, and I crawled quietly out of the tent to see if our belongings were safe. I moved carefully so as not to waken my companion. A curious excitement was on me.

I was half-way out, kneeling on all fours, when my eye first took in that the tops of the bushes opposite, with their moving tracery of leaves, made shapes against the sky. I sat back on my haunches and stared. It was incredible, surely, but there, opposite and slightly above me, were shapes of some indeterminate sort among the willows, and as the branches swayed in the wind they seemed to group themselves about these shapes, forming a series of monstrous outlines that shifted rapidly beneath the moon. Close, about fifty feet in front of me, I saw these things.

My first instinct was to waken my companion, that he too might see them, but something made me hesitate—the sudden realization, probably, that I should not welcome corroboration; and meanwhile I crouched there staring in amazement with smarting eyes. I was wide awake. I remember saying to myself that I was *not* dreaming.

They first became properly visible, these huge figures, just within the tops of the bushes—immense, bronze-coloured, moving, and wholly independent of the swaying of the branches. I saw them plainly and noted, now I came to examine them more calmly, that they were very much larger than human, and indeed that something in their appearance proclaimed them to be *not human* at all. Certainly they were not merely the moving tracery of the branches against the moonlight. They shifted independently. They rose upwards in a continuous stream from earth to sky, vanishing utterly as soon as they reached the dark of the sky. They were interlaced one with another, making a great column, and I saw their limbs and huge bodies melting in and out of each other, forming this serpentine line that bent and swayed and twisted spirally with the contortions of the wind-tossed trees. They were nude, fluid shapes, passing up the bushes, *within* the leaves almost—rising up in a living column into the heavens. Their faces I never could see. Unceasingly they poured upwards, swaying in great bending curves, with a hue of dull bronze upon their skins.

I stared, trying to force every atom of vision from my eyes. For a long time I thought they must every moment disappear and resolve themselves into the movements of the branches and prove to be an optical illusion. I searched everywhere for a proof of reality, when all the while I understood quite well that the standard of reality had changed. For the longer I looked the more certain I became that these figures were real and living, though perhaps not according to the standards that the camera and the biologist would insist upon.

Far from feeling fear, I was possessed with a sense of awe and wonder such as I have never known. I seemed to be gazing at the personified elemental forces of this haunted and primeval region. Our intrusion had stirred the powers of the place into activity. It was we who were the cause of the disturbance, and my brain filled to bursting with stories and legends of the spirits and deities of places that have been acknowledged and worshipped by men in all ages of the world's history. But, before I could arrive at any possible explanation, something impelled me to go farther out, and I crept forward on the sand and stood upright. I felt the ground still warm under my bare feet; the wind tore at my hair and face; and the sound of the river burst upon my ears with a sudden roar. These things, I knew, were real, and proved that my senses were acting normally. Yet the figures still rose from earth to heaven, silent, majestically, in a great spiral of grace and strength that overwhelmed me at length with a genuine deep emotion of worship. I felt that I must fall down and worship—absolutely worship.

Perhaps in another minute I might have done so, when a gust of wind swept against me with such force that it blew me sideways, and I nearly stumbled and fell. It seemed to shake the dream violently out of me. At least it gave me another point of view somehow. The figures still remained, still ascended into heaven from the heart of the night, but my reason at last began to assert itself. It must be a subjective experience, I argued—none the less real for that, but still subjective. The moonlight and the branches combined to work out these pictures upon the mirror of my imagination, and for some reason I projected them outwards and made them appear objective. I knew this must be the case, of course. I took courage, and began to move forward across the open patches of sand. By Jove, though, was it all hallucination? Was it merely subjective? Did not my reason argue in the old futile way from the little standard of the known?

I only know that great column of figures ascended darkly into the sky for what seemed a very long period of time, and with a very complete measure of reality as most men are accustomed to gauge reality. Then suddenly they were gone!

And, once they were gone and the immediate wonder of their great presence had passed, fear came down upon me with a cold rush. The esoteric meaning of this lonely and haunted region suddenly flamed up within me, and I began to tremble dreadfully. I took a quick look round—a look of horror that came near to panic—calculating vainly ways of escape; and then, realizing how helpless I was to achieve anything really effective, I crept back silently into the tent and lay down again upon my sandy mattress, first lowering the door-curtain to shut out the sight of the willows in the moonlight, and then burying my head as deeply as possible beneath the blankets to deaden the sound of the terrifying wind.

III

As though further to convince me that I had not been dreaming, I remember that it was a long time before I fell again into a troubled and restless sleep; and even then only the upper crust of me slept, and underneath there was something that never quite lost consciousness, but lay alert and on the watch.

But this second time I jumped up with a genuine start of terror. It was neither the wind nor the river that woke me, but the slow approach of something that caused the sleeping portion of me to grow smaller and smaller till at last it vanished altogether, and I found myself sitting bolt upright—listening.

Outside there was a sound of multitudinous little patterings. They had been coming, I was aware, for a long time, and in my sleep they had first become audible. I sat there nervously wide awake as though I had not slept at all. It seemed to me that my breathing came with difficulty, and that there was a great weight upon the surface of my body. In spite of the hot night, I felt clammy with cold and shivered. Something surely was pressing steadily against the sides of the tent and weighing down upon it from above. Was it the body of the wind? Was this the pattering rain, the dripping of the leaves? The spray blown from the river by the wind and gathering in big drops? I thought quickly of a dozen things.

Then suddenly the explanation leaped into my mind: a bough from the poplar, the only large tree on the island, had fallen with the wind. Still half caught by the other branches, it would fall with the next gust and crush us, and meanwhile its leaves brushed and tapped upon the tight canvas surface of the tent. I raised a loose flap and rushed out, calling to the Swede to follow.

But when I got out and stood upright I saw that the tent was free. There was no hanging bough; there was no rain or spray; nothing approached.

A cold, grey light filtered down through the bushes and lay on the faintly gleaming sand. Stars still crowded the sky directly overhead, and the wind howled magnificently, but the fire no longer gave out any glow, and I saw the east reddening in streaks through the trees. Several hours must have passed since I stood there before watching the ascending figures, and the memory of it now came back to me horribly, like an evil dream. Oh, how tired it made me feel, that ceaseless raging wind! Yet, though the deep lassitude of a sleepless night was on me, my nerves were tingling with the activity of an equally tireless apprehension, and all idea of repose was out of the question. The river I saw had risen further. Its thunder filled the air, and a fine spray made itself felt through my thin sleeping shirt.

Yet nowhere did I discover the slightest evidence of anything to cause alarm. This deep, prolonged disturbance in my heart remained wholly unaccounted for.

My companion had not stirred when I called him, and there was no need to waken him now. I looked about me carefully, noting everything; the turned-over canoe; the yellow paddles—two of them, I'm certain; the provision sack and the extra lantern hanging together from the tree; and, crowding everywhere about me, enveloping all, the willows, those endless, shaking willows. A bird uttered its morning cry, and a string of duck passed with whirring flight overhead in the twilight. The sand whirled, dry and stinging, about my bare feet in the wind.

I walked round the tent and then went out a little way into the bush, so that I could see across the river to the farther landscape, and the same profound yet indefinable emotion of distress seized upon me again as I saw the interminable sea of bushes stretching to the horizon, looking ghostly and unreal in the wan light of dawn. I walked softly here and there, still puzzling over that odd sound of infinite pattering, and of that pressure upon the tent that had wakened me. It *must* have been the wind, I reflected—the wind bearing upon the loose, hot sand, driving the dry particles smartly against the taut canvas—the wind dropping heavily upon our fragile roof.

Yet all the time my nervousness and malaise increased appreciably.

I crossed over to the farther shore and noted how the coast-line had altered in the night, and what masses of sand the river had torn away. I dipped my hands and feet into the cool current, and bathed my forehead. Already there was a glow of sunrise in the sky and the exquisite freshness of coming day. On my way back I passed purposely beneath the very bushes where I had seen the column of figures rising into the air, and midway among the clumps I suddenly found myself overtaken by a sense of vast terror. From the shadows a large figure went swiftly by. Someone passed me, as sure as ever man did . . .

It was a great staggering blow from the wind that helped me forward again, and once out in the more open space, the sense of terror diminished strangely. The winds were about and walking, I remember saying to myself, for the winds often move like great presences under the trees. And altogether the fear that hovered about me was such an unknown and immense kind of fear, so unlike anything I had ever felt before, that it woke a sense of awe and wonder in me that did much to counteract its worst effects; and when I reached a high point in the middle of the island from which I could see the wide stretch of river, crimson in the sunrise, the whole magical beauty of it all was so overpowering that a sort of wild yearning woke in me and almost brought a cry up into the throat.

But this cry found no expression, for as my eyes wandered from the plain beyond to the island round me and noted our little tent half hidden among the willows, a dreadful discovery leaped out at me, compared to which my terror of the walking winds seemed as nothing at all.

For a change, I thought, had somehow come about in the arrangement of the landscape. It was not that my point of vantage gave me a different view, but that an alteration had apparently been effected in the relation of the tent to the willows, and of the willows to the tent. Surely the bushes now crowded much closer—unnecessarily, unpleasantly close. *They had moved nearer.*

Creeping with silent feet over the shifting sands, drawing imperceptibly nearer by soft, unhurried movements, the willows had come closer during the night. But had the wind moved them, or had they moved of themselves? I recalled the sound of infinite small patterings and the pressure upon the tent and upon my own heart that caused me to wake in terror. I swayed for a moment in the wind like a tree, finding it hard to keep my upright position on the sandy hillock. There was a suggestion here of personal agency, of deliberate intention, of aggressive hostility, and it terrified me into a sort of rigidity.

Then the reaction followed quickly. The idea was so bizarre, so absurd, that I felt inclined to laugh. But the laughter came no more readily than the cry, for the knowledge that my mind was so receptive to such dangerous imaginings brought the additional terror that it was through our minds and not through our physical bodies that the attack would come, and was coming.

The wind buffeted me about, and, very quickly it seemed, the sun came up over the horizon, for it was after four o'clock, and I must have stood on that little pinnacle of sand longer than I knew, afraid to come down to close quarters with the willows. I returned quietly, creepily, to the tent, first taking another exhaustive look round and—yes, I confess it—making a few measurements. I paced out on the warm sand the distances between the willows and the tent, making a note of the shortest distance particularly.

I crawled stealthily into my blankets. My companion, to all appearances, still slept soundly, and I was glad that this was so. Provided my experiences were not corroborated, I could find strength somehow to deny them, perhaps. With the day-light I could persuade myself that it was all a subjective hallucination, a fantasy of the night, a projection of the excited imagination.

Nothing further came in to disturb me, and I fell asleep almost at once, utterly exhausted, yet still in dread of hearing again that weird sound of multitudinous pat-tering, or of feeling the pressure upon my heart that had made it difficult to breathe.

IV

The sun was high in the heavens when my companion woke me from a heavy sleep and announced that the porridge was cooked and there was just time to bathe. The grateful smell of frizzling bacon entered the tent door.

"River still rising," he said, "and several islands out in mid-stream have disap-peared altogether. Our own island's much smaller."

"Any wood left?" I asked sleepily.

"The wood and the island will finish to-morrow in a dead heat," he laughed, "but there's enough to last us till then."

I plunged in from the point of the island, which had indeed altered a lot in size and shape during the night, and was swept down in a moment to the landing-place opposite the tent. The water was icy, and the banks flew by like the country from an express train. Bathing under such conditions was an exhilarating operation, and the terror of the night seemed cleansed out of me by a process of evaporation in the brain. The sun was blazing hot; not a cloud showed itself anywhere; the wind, however, had not abated one little jot.

Quite suddenly then the implied meaning of the Swede's words flashed across me, showing that he no longer wished to leave post-haste, and had changed his mind. "Enough to last till to-morrow"—he assumed we should stay on the island another night. It struck me as odd. The night before he was so positive the other way. How had the change come about?

Great crumblings of the banks occurred at breakfast, with heavy splashings and clouds of spray which the wind brought into our frying-pan, and my fellow-traveler talked incessantly about the difficulty the Vienna-Pesth steamers must have to find the channel in flood. But the state of his mind interested and impressed me far more than the state of the river or the difficulties of the steamers. He had changed somehow since the evening before. His manner was different—a trifle excited, a trifle shy, with a sort of suspicion about his voice and gestures. I hardly know how to describe it now in cold blood, but at the time I remember being quite certain of one thing, viz., that he had become frightened?

He ate very little breakfast, and for once omitted to smoke his pipe. He had the map spread open beside him, and kept studying its markings.

"We'd better get off sharp in an hour," I said presently, feeling for an opening that must bring him indirectly to a partial confession at any rate. And his answer puzzled me uncomfortably: "Rather! If they'll let us."

"Who'll let us? The elements?" I asked quickly, with affected indifference.

"The powers of this awful place, whoever they are," he replied, keeping his eyes on the map. "The gods are here, if they are anywhere at all in the world."

"The elements are always the true immortals," I replied, laughing as naturally as I could manage, yet knowing quite well that my face reflected my true feelings when he looked up gravely at me and spoke across the smoke:

"We shall be fortunate if we get away without further disaster."

This was exactly what I had dreaded, and I screwed myself up to the point of the direct question. It was like agreeing to allow the dentist to extract the tooth; it *had* to come anyhow in the long run, and the rest was all pretence.

"Further disaster! Why, what's happened?"

"For one thing—the steering paddle's gone," he said quietly.

"The steering paddle gone!" I repeated, greatly excited, for this was our rudder, and the Danube in flood without a rudder was suicide. "But what—"

"And there's a tear in the bottom of the canoe," he added, with a genuine little tremor in his voice.

I continued staring at him, able only to repeat the words in his face somewhat foolishly. There, in the heat of the sun, and on this burning sand, I was aware of a freezing atmosphere descending round us. I got up to follow him, for he merely nodded his head gravely and led the way towards the tent a few yards on the other side of the fireplace. The canoe still lay there as I had last seen her in the night, ribs uppermost, the paddles, or rather, *the* paddle, on the sand beside her.

"There's only one," he said, stooping to pick it up. "And here's the rent in the base-board."

It was on the tip of my tongue to tell him that I had clearly noticed *two* paddles a few hours before, but a second impulse made me think better of it, and I said nothing. I approached to see.

There was a long, finely made tear in the bottom of the canoe where a little slither of wood had been neatly taken clean out; it looked as if the tooth of a sharp rock or snag had eaten down her length, and investigation showed that the hole went through. Had we launched out in her without observing it we must inevitably have foundered. At first the water would have made the wood swell so as to close the hole, but once out in mid-stream the water must have poured in, and the canoe, never more than two inches above the surface, would have filled and sunk very rapidly.

"There, you see an attempt to prepare a victim for the sacrifice," I heard him saying, more to himself than to me, "two victims rather," he added as he bent over and ran his fingers along the slit.

I began to whistle—a thing I always do unconsciously when utterly nonplussed—and purposely paid no attention to his words. I was determined to consider them foolish.

"It wasn't there last night," he said presently, straightening up from his examination and looking anywhere but at me.

"We must have scratched her in landing, of course," I stopped whistling to say. "The stones are very sharp—"

I stopped abruptly, for at that moment he turned round and met my eye squarely. I knew just as well as he did how impossible my explanation was. There were no stones, to begin with.

"And then there's this to explain too," he added quietly, handing me the paddle and pointing to the blade.

A new and curious emotion spread freezingly over me as I took and examined it. The blade was scraped down all over, beautifully scraped, as though someone had sand-papered it with care, making it so thin that the first vigorous stroke must have snapped it off at the elbow.

"One of us walked in his sleep and did this thing," I said feebly, "or—or it has been filed by the constant stream of sand particles blown against it by the wind, perhaps."

"Ah," said the Swede, turning away, laughing a little, "you can explain everything."

"The same wind that caught the steering paddle and flung it so near the bank that it fell in with the next lump that crumbled," I called out after him, absolutely determined to find an explanation for everything he showed me.

"I see," he shouted back, turning his head to look at me before disappearing among the willow bushes.

Once alone with these perplexing evidences of personal agency, I think my first thoughts took the form of "One of us must have done this thing, and it certainly was not I." But my second thought decided how impossible it was to suppose, under all the circumstances, that either of us had done it. That my companion, the trusted friend of a dozen similar expeditions, could have knowingly had a hand in it, was a suggestion not to be entertained for a moment. Equally absurd seemed the explanation that this imperturbable and densely practical nature had suddenly become insane and was busied with insane purposes.

Yet the fact remained that what disturbed me most, and kept my fear actively alive even in this blaze of sunshine and wild beauty, was the clear certainty that some curious alteration had come about in his *mind*—that he was nervous, timid, suspicious, aware of goings on he did not speak about, watching a series of secret and hitherto unmentionable events—waiting, in a word, for a climax that he expected, and, I thought, expected very soon. This grew up in my mind intuitively—I hardly knew how.

I made a hurried examination of the tent and its surroundings, but the measurements of the night remained the same. There were deep hollows formed in the sand I now noticed for the first time, basin-shaped and of various depths and sizes, varying from that of a tea-cup to a large bowl. The wind, no doubt, was responsible for these miniature craters, just as it was for lifting the paddle and tossing it towards the water. The rent in the canoe was the only thing that seemed quite inexplicable; and, after all, it *was* conceivable that a sharp point had caught it when we landed. The examination I made of the shore did not assist this theory, but all the same I clung to it with that diminishing portion of my intelligence which I called my "reason." An explanation of some kind was an absolute necessity, just as some working explanation of the universe is necessary—however absurd—to the happiness of every individual who seeks to do his duty in the world and face the problems of life. The simile seemed to me at the time an exact parallel.

I at once set the pitch melting, and presently the Swede joined me at the work, though under the best conditions in the world the canoe could not be safe for traveling till the following day. I drew his attention casually to the hollows in the sand.

"Yes," he said, "I know. They're all over the island. But *you* can explain them, no doubt!"

"Wind, of course," I answered without hesitation. "Have you never watched those little whirlwinds in the street that twist and twirl everything into a circle? This sand's loose enough to yield, that's all."

He made no reply, and we worked on in silence for a bit. I watched him surreptitiously all the time, and I had an idea he was watching me. He seemed, too, to be always listening attentively to something I could not hear, or perhaps for something that he expected to hear, for he kept turning about and staring into the bushes, and up into the sky, and out across the water where it was visible through the openings among the willows. Sometimes he even put his hand to his ear and held it there for several minutes. He said nothing to me, however, about it, and I asked no questions. And meanwhile, as he mended that torn canoe with the skill and address of a red Indian, I was glad to notice his absorption in the work, for there was a vague dread in my heart that he would speak of the changed aspect of the willows. And, if he had noticed that, my imagination could no longer be held a sufficient explanation of it.

At length, after a long pause, he began to talk.

"Queer thing," he added in a hurried sort of voice, as though he wanted to say something and get it over. "Queer thing. I mean, about that otter last night."

I had expected something so totally different that he caught me with surprise, and I looked up sharply.

"Shows how lonely this place is. Otters are awfully shy things—"

"I don't mean that, of course," he interrupted. "I mean—do you think—did you think it really *was* an otter?"

"What else, in the name of Heaven, what else?"

"You know, I saw it before you did, and at first it seemed—so *much* bigger than an otter."

"The sunset as you looked up-stream magnified it, or something," I replied.

He looked at me absently a moment, as though his mind were busy with other thoughts.

"It had such extraordinary yellow eyes," he went on half to himself.

"That was the sun too," I laughed, a trifle boisterously. "I suppose you'll wonder next if that fellow in the boat—"

I suddenly decided not to finish the sentence. He was in the act again of listening, turning his head to the wind, and something in the expression of his face made me halt. The subject dropped, and we went on with our caulking. Apparently he had not noticed my unfinished sentence. Five minutes later, however, he looked at me across the canoe, the smoking pitch in his hand, his face exceedingly grave.

"I *did* rather wonder, if you want to know," he said slowly, "what that thing in the boat was. I remember thinking at the time it was not a man. The whole business seemed to rise quite suddenly out of the water."

I laughed again boisterously in his face, but this time there was impatience, and a strain of anger too, in my feeling.

"Look here now," I cried, "this place is quite queer enough without going out of our way to imagine things! That boat was an ordinary boat, and the man in it was an ordinary man, and they were both going down-stream as fast as they could lick. And that otter *was* an otter, so don't let's play the fool about it!"

He looked steadily at me with the same grave expression. He was not in the least annoyed. I took courage from his silence.

"And, for Heaven's sake," I went on, "don't keep pretending you hear things, because it only gives me the jumps, and there's nothing to hear but the river and this cursed old thundering wind."

"You *fool!*" he answered in a low, shocked voice, "you utter fool. That's just the way all victims talk. As if you didn't understand just as well as I do!" he sneered with scorn in his voice, and a sort of resignation. "The best thing you can do is to keep quiet and try to hold your mind as firm as possible. This feeble attempt at self-deception only makes the truth harder when you're forced to meet it."

My little effort was over, and I found nothing more to say, for I knew quite well his words were true, and that I was the fool, not he. Up to a certain stage in the adventure he kept ahead of me easily, and I think I felt annoyed to be out of it, to be thus proved less psychic, less sensitive than himself to these extraordinary happenings, and half ignorant all the time of what was going on under my very nose. *He knew* from the very beginning, apparently. But at the moment I wholly missed the point of his words about the necessity of there being a victim, and that we ourselves were destined to satisfy the want. I dropped all pretence thenceforward, but thenceforward likewise my fear increased steadily to the climax.

"But you're quite right about one thing," he added, before the subject passed, "and that is that we're wiser not to talk about it, or even to think about it, because what one *thinks* finds expression in words, and what one *says,* happens."

That afternoon, while the canoe dried and hardened, we spent trying to fish, testing the leak, collecting wood, and watching the enormous flood of rising water. Masses of driftwood swept near our shores sometimes, and we fished for them with long willow branches. The island grew perceptibly smaller as the banks were torn away with great gulps and splashes. The weather kept brilliantly fine till about four o'clock, and then for the first time for three days the wind showed signs of abating. Clouds began to gather in the south-west, spreading thence slowly over the sky.

This lessening of the wind came as a great relief, for the incessant roaring, banging, and thundering had irritated our nerves. Yet the silence that came about five o'clock with its sudden cessation was in a manner quite as oppressive. The booming of the river had everything in its own way then; it filled the air with deep murmurs, more musical than the wind noises, but infinitely more monotonous. The wind held many notes, rising, falling always beating out some sort of great elemental tune; whereas the river's song lay between three notes at most—dull pedal notes, that held a lugubrious quality foreign to the wind, and somehow seemed to me, in my then nervous state, to sound wonderfully well the music of doom.

It was extraordinary, too, how the withdrawal suddenly of bright sunlight took everything out of the landscape that made for cheerfulness; and since this particular landscape had already managed to convey the suggestion of something sinister, the change of course was all the more unwelcome and noticeable. For me, I know, the darkening outlook became distinctly more alarming, and I found myself more than once calculating how soon after sunset the full moon would get up in the east, and whether the gathering clouds would greatly interfere with her lighting of the little island.

With this general hush of the wind—though it still indulged in occasional brief gusts—the river seemed to me to grow blacker, the willows to stand more densely together. The latter, too, kept up a sort of independent movement of their own, rustling among themselves when no wind stirred, and shaking oddly from the roots upwards. When common objects in this way be come charged with the suggestion of horror, they stimulate the imagination far more than things of unusual appearance; and these bushes, crowding huddled about us, assumed for me in the darkness a bizarre *grotesquerie* of appearance that lent to them somehow the aspect of purposeful and living creatures. Their very ordinariness, I felt, masked what was malignant and hostile to us. The forces of the region drew nearer with the coming of night. They were focusing upon our island, and more particularly upon ourselves. For thus, somehow, in the terms of the imagination, did my really indescribable sensations in this extraordinary place present themselves.

I had slept a good deal in the early afternoon, and had thus recovered somewhat from the exhaustion of a disturbed night, but this only served apparently to render me more susceptible than before to the obsessing spell of the haunting. I fought against it, laughing at my feelings as absurd and childish, with very obvious physiological explanations, yet, in spite of every effort, they gained in strength upon me so that I dreaded the night as a child lost in a forest must dread the approach of darkness.

The canoe we had carefully covered with a waterproof sheet during the day, and the one remaining paddle had been securely tied by the Swede to the base of a tree, lest the wind should rob us of that too. From five o'clock onwards I busied myself with the stew-pot and preparations for dinner, it being my turn to cook that night. We had potatoes, onions, bits of bacon fat to add flavor, and a general thick residue from former stews at the bottom of the pot; with black bread broken up into it the result was most excellent, and it was followed by a stew of plums with sugar and a brew of strong tea with dried milk. A good pile of wood lay close at hand, and the absence of wind made my duties easy. My companion sat lazily watching me, dividing his attentions between cleaning his pipe and giving useless advice—an admitted privilege of the off-duty man. He had been very quiet all the afternoon, engaged in re-caulking the canoe, strengthening the tent ropes, and fishing for driftwood while I slept. No more talk about undesirable things had passed between us, and I think his only remarks had to do with the gradual destruction of the island, which he declared was not fully a third smaller than when we first landed.

The pot had just begun to bubble when I heard his voice calling to me from the bank, where he had wandered away without my noticing. I ran up.

"Come and listen," he said, "and see what you make of it." He held his hand cupwise to his ear, as so often before.

"*Now* do you hear anything?" he asked, watching me curiously.

We stood there, listening attentively together. At first I heard only the deep note of the water and the hissings rising from its turbulent surface. The willows, for once, were motionless and silent. Then a sound began to reach my ears faintly, a peculiar sound—something like the humming of a distant gong. It seemed to come across to us in the darkness from the waste of swamps and willows opposite. It was repeated at regular intervals, but it was certainly neither the sound of a bell nor the hooting of a distant steamer. I can liken it to nothing so much as to the sound of an immense gong, suspended far up in the sky, repeating incessantly its muffled metallic note, soft and musical, as it was repeatedly struck. My heart quickened as I listened.

"I've heard it all day," said my companion. "While you slept this afternoon it came all round the island. I hunted it down, but could never get near enough to see—to localize it correctly. Sometimes it was overhead, and sometimes it seemed under the water. Once or twice, too, I could have sworn it was not outside at all, but *within myself*—you know—the way a sound in the fourth dimension is supposed to come."

I was too much puzzled to pay much attention to his words. I listened carefully, striving to associate it with any known familiar sound I could think of, but without success. It changed in the direction, too, coming nearer, and then sinking utterly away into remote distance. I cannot say that it was ominous in quality, because to me it seemed distinctly musical, yet I must admit it set going a distressing feeling that made me wish I had never heard it.

"The wind blowing in those sand-funnels," I said determined to find an explanation, "or the bushes rubbing together after the storm perhaps."

"It comes off the whole swamp," my friend answered. "It comes from everywhere at once." He ignored my explanations. "It comes from the willow bushes somehow—"

"But now the wind has dropped," I objected. "The willows can hardly make a noise by themselves, can they?"

His answer frightened me, first because I had dreaded it, and secondly, because I knew intuitively it was true.

"It is *because* the wind has dropped we now hear it. It was drowned before. It is the cry, I believe, of the—"

I dashed back to my fire, warned by the sound of bubbling that the stew was in danger, but determined at the same time to escape further conversation. I was resolute, if possible, to avoid the exchanging of views. I dreaded, too, that he would begin about the gods, or the elemental forces, or something else disquieting, and I wanted to keep myself well in hand for what might happen later. There was another night to be faced before we escaped from this distressing place, and there was no knowing yet what it might bring forth.

"Come and cut up bread for the pot," I called to him, vigorously stirring the appetizing mixture. That stew-pot held sanity for us both, and the thought made me laugh.

He came over slowly and took the provision sack from the tree, fumbling in its mysterious depths, and then emptying the entire contents upon the ground-sheet at his feet.

"Hurry up!" I cried; "it's boiling."

The Swede burst out into a roar of laughter that startled me. It was forced laughter, not artificial exactly, but mirthless.

"There's nothing here!" he shouted, holding his sides.

"Bread, I mean."

"It's gone. There is no bread. They've taken it!"

I dropped the long spoon and ran up. Everything the sack had contained lay upon the ground-sheet, but there was no loaf.

The whole dead weight of my growing fear fell upon me and shook me. Then I burst out laughing too. It was the only thing to do: and the sound of my laughter also made me understand his. The stain of psychical pressure caused it—this explosion of unnatural laughter in both of us; it was an effort of repressed forces to seek relief; it was a temporary safety-valve. And with both of us it ceased quite suddenly.

"How criminally stupid of me!" I cried, still determined to be consistent and find an explanation. "I clean forgot to buy a loaf at Pressburg. That chattering woman put everything out of my head, and I must have left it lying on the counter or—"

"The oatmeal, too, is much less than it was this morning," the Swede interrupted.

Why in the world need he draw attention to it? I thought angrily.

"There's enough for to-morrow," I said, stirring vigorously, "and we can get lots more at Komorn or Gran. In twenty-four hours we shall be miles from here."

"I hope so—to God," he muttered, putting the things back into the sack, "unless we're claimed first as victims for the sacrifice," he added with a foolish laugh. He dragged the sack into the tent, for safety's sake, I suppose, and I heard him mumbling to himself, but so indistinctly that it seemed quite natural for me to ignore his words.

Our meal was beyond question a gloomy one, and we ate it almost in silence, avoiding one another's eyes, and keeping the fire bright. Then we washed up and prepared for the night, and, once smoking, our minds unoccupied with any definite duties, the apprehension I had felt all day long became more and more acute. It was not then active fear, I think, but the very vagueness of its origin distressed me far more that if I had been able to ticket and face it squarely. The curious sound I have likened to the note of a gong became now almost incessant, and filled the stillness of the night with a faint, continuous ringing rather than a series of distinct notes. At one time it was behind and at another time in front of us. Sometimes I fancied it came from the bushes on our left, and then again from the clumps on our right. More often it hovered directly overhead like the whirring of wings. It was really everywhere at once, behind, in front, at our sides and over our heads, completely surrounding us. The sound really defies description. But nothing within my knowledge is like that ceaseless muffled humming rising off the deserted world of swamps and willows.

We sat smoking in comparative silence, the strain growing every minute greater. The worst feature of the situation seemed to me that we did not know what to expect, and could therefore make no sort of preparation by way of defence. We could anticipate nothing. My explanations made in the sunshine, moreover, now came to haunt me with their foolish and wholly unsatisfactory nature, and it was more and more clear to us that some kind of plain talk with my companion was inevitable, whether I liked it or not. After all, we had to spend the night together, and to sleep in the same tent side by side. I saw that I could not get along much longer without the support of his mind, and for that, of course, plain talk was imperative. As long as possible, however, I postponed this little climax, and tried to ignore or laugh at the occasional sentences he flung into the emptiness.

Some of these sentences, moreover, were confoundedly disquieting to me, coming as they did to corroborate much that I felt myself; corroboration, too—which made it so much more convincing—from a totally different point of view. He composed such curious sentences, and hurled them at me in such an inconsequential sort of way, as though his main line of thought was secret to himself, and these fragments were mere bits he found it impossible to digest. He got rid of them by uttering them. Speech relieved him. It was like being sick.

"There are things about us, I'm sure, that make for disorder, disintegration, destruction, our destruction," he said once, while the fire blazed between us. "We've strayed out of a safe line somewhere."

And, another time, when the gong sounds had come nearer, ringing much louder than before, and directly over our heads, he said as though talking to himself:

"I don't think a phonograph would show any record of that. The sound doesn't come to me by the ears at all. The vibrations reach me in another manner altogether, and seem to be within me, which is precisely how a fourth dimensional sound might be supposed to make itself heard."

I purposely made no reply to this, but I sat up a little closer to the fire and peered about me into the darkness. The clouds were massed all over the sky, and no trace of moonlight came through. Very still, too, everything was, so that the river and the frogs had things all their own way.

"It has that about it," he went on, "which is utterly out of common experience. It is *unknown*. Only one thing describes it really; it is a non-human sound; I mean a sound outside humanity."

Having rid himself of this indigestible morsel, he lay quiet for a time, but he had so admirably expressed my own feeling that it was a relief to have the thought out, and to have confined it by the limitation of words from dangerous wandering to and fro in the mind.

The solitude of that Danube camping-place, can I ever forget it? The feeling of being utterly alone on an empty planet! My thoughts ran incessantly upon cities and the haunts of men. I would have given my soul, as the saying is, for the "feel" of those Bavarian villages we had passed through by the score; for the normal, human commonplaces; peasants drinking beer, tables beneath the trees, hot sunshine, and a ruined castle on the rocks behind the red-roofed church. Even the tourists would have been welcome.

Yet what I felt of dread was no ordinary ghostly fear. It was infinitely greater, stranger, and seemed to arise from some dim ancestral sense of terror more profoundly disturbing than anything I had known or dreamed of. We had "strayed," as the

Swede put it, into some region or some set of conditions where the risks were great, yet unintelligible to us; where the frontiers of some unknown world lay close about us. It was a spot held by the dwellers in some outer space, a sort of peep-hole whence they could spy upon the earth, themselves unseen, a point where the veil between had worn a little thin. As the final result of too long a sojourn here, we should be carried over the border and deprived of what we called "our lives," yet by mental, not physical, processes. In that sense, as he said, we should be the victims of our adventure—a sacrifice.

It took us in different fashion, each according to the measure of his sensitiveness and powers of resistance. I translated it vaguely into a personification of the mightily disturbed elements, investing them with the horror of a deliberate and malefic purpose, resentful of our audacious intrusion into their breeding-place; whereas my friend threw it into the unoriginal form at first of a trespass on some ancient shrine, some place where the old gods still held sway, where the emotional forces of former worshippers still clung, and the ancestral portion of him yielded to the old pagan spell.

At any rate, here was a place unpolluted by men, kept clean by the winds from coarsening human influences, a place where spiritual agencies were within reach and aggressive. Never, before or since, have I been so attacked by indescribable suggestions of a "beyond region," of another scheme of life, another revolution not parallel to the human. And in the end our minds would succumb under the weight of the awful spell, and we should be drawn across the frontier into *their* world.

Small things testified to the amazing influence of the place, and now in the silence round the fire they allowed themselves to be noted by the mind. The very atmosphere had proved itself a magnifying medium to distort every indication: the otter rolling in the current, the hurrying boatman making signs, the shifting willows, one and all had been robbed of its natural character, and revealed in something of its other aspect—as it existed across the border to that other region. And this changed aspect I felt was now not merely to me, but to the race. The whole experience whose verge we touched was unknown to humanity at all. It was a new order of experience, and in the true sense of the word *unearthly*.

"It's the deliberate, calculating purpose that reduces one's courage to zero," the Swede said suddenly, as if he had been actually following my thoughts. "Otherwise imagination might count for much. But the paddle, the canoe, the lessening food—"

"Haven't I explained all that once?" I interrupted viciously.

"You have," he answered dryly; "you have indeed."

He made other remarks too, as usual, about what he called the "plain determination to provide a victim"; but, having now arranged my thoughts better, I recognized that this was simply the cry of his frightened soul against the knowledge that he was being attacked in a vital part, and that he would be somehow taken or destroyed. The situation called for a courage and calmness of reasoning that neither of us could compass, and I have never before been so clearly conscious of two persons in me—the one that explained everything, and the other that laughed at such foolish explanations, yet was horribly afraid.

Meanwhile, in the pitchy night the fire died down and the wood pile grew small. Neither of us moved to replenish the stock, and the darkness consequently came up very close to our faces. A few feet beyond the circle of firelight it was inky black. Occasionally a stray puff of wind set the willows shivering about us, but apart from this not very welcome sound a deep and depressing silence reigned, broken only by the gurgling of the river and the humming in the air overhead.

We both missed, I think, the shouting company of the winds.

At length, at a moment when a stray puff prolonged itself as though the wind were about to rise again, I reached the point for me of saturation, the point where it was absolutely necessary to find relief in plain speech, or else to betray myself by some hysterical extravagance that must have been far worse in its effect upon both of us. I kicked the fire into a blaze, and turned to my companion abruptly. He looked up with a start.

"I can't disguise it any longer," I said; "I don't like this place, and the darkness, and the noises, and the awful feelings I get. There's something here that beats me utterly. I'm in a blue funk, and that's the plain truth. If the other shore was—different, I swear I'd be inclined to swim for it!"

The Swede's face turned very white beneath the deep tan of sun and wind. He stared straight at me and answered quietly, but his voice betrayed his huge excitement by its unnatural calmness. For the moment, at any rate, he was the strong man of the two. He was more phlegmatic, for one thing.

"It's not a physical condition we can escape from by running away," he replied, in the tone of a doctor diagnosing some grave disease; "we must sit tight and wait. There are forces close here that could kill a herd of elephants in a second as easily as you or I could squash a fly. Our only chance is to keep perfectly still. Our insignificance perhaps may save us."

I put a dozen questions into my expression of face, but found no words. It was precisely like listening to an accurate description of a disease whose symptoms had puzzled me.

"I mean that so far, although aware of our disturbing presence, they have not *found* us—not 'located' us, as the Americans say," he went on. "They're blundering about like men hunting for a leak of gas. The paddle and canoe and provisions prove that. I think they *feel* us, but cannot actually see us. We must keep our minds quiet—it's our minds they feel. We must control our thoughts, or it's all up with us."

"Death, you mean?" I stammered, icy with the horror of his suggestion.

"Worse—by far," he said. "Death, according to one's belief, means either annihilation or release from the limitations of the senses, but it involves no change of character. You don't suddenly alter just because the body's gone. But this means a radical alteration, a complete change, a horrible loss of oneself by substitution—far worse than death, and not even annihilation. We happen to have camped in a spot where their region touches ours, where the veil between has worn thin"—horrors! he was using my very own phrase, my actual words—"so that they are aware of our being in their neighborhood."

"But *who* are aware?" I asked.

I forgot the shaking of the willows in the windless calm, the humming overhead, everything except that I was waiting for an answer that I dreaded more than I can possibly explain.

He lowered his voice at once to reply, leaning forward a little over the fire, an indefinable change in his face that made me avoid his eyes and look down upon the ground.

"All my life," he said, "I have been strangely, vividly conscious of another region—not far removed from our own world in one sense, yet wholly different in kind—where great things go on unceasingly, where immense and terrible personalities hurry by, intent on vast purposes compared to which earthly affairs, the rise and fall of nations, the destinies of empires, the fate of armies and continents, are all as dust in the balance; vast purposes, I mean, that deal directly with the soul, and not indirectly with more expressions of the soul—"

"I suggest just now—" I began, seeking to stop him, feeling as though I was face to face with a madman. But he instantly overbore me with his torrent that *had* to come.

"You think," he said, "it is the spirit of the elements, and I thought perhaps it was the old gods. But I tell you now it is—*neither*. These would be comprehensible entities, for they have relations with men, depending upon them for worship or sacrifice, whereas these beings who are now about us have absolutely nothing to do with mankind, and it is mere chance that their space happens just at this spot to touch our own."

The mere conception, which his words somehow made so convincing, as I listened to them there in the dark stillness of that lonely island, set me shaking a little all over. I found it impossible to control my movements.

"And what do you propose?" I began again.

"A sacrifice, a victim, might save us by distracting them until we could get away," he went on, "just as the wolves stop to devour the dogs and give the sleigh another start. But—I see no chance of any other victim now."

I stared blankly at him. The gleam in his eye was dreadful. Presently he continued.

"It's the willows, of course. The willows *mask* the others, but the others are feeling about for us. If we let our minds betray our fear, we're lost, lost utterly." He looked at me with an expression so calm, so determined, so sincere, that I no longer had any doubts as to his sanity. He was as sane as any man ever was. "If we can hold out through the night," he added, "we may get off in the daylight unnoticed, or rather, *undiscovered*."

"But you really think a sacrifice would—"

That gong-like humming came down very close over our heads as I spoke, but it was my friend's scared face that really stopped my mouth.

"Hush!" he whispered, holding up his hand. "Do not mention them more than you can help. Do not refer to them *by name*. To name is to reveal; it is the inevitable clue, and our only hope lies in ignoring them, in order that they may ignore us."

"Even in thought?" He was extraordinarily agitated.

"Especially in thought. Our thoughts make spirals in their world. We must keep them *out of our minds* at all costs if possible."

I raked the fire together to prevent the darkness having everything its own way. I never longed for the sun as I longed for it then in the awful blackness of that summer night.

"Were you awake all last night?" he went on suddenly.

"I slept badly a little after dawn," I replied evasively, trying to follow his instructions, which I knew instinctively were true, "but the wind, of course—"

"I know. But the wind won't account for all the noises."

"Then you heard it too?"

"The multiplying countless little footsteps I heard," he said, adding, after a moment's hesitation, "and that other sound—"

"You mean above the tent, and the pressing down upon us of something tremendous, gigantic?"

He nodded significantly.

"It was like the beginning of a sort of inner suffocation?" I said.

"Partly, yes. It seemed to me that the weight of the atmosphere had been altered—had increased enormously, so that we should have been crushed."

"And *that*," I went on, determined to have it all out, pointing upwards where the gong-like note hummed ceaselessly, rising and falling like wind. "What do you make of that?"

"It's *their* sound," he whispered gravely. "It's the sound of their world, the humming in their region. The division here is so thin that it leaks through somehow. But, if you listen carefully, you'll find it's not above so much as around us. It's in the willows. It's the willows themselves humming, because here the willows have been made symbols of the forces that are against us."

I could not follow exactly what he meant by this, yet the thought and idea in my mind were beyond question the thought and idea in his. I realized what he realized, only with less power of analysis than his. It was on the tip of my tongue to tell him at last about my hallucination of the ascending figures and the moving bushes, when he suddenly thrust his face again close into mine across the firelight and began to speak in a very earnest whisper. He amazed me by his calmness and pluck, his apparent control of the situation. This man I had for years deemed unimaginative, stolid!

"Now listen," he said. "The only thing for us to do is to go on as though nothing had happened, follow our usual habits, go to bed, and so forth; pretend we feel nothing and notice nothing. It is a question wholly of the mind, and the less we think about them the better our chance of escape. Above all, don't think, for what you *think* happens!"

"All right," I managed to reply, simply breathless with his words and the strangeness of it all; "all right, I'll try, but tell me one more thing first. Tell me what you make of those hollows in the ground all about us, those sand-funnels?"

"No!" he cried, forgetting to whisper in his excitement. "I dare not, simply dare not, put the thought into words. If you have not guessed I am glad. Don't try to. *They* have put it into my mind; try your hardest to prevent their putting it into yours."

He sank his voice again to a whisper before he finished, and I did not press him to explain. There was already just about as much horror in me as I could hold. The conversation came to an end, and we smoked our pipes busily in silence.

Then something happened, something unimportant apparently, as the way is when the nerves are in a very great state of tension, and this small thing for a brief space gave me an entirely different point of view. I chanced to look down at my sand-shoe—the sort we used for the canoe—and something to do with the hole at the toe suddenly recalled to me the London shop where I had bought them, the difficulty the man had in fitting me, and other details of the uninteresting but practical operation. At once, in its train, followed a wholesome view of the modern skeptical world I was accustomed to move in at home. I thought of roast beef, and ale, motor-cars, policemen, brass bands, and a dozen other things that proclaimed the soul of ordinariness or utility. The effect was immediate and astonishing even to myself. Psychologically, I suppose, it was simply a sudden and violent reaction after the strain of living in an atmosphere of things that to the normal consciousness must seem impossible and incredible. But, whatever the cause, it momentarily lifted the spell from my heart, and left me for the short space of a minute feeling free and utterly unafraid. I looked up at my friend opposite.

"You damned old pagan!" I cried, laughing aloud in his face. "You imaginative idiot! You superstitious idolater! You—"

I stopped in the middle, seized anew by the old horror. I tried to smother the sound of my voice as something sacrilegious. The Swede, of course, heard it too—the strange cry overhead in the darkness—and that sudden drop in the air as though something had come nearer.

He had turned ashen white under the tan. He stood bolt upright in front of the fire, stiff as a rod, staring at me.

"After that," he said in a sort of helpless, frantic way, "we must go! We can't stay now; we must strike camp this very instant and go on—down the river."

He was talking, I saw, quite wildly, his words dictated by abject terror—the terror he had resisted so long, but which had caught him at last.

"In the dark?" I exclaimed, shaking with fear after my hysterical outburst, but still realizing our position better than he did. "Sheer madness! The river's in flood, and we've only got a single paddle. Besides, we only go deeper into their country! There's nothing ahead for fifty miles but willows, willows, willows!"

He sat down again in a state of semi-collapse. The positions, by one of those kaleidoscopic changes nature loves, were suddenly reversed, and the control of our forces passed over into my hands. His mind at last had reached the point where it was beginning to weaken.

"What on earth possessed you to do such a thing?" he whispered with the awe of genuine terror in his voice and face.

I crossed round to his side of the fire. I took both his hands in mine, kneeling down beside him and looking straight into his frightened eyes.

"We'll make one more blaze," I said firmly, "and then turn in for the night. At sunrise we'll be off full speed for Komorn. Now, pull yourself together a bit, and remember your own advice about *not thinking fear!*"

He said no more, and I saw that he would agree and obey. In some measure, too, it was a sort of relief to get up and make an excursion into the darkness for more wood. We kept close together, almost touching, groping among the bushes and along the bank. The humming overhead never ceased, but seemed to me to grow louder as we increased our distance from the fire. It was shivery work!

We were grubbing away in the middle of a thickish clump of willows where some driftwood from a former flood had caught high among the branches, when my body was seized in a grip that made me half drop upon the sand. It was the Swede. He had fallen against me, and was clutching me for support. I heard his breath coming and going in short gasps.

"Look! By my soul!" he whispered, and for the first time in my experience I knew what it was to hear tears of terror in a human voice. He was pointing to the fire, some fifty feet away. I followed the direction of his finger, and I swear my heart missed a beat.

There, in front of the dim glow, *something was moving*.

I saw it through a veil that hung before my eyes like the gauze drop-curtain used at the back of a theater—hazily a little. It was neither a human figure nor an animal. To me it gave the strange impression of being as large as several animals grouped together, like horses, two or three, moving slowly. The Swede, too, got a similar result, though expressing it differently, for he thought it was shaped and sized like a clump of willow bushes, rounded at the top, and moving all over upon its surface— "coiling upon itself like smoke," he said afterwards.

"I watched it settle downwards through the bushes," he sobbed at me. "Look, by God! It's coming this way! Oh, oh!"—he gave a kind of whistling cry. "*They've found us.*"

I gave one terrified glance, which just enabled me to see that the shadowy form was swinging towards us through the bushes, and then I collapsed backwards with a crash into the branches. These failed, of course, to support my weight, so that with the Swede on top of me we fell in a struggling heap upon the sand. I really hardly knew what was happening. I was conscious only of a sort of enveloping sensation of icy fear that plucked the nerves out of their fleshly covering, twisted them this way and that, and replaced them quivering. My eyes were tightly shut; something in my throat choked me; a feeling that my consciousness was expanding, extending out into space, swiftly gave way to another feeling that I was losing it altogether, and about to die.

An acute spasm of pain passed through me, and I was aware that the Swede had hold of me in such a way that he hurt me abominably. It was the way he caught at me in falling.

But it was the pain, he declared afterwards, that saved me; it caused me to *forget them* and think of something else at the very instant when they were about to find me. It concealed my mind from them at the moment of discovery, yet just in time to evade their terrible seizing of me. He himself, he says, actually swooned at the same moment, and that was what saved him.

I only know that at a later date, how long or short is impossible to say, I found myself scrambling up out of the slippery network of willow branches, and saw my companion standing in front of me holding out a hand to assist me. I stared at him in a dazed way, rubbing the arm he had twisted for me. Nothing came to me to say, somehow.

"I lost consciousness for a moment or two," I heard him say. "That's what saved me. It made me stop thinking about them."

"You nearly broke my arm in two," I said, uttering my only connected thought at the moment. A numbness came over me.

"That's what saved *you!*" he replied. "Between us, we've managed to set them off on a false tack somewhere. The humming has ceased. It's gone—for the moment at any rate!"

A wave of hysterical laughter seized me again, and this time spread to my friend too—great healing gusts of shaking laughter that brought a tremendous sense of relief in their train. We made our way back to the fire and put the wood on so that it blazed at once. Then we saw that the tent had fallen over and lay in a tangled heap upon the ground.

We picked it up, and during the process tripped more than once and caught our feet in sand.

"It's those sand-funnels," exclaimed the Swede, when the tent was up again and the firelight lit up the ground for several yards about us. "And look at the size of them!"

All round the tent and about the fireplace where we had seen the moving shadows there were deep funnel-shaped hollows in the sand, exactly similar to the ones we had already found over the island, only far bigger and deeper, beautifully formed, and wide enough in some instances to admit the whole of my foot and leg.

Neither of us said a word. We both knew that sleep was the safest thing we could do, and to bed we went accordingly without further delay, having first thrown sand on the fire and taken the provision sack and the paddle inside the tent with us. The canoe, too, we propped in such a way at the end of the tent that our feet touched it, and the least motion would disturb and wake us.

In case of emergency, too, we again went to bed in our clothes, ready for a sudden start.

V

It was my firm intention to lie awake all night and watch, but the exhaustion of nerves and body decreed otherwise, and sleep after a while came over me with a welcome blanket of oblivion. The fact that my companion also slept quickened its approach. At first he fidgeted and constantly sat up, asking me if I "heard this" or "heard that." He tossed about on his cork mattress, and said the tent was moving and the river had risen over the point of the island, but each time I went out to look I returned with the report that all was well, and finally he grew calmer and lay still. Then at length his breathing became regular and I heard unmistakable sounds of snoring—the first and only time in my life when snoring has been a welcome and calming influence.

This, I remember, was the last thought in my mind before dozing off.

A difficulty in breathing woke me, and I found the blanket over my face. But something else besides the blanket was pressing upon me, and my first thought was that my companion had rolled off his mattress on to my own in his sleep. I called to him and sat up, and at the same moment it came to me that the tent was *surrounded*. That sound of multitudinous soft pattering was again audible outside, filling the night with horror.

I called again to him, louder than before. He did not answer, but I missed the sound of his snoring, and also noticed that the flap of the tent was down. This was the unpardonable sin. I crawled out in the darkness to hook it back securely, and it was then for the first time I realized positively that the Swede was not here. He had gone.

I dashed out in a mad run, seized by a dreadful agitation, and the moment I was out I plunged into a sort of torrent of humming that surrounded me completely and came out of every quarter of the heavens at once. It was that same familiar humming—gone mad! A swarm of great invisible bees might have been about me in the air. The sound seemed to thicken the very atmosphere, and I felt that my lungs worked with difficulty.

But my friend was in danger, and I could not hesitate.

The dawn was just about to break, and a faint whitish light spread upwards over the clouds from a thin strip of clear horizon. No wind stirred. I could just make out the bushes and river beyond, and the pale sandy patches. In my excitement I ran frantically to and fro about the island, calling him by name, shouting at the top of my voice the first words that came into my head. But the willows smothered my voice, and the humming muffled it, so that the sound only traveled a few feet round me. I plunged among the bushes, tripping headlong, tumbling over roots, and scraping my face as I tore this way and that among the preventing branches.

Then, quite unexpectedly, I came out upon the island's point and saw a dark figure outlined between the water and the sky. It was the Swede. And already he had one foot in the river! A moment more and he would have taken the plunge.

I threw myself upon him, flinging my arms about his waist and dragging him shorewards with all my strength. Of course he struggled furiously, making a noise all the time just like that cursed humming, and using the most outlandish phrases in his anger about "going *inside* to Them," and "taking the way of the water and the wind," and God only knows what more besides, that I tried in vain to recall afterwards, but which turned me sick with horror and amazement as I listened. But in the end I managed to get him into the comparative safety of the tent, and flung him breathless and cursing upon the mattress where I held him until the fit had passed.

I think the suddenness with which it all went and he grew calm, coinciding as it did with the equally abrupt cessation of the humming and pattering outside—I think this was almost the strangest part of the whole business perhaps. For he had just opened his eyes and turned his tired face up to me so that the dawn threw a pale light upon it through the doorway, and said, for all the world just like a frightened child:

"My life, old man—it's my life I owe you. But it's all over now anyhow. They've found a victim in our place!"

Then he dropped back upon his blankets and went to sleep literally under my eyes. He simply collapsed, and began to snore again as healthily as though nothing had happened and he had never tried to offer his own life as a sacrifice by drowning. And when the sunlight woke him three hours later—hours of ceaseless vigil for me—it became so clear to me that he remembered absolutely nothing of what he had attempted to do, that I deemed it wise to hold my peace and ask no dangerous questions.

He woke naturally and easily, as I have said, when the sun was already high in a windless hot sky, and he at once got up and set about the preparation of the fire for breakfast. I followed him anxiously at bathing, but he did not attempt to plunge in, merely dipping his head and making some remark about the extra coldness of the water.

"River's falling at last," he said, "and I'm glad of it."

"The humming has stopped too," I said.

He looked up at me quietly with his normal expression. Evidently he remembered everything except his own attempt at suicide.

"Everything has stopped," he said, "because—"

He hesitated. But I knew some reference to that remark he had made just before he fainted was in his mind, and I was determined to know it.

253

"Because 'They've found another victim'?" I said, forcing a little laugh.

"Exactly," he answered, "exactly! I feel as positive of it as though—as though—I feel quite safe again, I mean," he finished.

He began to look curiously about him. The sunlight lay in hot patches on the sand. There was no wind. The willows were motionless. He slowly rose to feet.

"Come," he said; "I think if we look, we shall find it."

He started off on a run, and I followed him. He kept to the banks, poking with a stick among the sandy bays and caves and little back-waters, myself always close on his heels.

"Ah!" he exclaimed presently, "ah!"

The tone of his voice somehow brought back to me a vivid sense of the horror of the last twenty-four hours, and I hurried up to join him. He was pointing with his stick at a large black object that lay half in the water and half on the sand. It appeared to be caught by some twisted willow roots so that the river could not sweep it away. A few hours before the spot must have been under water.

"See," he said quietly, "the victim that made our escape possible!"

And when I peered across his shoulder I saw that his stick rested on the body of a man. He turned it over. It was the corpse of a peasant, and the face was hidden in the sand. Clearly the man had been drowned, but a few hours before, and his body must have been swept down upon our island somewhere about the hour of the dawn—*at the very time the fit had passed.*

"We must give it a decent burial, you know."

"I suppose so," I replied. I shuddered a little in spite of myself, for there was something about the appearance of that poor drowned man that turned me cold.

The Swede glanced up sharply at me, an undecipherable expression on his face, and began clambering down the bank. I followed him more leisurely. The current, I noticed, had torn away much of the clothing from the body, so that the neck and part of the chest lay bare.

Halfway down the bank my companion suddenly stopped and held up his hand in warning; but either my foot slipped, or I had gained too much momentum to bring myself quickly to a halt, for I bumped into him and sent him forward with a sort of leap to save himself. We tumbled together on to the hard sand so that our feet splashed into the water. And, before anything could be done, we had collided a little heavily against the corpse.

The Swede uttered a sharp cry. And I sprang back as if I had been shot.

At the moment we touched the body there rose from its surface the loud sound of humming—the sound of several hummings—which passed with a vast commotion as of winged things in the air about us and disappeared upwards into the sky, growing fainter and fainter till they finally ceased in the distance. It was exactly as though we had disturbed some living yet invisible creatures at work.

My companion clutched me, and I think I clutched him, but before either of us had time properly to recover from the unexpected shock, we saw that a movement of the current was turning the corpse round so that it became released from the grip of the willow roots. A moment later it had turned completely over, the dead face uppermost, staring at the sky. It lay on the edge of the main stream. In another moment it would be swept away.

The Swede started to save it, shouting again something I did not catch about a "proper burial"—and then abruptly dropped upon his knees on the sand and covered his eyes with his hands. I was beside him in an instant.

I saw what he had seen.

For just as the body swung round to the current the face and the exposed chest turned full towards us, and showed plainly how the skin and flesh were indented with small hollows, beautifully formed, and exactly similar in shape and kind to the sand-funnels that we had found all over the island.

"Their mark!" I heard my companion mutter under his breath. "Their awful mark!"

And when I turned my eyes again from his ghastly face to the river, the current had done its work, and the body had been swept away into midstream and was already beyond our reach and almost out of sight, turning over and over on the waves like an otter.

THE VOICE IN THE NIGHT
WILLIAM HOPE HODGSON

WILLIAM HOPE HODGSON (1877-1918) SPENT MUCH OF HIS YOUTH AS A SAILOR, SO IT IS NOT SURPRISING THAT MANY OF HIS TALES OF HORROR, INCLUDING HIS NOVELS *THE BOATS OF THE GLEN CARRIG* (1907) AND *THE GHOST PIRATES* (1909), ARE SET ON SHIPS AND AT SEA. THIS STORY, PUBLISHED FIRST IN THE SEPTEMBER 1907 ISSUE OF *BLUE BOOK,* IS A FINE EXAMPLE OF HOW HODGSON IMAGINED HORRORS TOTALLY UNIQUE TO MARITIME SETTINGS. HODGSON IS ONE OF THE GENERATION OF BRITISH WRITERS WHOSE LIFE WAS CUT TRAGICALLY SHORT BY WORLD WAR I.

It was a dark, starless night. We were becalmed in the Northern Pacific. Our exact position I do not know; for the sun had been hidden during the course of a weary, breathless week, by a thin haze which had seemed to float above us, about the height of our mastheads, at whiles descending and shrouding the surrounding sea.

With there being no wind, we had steadied the tiller, and I was the only man on deck. crew, consisting of two men and a boy, were sleeping forrard in their den; while Will—my friend, and the master of our little craft—was aft in his bunk on the port side of the little cabin.

Suddenly, from out of the surrounding darkness, there came a hail: "Schooner, ahoy!"

The cry was so unexpected that I gave no immediate answer, because of my surprise.

It came again—a voice curiously throaty and inhuman, calling from somewhere upon the dark sea away on our port broadside: "Schooner, ahoy!"

"Hullo!" I sung out, having gathered my wits somewhat. "What are you? What do you want?"

"You need not be afraid," answered the queer voice, having probably noticed some trace of confusion in my tone. "I am only an old man."

The pause sounded oddly; but it was only afterwards that it came back to me with any significance.

"Why don't you come alongside, then?" I queried somewhat snappishly; for I liked not his hinting at my having been a trifle shaken.

"I—I—can't. It wouldn't be safe. I——" The voice broke off, and there was silence.

"What do you mean?" I asked, growing more and more astonished. "Why not safe? Where are you?"

I listened for a moment; but there came no answer. And then, a sudden indefinite suspicion, of I knew not what, coming to me, I stepped swiftly to the binnacle, and took out the lighted lamp. At the same time, I knocked on the deck with my heel to waken Will. Then I was back at the side, throwing the yellow funnel of light out into the silent immensity beyond our rail. As I did so, I heard a slight, muffled cry, and then the sound of a splash as though someone had dipped oars abruptly. Yet I cannot say that I saw anything with certainty; save, it seemed to me, that with the first flash of the light, there had been something upon the waters, where now there was nothing.

"Hullo, there!" I called. "What foolery is this!"

But there came only the indistinct sounds of a boat being pulled away into the night.

Then I heard Will's voice, from the direction of the after scuttle: "What's up, George?"

"Come here, Will!" I said.

"What is it?" he asked, coming across the deck.

I told him the queer thing which had happened. He put several questions; then, after a moment's silence, he raised his hands to his lips, and hailed: "Boat, ahoy!"

From a long distance away there came back to us a faint reply, and my companion repeated his call. Presently, after a short period of silence, there grew on our hearing the muffled sound of oars; at which Will hailed again.

This time there was a reply:—

"Put away the light."

"I'm damned if I will," I muttered; but Will told me to do as the voice bade, and I shoved it down under the bulwarks.

"Come nearer," he said, and the oar-strokes continued. Then, when apparently some half-dozen fathoms distant, they again ceased.

"Come alongside," exclaimed Will. "There's nothing to be frightened of aboard here!"

"Promise that you will not show the light?"

"What's to do with you," I burst out, "that you're so infernally afraid of the light?"

"Because—" began the voice, and stopped short.

"Because what?" I asked quickly.

Will put his hand on my shoulder.

"Shut up a minute, old man," he said, in a low voice. "Let me tackle him."

He leant more over the rail.

"See here, Mister," he said, "this is a pretty queer business, you coming upon us like this, right out in the middle of the blessed Pacific. How are we to know what sort of a hanky-panky trick you're up to? You say there's only one of you. How are we to know, unless we get a squint at you—eh? What's your objection to the light, anyway?"

As he finished, I heard the noise of the oars again, and then the voice came; but now from a greater distance, and sounding extremely hopeless and pathetic.

"I am sorry—sorry! I would not have troubled you, only I am hungry, and—so is she."

The voice died away, and the sound of the oars, dipping irregularly, was borne to us.

"Stop!" sung out Will. "I don't want to drive you away. Come back! We'll keep the light hidden, if you don't like it."

He turned to me:—

"It's a damned queer rig, this; but I think there's nothing to be afraid of?"

There was a question in his tone, and I replied.

"No, I think the poor devil's been wrecked around here, and gone crazy."

The sound of the oars drew nearer.

"Shove that lamp back in the binnacle," said Will; then he leaned over the rail and listened. I replaced the lamp, and came back to his side. The dipping of the oars ceased some dozen yards distant.

"Won't you come alongside now?" asked Will in an even voice. "I have had the lamp put back in the binnacle."

"I—I cannot," replied the voice. "I dare not come nearer. I dare not even pay you for the—the provisions."

"That's all right," said Will, and hesitated. "You're welcome to as much grub as you can take——" Again he hesitated.

"You are very good," exclaimed the voice. "May God, Who understands everything, reward you——" It broke off huskily.

"The—the lady?" said Will abruptly. "Is she——"

"I have left her behind upon the island," came the voice.

"What island?" I cut in.

"I know not its name," returned the voice. "I would to God——!" it began, and checked itself as suddenly.

"Could we not send a boat for her?" asked Will at this point.

"No!" said the voice, with extraordinary emphasis. "My God! No!" There was a moment's pause; then it added, in a tone which seemed a merited reproach:—

"It was because of our want I ventured—because her agony tortured me."

"I am a forgetful brute," exclaimed Will. "Just wait a minute, whoever you are, and I will bring you up something at once."

In a couple of minutes he was back again, and his arms were full of various edibles. He paused at the rail.

"Can't you come alongside for them?" he asked.

"No—I *dare not,*" replied the voice, and it seemed to me that in its tones I detected a note of stifled craving—as though the owner hushed a mortal desire. It came to me then in a flash, that poor old creature out there in the darkness, was *suffering* for actual need of that which Will held in his arms; and yet, because of some unintelligible dread, refraining from dashing to the side of our little schooner, and receiving it. And with the lightning-like conviction, there came the knowledge that the Invisible was not mad; but sanely facing some intolerable horror.

"Damn it, Will!" I said, full of many feelings, over which predominated a vast sympathy. "Get a box. We must float off the stuff to him in it."

This we did—propelling it away from the vessel, out into the darkness, by means of a boathook. In a minute, a slight cry from the Invisible came to us, and we knew that he had secured the box.

A little later, he called out a farewell to us, and so heartful a blessing, that I am sure we were the better for it. Then, without more ado, we heard the ply of oars across the darkness.

"Pretty soon off," remarked Will, with perhaps just a little sense of injury.

"Wait," I replied. "I think somehow he'll come back. He must have been badly needing that food."

"And the lady," said Will. For a moment he was silent; then he continued:—

"It's the queerest thing ever I've tumbled across, since I've been fishing."

"Yes," I said, and fell to pondering.

And so the time slipped away—an hour, another, and still Will stayed with me; for the queer adventure had knocked all desire for sleep out of him.

The third hour was three parts through, when we heard again the sound of oars across the silent ocean.

"Listen!" said Will, a low note of excitement in his voice.

"He's coming, just as I thought," I muttered.

The dipping of the oars grew nearer, and I noted that the strokes were firmer and longer. The food had been needed.

They came to a stop a little distance off the broadside, and the queer voice came again to us through the darkness:—

"Schooner, ahoy!"

"That you?" asked Will.

"Yes," replied the voice. "I left you suddenly; but—but there was great need."

"The lady?" questioned Will.

"The—lady is grateful now on earth. She will be more grateful soon in—in heaven."

Will began to make some reply, in a puzzled voice; but became confused, and broke off short. I said nothing. I was wondering at the curious pauses, and, apart from my wonder, I was full of a great sympathy.

The voice continued:—

"We—she and I, have talked, as we shared the result of God's tenderness and yours—"

Will interposed; but without coherence.

"I beg of you not to—to belittle your deed of Christian charity this night," said the voice. "Be sure that it has not escaped His notice."

It stopped, and there was a full minute's silence. Then it came again:—

"We have spoken together upon that which—which has befallen us. We had thought to go out, without telling any, of the terror which has come into our—lives. She is with me in believing that to-night's happenings are under a special ruling, and that it is God's wish that we should tell to you all that we have suffered since—since———"

"Yes?" said Will softly. "Since the sinking of the *Albatross*."

"Ah!" I exclaimed involuntarily. "She left Newcastle for 'Frisco some six months ago, and hasn't been heard of since."

"Yes," answered the voice. "But some few degrees to the North of the line she was caught in a terrible storm, and dismasted. When the day came, it was found that she was leaking badly, and, presently, it falling to a calm, the sailors took to the boats, leaving—leaving a young lady—my fiancée—and myself upon the wreck.

"We were below, gathering together a few of our belongings, when they left. They were entirely callous, through fear, and when we came up upon the deck, we saw them only as small shapes afar off upon the horizon. Yet we did not despair, but set to work and constructed a small raft. Upon this we put such few matters as it would hold including a quantity of water and some ship's biscuit. Then, the vessel being very deep in the water, we got ourselves on to the raft, and pushed off.

"It was later, when I observed that we seemed to be in the way of some tide or current, which bore us from the ship at an angle; so that in the course of three hours, by my watch, her hull became invisible to our sight, her broken masts remaining in view for a somewhat longer period. Then, towards evening, it grew misty, and so through the night. The next day we were still encompassed by the mist, the weather remaining quiet.

"For four days we drifted through this strange haze, until, on the evening of the fourth day, there grew upon our ears the murmur of breakers at a distance. Gradually it became plainer, and, somewhat after midnight, it appeared to sound upon either hand at no very great space. The raft was raised upon a swell several times, and then we were in smooth water, and the noise of the breakers was behind.

"When the morning came, we found that we were in a sort of great lagoon; but of this we noticed little at the time; for close before us, through the enshrouding mist, loomed the hull of a large sailing-vessel. With one accord, we fell upon our knees and thanked God; for we thought that here was an end to our perils. We had much to learn.

"The raft drew near to the ship, and we shouted on them to take us aboard; but none answered. Presently the raft touched against the side of the vessel, and, seeing a rope hanging downwards, I seized it and began to climb. Yet I had much ado to make my way up, because of a kind of grey, lichenous fungus which had seized upon the rope, and which blotched the side of the ship lividly.

"I reached the rail and clambered over it, on to the deck. Here I saw that the decks were covered, in great patches, with grey masses, some of them rising into nodules several feet in height; but at the time I thought less of this matter than of the possibility of there being people aboard the ship. I shouted; but none answered. Then I went to the door below the poop deck. I opened it, and peered in. There was a great smell of staleness, so that I knew in a moment that nothing living was within, and with the knowledge, I shut the door quickly; for I felt suddenly lonely.

"I went back to the side where I had scrambled up. My—my sweetheart was still sitting quietly upon the raft. Seeing me look down she called up to know whether there were any aboard of the ship. I replied that the vessel had the appearance of having been long deserted; but that if she would wait a little I would see whether there was anything in the shape of a ladder by which she could ascend to the deck. Then we would make a search through the vessel together. A little later, on the opposite side of the decks, I found a rope side-ladder. This I carried across, and a minute afterwards she was beside me.

"Together we explored the cabins and apartments in the after part of the ship; but nowhere was there any sign of life. Here and there within the cabins themselves, we came across odd patches of that queer fungus; but this, as my sweetheart said, could be cleansed away.

"In the end, having assured ourselves that the after portion of the vessel was empty, we picked our ways to the bows, between the ugly grey nodules of that strange growth; and here we made a further search which told us that there was indeed none aboard but ourselves.

"This being now beyond any doubt, we returned to the stern of the ship and proceeded to make ourselves as comfortable as possible. Together we cleared out and cleaned two of the cabins: and after that I made examination whether there was anything eatable in the ship. This I soon found was so, and thanked God in my heart for His goodness. In addition to this I discovered the whereabouts of the fresh-water pump, and having fixed it I found the water drinkable, though somewhat unpleasant to the taste.

"For several days we stayed aboard the ship, without attempting to get to the shore. We were busily engaged in making the place habitable. Yet even thus early we became aware that our lot was even less to be desired than might have been imagined; for though, as a first step, we scraped away the odd patches of growth that studded the floors and walls of the cabins and saloon, yet they returned almost to their original size within the space of twenty-four hours, which not only discouraged us, but gave us a feeling of vague unease.

"Still we would not admit ourselves beaten, so set to work afresh, and not only scraped away the fungus, but soaked the places where it had been, with carbolic, a can-full of which I had found in the pantry. Yet, by the end of the week the growth had returned in full strength, and, in addition, it had spread to other places, as though our touching it had allowed germs from it to travel elsewhere.

"On the seventh morning, my sweetheart woke to find a small patch of it growing on her pillow, close to her face. At that, she came to me, so soon as she could get her garments upon her. I was in the galley at the time lighting the fire for breakfast.

"'Come here, John,'" she said, and led me aft. When I saw the thing upon her pillow I shuddered, and then and there we agreed to go right out of the ship and see whether we could not fare to make ourselves more comfortable ashore.

"Hurriedly we gathered together our few belongings, and even among these I found that the fungus had been at work; for one of her shawls had a little lump of it growing near one edge. I threw the whole thing over the side, without saying anything to her.

"The raft was still alongside, but it was too clumsy to guide, and I lowered down a small boat that hung across the stern, and in this we made our way to the shore. Yet, as we drew near to it, I became gradually aware that here the vile fungus, which had driven us from the ship, was growing riot. In places it rose into horrible, fantastic mounds, which seemed almost to quiver, as with a quiet life, when the wind blew across them. Here and there it took on the forms of vast fingers, and in others it just spread out flat and smooth and treacherous. Odd places, it appeared as grotesque stunted trees, seeming extraordinarily kinked and gnarled—the whole quaking vilely at times.

"At first, it seemed to us that there was no single portion of the surrounding shore which was not hidden beneath the masses of the hideous lichen; yet, in this, I found we were mistaken; for somewhat later, coasting along the shore at a little distance, we descried a smooth white patch of what appeared to be fine sand, and there we landed. It was not sand. What it was I do not know. All that I have observed is that upon it the fungus will not grow; while everywhere else, save where the sand-like earth wanders oddly, path-wise, amid the grey desolation of the lichen, there is nothing but that loathsome greyness.

"It is difficult to make you understand how cheered we were to find one place that was absolutely free from the growth, and here we deposited our belongings. Then we went back to the ship for such things as it seemed to us we should need. Among other matters, I managed to bring ashore with me one of the ship's sails, with which I constructed two small tents, which, though exceedingly rough-shaped, served the purpose for which they were intended. In these we lived and stored our various necessities, and thus for a matter of some four weeks all went smoothly and without particular unhappiness. Indeed, I may say with much of happiness—for— for we were together.

"It was on the thumb of her right hand that the growth first showed. It was only a small circular spot, much like a little grey mole. My God! how the fear leapt to my

263

heart when she showed me the place. We cleansed it, between us, washing it with carbolic and water. In the morning of the following day she showed her hand to me again. The grey warty thing had returned. For a little while, we looked at one another in silence. Then, still wordless, we started again to remove it. In the midst of the operation she spoke suddenly.

"'What's that on the side of your face, dear?' Her voice was sharp with anxiety. I put my hand up to feel.

"'There! Under the hair by your ear. A little to the front a bit.' My finger rested upon the place, and then I knew.

"'Let us get your thumb done first,' I said. And she submitted, only because she was afraid to touch me until it was cleansed. I finished washing and disinfecting her thumb, and then she turned to my face. After it was finished we sat together and talked awhile of many things for there had come into our lives sudden, very terrible thoughts. We were, all at once, afraid of something worse than death. We spoke of loading the boat with provisions and water and making our way out on to the sea; yet we were helpless, for many causes, and—and the growth had attacked us already. We decided to stay. God would do with us what was His will. We would wait.

"A month, two months, three months passed and the places grew somewhat, and there had come others. Yet we fought so strenuously with the fear that its headway was but slow, comparatively speaking.

"Occasionally we ventured off to the ship for such stores as we needed. There we found that the fungus grew persistently. One of the nodules on the maindeck became soon as high as my head.

"We had now given up all thought or hope of leaving the island. We had realized that it would be unallowable to go among healthy humans, with the things from which we were suffering.

"With this determination and knowledge in our minds we knew that we should have to husband our food and water; for we did not know, at that time, but that we should possibly live for many years.

"This reminds me that I have told you that I am an old man. Judged by the years this is not so. But—but—"

He broke off; then continued somewhat abruptly: "As I was saying, we knew that we should have to use care in the matter of food. But we had no idea then how little food there was left of which to take care. It was a week later that I made the discovery that all the other bread tanks—which I had supposed full—were empty, and that (beyond odd tins of vegetables and meat, and some other matters) we had nothing on which to depend, but the bread in the tank which I had already opened.

"After learning this I bestirred myself to do what I could, and set to work at fishing in the lagoon; but with no success. At this I was somewhat inclined to feel desperate until the thought came to me to try outside the lagoon, in the open sea.

"Here, at times, I caught odd fish; but so infrequently that they proved of but little help in keeping us from the hunger which threatened.

It seemed to me that our deaths were likely to come by hunger, and not by the growth of the thing which had seized upon our bodies.

"We were in this state of mind when the fourth month wore out. When I made a very horrible discovery. One morning, a little before midday. I came off from the ship with a portion of the biscuits which were left. In the mouth of her tent I saw my sweetheart sitting, eating something.

" 'What is it, my dear?' I called out as I leapt ashore. Yet, on hearing my voice, she seemed confused, and, turning, slyly threw something towards the edge of the little clearing. It fell short, and a vague suspicion having arisen within me, I walked across and picked it up. It was a piece of the grey fungus.

"As I went to her with it in my hand, she turned deadly pale; then rose red.

"I felt strangely dazed and frightened.

"'My dear! My dear!' I said, and could say no more. Yet at words she broke down and cried bitterly. Gradually, as she calmed, I got from her the news that she had tried it the preceding day, and—and liked it. I got her to promise on her knees not to touch it again, however great our hunger. After she had promised she told me that the desire for it had come suddenly, and that, until the moment of desire, she had experienced nothing towards it but the most extreme repulsion.

"Later in the day, feeling strangely restless, and much shaken with the thing which I had discovered, I made my way along one of the twisted paths—formed by the white, sand-like substance—which led among the fungoid growth. I had, once before, ventured along there; but not to any great distance. This time, being involved in perplexing thought, I went much further than hitherto.

"Suddenly I was called to myself by a queer hoarse sound on my left. Turning quickly I saw that there was movement among an extraordinarily shaped mass of fungus, close to my elbow. It was swaying uneasily, as though it possessed life of its own. Abruptly, as I stared, the thought came to me that the thing had a grotesque resemblance to the figure of a distorted human creature. Even as the fancy flashed into my brain, there was a slight, sickening noise of tearing, and I saw that one of the branch-like arms was detaching itself from the surrounding grey masses, and coming towards me. The head of the thing—a shapeless grey ball, inclined in my direction. I stood stupidly, and the vile arm brushed across my face. I gave out a frightened cry, and ran back a few paces. There was a sweetish taste upon my lips where the thing had touched me. I licked them, and was immediately filled with an inhuman desire. I turned and seized a mass of the fungus. Then more and—more. I was insatiable. In the midst of devouring, the remembrance of the morning's discovery swept into my mazed brain. It was sent by God. I dashed the fragment I held to the ground. Then, utterly wretched and feeling a dreadful guiltiness, I made my way back to the little encampment.

"I think she knew, by some marvellous intuition which love must have given, so soon as she set eyes on me. Her quiet sympathy made it easier for me, and I told her of my sudden weakness; yet omitted to mention the extraordinary thing which had gone before. I desired to spare her all unnecessary terror.

"But, for myself, I had added an intolerable knowledge, to breed an incessant terror in my brain; for I doubted not but that I had seen the end of one of those men who had come to the island in the ship in the lagoon; and in that monstrous ending I had seen our own.

"Thereafter we kept from the abominable food, though the desire for it had entered into our blood. Yet our drear punishment was upon us; for, day by day, with monstrous rapidity, the fungoid growth took hold of our poor bodies. Nothing we could do would check it materially, and so—and so—we who had been human, became— Well, it matters less each day. Only—only we had been man and maid!

"And day by day the fight is more dreadful, to withstand the hungerlust for the terrible lichen.

"A week ago we ate the last of the biscuit, and since that time I have caught three fish. I was out here fishing tonight when your schooner drifted upon me out of the mist. I hailed you. You know the rest, and may God, out of His great heart, bless you for your goodness to a—a couple of poor outcast souls."

There was the dip of an oar—another. Then the voice came again, and for the last time, sounding through the slight surrounding mist, ghostly and mournful.

"God bless you! Good-bye!"

"Good-bye," we shouted together, hoarsely, our hearts full of many emotions.

I glanced about me. I became aware that the dawn was upon us.

The sun flung a stray beam across the hidden sea; pierced the mist dully, and lit up the receding boat with a gloomy fire. Indistinctly I saw something nodding between the oars. I thought of a sponge—a great, grey nodding sponge—

The oars continued to ply. They were grey—as was the boat—and my eyes searched a moment vainly for the conjunction of hand and oar. My gaze flashed back to the—head. It nodded forward as the oars went backward for the stroke. Then the oars were dipped, the boat shot out of the patch of light, and the—the thing went nodding into the mist.

THURNLEY ABBEY

PERCEVAL LANDON

PERCEVAL LANDON (1869–1927) WROTE ONLY A
HANDFUL OF SUPERNATURAL TALES, BUT THIS STORY HAS
BECOME A FIXTURE IN THE GHOST STORY CANON OWING
TO ITS MIX OF CLASSIC GHOST STORY ATMOSPHERICS
AND PHYSICAL HORROR. A SHORTER VERSION OF THIS
STORY WAS FIRST PUBLISHED IN *McCLURE'S MAGAZINE*
IN 1907. THIS LONGER TREATMENT APPEARED IN HIS
COLLECTION *RAW EDGES* THE FOLLOWING YEAR.

Three years ago I was on my way out to the East, and as an extra day in London was of some importance, I took the Friday evening mail-train to Brindisi instead of the usual Thursday morning Marseilles express. Many people shrink from the long forty-eight-hour train journey through Europe, and the subsequent rush across the Mediterranean on the nineteen-knot *Isis* or *Osiris*; but there is really very little discomfort on either the train or the mail-boat, and unless there is actually nothing for me to do, I always like to save the extra day and a half in London before I say goodbye to her for one of my longer tramps. This time—it was early, I remember, in the shipping season, probably about the beginning of September—there were few passengers, and I had a compartment in the P. & O. Indian express to myself all the way from Calais. All Sunday I watched the blue waves dimpling the Adriatic, and the pale rosemary along the cuttings; the plain white towns, with their flat roofs and their bold "duomos," and the grey-green gnarled olive orchards of Apulia. The journey was just like any other. We ate in the dining-car as often and as long as we decently could. We slept after luncheon; we dawdled the afternoon away with yellow-backed novels; sometimes we exchanged platitudes in the smoking-room, and it was there that I met Alastair Colvin.

Colvin was a man of middle height, with a resolute, well-cut jaw; his hair was turning grey; his moustache was sun-whitened, otherwise he was clean-shaven—obviously a gentleman, and obviously also a pre-occupied man. He had no great wit. When spoken to, he made the usual remarks in the right way, and I dare say he refrained from banalities only because he spoke less than the rest of us; most of the time he buried himself in the Wagonlit Company's Time-table, but seemed unable to concentrate his attention on any one page of it. He found that I had been over the Siberian railway, and for a quarter of an hour he discussed it with me. Then he lost interest in it, and rose to go to his compartment. But he came back again very soon, and seemed glad to pick up the conversation again.

Of course this did not seem to me to be of any importance. Most travellers by train become a trifle infirm of purpose after thirty-six hours' rattling. But Colvin's restless way I noticed in somewhat marked contrast with the man's personal importance and dignity; especially ill suited was it to his finely made large hand with strong, broad, regular nails and its few lines. As I looked at his hand I noticed a long, deep, and recent scar of ragged shape. However, it is absurd to pretend that I thought anything was unusual. I went off at five o'clock on Sunday afternoon to sleep away the hour or two that had still to be got through before we arrived at Brindisi.

Once there, we few passengers transhipped our hand baggage, verified our berths—there were only a score of us in all—and then, after an aimless ramble of half an hour in Brindisi, we returned to dinner at the Hôtel International, not wholly surprised that the town had been the death of Virgil. If I remember rightly, there is a gaily painted hall at the International—I do not wish to advertise anything, but there is no other place in Brindisi at which to await the coming of the mails—and after dinner I was looking with awe at a trellis overgrown with blue vines, when Colvin moved across the room to my table. He picked up *Il Secolo*, but almost immediately gave up the pretence of reading it. He turned squarely to me and said:

"Would you do me a favour?"

One doesn't do favours to stray acquaintances on Continental expresses without knowing something more of them than I knew of Colvin. But I smiled in a noncommittal way, and asked him what he wanted. I wasn't wrong in part of my estimate of him; he said bluntly:

"Will you let me sleep in your cabin on the *Osiris*?" And he coloured a little as he said it.

Now, there is nothing more tiresome than having to put up with a stable-companion at sea, and I asked him rather pointedly:

"Surely there is room for all of us?" I thought that perhaps he had been partnered off with some mangy Levantine, and wanted to escape from him at all hazards.

Colvin, still somewhat confused, said: "Yes; I am in a cabin by myself. But you would do me the greatest favour if you would allow me to share yours."

This was all very well, but, besides the fact that I always sleep better when alone, there had been some recent thefts on board English liners, and I hesitated, frank and honest and self-conscious as Colvin was. Just then the mail-train came in with a clatter and a rush of escaping steam, and I asked him to see me again about it on the boat when we started. He answered me curtly—I suppose he saw the mistrust in my manner—"I am a member of White's and the Beefsteak." I smiled to myself as he said it, but I remembered in a moment that the man—if he were really what he claimed to be, and I make no doubt that he was—must have been sorely put to it before he urged the fact as a guarantee of his respectability to a total stranger at a Brindisi hotel.

That evening, as we cleared the red and green harbour-lights of Brindisi, Colvin explained. This is his story in his own words:

"When I was travelling in India some years ago, I made the acquaintance of a youngish man in the Woods and Forests. We camped out together for a week, and I found him a pleasant companion. John Broughton was a light-hearted soul when off duty, but a steady and capable man in any of the small emergencies that continually arise in that department. He was liked and trusted by the natives, and though a trifle over-pleased with himself when he escaped to civilisation at Simla or Calcutta, Broughton's future was well assured in Government service, when a fair-sized estate was unexpectedly left to him, and he joyfully shook the dust of the Indian plains from his feet and returned to England. For five years he drifted about London. I saw him now and then. We dined together about every eighteen months, and I could trace pretty exactly the gradual sickening of Broughton with a merely idle life. He then set out on a couple of long voyages, returned as restless as before, and at last told me that he had decided to marry and settle down at his place, Thurnley Abbey, which had long been empty. He spoke about looking after the property and standing for his constituency in the usual way. Vivien Wilde, his fiancée, had, I suppose, begun to take him in hand. She was a pretty girl with a deal of fair hair and rather an exclusive manner; deeply religious in a narrow school, she was still kindly and high-spirited, and I thought that Broughton was in luck. He was quite happy and full of information about his future.

"Among other things, I asked him about Thurnley Abbey. He confessed that he hardly knew the place. The last tenant, a man called Clarke, had lived in one wing for fifteen years and seen no one. He had been a miser and a hermit. It was the rarest thing for a light to be seen at the Abbey after dark. Only the barest necessities of life were ordered, and the tenant himself received them at the side-door. His one half-caste manservant, after a month's stay in the house, had abruptly left without warning, and had returned to the Southern States. One thing Broughton complained bitterly about: Clarke had wilfully spread the rumour among the villagers that the Abbey was haunted, and had even condescended to play childish tricks with spirit-lamps and salt in order to scare trespassers away at night. He had been detected in the act of this tomfoolery, but the story spread, and no one, said Broughton, would venture near the house except in broad daylight. The hauntedness of Thurnley Abbey was now, he said with a grin, part of the gospel of the countryside, but he and his young wife were going to change all that. Would I propose myself any time I liked? I, of course, said I would, and equally, of course, intended to do nothing of the sort without a definite invitation.

"The house was put in thorough repair, though not a stick of the old furniture and tapestry were removed. Floors and ceilings were relaid; the roof was made watertight again, and the dust of half a century was scoured out. He showed me some photographs of the place. It was called an Abbey, though as a matter of fact it had been only the infirmary of the long-vanished Abbey of Clouster some five miles away. The larger part of the building remained as it had been in pre-Reformation days, but a wing had been added in Jacobean times, and that part of the house had been kept in something like repair by Mr. Clarke. He had in both the ground and first floors set a heavy timber door, strongly barred with iron, in the passage between the earlier and the Jacobean parts of the house, and had entirely neglected the former. So there had been a good deal of work to be done.

"Broughton, whom I saw in London two or three times about this period, made a deal of fun over the positive refusal of the workmen to remain after sundown. Even after the electric light had been put into every room, nothing would induce them to remain, though, as Broughton observed, electric light was death on ghosts. The legend of the Abbey's ghosts had gone far and wide, and the men would take no risks. They went home in batches of five and six, and even during the daylight hours there was an inordinate amount of talking between one and another, if either happened to be out of sight of his companion. On the whole, though nothing of any sort or kind had been conjured up even by their heated imaginations during their five months' work upon the Abbey, the belief in the ghosts was rather

strengthened than otherwise in Thurnley because of the men's confessed nervousness, and local tradition declared itself in favour of the ghost of an immured nun.

"'Good old nun!' said Broughton.

"I asked him whether in general he believed in the possibility of ghosts, and,
rather to my surprise, he said that he couldn't say he entirely disbelieved in them.
A man in India had told him one morning in camp that he believed that his mother
was dead in England, as her vision had come to his tent the night before. He had not
been alarmed, but had said nothing, and the figure vanished again. As a matter of fact,
the next possible dak-walla brought on a telegram announcing the mother's death.
'There the thing was,' said Broughton. But at Thurnley he was practical enough. He
roundly cursed the idiotic selfishness of Clarke, whose silly antics had caused all the
inconvenience. At the same time, he couldn't refuse to sympathise to some extent
with the ignorant workmen. " 'My own idea,' said he, 'is that if a ghost ever does
come in one's way, one ought to speak to it.'

"I agreed. Little as I knew of the ghost world and its conventions, I had always
remembered that a spook was in honour bound to wait to be spoken to. It didn't
seem much to do, and I felt that the sound of one's own voice would at any rate
reassure oneself as to one's wakefulness. But there are few ghosts outside Europe—
few, that is, that a white man can see—and I had never been troubled with any.
However, as I have said, I told Broughton that I agreed.

"So the wedding took place, and I went to it in a tall hat which I bought for
the occasion, and the new Mrs. Broughton smiled very nicely at me afterwards. As
it had to happen, I took the Orient Express that evening and was not in England
again for nearly six months. Just before I came back I got a letter from Broughton.
He asked if I could see him in London or come to Thurnley, as he thought I should
be better able to help him than anyone else he knew. His wife sent a nice message
to me at the end, so I was reassured about at least one thing. I wrote from Budapest
that I would come and see him at Thurnley two days after my arrival in London,
and as I sauntered out of the Pannonia into the Kerepesi Utcza to post my letters,
I wondered of what earthly service I could be to Broughton. I had been out with
him after tiger on foot, and I could imagine few men better able at a pinch to manage their own business. However, I had nothing to do, so after dealing with some
small accumulations of business during my absence, I packed a kit-bag and departed
to Euston.

"I was met by Broughton's great limousine at Thurnley Road station, and after
a drive of nearly seven miles we echoed through the sleepy streets of Thurnley village, into which the main gates of the park thrust themselves, splendid with pillars

and spread-eagles and tom-cats rampant atop of them. I never was a herald, but I know that the Broughtons have the right to supporters—Heaven knows why! From the gates a quadruple avenue of beech-trees led inwards for a quarter of a mile. Beneath them a neat strip of fine turf edged the road and ran back until the poison of the dead beech-leaves killed it under the trees. There were many wheel-tracks on the road, and a comfortable little pony trap jogged past me laden with a country parson and his wife and daughter. Evidently there was some garden party going on at the Abbey. The road dropped away to the right at the end of the avenue, and I could see the Abbey across a wide pasturage and a broad lawn thickly dotted with guests.

"The end of the building was plain. It must have been almost mercilessly austere when it was first built, but time had crumbled the edges and toned the stone down to an orange-lichened grey wherever it showed behind its curtain of magnolia, jasmine, and ivy. Farther on was the three-storied Jacobean house, tall and hand-some. There had not been the slightest attempt to adapt the one to the other, but the kindly ivy had glossed over the touching-point. There was a tall flèche in the middle of the building, surmounting a small bell tower. Behind the house there rose the mountainous verdure of Spanish chestnuts all the way up the hill.

"Broughton had seen me coming from afar, and walked across from his other guests to welcome me before turning me over to the butler's care. This man was sandy-haired and rather inclined to be talkative. He could, however, answer hardly any questions about the house; he had, he said, only been there three weeks. Mindful of what Broughton had told me, I made no inquiries about ghosts, though the room into which I was shown might have justified anything. It was a very large low room with oak beams projecting from the white ceiling. Every inch of the walls, including the doors, was covered with tapestry, and a remarkably fine Italian fourpost bedstead, heavily draped, added to the darkness and dignity of the place. All the furniture was old, well made, and dark. Underfoot there was a plain green pile carpet, the only new thing about the room except the electric light fittings and the jugs and basins. Even the looking-glass on the dressing-table was an old pyramidal Venetian glass set in heavy repoussé frame of tarnished silver.

"After a few minutes' cleaning up, I went downstairs and out upon the lawn, where I greeted my hostess. The people gathered there were of the usual country type, all anxious to be pleased and roundly curious as to the new master of the Abbey. Rather to my surprise, and quite to my pleasure, I rediscovered Glenham, whom I had known well in old days in Barotseland: he lived quite close, as, he remarked with a grin, I ought to have known. 'But,' he added, 'I don't live in a place like this.' He swept his hand to the long, low lines of the Abbey in obvious admiration, and then, to my intense interest, muttered beneath his breath, 'Thank God!' He saw that I had overheard him, and turning to me said decidedly, 'Yes, "thank God" ' I said, and I meant it. I wouldn't live at the Abbey for all Broughton's money.'

"'But surely,' I demurred, 'you know that old Clarke was discovered in the very act of setting light on his bug-a-boos?'

"Glenham shrugged his shoulders. 'Yes, I know about that. But there is something wrong with the place still. All I can say is that Broughton is a different man since he has lived there. I don't believe that he will remain much longer. But—you're staying here?—Well, you'll hear all about it to-night. There's a big dinner, I understand.' The conversation turned off to old reminiscences, and Glenham soon after had to go.

"Before I went to dress that evening I had twenty minutes' talk with Broughton in his library. There was no doubt that the man was altered, gravely altered. He was nervous and fidgety, and I found him looking at me only when my eye was off him. I naturally asked him what he wanted of me. I told him I would do anything I could, but that I couldn't conceive what he lacked that I could provide. He said with a lustreless smile that there was, however, something, and that he would tell me the following morning. It struck me that he was somehow ashamed of himself, and perhaps ashamed of the part he was asking me to play. However, I dismissed the subject from my mind and went up to dress in my palatial room. As I shut the door a draught blew out the Queen of Sheba from the wall, and I noticed that the tapestries were not fastened to the wall at the bottom. I have always held very practical views about spooks, and it has often seemed to me that the slow waving in firelight of loose tapestry upon a wall would account for ninety-nine per cent. of the stories one hears. Certainly the dignified undulation of this lady with her attendants and huntsmen—one of whom was untidily cutting the throat of a fallow deer upon the very steps on which King Solomon, a grey-faced Flemish nobleman with the order of the Golden Fleece, awaited his fair visitor—gave colour to my hypothesis.

"Nothing much happened at dinner. The people were very much like those of the garden party. A young woman next me seemed anxious to know what was being read in London. As she was far more familiar than I with the most recent magazines and literary supplements, I found salvation in being myself instructed in the tendencies of modern fiction. All true art, she said, was shot through and through with melancholy. How vulgar were the attempts at wit that marked so many modern books! From the beginning of literature it had always been tragedy that embodied the highest attainment of every age. To call such works morbid merely begged the question. No thoughtful man—she looked sternly at me through the steel rim of her glasses—could fail to agree with me. Of course, as one would, I immediately and properly said that I slept with Pett Ridge and Jacobs under my pillow at night, and that if Jorrocks weren't quite so large and cornery, I would add him to the company. She hadn't read any of them, so I was saved—for a time. But I remember grimly that she said that the dearest wish of her life was to be in some awful and soul-freezing situation of horror, and I remember that she dealt hardly with the hero of Nat Paynter's vampire story, between nibbles at her brown-bread ice. She was a cheerless soul, and I couldn't help thinking that if there were many such in the neighbourhood, it was not surprising that old Glenham had been stuffed with some nonsense or other about the Abbey. Yet nothing could well have been less creepy than the glitter of silver and glass, and the subdued lights and cackle of conversation all round the dinner-table.

"After the ladies had gone I found myself talking to the rural dean. He was a thin, earnest man, who at once turned the conversation to old Clarke's buffooneries. But, he said, Mr. Broughton had introduced such a new and cheerful spirit, not only into the Abbey, but, he might say, into the whole neighbourhood, that he had great hopes that the ignorant superstitions of the past were from henceforth destined to oblivion. Thereupon his other neighbour, a portly gentleman of independent means and position, audibly remarked 'Amen,' which damped the rural dean, and we talked to partridges past, partridges present, and pheasants to come. At the other end of the table Broughton sat with a couple of his friends, red-faced hunting men. Once I noticed that they were discussing me, but I paid no attention to it at the time. I remembered it a few hours later.

"By eleven all the guests were gone, and Broughton, his wife, and I were alone together under the fine plaster ceiling of the Jacobean drawing-room. Mrs. Broughton talked about one or two of the neighbours, and then, with a smile, said that she knew I would excuse her, shook hands with me, and went off to bed. I am not very good at analysing things, but I felt that she talked a little uncomfortably and with a suspicion of effort, smiled rather conventionally, and was obviously glad to go. These things seem trifling enough to repeat, but I had throughout the faint feeling that everything was not quite square. Under the circumstances, this was enough to set me wondering what on earth the service could be that I was to render—wondering also whether the whole business were not some ill-advised jest in order to make me come down from London for a mere shooting-party.

"Broughton said little after she had gone. But he was evidently labouring to bring the conversation round to the so-called haunting of the Abbey. As soon as I saw this, of course I asked him directly about it. He then seemed at once to lose interest in the matter. There was no doubt about it: Broughton was somehow a changed man, and to my mind he had changed in no way for the better. Mrs. Broughton seemed no sufficient cause. He was clearly very fond of her, and she of him. I reminded him that he was going to tell me what I could do for him in the morning, pleaded my journey, lighted a candle, and went upstairs with him. At the end of the passage leading into the old house he grinned weakly and said, 'Mind, if you see a ghost, do talk to it; you said you would.' He stood irresolutely a moment and then turned away. At the door of his dressing-room he paused once more: 'I'm here,' he called out, 'if you should want anything. Good night,' and he shut the door.

"I went along the passage to my room, undressed, switched on a lamp beside my bed, read a few pages of *The Jungle Book,* and then, more than ready for sleep, turned the light off and went fast asleep.

"Three hours later I woke up. There was not a breath of wind outside. There was not even a flicker of light from the fireplace. As I lay there, an ash tinkled slightly as it cooled, but there was hardly a gleam of the dullest red in the grate. An owl cried among the silent Spanish chestnuts on the slope outside. I idly reviewed the events of the day, hoping that I should fall off to sleep again before I reached dinner. But at the end I seemed as wakeful as ever. There was no help for it. I must read my *Jungle Book* again till I felt ready to go off, so I fumbled for the pear at the end of the cord that hung down inside the bed, and I switched on the bedside lamp. The sudden glory dazzled me for a moment. I felt under my pillow for my book with half-shut eyes. Then, growing used to the light, I happened to look down to the foot of my bed.

"I can never tell you really when happened then. Nothing I could ever confess in the most abject words could even faintly picture to you what I felt. I know that my heart stopped dead, and my throat shut automatically. In one instinctive movement I crouched back up against the head-boards of the bed, staring at the horror. The movement set my heart going again, and the sweat dripped from every pore. I am not a particularly religious man, but I had always believed that God would never allow any supernatural appearance to present itself to man in such a guise and in such circumstances that harm, either bodily or mental, could result to him. I can only tell you that at the moment both my life and my reason rocked unsteadily on their seats."

The other *Osiris* passengers had gone to bed. Only he and I remained leaning over the starboard railing, which rattled uneasily now and then under the fierce vibration of the over-engined mail-boat. Far over, there were the lights of a few fishing-smacks riding out the night, and a great rush of white combing and seething water fell out and away from us overside.

At last Colvin went on:

"Leaning over the foot of my bed, looking at me, was a figure swathed in a rotten and tattered veiling. This shroud passed over the head, but left both eyes and the right side of the face bare. It then followed the line of the arm down to where the hand grasped the bed-end. The face was not entirely that of a skull, though the eyes and the flesh of the face were totally gone. There was a thin, dry skin drawn tightly over the features, and there was some skin left on the hand. One wisp of hair crossed the forehead. It was perfectly still. I looked at it, and it looked at me, and my brains turned dry and hot in my head. I had still got the pear of the electric lamp in my hand, and I played idly with it; only I dared not turn the light out again. I shut my eyes, only to open them in a hideous terror the same second. The thing had not moved. My heart was thumping, and the sweat cooled me as it evaporated. Another cinder tinkled in the grate, and a panel creaked in the wall.

"My reason failed me. For twenty minutes, or twenty seconds, I was able to think of nothing else but this awful figure, till there came, hurtling through the empty channels of my senses, the remembrances that Broughton and his friends had discussed me furtively at dinner. The dim possibility of its being a hoax stole gratefully into my unhappy mind, and once there, one's pluck came creeping back along a thousand tiny veins. My first sensation was one of blind unreasoning thankfulness that my brain was going to stand the trial. I am not a timid man, but the best of us needs some human handle to steady him in time of extremity, and in this faint but growing hope that after all it might be only a brutal hoax, I found the fulcrum that I needed. At last I moved.

"How I managed to do it I cannot tell you, but with one spring towards the foot of the bed I got within arm's-length and struck out one fearful blow with my fist at the thing. It crumbled under it, and my hand was cut to the bone. With a sickening revulsion after my terror, I dropped half-fainting across the end of the bed. So it was merely a foul trick after all. No doubt the trick had been played many a time before: no doubt Broughton and his friends had had some large bet among themselves as to what I should do when I discovered the gruesome thing. From my state of abject terror I found myself transported into an insensate anger. I shouted curses upon Broughton. I dived rather than climbed over the bed-end of the sofa. I tore at the robed skeleton—how well the whole thing had been carried out, I thought—I broke the skull against the floor, and stamped upon its dry bones. I flung the head away under the bed, and rent the brittle bones of the trunk in pieces. I snapped the thin thigh-bones across my knee, and flung them in different directions. The shin-bones I set up against a stool and broke with my heel. I raged like a Berserker against the loathly thing, and stripped the ribs from the backbone and slung the breastbone against the cupboard. My fury increased as the work of destruction went on. I tore the frail rotten veil into twenty pieces, and the dust went up over everything, over the clean blotting-paper and the silver inkstand. At last my work was done. There was but a raffle of broken bones and strips of parchment and crumbling wool. Then, picking up a piece of the skull—it was the cheek and temple bone of the right side, I remember—I opened the door and went down the passage to Broughton's dressing-room. I remember still how my sweat-dripping pyjamas clung to me as I walked. At the door I kicked and entered.

"Broughton was in bed. He had already turned the light on and seemed shrunken and horrified. For a moment he could hardly pull himself together. Then I spoke. I don't know what I said. Only I know that from a heart full and over-full with hatred and contempt, spurred on by shame of my own recent cowardice, I let my tongue run on. He answered nothing. I was amazed at my own fluency. My hair still clung lankily to my wet temples, my hand was bleeding profusely, and I must have looked a strange sight. Broughton huddled himself up at the head of the bed just as I had. Still he made no answer, no defence. He seemed preoccupied with something besides my reproaches, and once or twice moistened his lips with his tongue. But he could say nothing though he moved his hands now and then, just as a baby who cannot speak moves its hands.

"At last the door into Mrs. Broughton's rooms opened and she came in, white and terrified. 'What is it? What is it? Oh, in God's name! what is it?' she cried again and again, and then she went up to her husband and sat on the bed in her night-dress, and the two faced me. I told her what the matter was. I spared her husband not a word for her presence there. Yet he seemed hardly to understand. I told the pair that I had spoiled their cowardly joke for them. Broughton looked up.

"'I have smashed the foul thing into a hundred pieces,' I said. Broughton licked his lips again and his mouth worked. 'By God!' I shouted, 'it would serve you right if I thrashed you within an inch of your life. I will take care that not a decent man or woman of my acquaintance ever speaks to you again. And there,' I added, throwing the broken piece of the skull upon the floor beside his bed, 'there is a souvenir for you, of your damned work to-night!'

278

"Broughton saw the bone, and in a moment it was his turn to frighten me. He squealed like a hare caught in a trap. He screamed and screamed till Mrs. Broughton, almost as bewildered as myself, held on to him and coaxed him like a child to be quiet. But Broughton—and as he moved I thought that ten minutes ago I perhaps looked as terribly ill as he did—thrust her from him, and scrambled out of bed on to the floor, and still screaming put out his hand to the bone. It had blood on it from my hand. He paid no attention to me whatever. In truth I said nothing. This was a new turn indeed to the horrors of the evening. He rose from the floor with the bone in his hand and stood silent. He seemed to be listening. 'Time, time, perhaps,' he muttered, and almost at the same moment fell at full length on the carpet, cutting his head against the fender. The bone flew from his hand and came to rest near the door. I picked Broughton up, haggard and broken, with blood over his face. He whispered hoarsely and quickly, 'Listen, listen!' We listened.

"After ten seconds' utter quiet, I seemed to hear something. I could not be sure, but at last there was no doubt. There was a quiet sound as one moving along the passage. Little regular steps came towards us over the hard oak flooring. Broughton moved to where his wife sat, white and speechless, on the bed, and pressed her face into his shoulder.

"Then, the last thing that I could see as he turned the light out, he fell forward with his own head pressed into the pillow of the bed. Something in their company, something in their cowardice, helped me, and I faced the open doorway of the room, which was outlined fairly clearly against the dimly lighted passage. I put out one hand and touched Mrs. Broughton's shoulder in the darkness. But at the last moment I too failed. I sank on my knees and put my face in the bed. Only we all heard. The footsteps came to the door and there they stopped. The piece of bone was lying a yard inside the door. There was a rustle of moving stuff, and the thing was in the room. Mrs. Broughton was silent: I could hear Broughton's voice praying, muffled in the pillow: I was cursing my own cowardice. Then the steps moved out again on the oak boards of the passage, and I heard the sounds dying away. In a flash of remorse I went to the door and looked out. At the end of the corridor I thought I saw something that moved away. A moment later the passage was empty. I stood with my forehead against the jamb of the door almost physically sick.

"'You can turn the light on,' I said, and there was an answering flare. There was no bone at my feet. Mrs. Broughton had fainted. Broughton was almost useless, and it took me ten minutes to bring her to. Broughton only said one thing worth remembering. For the most part he went on muttering prayers. But I was glad afterwards to recollect that he had said that thing. He said in a colourless voice, half as a question, half as a reproach, 'You didn't speak to her.'

"We spent the remainder of the night together. Mrs. Broughton actually fell off into a kind of sleep before dawn, but she suffered so horribly in her dreams that I shook her into consciousness again. Never was dawn so long in coming. Three or four times Broughton spoke to himself. Mrs. Broughton would then just tighten her hold on his arm, but she could say nothing. As for me, I can honestly say that I grew worse as the hours passed and the light strengthened. The two violent reactions had battered down my steadiness of view, and I felt that the foundations of my life had been built upon the sand. I said nothing, and after binding up my hand with a towel, I did not move. It was better so. They helped me and I helped them, and we all three knew that our reason had gone very near to ruin that night. At last, when the light came in pretty strongly, and the birds outside were chattering and singing, we felt that we must do something. Yet we never moved. You might have thought that we should particularly dislike being found as we were by the servants: yet nothing of that kind mattered a straw, and an overpowering listlessness bound us as we sat, until Chapman, Broughton's man, actually knocked and opened the door. None of us moved. Broughton, speaking hardly and stiffly, said, 'Chapman you can come back in five minutes.' Chapman, was a discreet man, but it would have made no difference to us if he had carried his news to the 'room' at once.

"We looked at each other and I said I must go back. I meant to wait outside till Chapman returned. I simply dared not re-enter my bedroom alone. Broughton roused himself and said that he would come with me. Mrs. Broughton agreed to remain in her own room for five minutes if the blinds were drawn up and all the doors left open.

"So Broughton and I, leaning stiffly one against the other, went down to my room. By the morning light that filtered past the blinds we could see our way, and I released the blinds. There was nothing wrong with the room from end to end, except smears of my own blood on the end of the bed, on the sofa, and on the carpet where I had torn the thing to pieces."

Colvin had finished his story. There was nothing to say. Seven bells stuttered out from the fo'c'sle, and the answering cry wailed through the darkness. I took him downstairs.

"Of course I am much better now, but it is a kindness of you to let me sleep in your cabin."

THE SNOUT

EDWARD LUCAS WHITE

In his collection *Lukundoo and Other Stories,* where this tale from 1909 was first collected, American writer Edward Lucas White (1866–1934) claimed much of his macabre fiction was inspired by his dreams. While it does have a surreal, nightmarish quality, "The Snout" is equally memorable for its blend of hardboiled crime and supernatural horror.

I

I was not so much conning the specimens in the Zoölogical Garden as idly basking in the agreeable morning sunshine and relishing at leisure the perfect weather. So I saw him the instant he turned the corner of the building. At first, I thought I recognized him, then I hesitated. At first he seemed to know me and to be just about to greet me; then he saw past me into the cage. His eyes bulged; his mouth opened into a long egg-shaped oval, till you might almost have said that his jaw dropped; he made an inarticulate sound, partly a grunt, partly the ghost of a howl, and collapsed in a limp heap on the gravel. I had not seen a human being since I passed the gate, some distance away. No one came when I called. So I dragged him to the grass by a bench, untied his faded, shiny cravat, took off his frayed collar and unbuttoned his soiled neckband. Then I peeled his coat off him, rolled it up, and put it under his knees as he lay on his back. I tried to find some water, but could see none. So I sat down on the bench near him. There he lay, his legs and body on the grass, his head in the dry gutter, his arms on the pebbles of the path. I was sure I knew him, but I could not recall when or where we had encountered each other before. Presently he answered to my rough and ready treatment and opened his eyes, blinking at me heavily. He drew up his arms to his shoulders and sighed.

"Queer," he muttered, "I come here because of you and I meet you. Still I could not remember him and he had revived enough to read my face. He sat up.

281

"Don't try to stand up!" I warned him.

He did not need the admonition, but clung to the end of the bench, his head bowed wagglingly over his arms.

"Don't you remember," he asked thickly. "You said I had a pretty good smattering of an education on everything except Natural History and Ancient History. I'm hoping for a job in a few days, and I thought I'd put in the time and keep out of mischief brushing up. So I started on Natural History first and—"

He broke off and glared up at me. I remembered him now. I should have recognized him the moment I saw him, for he was daily in my mind. But his luxuriant hair, his tanned skin and above all his changed expression, a sort of look of acquired cosmopolitanism, had baffled me.

"Natural History!" he repeated, in a hoarse whisper. His fingers digging in the slats of the bench he wrenched himself round to face the cage.

"Hell!" he screamed. "There it is yet!"

He held on by the end iron-arm of the bench, shaking, almost sobbing. "What's wrong with you?" I queried. "What do think you see in that cage?"

"Do you see anything in that cage?" he demanded in reply.

"Certainly," I told him.

"Then for God's sake," he pleaded. "What do you see?"

I told him briefly.

"Good Lord," he ejaculated. "Are we both crazy'?"

"Nothing crazy about either of us," I assured him. "What we see in the cage is what is in the cage."

"Is there such a critter as that, honest?" he pressed me. I gave him a pretty full account of the animal, its habits and relationships.

"Well," he said, weakly, "I suppose you're telling the truth. If there is such a critter let's get where I can't see it."

I helped him to his feet and assisted him to a bench altogether out of sight of that building. He put 'on his collar and knotted his cravat. While I had held it I had noticed that, through its greasy condition, it showed plainly having been a very expensive cravat. His clothes I remarked were seedy, but had been of the very best when new.

"Let's find a drinking fountain," he suggested, "I can walk now." We found one not far away and at no great distance from it a shaded bench facing an agreeable view. I offered him a cigarette and we smoked. I meant to let him do most of the talking.

"Do you know," he began presently. "Things you said to me run in my head more than anything anybody ever said to me. I suppose it's because you're a sort of philosopher and student of human nature and what you say is true. For instance,

282

you said that criminals would get off clear three times out of four, if they just kept their mouths shut, but they have to confide in some one, even against all reason. That's just the way with me now."

"You aren't a criminal," I interrupted him. "You lost your temper and made a fool of yourself just once. If you'd been a criminal and had done what you did, you'd have likely enough got off, because you'd have calculated how to do it. As it was you put yourself in a position where everything was against you and you had no chance. We were all sorry for you."

"You most of all," he amplified. "You treated me bully."

"But we were all sorry for you," I repeated, "and all the jury too, and the judge. You're no criminal."

"How do you know," he demanded defiantly, "what I have done since I got out?"

"You've grown a pretty good head of hair," I commented.

"I've had time," he said. "I've been all over the world and blown in ten thousand dollars."

"And never seen—" I began.

He interrupted me at the third word.

"Don't say it," he shuddered. "I never had, nor heard of one. But I wasn't after caged animals while I had any money left. I didn't remember your advice and your other talk till I was broke. Now, it's just as you said, I've just got to tell you. That's the criminal in me, I suppose."

"You're no criminal," I repeated soothingly.

"Hell," he snarled, "a year in the pen makes a man a criminal, if he never was before."

"Not necessarily," I encouraged him.

"It's pretty sure to," he sighed. "They treated me mighty well and put me to bookkeeping, and I got my full good-conduct allowance. But I met professionals, and they never forget a man."

"Now it don't make any difference what I did when I got out, nor what I tried to do nor how I met Rivvin, nor how he put Thwaite after me.. No, nor how Thwaite got hold of me, nor what he said to me, nor anything, right up to the very night, till after we had started."

He looked me in the eye. His attitude became alert. I could see him warming to his narrative. In fact, when after very little rumination he began it, his early self dropped from him with his boyhood dialect and the jargon of his late associates. He was all the easy cosmopolitan telling his tale with conscious zest.

II

As if it had been broad day Thwaite drove the car at a terrific pace for nearly an hour. Then he stopped it while Rivvin put out every lamp. We had not met or overtaken anything, but when we started again through the moist, starless blackness it was too much for my nerves. Thwaite was as cool as if he could see. I could not so much as guess at him in front of me, but I could feel his self-confidence in every quiver of the car. It was one of those super-expensive makes which are, on any gear, at any speed, on any grade, as noiseless as a puma. Thwaite never hesitated in the gloom; he kept straight or swerved, crept or darted, whizzed or crawled for nearly an hour more. Then he turned sharp to the left and uphill. I could feel and smell the soaked, hanging boughs close above and about me, the wet foliage on them, and the deep sodden earth mold that squelched under the tires. We climbed steeply, came to a level and then backed and went forward a length or so a half dozen times, turning. Then we stopped dead. Thwaite moved things that clicked or thumped and presently said:

"Now I'll demonstrate how a man can fill his gasoline tank in the pitch dark if he knows the touch system."

After some more time he said: "Rivvin, go bury this."

Rivvin swore, but went. Thwaite climbed in beside me. When Rivvin returned he climbed in on the other side of me. He lit his pipe, Thwaite lit a cigar and looked at his watch. After I had lit too, Thwaite said:

"We've plenty of time to talk here and all you have to do is to listen. I'll begin at the beginning. When old Hiram Eversleigh died—"

"You don't mean—" I interrupted him.

"Shut up!" he snapped, "and keep your mouth shut. You'll have your say when I've done." I shut up.

"When old man Eversleigh died," he resumed, "the income of the fortune was divided equally among his sons. You know what the others did with their shares: palaces in New York and London and Paris, chateaux on the Breton Coast, deer and grouse moors in Scotland, steam yachts and all the rest of it, the same as they have kept it up ever since. At first Vortigern Eversleigh went in for all that sort of thing harder than any one of his brothers. But when his wife died, more than forty years ago, he stopped all that at once. He sold everything else, bought this place, put the wall round it and built that infinity of structures inside. You've seen the pinnacles and roofs of them, and that's all anybody I ever talked to has ever seen of them since they were finished about five years after his wife's death. You've seen the two gatehouses and you know each is big even for a millionaire's mansion. You can judge of the size and extent of the complication of buildings that make up the castle or

284

mansion-house or whatever you choose to call it. There Vortigern Eversleigh lived. Not once did he ever leave it that I can learn of. There he died. Since his death, full twenty years ago, his share of the Eversleigh income has been paid to his heir. No one has ever seen that heir. From what I'll tell you presently you'll see as I have that the heir is probably not a woman. But nobody knows anything about him, he has never been outside these miles of wall. Yet not one of the greedy, selfish Eversleigh grandsons and grand-daughters, and sons-in-law and daughters-in-law, has ever objected to the payment to that heir of the full entire portion of Vortigern Eversleigh, and that portion has been two hundred thousand dollars a month, paid in gold on the first banking day of each month. I found that out for sure, for there have been disputes about the division of Wulfstan Eversleigh's share and of Cedric Eversleigh's share and I made certain from the papers in the suits. All that money, or the value of it, has been either reinvested or spent inside that park wall. Not much has been reinvested. I got on the track of the heir's purchases. He buys musical instruments any quantity and at any price. Those were the first things I made sure of. And artists' materials, paints, brushes, canvas, tools, woods, clay, marble, tons of clay and great blocks of superfine-grained marble. He's no magpie collecting expensive trash for a whim; he knows what he wants and why; he has taste. He buys horses and saddlery and carriages, furniture and carpets and tapestries, pictures, all landscapes, never any figure pictures, he buys photographs of pictures by the ten thousand, and he buys fine porcelains, rare vases, table silver, ornaments of Venetian glass, silver and gold filigree, jewelry, watches, chains, gems, pearls, rubies, emeralds and—diamonds; diamonds!"

Thwaite's voice shook with excitement, though he kept it soft and even.

"Oh, I did two years investigating," he went on, "I know. People blabbed. But not any of the servants or grooms or gardeners. Not a word could I get, at first or second or third hand, from them or any of their relatives or friends. They keep dumb. They know which side their bread is buttered on. But some of the discharged tradesmen's assistants told all I wanted to know and I got it straight, though not direct. No one from outside ever gets into that place beyond the big paved courtyards of the gate-houses. Every bit of supplies for all that regiment of servants goes into the brownstone gate-house. The outer gates open and the wagon or whatever it is drives under the archway. There it halts. The outer gates shut and the inner gates open. It drives into the courtyard. Then the Major-domo (I suppose that wouldn't be too big a name for him) makes his selections. The inner gates of the other gateway open and the wagon drives under the archway and halts. The inner gates close fast and the outer gates open. That's the way with every wagon and only one enters at a time. Everything is carried through the gate-house to the smaller inner courtyard and loaded on the wagons of the estate to be driven up to the mansion.

"Everything like furniture, for instance, comes into the courtyard of the green-stone gate- house. There a sort of auditor verifies the inventory and receipts for the goods before two witnesses from the dealers and two for the estate. The consignment may be kept a day or a month; it may be returned intact or kept entire; any difference is settled for at once upon return of what is rejected. So with jewelry. I had luck. I found out for certain that more than a million dollars worth of diamonds alone have gone into this place in the last ten years and stayed there."

Thwaite paused dramatically. I never said a word and we sat there in the rear seat of that stationary auto, the leather creaking as we breathed, Rivyin sucking at his pipe, and the leaves dripping above us; not another sound.

"It's all in there," Thwaite began again. "The biggest stack of loot in North America. And this is going to be the biggest and most successful burglary ever perpetrated on this continent. And no one will ever be convicted for it or so much as suspected of it. Mark my words."

"I do," I broke in, "and I don't feel a bit better than when we started. You promised to explain and you said I'd be as eager and confident as you and Rivvin. I acknowledge the bait, admitting all you say is true, and it doesn't seem likely. But do you suppose any recluse millionaire eccentric is going to live unguarded? If he is careless himself his household are the reverse. By what you tell of the gate-houses there are precautions enough. Diamonds are tempting if you like, but so is the bullion in the mint. By your account all this accumulation of treasure you imagine is as safe where it is as the gold reserve in the United States Treasury. You scare me, you don't reassure me."

"Keep your head," Thwaite interrupted. "I'm no fool. I've spent years on this scheme. After I was sure of the prize I made sure of the means. There are precautions a-many, but not enough. How simple to put a watchman's cottage every hundred yards on the other side of the road across from the wall? They haven't done it. How simple to light the road and the outside of the wall? They haven't done that. Nor have they thought of any one of the twenty other simple outside precautions. The park's big enough to be lonely. And outside the wall is all dark, lonely road and unfenced, empty woods like this. They're overconfident. They think their wall and their gate-houses are enough. And they are not. They think their outside precautions are perfect. They are not. I know. I've been over that wall ten times, twenty times, fifty times. I've risked it and I have risked man-traps and spring guns and alarm wires. There aren't any. There isn't any night patrol, nor any regular day patrol, only casual gardeners and such. I know. I made sure of it by crawling all over the place on my belly like an Iroquois Indian in one of Cooper's novels. They are so confident of the potency of their wall that they haven't so much as a watch dog, nor any dog of any kind."

I was certainly startled. "No dog!" I exclaimed. "Are you sure?"

"Dead sure!" Thwaite returned, triumphantly, "And sure there never has been a dog on the place."

"How could you be sure of that?" I cavilled.

"I'm coming to that," Thwaite went on, "I could not get anybody that ever belonged to the place to talk, but I managed to arrange to overhear two of them talking to each other; and more than once, too. Most of what they said was no use to me, but I overheard scraps I could piece together. There's a cross-wall that divides the park. In the smaller division, into which the lodge gates lead, are the homes of all the caretakers and servants, of the overseers and manager and of the estate doctor; for there is an estate doctor. He has two assistants, young men, frequently changed. He is married like most of the retinue. There is a sort of village of them inside the outer wall, outside the inner cross-wall. Some of them have been there thirty-five years. When they get too old they are pensioned off and sent away, somewhere; far off, for I could not get a clue to any pensioner.

"The valets or keepers, whichever they are, and there are many of them, to relieve each other, are all unmarried except two or three of the most trusted. The rest are all brought over from England and shipped back usually after four or five years of service. The men I overheard were two of these, an old hand soon to finish his enlistment, as he called it, and go home, and the lad he was training to take his place. All these specials have plenty of time off to spend outside. They'd sit over their beer for two or three hours at a time, chatting on, Appleshaw giving points to Kitworth or Kitworth asking questions. I learnt from them about the cross-wall."

"Never's been a woman t' other side of it since it was built," Appleshaw said. "I shouldn't have thought it," Kitworth ruminated.

"Can you imagine a woman," Appleshaw asked, "standin' him?"

"No," Kitworth admitted, "I hardly can. But some women'll stand more'n a man."

"Anyhow," Appleshaw added, "he can't abide the sight of a woman."

"Odd," said Kitworth, "I've heard his kind are all the other way."

"They are, as we know," Appleshaw replied, "havin' watched 'em; but he ain't. He can't endure 'em."

"I suppose it's the same way about dogs," Kit-worth reflected.

287

"No dog'd ever get used to him," Appleshaw agreed, "and he's that afraid of dogs, they're not allowed inside the place anywhere. Never's been one here since he was born, I'm told. No, nor any cat, either, not one even."

Another time I heard Appleshaw say:

"He built the museums, and the pavilion and the towers, the rest was built before he grew up."

Generally I could not hear much of Kitworth's utterances, he talked so low. I once heard Appleshaw reply:

'Sometimes nights and nights he'll be quiet as anybody, lights out early and sleep sound for all we know. Again he'll be up all night, every window blazin', or up late, till after midnight.

Whoever's on duty sees the night out, nobody else's business, unless they send an alarm for help, and that ain't often; not twice a year. Mostly he's as quiet as you or me, as long as he's obeyed.

"His temper's short though. Now he'll fly into a rage if he's not answered quick; again he'll storm if the watchers come near him uncalled."

Of long inaudible whispers I caught fragments.

Once:

"Oh, then he'll have no one near. You can hear him sobbing like a child. When he's worst you'll hear him, still nights, howlin' and screamin' like a lost soul."

Again:

"Clean-fleshed as a child and no more hairy than you or me." Again:

"Fiddle? No violinist can beat him. I've listened hours. It makes you think of your sins. An' then it'll change an' you remember your first sweetheart, an' spring rains and flowers, an' when you was a child on your mother's knee. It tears your heart out."

The two phrases that seemed to mean most were: "He won't stan' any interference."

And:

"Never a lock touched till daylight after he's once locked in."

"Now what do you think?" Thwaite asked me.

"It sounds," I said, "as if the place were a one-patient asylum for a lunatic with long lucid intervals."

"Something like that," Thwaite answered, "but there seems to be more in it than that. I can't make all the things I hear fit. Appleshaw said one thing that runs in my head:

"Seem' him in the suds give me a turn:'

And Kitworth said once:

"It was the bright colors alongside of it that made my blood run cold." And Appleshaw said more than once, in varying words, but always with the same meaning tone:

"You'll never get over bein' afraid of him. But you'll respect him more and more, you'll almost love him. You won't fear him for his looks, but for his awful wisdom. He's that wise, no man is more so."

Once Kitworth answered: "I don't envy Sturry locked in there with him."

"Sturry nor none of us that's his most trusted man for the time bein' is not to be envied," Appleshaw agreed. "But you'll come to it, as I have, if you're the man I take you for."

"That's about all I got from listening," Thwaite went on, "the rest I got from watching and scouting. I made sure of the building they call the Pavilion, that's his usual home. But sometimes he spends his nights in one or the other of the towers, they stand all by themselves. Sometimes the lights are all out after ten o'clock or even nine; then again they're on till after midnight. Sometimes they come on late, two o'clock or three. I have heard music too, violin music, as Appleshaw described it, and organ music, too; but no howling. He is certainly a lunatic, judging by the statuary."

"Statuary?" I queried.

"Yes," Thwaite said, "statuary. Big figures and groups, all crazy men with heads like elephants or American eagles, perfectly crazy statuary. But all well-done. They stand all about the park. The little, square building between the Pavilion and the green tower is his sculpture studio."

"You seem to know the place mighty well," I said.

"I do," Thwaite assented, "I've gotten to know it well. At first I tried nights like this. Then I dared starlight. Then I dared even moonlight. I've never had a scare. I've sat on the front steps of the Pavilion at one o'clock of starlight night and never been challenged. I even tried staying in all day, hiding in some bushes, hoping to see him."

"Ever see him?" I inquired.

"Never," Thwaite answered, "I've heard him though. He rides horseback after dark. I've watched the horse being led up and down in front of the Pavilion, till it got too dark to see it from where I was hid. I've heard it pass me in the dark. But I could never get the horse against the sky to see what was on it. Hiding and getting downhill of a road, close to it, don't go together."

"You didn't see him the day you spent there?" I insisted.

"No," Thwaite said, "I didn't. I was disappointed too. For a big auto purred up to the Pavilion entrance and stood under the porte cochère. But when it spun round the park there was nobody in it, only the chauffeur in front and a pet monkey on the back seat."

"A pet monkey!" I exclaimed.

"Yes," he said. "You know how a dog, a Newfoundland, or a terrier, will sit up in an auto and look grand and superior and enjoy himself? Well, that monkey sat there just like that turning his head one way and the other taking in the view."

"What was he like?" I asked.

"Sort of dog-faced ape," Thwaite told me, "more like a mastiff." Rivvin grunted.

"This isn't business," Thwaite went on, "we've got to get down to business. The point is the wall is their only guard, there's no dog, perhaps because of the pet monkey as much as anything else. They lock Mr. Eversleigh up every night with only one valet to take care of him. They never interfere whatever noise they hear or light they see, unless the alarm is sent out and I have located the alarm wires you are to cut. That's all. Do you go?"

Rivvin was sitting close to me, half on me. I could feel his great muscles and the butt of his pistol against my hip.

"I come with you," I said. "Of your own accord?" Thwaite insisted. The butt of that pistol moved as Rivvin breathed. "I come of my own accord," I said.

III

Afoot Thwaite led as confidently as he had driven the car. It was the stillest, pitchiest night I ever experienced, without light, air, sound or smell to guide anyone: through that fog Thwaite sped like a man moving about his own bedroom, never for a second at a loss.

"Here's the place," he said at the wall, and guided my hand to feel the ring-bolt in the grass at its foot. Rivvin made a back for him and I scrambled up on the two. Tip-toe on Thwaite's shoulders I could just finger the coping.

"Stand on my head, you fool!" he whispered.

I clutched the coping. Once astraddle of it I let down one end of the silk ladder. "Fast!" breathed Thwaite from below.

I drew it taut and went down. The first sweep of my fingers in the grass found the other ring-bolt. I made the ladder fast and gave it the signal twitches. Rivvin came over first, then Thwaite. Through the park he led evenly. When he halted he caught me by the elbow and asked:

"Can you see any lights?"

"Not a light," I told him.

"Same here," he said, "there are no lights. Every window is dark. We're in luck."
He led again for a while. Stopping he said only:

"Here's where you shin up. Cut every wire, but don't waste time cutting any twice. The details of his directions were exact. I found every handhold and foothold as he had schooled me. But I needed all my nerve. I realized that no heavyweight like Rivvin or Thwaite could have done it. When I came down I was limp and tottery.

"Just one swallow!" Thwaite said, putting a flask to my lips. Then we went on. The night was so black and the fog so thick that I saw no loom of the building till we were against its wall.

"Here's where you go in," Thwaite directed.

Doubly I understood why I was with them. Neither could have squeezed through that aperture in the stone. I barely managed it. Inside, instead of the sliding crash I had dreaded, I landed with a mere crunch, the coal in that bin was not anthracite. Likewise the bin under the window was for soft-coal. I blessed my luck and felt encouraged. The window I got open without too much work. Rivvin and Thwaite slid in. We crunched downhill four or five steps and stood on a firm floor. Rivvin flashed his electric candle boldly round. We were between a suite of trim coal-bins and a battery of serried furnaces. There was no door at either end of the open space in which we stood. I had a momentary vision of the alternate windows and coal-chutes above the bins, of two big panels of shiny, colored tiling, of clear brick-work, fresh-painted, jetty iron and dazzling-white brass-ringed asbestos, of a black vacancy between two furnaces. Toward that I half heard, half felt Rivvin turn. During the rest of our adventure he led, Thwaite followed and I mostly tagged or groped after Thwaite, often judging of their position or movement by that combination of senses which is neither hearing nor touch, though partly both.

Rivvin's torch flashed again. We were in a cement-floored, brick-walled passage, with a door at each end and on the side facing us doors in a bewildering row. In the darkness that came after the flash I followed the others to the right. Well through the doorway we stood still, breathing and listening. When Rivvin illuminated our environment we saw about us thousands of bottles, all set aslant, neck down, in tiers of racks that reached to the ceiling. Edging between them we made the circuit of the cellar, but found no sign of any door save that by which we had entered. A whispered growl from Rivvin, a nudge from Thwaite and we went back the full length of the passage. Again we found ourselves in a wine vault, the duplicate of that we had left, and with the same peculiarity.

Our curiosity overcame any prudence. Rivvin, instead of flashing his torch at intervals, kept the light steady, and we scrutinized, examined and whispered our astonishment. As in its fellow there was not in all this vault any spare space, the aisles were narrow, the racks reached the girders supporting the flat arches, every rack was so full that a holder empty of its bottle was scarcely findable. And there was not in all that great cellar, there was not among all those tens of thousands of bottles a magnum, or a quart or even a pint. They were all splits. We handled a number and all had the same label. I know now what the device was, from seeing it so often and so much larger afterwards, but there it seemed a picture of a skirt-dancer leading an alligator by a dog chain. There was no name of any wine or liquor on any bottle, but each label had a red number, 17, or 45 or 328, above the picture, and under it:

"Bottled for Hengist Eversleigh."

"We know his name now," Thwaite whispered. Back in the passage Rivvin took the first door to the left. It brought us to an easy stone stair between walls, which turned twice to the left at broad landings.

When we trod a softer footing we stood a long time breathing cautiously and listening. Presently Rivvin flashed his light. It showed to our left a carpeted stair, the dull red carpet bulging up over thick pads and held down by brass stair-rods; the polished quartered oak of the molded door-jamb or end of wainscot beyond it; the floor-covering of brownish-yellow or yellowish brown linoleum or something similar, made to look like inlaid wood; and the feet, legs and thighs of a big stocky man. The light shone but the fraction of a second, yet it showed plain his knee-breeches, tight stockings on his big calves, and bright buckles at his knees and on his low shoes.

There was no loud sound, but the blurred brushy noise of a mute struggle. I backed against a window-sill and could back no further. All I could hear was the shuffling, rasping sounds of the fight, and panting that became a sort of gurgle.

Again the light flashed and stayed full bright. I saw that it was Thwaite struggling with the man, and that one of his big hands was on Thwaite's throat. Thwaite had him round the neck and his face was against Thwaite's chest. His hair was brownish. Rivvin's slung-shot crunched horribly on his skull. Instantly the light went out.

Thwaite, radiating heat like a stove, stood gasping close by me. I heard no other noise after the body thudded on the floor except that on the carpeted stair I seemed to hear light treads, as it were of a big dog or of a frightened child, padding away upward.

"Did you hear anything?" I whispered.

Rivvin punched me.

After Thwaite was breathing naturally, he turned on his torch and Rivvin did the same. The dead man was oldish, over fifty I should judge, tall, large in all his dimensions, and spare, though heavy. His clothing was a gold-laced livery of green velvet, with green velvet knee breeches, green silk stockings and green leather pumps. The four buckles were gold.

Thwaite startled me by speaking out loud.

"I take it, Rivvin," he said, "this is the trusted valet. He would have yelled if there had been anybody to call. Either we have this building to ourselves or we have no one to deal with except Mr. Hengist Eversleigh."

Rivvin grunted.

"If he is here," Thwaite went on, "he's trying to send the alarm over the cut wires, or he's frightened and hiding. Let's find him and finish him, if he's here, and then find his diamonds. Anyway let's find those diamonds."

Rivvin grunted.

Swiftly they led from room to room and floor to floor. Not a door resisted. We had been curious and astonished in the wine-vaults; above we were electrified and numb. We were in a palace of wonders, among such a profusion of valuables that even Rivvin, after the second or third opportunity, ceased any attempt to pocket or bag anything. We came upon nothing living, found no door locked and apparently made the tour of the entire building.

When they halted, I halted. We were delirious with amazement, frantic with inquisitiveness, frenzied with curiosity, incredulous, hysterical, dazed and quivering.

Thwaite spoke in the dark.

"I'm going to see this place plain, all over it, if I die for it."

They flashed their torches. We were right beside the body of the murdered footman. Rivvin and Thwaite did not seem to mind the corpse. They waved their torches until one fell on an electric-light button.

"Hope those wires are underground," Thwaite remarked. He pushed the button and the electric lights came on full and strong. We were apparently at the foot of the back stairs, in a sort of lobby, an expanded passage-way out of which opened several doors.

We all three regarded the knobs of those doors. As we had half seen by flash-light on every door everywhere each door had two knobs, one like any door-knob, the other about half way between it and the floor. Rivvin opened one which proved to lead into a broom closet. He tried the knobs, Thwaite and I watching too. The lock and latch were at the upper knob, but controlled by either knob indifferently. They tried another door, but my eyes would roam to the dead body.

Rivvin and Thwaite paid no more attention to it than if it had not been there. I had never seen but one killed man before and neither wanted to be reminded of that one nor relished the sight of this one. I stared down the blackness of the stone stair up which we had come or glanced into the dimness of the padded stairway.

Then Rivvin, feeling inside the open door, found the button and turned on the lights. It was a biggish dining-room, the four corners cut off by inset glass-framed shelved closets, full of china and glassware. The furniture was oak.

"Servants dining-room," Thwaite commented.

Turning on the lights in each we went through a series of rooms; a sort of sitting-room, with card-tables and checker-boards; a library walled with bookcases and open book-shelves, its two stout oak tables littered with magazines and news-papers; a billiard room with three tables, a billiard-table, a pool-table and one for bagatelle; a sort of lounging room, all leather-covered sofas and deep armchairs; an entry with hat-hooks and umbrella-stands, the outer door dark oak with a great deal of stained glass set in and around it.

"All servants' rooms," Thwaite commented. "Every bit of the furniture is natural man-size. Let's go on."

Back we went along a passage and into a big kitchen beyond the dining-room. "Never mind the pantries till we come down again," Thwaite commanded. "Let's go upstairs. We'll do the banqueting-hall after those bedrooms, and the writing rooms and study last. I want a real sight of those pictures."

They passed the dead flunkey as if he had not been there at all. On the floor above Thwaite touched Rivvins' elbow.

"I forgot these," he said.

We inspected a medium-sized sitting-room with a round center-table, an arm-chair drawn up by it, and in the armchair a magazine and a sort of wadded smoking-jacket. Next this room was a bedroom and a bathroom.

"Mr. Footman's quarters," Thwaite remarked, staring unconcernedly at a pho-tograph of a dumpy young woman and two small children, set on the bureau. "All man-size furniture here, too."

Rivvin nodded.

Up the second flight of that back-stair we went again. It ended in a squarish hallway or lobby or room with nothing in it but two settees. It had two doors.

Rivvin pushed one open, felt up and down for the electric button and found it. We all three gasped; we almost shouted. We had had glimpses of this gallery before, but the flood of light from a thousand bulbs under inverted trough-reflectors dazzled us; the pictures fairly petrified us.

The glare terrified me.

"Surely we are crazy," I objected, "to make all this illumination. It's certain to give the alarm."

"Alarm nothing," Thwaite snapped. "Haven't I watched these buildings night after night. I told you he is never disturbed at any hour, lights or no lights."

My feeble protest thus brushed away I became absorbed, like the others, in those incredible paintings. Rivvin was merely stupidly dazed in uncomprehending wonder, Thwaite keenly speculative, questing for a clue to the origin of their peculiarities, I totally bewildered at the perfection of their execution, shivering at their uncanniness.

The gallery was all of ninety feet long, nearly thirty wide and high. Apparently it had a glass roof above the rectangle of reflectors. The pictures covered all four walls, except the little door at either end. None was very small and several were very large. A few were landscapes, but all had figures in them, most were crowded with figures.

Those figures.

They were human figures, but not one had a human head. The heads were invariably those of birds, animals or fishes, generally of animals, some of common animals, many of creatures I had seen pictures of or had heard of, some of imaginary creatures like dragons or griffons, more than half of the heads either of animals I knew nothing of or which had been invented by the painter.

Close to me when the lights blazed out was a sea picture, blurred grayish foggy weather and a heavy ground-swell; a strange other-world open boat with fish heaped in the bottom of it and standing among them four human figures in shining boots like rubber boots and wet, shiny, loose coats like oilskins, only the boots and skins were red as claret, and the four figures had hyenas' heads. One was steering and the others were hauling at a net. Caught in the net was a sort of merman, but different from the pictures of mermaids. His shape was all human except the head and hands and feet; every bit of him was covered with fish-scales all rainbowy. He had flat broad fins in place of hands and feet and his head was the head of a fat hog. He was thrashing about in the net in an agony of impotent effort. Queer as the picture was it had a compelling impression of reality, as if the scene were actually happening before our eyes.

Next it was a picnic in a little meadow by a pond between woods with mountains behind it higher up. Every one of the picnickers about the white tablecloth spread on the grass had the head of a different animal, one of a sheep, one of a camel, and the rest of animals like deer, not one of them known to me.

Then next to that was a fight of two compound creatures shaped like centaurs, only they had bulls' bodies, with human torsos growing out of them, where the necks ought to be, the arms scaly snakes with open-mouthed, biting heads in place of hands; and instead of human heads roosters' heads, bills open and pecking. Under the creatures in place of bulls' hoofs were yellow roosters' legs, stouter than chickens' legs and with short thick toes, and long sharp spurs like game roosters'. Yet these fantastic chimeras appeared altogether alive and their movements looked natural, yes that's the word, natural.

Every picture was as complete a staggerer as these first three. Every one was signed in the lower left hand corner in neat smallish letters of bright gold paint:

"Hengist Eversleigh"

and a date.

"Mr. Hengist Eversleigh is a lunatic that's certain," Thwaite commented, "but he unquestionably knows how to paint."

There must have been more than fifty pictures in that gallery, maybe as many as seventy-five, and every one a nightmare.

Beyond was a shorter gallery of the same width, end on to the side of the first, and beyond that the duplicate of the first; the three taking up three sides of the building. The fourth side was a studio, the size of the second gallery; it had a great skylight of glass tilted sideways all along over one whole wall. It was white-washed, very plain and empty-looking, with two easels, a big one and a little one.

On the little one was a picture of some vegetables and five or six little fairies, as it were, with children's bodies and mice's heads, nibbling at a carrot.

On the big one was a canvas mostly blank. One side of it had a palm-tree in splashy, thick slaps of paint and under it three big crabs with cocoanuts in their claws. A man's feet and legs showed beside them and the rest was unfinished.

The three galleries had fully three hundred paintings, for the smaller gallery contained only small canvases. Besides being impressed with the grotesqueness of the subjects and the perfection of the drawing and coloring, two things struck me as to the pictures collectively.

First, there was not represented in any one of all those paintings any figure of a woman or any female shape of any kind. The beast-headed figures were all, whether clothed or nude, figures of men. The animals, as far as I could see, were all males.

Secondly, nearly half of the pictures were modifications, or parallels or emulations (I could hardly say travesties or imitations), of well-known pictures by great artists, paintings I had seen in public galleries or knew from engravings or photographs or reproductions in books or magazines.

There was a picture like Washington crossing the Delaware and another like Washington saying farewell to his generals. There was a batch of Napoleon pictures; after the paintings of Napoleon at Austerlitz, at Friedland, giving the eagles to his regiments, on the morning of Waterloo, coming down the steps at Fontainebleau, and on the deck of the ship going to St. Helena. There were dozens of other pictures of generals or kings or emperors reviewing victorious armies; two or three of Lincoln. One that hit me hardest, obviously after some picture I had never seen or heard of, of the ghost of Lincoln, far larger than a life-size man, towering above the surviving notabilities of his time on the grandstand reviewing the homecoming Federal army marching through Washington.

In every one of these pictures, the dominant figure, whether it stood for Lincoln, Napoleon, Washington, or some other general or ruler; whatever uniform or regalia clothed its human shape, had the same head. The heads of the fighting men in all these pictures were those of dogs, all alike in any one picture, but differing from one to another; terriers or wolf-hounds or mastiffs or what not. The heads of any men not soldiers were those of oxen or sheep or horses or some other mild sort of animal. The head of the dominant figure I then took to be invented, legendary, fabulous—oh, that's not the word I want."

"Mythological?" I suggested, the only interruption I interjected into his entire narrative.

Yes, mythological, he returned. I thought it was a mythological creature. The long-jawed head, like a hound's; the little pointed yellow beard under the chin; the black, naked ears, like a hairless dog's ears and yet not doggy, either; the ridge of hair on top of the skull; the triangular shape of the whole head; the close-set, small, beady, terribly knowing eyes; the brilliant patches of color on either side of the muzzle; all these made a piercing impression of individuality and yet seemed not so much actual as mythological.

It takes a great deal longer to tell what we saw on that third floor than it took to see it. All round the galleries under the pictures were cases of drawers, solidly built in one length like a counter and about as high. Thwaite went down one side of the gallery and Rivvin down the other, pulling them out and slamming them shut again. All I saw held photographs of pictures. But Rivvin and Thwaite were taking no chances and looked into every drawer. I had plenty of time to gaze about me and circulated at a sort of cantering trot around the green-velvet miniature sofas and settees placed back to back down the middle of the floor-space. It seemed to me that Mr. Hengist Eversleigh was a great master of figure and landscape drawing, color, light and perspective.

As we went down the duplicate staircase at the other corner from where we came up Thwaite said:

"Now for those bedrooms."

By the stair we found another valet's or footman's apartment, sitting-room, bed-room and bathroom, just like the one by the other stair. And there were four more between them, under the studio and over the lounging-rooms.

On the east and west sides of the building were "the" bedrooms, twelve apart-ments, six on each side; each of the twelve made up of a bedroom, a dressing-room and a bathroom.

The beds were about three feet long, and proportionately narrow and low. The furniture, bureaus, tables, chairs, chests-of-drawers and the rest, harmonized with the dimensions of the beds, except the cheval-glasses and wall-mirrors which reached the ceilings. The bathtubs were almost pools, about nine feet by six and all of three feet deep, each a single block of porcelain.

The shapes and sizes and styles of the furniture were duplicated all through, but the colors varied, so that the twelve suites were in twelve colors; black, white, gray and brown, and light and dark yellow, red, green and blue; wall coverings, hangings, carpets and rugs all to match in each suite. The panels of the walls had the same picture, how-ever, repeated over and over, two, four or six times to a room and in every suite alike.

This picture was the design I had failed to make out on the labels of the bottles. It was set as a medallion in each panel of the blue or red walls, or whatever other color they were. The background of the picture was a vague sort of palish sky and blurred, hazy clouds above tropical-looking foliage. The chief figure was an angel, in flowing white robes, floating on silvery-plumed wings widespread. The angel's face was a human face, the only human face in any picture in that palace, the face of a grave, gentle, rather girlish young man.

The creature the angel was leading was a huge, bulky crocodile, with a gold col-lar about its neck, and a gold chain from that, not to the angel's hand, but to a gold fetter about his wrist.

Under each picture was a verse of four lines, always the same.

> "Let not your baser nature drag you down.
> Utter no whimper, not one sigh or moan,
> Hopeless of respite, solace, palm or crown
> Live out your life unflinching and alone."

I saw it so often I shall never forget it.

The bathrooms were luxurious in the extreme, a needle-bath, a shower-bath, two basins of different sizes in each, besides the sunk pool-tub. The dressing-rooms has each a variety of wardrobes. One or two we opened, finding in each several suits of little clothes, as if for a boy under six years old. One closet had shelf above shelf of small shoes, not much over four inches long.

"Evidently," Thwaite remarked, "Hengist Eversleigh is a dwarf, whatever else he is." Rivvin left the wardrobes and closets alone after the first few.

Each bedroom had in it nothing but the bed and on each side of it a sort of wine-cooler, like a pail with a lid, but bigger, set on three short legs so that its top was level with the bed. We opened most of them; every one we opened was filled with ice, bedded in which were several half-pint bottles. Every one of the twelve beds had the covers carefully turned down. Not one showed any sign of having been occupied. The wine-coolers were solid silver but we left them where they were. As Thwaite remarked, it would have taken two full-sized freight cars to contain the silver we had seen.

In the dressing-rooms the articles like brushes and combs on the bureaus were all of gold, and most set with jewels. Rivvin began to fill a bag with those entirely of metal, but even he made no attempt to tear the backs off the brushes or to waste energy on any other breakage. By the time we had scanned the twelve suites Rivvin could barely carry his bag.

The front room on the south side of the building was a library full of small, showily-bound books in glass-fronted cases all the way to the ceiling, covering every wall except where the two doors and six windows opened. There were small, narrow tables, the height of those in the dressing-rooms. There were magazines on them and papers. Thwaite opened a bookcase and I another and we looked at three or four books. Each had in it a book-plate with the device of the angel and the crocodile.

Rivvin did not find the electric button in the main hallway and we went down the great broad, curving stair by our electric candles. Rivvin turned to the left and we found ourselves in the banquet hall as Thwaite had called it, a room all of forty by thirty and gorgeous beyond any description.

The diminutive table, not three feet square, was a slab of crystal-white glass set on silver-covered legs. The tiny armchair, the only chair in the big room, was solid silver, with a crimson cushion loose in it.

The sideboards and glass-fronted closets paralyzed us. One had fine china and cut glass; wonderful china and glass. But four held a table service of gold, all of pure gold; forks, knives, spoons, plates, bowls, platters, cups, everything; all miniature, but a profusion of everything. We hefted the pieces. They were gold. All the pieces were normal in shape except that instead of wine-glasses, goblets and tumblers were things like broad gravy-boats on stems or short feet, all lopsided, with one project-ing edge like the mouth of a pitcher, only broader and flatter. There were dozens of these. Rivvin filled two bags with what two bags would hold. The three bags were all we three could carry, must have been over a hundred and fifty pounds apiece.

"We'll have to make two trips to the wall," Thwaite said. "You brought six bags, didn't you, Rivvin?"

Rivvin grunted.

At the foot of the grand staircase Rivvin found the electric button and flooded the magnificent stairway with light.

The stair itself was all white marble, the rails yellow marble, and the paneling of the dado malachite. But the main feature was the painting above the landing. This was the most amazing of all the paintings we had come upon.

I remembered something like it, an advertisement of a root-beer or talcum pow-der, or some other proprietary article, representing all the nations of the earth and their rulers in the foreground congratulating the orator.

This picture was about twenty feet wide and higher than its width. There was a throne, a carved and jeweled throne, set on an eminence. There was a wide view on either side of the throne, and all filled with human figures with animal heads, an infinite throng, all facing the throne. Nearest it were figures that seemed meant for all the presidents and kings and queens and emperors of the world. I recognized the robes or uniforms of some of them. Some had heads taken from their national coat of arms, like the heads of the Austrian and Russian eagles. All these figures were paying homage to the figure that stood before the throne; the same monster we had seen in place of Lincoln or Washington or Napoleon in the paintings upstairs.

He stood proudly with one foot on a massive crocodile. He was dressed in a sort of revolutionary uniform, low shoes, with gold buckles, white stockings and knee-breeches, a red waistcoat, and a bright blue coat. His head was the same beast-head of the other pictures, triangular and strange, which I then though mythological.

Above and behind the throne floated on outspread silver wings the white-robed angel with the Sir Galahad face.

Rivvin shut off the lights almost instantly, but even in the few breaths while I looked I saw it all.

The three sacks of swag we put down by the front door. The room opposite the banquet-hall was a music room, with an organ and a piano, both with keys and keyboards far smaller than usual; great cases of music books; an array of brass instruments and cellos and more than a hundred violin cases. Thwaite opened one or two.

"These'd be enough to make our fortune," he said. "If we could get away with them." Beyond the music-room was the study. It had in it four desks, miniature in size and the old-fashioned model with drawers below, a lid to turn down and form a writing surface, and a sort of bookcase above with a peaked top. All were carved and on the lids in the carving we read:

JOURNAL

MUSIC

CRITICISM

BUSINESS

Thwaite opened the desk marked BUSINESS and pulled open the drawers. In pigeon-holes of the desk were bundles of new, clean greenbacks and treasury notes of higher denominations; five each of fives, tens, twenties, fifties and hundreds. Thwaite tossed one bundle of each to me and Rivvin and pocketed the rest.

He bulged.

One drawer had a division down the middle. One half was full of ten-dollar gold pieces, the other half of twenties.

"I've heard of misers," said Thwaite, "but this beats hell. Think of that crazy dwarf, a prisoner in this palace, running his hands through this and gloating over the cash he can never use.

Rivvin loaded a bag with the coin and when he had them all he could barely lift the bag. Leaving it where it lay before the desk he strode the length of the room and tried the door at the end.

It was fast.

Instantly Rivvin and Thwaite were like two terriers after a rat.

"This is where the diamonds are," Thwaite declared, "and Mr. Hengist Eversleigh is in there with them."

He and Rivvin conferred a while together.

"You kneel low," Thwaite whispered. "Duck when you open it. He'll fire over you. Then you've got him. See?"

Rivvin tip-toed to the door, knelt and tried key after key in the lock. There were at least twenty bulbs in the chandelier of that room and the light beat down on him. His red neck dew-lapped over the low collar of his lavenderish shirt, his great broad back showed vast and powerful.

On the other side of the doorway Thwaite stood, his finger at the electric button. Each had his slung-shot in his left hand. They had spun the cylinders of their revolvers and stuck them in their belts in front before Rivvin began work on the lock.

I heard a click.

Rivvin put up his hand.

The lights went out.

In the black dark we stood, stood until I could almost see the outlines of the windows; less black against the intenser blackness.

Soon I heard another click, and the grate of an opened door. Then a kind of snarl, a thump like a blow, a sort of strangling gasp, and the cushiony sounds of a struggle.

Thwaite turned on the lights.

Rivvin was in the act of staggering up from his knees. I saw a pair of small, pink hands, the fingers intertwined, locked behind Rivvin's neck. They slipped apart as I caught sight of them.

I had a vision of small feet in little patent leather silver-buckled low-shoes, of green socks, of diminutive legs in white trousers flashing right and left in front of Rivvin, as if he held by the throat a struggling child.

Next I saw that his arms were thrown up, wide apart.

He collapsed and fell back his full length with a dull crash. Then I saw the snout! Saw the wolf-jaws vised on his throat!

Saw the blood welling round the dazzling white fangs, and recognized the reality of the sinister head I had seen over and over in his pictures.

Rivvin made the fish-out-of-water contortions of a man being killed. Thwaite brought his slung-shot down on the beast-head skull.

The blow was enough to crush in a steel cylinder. The beast wrinkled its snout and shook its head from side to side, worrying like a bull-dog at Rivvin's throat.

Again Thwaite struck and again and again. At each blow the portentous head oscillated viciously. The awful thing about it to me was the two blue bosses on each side of the muzzle, like enamel, shiny and hard looking; and the hideous welt of red, like fresh sealing-wax, down between them and along the snout.

Rivvin's struggles grew weaker as the great teeth tore at his throat. He was dead before Thwaite's repeated blows drove in the splintered skull and the clenched jaws relaxed, the snout crinkling and contracting as the dog-teeth slid from their hold.

Thwaite gave the monster two or three more blows, touched Rivvin and fairly dashed out of the room, shouting.

"You stay here!"

I heard the sound of prying and sawing. There alone I looked but once at the dead cracksman. The thing that had killed him was the size of a four to six year old child, but more stockily built, looked entirely human up to the neck, and was dressed in a coat of bright dark blue, a vest of crimson velvet, and white duck trousers. As I looked the muzzle wriggled for the last time, the jaws fell apart and the carcass rolled sideways. It was the very duplicate in miniature of the figure in the big picture on the staircase landing.

Thwaite came dashing back. Without any sign of any qualm he searched Rivvin and tossed me two or three bundles of greenbacks.

He stood up.

He laughed.

"Curiosity," he said, "will be the death of me." Then he stripped the clothing from the dead monster, kneeling by it.

The beast-hair stopped at the shirt collar. Below that the skin was human, as was the shape, the shape of a forty-year-old man, strong and vigorous and well-made, only dwarfed to the smallness of a child.

Across the hairy breast was tatooed in blue,

"HENGIST EVERSLEIGH."

"Hell," said Thwaite.

He stood up and went to the fatal door. Inside he found the electric button. The room was small and lined with cases of little drawers, tier on tier, rows of brass knobs on mahogany.

Thwaite opened one.

It was velvet lined and grooved like a jeweler's tray and contained rings, the settings apparently emeralds.

Thwaite dumped them into one of the empty bags he had taken from Rivvin's corpse. The next case was of similar drawers of rings set with rubies. The first of these Thwaite dumped in with the emeralds.

But then he flew round the room pulling out drawers and slamming them shut, until he came upon trays of unset diamonds. These he emptied into his sack to the last of them, then diamond rings on them, other jewelry set with diamonds, then rubies and emeralds till the sack was full.

He tied its neck, had me open a second sack and was dumping drawer after drawer into that when suddenly he stopped.

His nose worked, worked horridly like that of the dead monster.

I thought he was going crazy and was beginning to laugh nervously, was on the verge of hysterics when he said:

"Smell! Try what you smell." I sniffed. "I smell smoke," I said.

"So do I," he agreed. "This place is afire."

"And we locked in!" I exclaimed.

"Locked in?" he sneered. "Bosh. I broke open the front door the instant I was sure they were dead. Come! Drop that empty bag. This is no time for haggling."

We had to step between the two corpses. Rivvin was horridly dead. The colors had all faded from the snout. The muzzle was all mouse-color.

When we had hold of the bag of coin, Thwaite turned off the electric lights and we struggled out with that and the bag of jewels, and went out into the hallway full of smoke.

"We can carry only these," Thwaite warned me. "We'll have to leave the rest." I shouldered the bag of coin, and followed him down the steps, across a gravel road, and, oh the relief of treading turf and feeling the fog all about me.

At the wall Thwaite turned and looked back. "No chance to try for those other bags," he said. In fact the red glow was visible at that distance and was fast becoming a glare. I heard shouts.

We got the bags over the wall and reached the car. Thwaite cranked up at once and we were off.

How we went I could not guess, nor in what directions, nor even how long. Ours was the only vehicle on the roads we darted along.

When the dawn light was near enough for me to see Thwaite stopped the car. He turned to me.

"Get out!" he said.

"What?" I asked.

He shoved his pistol muzzle in my face. "You've fifty thousand dollars in bank bills in your pockets," he said. "It's a half a mile down that road to a railway station. Do you understand English? Get out!"

I got out.

The car shot forward into the morning fog and was gone.

IV

He was silent a long time.

"What did you do then?" I asked.

"Headed for New York," he said, "and got on a drunk. When I came round I had barely eleven thousand dollars. I headed for Cook's office and bargained for a ten thousand dollar tour of the world, the most places and the longest time they'd give for the money; the whole cost on them. I not to need a cent after I started."

"What date was that?" I asked.

He meditated and gave me some approximate indications rather rambling and roundabout. "What did you do after you left Cook's?" I asked.

"I put a hundred dollars in a savings bank," he said. "Bought a lot of clothes and things and started.

"I kept pretty sober all round the world because the only way to get full was by being treated and I had no cash to treat back with.

"When I landed in New York I thought I was all right for life. But no sooner did I have my hundred and odd dollars in my pockets than I got full again. I don't seem able to keep sober."

"Are you sober now?" I asked.

"Sure," he asserted.

He seemed to shed his cosmopolitan vocabulary the moment he came back to everyday matters.

"Let's see you write what I tell you on this," I suggested, handing him a fountain-pen and a torn envelope, turned inside out.

Word by word after my dictation he wrote.

"Until you hear from me again

     Yours truly,

        No Name."

I took the paper from him and studied the handwriting. "How long were you on that spree?" I asked.

"Which?" he twinkled.

"Before you came to and had but eleven thousand dollars left," I explained. "I don't know," he said, "I didn't know anything I had been doing."

"I can tell you one thing you did," I said.

"What?" he queried.

"You put four packets, each of one hundred hundred-dollar bills, in a thin manila clasp-envelope, directed it to a New York lawyer and mailed the envelope to him with no letter in it, only a half sheet of dirty paper with nothing on it except: 'Keep this for me until I ask for it,' and the signature you have just written."

"Honest?" he enunciated incredulously. "Fact!" I said.

"Then you believe what I've told you," he exclaimed joyfully. "Not a bit I don't," I asseverated.

"How's that?" he asked.

"If you were drunk enough," I explained, "to risk forty thousand dollars in that crazy way, you were drunk enough to dream all the complicated nightmare you have spun out to me.

"If I did," he argued, "how did I get the fifty thousand odd dollars?"

"I'm willing to suppose you got it with no more dishonesty on your part," I told him, "than if you had come by it as you described."

"It makes me mad you won't believe me," he said. "I don't," I finished.

He gloomed in silence. Presently he said: "I can stand looking at him now," and led the way to the cage where the big blue-nosed mandril chattered his inarticulate bestialities and scratched himself intermittently.

He stared at the brute. "And you don't believe me?" he regretted.

"No, I don't," I repeated, "and I'm not going to. The thing's incredible."

"Couldn't there be a mongrel, a hybrid?" he suggested.

"Put that out of your head," I told him, "the whole thing's incredible."

"Suppose she'd seen a critter like this," he persisted, "just at the wrong time?"

"Bosh!" I said. "Old wives' tales! Superstition! Impossibility!"

"His head," he declared, "was just like that." He shuddered.

"Somebody put drops in some of your drink," I suggested. "Anyhow, let's talk about something else. Come and have lunch with me."

Over the lunch I asked him:

"What city did you like best of all you saw?"

"Paris for mine," he grinned, "Paris forever."

"I tell you what I advise you to do," I said.

"What's that?" he asked, his eyes bright on mine. "Let me buy you an annuity with your forty thousand," I explained, "an annuity payable in Paris. There's enough interest already to pay your way to Paris and leave you some cash till the first quarterly payment comes due."

"You wouldn't feel yourself defrauding the Eversleighs?" he questioned. "If I'm defrauding any people," I said, "I don't know who they are."

"How about the fire?" he insisted. "I'll bet you heard of it. Don't the dates agree?"

"The dates agree," I admitted. "And the servants were all dismissed, the remaining buildings and walls torn down and the place cut up and sold in portions just about as it would have been if your story were true."

"There now!" he ejaculated. "You do believe me!"

"I do not!" I insisted. "And the proof is that I'm ready to carry out my annuity plan for you."

"I agree," he said, and stood up from the lunch table.

"Where are we going now?" he inquired as we left the restaurant.

"Just you come with me," I told him, "and ask no questions."

I piloted him to the Museum of Archæology and led him circuitously to what I meant for an experiment on him. I dwelt on other subjects nearby and waited for him to see it himself.

He saw.

He grabbed me by the arm. "That's him!" he whispered. "Not the size, but his very expression, in all his pictures." He pointed to that magnificent, enigmatical black-diorite twelfth-dynasty statue which represents neither Anubis nor Seth, but some nameless cynocephalus god.

"That's him," he repeated. "Look at the awful wisdom of him." I said nothing.

"And you brought me here!" he cried. "You meant me to see this! You do believe!"

"No," I maintained. "I do not believe."

V

After I waved a farewell to him from the pier I never saw him again.

We had an extensive correspondence six months later when he wanted his annuity exchanged for a joint-life annuity for himself and his bride. I arranged it for him with less difficulty than I had anticipated. His letter of thanks, explaining that a French wife was so great an economy that the shrinkage in his income was more than made up for, was the last I heard from him.

As he died more than a year ago and his widow is already married, this story can do him no harm. If the Eversleighs were defrauded they will never feel it and my conscience, at least, gives me no twinges.

AUGUST HEAT

WILLIAM FRYER HARVEY

WILLIAM FRYER HARVEY (1885-1937) IS BEST KNOWN AS
THE AUTHOR OF "THE BEAST WITH FIVE FINGERS," THE TITLE
STORY FOR ONE OF HIS COLLECTIONS OF MACABRE FICTION. THIS
TALE, WHICH APPEARED FIRST IN HIS 1910 DEBUT COLLECTION
MIDNIGHT HOUSE AND OTHER TALES, IS PROBABLY HIS MOST
REPRINTED. A MASTERPIECE OF CONCISION AND DRAMATIC
TENSION, IT BUILDS TO A HORROR THAT CLIMAXES *AFTER* THE
STORY'S END.

PENISTONE ROAD, CLAPHAM,
August 20th, 190—.

I have had what I believe to be the most remarkable day in my life, and while the events are still fresh in my mind, I wish to put them down on paper as clearly as possible.

Let me say at the outset that my name is James Clarence Withencroft.

I am forty years old, in perfect health, never having known a day's illness.

By profession I am an artist, not a very successful one, but I earn enough money by my black-and-white work to satisfy my necessary wants.

My only near relative, a sister, died five years ago, so that I am independent. I breakfasted this morning at nine, and after glancing through the morning paper I lighted my pipe and proceeded to let my mind wander in the hope that I might chance upon some subject for my pencil.

The room, though door and windows were open, was oppressively hot, and I had just made up my mind that the coolest and most comfortable place in the neighbourhood would be the deep end of the public swimming bath, when the idea came.

I began to draw. So intent was I on my work that I left my lunch untouched, only stopping work when the clock of St. Jude's struck four.

The final result, for a hurried sketch, was, I felt sure, the best thing I had done. It showed a criminal in the dock immediately after the judge had pronounced sentence. The man was fat—enormously fat. The flesh hung in rolls about his chin; it creased his huge, stumpy neck. He was clean shaven (perhaps I should say a few days before he must have been clean shaven) and almost bald. He stood in the dock, his short, clumsy fingers clasping the rail, looking straight in front of him. The feeling that his expression conveyed was not so much one of horror as of utter, absolute collapse.

There seemed nothing in the man strong enough to sustain that mountain of flesh.

I rolled up the sketch, and without quite knowing why, placed it in my pocket. Then with the rare sense of happiness which the knowledge of a good thing well done gives, I left the house.

I believe that I set out with the idea of calling upon Trenton, for I remember walking along Lytton Street and turning to the right along Gilchrist Road at the bottom of the hill where the men were at work on the new tram lines.

From there onwards I have only the vaguest recollection of where I went. The one thing of which I was fully conscious was the awful heat, that came up from the dusty asphalt pavement as an almost palpable wave. I longed for the thunder promised by the great banks of copper-coloured cloud that hung low over the western sky.

I must have walked five or six miles, when a small boy roused me from my reverie by asking the time.

It was twenty minutes to seven.

When he left me I began to take stock of my bearings. I found myself standing before a gate that led into a yard bordered by a strip of thirsty earth, where there were flowers, purple stock and scarlet geranium. Above the entrance was a board with the inscription—

CHS. ATKINSON.   MONUMENTAL MASON.
WORKER IN ENGLISH AND ITALIAN MARBLES.

From the yard itself came a cheery whistle, the noise of hammer blows, and the cold sound of steel meeting stone.

A sudden impulse made me enter.

A man was sitting with his back towards me, busy at work on a slab of curiously veined marble. He turned round as he heard my steps and I stopped short.

It was the man I had been drawing, whose portrait lay in my pocket.

He sat there, huge and elephantine, the sweat pouring from his scalp, which he wiped with a red silk handkerchief. But though the face was the same, the expression was absolutely different.

He greeted me smiling, as if we were old friends, and shook my hand.

I apologised for my intrusion.

"Everything is hot and glary outside," I said. "This seems an oasis in the wilderness."

"I don't know about the oasis," he replied, "but it certainly is hot, as hot as hell. Take a seat, sir!"

He pointed to the end of the gravestone on which he was at work, and I sat down.

"That's a beautiful piece of stone you've got hold of," I said.

He shook his head. "In a way it is," he answered; "the surface here is as fine as anything you could wish, but there's a big flaw at the back, though I don't expect you'd ever notice it. I could never make really a good job of a bit of marble like that. It would be all right in the summer like this; it wouldn't mind the blasted heat. But wait till the winter comes. There's nothing quite like frost to find out the weak points in stone."

"Then what's it for?" I asked.

The man burst out laughing.

"You'd hardly believe me if I was to tell you it's for an exhibition, but it's the truth. Artists have exhibitions: so do grocers and butchers; we have them too. All the latest little things in headstones, you know."

He went on to talk of marbles, which sort best withstood wind and rain, and which were easiest to work; then of his garden and a new sort of carnation he had bought. At the end of every other minute he would drop his tools, wipe his shining head, and curse the heat.

I said little, for I felt uneasy. There was something unnatural, uncanny, in meeting this man.

I tried at first to persuade myself that I had seen him before, that his face, unknown to me, had found a place in some out-of-the-way corner of my memory, but I knew that I was practising little more than a plausible piece of self-deception.

Mr. Atkinson finished his work, spat on the ground, and got up with a sigh of relief.

"There! what do you think of that?" he said, with an air of evident pride. The inscription which I read for the first time was this—

SACRED TO THE MEMORY

OF

JAMES CLARENCE WITHENCROFT.

BORN JAN, 18TH, 1860.

HE PASSED AWAY VERY SUDDENLY

ON AUGUST 20TH, 190—

"In the midst of life we are in death."

For some time I sat in silence. Then a cold shudder ran down my spine. I asked him where he had seen the name.

"Oh, I didn't see it anywhere," replied Mr. Atkinson. "I wanted some name, and I put down the first that came into my head. Why do you want to know?"

"It's a strange coincidence, but it happens to be mine." He gave a long, low whistle.

"And the dates?"

"I can only answer for one of them, and that's correct."

"It's a rum go!" he said.

But he knew less than I did. I told him of my morning's work. I took the sketch from my pocket and showed it to him. As he looked, the expression of his face altered until it became more and more like that of the man I had drawn.

"And it was only the day before yesterday," he said, "that I told Maria there were no such things as ghosts!"

Neither of us had seen a ghost, but I knew what he meant.

"You probably heard my name," I said.

"And you must have seen me somewhere and have forgotten it! Were you at Clacton-on-Sea last July?"

I had never been to Clacton in my life. We were silent for some time. We were both looking at the same thing, the two dates on the gravestone, and one was right.

"Come inside and have some supper," said Mr. Atkinson.

His wife was a cheerful little woman, with the flaky red cheeks of the country-bred. Her husband introduced me as a friend of his who was an artist. The result was unfortunate, for after the sardines and watercress had been removed, she brought out a Doré Bible, and I had to sit and express my admiration for nearly half an hour.

I went outside, and found Atkinson sitting on the gravestone smoking.

We resumed the conversation at the point we had left off. "You must excuse my asking," I said, "but do you know of anything you've done for which you could be put on trial?"

He shook his head. "I'm not a bankrupt, the business is prosperous enough. Three years ago I gave turkeys to some of the guardians at Christmas, but that's all I can think of. And they were small ones, too," he added as an afterthought.

He got up, fetched a can from the porch, and began to water the flowers. "Twice a day regular in the hot weather," he said, "and then the heat sometimes gets the better of the delicate ones.

And ferns, good Lord! they could never stand it. Where do you live?"

I told him my address. It would take an hour's quick walk to get back home.

"It's like this," he said. "We'll look at the matter straight. If you go back home to-night, you take your chance of accidents. A cart may run over you, and there's always banana skins and orange peel, to say nothing of fallen ladders."

He spoke of the improbable with an intense seriousness that would have been laughable six hours before. But I did not laugh.

"The best thing we can do," he continued, "is for you to stay here till twelve o'clock. We'll go upstairs and smoke, it may be cooler inside."

To my surprise I agreed.

★ ★ ★

We are sitting now in a long, low room beneath the eaves. Atkinson has sent his wife to bed. He himself is busy sharpening some tools at a little oilstone, smoking one of my cigars the while.

The air seems charged with thunder. I am writing this at a shaky table before the open window.

The leg is cracked, and Atkinson, who seems a handy man with his tools, is going to mend it as soon as he has finished putting an edge on his chisel.

It is after eleven now. I shall be gone in less than an hour.

But the heat is stifling.

It is enough to send a man mad.

THE GROVE OF ASHTAROTH

JOHN BUCHAN

<small>Best known as the author of the classic mystery novel *The 39 Steps,* John Buchan (1875-1940) wrote prolifically in a number of genres, including horror and the supernatural. This story, first published in the June 1910 issue of the venerable British magazine *Blackwood's,* alternates between horror and romance in its depiction of a pagan survival into modern times.</small>

> *C'est enfin que dans leurs prunelles*
> *Rit et pleure—fastidieux—*
> *L'amour des choses éternelles,*
> *Des vieux morts et des anciens dieux!*
> —PAUL VERLAINE

I

We were sitting around the camp-fire, some thirty miles north of a place called Taqui, when Lawson announced his intention of finding a home. He had spoken little the last day or two, and I had guessed that he had struck a vein of private reflection. I thought it might be a new mine or irrigation scheme, and I was surprised to find that it was a country-house.

"I don't think I shall go back to England," he said, kicking a sputtering log into place. "I don't see why I should. For business purposes I am far more useful to the firm in South Africa than in Throgmorton Street. I have no relation left except a third cousin, and I have never cared a rush for living in town. That beastly house of mine in Hill Street will fetch what I gave for it—Isaacson cabled about it the other day, offering for furniture and all. I don't want to go into Parliament, and I hate shooting little birds and tame deer. I am one of those fellows who are born Colonial at heart, and I don't see why I shouldn't arrange my life as I please. Besides, for ten years I have been falling in love with this country, and now I am up to the neck."

He flung himself back in the camp-chair till the canvas creaked, and looked at me below his eyelids. I remember glancing at the lines of him, and thinking what a fine make of a man he was. In his untanned field-boots, breeches, and grey shirt, he looked the born wilderness-hunter, though less than two months before he had been driving down to the City every morning in the sombre regimentals of his class. Being a fair man, he was gloriously tanned, and there was a clear line at his shirt-collar to mark the limits of his sunburn. I had first known him years ago, when he was a broker's clerk working on half-commission. Then he had gone to South Africa, and soon I heard he was a partner in a mining house which was doing wonders with some gold areas in the North. The next step was his return to London as the new millionaire—young, good-looking, wholesome in mind and body, and much sought after by the mothers of marriageable girls. We played polo together, and hunted a little in the season, but there were signs that he did not propose to become the conventional English gentleman. He refused to buy a place in the country, though half the Homes of England were at his disposal. He was a very busy man, he declared, and had not time to be a squire. Besides, every few months he used to rush out to South Africa. I saw that he was restless, for he was always badgering me to go big-game hunting with him in some remote part of the earth. There was that in his eyes, too, which marked him out from the ordinary blond type of our countrymen. They were large and brown and mysterious, and the light of another race was in their odd depths.

To hint such a thing would have meant a breach of friendship, for Lawson was very proud of his birth. When he first made his fortune he had gone to the Heralds to discover his family, and these obliging gentlemen had provided a pedigree. It appeared that he was a scion of the house of Lowson or Lowieson, an ancient and rather disreputable clan on the Scottish side of the Border. He took a shooting in Teviotdale on the strength of it, and used to commit lengthy Border ballads to memory. But I had known his father, a financial journalist who never quite succeeded, and I had heard of a grandfather who sold antiques in a back street at Brighton. The latter, I think, had not changed his name, and still frequented the synagogue. The father was a progressive Christian, and the mother had been a blonde Saxon from the Midlands. In my mind there was no doubt, as I caught Lawson's heavy-lidded eyes fixed on me. My friend was of a more ancient race than the Lowsons of the Border.

"Where are you thinking of looking for your house?" I asked. "In Natal or in the Cape Peninsula? You might get the Fishers' place if you paid a price."

"The Fishers' place be hanged!" he said crossly. "I don't want any stuccoed, over-grown Dutch farm. I might as well be at Roehampton as in the Cape."

He got up and walked to the far side of the fire, where a lane ran down through the thorn-scrub to a gully of the hills. The moon was silvering the bush of the plains, forty miles off and three thousand feet below us.

"I am going to live somewhere hereabouts," he answered at last. I whistled. "Then you've got to put your hand in your pocket, old man. You'll have to make everything, including a map of the countryside."

"I know," he said; "that's where the fun comes in. Hang it all, why shouldn't I indulge my fancy? I'm uncommonly well off, and I haven't chick or child to leave it to. Supposing I'm a hundred miles from rail-head, what about it? I'll make a motor-road and fix up a telephone. I'll grow most of my supplies, and start a colony to provide labour. When you come and stay with me, you'll get the best food and drink on earth, and sport that will make your mouth water. I'll put Lochleven trout in these streams—at 6,000 feet you can do anything. We'll have a pack of hounds, too, and we can drive pig in the woods, and if we want big game there are the Mangwe flats at our feet. I tell you I'll make such a country-house as nobody ever dreamed of. A man will come plumb out of stark savagery into lawns and rose-gardens." Lawson flung himself into his chair again and smiled dreamily at the fire.

"But why here, of all places?" I persisted. I was not feeling very well and did not care for the country.

"I can't quite explain. I think it's the sort of land I have always been looking for. I always fancied a house on a green plateau in a decent climate looking down on the tropics. I like heat and colour, you know, but I like hills too, and greenery, and the things that bring back Scotland. Give me a cross between Teviotdale and the Orinoco, and, by Gad! I think I've got it here."

I watched my friend curiously, as with bright eyes and eager voice he talked of his new fad. The two races were very clear in him—the one desiring gorgeous-ness, the other athirst for the soothing spaces of the North. He began to plan out the house. He would get Adamson to design it, and it was to grow out of the landscape like a stone on the hillside. There would be wide verandahs and cool halls, but great fireplaces against winter time. It would all be very simple and fresh—"clean as morning" was his odd phrase; but then another idea supervened, and he talked of bringing the Tintorets from Hill Street. "I want it to be a civilised house, you know. No silly luxury, but the best pictures and china and books. I'll have all the furniture made after the old plain English models out of native woods. I don't want second-hand sticks in a new country. Yes, by Jove, the Tintorets are a great idea, and all those Ming pots I bought. I had meant to sell them, but I'll have them out here."

He talked for a good hour of what he would do, and his dream grew richer as he talked, till by the time we went to bed he had sketched something more like a palace than a country-house. Lawson was by no means a luxurious man. At present he was well content with a Wolseley valise, and shaved cheerfully out of a tin mug. It struck me as odd that a man so simple in his habits should have so sumptuous a taste in bric-à-brac. I told myself, as I turned in, that the Saxon mother from the Midlands had done little to dilute the strong wine of the East.

It drizzled next morning when we inspanned, and I mounted my horse in a bad temper. I had some fever on me, I think, and I hated this lush yet frigid tableland, where all the winds on earth lay in wait for one's marrow. Lawson was, as usual, in great spirits. We were not hunting, but shifting our hunting-ground, so all morning we travelled fast to the north along the rim of the uplands.

At mid-day it cleared, and the afternoon was a pageant of pure colour. The wind sank to a low breeze; the sun lit the infinite green spaces, and kindled the wet forest to a jewelled coronal. Lawson gaspingly admired it all, as he cantered bareheaded up a bracken-clad slope. "God's country," he said twenty times. "I've found it." Take a piece of Sussex downland; put a stream in every hollow and a patch of wood; and at the edge, where the cliffs at home would fall to the sea, put a cloak of forest muffling the scarp and dropping thousands of feet to the blue plains. Take the diamond air of the Gornergrat, and the riot of colour which you get by a West Highland lochside in late September. Put flowers everywhere, the things we grow in hothouses, geraniums like sun-shades and arums like trumpets. That will give you a notion of the countryside we were in. I began to see that after all it was out of the common.

And just before sunset we came over a ridge and found something better. It was a shallow glen, half a mile wide, down which ran a blue-grey stream in lings like the Spean, till at the edge of the plateau it leaped into the dim forest in a snowy cascade. The opposite side ran up in gentle slopes to a rocky knell, from which the eye had a noble prospect of the plains. All down the glen were little copses, half-moons of green edging some silvery shore of the burn, or delicate clusters of tall trees nodding on the hill brow. The place so satisfied the eye that for the sheer wonder of its perfection we stopped and stared in silence for many minutes.

Then "The House," I said, and Lawson replied softly, "The House!"

We rode slowly into the glen in the mulberry gloaming. Our transport waggons were half an hour behind, so we had time to explore. Lawson dismounted and plucked handfuls of flowers from the water meadows. He was singing to himself all the time—an old French catch about *Cadet Rousselle* and his *trois maisons*.

"Who owns it?" I asked.

"My firm, as like as not. We have miles of land about here. But whoever the man is, he has got to sell. Here I build my tabernacle, old man. Here, and nowhere else!"

In the very centre of the glen, in a loop of the stream, was one copse which even in that half light struck me as different from the others. It was of tall, slim, fairy-like trees, the kind of wood the monks painted in old missals. No, I rejected the thought. It was no Christian wood. It was not a copse, but a "grove"—one such as Artemis may have flitted through in the moonlight. It was small, forty or fifty yards in diameter, and there was a dark something at the heart of it which for a second I thought was a house.

We turned between the slender trees, and—was it fancy?—an odd tremor went through me. I felt as if I were penetrating the *temenos* of some strange and lovely divinity, the goddess of this pleasant vale. There was a spell in the air, it seemed, and an odd dead silence.

Suddenly my horse started at a flutter of light wings. A flock of doves rose from the branches, and I saw the burnished green of their plumes against the opal sky. Lawson did not seem to notice them. I saw his keen eyes staring at the centre of the grove and what stood there.

It was a little conical tower, ancient and lichened, but, so far as I could judge, quite flawless. You know the famous Conical Temple at Zimbabwe, of which prints are in every guide-book. This was of the same type, but a thousandfold more perfect. It stood about thirty feet high, of solid masonry, without door or window or cranny, as shapely as when it first came from the hands of the old builders. Again I had the sense of breaking in on a sanctuary. What right had I, a common vulgar modern, to be looking at this fair thing, among these delicate trees, which some white goddess had once taken for her shrine?

Lawson broke in on my absorption. "Let's get out of this," he said hoarsely and he took my horse's bridle (he had left his own beast at the edge) and led him back to the open. But I noticed that his eyes were always turning back and that his hand trembled.

"That settles it," I said after supper. "What do you want with your mediæval Venetians and your Chinese pots now? You will have the finest antique in the world in your garden—a temple as old as time, and in a land which they say has no history. You had the right inspiration this time."

I think I have said that Lawson had hungry eyes. In his enthusiasm they used to glow and brighten; but now, as he sat looking down at the olive shades of the glen, they seemed ravenous in their fire. He had hardly spoken a word since we left the wood.

"Where can I read about these things?" he asked, and I gave him the names of books. Then, an hour later, he asked me who were the builders. I told him the little I knew about Phœnician and Sabæn wanderings, and the ritual of Sidon and Tyre. He repeated some names to himself and went soon to bed.

As I turned in, I had one last look over the glen, which lay ivory and black in the moon. I seemed to hear a faint echo of wings, and to see over the little grove a cloud of light visitants. "The Doves of Ashtaroth have come back," I said to myself. "It is a good omen. They accept the new tenant." But as I fell asleep I had a sudden thought that I was saying something rather terrible.

II

Three years later, pretty nearly to a day, I came back to see what Lawson had made of his hobby. He had bidden me often to Welgevonden, as he chose to call it—though I do not know why he should have fixed a Dutch name to a countryside where Boer never trod. At the last there had been some confusion about dates, and I wired the time of my arrival, and set off without an answer. A motor met me at the queer little wayside station of Taqui, and after many miles on a doubtful highway I came to the gates of the park, and a road on which it was a delight to move. Three years had wrought little difference in the landscape. Lawson had done some planting—conifers and flowering shrubs and suchlike—but wisely he had resolved that Nature had for the most part forestalled him. All the same, he must have spent a mint of money. The drive could not have been beaten in England, and fringes of mown turf on either hand had been pared out of the lush meadows. When we came over the edge of the hill and looked down on the secret glen, I could not repress a cry of pleasure. The house stood on the farther ridge, the viewpoint of the whole neighbourhood; and its brown timbers and white rough-cast walls melted into the hillside as if it had been there from the beginning of things. The vale below was ordered in lawns and gardens. A blue lake received the rapids of the stream, and its banks were a maze of green shades and glorious masses of blossom. I noticed, too, that the little grove we had explored on our first visit stood alone in a big stretch of lawn, so that its perfection might be clearly seen. Lawson had excellent taste, or he had had the best advice.

The butler told me that his master was expected home shortly, and took me into the library for tea. Lawson had left his Tintorets and Ming pots at home after all. It was a long, low room, panelled in teak half-way up the walls, and the shelves held a multitude of fine bindings. There were good rugs on the parquet door, but no ornaments anywhere, save three. On the carved mantelpiece stood two of the old soapstone birds which they used to find at Zimbabwe, and between, on an ebony stand, a half moon of alabaster, curiously carved with zodiacal figures. My host had altered his scheme of furnishing, but I approved the change.

He came in about half-past six, after I had consumed two cigars and all but fallen asleep. Three years make a difference in most men, but I was not prepared for the change in Lawson. For one thing, he had grown fat. In place of the lean young man I had known, I saw a heavy, flaccid being, who shuffled in his gait, and seemed tired and listless. His sunburn had gone, and his face was as pasty as a city clerk's. He had been walking, and wore shapeless flannel clothes, which hung loose even on his enlarged figure. And the worst of it was, that he did not seem over-pleased to see me. He murmured something about my journey, and then flung himself into an arm-chair and looked out of the window.

I asked him if he had been ill.

"Ill! No!" he said crossly. "Nothing of the kind. I'm perfectly well."

"You don't look as fit as this place should make you. What do you do with yourself? Is the shooting as good as you hoped?"

He did not answer, but I thought I heard him mutter something like "shooting be damned."

Then I tried the subject of the house. I praised it extravagantly, but with conviction. "There can be no place like it in the world," I said.

He turned his eyes on me at last, and I saw that they were as deep and restless as ever. With his pallid face they made him look curiously Semitic. I had been right in my theory about his ancestry.

"Yes," he said slowly, "there is no place like it—in the world."

Then he pulled himself to his feet. "I'm going to change," he said. "Dinner is at eight. Ring for Travers, and he'll show you your room."

I dressed in a noble bedroom, with an outlook over the garden-vale and the escarpment to the far line of the plains, now blue and saffron in the sunset. I dressed in an ill temper, for I was seriously offended with Lawson, and also seriously alarmed. He was either very unwell or going out of his mind, and it was clear, too, that he would resent any anxiety on his account. I ransacked my memory for rumours, but found none. I had heard nothing of him except that he had been extraordinarily

successful in his speculations, and that from his hill-top he directed his firm's opera-
tions with uncommon skill. If Lawson was sick or mad, nobody knew of it.

Dinner was a trying ceremony. Lawson, who used to be rather particular in
his dress, appeared in a kind of smoking suit with a flannel collar. He spoke scarcely
a word to me, but cursed the servants with a brutality which left me aghast. A
wretched footman in his nervousness spilt some sauce over his sleeve. Lawson dashed
the dish from his hand and volleyed abuse with a sort of epileptic fury. Also he, who
had been the most abstemious of men, swallowed disgusting quantities of cham-
pagne and old brandy.

He had given up smoking, and half an hour after we left the dining-room he
announced his intention of going to bed. I watched him as he waddled upstairs with
a feeling of angry bewilderment. Then I went to the library and lit a pipe. I would
leave first thing in the morning—on that I was determined. But as I sat gazing at the
moon of alabaster and the soapstone birds my anger evaporated, and concern took
its place. I remembered what a fine fellow Lawson had been, what good times we
had had together. I remembered especially that evening when we had found this
valley and given rein to our fancies. What horrid alchemy in the place had turned
a gentleman into a brute? I thought of drink and drugs and madness and insomnia,
but I could fit none of them into my conception of my friend. I did not consciously
rescind my resolve to depart, but I had a notion that I would not act on it.

The sleepy butler met me as I went to bed. "Mr. Lawson's room is at the end
of your corridor, sir," he said. "He don't sleep over well, so you may hear him stirring in the night. At what hour would you like breakfast, sir? Mr. Lawson mostly
has his in bed."

My room opened from the great corridor, which ran the full length of the front
of the house. So far as I could make out, Lawson was three rooms off, a vacant bedroom and his servant's room being between us. I felt tired and cross, and tumbled
into bed as fast as possible. Usually I sleep well, but now I was soon conscious that
my drowsiness was wearing off and that I was in for a restless night. I got up and
laved my face, turned the pillows, thought of sheep coming over a hill and clouds
crossing the sky; but none of the old devices were of any use. After about an hour
of make-believe I surrendered myself to facts, and, lying on my back, stared at the
white ceiling and the patches of moonshine on the walls.

It certainly was an amazing night. I got up, put on a dressing-gown, and drew
a chair to the window. The moon was almost at its full, and the whole plateau
swam in a radiance of ivory and silver. The banks of the stream were black, but
the lake had a great belt of light athwart it, which made it seem like a horizon and

the rim of land beyond it like a contorted cloud. Far to the right I saw the delicate outlines of the little wood which I had come to think of as the Grove of Ashtaroth. I listened. There was not a sound in the air. The land seemed to sleep peacefully beneath the moon, and yet I had a sense that the peace was an illusion. The place was feverishly restless.

I could have given no reason for my impression but there it was. Something was stirring in the wide moonlit landscape under its deep mask of silence. I felt as I had felt on the evening three years ago when I had ridden into the grove. I did not think that the influence, whatever it was, was maleficent. I only knew that it was very strange, and kept me wakeful.

By-and-by I bethought me of a book. There was no lamp in the corridor save the moon, but the whole house was bright as I slipped down the great staircase and across the hall to the library. I switched on the lights and then switched them off. They seemed profanation, and I did not need them.

I found a French novel, but the place held me and I stayed. I sat down in an arm-chair before the fireplace and the stone birds. Very odd those gawky things, like prehistoric Great Auks, looked in the moonlight. I remember that the alabaster moon shimmered like translucent pearl, and I fell to wondering about its history. Had the old Sabæns used such a jewel in their rites in the Grove of Ashtaroth?

Then I heard footsteps pass the window. A great house like this would have a watchman, but these quick shuffling footsteps were surely not the dull plod of a servant. They passed on to the grass and died away. I began to think of getting back to my room.

In the corridor I noticed that Lawson's door was ajar, and that a light had been left burning. I had the unpardonable curiosity to peep in. The room was empty, and the bed had not been slept in. Now I knew whose were the footsteps outside the library window.

I lit a reading-lamp and tried to interest myself in *La Cruelle Enigme*. But my wits were restless, and I could not keep my eyes on the page. I flung the book aside and sat down again by the window. The feeling came over me that I was sitting in a box at some play. The glen was a huge stage, and at any moment the players might appear on it. My attention was strung as high as if I had been waiting for the advent of some world-famous actress. But nothing came. Only the shadows shifted and lengthened as the moon moved across the sky.

Then quite suddenly the restlessness left me and at the same moment the silence was broken by the crow of a cock and the rustling of trees in a light wind. I felt very sleepy, and was turning to bed when again I heard footsteps without. From the window I could see a figure moving across the garden towards the house. It was Lawson, got up in the sort of towel dressing-gown that one wears on board ship. He was walking slowly and painfully, as if very weary. I did not see his face, but the man's whole air was that of extreme fatigue and dejection.

I tumbled into bed and slept profoundly till long after daylight.

III

The man who valeted me was Lawson's own servant. As he was laying out my clothes I asked after the health of his master, and was told that he had slept ill and would not rise till late. Then the man, an anxious-faced Englishman, gave me some information on his own account. Mr. Lawson was having one of his bad turns. It would pass away in a day or two, but till it had gone he was fit for nothing. He advised me to see Mr. Jobson, the factor, who would look to my entertainment in his master's absence.

Jobson arrived before luncheon, and the sight of him was the first satisfactory thing about Welgevonden. He was a big, gruff Scot from Roxburghshire, engaged, no doubt, by Lawson as a duty to his Border ancestry. He had short grizzled whiskers, a weatherworn face, and a shrewd, calm blue eye. I knew now why the place was in such perfect order.

We began with sport, and Jobson explained what I could have in the way of fishing and shooting. His exposition was brief and business-like, and all the while I could see his eye searching me. It was clear that he had much to say on other matters than sport.

I told him that I had come here with Lawson three years before, when he chose the site. Jobson continued to regard me curiously. "I've heard tell of ye from Mr. Lawson. Ye're an old friend of his, I understand."

"The oldest," I said. "And I am sorry to find that the place does not agree with him. Why it doesn't I cannot imagine, for you look fit enough. Has he been seedy for long?"

"It comes and it goes," said Mr. Jobson. "Maybe once a month he has a bad turn. But on the whole it agrees with him badly. He's no' the man he was when I first came here."

Jobson was looking at me very seriously and frankly. I risked a question.

"What do you suppose is the matter?"

He did not reply at once, but leaned forward and tapped my knee. "I think it's something that doctors canna cure. Look at me, sir. I've always been counted a sensible man, but if I told you what was in my head you would think me daft. But

322

I have one word for you. Bide till to-night is past and then speir your question. Maybe you and me will be agreed."

The factor rose to go. As he left the room he flung me back a remark over his shoulder—"Read the eleventh chapter of the First Book of Kings."

After luncheon I went for a walk. First I mounted to the crown of the hill and feasted my eyes on the unequalled loveliness of the view. I saw the far hills in Portuguese territory, a hundred miles away, lifting up thin blue fingers into the sky. The wind blew light and fresh, and the place was fragrant with a thousand delicate scents. Then I descended to the vale, and followed the stream up through the garden. Poinsettias and oleanders were blazing in coverts, and there was a paradise of tinted water-lilies in the slacker reaches. I saw good trout rise at the fly, but I did not think about fishing. I was searching my memory for a recollection which would not come. By-and-by I found myself beyond the garden, where the lawns ran to the fringe of Ashtaroth's Grove.

It was like something I remembered in an old Italian picture. Only, as my memory drew it, it should have been peopled with strange figures-nymphs dancing on the sward, and a prick-eared faun peeping from the covert. In the warm afternoon sunlight it stood, ineffably gracious and beautiful, tantalising with a sense of some deep hidden loveliness. Very reverently I walked between the slim trees, to where the little conical tower stood half in the sun and half in shadow. Then I noticed something new. Round the tower ran a narrow path, worn in the grass by human feet. There had been no such path on my first visit, for I remembered the grass growing tall to the edge of the stone. Had the Kaffirs made a shrine of it, or were there other and strange votaries?

When I returned to the house I found Travers with a message for me. Mr. Lawson was still in bed, but he would like me to go to him. I found my friend sitting up and drinking strong tea—a bad thing, I should have thought, for a man in his condition. I remember that I looked about the room for some sign of the pernicious habit of which I believed him a victim. But the place was fresh and clean, with the windows wide open, and, though I could not have given my reasons, I was convinced that drugs or drink had nothing to do with the sickness.

He received me more civilly, but I was shocked by his looks. There were great bags below his eyes, and his skin had the wrinkled puffy appearance of a man in dropsy. His voice, too, was reedy and thin. Only his great eyes burned with some feverish life.

"I am a shocking bad host," he said, "but I'm going to be still more inhospitable. I want you to go away. I hate anybody here when I'm off colour."

"Nonsense," I said; "you want looking after. I want to know about this sickness. Have you had a doctor?"

He smiled wearily. "Doctors are no earthly use to me. There's nothing much the matter I tell you. I'll be all right in a day or two, and then you can come back. I want you to go off with Jobson and hunt in the plains till the end of the week. It will be better fun for you, and I'll feel less guilty."

Of course I pooh-poohed the idea, and Lawson got angry. "Damn it, man," he cried, "why do you force yourself on me when I don't want you? I tell you your presence here makes me worse. In a week I'll be as right as the mail and then I'll be thankful for you. But get away now; get away, I tell you."

I saw that he was fretting himself into a passion. "All right," I said soothingly; "Jobson and I will go off hunting. But I am horribly anxious about you, old man."

He lay back on his pillows. "You needn't trouble. I only want a little rest. Jobson will make all arrangements, and Travers will get you anything you want. Good-bye."

I saw it was useless to stay longer, so I left the room. Outside I found the anxious-faced servant "Look here," I said, "Mr. Lawson thinks I ought to go, but I mean to stay. Tell him I'm gone if he asks you. And for Heaven's sake keep him in bed."

The man promised, and I thought I saw some relief in his face.

I went to the library, and on the way remembered Jobson's remark about 1st Kings. With some searching I found a Bible and turned up the passage. It was a long screed about the misdeeds of Solomon, and I read it through without enlightenment. I began to re-read it, and a word suddenly caught my attention—

"For Solomon went after Ashtaroth, the goddess of the Zidonians."

That was all, but it was like a key to a cipher. Instantly there flashed over my mind all that I had heard or read of that strange ritual which seduced Israel to sin. I saw a sunburnt land and a people vowed to the stern service of Jehovah. But I saw, too, eyes turning from the austere sacrifice to lonely hill-top groves and towers and images, where dwelt some subtle and evil mystery. I saw the fierce prophets, scourging the votaries with rods, and a nation Penitent before the Lord; but always the backsliding again, and the hankering after forbidden joys. Ashtaroth was the old goddess of the East. Was it not possible that in all Semitic blood there remained transmitted through the dim generations, some craving for her spell? I thought of the grandfather in the back street at Brighten and of those burning eyes upstairs.

As I sat and mused my glance fell on the inscrutable stone birds. They knew all those old secrets of joy and terror. And that moon of alabaster! Some dark priest had worn it on his forehead when he worshipped, like Ahab, "all the host of Heaven." And then I honestly began to be afraid. I, a prosaic, modern Christian gentleman, a half-believer in casual faiths, was in the presence of some hoary mystery of sin far older than creeds or Christendom. There was fear in my heart—a kind of uneasy disgust, and above all a nervous eerie disquiet. Now I wanted to go away and yet I was ashamed of the cowardly thought. I pictured Ashtaroth's Grove with sheer horror. What tragedy was in the air? What secret awaited twilight? For the night was coming, the night of the Full Moon, the season of ecstasy and sacrifice.

I do not know how I got through that evening. I was disinclined for dinner, so I had a cutlet in the library and sat smoking till my tongue ached. But as the hours passed a more manly resolution grew up in my mind. I owed it to old friendship to stand by Lawson in this extremity. I could not interfere—God knows, his reason seemed already rocking—but I could be at hand in case my chance came. I determined not to undress, but to watch through the night. I had a bath, and changed into light flannels and slippers. Then I took up my position in a corner of the library close to the window, so that I could not fail to hear Lawson's footsteps if he passed.

Fortunately I left the lights unlit, for as I waited I grew drowsy, and fell asleep. When I woke the moon had risen, and I knew from the feel of the air that the hour was late. I sat very still, straining my ears, and as I listened I caught the sound of steps. They were crossing the hall stealthily, and nearing the library door. I huddled into my corner as Lawson entered.

He wore the same towel dressing-gown, and he moved swiftly and silently as if in a trance. I watched him take the alabaster moon from the mantelpiece and drop it in his pocket. A glimpse of white skin showed that the gown was his only clothing. Then he moved past me to the window, opened it, and went out.

Without any conscious purpose I rose and followed, kicking off my slippers that I might go quietly. He was running, running fast, across the lawns in the direction of the Grove—an odd shapeless antic in the moonlight. I stopped, for there was no cover, and I feared for his reason if he saw me. When I looked again he had disappeared among the trees.

I saw nothing for it but to crawl, so on my belly I wormed my way over the dripping sward. There was a ridiculous suggestion of deer-stalking about the game which tickled me and dispelled my uneasiness. Almost I persuaded myself I was tracking an ordinary sleep-walker. The lawns were broader than I imagined, and it seemed an age before I reached the edge of the Grove. The world was so still that

I appeared to be making a most ghastly amount of noise. I remember that once I heard a rustling in the air, and looked up to see the green doves circling about the tree-tops.

There was no sign of Lawson. On the edge of the Grove I think that all my assurance vanished. I could see between the trunks to the little tower, but it was quiet as the grave, save for the wings above. Once more there came over me the unbearable sense of anticipation I had felt the night before. My nerves tingled with mingled expectation and dread. I did not think that any harm would come to me, for the powers of the air seemed not malignant. But I knew them for powers, and felt awed and abased. I was in the presence of the "host of Heaven," and I was no stern Israelitish prophet to prevail against them.

I must have lain for hours waiting in that spectral place, my eyes riveted on the tower and its golden cap of moonshine. I remember that my head felt void and light, as if my spirit were becoming disembodied and leaving its dew-drenched sheath far below. But the most curious sensation was of something drawing me to the tower, something mild and kindly and rather feeble, for there was some other and stronger force keeping me back. I yearned to move nearer, but I could not drag my limbs an inch. There was a spell somewhere which I could not break. I do not think I was in any way frightened now. The starry influence was playing tricks with me, but my mind was half asleep. Only I never took my eyes from the little tower. I think I could not, if I had wanted to.

Then suddenly from the shadows came Lawson. He was stark-naked, and he wore, bound across his brow, the half-moon of alabaster. He had something, too, in his hand—something which glittered.

He ran round the tower, crooning to himself, and flinging wild arms to the skies. Sometimes the crooning changed to a shrill cry of passion, such as a manad may have uttered in the train of Bacchus. I could make out no words, but the sound told its own tale. He was absorbed in some infernal ecstasy. And as he ran, he drew his right hand across his breast and arms, and I saw that it held a knife.

I grew sick with disgust—not terror, but honest physical loathing. Lawson, gashing his fat body, affected me with an overpowering repugnance. I wanted to go forward and stop him, and I wanted, too, to be a hundred miles away. And the result was that I stayed still. I believe my own will held me there, but I doubt if in any case I could have moved my legs.

The dance grew swifter and fiercer. I saw the blood dripping from Lawson's body, and his face ghastly white above his scarred breast. And then suddenly the horror left me; my head swam; and for one second—one brief second—I seemed to peer into a new world. A strange passion surged up in my heart. I seemed to see the earth peopled with forms not human, scarcely divine, but more desirable than man or god. The calm face of Nature broke up for me into wrinkles of wild knowledge. I saw the things which brush against the soul in dreams, and found them lovely. There seemed no cruelty in the knife or the blood. It was a delicate mystery of worship, as wholesome as the morning song of birds. I do not know how the Semites found Ashtaroth's ritual; to them it may well have been more rapt and passionate than it seemed to me. For I saw in it only the sweet simplicity of Nature, and all riddles of lust and terror soothed away as a child's nightmares are calmed by a mother. I found my legs able to move, and I think I took two steps through the dusk towards the tower.

And then it all ended. A cock crew, and the homely noises of earth were renewed. While I stood dazed and shivering, Lawson plunged through the Grove toward me. The impetus carried him to the edge, and he fell fainting just outside the shade.

My wits and common-sense came back to me with my bodily strength. I got my friend on my back, and staggered with him towards the house. I was afraid in real earnest now, and what frightened me most was the thought that I had not been afraid sooner. I had come very near the "abomination of the Zidonians."

At the door I found the scared valet waiting. He had apparently done this sort of thing before.

"Your master has been sleep-walking and has had a fall," I said. "We must get him to bed at once."

We bathed the wounds as he lay in a deep stupor, and I dressed them as well as I could. The only danger lay in his utter exhaustion, for happily the gashes were not serious, and no artery had been touched. Sleep and rest would make him well, for he had the constitution of a strong man. I was leaving the room when he opened his eyes and spoke. He did not recognize me, but I noticed that his face had lost its strangeness, and was once more that of the friend I had known. Then I suddenly bethought me of an old hunting remedy which he and I always carried on our expeditions. It is a pill made up from an ancient Portuguese prescription. One is an excellent specific for fever. Two are invaluable if you are lost in the bush, for they send a man for many hours into a deep sleep, which prevents suffering and madness, till help comes. Three give a painless death. I went to my room and found the little box in my jewel-case. Lawson swallowed two, and turned wearily on his side. I bade his man let him sleep till he woke, and went off in search of food.

IV

I had business on hand which would not wait. By seven, Jobson, who had been sent for, was waiting for me in the library. I knew by his grim face that here I had a very good substitute for a prophet of the Lord.

"You were right," I said. "I have read the 11th chapter of 1st Kings, and I have spent such a night as I pray God I shall never spend again."

"I thought you would," he replied. "I've had the same experience myself."

"The Grove?" I said.

"Ay, the wud," was the answer in broad Scots.

I wanted to see how much he understood. "Mr. Lawson's family is from the Scottish Border?"

"Ay. I understand they come off Borthwick Water side," he replied, but I saw by his eyes that he knew what I meant.

"Mr. Lawson is my oldest friend," I went on, "and I am going to take measures to cure him. For what I am going to do I take the sole responsibility. I will make that plain to your master. But if I am to succeed I want your help. Will you give it me? It sounds like madness and you are a sensible man and may like to keep out of it. I leave it to your discretion."

Jobson looked me straight in the face. "Have no fear for me," he said; "there is an unholy thing in that place, and if I have the strength in me I will destroy it. He has been a good master to me, and, forbye I am a believing Christian. So say on, sir."

There was no mistaking the air. I had found my Tishbite.

"I want men," I said, "—as many as we can get."

Jobson mused. "The Kaffirs will no' gang near the place, but there's some thirty white men on the tobacco farm. They'll do your will, if you give them an indemnity in writing."

"Good," said I. "Then we will take our instructions from the only authority which meets the case. We will follow the example of King Josiah. I turned up the 23rd chapter of 2nd Kings, and read—

> "And the high places that were before Jerusalem, which were on the right hand of the Mount of Corruption, which Solomon the king of Israel had builded for Ashtaroth the abomination of the Zidonians. . . did the king defile.
>
> "And he brake in Pieces the images, and cut down the groves, and filled their places with the bones of men. . . .

"Moreover the altar that was at Beth-el, and the high place which Jeroboam the son of Nebat, who made Israel to sin, had made, both that altar and the high place he brake down, and burned the high place, and stamped it small to powder, and burned the grove."

Jobson nodded. "It'll need dinnymite. But I've plenty of yon down at the workshops. I'll be off to collect the lads."

Before nine the men had assembled at Jobson's house. They were a hardy lot of young farmers from home, who took their instructions docilely from the masterful factor. On my orders they had brought their shotguns. We armed them with spades and woodmen's axes, and one man wheeled some coils of rope in a handcart.

In the clear, windless air of morning the Grove, set amid its lawns, looked too innocent and exquisite for ill. I had a pang of regret that a thing so fair should suffer; nay, if I had come alone, I think I might have repented. But the men were there, and the grim-faced Jobson was waiting for orders. I placed the guns, and sent beaters to the far side. I told them that every dove must be shot.

It was only a small flock, and we killed fifteen at the first drive. The poor birds flew over the glen to another spinney, but we brought them back over the guns and seven fell. Four more were got in the trees, and the last I killed myself with a long shot. In half an hour there was a pile of little green bodies on the sward.

Then we went to work to cut down the trees. The slim stems were an easy task to a good woodman, and one after another they toppled to the ground. And meantime, as I watched, I became conscious of a strange emotion.

It was as if someone were pleading with me. A gentle voice, not threatening, but pleading—something too fine for the sensual ear, but touching inner chords of the spirit. So tenuous it was and distant that I could think of no personality behind it. Rather it was the viewless, bodiless grace of this delectable vale, some old exquisite divinity of the groves. There was the heart of all sorrow in it, and the soul of all loveliness. It seemed a woman's voice, some lost lady who had brought nothing but goodness unrepaid to the world. And what the voice told me was that I was destroying her last shelter.

That was the pathos of it—the voice was homeless. As the axes flashed in the sunlight and the wood grew thin, that gentle spirit was pleading with me for mercy and a brief respite. It seemed to be telling of a world for centuries grown coarse and pitiless, of long sad wanderings, of hardly-won shelter, and a peace which was the little all she sought from men. There was nothing terrible in it. No thought of wrong-doing. The spell, which to Semitic blood held the mystery of evil, was to me, of the Northern race, only delicate and rare and beautiful. Jobson and the rest did not feel it, I with my finer senses caught nothing but the hopeless sadness of it. That which had stirred the passion in Lawson was only wringing my heart. It was almost too pitiful to bear. As the trees crashed down and the men wiped the sweat from their brows, I seemed to myself like the murderer of fair women and innocent children. I remember that the tears were running over my cheeks. More than once I opened my mouth to countermand the work, but the face of Jobson, that grim Tishbite, held me back.

I knew now what gave the Prophets of the Lord their mastery, and I knew also why the people sometimes stoned them.

The last tree fell, and the little tower stood like a ravished shrine, stripped of all defence against the world. I heard Jobson's voice speaking. "We'd better blast that stane thing now. We'll trench on four sides and lay the dinnymite. Ye're no' looking weel, sir. Ye'd better go and sit down on the brae-face."

I went up the hillside and lay down. Below me, in the waste of shorn trunks, men were running about, and I saw the mining begin. It all seemed like an aimless dream in which I had no part. The voice of that homeless goddess was still pleading. It was the innocence of it that tortured me Even so must a merciful Inquisitor have suffered from the plea of some fair girl with the aureole of death on her hair. I knew I was killing rare and unrecoverable beauty. As I sat dazed and heartsick, the whole loveliness of Nature seemed to plead for its divinity. The sun in the heavens, the mellow lines of upland, the blue mystery of the far plains, were all part of that soft voice. I felt bitter scorn for myself. I was guilty of blood; nay, I was guilty of the sin against light which knows no forgiveness. I was murdering innocent gentleness— and there would be no peace on earth for me. Yet I sat helpless. The power of a sterner will constrained me. And all the while the voice was growing fainter and dying away into unutterable sorrow.

Suddenly a great flame sprang to heaven, and a pall of smoke. I heard men crying out, and fragments of stone fell around the ruins of the grove. When the air cleared, the little tower had gone out of sight.

The voice had ceased and there seemed to me to be a bereaved silence in the world. The shock moved me to my feet, and I ran down the slope to where Jobson stood rubbing his eyes.

"That's done the job. Now we maun get up the tree roots. We've no time to howk. We'll just blast the feck o' them."

The work of destruction went on, but I was coming back to my senses. I forced myself to be practical and reasonable. I thought of the night's experience and Lawson's haggard eyes, and I screwed myself into a determination to see the thing through. I had done the deed; it was my business to make it complete. A text in Jeremiah came into my head:

> Their children remember their altars and their groves by the green trees upon the high hills.

I would see to it that this grove should be utterly forgotten.

We blasted the tree-roots, and, yolking oxen, dragged the debris into a great heap. Then the men set to work with their spades, and roughly levelled the ground. I was getting back to my old self, and Jobson's spirit was becoming mine.

"There is one thing more," I told him "Get ready a couple of ploughs. We will improve upon King Josiah." My brain was a medley of Scripture precedents, and I was determined that no safeguard should be wanting.

We yoked the oxen again and drove the ploughs over the site of the grove. It was rough ploughing, for the place was thick with bits of stone from the tower, but the slow Afrikaner oxen plodded on, and sometime in the afternoon the work was finished. Then I sent down to the farm for bags of rock-salt, such as they use for cattle. Jobson and I took a sack apiece, and walked up and down the furrows, sowing them with salt.

The last act was to set fire to the pile of tree trunks. They burned well, and on the top we flung the bodies of the green doves. The birds of Ashtaroth had an honourable pyre.

Then I dismissed the much-perplexed men, and gravely shook hands with Jobson. Black with dust and smoke I went back to the house, where I bade Travers pack my bags and order the motor. I found Lawson's servant, and heard from him that his master was sleeping peacefully. I gave him some directions, and then went to wash and change.

Before I left I wrote a line to Lawson. I began by transcribing the verses from the 23rd chapter of 2nd Kings. I told him what I had done, and my reason. "I take the whole responsibility upon myself," I wrote. "No man in the place had anything to do with it but me. I acted as I did for the sake of our old friendship, and you will believe it was no easy task for me. I hope you will understand. Whenever you are able to see me send me word, and I will come back and settle with you. But I think you will realise that I have saved your soul."

The afternoon was merging into twilight as I left the house on the road to Taqui. The great fire, where the Grove had been, was still blazing fiercely, and the smoke made a cloud over the upper glen, and filled all the air with a soft violet haze. I knew that I had done well for my friend, and that he would come to his senses and be grateful. My mind was at ease on that score, and in something like comfort I faced the future. But as the car reached the ridge I looked back to the vale I had outraged. The moon was rising and silvering the smoke, and through the gaps I could see the tongues of fire. Somehow, I know not why, the lake, the stream, the garden-coverts, even the green slopes of hill, wore an air of loneliness and desecration. And then my heartache returned, and I knew that I had driven something lovely and adorable from its last refuge on earth.

ROOUM

OLIVER ONIONS

OLIVER ONIONS (1872–1943) IS THE AUTHOR OF "THE
BECKONING FAIR ONE," ONE OF THE MOST HIGHLY REGARDED
GHOST STORIES IN THE CLASSIC TRADITION AND THE ANCHOR
OF HIS LANDMARK COLLECTION OF SUPERNATURAL TALES
WIDDERSHINS (1911). THAT COLLECTION ALSO INCLUDED
THIS STORY, FIRST PUBLISHED IN THE FORTNIGHTLY REVIEW
OF DECEMBER 1910 AND ONE OF THE EERIEST STORIES TO
SUGGEST AN OTHERWORLD THAT, ALONG WITH ITS MACABRE
ENTITIES, CAN BE PERCEIVED ONLY BY AN UNLUCKY FEW.

For all I ever knew to the contrary, it was his own name; and something about him, name or man or both, always put me in mind, I can't tell you how, of negroes. As regards the name, I dare say it was something huggermugger in the mere sound—something that I classed, for no particular reason, with the dark and ignorant sort of words, such as "Obi" and "Hoodoo." I only know that after I learned that his name was Rooum, I couldn't for the life of me have thought of him as being called anything else.

The first impression that you got of his head was that it was a patchwork of black and white—black bushy hair and short white beard, or else the other way about. As a matter of fact, both hair and beard were piebald, so that if you saw him in the gloom a dim patch of white showed down one side of his head, and dark tufts cropped up here and there in his beard. His eyebrows alone were entirely black, with a little sprouting of hair almost joining them. And perhaps his skin helped to make me think of negroes, for it was very dark, of the dark brown that always seems to have more than a hint of green behind it. His forehead was low, and scored across with deep horizontal furrows.

We never knew when he was going to turn up on a job. We might not have seen him for weeks, but his face was always as likely as not to appear over the edge of a crane-platform just when that marvellous mechanical intuition of his was badly needed. He wasn't certificated. He wasn't even trained, as the rest of us understood training; and he scoffed at the drawing-office, and laughed outright at logarithms and our laborious methods of getting out quantities. But he could set sheers and tackle in a way that made the rest of us look silly. I remember once how, through the parting of a chain, a sixty-foot girder had come down and lay under a ruck of other stuff, as the bottom chip lies under a pile of spellikins—a hopeless-looking smash. Myself, I'm certificated twice or three times over; but I can only assure you that I wanted to kick myself when, after I'd spent a day and a sleepless night over the job, I saw the game of tit-tat-toe that Rooum made of it in an hour or two. Certificated or not, a man isn't a fool who can do that sort of thing. And he was one of these fellows, too, who can "find water"—tell you where water is and what amount of getting it is likely to take, by just walking over the place. We aren't certificated up to that yet.

He was offered good money to stick to us—to stick to our firm—but he always shook his black-and-white piebald head. He'd never be able to keep the bargain if he were to make it, he told us quite fairly. I know there are these chaps who can't endure to be clocked to their work with a patent time-clock in the morning and released of an evening with a whistle—and it's one of the things no master can ever understand. So Rooum came and went erratically, showing up maybe in Leeds or Liverpool, perhaps next on Plymouth breakwater, and once he turned up in an out-of-the-way place in Glamorganshire just when I was wondering what had become of him.

The way I got to know him (got to know him, I mean, more than just to nod) was that he tacked himself on to me one night down Vauxhall way, where we were setting up some small plant or other. We had knocked off for the day, and I was walking in the direction of the bridge when he came up. We walked along together; and we had not gone far before it appeared that his reason for joining me was that he wanted to know "what a molecule was."

I stared at him a bit.

"What do you want to know that for?" I said. "What does a chap like you, who can do it all backwards, want with molecules?"

Oh, he just wanted to know, he said.

So, on the way across the bridge, I gave it him more or less from the book—Molecular Theory and all the rest of it. But, from the childish questions he put, it was plain that he hadn't got the hang of it at all. "Did the Molecular Theory allow things to pass through one another?" he wanted to know; "*Could* things pass through one another?" and a lot of ridiculous things like that. I gave it up.

"You're a genius in your own way, Rooum," I said finally; "you know these things without the books we plodders have to depend on. If I'd luck like that, I think I should be content with it."

But he didn't seem satisfied, though he dropped the matter for that time. But I had his acquaintance, which was more than most of us had. He asked me, rather timidly, if I'd lend him a book or two. I did so, but they didn't seem to contain what he wanted to know, and he soon returned them, without remark.

Now you'd expect a fellow to be specially sensitive, one way or another, who can tell when there's water a hundred feet beneath him; and as you know, the big men are squabbling yet about this water-finding business. But, somehow, the water-finding puzzled me less than it did that Rooum should be extraordinarily sensitive to something far commoner and easier to understand—ordinary echoes. He couldn't stand echoes. He'd go a mile round rather than pass a place that he knew had an echo; and if he came on one by chance, sometimes he'd hurry through as quick as he could, and sometimes he'd loiter and listen very intently. I rather joked about this at first, till I found it really distressed him; then, of course, I pretended not to notice. We're all cranky somewhere, and for that matter, I can't touch a spider myself.

For the remarkable thing that overtook Rooum—(that, by the way, is an odd way to put it, as you'll see presently; but the words came that way into my head, so let them stand)—for the remarkable thing that overtook Rooum, I don't think I can begin better than with the first time, or very soon after the first time, that I noticed this peculiarity about the echoes.

It was early on a particularly dismal November evening, and this time we were somewhere out south-east London way, just beyond what they are pleased to call the building-line—you know these districts of wretched trees and grimy fields and market-gardens that are about the same to real country that a slum is to a town. It rained that night; rain was the most appropriate weather for the brickfields and sewage-farms and yards of old carts and railway-sleepers we were passing. The rain shone on the black hand-bag that Rooum always carried; and I sucked at the dottle of a pipe that it was too much trouble to fill and light again. We were walking in the direction of Lewisham (I think it would be), and were still a little way from that eruption of red-brick houses that . . . but you've doubtless seen them.

You know how, when they're laying out new roads, they lay down the narrow strip of kerb first, with neither setts on the one hand nor flagstones on the other? We had come upon one of these. (I had noticed how, as we had come a few minutes before under a tall hollow-ringing railway arch, Rooum had all at once stopped talking—it was the echo, of course, that bothered him.) The unmade road to which we had come had headless lamp-standards at intervals, and ramparts of grey road-metal ready for use; and save for the strip of kerb, it was a broth of mud and stiff clay. A red light or two showed where the road-barriers were—they were laying the mains; a green railway light showed on an embankment; and the Lewisham lamps made a rusty glare through the rain. Rooum went first, walking along the narrow strip of kerb.

The lamp-standards were a little difficult to see, and when I heard Rooum stop suddenly and draw in his breath sharply, I thought he had walked into one of them.

"Hurt yourself?" I said.

He walked on without replying; but half a dozen yards farther on he stopped again. He was listening again. He waited for me to come up.

"I say—" he said, in an odd sort of voice, "—go a yard or two ahead, will you?"

"What's the matter?" I asked, as I passed ahead. He didn't answer.

Well, I hadn't been leading for more than a minute before he wanted to change again. He was breathing very quick and short.

"Why, what ails you?" I demanded, stopping.

"It's all right. . . . You're not playing any tricks, are you? . . ."

I saw him pass his hand over his brow.

"Come, get on," I said shortly; and we didn't speak again till we struck the pavement with the lighted lamps. Then I happened to glance at him.

"Here," I said brusquely, taking him by the sleeve, "you're not well. We'll call somewhere and get a drink."

"Yes," he said, again wiping his brow. "I say . . . did you hear?"

"Hear what?"

"Ah, you didn't . . . and, of course, you didn't feel anything. . . ."

"Come, you're shaking."

When presently we came to a brightly lighted public-house or hotel, I saw that he was shaking even worse than I had thought. The shirt-sleeved barman noticed it too, and watched us curiously. I made Rooum sit down, and got him some brandy.

"What was the matter?" I asked, as I held the glass to his lips.

But I could get nothing out of him except that it was "All right—all right—" with his head twitching over his shoulder almost as if he had touch of the dance.

He began to come round a little. He wasn't the kind of man you'd press for explanations, and presently we set out again. He walked with me as far as my lodgings, refused to come in, but for all that lingered at the gate as if loath to leave. I watched him turn the corner in the rain.

We came home together again the next evening, but by a different way, quite half a mile longer. He had waited for me a little pertinaciously. It seemed he wanted to talk about molecules again.

Well, when a man of his age—he'd be near fifty—begins to ask questions, he's rather worse than a child who wants to know where Heaven is or some such thing—for you can't put him off as you can the child. Somewhere or other he'd picked up the word "osmosis," and seemed to have some glimmering of its meaning. He dropped the molecules, and began to ask me about osmosis.

"It means, doesn't it," he demanded, "that liquids will work their way into one another—through a bladder or something? Say a thick fluid and a thin: you'll find some of the thick in the thin, and the thin in the thick?"

"Yes. The thick into the thin is ex-osmosis, and the other end-osmosis. That takes place more quickly. But I don't know a deal about it."

"Does it ever take place with solids?" he next asked.

What was he driving at? I thought; but replied: "I believe that what is commonly called 'adhesion' is something of the sort, under another name."

"A good deal of this bookwork seems to be finding a dozen names for the same thing," he grunted; and continued to ask his questions.

But what it was he really wanted to know I couldn't for the life of me make out.

Well, he was due any time now to disappear again, having worked quite six weeks in one place; and he disappeared. He disappeared for a good many weeks. I think it would be about February before I saw or heard of him again.

It was February weather, anyway, and in an echoing enough place that I found him—the subway of one of the Metropolitan stations. He'd probably forgotten the echoes when he'd taken the train; but, of course, the railway folk won't let a man who happens to dislike echoes go wandering across the metals where he likes.

He was twenty yards ahead when I saw him. I recognised him by his patched head and black handbag. I ran along the subway after him.

It was very curious. He'd been walking close to the white-tiled wall, and I saw him suddenly stop; but he didn't turn. He didn't even turn when I pulled up, close behind him; he put out one hand to the wall, as if to steady himself. But, the moment I touched his shoulder, he just dropped—just dropped, half on his knees against the white tiling. The face he turned round and up to me was transfixed with fright.

There were half a hundred people about—a train was just in—and it isn't a difficult matter in London to get a crowd for much less than a man crouching terrified against a wall, looking over his shoulder as Rooum looked, at another man almost as terrified. I felt somebody's hand on my own arm. Evidently somebody thought I'd knocked Rooum down.

The terror went slowly from his face. He stumbled to his feet. I shook myself free of the man who held me and stepped up to Rooum.

"What the devil's all this about?" I demanded, roughly enough.

"It's all right . . . it's all right . . ." he stammered.

"Heavens, man, you shouldn't play tricks like that!"

"No . . . no . . . but for the love of God don't do it again!. . ."

"We'll not explain here," I said, still in a good deal of a huff; and the small crowd melted away—disappointed, I dare say, that it wasn't a fight.

"Now," I said, when we were outside in the crowded street, "you might let me know what all this is about, and what it is that for the love of God I'm not to do again."

He was half apologetic, but at the same time half blustering, as if I had committed some sort of an outrage.

"A senseless thing like that!" he mumbled to himself. "But there: you didn't know. . . . You *don't* know, do you? . . . I tell you, d'you hear, *you're not to run at all when I'm about!* You're a nice fellow and all that, and get your quantities somewhere near right, if you do go a long way round to do it—but I'll not answer for myself *if you run,* d'you hear? . . . Putting your hand on a man's shoulder like that, just when . . ."

"Certainly I might have spoken," I agreed, a little stiffly.

"Of course, you ought to have spoken! Just you see you don't do it again. It's monstrous!"

I put a curt question.

"Are you sure you're quite right in your head, Rooum?"

"Ah," he cried, "don't you think I just fancy it, my lad! Nothing so easy! I thought you guessed that other time, on the new road . . . it's as plain as a pikestaff . . . no, no, no! *I* shall be telling *you* something about molecules one of these days!"

We walked for a time in silence.

Suddenly he asked: "What are you doing now?"

"I myself, do you mean? Oh, the firm.—A railway job, past Pinner. But we've a big contract coming on in the West End soon they might want you for. They call it 'alterations,' but it's one of these big shop-rebuildings."

"I'll come along."

"Oh, it isn't for a month or two yet."

"I don't mean that. I mean I'll come along to Pinner with you now, to-night, or whenever you go."

"Oh!" I said.

I don't know that I specially wanted him. It's a little wearing, the company of a chap like that. You never know what he's going to let you in for next. But, as this didn't seem to occur to him, I didn't say anything. If he really liked catching the last train down, a three-mile walk, and then sharing a double-bedded room at a poor sort of alehouse (which was my own programme), he was welcome. We walked a little farther; then I told him the time of the train and left him.

He turned up at Euston, a little after twelve. We went down together. It was getting on for one when we left the station at the other end, and then we began the tramp across the Weald to the inn. A little to my surprise (for I had begun to expect unaccountable behaviour from him) we reached the inn without Rooum having dodged about changing places with me, or having fallen cowering under a gorse-bush, or anything of that kind. Our talk, too, was about work, not molecules and osmosis.

The inn was only a roadside beerhouse—I have forgotten its name—and all its sleeping accomodation was the one double-bedded room. Over the head of my own bed the ceiling was cut away, following the roof-line; and the wallpaper was perfectly shocking—faded bouquets that made V's and A's, interlacing everywhere. The other bed was made up, and lay across the room.

I think I only spoke once while we were making ready for bed, and that was when Rooum took from his black handbag a brush and a torn night-gown.

"That's what you always carry about, is it?" I remarked; and Rooum grunted something: Yes . . . never knew where you'd be next . . . no harm, was it?—We tumbled into bed.

But, for all the lateness of the hour, I wasn't sleepy; so from my own bag I took a book, set the candle on the end of the mantel, and began to read. Mark you, I don't say I was much better informed for the reading I did, for I was watching the V's on the wallpaper mostly—that, and wondering what was wrong with the man in the other bed who had fallen down at a touch in the subway. He was already asleep.

Now I don't know whether I can make the next clear to you. I'm quite certain he was sound asleep, so that it wasn't just the fact that he spoke. Even that is a little unpleasant, I always think, any sort of sleep-talking; but it's a very queer sort of sensation when a man actually answers a question that's put to him, knowing nothing whatever about it in the morning. Perhaps I ought not to have put that question; having put it, I did the next best thing afterwards, as you'll see in a moment . . . but let me tell you.

He'd been asleep perhaps an hour, and I woolgathering about the wallpaper, when suddenly, in a far more clear and loud voice than he ever used when awake, he said:

"*What the devil is it prevents me seeing him, then?*"

That startled me, rather, for the second time that evening; and I really think I had spoken before I had fully realised what was happening.

"From seeing whom?" I said, sitting up in bed.

"Whom? . . . You're not attending. The fellow I'm telling you about, who runs after me," he answered—answered perfectly plainly.

I could see his head there on the pillow, black and white, and his eyes were closed. He made a slight movement with his arm, but that did not wake him. Then it came to me, with a sort of start, what was happening. I slipped half out of bed. Would he—would he?—answer another question? . . . I risked it, breathlessly.

"Have you any idea who he is?"

Well, that too he answered.

"Who he is? The Runner? . . . Don't be silly. *Who else should it be?*"

With every nerve in me tingling, I tried again.

"What happens, then, when he catches you?"

This time, I really don't know whether his words were an answer or not; they were these:

"To hear him catching you up . . . and then padding away ahead again! All right, all right . . . but I guess it's weakening him a bit, too. . . ."

Without noticing it, I had got out of bed, and had advanced quite to the middle of the floor.

"What did you say his name was?" I breathed.

—But that was a dead failure. He muttered brokenly for a moment, gave a deep troubled sigh, and then began to snore loudly and regularly.

I made my way back to bed; but I assure you that before I did so I filled my basin with water, dipped my face into it, and then set the candlestick afloat in it, leaving the candle burning. I thought I'd like to have a light. . . . It had burned down by morning. Rooum, I remember, remarked on the silly practice of reading in bed.

Well, it was a pretty kind of obsession for a man to have, wasn't it? Somebody running after him all the time, and then . . . running on ahead? And, of course, on a broad pavement there would be plenty of room for this running gentleman to run round; but on an eight- or nine-inch kerb, such as that of the new road out Lewisham way . . . but perhaps he was a jumping gentleman too, and could jump over a man's head. You'd think he'd have to get past some way, wouldn't you? . . . I remember vaguely wondering whether the name of that Runner was not Conscience; but Conscience isn't a matter of molecules and osmosis. . . .

One thing, however, was clear; I'd got to tell Rooum what I'd learned: for you can't get hold of a fellow's secrets in ways like that. I lost no time about it. I told him, in fact, soon after we'd left the inn the next morning—told him how he'd answered in his sleep.

And—what do you think of this?—he seemed to think I ought to have guessed it! *Guessed* a monstrous thing like that!

"You're less clever than I thought, with your books and that, if you didn't," he grunted.

"But . . . Good God, man!—"

"Queer, isn't it? But you don't know the queerest—"

He pondered for a moment, and then suddenly put his lips to my ear.

"I'll tell you," he whispered. "*It gets harder every time!* . . . At first, he just slipped through: a bit of a catch at my heart, like when you nod off to sleep in a chair and jerk up awake again; and away he went. But now it's getting grinding, sluggish; and the pain. . . . You'd notice, that night on the road, the little check it gave me; that's past long since; and last night, when I'd just braced myself up stiff to meet it, and you tapped me on the shoulder. . . ." He passed the back of his hand over his brow.

"I tell you," he continued, "it's an agony each time. I could scream at the thought of it. It's oftener, too, now, and he's getting stronger. The end-osmosis—is getting to be ex-osmosis—is that right? Just let me tell you one more thing—"

But I'd had enough. I'd asked questions the night before, but now—well, I knew quite as much as, and more than, I wanted.

"Stop, please," I said. "You're either off your head, or worse. Let's call it the first. Don't tell me any more, please."

"Frightened, what? Well, I don't blame you. But what would *you* do?"

"I should see a doctor; I'm only an engineer," I replied.

"Doctors? . . . Bah!" he said, and spat.

I hope you see how the matter stood with Rooum. What do you make of it? Could you have believed it—*do* you believe it?... He'd made a nearish guess when he'd said that much of our knowledge is giving names to things we know nothing about; only rule-of-thumb Physics thinks everything's explained in the Manual; and you've always got to remember one thing:—You can call it Force or what you like, but it's a certainty that things, solid things of wood and iron and stone, would explode, just go off in a puff into space, if it wasn't for something just as inexplicable as that that Rooum said he felt in his own person. And if you can swallow that, it's a relatively small matter whether Rooum's light-footed Familiar slipped through him unperceived, or had to struggle through obstinately. You see now why I said that "a queer thing overtook Rooum."

More: I saw it. This thing, that outrages reason—I saw it happen. That is to say, I saw its effects, and it was in broad daylight, on an ordinary afternoon, in the middle of Oxford Street, of all places. There wasn't a shadow of doubt about it. People were pressing and jostling about him, and suddenly I saw him turn his head and listen, as I'd seen him before. I tell you, an icy creeping ran all over my skin. I fancied *I* felt it approaching too, nearer and nearer. . . . The next moment he had made a sort of gathering of himself, as if against a gust. He stumbled and thrust—thrust with his body. He swayed, physically, as a tree sways in a wind; he clutched my arm and gave a loud scream. Then, after seconds—minutes—I don't know how long—he was free again.

And for the colour of his face when by and bye I glanced at it . . . well, I once saw a swarthy Italian fall under a sunstroke, and *his* face was much the same colour that Rooum's negro face had gone: a cloudy, whitish green.

"Well—you've seen it—what do you think of it?" he gasped presently, turning a ghastly grin on me.

But it was night before the full horror of it had soaked into me.

Soon after that he disappeared again. I wasn't sorry.

* * *

Our big contract in the West End came on. It was a time-contract, with all manner of penalty clauses if we didn't get through; and I assure you that we were busy. I myself was far too busy to think of Rooum.

It's a shop now, the place we were working at, or rather one of these huge weldings of fifty shops where you can buy anything; and if you'd seen us there . . . but perhaps you did see us, for people stood up on the tops of omnibuses as they passed,

342

to look over the mud-splashed hoarding into the great excavation we'd made. It was a sight. Staging rose on staging, tier on tier, with interminable ladders all over the steel structure. Three or four squat Otis lifts crouched like iron turtles on top, and a lattice-crane on a towering three-cornered platform rose a hundred and twenty feet into the air. At one end of the vast quarry was a demolished house, showing flues and fireplaces and a score of thicknesses of old wallpaper; and at night—they might well have stood up on the tops of the buses! A dozen great spluttering violet arc-lights half-blinded you; down below were the watchmen's fires; overhead, the riveters had their fire-baskets; and in odd corners naphtha-lights guttered and flared. And the steel rang with the riveters' hammers, and the crane-chains rattled and clashed. . . . There's not much doubt in *my* mind, it's the engineers who are the architects nowadays. The chaps who think they're the architects are only a sort of paperhangers, who hang brick and terra-cotta on our work and clap a pinnacle or two on top—but never mind that. There we were, sweating and clanging and navvying, till the day shift came to relieve us.

And I ought to say that fifty feet above our great gap, and from end to end across it, there ran a travelling crane on a skeleton line, with platform, engine, and wooden cab all compact in one.

It happened that they had pitched in as one of the foremen some fellow or other, a friend of the firm's, a rank duffer, who pestered me incessantly with his questions. I did half his work and all my own, and it hadn't improved my temper much. On this night that I'm telling about, he'd been playing the fool with his questions as if a time-contract was a sort of summer holiday; and he'd filled me up to that point that I really can't say just when it was that Rooum put in an appearance again. I think I *had* heard somebody mention his name, but I'd paid no attention.

Well, our Johnnie Fresh came up to me for the twentieth time that night, this time wanting to know something about the overhead crane. At that I fairly lost my temper.

"What ails the crane?" I cried. "It's doing its work, isn't it? Isn't everybody doing their work except you? Why can't you ask Hopkins; isn't Hopkins there?"

"I don't know," he said.

"Then," I snapped, "in that particular I'm as ignorant as you, and I hope it's the only one."

But he grabbed my arm.

"Look at it now!" he cried, pointing; and I looked up.

Either Hopkins or somebody was dangerously exceeding the speed-limit. The thing was flying along its thirty yards of rail as fast as a tram, and the heavy fall-blocks swung like a ponderous kite-tail, thirty feet below. As I watched, the engine brought up within a yard of the end of the way, the blocks crashed like a ram into the broken house end, fetching down plaster and brick, and then the mechanism was reversed. The crane set off at a tear back.

"Who in Hell . . ." I began; but it wasn't a time to talk. "*Hi!*" I yelled, and made a spring for a ladder.

The others had noticed it, too, for there were shouts all over the place. By that time I was halfway up the second stage. Again the crane tore past, with the massive tackle sweeping behind it, and again I heard the crash at the other end. Whoever had the handling of it was managing it skilfully, for there was barely a foot to spare when it turned again.

On the fourth platform, at the end of the way, I found Hopkins. He was white, and seemed to be counting on his fingers.

"What's the matter here?" I cried.

"It's Rooum," he answered. "I hadn't stepped out of the cab, not a minute, when I heard the lever go. He's running somebody down, he says; he'll run the whole shoot down in a minute—look! —"

The crane was coming back again. Half out of the cab I could see Rooum's mottled hair and beard. His brow was ribbed like a gridiron, and as he ripped past one of the arcs his face shone like porcelain with the sweat that bathed it.

"Now . . . you! . . . *Now*, damn you! . . ." he was shouting.

"Get ready to board him when he reverses!" I shouted to Hopkins.

Just how we scrambled on I don't know. I got one arm over the lifting-gear (which, of course, wasn't going), and heard Hopkins on the other footplate. Rooum put the brakes down and reversed; again came the thud of the fall-blocks; and we were speeding back again over the gulf of misty orange light. The stagings were thronged with gaping men.

"Ready?—Now!" I cried to Hopkins; and we sprang into the cab.

Hopkins hit Rooum's wrist with a spanner. Then he seized the lever, jammed the brake down and tripped Rooum, all, as it seemed, in one movement. I fell on top of Rooum. The crane came to a standstill half way down the line. I held Rooum panting.

But either Rooum was stronger than I, or else he took me very much unawares. All at once he twisted clear from my grasp and stumbled on his knees to the rear door of the cab. He threw up one elbow, and staggered to his feet as I made another clutch at him.

"Keep still, you fool!" I bawled. "Hit him over the head, Hopkins!"

Rooum screamed in a high voice.

"Run him down—cut him up with the wheels—down, you!—down, I say!—Oh, my good... *Ha!*"

He sprang clear out from the crane door, well-nigh taking me with him.

I told you it was a skeleton line, two rails and a tie or two. He'd actually jumped to the right-hand rail. And he was running along it—running along that iron tightrope, out over that well of light and watching men. Hopkins had started the travelling-gear, as if with some insane idea of catching him; but there was only one possible end to it. He'd gone fully a dozen yards, while I watched, horribly fascinated; and then I saw the turn of his head....

He didn't meet it this time; he sprang to the other rail, *as if to evade it.* ...

Even at the take-off he missed. As far as I could see, he made no attempt to save himself with his hands. He just went down out of the field of my vision. There was an awful silence; then, from far below....

★ ★ ★

They weren't the men on the lower stages who moved first. The men above went a little way down, and then they too stopped. Presently two of them descended, but by a distant way. They returned, with two bottles of brandy, and there was a hasty consultation. Two men drank the brandy off there and then—getting on for a pint of brandy apiece; then they went down, drunk.

I, Hopkins tells me, had got down on my knees in the crane cab, and was jabbering away cheerfully to myself. When I asked him what I said, he hesitated, and then said: "Oh, you don't want to know that, sir," and I haven't asked him since.

What do *you* make of it?

THE MUSIC ON THE HILL

SAKI

UNDER THE PEN NAME "SAKI," HECTOR HUGH MONROE
(1870–1916) WROTE SEVERAL COLLECTIONS OF SHORT STORIES
MEMORABLE FOR THEIR SHARP, SARDONIC WIT AND DARKLY
COMIC DEPICTIONS OF OUTRAGEOUS BEHAVIOR BY THEIR
SOPHISTICATED PROTAGONISTS. THIS UNCOMMONLY HUMORLESS
STORY FROM HIS 1911 COLLECTION *THE CHRONICLES OF CLOVIS*
IS ONE OF A SUBGENRE OF TALES WRITTEN BY VICTORIAN
AUTHORS ON THE THEME OF THE PAGAN GOD PAN'S SURVIVAL
INTO MODERN TIMES.

Sylvia Seltoun ate her breakfast in the morning-room at Yessney with a pleasant sense of ultimate victory, such as a fervent Ironside might have permitted himself on the morrow of Worcester fight. She was scarcely pugnacious by temperament, but belonged to that more successful class of fighters who are pugnacious by circumstance. Fate had willed that her life should be occupied with a series of small struggles, usually with the odds slightly against her, and usually she had just managed to come through winning. And now she felt that she had brought her hardest and certainly her most important struggle to a successful issue. To have married Mortimer Seltoun, "Dead Mortimer" as his more intimate enemies called him, in the teeth of the cold hostility of his family, and in spite of his unaffected indifference to women, was indeed an achievement that had needed some determination and adroitness to carry through; yesterday she had brought her victory to its concluding stage by wrenching her husband away from Town and its group of satellite watering-places and "settling him down," in the vocabulary of her kind, in this remote wood-girt manor farm which was his country house.

"You will never get Mortimer to go," his mother had said carpingly, "but if he once goes he'll stay; Yessney throws almost as much a spell over him as Town does. One can understand what holds him to Town, but Yessney—" and the dowager had shrugged her shoulders.

There was a sombre almost savage wildness about Yessney that was certainly not likely to appeal to town-bred tastes, and Sylvia, notwithstanding her name, was accustomed to nothing much more sylvan than "leafy Kensington." She looked on the country as something excellent and wholesome in its way, which was apt to become troublesome if you encouraged it overmuch. Distrust of town-life had been a new thing with her, born of her marriage with Mortimer, and she had watched with satisfaction the gradual fading of what she called "the Jermyn-Street-look" in his eyes as the woods and heather of Yessney had closed in on them yesternight. Her will-power and strategy had prevailed; Mortimer would stay.

Outside the morning-room windows was a triangular slope of turf, which the indulgent might call a lawn, and beyond its low hedge of neglected fuschia bushes a steeper slope of heather and bracken dropped down into cavernous combes overgrown with oak and yew. In its wild open savagery there seemed a stealthy linking of the joy of life with the terror of unseen things. Sylvia smiled complacently as she gazed with a School-of-Art appreciation at the landscape, and then of a sudden she almost shuddered.

"It is very wild," she said to Mortimer, who had joined her; "one could almost think that in such a place the worship of Pan had never quite died out."

"The worship of Pan never has died out," said Mortimer. "Other newer gods have drawn aside his votaries from time to time, but he is the Nature-God to whom all must come back at last. He has been called the Father of all the Gods, but most of his children have been stillborn."

Sylvia was religious in an honest, vaguely devotional kind of way, and did not like to hear her beliefs spoken of as mere aftergrowths, but it was at least something new and hopeful to hear Dead Mortimer speak with such energy and conviction on any subject.

"You don't really believe in Pan?" she asked incredulously.

"I've been a fool in most things," said Mortimer quietly, "but I'm not such a fool as not to believe in Pan when I'm down here. And if you're wise you won't disbelieve in him too boastfully while you're in his country."

It was not till a week later, when Sylvia had exhausted the attractions of the woodland walks round Yessney, that she ventured on a tour of inspection of the farm buildings. A farmyard suggested in her mind a scene of cheerful bustle, with churns and flails and smiling dairymaids, and teams of horses drinking knee-deep in duck-crowded ponds. As she wandered among the gaunt grey buildings of Yessney manor farm her first impression was one of crushing stillness and desolation, as though she had happened on some lone deserted homestead long given over to owls and cobwebs; then came a sense of furtive watchful hostility, the same shadow of unseen things that seemed to lurk in the wooded combes and coppices. From behind heavy doors and shuttered windows came the restless stamp of hoof or rasp of chain halter, and at times a muffled bellow from some stalled beast. From a distant corner a shaggy dog watched her with intent unfriendly eyes; as she drew near it slipped quietly into its kennel, and slipped out again as noiselessly when she had passed by. A few hens, questing for food under a rick, stole away under a gate at her approach. Sylvia felt that if she had come across any human beings in this wilderness of barn and byre they would have fled wraith-like from her gaze. At last, turning a corner quickly, she came upon a living thing that did not fly from her. A stretch in a pool of mud was an enormous sow, gigantic beyond the town-woman's wildest computation of swine-flesh, and speedily alert to resent and if necessary repel the unwonted intrusion. It was Sylvia's turn to make an unobtrusive retreat. As she threaded her way past rickyards and cowsheds and long blank walls, she started suddenly at a strange sound—the echo of a boy's laughter, golden and equivocal. Jan, the only boy employed on the farm, a tow-headed, wizen-faced yokel, was visibly at work on a potato clearing half-way up the nearest hill-side, and Mortimer, when questioned, knew of no other probable or possible begetter of the hidden mockery that had ambushed Sylvia's retreat. The memory of that untraceable echo was added to her other impressions of a furtive sinister "something" that hung around Yessney.

Of Mortimer she saw very little; farm and woods and trout- streams seemed to swallow him up from dawn till dusk. Once, following the direction she had seen him take in the morning, she came to an open space in a nut copse, further shut in by huge yew trees, in the centre of which stood a stone pedestal surmounted by a small bronze figure of a youthful Pan. It was a beautiful piece of workmanship, but her attention was chiefly held by the fact that a newly cut bunch of grapes had been placed as an offering at its feet. Grapes were none too plentiful at the manor house, and Sylvia snatched the bunch angrily from the pedestal. Contemptuous annoy-ance dominated her thoughts as she strolled slowly homeward, and then gave way to a sharp feeling of something that was very near fright; across a thick tangle of undergrowth a boy's face was scowling at her, brown and beautiful, with unutterably evil eyes. It was a lonely pathway, all pathways round Yessney were lonely for the matter of that, and she sped forward without waiting to give a closer scrutiny to this sudden apparition. It was not till she had reached the house that she discovered that she had dropped the bunch of grapes in her flight.

"I saw a youth in the wood today," she told Mortimer that evening, "brown-faced and rather handsome, but a scoundrel to look at. A gipsy lad, I suppose."

"A reasonable theory," said Mortimer, "only there aren't any gipsies in these parts at present."

"Then who was he?" asked Sylvia, and as Mortimer appeared to have no theory of his own she passed on to recount her finding of the votive offering.

"I suppose it was your doing," she observed; "it's a harmless piece of lunacy, but people would think you dreadfully silly if they knew of it."

"Did you meddle with it in any way?" asked Mortimer.

"I—I threw the grapes away. It seemed so silly," said Sylvia, watching Mortimer's impassive face for a sign of annoyance.

"I don't think you were wise to do that," he said reflectively. "I've heard it said that the Wood Gods are rather horrible to those who molest them."

"Horrible perhaps to those that believe in them, but you see I don't," retorted Sylvia.

"All the same," said Mortimer in his even, dispassionate tone, "I should avoid the woods and orchards if I were you, and give a wide berth to the horned beasts on the farm."

It was all nonsense, of course, but in that lonely wood-girt spot nonsense seemed able to rear a bastard brood of uneasiness.

"Mortimer," said Sylvia suddenly, "I think we will go back to Town some time soon."

Her victory had not been so complete as she had supposed; it had carried her on to ground that she was already anxious to quit.

"I don't think you will ever go back to Town," said Mortimer. He seemed to be paraphrasing his mother's prediction as to himself.

Sylvia noted with dissatisfaction and some self-contempt that the course of her next afternoon's ramble took her instinctively clear of the network of woods. As to the horned cattle, Mortimer's warning was scarcely needed, for she had always regarded them as of doubtful neutrality at the best: her imagination unsexed the most matronly dairy cows and turned them into bulls liable to "see red" at any moment. The ram who fed in the narrow paddock below the orchards she had adjudged, after ample and cautious probation, to be of docile temper; today, how-ever, she decided to leave his docility untested, for the usually tranquil beast was roaming with every sign of restlessness from corner to corner of his meadow. A

low, fitful piping, as of some reedy flute, was coming from the depth of a neighbouring copse, and there seemed to be some subtle connection between the animal's restless pacing and the wild music from the wood. Sylvia turned her steps in an upward
direction and climbed the heather-clad slopes that stretched in rolling shoulders
high above Yessney. She had left the piping notes behind her, but across the wooded
combes at her feet the wind brought her another kind of music, the straining bay of
hounds in full chase. Yessney was just on the outskirts of the Devon-and-Somerset
country, and the hunted deer sometimes came that way. Sylvia could presently see
a dark body, breasting hill after hill, and sinking again and again out of sight as he
crossed the combes, while behind him steadily swelled that relentless chorus, and
she grew tense with the excited sympathy that one feels for any hunted thing in
whose capture one is not directly interested. And at last he broke through the out-
ermost line of oak scrub and fern and stood panting in the open, a fat September
stag carrying a well-furnished head. His obvious course was to drop down to the
brown pools of Undercombe, and thence make his way towards the red deer's
favoured sanctuary, the sea. To Sylvia's surprise, however, he turned his head to the
upland slope and came lumbering resolutely onward over the heather. "It will be
dreadful," she thought, "the hounds will pull him down under my very eyes." But
the music of the pack seemed to have died away for a moment, and in its place she
heard again that wild piping, which rose now on this side, now on that, as though
urging the failing stag to a final effort. Sylvia stood well aside from his path, half
hidden in a thick growth of whortle bushes, and watched him swing stiffly upward,
his flanks dark with sweat, the coarse hair on his neck showing light by contrast. The
pipe music shrilled suddenly around her, seeming to come from the bushes at her
very feet, and at the same moment the great beast slewed round and bore directly
down upon her. In an instant her pity for the hunted animal was changed to wild
terror at her own danger; the thick heather roots mocked her scrambling efforts at
flight, and she looked frantically downward for a glimpse of oncoming hounds. The
huge antler spikes were within a few yards of her, and in a flash of numbing fear
she remembered Mortimer's warning, to beware of horned beasts on the farm. And
then with a quick throb of joy she saw that she was not alone; a human figure stood
a few paces aside, knee-deep in the whortle bushes.

"Drive it off!" she shrieked. But the figure made no answering movement.

The antlers drove straight at her breast, the acrid smell of the hunted animal was
in her nostrils, but her eyes were filled with the horror of something she saw other
than her oncoming death. And in her ears rang the echo of a boy's laughter, golden
and equivocal.

THE PEOPLE OF THE PIT

A. MERRITT

In the pulp fiction magazines of the early twentieth century, Abraham Merritt (1884–1943) was the undisputed master of the lost race fantasy. Typically, in his stories and novels, intrepid explorers of remote lands stumble upon forgotten civilizations shaped by esoteric science, magic, and mystery. Occasionally, as in this tale from the January 5, 1918 issue of *All-Story Weekly*, they have adventures that are more terrifying than marvelous.

North of us a shaft of light shot half way to the zenith. It came from behind the five peaks. The beam drove up through a column of blue haze whose edges were marked as sharply as the rain that streams from the edges of a thunder cloud. It was like the flash of a searchlight through an azure mist. It cast no shadows.

As it struck upward the summits were outlined hard and black and I saw that the whole mountain was shaped like a hand. As the light silhouetted it, the gigantic fingers stretched, the hand seemed to thrust itself forward. It was exactly as though it moved to push something back. The shining beam held steady for a moment; then broke into myriads of little luminous globes that swung to and fro and dropped gently. They seemed to be searching.

The forest had become very still. Every wood noise held its breath. I felt the dogs pressing against my legs. They too were silent; but every muscle in their bodies trembled, their hair was stiff along their backs and their eyes, fixed on the falling lights, were filmed with the terror glaze.

I looked at Anderson. He was staring at the North where once more the beam had pulsed upward.

"It can't be the aurora," I spoke without moving my lips. My mouth was as dry as though Lao T'zai had poured his fear dust down my throat.

"If it is I never saw one like it," he answered in the same tone. "Besides who ever heard of an aurora at this time of the year?"

He voiced the thought that was in my own mind.

"It makes me think something is being hunted up there," he said, "an unholy sort of hunt—it's well for us to be out of range."

"The mountain seems to move each time the shaft shoots up," I said. "What's it keeping back, Starr? It makes me think of the frozen hand of cloud that Shan Nadour set before the Gate of Ghouls to keep them in the lairs that Eblis cut for them."

He raised a hand—listening.

From the North and high overhead there came a whispering. It was not the rustling of the aurora, that rushing, crackling sound like the ghosts of winds that blew at Creation racing through the skeleton leaves of ancient trees that sheltered Lilith. It was a whispering that held in it a demand. It was eager. It called us to come up where the beam was flashing. It drew. There was in it a note of inexorable insistence. It touched my heart with a thousand tiny fear-tipped fingers and it filled me with a vast longing to race on and merge myself in the light. It must have been so that Ulysses felt when he strained at the mast and strove to obey the crystal sweet singing of the Sirens.

The whispering grew louder.

"What the hell's the matter with those dogs?" cried Anderson savagely. "Look at them!"

The malemutes, whining, were racing away toward the light. We saw them disappear among the trees. There came back to us a mournful howling. Then that too died away and left nothing but the insistent murmuring overhead.

The glade we had camped in looked straight to the North. We had reached I suppose three hundred mile above the first great bend of the Koskokwim toward the Yukon. Certainly we were in an untrodden part of the wilderness. We had pushed through from Dawson at the breaking of the Spring, on a fair lead to the lost five peaks between which, so the Athabasean medicine man had told us, the gold streams out like putty from a clenched fist. Not an Indian were we able to get to go with us. The land of the Hand Mountain was accursed they said. We had sighted the peaks the night before, their tops faintly outlined against a pulsing glow. And now we saw the light that had led us to them.

Anderson stiffened. Through the whispering had broken a curious pad-pad and a rustling. It sounded as though a small bear were moving towards us. I threw a pile of wood on the fire and, as it blazed up, saw something break through the bushes. It walked on all fours, but it did not walk like a bear. All at once it flashed upon me—it was like a baby crawling upstairs. The forepaws lifted themselves in grotesquely infantile fashion. It was grotesque but it was—terrible. It grew closer. We reached for our guns—and dropped them. Suddenly we knew that this crawling thing was a man!

It was a man. Still with the high climbing pad-pad he swayed to the fire. He stopped.

"Safe," whispered the crawling man, in a voice that was an echo of the murmur overhead. "Quite safe here. They can't get out of the blue, you know. They can't get you—unless you go to them—"

He fell over on his side. We ran to him. Anderson knelt.

"God's love!" he said. "Frank, look at this!" He pointed to the hands. The wrists were covered with torn rags of a heavy shirt. The hands themselves were stumps! The fingers had been bent into the palms and the flesh had been worn to the bone. They looked like the feet of a little black elephant! My eyes traveled down the body. Around the waist was a heavy band of yellow metal. From it fell a ring and a dozen links of shining white chain!

"What is he? Where did he come from?" said Anderson. "Look, he's fast asleep—yet even in his sleep his arms try to climb and his feet draw themselves up one after the other! And his knees—how in God's name was he ever able to move on them?"

It was even as he said. In the deep sleep that had come upon the crawler arms and legs kept raising in a deliberate, dreadful climbing motion. It was as though they had a life of their own—they kept their movement independently of the motionless body. They were semaphoric motions. If you have ever stood at the back of a train and had watched the semaphores rise and fall you will know exactly what I mean.

Abruptly the overhead whispering ceased. The shaft of light dropped and did not rise again. The crawling man became still. A gentle glow began to grow around us. It was dawn, and the short Alaskan summer night was over. Anderson rubbed his eyes and turned to me a haggard face.

"Man!" he exclaimed. "You look as though you have been through a spell of sickness!"

"No more than you, Starr," I said. "What do you make of it all?"

"I'm thinking our only answer lies there," he answered, pointing to the figure that lay so motionless under the blankets we had thrown over him. "Whatever it

353

was—that's what it was after. There was no aurora about that light, Frank. It was like the flaring up of some queer hell the preacher folk never frightened us with."

"We'll go no further today," I said. "I wouldn't wake him for all the gold that runs between the fingers of the five peaks—nor for all the devils that may be behind them."

The crawling man lay in a sleep as deep as the Styx. We bathed and bandaged the pads that had been his hands. Arms and legs were as rigid as though they were crutches. He did not move while we worked over him. He lay as he had fallen, the arms a trifle raised, the knees bent.

"Why did he crawl?" whispered Anderson. "Why didn't he walk?"

I was filing the band about the waist. It was gold, but it was like no gold I had ever handled. Pure gold is soft. This was soft, but it had an unclean, viscid life of its own. It clung to the file. I gashed through it, bent it away from the body and hurled it far off. It was—loathsome!

All that day he slept. Darkness came and still he slept. That night there was no shaft of light, no questing globe, no whispering. Some spell of horror seemed lifted from the land. It was noon when the crawling man awoke. I jumped as the pleasant drawling voice sounded.

"How long have I slept?" he asked. His pale blue eyes grew quizzical as I stared at him.

"A night—and almost two days," I said.

"Was there any light up there last night?" He nodded to the North eagerly. "Any whispering?"

"Neither," I answered. His head fell back and he stared up at the sky.

"They've given it up, then?" he said at last.

"Who have given it up?" asked Anderson.

"Why, the people of the pit," replied the crawling man quietly.

We stared at him.

"The people of the pit," he said. "Things that the Devil made before the Flood and that somehow have escaped God's vengeance. You weren't in any danger from them—unless you had followed their call. They can't get any further than the blue haze. I was their prisoner," he added simply. "They were trying to whisper me back to them!"

Anderson and I looked at each other, the same thought in both our minds.

"You're wrong," said the crawling man. "I'm not insane. Give me a very little to drink. I'm going to die soon, but I want you to take me as far South as you can before I die, and afterwards I want you to build a big fire and burn me. I want to be in such shape that no infernal spell of theirs can drag my body back to them.

You'll do it too, when I've told you about them—" he hesitated. "I think their chain is off me?" he said.

"I cut it off," I answered shortly.

"Thank God for that too," whispered the crawling man.

He drank the brandy and water we lifted to his lips.

"Arms and legs quite dead," he said. "Dead as I'll be soon. Well, they did well for me. Now I'll tell you what's up there behind that hand. Hell!"

"Now listen. My name is Stanton—Sinclair Stanton. Class 1900, Yale. Explorer. I started away from Dawson last year to hunt for five peaks that rise like a hand in a haunted country and run pure gold between them. Same thing you were after? I thought so. Late last fall my comrade sickened. Sent him back with some Indians. Little later all my Indians ran away from me. I decided I'd stick, built a cabin, stocked myself with food and lay down to winter it. In the Spring I started off again. Little less than two weeks ago I sighted the five peaks. Not from this side though—the other. Give me some more brandy.

"I'd made too wide a detour," he went on. "I'd gotten too far North. I beat back. From this side you see nothing but forest straight up to the base of the Hand Mountain. Over on the other side—"

He was silent for a moment.

"Over there is forest too. But it doesn't reach so far. No! I came out of it. Stretching miles in front of me was a level plain. It was as worn and ancient looking as the desert around the ruins of Babylon. At its end rose the peaks. Between me and them—far off—was what looked like a low dike of rocks. Then—I ran across the road!

"The road!" cried Anderson incredulously.

"The road," said the crawling man. "A fine smooth stone road. It ran straight on to the mountain. Oh, it was road all right—and worn as though millions and millions of feet had passed over it for thousands of years. On each side of it were sand and heaps of stones. After while I began to notice these stones. They were cut, and the shape of the heaps somehow gave me the idea that a hundred thousand years ago they might have been houses. I sensed man about them and at the same time they smelled of immemorial antiquity. Well—

"The peaks grew closer. The heaps of ruins thicker. Something inexpressibly desolate hovered over them; something reached from them that struck my heart like the touch of ghosts so old that they could be only the ghosts of ghosts. I went on.

"And now I saw that what I had thought to be the low rock range at the base of the peaks was a thicker litter of ruins. The Hand Mountain was really much farther off. The road passed between two high rocks that raised themselves like a gateway."

The crawling man paused.

"They were a gateway," he said. "I reached them. I went between them. And then I sprawled and clutched the earth in sheer awe! I was on a broad stone platform. Before me was—sheer space! Imagine the Grand Canyon five times as wide and with the bottom dropped out. That is what I was looking into. It was like peeping over the edge of a cleft world down into the infinity where the planets roll! On the far side stood the five peaks. They looked like a gigantic warning hand stretched up to the sky. The lip of the abyss curved away on each side of me.

"I could see down perhaps a thousand feet. Then a thick blue haze shut out the eye. It was like the blue you see gather on the high hills at dusk. And the pit—it was awesome; awesome as the Maori Gulf of Ranalak, that sinks between the living and the dead and that only the freshly released soul has strength to leap—but never strength to cross again.

"I crept back from the verge and stood up, weak. My hand rested against one of the pillars of the gateway. There was carving upon it. It bore in still sharp outlines the heroic figure of a man. His back was turned. His arms were outstretched. There was an odd peaked headdress upon him. I looked at the opposite pillar. It bore a figure exactly similar. The pillars were triangular and the carvings were on the side away from the pit. The figures seemed to be holding something back. I looked closer. Behind the outstretched hands I seemed to see other shapes.

"I traced them out vaguely. Suddenly I felt unaccountably sick. There had come to me an impression of enormous upright slugs. Their swollen bodies were faintly cut—all except the heads which were well marked globes. They were—unutterably loathsome. I turned from the gates back to the void. I stretched myself upon the slab and looked over the edge.

"A stairway led down into the pit!"

"A stairway!" we cried.

"A stairway," repeated the crawling man as patiently as before. "It seemed not so much carved out of the rock as built into it. The slabs were about six feet long and three feet wide. It ran down from the platform and vanished into the blue haze."

"But who could build such a stairway as that?" I said. "A stairway built into the wall of a precipice and leading down into a bottomless pit!"

"Not bottomless," said the crawling man quietly. "There was a bottom. I reached it!"

"Reached it?" we repeated.

"Yes, by the stairway," answered the crawling man. "You see—I went down it!

"Yes," he said. "I went down the stairway. But not that day. I made my camp back of the gates. At dawn I filled my knapsack with food, my two canteens with water from a spring that wells up there by the gateway, walked between the carved monoliths and stepped over the edge of the pit.

"The steps ran along the side of the rock at a forty degree pitch. As I went down and down I studied them. They were of a greenish rock quite different from the granitic porphyry that formed the wall of the precipice. At first I thought that the builders had taken advantage of an outcropping stratum, and had carved from it their gigantic flight. But the regularity of the angle at which it fell made me doubtful of this theory.

"After I had gone perhaps half a mile I stepped out upon a landing. From this landing the stairs made a V shaped turn and ran on downward, clinging to the cliff at the same angle as the first flight; it was a zig-zag, and after I had made three of these turns I knew that the steps dropped straight down in a succession of such angles. No strata could be so regular as that. No, the stairway was built by hands! But whose? The answer is in those ruins around the edge, I think—never to be read.

"By noon I had lost sight of the five peaks and the lip of the abyss. Above me, below me, was nothing but the blue haze. Beside me, too, was nothingness, for the further breast of rock had long since vanished. I felt no dizziness, and any trace of fear was swallowed in a vast curiosity. What was I to discover? Some ancient and wonderful civilization that had ruled when the Poles were tropical gardens? Nothing living, I felt sure—all was too old for life. Still, a stairway so wonderful must lead to something quite as wonderful I knew. What was it? I went on.

"At regular intervals I had passed the mouths of small caves. There would be two thousand steps and then an opening, two thousand more steps and an opening—and so on and on. Late that afternoon I stopped before one of these clefts. I suppose I had gone then three miles down the pit, although the angles were such that I had walked in all fully ten miles. I examined the entrance. On each side were carved the figures of the great portal above, only now they were standing face forward, the arms outstretched as though to hold something back from the outer depths. Their faces were covered with veils. There were no hideous shapes behind them. I went inside. The fissure ran back for twenty yards like a burrow. It was dry and perfectly light. Outside I could see the blue haze rising upward like a column, its edges clearly marked. I felt an extraordinary sense of security, although I had not been conscious of any fear. I felt that the figures at the entrance were guardians—but against what?

357

"The blue haze thickened and grew faintly luminescent. I fancied that it was dusk above. I ate and drank a little and slept. When I awoke the blue had lightened again, and I fancied it was dawn above. I went on. I forgot the gulf yawning at my side. I felt no fatigue and little hunger or thirst, although I had drunk and eaten sparingly. That night I spent within another of the caves, and at dawn I descended again.

"It was late that day when I first saw the city—."

He was silent for a time.

"The city," he said at last, "there is a city you know. But not such a city as you have ever seen—nor any other man who has lived to tell of it. The pit, I think, is shaped like a bottle; the opening before the five peaks is the neck. But how wide the bottom is I do not know—thousands of miles maybe. I had begun to catch little glints of light far down in the blue. Then I saw the tops of—trees, I suppose they are. But not our kind of trees—unpleasant, snaky kind of trees. They reared themselves on high thin trunks and their tops were nests of thick tendrils with ugly little leaves like arrow heads. The trees were red, a vivid angry red. Here and there I glimpsed spots of shining yellow. I knew these were water because I could see things breaking through their surface—or at least I could see the splash and ripple, but what it was that disturbed them I never saw.

"Straight beneath me was the—city. I looked down upon mile after mile of closely packed cylinders. They lay upon their sides in pyramids of three, of five— of dozens—piled upon each other. It is hard to make you see what that city is like—look, suppose you have water pipes of a certain length and first you lay three of them side by side and on top of them you place two and on these two one; or suppose you take five for a foundation and place on these four and then three, then two and then one. Do you see? That was the way they looked. But they were topped by towers, by minarets, by flares, by fans, and twisted monstrosities. They gleamed as though coated with pale rose flame. Beside them the venomous red trees raised themselves like the heads of hydras guarding nests of gigantic, jeweled and sleeping worms!

"A few feet beneath me the stairway jutted out into a Titanic arch, unearthly as the span that bridges Hell and leads to Asgard. It curved out and down straight through the top of the highest pile of carven cylinders and then it vanished through it. It was appalling—it was demonic—"

The crawling man stopped. His eyes rolled up into his head. He trembled and his arms and legs began their horrible crawling movement. From his lips came a whispering. It was an echo of the high murmuring we had heard the night he came to us. I put my hands over his eyes. He quieted.

"The Things Accursed!" he said. "The People of the Pit! Did I whisper. Yes—but they can't get me now—they can't!"

After a time he began as quietly as before.

"I crossed the span. I went down through the top of that—building. Blue darkness shrouded me for a moment and I felt the steps twist into a spiral. I wound down and then—I was standing high up in—I can't tell you in what, I'll have to call it a room. We have no images for what is in the pit. A hundred feet below me was the floor. The walls sloped down and out from where I stood in a series of widening crescents. The place was colossal—and it was filled with a curious mottled red light. It was like the light inside a green and gold flecked fire opal. I went down to the last step. Far in front of me rose a high, columned altar. Its pillars were carved in monstrous scrolls—like mad octopuses with a thousand drunken tentacles; they rested on the backs of shapeless monstrosities carved in crimson stone. The altar front was a gigantic slab of purple covered with carvings.

"I can't describe these carvings! No human being could—the human eye cannot grasp them any more than it can grasp the shapes that haunt the fourth dimension. Only a subtle sense in the back of the brain sensed them vaguely. They were formless things that gave no conscious image, yet pressed into the mind like small hot seals—ideas of hate—of combats between unthinkable monstrous things—victories in a nebulous hell of steaming, obscene jungles—aspirations and ideals immeasurably loathsome—

"And as I stood I grew aware of something that lay behind the lip of the altar fifty feet above me. I knew it was there—I felt it with every hair and every tiny bit of my skin. Something infinitely malignant, infinitely horrible, infinitely ancient. It lurked, it brooded, it threatened and it—was invisible!

"Behind me was a circle of blue light. I ran for it. Something urged me to turn back, to climb the stairs and make away. It was impossible. Repulsion for that unseen Thing raced me onward as though a current had my feet. I passed through the circle. I was out on a street that stretched on into dim distance between rows of the carven cylinders.

"Here and there the red trees arose. Between them rolled the stone burrows. And now I could take in the amazing ornamentation that clothed them. They were like the trunks of smooth skinned trees that had fallen and had been clothed with high reaching noxious orchids. Yes—those cylinders were like that—and more. They should have gone out with the dinosaurs. They were—monstrous. They struck the eyes like a blow and they passed across the nerves like a rasp. And nowhere was there sight or sound of living thing.

"There were circular openings in the cylinders like the circle in the Temple of the Stairway. I passed through one of them. I was in a long, bare vaulted room whose curving sides half closed twenty feet over my head, leaving a wide slit that opened into another vaulted chamber above. There was absolutely nothing in the room save the same mottled reddish light that I had seen in the Temple. I stumbled. I still could see nothing, but there was something on the floor over which I had tripped. I reached down—and my hand touched a thing cold and smooth—that moved under it—I turned and ran out of that place—I was filled with a loathing that had in it something of madness—I ran on and on blindly—wringing my hands—weeping with horror—

"When I came to myself I was still among the stone cylinders and red trees. I tried to retrace my steps; to find the Temple. I was more than afraid. I was like a new loosed soul panic-stricken with the first terrors of hell. I could not find the Temple! Then the haze began to thicken and glow; the cylinders to shine more brightly. I knew that it was dusk in the world above and I felt that with dusk my time of peril had come; that the thickening of the haze was the signal for the awakening of whatever things lived in this pit.

"I scrambled up the sides of one of the burrows. I hid behind a twisted nightmare of stone. Perhaps, I thought, there was a chance of remaining hidden until the blue lightened and the peril passed. There began to grow around me a murmur. It was everywhere—and it grew and grew into a great whispering. I peeped from the side of the stone down into the street. I saw lights passing and repassing. More and more lights—they swam out of the circular doorways and they thronged the street. The highest were eight feet above the pave; the lowest perhaps two. They hurried, they sauntered, they bowed, they stopped and whispered—and there was nothing under them!"

"Nothing under them!" breathed Anderson.

"No," he went on, "that was the terrible part of it—there was nothing under them. Yet certainly the lights were living things. They had consciousness, volition, thought—what else I did not know. They were nearly two feet across—the largest. Their center was a bright nucleus—red, blue, green. This nucleus faded off, gradually, into a misty glow that did not end abruptly. It too seemed to fade off into nothingness—but a nothingness that had under it a somethingness. I strained my eyes trying to grasp this body into which the lights merged and which one could only feel was there, but could not see.

"And all at once I grew rigid. Something cold, and thin like a whip, had touched my face. I turned my head. Close behind were three of the lights. They were a pale blue. They looked at me—if you can imagine lights that are eyes. Another whiplash gripped my shoulder. Under the closest light came a shrill whispering. I shrieked. Abruptly the murmuring in the street ceased. I dragged my eyes from the pale blue globe that held them and looked out—the lights in the streets were rising by myriads to the level of where I stood! There they stopped and peered at me. They crowded and jostled as though they were a crowd of curious people—on Broadway. I felt a score of the lashes touch me—

"When I came to myself I was again in the great Place of the Stairway, lying at the foot of the altar. All was silent. There were no lights—only the mottled red glow. I jumped to my feet and ran toward the steps. Something jerked me back to my knees. And then I saw that around my waist had been fastened a yellow ring of metal. From it hung a chain and this chain passed up over the lip of the high ledge. I was chained to the altar!

"I reached into my pockets for my knife to cut through the ring. It was not there! I had been stripped of everything except one of the canteens that I had hung around my neck and which I suppose They had thought was—part of me. I tried to break the ring. It seemed alive. It writhed in my hands and it drew itself closer around me! I pulled at the chain. It was immovable. There came to me the consciousness of the unseen Thing above the altar. I groveled at the foot of the slab and wept. Think—alone in that place of strange light with the brooding ancient Horror above me—a monstrous Thing, a Thing unthinkable—an unseen Thing that poured forth horror—

"After awhile I gripped myself. Then I saw beside one of the pillars a yellow bowl filled with a thick white liquid. I drank it. If it killed I did not care. But its taste was pleasant and as I drank my strength came back to me with a rush. Clearly I was not to be starved. The lights, whatever they were, had a conception of human needs.

"And now the reddish mottled gleam began to deepen. Outside arose the humming and through the circle that was the entrance came streaming the globes. They ranged themselves in ranks until they filled the Temple. Their whispering grew into a chant, a cadenced whispering chant that rose and fell, rose and fell, while to its rhythm the globes lifted and sank, lifted and sank.

"All that night the lights came and went—and all that night the chant sounded as they rose and fell. At the last I felt myself only an atom of consciousness in a sea of cadenced whispering; an atom that rose and fell with the bowing globes. I tell you that even my heart pulsed in unison with them! The red glow faded, the lights streamed out; the whispering died. I was again alone and I knew that once again day had broken in my own world.

"I slept. When I awoke I found beside the pillar more of the white liquid. I scrutinized the chain that held me to the altar. I began to rub two of the links together.

I did this for hours. When the red began to thicken there was a ridge worn in the links. Hope rushed up within me. There was, then, a chance to escape.

"With the thickening the lights came again. All through that night the whispering chant sounded, and the globes rose and fell. The chant seized me. It pulsed through me until every nerve and muscle quivered to it. My lips began to quiver. They strove like a man trying to cry out on a nightmare. And at last they too were whispering the chant of the people of the pit. My body bowed in unison with the lights—I was, in movement and sound, one with the nameless things while my soul sank back sick with horror and powerless. While I whispered I—saw Them!"

"Saw the lights?" I asked stupidly.

"Saw the Things under the lights," he answered. "Great transparent snail-like bodies—dozens of waving tentacles stretching from them—round gaping mouths under the luminous seeing globes. They were like the ghosts of inconceivably monstrous slugs! I could see through them. And as I stared, still bowing and whispering, the dawn came and they streamed to and through the entrance. They did not crawl or walk—they floated! They floated and were—gone!

"I did not sleep. I worked all that day at my chain. By the thickening of the red I had worn it a sixth through. And all that night I whispered and bowed with the pit people, joining in their chant to the Thing that brooded above me!

"Twice again the red thickened and the chant held me—then on the morning of the fifth day I broke through the worn links of the chain. I was free! I drank from the bowl of white liquid and poured what was left in my flask. I ran to the Stairway. I rushed up and past that unseen Horror behind the altar ledge and was out upon the Bridge. I raced across the span and up the Stairway.

"Can you think what it is to climb straight up the verge of a cleft-world—with hell behind you? Hell was behind me and terror rode me. The city had long been lost in the blue haze before I knew that I could climb no more. My heart beat upon my ears like a sledge. I fell before one of the little caves feeling that here at last was sanctuary. I crept far back within it and waited for the haze to thicken. Almost at once it did so. From far below me came a vast and angry murmur. At the mouth of the rift I saw a light pulse up through the blue; die down and as it dimmed I saw myriads of the globes that are the eyes of the pit people swing downward into the abyss. Again and again the light pulsed and the globes fell. They were hunting me. The whispering grew louder, more insistent.

"There grew in me the dreadful desire to join in the whispering as I had done in the Temple. I bit my lips through and through to still them. All that night the beam shot up through the abyss, the globes swung and the whispering sounded—and now

I knew the purpose of the caves and of the sculptured figures that still had power to guard them. But what were the people who had carved them? Why had they built their city around the verge and why had they set that Stairway in the pit? What had they been to those Things that dwelt at the bottom and what use had the Things been to them that they should live beside their dwelling place? That there had been some purpose was certain. No work so prodigious as the Stairway would have been undertaken otherwise. But what was the purpose? And why was it that those who had dwelt about the abyss had passed away ages gone, and the dwellers in the abyss still lived? I could find no answer—nor can I find any now. I have not the shred of a theory.

"Dawn came as I wondered and with it silence. I drank what was left of the liquid in my canteen, crept from the cave and began to climb again. That afternoon my legs gave out. I tore off my shirt, made from it pads for my knees and coverings for my hands. I crawled upward. I crawled up and up. And again I crept into one of the caves and waited until again the blue thickened, the shaft of light shot through it and the whispering came.

"But now there was a new note in the whispering. It was no longer threatening. It called and coaxed. It drew.

"A new terror gripped me. There had come upon me a mighty desire to leave the cave and go out where the lights swung; to let them do with me as they pleased, carry me where they wished. The desire grew. It gained fresh impulse with every rise of the beam until at last I vibrated with the desire as I had vibrated to the chant in the Temple. My body was a pendulum. Up would go the beam and I would swing toward it! Only my soul kept steady. It held me fast to the floor of the cave; And all that night it fought with my body against the spell of the pit people.

"Dawn came. Again I crept from the cave and faced the Stairway. I could not rise. My hands were torn and bleeding; my knees an agony. I forced myself upward step by step. After a while my hands became numb, the pain left my knees. They deadened. Step by step my will drove my body upward upon them.

"And then—a nightmare of crawling up infinite stretches of steps—memories of dull horror while hidden within caves with the lights pulsing without and whisperings that called and called me—memory of a time when I awoke to find that my body was obeying the call and had carried me half way out between the guardians of the portals while thousands of gleaming globes rested in the blue haze and watched me."

"Glimpses of bitter fights against sleep and always, always—a climb up and up along infinite distances of steps that led from Abaddon to a Paradise of blue sky and open world!

"At last a consciousness of the clear sky close above me, the lip of the pit before me—memory of passing between the great portals of the pit and of steady withdrawal from it—dreams of giant men with strange peaked crowns and veiled faces who pushed me onward and onward and held back Roman Candle globules of light that sought to draw me back to a gulf wherein planets swam between the branches of red trees that had snakes for crowns.

"And then a long, long sleep—how long God alone knows—in a cleft of rocks; an awakening to see far in the North the beam still rising and falling, the lights still hunting, the whispering high above me calling.

"Again crawling on dead arms and legs that moved—that moved—like the Ancient Mariner's ship—without volition of mine, but that carried me from a haunted place. And then—your fire—and this—safety!"

The crawling man smiled at us for a moment. Then swiftly life faded from his face. He slept.

That afternoon we struck camp and carrying the crawling man started back South. For three days we carried him and still he slept. And on the third day, still sleeping, he died. We built a great pile of wood and we burned his body as he had asked. We scattered his ashes about the forest with the ashes of the trees that had consumed him. It must be a great magic indeed that could disentangle those ashes and draw him back in a rushing cloud to the pit he called Accursed. I do not think that even the People of the Pit have such a spell. No.

But we did not return to the five peaks to see.

SILENT, WHITE
AND BEAUTIFUL

TOD ROBBINS

TOD ROBBINS (1888-1949) WROTE THE NOVEL *THE UNHOLY THREE* AND THE SHORT STORY "SPURS," BOTH ADAPTED FOR THE SCREEN BY DIRECTOR TOD BROWNING, THE LATTER AS THE CULT CLASSIC *FREAKS*. THIS STORY, THE TITLE TALE OF HIS 1920 COLLECTION OF MACABRE FICTION, SHOWS THE INFLUENCE OF EDGAR ALLAN POE IN ITS DEPICTION OF A MADMAN WHOSE INSANITY EXPLODES INTO SOCIOPATHY.

I

To-morrow at this time I shall be dead! I have repeated this phrase over and over since breakfast with the utmost calmness, with the utmost resignation. In no way have I attempted to blind myself to the truth. He who does that is lost. The philosopher alone is wise. Before the clear calm eyes of reason, the imaginary terrors of dissolution become infinitesimal specks of dust. I breathe upon them and they are gone.

And yet I cannot visualize my death. I have tried to many times, but have failed. Sitting down on the left hand corner of my cot, I attempt to picture the execution. My imagination has always been supernaturally acute. I can see the room and the chair—the chair dreaded by so many. And the witnesses? Yes, I can see them—all those sensation-mongers. There is one fat old gentleman in a striped flannel waist-coat—an old gentleman who keeps on smiling and smiling. One would think he were at a wedding, his smile is so forced and unreal. And the others are like statues, grouped together to represent something.

Yes, I can see them all. But they are not looking at me. No, they are looking at another man—a man who has seated himself in the chair. But this man is not I.

365

No, though he sits in my place, wears the new suit which was given me, bears my dishonored name, he is not I. And although I attempt to analyze this man's emotions, read the secret workings of that brain, understand the feelings of one in the shadow, the blade of imagination bends in my mind, becoming useless and dull.

To-morrow at this time I shall be dead! This phrase no longer conjures up anything. Like a child who has repeated the Lord's Prayer over and over, so have I repeated, "To-morrow at this time I shall be dead," till the words have become meaningless, sinking back into the black unexplored caverns of sound. And that this hand which guides the pencil—this live human hand—will in so short a space be motionless and powerless, cold and senseless, seems as impossible as the wildest dream. The voice of reason pounds dully against my ear-drums, but cannot gain admittance. Perhaps it is better so.

Am I afraid of death? No. Then why have I taken up the pencil? Because, although I am not afraid of death, I am afraid of something which lurks on the invisible frontier—something which is quite apart from, both life and death—something which reads my words, my looks, my gestures. And because of this silent sentinel in my cell, I have become a stranger to myself—an uncouth awkward stranger. The egoist has fled, the artist who crushed conventionality beneath his heel; and in his place stands an unknown, terrible fellow—a fellow who needs watching. I could have pleaded insanity at my trial and escaped the chair. It is so easy for me to act. But now—Why could not the judge and jury see me now?

But I must not peer too long into my soul. Introspection looks down the shaft, and soon sees the grinning face of Madness floating on the black water. The austere countenance of the philosopher casts back a reflection which he recognizes with a shudder. The moon may be— But I must not wander.

One source of solace has been with me constantly during my days of imprisonment. To a man such as I—a man condemned to death—the daily newspapers are of great value. It is comforting to realize that there are thousands, nay millions, of human beings who are cognizant of my existence, perhaps intimately interested in the outcome of my career. During these last few weeks, as never before, I have felt myself to be an important link in the human chain—a link which daily holds the attention of a multitude of minds. I, the unknown sculptor, the young man of limited means and limited reputation, am now something of a celebrity. What an enduring hold has egotism! I caught myself smiling a self-satisfied smile when I wrote, "something of a celebrity." Avaunt, False Pride! You are in the presence of the shadow. Back, back to the highway of life, where the multitude sit in the sunlight. I have no need of you here.

I realize perfectly what a storm of curiosity my actions have aroused and it is not my purpose to leave this planet without a satisfying answer to the question which I myself have raised. You, who have so often studied my striking portrait in the papers, you, who have so puzzled over my whimsical acts during the ill-fated month of March, you, my friends and admirers, shall learn of everything which prompted me to a series of crimes destined to set the world of sensation agog. And you, my fair readers, you, whose soft cheeks so quickly change from rose to lily, you, who shudder and turn away, look again into the face which you have covertly abstracted from the newspaper—the face of René Galien, your humble servant; René Galien who created that group "The Happy Family." Respect is akin to fear, is it not? You shall respect me.

II

I come of an old French family. There is the blood of kings in my veins. You smile; but it is a fact, I assure you. Have you not noted in my many portraits, the finely chiseled features, the aristocratic curl to the lips, the small shell-like ears? But my hands! They are what tell the story. The long tapering fingers, the delicacy of wrist and palm—yes, these are the hands of one refined by the gradual process of centuries. Why do my eyes hold your attention then, when I have such hands as these?

After the Revolution, my great grandfather emigrated to America. Since then the Galiens have been bobbing up and down like corks. You know how it is—one year a mansion, servants, horses, dogs; another year a boarding house, genteel respectability, a single suit shiny at the elbows and knees. That comes from an excess of aristocratic blood in a plebeian age. The male members of my family have never been saving with their money. My father cried out on his deathbed:

"It is glorious to die in debt. One has succeeded in cheating one's enemy, the world."

A strange man was he, with a laugh like the cackling of a frightened hen and dry, shriveled hands which rustled in the empty pockets of his frock-coat like banknotes.

My mother died before I can remember. At an early age I was sent to a school in Paris. Once a year I was allowed to cross the sea and visit my father in New York. He would meet me each time at the pier, looking very somber in his frock-coat. I remember that towards the last his face seemed as yellow as the pale bloodless oranges one buys.

He resided at a small boarding-house in Thirty-third street—a French boarding-house where one encountered all manner of odd characters. Madame Fabien, the landlady, was a woman well on in middle life. At the time of which I speak, she attempted to maintain a semblance of youth by a plentiful use of cosmetics. Her face, as haggard as a death's head, had a vivid splash of color beneath each prominent cheek-bone; and above it, her hair, yellow and fuzzy, reminded me of sundried weeds. Her eyes were a bitter blue, but they softened when they looked upon my father.

In some way—perhaps by his glib tongue and polished manners—he had wormed himself into the landlady's good grace. The pitcher of cream always stood beside his place at the breakfast table; and, when he came to die, for many nights she went about the house mewing like a sick cat. No doubt with him was buried the last romance of her checkered career. Perhaps the realization of this added to the poignancy of her grief.

Madame Fabien had a daughter of about my own age who did much to make my visits to New York agreeable. She was a pretty vivacious child, with a mind far too precocious for her years. Looking through keyholes had given one of her eye-lids an unconscious droop. She had made herself the bane of the boarders' existence. It is needless to say that what youthful innocence a French boarding-school had left me, vanished after a month's sojourn at Madame Fabien's.

After my father's death, I returned to Paris with a letter of introduction to an old friend of the landlady's—a certain Paul Montaigne. He was a successful sculptor of the period—a man, who, if he had not been addicted to drugs, might have reached high places. From the first I loved him. There was something restful in his companionship—something which reminded me of a calm autumn day. He gave me the key which opened the door to a new resplendent world. Art was his mistress. She soon became mine. Before long I, too, could see the beauty in ugliness, the joy in tears. If he had lived, what might I not have done?

Paul Montaigne adopted me. I posed for him; I swept up the studio; I enlivened him when he waa plunged into one of those fits of melancholy which followed his excesses. In return for this, he taught me his art. I was an apt pupil. Soon I conceived several small pieces of my own, which I sold on the Paris streets. Once a week I took my stand on the Rue Montmartre and peddled my wares to any passerby.

One afternoon I returned to the studio and found my benefactor dead. He was lying at the feet of a statue upon which he had been working—a statue representing Justice. His body seemed to be in an attitude of supplication. A thin ribbon of blood crawled towards the door like a miniature river of red. He had cut his throat. It seemed unbelievable at first. When I saw him lying thus, I felt that I had lost everything in the world. Dropping the bag which contained several tiny statues I had not sold, I sank to my knees and began to blubber like a baby. There the concierge found me an hour later, sobbing as though my heart would break.

After Paul Montaigne's death, I returned to America. It seemed to me that I could make my fortune there much more readily. Surely in the United States competition was not so great. My four years with the sculptor had given me a foundation few could boast of. Montaigne had often told me that I possessed a talent which was in no way inferior to his own. It was with high hopes that I set sail from France.

On arriving in New York, I took a cab to the familiar boarding-house. Madame Fabien opened the door for me. I scarcely recognized her. In the four years which had elapsed she had become an old hag and looked every day of sixty. After my father's death she had evidently buried her cosmetics. Her face, wrinkled and yellow, was so thin that the sharp protruding cheekbones seemed at any moment about to penetrate the skin; her scanty hair was now a splotched grey; and she leaned heavily on her cane in the doorway, reminding me of the witches in Macbeth. But her eyes had not changed. No, they were that same bitter blue. Now they looked at me suspiciously from beneath a ragged boudoir cap.

"Well?" said she.

"Is this Madame Fabien?" I asked, suspecting that my memory had played me tricks.

"Yes, this is Madame Fabien. What is it you wish of me, young man?"

"I am René Galien," I answered, stepping forward. "Do you not remember me?"

"Mon Dieu!" The old woman's expression changed from suspicion to joy. She tapped me playfully on the shoulder with her cane. "Come in, come in! Of course it is René. Why, you are your father over again! The same carriage of the head, the same air distingue. Only the eyes are different. But come to these old arms. I have heard such things of you from Paul! *You* are the great sculptor now, is it not so?"

In spite of an inner qualm, I submitted myself to the old hag's embraces. She pinched my cheeks with fingers as yellow as sticks of cinnamon; she rose on tiptoe to press her lips to my forehead; she smoothed my silky hair with the palm of her hand—a palm which was as rough as a nutmeg grater. She was like the cracked dusty vase in which lies buried the trampled rose-leaves of the preceding spring. Once a vessel of desire, she had been quaffed to the very dregs.

"Louise will be delighted to see you, René," she said, leering up at me. "Ah, you blush, eh! You remember her—the little cat that she was. But now! How she has changed! Like you, she has grown tall and beautiful. And such a figure! The art students draw her twice during the week. How the pencils shake in their hands, how their eyes stare and stare! They are like men in a trance—so beautiful is she!"

"Is she a model?" I asked.

"Yes; but there is none other like her in New York. When my last boarder left, it was necessary that she do something. We must live, is it not so? But I will tell her that you are here. She will be overjoyed."

Madame Fabien hobbled down the passageway, leaving me standing in the hot stuffy hall. As I watched her figure receding in the shadows, I made up my mind to remain in her good graces. I had been barely able to scrape up enough money in Paris to pay for my passage; I was now in a wellnigh penniless condition. Of course I would soon be successful, but in the meantime I must not neglect any slight smile of fortune. Before the old woman returned with her daughter, I had made up my mind to be enthusiastic.

Louise did not make my role difficult to play. She had, indeed, matured into a kind of rare if sulky beauty. Her full lips, although pouting and discontented, were still inviting; and, although her figure was rather buxom according to my standard, still there were men who would have thought it perfect. My raised hands and upturned eyes therefore, while delighting both mother and daughter, even to myself had no savor of the ludicrous.

"Is she not changed?" asked Madame Fabien.

"Changed!" I cried. *"Ma Foi!* she is transfigured!"

Louise blushed and smiled. Evidently I had pleased her.

"You, yourself, have altered for the better," she said, looking at me quaintly, "You are no longer the ugly duckling."

I murmured a graceful acknowledgment, then, turning to her mother, immediately reverted to the point in hand.

"Do you still take boarders?" I asked. "If so, I would consider myself fortunate in securing—"

"Most certainly you may board here," the old woman answered. "At present there is no one, and we can give you the better attention. My fees are moderate to the son of an old friend."

Again Louise smiled, disclosing two rows of large white teeth.

"Follow me," she said, picking up my valise in spite of my protests. "I will show you to your room."

Madame Fabien leered at me as I passed her. She again reached up and pinched my cheek. It nauseated me. Without the slightest compunction, I could have put my hands on her weed-like throat and choked the life out of her. Even then I felt that she and I could not live under the same roof without disastrous results. I hesitated for a moment on the landing before I followed Louise up the creaking staircase.

III

I must break off for the time. Father Flynn has been shown into my cell. Why does he insist on offering ghostly consolation to me? Can he not realize that I am a man of adamant will, of unshakable determination?

This priest in the sunshine dares to come to me in the shadow—dares to come to me and cry:

"See, there is everlasting life!"

Everlasting life? Bah! Rather everlasting death—everlasting death with its calm immobility—everlasting death with its enigmatic smile. Yes, there I will be reigning like a mountain peak, cold, still and thoughtful

But now Father Flynn is approaching. Hia long black robe brushes over the floor of my cell with a swishing sound. His solemn eyes are fixed upon my face. About his neck a crucifix is suspended. Christ hangs on this crucifix, tiny, weak, and helpless—Christ made into a doll. When he speaks of life everlasting, I shall point at his toy Christ and laugh.

IV

Father Flynn has left me. His brain, heavy and ponderous as a mediæval battle-ax, was no match for the lightning thrusts of mine. I have hurt him in a sensitive spot beneath his armor of religion; I have penetrated his self-esteem. He now doubts himself, which is far worse than doubting God. Like an old woman who suddenly encounters a mouse in her bedroom, like an old woman with dragging skirts and downcast eyes, he has hurried from the cell. In his opinion, I am eternally damned—a man for whom the jaws of Hell are yawning. I have refused to reverence the doll dangling from his neck, therefore I am as one lost.

Poor old man! I pity him for his childish credulity, while I envy him his simple trust. But if I had had a Christ, if I had had a sacred symbol of something greater than myself, I would not hang it about my neck and be content. Ah no! I would build for it a pedestal; and on this pedestal I would place it so that it could sneer down on the passing people, sneer down on the passing people in the dust. And in its eyes would be hot anger; and in its hand, a reeking sword. Away with your tiny toy Christ, Father Flynn. Mine would be gigantic and terrible—gigantic, terrible, and red!

But I must compose myself. Already night stretches out her ebony wings over the world. When the first rays of dawn creep into my cell, they will come and take me away. Meanwhile Death is waiting in the corner. He, alone, does not fear me; He, alone, can return the look in my eyes. Before that grim sentinel my glance wavers and falls. I will take up the pencil and finish my record; yes, although the pitiless spectre continues to stare at me with his dull lack-lustre eyes.

V

When I took up my residence with Madame Fabien, I intended remaining there only a short time. It seemed to me that my genius would find recognition before many weeks went by. In the meanwhile it was necessary for me to live—and where could I live on credit except at Madame Fabien's?

The old Frenchwoman ensconced me in a large room on the topmost floor—a room which had once served as an artist's studio. It had a north light; and was in every way suitable for a work-shop. I had brought over with me from Paris the tools of my trade; and it was not long before I started working in dead earnest. Ere a month, went by, I had created several miniatures which I thought I could dispose of for a fair sum.

My moments of leisure were spent with Louise and her mother. I felt it necessary to keep in the good graces of both women. But what a bore it was! My flesh fairly crawled when Madame Fabien touched me. It was as much as I could do to submit to her caresses. And then the atmosphere of the house began to get on my nerves. It was so hot and stuffy downstairs, and a sweet sickening odor hovered about everything. In the parlor there were a multitude of photographs, representing Madame Fabien in her youth. She had evidently been a vaudeville performer of versatile repertoire. There were pictures of her walking a tightrope, a parasol above her head, smiling sentimentally at space; pictures of her in knickerbockers, riding an old-fashioned bicycle; pictures of her in tights, toe-dancing on a horse's back. And in all these photographs she resembled Louise. Yes, there was the same haggard face with high cheek-bones and petulant lips, the same full-bosomed, broad-hipped figure, the same sensual drooping eyelids. Thirty years ago my landlady had been another Louise. And, when I realized this, what little affection I had for the girl faded. Although I continued to ply her assiduously with compliments, my words no longer had the slightest ring of truth.

And as the weeks went by, I came to realize that it would be difficult to escape my environment. Daily a web of attachment took shape. Both these women regarded me now with an air of ownership. To Madame Fabien, I was a living embodiment of one to whom she had given the last dying sparks of passion; to Louise I was a companion of childhood suddenly transformed into a fairy prince who had crossed the seas to win her.

And I? Why, struggle as I might to free myself, my feet were sinking in the quicksand. A month passed, and I had not sold a single piece of work. Where else could I go? I was penniless and in debt. Contrary to my expectations, my miniatures went begging. These imaginative figures which I had sold so easily in Paris—these weird gargoyles, nymphs and satyrs, were shuddered at, but never bought.

I found myself battering my head against an obstinate senseless wall of optimism. The beauty which lurks in ugliness, the transcending horror depicted in my work, the morbid terror which enwrapped those tiny figures—all was quite lost on the stupid smiling people who passed me by. They hurried on, these people; hurried on through the tunnel of life unheedingly, looking neither up nor down, quite immersed in their own -bright dreams and unwilling to contemplate the stern austere countenance of Art. I might have gone on for centuries in my garret, striving, creating, and quite unnoticed, were it not for that group "The Happy Family."

At last my affairs reached a climax. I could no longer avoid Fate. I married Louise. Yes, loathing her with all my soul, seeing in her a future Madame Fabien, I married her. It came about like this:

One afternoon, while I was at work, a knock sounded on my door. It was Louise. The night before she had heard me express a wish for a female model. She had come to offer her services. Yes, she was quite willing to pose for me. It was no trouble at all. She would be ready in a moment now.

With brazenness, even for a professional model, she began to disrobe. I attempted to detain her. I put my hand on her arm, but she only kissed me and called me a foolish boy.

"Are we not already as good as married?" said she.

I did not realize how truly she spoke until I looked over her shoulder and saw Madame Fabien standing in the doorway. I was positive that something was about to happen. My landlady, among her other accomplishments, had at one time been a melodramatic tragedienne. On her face was mirrored the rôle which she was about to play.

"So!" she cried in a voice which squeaked like a violin out of tune. "So! I find you thus! Is this how you repay me, René? Has it not been enough to live here week after week, to take board and lodging from me gratis, to receive from my hands all the attention of a mother, without attacking the virtue of my daughter? No, don't attempt to explain away your guilt. Thank God my eyes can still be trusted! Louise, go to your room! I will talk to this young man alone."

Fifteen minutes later, all was over. I had agreed to marry Louise on the following day. That old virago Had so battered me with words that my brain was reeling. I would have signed my death-warrant to have gotten rid of her. And she, when the victory had been won, when my promise had been gained, immediately relapsed into a sickly sentimental air. She pinched my cheek and lavished me with endearments; she called me her own beautiful boy; she bade Louise fetch a bottle of Madeira from the cellar, and pledged my health in the sweet wine till her eyes grew misty and her voice sounded dull and indistinct.

And I? Why, I bowed and smiled, and kept on bowing and smiling till I felt like a mechanical doll attached to a giant's finger. And the smile seemed to grow and grow till it covered my face with painful agitated wrinkles; and my head grew heavy and bulbous, so that it became difficult to raise and lower it in time to the old woman's eager, querulous questions.

At last they left me to myself.

VI

On the following day Louise and I were married. What a mockery! As the words fell slowly from the priest's mouth—words which weighed me down as though they had been so many pellets of lead—I had a wild impulse to leap to my feet, to shake the girl's hand from my arm and dash out of that church never to return. My one cowardly trait, my dread of penury and hunger, forced me to remain. And as I knelt before the altar, looking up into the priest's wrinkled face, I became unpleasantly conscious of Madame Fabien's proximity. I felt her breath fanning the back of my neck. Involuntarily I shuddered and yet beads of perspiration dotted my forehead. At last the ceremony was over, and we returned home.

Home! What a blasphemous title to apply to such a place! And yet the roof sheltered my head, the walls shut out the darkness and the cold. Where else could I find as much, I asked myself. Think of the irony of it! I, a young man of talent, an individualist, an artist, and yet forced to acknowledge such a defeat. It was then I came to the realization that there was something wrong with the world. Surely it had been rolling downhill for ages—a wicked ball bent on destruction. In vain we Supermen seek to push it up, to place it on the heights—it evades our eager hands and descends into the black depths. To this day, I cannot contemplate its final degradation without a feeling of regret, even of horror.

It is not my purpose to dwell too long on my married life. Suffice it to say, that it soon became unendurable to me. Living with one woman constantly is prone to wear on the nerves of the sensitive man; but, when this woman is lacking in both mentality and feeling, artistic appreciation and higher aspirations, she becomes a burning coal of agony which one is forced to hold to one's bare breast. Before a week had passed, I hated Louise as I had never thought to hate any human being.

What made it worse, the girl positively adored me. She gave me no peace. She would break into my studio while I was at work, and shower me with loathsome caresses. I had no solitude of the soul so necessary to an artist. She sought to occupy every cranny of my life. If I reprimanded her, if, driven to desperation, I struck her, waves of hysterics would follow—hysterics, that abomination of woman—and to avoid this shrieking inferno it was necessary for me to calm her with kisses and protestations of affection.

Then there was Madame Fabien—Madame Fabien with her fishy eyes! How her tongue clattered! I have often thought that she must have assassinated my father with it. And life was still strong in this bag of old bones! It shown evilly out of her bitter blue eyes; it spoke volubly through her dry, shriveled lips. She might live twenty years more—live and persecute me.

One night inspiration touched me—the inspiration of "The Happy Family." True perception springs from contrast. It has always been my experience that in the city one can visualize the country with an acute clarity. So it is with all things. The musician composes a dirge on a bright spring day; the starving poet writes an ode to sparkling wine and luscious fruit. Thus it was in my case. From a confirmed unbeliever in marriage, I could now see the joys of wedlock. My own unfortunate affair had conjured up in my mind an ideal picture of wedded bliss—a happy family, united in thought and deed; a silent, happy family who found mere speech unnecessary to a complete mental understanding.

And as I sat at dinner, listening to the shrill voices of the women, watching their distorted mouths and glistening eyes, in an instant it became apparent what made them so hideous, so revolting. It was life that marred them; hot, noisy life which twisted them into repellent shapes; life which made them detestable and unforgivable. As statues—deprived of breath, motion, speech—they would no longer cause me any pain. On the contrary, I might be proud of them. Madame Fabien could very well have been Rodin's "Courtesan," alive, clothed and speaking. Such ugliness was beautiful in art. It was only when it stepped down from its pedestal that it became loathsome and degraded. And Louise? If she would not speak in that whining tone, if her face could always remain calm and placid, if she could be placed in an artistic posture with her chin resting on her hand—why, she would be beautiful!

And then in my imagination I saw them as statues; saw them sitting there, silent, white and beautiful; saw them sitting on a pedestal, united and peaceful, cleansed of life's impurities, quietly waiting for the children yet unborn—I saw "The Happy Family"!

Why was it not possible to make them so? A few drops of poison in their coffee, and life would quickly fade away. And then? Why, then I would carry them up to my studio where I had so often werked before. But this time I would not work in vain. No, I would make statues of them—enclose them in a special preparation of clay which might last through all the centuries. Their bodies would not decompose in such a covering. It would be easy—easy! Perhaps I could sell them to an art dealer. At this thought, I laughed aloud.

"Why are you laughing, René?" asked Madame Fabien with one of her quick, suspicious looks.

"I was thinking of what an excellent statue you would make, mama. May I use you for a model?"

She shook her bony head at me like an old vulture.

"Careful, René, careful," she mumbled. "Don't bite the hand that feeds you. Youth should respect age."

"But I was in earnest, mama," I assured her.

"Bah!" She rose and hobbled off on her cane, leaving Louise to wash up the dinner things.

For the moment I was free.

Telling my wife that I had to post a letter, I put on my hat and left the house.

When I returned I had a small vial of poison in my waistcoat pocket.;

As I lay beside Louise that night, I dreamed peacefully of "The Happy Family."

VII

Have you ever considered what a childishly simple thing it is to take a human life? We are all so trusting with our fellows, so guileless and trusting, that, when the murderous hand reaches out to cut the cord of existence, we stand blinking our eyes stupidly, quite unable to realize the danger. If it were not for the bodies of his victims—bodies which, although silent, bear unfaltering testimony to the truth—the assassin might stalk unmolested through the world. Our immortality seems so assured to us, that we seldom question the eyes of those who may have it in their keeping.

Louise and her mother suspected nothing. On the following evening, when I suggested that I prepare their coffee in a manner new to them—a method which

I had picked up in Paris—they assented readily. It was only when I placed the two steaming cups upon the table that any difficulty arose.

"I should not drink any coffee," said Madame Fabien, shaking her head sorrowfully.

I felt a sudden flicker of fear.

"Why not, mama?" I murmured, bending over her solicitously.

"It keeps me awake at night. I cannot sleep when I drink coffee."

I could not refrain from smiling.

"Never fear, mama," I answered reassuringly. "This coffee is so prepared that you will not be troubled by insomnia. I guarantee that you will sleep soundly to-night—very soundly."

And then, without hesitation, without fear, almost without taking breath, these two women drank their poisoned coffee. I watched them with a calm, impersonal curiosity. And yet the next few moments were the most embarrassing moments of my life. I felt that I was conversing with spectres. Everything I said rang out of tune when I attempted to joke, and my witticisms fell far below humor. I attempted to laugh, and my own familiar laugh sounded as hoarse and guttural as the cawing of a crow. And these two women seemed like stiff formal strangers who could not in any way be amused.

Madame Fabien was the first to go. One side of her shriveled face drew up into knots, as though a cord in her cheek had been suddenly pulled. She clapped her hand to her stomach.

"Oh!" she cried. "I suffer! I—I—. Get the doctor. Get the "

She rolled to the floor, and lay there kicking and clawing like a wounded wildcat.

Louise rose and bent over her.

"René, run out and get Dr. Milburn," she called over her shoulder in an agitated voice.

I had no desire to see them die. A wanton taste for cruelty has never been one of my characteristics. I quitted the room, and, mounting the stairs to my studio, spent a few peaceful moments over a cigar. When I returned to the dining room, I found both women dead. Louise's body lay across her mother's. Her upturned face wore an expression of amazement. It was as though I had given her a sudden surprise.

Then the real work began. That night I toiled like a galley-slave. I carried the bodies up to my studio; I disrobed them; I burned the clothing piecemeal; and then I commenced my famous group, "The Happy Family."

With the firm, sure hand of an artist, I enclosed them in clinging garments of clay; I gave them immortal skins which might last through all eternity. And now that the life had gone out of them, these women were no longer repulsive to me. No, on the contrary, I felt a sensation of ennobling pride as I busied myself about them, placing them on the pedestal, making of them enduring works of art. When the sun finally peered in at me through the blind, two statues confronted me—two statues so lifelike, so virile, that the hand of Rodin himself could not have done better.

My work enraptured me. At last I had created something which might live. What a contrast was this!—Madame Fabien so thin and withered, cowering in the early light; and beside her, Louise, so strong and buxom, her chin resting in the hollow of her hand. This was art! For the first time in my life I loved them. I was so proud of them that it was all I could do to refrain from running out into the street and bringing back with me the first passerby to see what I had done. For the moment I was living on the sunlit heights of great achievement.

VIII

Unfortunately the artist is never satisfied with his first creation. He must go on and on, enlarging his original conception, until sometimes it winds itself about him like a many-membered octopus and sucks the life out of him.

So it was with me. For a week I busied myself in the studio, constructing a large pedestal for my statues; but at the end of that time, I found myself longing to add to the group. What was a happy family without children, I asked myself. A mother-in-law and a wife were all very well; but surely, without tender human plants sprouting up about them, they were meaningless and thrown away. Yes, both were lonely and must have childish companionship. The longing look on Louise's face touched my heart.

It was shortly after this that I began to visit the park. With bags of candy in my pocket, I soon made friends with a multitude of children. Finally I selected two rosy-cheeked little dears—a boy and a girl of four and five, who seemed worthy to join "The Happy Family." By promises of sweets beyond their wildest dreams, I enticed them to my house one afternoon. The rest was easy. Two sticks of peppermint, the vial—and that night, cleansed and beautiful, white and spotless, turned into tiny statues, they knelt at Louise's feet.

Another week of blissful contemplation went by; and then the loneliness on Louise's face again caused me an acute pain. Madame Fabien, of course, was perfectly content to sit silent in the sunlight with her grandchildren about her; but Louise was still young, still imbued with thoughts of love, still desirous of male companionship.

She must have a husband. It was necessary that I procure her one. Then indeed "The Happy Family" would be complete.

One afternoon, as I sat pondering in my studio, the door-bell rang. When I answered it, I found a tall good-looking young man on the stoop. Evidently fate was again playing into my hand. This young man would make an ideal husband for Louise. I could not refrain from smiling, as I stood aside and bade him enter.

"Is this Madame Fabien's house?" he asked, stepping into the hallway.

"Yes."

"Is she at home? May I see her?"

"No, she has gone to the country for a month," I murmured. "She may be away even longer." I shrugged my shoulders.

"Well," said the young man, eyeing me suspiciously, "I have a warrant to search the house. I am a police officer. See this." He threw back his coat, disclosing a metal badge.

In spite of myself, my voice was a trifle unsteady when I spoke.

"But why do you wish to search the house?"

"For evidence," the young man answered. "Several children have been kidnapped lately. Two of them were seen entering this house."

He pushed past me and began mounting the stairs. I followed him. My heart was beating wildly; but my face, I feel convinced, was as expressionless as a bare wall. As he searched the different rooms on the second floor, it became quite clear to me that I was perfectly safe. How could he suspect my statues of concealing what he sought? Soon I would lead him to my studio and thus divert all suspicion from "The Happy Family." And afterwards, when he had found nothing, I would offer him a cooling drink of my own concoction—a drink which would contain an everlasting sleeping potion. Already I could see him on the pedestal beside Louise—a silent, loving husband.

"If you are ready," I said to the young man, "I will show you my studio. I am a sculptor. You will find children there, but they are only statues."

He ignored my pleasantry and merely nodded. He was a very brusque young man.

"Show me your studio," he said.

I conducted him to it in silence. Opening the door, I stood aside and motioned him to enter. My heart was now beating calmly and evenly. No fear lurked in my soul. I would show this young man my statues, and perhaps he would appreciate what art could do. I was introducing him to his future family. Soon he would be sitting there, white, motionless, and smiling.

He looked about the room carelessly, and finally his eyes became fixed on the statues.

"They're good," he muttered, "—damnably good!"

And then turning to me with a new respect, he said:

"I had an ambition to become a sculptor myself. I studied at the school, but couldn't make a go of it. I know enough about the game though, to realize how good these are. Rodin himself wouldn't be ashamed of that old woman. What do you call this group?"

"'The Happy Family,'" I answered.

"'The Happy Family'?" he repeated thoughtfully. "They don't look very happy—any of them. They look as if they had just been surprised by something—unpleasantly surprised. Take that old woman, for instance. She looks—"

"Nonsense!" I broke in angrily. "They *are* happy—happy." This young man's stupidity began to aggravate me. "In life they would have been loathsome and repulsive. But here? Look at this old woman!"

I approached and put my hand proudly on her shriveled shoulder. "She is a masterpiece. She—"

"Look out!" cried the detective suddenly. "Look out! She's falling!"

I uttered a cry of horror and clutched at Madame Fabien. But it was too late! Unconsciously I had leaned my full weight for an instant on her shoulder; and now, swaying once or twice, she was falling forward. In vain I sought to clasp her in my arms, to shield her body with mine, she bore me over backwards and we both came toppling to the floor. The plaster, covering her face, was broken into a thousand bits; and then the head of Madame Fabien—the head with its ghastly grin and glassy eyes—like some evil Jack-in-the-box, popped out into the sunlight.

I remembered nothing more. The room, the detective, the statues, were swallowed up in blackness. I fainted. When I regained consciousness, it was to find myself jolting through the streets on my way to prison.

IX

It is morning. Already the grey light of dawn is sifting through the window. My task is over. I have told you faithfully the story of "The Happy Family." And now that the tale is told, now that the time grows short, I want to impress upon you, the reading public, you who have become so interested in my fate, that I, René Galien, am not afraid of death.

To-morrow they may lie about me in the papers; they may say I had to be carried to the chair, that I wept, that I pleaded, that I even prayed. But you, my admirers, my friends, my brothers, shall not believe them. No, I only fear something which lurks on the invisible frontier; something which is approaching steadily and relentlessly. What is this something? I do not know. But it is not death. . . . No, it is not death.

THE BAD LANDS

JOHN METCALFE

In many of his tales of horror, John Metcalfe (1891–1965) blurred the boundary between supernatural and psychological horror. "The Bad Lands," which first appeared in the April 15, 1920 issue of *Land and Water,* is an imaginative treatment of that classic horror theme, the "bad place."

It is now perhaps fifteen years ago that Brent Ormerod, seeking the rest and change of scene that should help him to slay the demon neurosis, arrived in Todd towards the close of a mid-October day. A decrepit fly bore him to the one hotel, where his rooms were duly engaged, and it is this vision of himself sitting in the appalling vehicle that makes him think it was October or thereabouts, for he distinctly remembers the determined settling down of the dusk that forced him to drive when he would have preferred to follow his luggage on foot.

He decided immediately that five o'clock was an unsuitable time to arrive in Todd. The atmosphere, as it were, was not receptive. There was a certain repellent quality about the frore autumn air, and something peculiarly shocking in the way in which desultory little winds would spring up in darkening streets to send the fallen leaves scurrying about in hateful, furtive whirlpools.

Dinner, too, at the hotel hardly brought the consolation he had counted on. The meal itself was unexceptionable, and the room cheerful and sufficiently well filled for that time of year, yet one trivial circumstance was enough to send him upstairs with his temper ruffled and his nerves on edge. They had put him to a table with a one-eyed man, and that night the blank eye haunted all his dreams.

But for the first eight or nine days at Todd things went fairly well with him. He took frequent cold baths and regular exercise and made a point of coming back to the hotel so physically tired that to get into bed was usually to drop immediately into sleep. He wrote back to his sister Joan, at Kensington, that his nerves were already much improved and that only another fortnight seemed needed to complete the cure. "Altogether a highly satisfactory week."

Those who have been to Todd remember it as a quiet, secretive watering-place, couched watchfully in a fold of a long range of low hills along the Norfolk coast. It has been pronounced "restful" by those in high authority, for time there has a way of passing dreamily as if the days, too, were being blown past like the lazy clouds on the wings of wandering breezes. At the back, the look of the land is somehow strangely forbidding, and it is wiser to keep to the shore and the more neighbouring villages. Salterton, for instance, has been found quite safe and normal.

There are long stretches of sand dunes to the west, and by their side a nine-hole golf-course.

Here, at the time of Brent's visit, stood an old and crumbling tower, an enigmatic structure which he found interesting from its sheer futility. Behind it an inexplicable road seemed to lead with great decision most uncomfortably to nowhere. . . . Todd, he thought, was in many ways a nice spot, but he detected in it a tendency to grow on one unpleasantly.

He came to this conclusion at the end of the ninth day, for it was then that he became aware of a peculiar uneasiness, an indescribable *malaise.*

This feeling of disquiet he at first found himself quite unable to explain or analyse. His nerves he had thought greatly improved since he had left Kensington, and his general health was good.

He decided, however, that perhaps yet more exercise was necessary, and so he walked along the links and the sand dunes to the queer tower and the inexplicable road that lay behind it three times a day instead of twice.

His discomfort rapidly increased. He would become conscious, as he set out for his walk, of a strange sinking at his heart and of a peculiar moral disturbance which was very difficult to describe. These sensations attained their maximum when he had reached his goal upon the dunes, and he suffered then what something seemed to tell him was very near the pangs of spiritual dissolution.

It was on the eleventh day that some faint hint of the meaning of these peculiar symptoms crossed his mind. For the first time he asked himself why it was that of all the many rambles he had taken in Todd since his arrival each one seemed inevitably to bring him to the same place—the yellow sand dunes with the mysterious looking tower in the background. Something in the bland foolishness of the structure seemed to have magnetised him, and in the unaccountable excitement which the sight of it invariably produced, he had found himself endowing it with almost human characteristics.

With its white nightcap dome and its sides of pale yellow stucco it might seem at one moment to be something extravagantly ridiculous, a figure of fun at which one should laugh and point.

Then, as likely as not, its character would change a little, and it would take on the abashed and crestfallen look of a jester whose best joke has fallen deadly flat, while finally, perhaps, it would develop with startling rapidity into a jovial old gentleman laughing madly at Ormerod from the middle distance out of infinite funds of merriment.

Now Brent was well aware of the dangers of an obsession such as this, and he immediately resolved to rob the tower of its unwholesome fascination by simply walking straight up to it, past it, and onwards along the road that stretched behind it.

It was on the morning of one of the last October days that he set out from the hotel with this intention in his mind. He reached the dunes at about ten, and plodded with some difficulty across them in the direction of the tower. As he neared it his accustomed sensations became painfully apparent, and presently increased to such a pitch that it was all he could do to continue on his way.

He remembered being struck again with the peculiar character of the winding road that stretched before him into a hazy distance where everything seemed to melt and swim in shadowy vagueness. On his left the gate stood open, to his right the grotesque form of the tower threatened. . . .

Now he had reached it, and its shadow fell straight across his path. He did not halt to examine it, but strode forward through the open gate and entered upon the winding road. At the same moment he was astonished to notice that the painful clutch at his heart was immediately lifted, and that with it, too, all the indescribable uneasiness which he had characterised to himself as "moral" had utterly disappeared.

He had walked on for some little distance before another rather remarkable fact struck his attention. The country was no longer vague; rather, it was peculiarly distinct, and he was able to see for long distances over what seemed considerable stretches of park-like land, grey, indeed, in tone and somehow sad with a most poignant melancholy, yet superficially, at least, well cultivated and in some parts richly timbered. He looked behind him to catch a glimpse of Todd and of the sea, but was surprised to find that in that direction the whole landscape was become astonishingly indistinct and shadowy.

It was not long before the mournful aspect of the country about him began so to depress him and work upon his nerves that he debated with himself the advisability of returning at once to the hotel. He found that the ordinary, insignificant things about him were becoming charged with sinister suggestion and that the scenery on all sides was rapidly developing an unpleasant tendency to the *macabre*. Moreover his watch told him that it was now half-past eleven—and lunch was at one. Almost hastily he turned about and began to descend the winding road.

It was about an hour later that he again reached the tower and saw the familiar dunes stretching once more before him. For some reason or other he seemed to have found the way back much longer and more difficult than the outward journey, and it was with a feeling of distinct relief that he actually passed through the gate and set his face towards Todd.

He did not go out again that afternoon, but sat smoking and thinking in the hotel. In the lounge he spoke to a man who sat in a chair beside him.

"What a queer place that is all at the back there behind the dunes!"

His companion's only comment was a somewhat drowsy grunt.

"Behind the tower," pursued Ormerod, "the funny tower at the other end of the links. The most God-forsaken, dismal place you can imagine. And simply miles of it!"

The other, roused to coherence much against his will, turned slowly round. "Don't know it," he said. "There's a large farm where you say, and the other side of that is a river, and then you come to Harkaby or somewhere."

He closed his eyes and Ormerod was left to ponder the many difficulties of his remarks.

At dinner he found a more sympathetic listener. Mr. Stanton-Boyle had been in Todd a week when Brent arrived, and his sensitive, young-old face with the eager eyes and the quick, nervous contraction of the brows had caught the newcomer's attention from the first. Up to now, indeed, they had only exchanged commonplaces, but to-night each seemed more disposed towards intimacy. Ormerod began.

"I suppose you've walked around the country at the back here a good deal?" he said.

"No," replied the other. "I never go there now. I went there once or twice and that was enough."

"Why?"

"Oh, it gets on my nerves, that's all. Do you get any golf here?"

The conversation passed to other subjects, and it was not until both were smoking together over liqueur brandies in the lounge that it returned to the same theme. And then they came to a remarkable conclusion.

"The country at the back of this place," said Brent's companion, "is somehow abominable. It ought to be blown up or something. I don't say it was always like that. Last year, for instance, I don't remember noticing it at all. I fancy it may have been depressing enough, but it was not—not abominable. It's gone abominable since then, particularly to the south-west!"

They said good-night after agreeing to compare notes on Todd, S.W., and Ormerod had a most desolating dream wherein he walked up and up into a strange dim country, full of sighs and whisperings and crowding, sombre trees, where hollow breezes blew fitfully, and a queer house set with lofty pine shone out white against a lurid sky. . . . .

On the next day he walked again past the tower and through the gate and along the winding road. As he left Todd behind him and began the slow ascent among the hills he became conscious of some strange influence that hung over the country like a brooding spirit. The clearness of the preceding day was absent; instead, all seemed nebulous and indistinct, and the sad landscape dropped behind and below him in the numb, unreal recession of a dream.

It was about four o'clock, and as he slowly ascended into the mournful tracts the greyness of the late autumn day was deepening into dusk. All the morning, clouds had been gathering in the west, and now the dull ache of the damp sky gave the uneasy sense of impending rain. Here a fitful wind blew the gold flame of a sear leaf athwart the November gloom, and out along the horizon great leaden masses were marching out to sea.

A terrible sense of loneliness fell upon the solitary walker trudging up into the sighing country, and even the sight of scattered habitations, visible here and there among the shadows, seemed only to intensify his feeling of dream and unreality. Everywhere the uplands strained in the moist wind, and the lines of gaunt firs that marched against the horizon gloom pointed ever out to sea.

The wan crowding on of the weeping heavens, the settled pack of those leaning firs, and the fitful scurry of the leaves in the chill blast down the lane smote upon his spirit as something unutterably sad and terrible. On his right a skinny black thorn shot up hard and wiry towards the dull, grey sky; there ahead trees in a wood fluttered ragged, yellow flags against the dimness.

A human figure appeared before him, and presently he saw that it was a man, apparently a labourer. He carried tools upon his shoulders, and his head was bent so that it was only when Ormerod addressed him that he looked up and showed a withered countenance. "What is the name of all this place?" said Brent, with a wide sweep of his arm.

"This," said the labourer, in a voice so thin and tired that it seemed almost like the cold breath of the wind that drove beside them, "is Hayes-in-the-Up. Of course, though, it'll be a mile further on for you before you get to Fennington." He pointed in the direction from which he had just come, turned his sunken eyes again for a moment upon Ormerod, and then quickly faded down the descending path.

Brent looked after him wondering, but as he swept his gaze about him much of his wonder vanished. All around, the wan country seemed to rock giddily beneath those lowering skies, so heavy with the rain that never fell; all around, the sailing uplands seemed to heave and yearn under the sad tooting of the damp November wind. Oh, he could well imagine that the men of this weary, twilight region would be worn and old before their time, with its sinister stare in their eyes and its haggard gloom abroad in their pinched faces!

Thinking thus, he walked on steadily, and it was not long before certain words of the man he had met rose with uneasy suggestion to the surface of his mind. What, he asked himself, was Fennington? Somehow he did not think that the name stood for another village; rather, the word seemed to connect itself ominously with the dream he had had some little time ago. He shuddered, and had not walked many paces further before he found that his instinct was correct.

Opposite him, across a shallow valley, stood that white house, dimly set in giant pine. Here the winds seemed almost visible as they strove in those lofty trees and the constant rush by of the weeping sky behind made all the view seem to tear giddily through some unreal, watery medium.

A striking resemblance of the pines to palm-trees and a queer effect of light which brought the white façade shaking bright against the sailing cloud-banks gave the whole a strangely exotic look.

Gazing at it across the little valley, Ormerod felt somehow that this, indeed, was the centre and hub of the wicked country, the very kernel and essence of this sad, unwholesome land that he saw flung wide in weariness about him. This abomination was it that magnetised him, that attracted him from afar with fatal fascination, and threatened him with untold disaster. Almost sobbing, he descended his side of the valley and then rose again to meet the house.

Park-like land surrounded the building, and from the smooth turf arose the pines and some clusters of shrubs. Amongst these Ormerod walked carefully till he was suddenly so near that he could look into a small room through its open window whilst he sheltered in a large yew whose dusky skirts swept the ground.

The room seemed strangely bare and deserted. A small table was pushed to one side, and dust lay thick upon it. Nearer Ormerod a chair or two appeared, and, opposite, a great black mantelpiece glowered in much gloom. In the centre of the floor was set the object that seemed to dominate the whole.

This was a large and cumbrous spinning-wheel of forbidding mien. It glistened foully in the dim light, and its many moulded points pricked the air in very awful fashion. Waiting there in the close stillness, the watcher fancied he could see the treadle stir. Quickly, with beating heart, beset by sudden dread, he turned away, retraced his steps among the sheltering shrubs, and descended to the valley bottom.

He climbed up the other side, and was glad to walk rapidly away down the winding path till, on turning his head, it was no longer possible to see the evil house he had just left.

It must have been near six o'clock when, on approaching the gate and tower, weary from his walk and anxious to reach the familiar and reassuring atmosphere of the hotel, he came suddenly upon a man walking through the darkness in the same direction as himself. It was Stanton-Boyle.

Ormerod quickly overtook him and spoke. "You have no idea," he said, "how glad I am to see you. We can walk back together now."

As they strolled to the hotel Brent described his walk, and he saw the other trembling.

Presently Stanton-Boyle looked at him earnestly and spoke. "I've been there too," he said, "and I feel just as you do about it. I feel that that place Fennington is the centre of the rottenness. I looked through the window, too, and saw the spinning-wheel and—" He stopped suddenly.

"No," he went on quietly a moment later, "I won't tell you what else I saw!"

"It ought to be destroyed!" shouted Ormerod. A curious excitement tingled in his blood. His voice was loud, so that people passing them in the street turned and gazed after them. His eyes were very bright. He went on, pulling Stanton-Boyle's arm impressively. "I shall destroy it!" he said. "I shall burn it and I shall most assuredly smash that old spinning-wheel and break off its horrid spiky points!" He had a vague sense of saying curious and unusual things, but this increased rather than moderated his unaccountable elation.

Stanton-Boyle seemed somewhat abnormal too. He seemed to be gliding along the pavement with altogether unexampled smoothness and nobility as he turned his glowing eyes on Brent. "Destroy it!" he said. "Burn it! Before it is too late and it destroys you. Do this and you will be an unutterably brave man!"

When they reached the hotel Ormerod found a telegram awaiting him from Joan. He had not written to her for some time and she had grown anxious and was coming down herself on the following day. He must act quickly, before she came, for her mind in this matter would be unsympathetic. That night as he parted from Stanton-Boyle his eyes blazed in a high resolve. "To-morrow," he said, as he shook the other's hand, "I shall attempt it."

The following morning found the neurotic as good as his word. He carried matches and a tin of oil. His usually pale cheeks were flushed and his eyes sparkled strangely. Those who saw him leave the hotel remembered afterwards how his limbs had trembled and his speech halted. Stanton-Boyle, who was to see him off at the tower, reflected these symptoms in a less degree. Both men were observed to set out arm-in-arm engaged in earnest conversation.

At about noon Stanton-Boyle returned. He had walked with Ormerod to the sand dunes, and there left him to continue on his strange mission alone. He had seen him pass the tower, strike the fatal gate in the slanting morning sun, and then dwindle up the winding path till he was no more than an intense, pathetic dot along that way of mystery.

As he returned he was aware of companionship along the street. He looked round and noticed a policeman strolling in much abstraction some fifty yards behind him. Again at the hotel-entrance he turned about. The same figure in blue uniform was visible, admiring the houses opposite from the shade of an adjacent lamp-post. Stanton-Boyle frowned and withdrew to lunch.

At half-past two Joan arrived. She inquired nervously for Ormerod, and was once addressed by Stanton-Boyle, who had waited for her in the entrance hall as desired by Brent. "Mr. Ormerod," he told her, "is out. He is very sorry. Will you allow me the impropriety of introducing myself? My name is Stanton-Boyle. . . ."

Joan tore open the note which had been left for her by Ormerod. She seemed to find the contents unsatisfactory, for she proceeded to catechise Stanton-Boyle upon her brother's health and general habit of life at Todd. Following this she left the hotel hastily after ascertaining the direction from which Ormerod might be expected to return.

Stanton-Boyle waited. The moments passed, heavy, anxious, weighted with the sense of coming trouble. He sat and smoked. Discreet and muffled noises from within the hotel seemed full somehow of uneasy suggestion and foreboding. Outside, the street looked very gloomy in the November darkness. Something, assuredly, would happen directly.

It came, suddenly. A sound of tramping feet and excited cries that grew rapidly in volume and woke strange echoes in the reserved autumnal roads. Presently the tumult lessened abruptly, and only broken, fitful shouts and staccato ejaculations stabbed the silence. Stanton-Boyle jumped to his feet and walked hurriedly to the entrance hall.

Here there were cries and hustlings and presently strong odours and much suppressed excitement. He saw Joan talking very quickly to the manager of the hotel. She seemed to be developing a Point-of-View, and it was evident that it was not the manager's. For some time the press of people prevented him from discovering the cause of the commotion, but here and there he could make out detached sentences: "Tried to set old Hackney's farm on fire—" "But they'd seen him before and another man too, so—" "Asleep in the barn several times."

Before long, all but the hotel residents had dispersed, and in the centre of the considerable confusion which still remained it was now possible to see Ormerod supported by two policemen. A third hovered in the background with a large notebook. As Stanton-Boyle gazed, Brent lifted his bowed head so that their eyes met. "I have done it," he said. "I smashed it up. I brought back one of its points in my pocket . . . Overcoat, left hand . . . as a proof." Having pronounced which words Mr. Ormerod fainted very quietly.

For some time there was much disturbance. The necessary arrangements for the temporary pacification of the Law and of the Hotel had to be carried through, and after that Ormerod had to be got to bed. It was only after the initial excitement had in large measure abated that Stanton-Boyle ventured to discuss the matter over the after-dinner coffee. He had recognised one of the three policemen as the man whom he had noticed in the morning, and had found it well to retire from observation until he and his companions had left the hotel. Now, however, he felt at liberty to explain his theories of the situation to such as chose to listen.

He held forth with peculiar vehemence and with appropriate gestures. He spoke of a new kind of *terre-mauvaise*, of strange regions, connected, indeed, with definite geographical limits upon the earth, yet somehow apart from them and beyond them. "The relation," he said, "is rather one of parallelism and correspondence than of actual connection. I honestly believe that these regions do exist, and are quite as 'real' in their way as the ordinary world we know. We might say they consist in a special and separated set of stimuli to which only certain minds in certain conditions are able to respond. Such a district seems to be superimposed upon the country to the south-west of this place."

A laugh arose. "You won't get the magistrate to believe that," said someone. "Why, all where you speak of past that gate by the dunes is just old Hackney's farm and nothing else."

"Of course," said another. "It was one of old Hackney's barns he was setting alight, I understand. I was speaking to one of the policemen about it. He said that fellow Ormerod had always been fossicking around there, and had gone to sleep in the barn twice. I expect it's all bad dreams."

A third spoke derisively. "Surely," he said, "you don't really expect us to believe in your Bad Lands. It's like Jack-in-the-Beanstalk."

"All right!" said Stanton-Boyle. "Have it your own way! I know my use of the term 'Bad Lands' may be called incorrect, because it usually means that bit in the States, you know—but that's a detail. I tell you I've run up against things like this before. There was the case of Dolly Wishart, but no, I won't say anything about that—you wouldn't believe it."

The group around looked at him oddly. Suddenly there was a stir, and a man appeared in the doorway. He carried Ormerod's overcoat.

"This may settle the matter," he said. "I heard him say he'd put something in the pocket. He said—"

Stanton-Boyle interrupted him excitedly. "Why, yes," he said. "I'd forgotten that. What I was telling you about—the spinning-wheel. It will be interesting to see if—" He stopped and fumbled in the pockets. In another moment he brought out something which he held in his extended hand for all to see.

It was part of the handle of a patent separator—an object familiar enough to any who held even meagre acquaintance with the life of farms, and upon it could still be discerned the branded letters G. P. H.

"George Philip Hackney," interpreted the unbelievers with many smiles.

THE HORROR-HORN

E.F. BENSON

EDWARD FREDRIC BENSON (1867–1940) WAS THE OLDEST OF
THREE BROTHERS (INCLUDING ROBERT HUGH BENSON AND
ARTHUR C. BENSON) WHO CONTRIBUTED TO THE ENGLISH
GHOST STORY TRADITION. THE FOUR COLLECTIONS OF HORROR
TALES HE PUBLISHED IN HIS LIFETIME FEATURE SOME OF THE
MOST MONSTROUS MANIFESTATIONS OF THE SUPERNATURAL
TO APPEAR IN THE FIRST HALF OF THE TWENTIETH CENTURY,
INCLUDING THIS STORY, FIRST PUBLISHED IN THE SEPTEMBER
1922 ISSUE OF *HUTCHINSON'S MAGAZINE*, ABOUT A TERRIFYING
CREATURE THAT LIES IN WAIT IN THE SWISS ALPS.

For the past ten days Alhubel had basked in the radiant midwinter weather proper to its eminence of over 6,000 feet. From rising to setting the sun (so surprising to those who have hitherto associated it with a pale, tepid plate indistinctly shining through the murky air of England) had blazed its way across the sparkling blue, and every night the serene and windless frost had made the stars sparkle like illuminated diamond dust. Sufficient snow had fallen before Christmas to content the skiers, and the big rink, sprinkled every evening, had given the skaters each morning a fresh surface on which to perform their slippery antics. Bridge and dancing served to while away the greater part of the night, and to me, now for the first time tasting the joys of a winter in the Engadine, it seemed that a new heaven and a new earth had been lighted, warmed, and refrigerated for the special benefit of those who like myself had been wise enough to save up their days of holiday for the winter.

But a break came in these ideal conditions: one afternoon the sun grew vapour-veiled and up the valley from the north-west a wind frozen with miles of travel over ice-bound hill-sides began scouting through the calm halls of the heavens. Soon it grew dusted with snow, first in small flakes driven almost horizontally before its congealing breath and then in larger tufts as of swansdown. And though all day for a fortnight before the fate of nations and life and death had seemed to me of far less importance than to get certain tracings of the skate-blades on the ice of proper shape and size, it now seemed that the one paramount consideration was to hurry back to the hotel for shelter: it was wiser to leave rocking-turns alone than to be frozen in their quest.

I had come out here with my cousin, Professor Ingram, the celebrated physiologist and Alpine climber. During the serenity of the last fortnight he had made a couple of notable winter ascents, but this morning his weather-wisdom had mistrusted the signs of the heavens, and instead of attempting the ascent of the Piz Passug he had waited to see whether his misgivings justified themselves. So there he sat now in the hall of the admirable hotel with his feet on the hot-water pipes and the latest delivery of the English post in his hands. This contained a pamphlet concerning the result of the Mount Everest expedition, of which he had just finished the perusal when I entered.

"A very interesting report," he said, passing it to me, "and they certainly deserve to succeed next year. But who can tell, what that final six thousand feet may entail? Six thousand feet more when you have already accomplished twenty-three thousand does not seem much, but at present no one knows whether the human frame can stand exertion at such a height. It may affect not the lungs and heart only, but possibly the brain. Delirious hallucinations may occur. In fact, if I did not know better, I should have said that one such hallucination had occurred to the climbers already."

"And what was that?" I asked.

"You will find that they thought they came across the tracks of some naked human foot at a great altitude. That looks at first sight like an hallucination. What more natural than that a brain excited and exhilarated by the extreme height should have interpreted certain marks in the snow as the footprints of a human being? Every bodily organ at these altitudes is exerting itself to the utmost to do its work, and the brain seizes on those marks in the snow and says 'Yes, I'm all right, I'm doing my job, and I perceive marks in the snow which I affirm are human footprints.' You know, even at this altitude, how restless and eager the brain is, how vividly, as you told me, you dream at night. Multiply that stimulus and that consequent eagerness and restlessness by three, and how natural that the brain should harbour illusions! What after all is the delirium which often accompanies high fever but the effort of the brain to do its work under the pressure of feverish conditions? It is so eager to continue perceiving that it perceives things which have no existence!"

"And yet you don't think that these naked human footprints were illusions," said I. "You told me you would have thought so, if you had not known better."

He shifted in his chair and looked out of the window a moment. The air was thick now with the density of the big snow-flakes that were driven along by the squealing north-west gale.

"Quite so," he said. "In all probability the human footprints were real human footprints. I expect that they were the footprints, anyhow, of a being more nearly a man than anything else.

My reason for saying so is that I know such beings exist. I have even seen quite near at hand—and I assure you I did not wish to be nearer in spite of my intense curiosity—the creature, shall we say, which would make such footprints. And if the snow was not so dense, I could show you the place where I saw him."

He pointed straight out of the window, where across the valley lies the huge tower of the Ungeheuerhorn with the carved pinnacle of rock at the top like some gigantic rhinoceros-horn.

On one side only, as I knew, was the mountain practicable, and that for none but the finest climbers; on the other three a succession of ledges and precipices rendered it unscalable. Two thousand feet of sheer rock form the tower; below are five hundred feet of fallen boulders, up to the edge of which grow dense woods of larch and pine.

"Upon the Ungeheuerhorn?" I asked.

"Yes. Up till twenty years ago it had never been ascended, and I, like several others, spent a lot of time in trying to find a route up it. My guide and I sometimes spent three nights together at the hut beside the Blumen glacier, prowling round it, and it was by luck really that we found the route, for the mountain looks even more impracticable from the far side than it does from this. But one day we found a long, transverse fissure in the side which led to a negotiable ledge; then there came a slanting ice couloir which you could not see till you got to the foot of it. However, I need not go into that."

The big room where we sat was filling up with cheerful groups driven indoors by this sudden gale and snowfall, and the cackle of merry tongues grew loud. The band, too, that invariable appanage of tea-time at Swiss resorts, had begun to tune up for the usual *potpourri* from the works of Puccini. Next moment the sugary, sentimental melodies began.

"Strange contrast!" said Ingram. "Here are we sitting warm and cosy, our ears pleasantly tickled with these little baby tunes and outside is the great storm growing more violent every moment, and swirling round the austere cliffs of the Ungeheuerhorn: the Horror-horn, as indeed it was to me."

"I want to hear all about it," I said. "Every detail: make a short story long, if it's short. I want to know why it's *your* Horror-horn?"

"Well, Chanton and I (he was my guide) used to spend days prowling about the cliffs, making a little progress on one side and then being stopped, and gaining perhaps five hundred feet on another side and then being confronted by some insuperable obstacle, till the day when by luck we found the route. Chanton never liked the job, for some reason that I could not fathom.

It was not because of the difficulty or danger of the climbing, for he was the most fearless man I have ever met when dealing with rocks and ice, but he was always insistent that we should get.off the mountain and back to the Blumen hut before sunset. He was scarcely easy even when we had got back to shelter and locked and barred the door, and I well remember one night when, as we ate our supper, we heard some animal, a wolf probably, howling somewhere out in the night. A positive panic seized him, and I don't think he closed his eyes till morning. It struck me then that there might be some grisly legend about the mountain, connected possibly with its name, and next day I asked him why the peak was called the Horror-horn. He put the question off at first, and said that, like the Schreckhorn, its name was due to its precipices and falling stones; but when I pressed him further he acknowledged that there was a legend about it, which his father had told him. There were creatures, so it was supposed, that lived in its caves, things human in shape, and covered, except for the face and hands, with long black hair. They were dwarfs in size, four feet high or thereabouts, but of prodigious strength and agility, remnants of some wild primeval race. It seemed that they were still in an upward stage of evolution, or so I guessed, for the story ran that sometimes girls had been carried off by them, not as prey, and not for any such fate as for those captured by cannibals, but to be bred from. Young men also had been raped by them, to be mated with the females of their tribe. All this looked as if the creatures, as I said, were tending towards humanity. But naturally I did not believe a word of it, as applied to the conditions of the present day. Centuries ago, conceivably, there may have been such beings, and, with the extraordinary tenacity of tradition, the news of this had been handed down and was still current round the hearths of the peasants. As for their numbers, Chanton told me that three had been once seen together by a man who owing to his swiftness on skis had escaped to tell the tale. This man, he averred, was no other than his grand-father, who had been benighted one winter evening as he passed through the dense woods below the Ungeheuerhorn, and Chanton supposed that they had been driven down to these lower altitudes in search of food during severe winter weather, for otherwise the recorded sights of them had always taken place among the rocks of the peak itself. They had pursued his grandfather, then a young man, at an extraordinarily swift canter, running sometimes upright as men run, sometimes on all-fours in the manner of beasts, and their howls were just such as that we had heard that night in the Blumen hut. Such at any rate was the story Chanton told me, and, like you, I regarded it as the very moonshine of superstition. But the very next day I had reason to reconsider my judgment about it.

"It was on that day that after a week of exploration we hit on the only route at present known to the top of our peak. We started as soon as there was light enough to climb by, for, as you may guess, on very difficult rocks it is impossible to climb by lantern or moonlight. We hit on the long fissure I have spoken of, we explored the ledge which from below seemed to end in nothingness, and with an hour's stepcutting ascended the couloir which led upwards from it. From there onwards it was a rock-climb, certainly of considerable difficulty, but with no heart-breaking discoveries ahead, and it was about nine in the morning that we stood on the top. We did not wait there long, for that side of the mountain is raked by falling stones loosened, when the sun grows hot, from the ice that holds them, and we made haste to pass the ledge where the falls are most frequent. After that there was the long fissure to descend, a matter of no great difficulty, and we were at the end of our work by midday, both of us, as you may imagine, in the state of the highest elation.

"A long and tiresome scramble among the huge boulders at the foot of the cliff then lay before us. Here the hill-side is very porous and great caves extend far into the mountain. We had unroped at the base of the fissure, and were picking our way as seemed good to either of us among these fallen rocks, many of them bigger than an ordinary house, when, on coming round the corner of one of these, I saw that which made it clear that the stories Chanton had told me were no figment of traditional superstition.

"Not twenty yards in front of me lay one of the beings of which he had spoken. There it sprawled naked and basking on its back with face turned up to the sun, which its narrow eyes regarded unwinking. In form it was completely human, but the growth of hair that covered limbs and trunk alike almost completely hid the sun-tanned skin beneath. But its face, save for the down on its cheeks and chin, was hairless, and I looked on a countenance the sensual and malevolent bestiality of which froze me with horror. Had the creature been an animal, one would have felt scarcely a shudder at the gross animalism of it; the horror lay in the fact that it was a man. There lay by it a couple of gnawed bones, and, its meal finished, it was lazily licking its protuberant lips, from which came a purring murmur of content. With one hand it scratched the thick hair on its belly, in the other it held one of these bones, which presently split in half beneath the pressure of its finger and thumb. But my horror was not based on the information of what happened to those men whom these creatures caught, it was due only to my proximity to a thing so human and so infernal. The peak, of which the ascent had a moment ago filled us with such elated satisfaction, became to me an Ungeheuerhorn indeed, for it was the home of beings more awful than the delirium of nightmare could ever have conceived.

"Chanton was a dozen paces behind me, and with a backward wave of my hand I caused him to halt. Then withdrawing myself with infinite precaution, so as not to attract the gaze of that basking creature, I slipped back round the rock, whispered to him what I had seen, and with blanched faces we made a long detour, peering round every corner, and crouching low, not knowing that at any step we might not come upon another of these beings, or that from the mouth of one of these caves in the mountain-side there might not appear another of those hairless and dreadful faces, with perhaps this time the breasts and insignia of womanhood. That would have been the worst of all.

"Luck favoured us, for we made our way among the boulders and shifting stones, the rattle of which might at any moment have betrayed us, without a repetition of my experience, and once among the trees we ran as if the Furies themselves were in pursuit. Well now did I understand, though I dare say I cannot convey, the qualms of Chanton's mind when he spoke to me of these creatures. Their very humanity was what made them so terrible, the fact that they were of the same race as ourselves, but of a type so abysmally degraded that the most brutal and inhuman of men would have seemed angelic in comparison."

The music of the small band was over before he had finished the narrative, and the chattering groups round the tea-table had dispersed. He paused a moment.

"There was a horror of the spirit," he said, "which I experienced then, from which, I verily believe, I have never entirely recovered. I saw then how terrible a living thing could be, and how terrible, in consequence, was life itself. In us all I suppose lurks some inherited germ of that ineffable bestiality, and who knows whether, sterile as it has apparently become in the course of centuries, it might not fructify again. When I saw that creature sun itself, I looked into the abyss out of which we have crawled. And these creatures are trying to crawl out of it now, if they exist any longer. Certainly for the last twenty years there has been no record of their being seen, until we come to this story of the footprint seen by the climbers on Everest. If that is authentic, if the party did not mistake the footprint of some bear, or what not, for a human tread, it seems as if still this bestranded remnant of mankind is in existence."

Now, Ingram, had told his story well; but sitting in this warm and civilised room, the horror which he had clearly felt had not communicated itself to me in any very vivid manner.

Intellectually, I agreed, I could appreciate his horror, but certainly my spirit felt no shudder of interior comprehension.

"But it is odd," I said, "that your keen interest in physiology did not disperse your qualms.

You were looking, so I take it, at some form of man more remote probably than the earliest human remains. Did not something inside you say 'This is of absorbing significance'?"

He shook his head.

"No: I only wanted to get away," said he. "It was not, as I have told you, the terror of what according to Chanton's story, might—await us if we were captured; it was sheer horror at the creature itself. I quaked at it."

The snowstorm and the gale increased in violence that night, and I slept uneasily, plucked again and again from slumber by the fierce battling of the wind that shook my windows as if with an imperious demand for admittance. It came in billowy gusts, with strange noises intermingled with it as for a moment it abated, with flut-ings and moanings that rose to shrieks as the fury of it returned. These noises, no doubt, mingled themselves with my drowsed and sleepy consciousness, and once I tore myself out of nightmare, imagining that the creatures of the Horror-horn had gained footing on my balcony and were rattling at the window-bolts. But before morning the gale had died away, and I awoke to see the snow falling dense and fast in a windless air. For three days it continued, without intermission, and with its cessation there came a frost such as I have never felt before. Fifty degrees were registered one night, and more the next, and what the cold must have been on the cliffs of the Ungeheuerborn I cannot imagine. Sufficient, so I thought, to have made an end altogether of its secret inhabitants: my cousin, on that day twenty years ago, had missed an opportunity for study which would probably never fall again either to him or another.

I received one morning a letter from a friend saying that he had arrived at the neighbouring winter resort of St. Luigi, and proposing that I should come over for a morning's skating and lunch afterwards. The place was not more than a couple of miles off, if one took the path over the low, pine-clad foot-hills above which lay the steep woods below the first rocky slopes of the Ungeheuerhorn; and accordingly, with a knapsack containing skates on my back, I went on skis over the wooded slopes and down by an easy descent again on to St. Luigi. The day was overcast, clouds entirely obscured the higher peaks though the sun was visible, pale and unluminous, through the mists. But as the morning went on, it gained the upper hand, and I slid down into St. Luigi beneath a sparkling firmament. We skated and lunched, and then, since it looked as if thick weather was coming up again, I set out early about three o'clock for my return journey.

Hardly had I got into the woods when the clouds gathered thick above, and streamers and skeins of them began to descend among the pines through which my path threaded its way. In ten minutes more their opacity had so increased that I could hardly see a couple of yards in front of me. Very soon I became aware that I must have got off the path, for snow-cowled shrubs lay directly in my way, and, casting back to find it again, I got altogether confused as to direction. But, though progress was difficult, I knew I had only to keep on the ascent, and presently I should come to the brow of these low foot-hills, and descend into the open valley where Alhubel stood. So on I went, stumbling and sliding over obstacles, and unable, owing to the thickness of the snow, to take off my skis, for I should have sunk over the knees at each step. Still the ascent continued, and looking at my watch I saw that I had already been near an hour on my way from St. Luigi, a period more than sufficient to complete my whole journey. But still I stuck to my idea that though I had certainly strayed far from my proper route a few minutes more must surely see me over the top of the upward way, and I should find the ground declining into the next valley. About now, too, I noticed that the mists were growing suffused with rose-colour, and, though the inference was that it must be close on sunset, there was consolation in the fact that they were there and might lift at any moment and disclose to me my whereabouts. But the fact that night would soon be on me made it needful to bar my mind against that despair of loneliness which so eats out the heart of a man who is lost in woods or on mountain-side, that, though still there is plenty of vigour in his limbs, his nervous force is sapped, and he can do no more than lie down and abandon himself to whatever fate may await him. . . . And then I heard that which made the thought of loneliness seem bliss indeed, for there was a worse fate than loneliness. What I heard resembled the howl of a wolf, and it came from not far in front of me where the ridge—was it a ridge?—still rose higher in vestment of pines.

From behind me came a sudden puff of wind, which shook the frozen snow from the drooping pine-branches, and swept away the mists as a broom sweeps the dust from the floor. Radiant above me were the unclouded skies, already charged with the red of the sunset, and in front I saw that I had come to the very edge of the wood through which I had wandered so long. But it was no valley into which I had penetrated, for there right ahead of me rose the steep slope of boulders and rocks soaring upwards to the foot of the Ungeheuerhorn. What, then, was that cry of a wolf which had made my heart stand still? I saw.

Not twenty yards from me was a fallen tree, and leaning against the trunk of it was one of the denizens of the Horror-horn, and it was a woman. She was enveloped in a thick growth of hair grey and tufted, and from her head it streamed down over her shoulders and her bosom, from which hung withered and pendulous breasts. And looking on her face I comprehended not with my mind alone, but with a shudder of my spirit, what Ingram had felt. Never had nightmare fashioned so terrible a countenance; the beauty of sun and stars and of the beasts of the field and the kindly race of men could not atone for so hellish an incarnation of the spirit of life. A fathomless bestiality modelled the slavering mouth and the narrow eyes; I looked into the abyss itself and knew that out of that abyss on the edge of which I leaned the generations of men had climbed. What if that ledge crumbled in front of me and pitched me headlong into its nethermost depths? . . .

In one hand she held by the horns a chamois that kicked and struggled. A blow from its hindleg caught her withered thigh, and with a grunt of anger she seized the leg in her other hand, and, as a man may pull from its sheath a stem of meadow-grass, she plucked it off the body, leaving the torn skin hanging round the gaping wound. Then putting the red, bleeding member to her mouth she sucked at it as a child sucks a stick of sweetmeat. Through flesh and gristle her short, brown teeth penetrated, and she licked her lips with a sound of purring. Then dropping the leg by her side, she looked again at the body of the prey now quivering in its death-convulsion, and with finger and thumb gouged out one of its eyes. She snapped her teeth on it, and it cracked like a soft-shelled nut.

It must have been but a few seconds that I stood watching her, in some indescribable catalepsy of terror, while through my brain there pealed the panic-command of my mind to my stricken limbs "Begone, begone, while there is time." Then, recovering the power of my joints and muscles, I tried to slip behind a tree and hide myself from this apparition. But the woman—shall I say?—must have caught my stir of movement, for she raised her eyes from her living feast and saw me. She craned forward her neck, she dropped her prey, and half rising began to move towards me.

As she did this, she opened her mouth, and gave forth a howl such as I had heard a moment before. It was answered by another, but faintly and distantly.

Sliding and slipping, with the toes of my skis tripping in the obstacles below the snow, I plunged forward down the hill between the pine-trunks. The low sun already sinking behind some rampart of mountain in the west reddened the snow and the pines with its ultimate rays. My knapsack with the skates in it swung to and fro on my back, one ski-stick had already been twitched out of my hand by a fallen branch of pine, but not a second's pause could I allow myself to recover it. I gave no glance behind, and I knew not at what pace my pursuer was on my track, or indeed whether any pursued at all, for my whole mind and energy, now working at full power again under the stress of my panic, was devoted to getting away down the hill and out of the wood as swiftly as my limbs could bear me. For a little while I heard nothing but the hissing snow of my headlong passage, and the rustle of the covered undergrowth beneath my feet, and then, from close at hand behind me, once more the wolf-howl sounded and I heard the plunging of footsteps other than my own.

The strap of my knapsack had shifted, and as my skates swung to and fro on my back it chafed and pressed on my throat, hindering free passage of air, of which, God knew, my labouring lungs were in dire need, and without pausing I slipped it free from my neck, and held it in the hand from which my ski-stick had been jerked. I seemed to go a little more easily for this adjustment, and now, not so far distant, I could see below me the path from which I had strayed. If only I could reach that, the smoother going would surely enable me to outdistance my pursuer, who even on the rougher ground was but slowly overhauling me, and at the sight of that riband stretching unimpeded downhill, a ray of hope pierced the black panic of my soul. With that came the desire, keen and insistent, to see who or what it was that was on my tracks, and I spared a backward glance. It was she, the hag whom I had seen at her gruesome meal; her long grey hair flew out behind her, her mouth chattered and gibbered, her fingers made grabbing movements, as if already they closed on me.

But the path was now at hand, and the nearness of it I suppose made me incautious. A hump of snow-covered bush lay in my path, and, thinking I could jump over it, I tripped and fell, smothering myself in snow. I heard a maniac noise, half scream, half laugh, from close behind, and before I could recover myself the grabbing fingers were at my neck, as if a steel vice had closed there. But my right hand in which I held my knapsack of skates was free, and with a blind back-handed movement I whirled it behind me at the full length of its strap, and knew that my desperate blow had found its billet somewhere. Even before I could look round I felt the grip on my neck relax, and something subsided into the very bush which had entangled me. I recovered my feet and turned.

There she lay, twitching and quivering. The heel of one of my skates piercing the thin alpaca of the knapsack had hit her full on the temple, from which the blood was pouring, but a hundred yards away I could see another such figure coming downwards on my tracks, leaping and bounding. At that panic rose again within me, and I sped off down the white smooth path that led to the lights of the village already beckoning. Never once did I pause in my headlong going: there was no safety until I was back among the haunts of men. I flung myself against the door of the hotel, and screamed for admittance, though I had but to turn the handle and enter; and once more as when Ingram had told his tale, there was the sound of the band, and the chatter of voices, and there, too, was he himself, who looked up and then rose swiftly to his feet as I made my clattering entrance.

"I have seen them too," I cried. "Look at my knapsack. Is there not blood on it? It is the blood of one of them, a woman, a hag, who tore off the leg of a chamois as I looked, and pursued me through the accursed wood. I—"

Whether it was I who spun round, or the room which seemed to spin round me, I knew not, but I heard myself falling, collapsed on the floor, and the next time that I was conscious at all I was in bed. There was Ingram there, who told me that I was quite safe, and another man, a stranger, who pricked my arm with the nozzle of a syringe, and reassured me. . . .

A day or two later I gave a coherent account of my adventure, and three or four men, armed with guns, went over my traces. They found the bush in which I had stumbled, with a pool of blood which had soaked into the snow, and, still following my ski-tracks, they came on the body of a chamois, from which had been torn one of its hindlegs and one eye-socket was empty. That is all the corroboration of my story that I can give the reader, and for myself I imagine that the creature which pursued me was either not killed by my blow or that her fellows removed her body. . . . Anyhow, it is open to the incredulous to prowl about the caves of the Ungeheuerhorn, and see if anything occurs that may convince them.

402

THE OUTSIDER

H.P. LOVECRAFT

To most students of supernatural literature, the
fiction of H.P. Lovecraft (1890-1937) is the nexus
between the classic and the modern tale of horror.
In the influential stories that Lovecraft published
in *Weird Tales* and other pulp fiction magazines
in the 1920s and '30s he invented a cosmology of
otherworldly monsters and locales and an influential
approach to horror that blended supernatural horror,
science fiction, and fantasy. The greatest influence
on Lovecraft's writing was the fiction of Edgar
Allan Poe, and this tale, published in the April 1926
Weird Tales and reprinted later as the title story
of his landmark first short fiction collection, is
Lovecraft's homage to Poe's type of horror tale.

> That night the Baron dreamt of many a woe;
> And all his warrior-guests, with shade and form
> Of witch, and demon, and large coffin-worm,
> Were long be-nightmared.
> —*Keats*

Unhappy is he to whom the memories of childhood bring only fear and sadness.
Wretched is he who looks back upon lone hours in vast and dismal chambers
with brown hangings and maddening rows of antique books, or upon awed watches
in twilight groves of grotesque, gigantic, and vine-encumbered trees that silently

wave twisted branches far aloft. Such a lot the gods gave to me—to me, the dazed, the disappointed; the barren, the broken. And yet I am strangely content, and cling desperately to those sere memories, when my mind momentarily threatens to reach beyond to *the other.*

I know not where I was born, save that the castle was infinitely old and infinitely horrible; full of dark passages and having high ceilings where the eye could find only cobwebs and shadows. The stones in the crumbling corridors seemed always hideously damp, and there was an accursed smell everywhere, as of the piled-up corpses of dead generations. It was never light, so that I used sometimes to light candles and gaze steadily at them for relief; nor was there any sun outdoors, since the terrible trees grew high above the topmost accessible tower. There was one black tower which reached above the trees into the unknown outer sky, but that was partly ruined and could not be ascended save by a well-nigh impossible climb up the sheer wall, stone by stone.

I must have lived years in this place, but I cannot measure the time. Beings must have cared for my needs, yet I cannot recall any person except myself; or anything alive but the noiseless rats and bats and spiders. I think that whoever nursed me must have been shockingly aged, since my first conception of a living person was that of something mockingly like myself, yet distorted, shrivelled, and decaying like the castle. To me there was nothing grotesque in the bones and skeletons that strowed some of the stone crypts deep down among the foundations. I fantastically associated these things with every-day events, and thought them more natural than the coloured pictures of living beings which I found in many of the mouldy books. From such books I learned all that I know. No teacher urged or guided me, and I do not recall hearing any human voice in all those years—not even my own; for although I had read of speech, I had never thought to try to speak aloud. My aspect was a matter equally unthought of, for there were no mirrors in the castle, and I merely regarded myself by instinct as akin to the youthful figures I saw drawn and painted in the books. I felt conscious of youth because I remembered so little.

Outside, across the putrid moat and under the dark mute trees, I would often lie and dream for hours about what I read in the books; and would longingly picture myself amidst gay crowds in the sunny world beyond the endless forest. Once I tried to escape from the forest, but as I went farther from the castle the shade grew denser and the air more filled with brooding fear; so that I ran frantically back lest I lose my way in a labyrinth of nighted silence.

So through endless twilights I dreamed and waited, though I knew not what I waited for. Then in the shadowy solitude my longing for light grew so frantic that

I could rest no more, and I lifted entreating hands to the single black ruined tower that reached above the forest into the unknown outer sky. And at last I resolved to scale that tower, fall though I might; since it were better to glimpse the sky and perish, than to live without ever beholding day.

In the dank twilight I climbed the worn and aged stone stairs till I reached the level where they ceased, and thereafter clung perilously to small foot-holds leading upward. Ghastly and terrible was that dead, stairless cylinder of rock; black, ruined, and deserted, and sinister with startled bats whose wings made no noise. But more ghastly and terrible still was the slowness of my progress; for climb as I might, the darkness overhead grew no thinner, and a new chill as of haunted and venerable mould assailed me. I shivered as I wondered why I did not reach the light, and would have looked down had I dared. I fancied that night had come suddenly upon me, and vainly groped with one free hand for a window embrasure, that I might peer out and above, and try to judge the height I had attained.

All at once, after an infinity of awesome, sightless crawling up that concave and desperate precipice, I felt my head touch a solid thing, and knew that I must have gained the roof, or at least some kind of floor. In the darkness I raised my free hand and tested the barrier, finding it stone and immovable. Then came a deadly circuit of the tower, clinging to whatever holds the slimy wall could give; till finally my testing hand found the barrier yielding, and I turned upward again, pushing the slab or door with my head as I used both hands in my fearful ascent. There was no light revealed above, and as my hands went higher I knew that my climb was for the nonce ended; since the slab was the trap-door of an aperture leading to a level stone surface of greater circumference than the lower tower, no doubt the floor of some lofty and capacious observation chamber. I crawled through carefully, and tried to prevent the heavy slab from falling back into place; but failed in the latter attempt. As I lay exhausted on the stone floor I heard the eerie echoes of its fall, but hoped when necessary to pry it open again.

Believing I was now at a prodigious height, far above the accursed branches of the wood, I dragged myself up from the floor and fumbled about for windows, that I might look for the first time upon the sky, and the moon and stars of which I had read. But on every hand I was disappointed; since all that I found were vast shelves of marble, bearing odious oblong boxes of disturbing size. More and more I reflected, and wondered what hoary secrets might abide in this high apartment so many aeons cut off from the castle below. Then unexpectedly my hands came upon a doorway, where hung a portal of stone, rough with strange chiselling. Trying it, I found it locked; but with a supreme burst of strength I overcame all obstacles and dragged it open inward. As I did so there came to me the purest ecstasy I have ever known; for shining tranquilly through an ornate grating of iron, and down a short stone passageway of steps that ascended from the newly found doorway, was the radiant full moon, which I had never before seen save in dreams and in vague visions I dared not call memories.

Fancying now that I had attained the very pinnacle of the castle, I commenced to rush up the few steps beyond the door; but the sudden veiling of the moon by a cloud caused me to stumble, and I felt my way more slowly in the dark. It was still very dark when I reached the grating—which I tried carefully and found unlocked, but which I did not open for fear of falling from the amazing height to which I had climbed. Then the moon came out.

Most daemoniacal of all shocks is that of the abysmally unexpected and grotesquely unbelievable. Nothing I had before undergone could compare in terror with what I now saw; with the bizarre marvels that sight implied. The sight itself was as simple as it was stupefying, for it was merely this: instead of a dizzying prospect of treetops seen from a lofty eminence, there stretched around me on a level through the grating nothing less than *the solid ground,* decked and diversified by marble slabs and columns, and overshadowed by an ancient stone church, whose ruined spire gleamed spectrally in the moonlight.

Half unconscious, I opened the grating and staggered out upon the white gravel path that stretched away in two directions. My mind, stunned and chaotic as it was, still held the frantic craving for light; and not even the fantastic wonder which had happened could stay my course. I neither knew nor cared whether my experience was insanity, dreaming, or magic; but was determined to gaze on brilliance and gaiety at any cost. I knew not who I was or what I was, or what my surroundings might be; though as I continued to stumble along I became conscious of a kind of fearsome latent memory that made my progress not wholly fortuitous. I passed under an arch out of that region of slabs and columns, and wandered through the open country; sometimes following the visible road, but sometimes leaving it curiously to tread across meadows where only occasional ruins bespoke the ancient presence of a forgotten road. Once I swam across a swift river where crumbling, mossy masonry told of a bridge long vanished.

Over two hours must have passed before I reached what seemed to be my goal, a venerable ivied castle in a thickly wooded park; maddeningly familiar, yet full of perplexing strangeness to me. I saw that the moat was filled in, and that some of the well-known towers were demolished; whilst new wings existed to confuse the beholder. But what I observed with chief interest and delight were the open windows—gorgeously ablaze with light and sending forth sound of the gayest revelry. Advancing to one of these I looked in and saw an oddly dressed company, indeed; making merry, and speaking brightly to one another. I had never, seemingly, heard human speech before; and could guess only vaguely what was said. Some of the faces seemed to hold expressions that brought up incredibly remote recollections; others were utterly alien.

I now stepped through the low window into the brilliantly lighted room, stepping as I did so from my single bright moment of hope to my blackest convulsion of despair and realisation. The nightmare was quick to come; for as I entered, there occurred immediately one of the most terrifying demonstrations I had ever conceived. Scarcely had I crossed the sill when there descended upon the whole company a sudden and unheralded fear of hideous intensity, distorting every face and evoking the most horrible screams from nearly every throat. Flight was universal, and in the clamour and panic several fell in a swoon and were dragged away by their madly fleeing companions. Many covered their eyes with their hands, and plunged blindly and awkwardly in their race to escape; overturning furniture and stumbling against the walls before they managed to reach one of the many doors.

The cries were shocking; and as I stood in the brilliant apartment alone and dazed, listening to their vanishing echoes, I trembled at the thought of what might be lurking near me unseen. At a casual inspection the room seemed deserted, but when I moved toward one of the alcoves I thought I detected a presence there—a hint of motion beyond the golden-arched doorway leading to another and somewhat similar room. As I approached the arch I began to perceive the presence more clearly; and then, with the first and last sound I ever uttered—a ghastly ululation that revolted me almost as poignantly as its noxious cause—I beheld in full, frightful vividness the inconceivable, indescribable, and unmentionable monstrosity which had by its simple appearance changed a merry company to a herd of delirious fugitives.

I cannot even hint what it was like, for it was a compound of all that is unclean, uncanny, unwelcome, abnormal, and detestable. It was the ghoulish shade of decay, antiquity, and desolation; the putrid, dripping eidolon of unwholesome revelation; the awful baring of that which the merciful earth should always hide. God knows it was not of this world—or no longer of this world—yet to my horror I saw in its eaten-away and bone-revealing outlines a leering, abhorrent travesty on the human shape; and in its mouldy, disintegrating apparel an unspeakable quality that chilled me even more.

I was almost paralysed, but not too much so to make a feeble effort toward flight; a backward stumble which failed to break the spell in which the nameless, voiceless monster held me. My eyes, bewitched by the glassy orbs which stared loathsomely into them, refused to close; though they were mercifully blurred, and shewed the terrible object but indistinctly after the first shock. I tried to raise my hand to shut out the sight, yet so stunned were my nerves that my arm could not fully obey my will. The attempt, however, was enough to disturb my balance; so that I had to stagger forward several steps to avoid falling. As I did so I became suddenly and agonisingly aware of the *nearness* of the carrion thing, whose hideous hollow breathing I half fancied I could hear. Nearly mad, I found myself yet able to throw out a hand to ward off the foetid apparition which pressed so close; when in one cataclysmic second of cosmic nightmarishness and hellish accident *my fingers touched the rotting outstretched paw of the monster beneath the golden arch.*

I did not shriek, but all the fiendish ghouls that ride the night-wind shrieked for me as in that same second there crashed down upon my mind a single and fleeting avalanche of soul-annihilating memory. I knew in that second all that had been; I remembered beyond the frightful castle and the trees, and recognised the altered edifice in which I now stood; I recognised, most terrible of all, the unholy abomination that stood leering before me as I withdrew my sullied fingers from its own.

But in the cosmos there is balm as well as bitterness, and that balm is nepenthe. In the supreme horror of that second I forgot what had horrified me, and the burst of black memory vanished in a chaos of echoing images. In a dream I fled from that haunted and accursed pile, and ran swiftly and silently in the moonlight. When I returned to the churchyard place of marble and went down the steps I found the stone trap-door immovable; but I was not sorry, for I had hated the antique castle and the trees. Now I ride with the mocking and friendly ghouls on the night-wind, and play by day amongst the catacombs of Nephren-Ka in the sealed and unknown valley of Hadoth by the Nile. I know that light is not for me, save that of the moon over the rock tombs of Neb, nor any gaiety save the unnamed feasts of Nitokris beneath the Great Pyramid; yet in my new wildness and freedom I almost welcome the bitterness of alienage.

For although nepenthe has calmed me, I know always that I am an outsider; a stranger in this century and among those who are still men. This I have known ever since I stretched out my fingers to the abomination within that great gilded frame; stretched out my fingers and touched *a cold and unyielding surface of polished glass.*